A Dance to the Music of Time
I

Spring

Anthony Powell was born in 1905. After working in publishing and as a scriptwriter, he began to write for the *Daily Telegraph* in the mid-1930s. He served in the army during World War II and subsequently became the fiction reviewer on the *TLS*. Next came five years as literary editor of *Punch*. He was appointed a Companion of Honour in 1988. In addition to the twelve-novel sequence, *A Dance to the Music of Time*, Anthony Powell is the author of seven other novels, and four volumes of memoirs, *To Keep the Ball Rolling*.

Books by Anthony Powell

Fiction

Afternoon Men
Venusberg
From a View to a Death
Agents and Patients
What's Become of Waring

A Dance to the Music of Time
Summer
At Lady Molly's
Casanova's Chinese Restaurant
The Kindly Ones
Autumn
The Valley of Bones
The Soldier's Art
The Military Philosophers
Winter
Books Do Furnish a Room
Temporary Kings
Hearing Secret Harmonies

O, How the Wheel Becomes It!
The Fisher King

Non Fiction

The Barnard Letters
John Aubrey and His Friends
Brief Lives and Other Selected Writings by John Aubrey
Miscellaneous Verdicts: Writings on Writers 1946–1989
Under Review: Further Writings on Writers 1946–1989

To Keep the Ball Rolling (memoirs)
Vol. I – Infants of the Spring
Vol. II – Messengers of Day
Vol. III – Faces in My Time
Vol. IV – The Strangers All Are Gone
Journals 1982–1986
Journals 1987–1989
Journals 1990–1992
A Writer's Notebook

Plays

The Garden God
The Rest I'll Whistle

ANTHONY POWELL

A Dance to the Music of Time
I

Spring

A Question of Upbringing

A Buyer's Market

The Acceptance World

arrow books

Reprinted in Arrow Books, 2000

13 15 17 19 20 18 16 14

A Question of Upbringing first published in Great Britain 1951
by William Heinemann Ltd

A Buyer's Market first published in Great Britain 1952
by William Heinemann Ltd

The Acceptance World first published in Great Britain 1955
by William Heinemann Ltd

This edition first published in the United Kingdom in 1997 by Mandarin
and reprinted 4 times

Arrow Books
The Random House Group Limited
20 Vauxhall Bridge Road, London SW1V 2SA

www.randomhouse.co.uk

Addresses for companies within The Random House Group Limited
can be found at:
www.randomhouse.co.uk/offices.htm

The Random House Group Limited Reg. No. 954009

A CIP catalogue record for this book
is available from the British Library

ISBN 9780099436683

The Random House Group Limited supports The Forest Stewardship
Council® (FSC®), the leading international forest certification organisation.
All our titles that are printed on Greenpeace approved FSC® certified paper
carry the FSC® logo. Our paper procurement policy can be found at:
www.randomhouse.co.uk/environment

Printed and bound in Great Britain by
CPI Cox & Wyman, Reading, RG1 8EX

A Question of Upbringing

For T.R.D.P.

1.

THE men at work at the corner of the street had made a kind of camp for themselves, where, marked out by tripods hung with red hurricane-lamps, an abyss in the road led down to a network of subterranean drain-pipes. Gathered round the bucket of coke that burned in front of the shelter, several figures were swinging arms against bodies and rubbing hands together with large, pantomimic gestures: like comedians giving formal expression to the concept of extreme cold. One of them, a spare fellow in blue overalls, taller than the rest, with a jocular demeanour and long, pointed nose like that of a Shakespearian clown, suddenly stepped forward, and, as if performing a rite, cast some substance—apparently the remains of two kippers, loosely wrapped in newspaper—on the bright coals of the fire, causing flames to leap fiercely upward, smoke curling about in eddies of the north-east wind. As the dark fumes floated above the houses, snow began to fall gently from a dull sky, each flake giving a small hiss as it reached the bucket. The flames died down again; and the men, as if required observances were for the moment at an end, all turned away from the fire, lowering themselves laboriously into the pit, or withdrawing to the shadows of their tarpaulin shelter. The grey, undecided flakes continued to come down, though not heavily, while a harsh odour, bitter and gaseous, penetrated the air. The day was drawing in.

For some reason, the sight of snow descending on fire always makes me think of the ancient world—legionaries in sheepskin warming themselves at a brazier: mountain altars where offerings glow between wintry pillars; centaurs with torches cantering beside a frozen sea—scattered, unco-ordinated shapes from a fabulous past, infinitely removed from life; and yet bringing with them memories of things real and imagined. These classical projections, and something in the physical attitudes of the men themselves as they turned from the fire, suddenly suggested Poussin's scene in which the Seasons, hand in hand and facing outward, tread in rhythm to the notes of the lyre that the winged and naked greybeard plays. The image of Time brought thoughts of mortality: of human beings, facing outward like the Seasons, moving hand in hand in intricate measure: stepping slowly, methodically, sometimes a trifle awkwardly, in evolutions that take recognisable shape: or breaking into seemingly meaningless gyrations, while partners disappear only to reappear again, once more giving pattern to the spectacle: unable to control the melody, unable, perhaps, to control the steps of the dance. Classical associations made me think, too, of days at school, where so many forces, hitherto unfamiliar, had become in due course uncompromisingly clear.

As winter advanced in that river valley, mist used to rise in late afternoon and spread over the flooded grass; until the house and all the outskirts of the town were enveloped in opaque, chilly vapour, tinted like cigar-smoke. The house looked on to other tenement-like structures, experiments in architectural insignificance, that intruded upon a central concentration of buildings, commanding and antiquated, laid out in a quadrilateral, though irregular, style. Silted-up residues of the years smouldered uninterruptedly—and not without melancholy—in the maroon brickwork of these medieval closes: beyond the cobbles and archways of which (in a more northerly direction) memory also brooded, no less enigmatic and inconsolable, among water-meadows and avenues of trees: the sombre demands of the past becoming at times almost suffocating in their insistence.

Running westward in front of the door, a metalled road continued into open country of a coarser sort than these gothic parklands—fields: railway arches: a gas-works: and then more fields—a kind of steppe where the climate seemed at all times extreme: sleet: wind: or sultry heat; a wide territory, loosely enclosed by inflexions of the river, over which the smells of the gasometer, recalled perhaps by the fumes of the coke fire, would come and go with intermittent strength. Earlier in the month droves of boys could be seen drifting in bands, and singly, along this trail, migrating tribes of the region, for ever on the move: trudging into exile until the hour when damp clouds began once more to overwhelm the red houses, and to contort or veil crenellations and pinnacles beyond. Then, with the return of the mist, these nomads would reappear again, straggling disconsolately back to their deserted habitations.

By this stage of the year—exercise no longer contestable five days a week—the road was empty; except for Widmerpool, in a sweater once white and cap at least a size too small, hobbling unevenly, though with determination, on the flat heels of spiked running-shoes. Slowly but surely he loomed through the dusk towards me as I walked back—well wrapped-up, I remember—from an expedition to the High Street. Widmerpool was known to go voluntarily for 'a run' by himself every afternoon. This was his return from trotting across the plough in drizzle that had been falling since early school. I had, of course, often seen him before, because we were in the same house; even spoken with him, though he was a bit older than myself. Anecdotes relating to his acknowledged oddness were also familiar;

but before that moment such stories had not made him live. It was on the bleak December tarmac of that Saturday afternoon in, I suppose, the year 1921 that Widmerpool, fairly heavily built, thick lips and metal-rimmed spectacles giving his face as usual an aggrieved expression, first took coherent form in my mind. As the damp, insistent cold struck up from the road, two thin jets of steam drifted out of his nostrils, by nature much distended, and all at once he seemed to possess a painful solidarity that talk about him had never conveyed. Something comfortless and inelegant in his appearance suddenly impressed itself on the observer, as stiffly, almost majestically, Widmerpool moved on his heels out of the mist.

His status was not high. He had no colours, and, although far from being a dunce, there was nothing notable about his work. At this or any other time of year he could be seen training for any games that were in season: in winter solitary running, with or without a football: in summer, rowing 'courses' on the river, breathing heavily, the sweat clouding his thick lenses, while he dragged his rigger through the water. So far as I know he never reached even the semi-finals of the events for which he used to enter. Most of the time he was alone, and even when he walked with other boys he seemed in some way separate from them. About the house he was more noticeable than in the open air, because his voice was pitched high and he articulated poorly: as if tongue were too big for mouth. This delivery made his words always appear to protest, a manner of speaking almost predictable from his face. In addition to that distinctly noisy manner of utterance, thick rubber reinforcements on soles and heels caused his boots—he wore boots more often than what Stringham used to call 'Widmerpool's good sensible shoes'—to squeal incessantly: their shrill rhythmic bursts of sound, limited in compass like the notes of a barbaric orchestra, giving warning of his approach along the linoleum of distant passages; their sullen whining dirge seeming designed to express in musical terms the mysteries of an existence of toil and abnegation lived apart from the daily life of the tribe. Perhaps he sounds a grotesque and conspicuous figure. In excess, Widmerpool was neither. He had his being, like many others, in obscurity. The gap in age caused most of my knowledge of him to have come second-hand; and, in spite of this abrupt realisation of him as a person that took place on that winter evening, he would have remained a dim outline to me if he had not at an earlier date, and before my own arrival, made himself already memorable, as a new boy, by wearing the wrong kind of overcoat.

At this distance of time I cannot remember precisely what sort of an overcoat Widmerpool was said to have worn in the first instance. Stories about it had grown into legend: so much so that even five or six years later you might still occasionally hear an obtrusive or inappropriate garment referred to as 'a Widmerpool'; and Templer, for example, would sometimes say: 'I am afraid I'm wearing rather Widmerpool socks today', or, 'I've bought a wonderfully Widmerpool tie to go home in'. My impression is that the overcoat's initial deviation from normal was slight, depending on the existence or absence of a belt at the back, the fact that the cut was single- or double-breasted, or, again, irregularity may have had something to do with the collar; perhaps the cloth, even, was of the wrong colour or texture.

As a matter of fact the overcoat was only remarkable in itself as a vehicle for the comment it aroused, insomuch that an element in Widmerpool himself had proved indigestible to the community. An overcoat (which never achieved the smallest notoriety) belonging to a boy called Offord whose parents lived in Madeira, where they had possibly purchased the garment, was indeed once pointed out to me as 'very like Widmerpool's'. There was on no occasion the slightest question of Widmerpool being bullied, or even seriously ragged about the matter. On the contrary, his deviation seems scarcely to have been mentioned to him, except by cruder spirits: the coat becoming recognised almost immediately as a traditionally ludicrous aspect of everyday life. Years later, if you questioned his contemporaries on the subject, they were vague in their answers, and would only laugh and say that he wore the coat for a couple of terms; and then, by the time winter came round again, he was found to possess an overcoat of a more conventional sort.

This overcoat gave Widmerpool a lasting notoriety which his otherwise unscintillating career at school could never wholly dispel. How fully he was aware of this reputation it was hard to say. His behaviour certainly indicated that he hoped for more substantial credit with other people than to be known solely on account of a few months given over to out-of-the-way dress. If such was his aim, he was unsuccessful; and the only occasion when I heard these exertions of his receive some small amount of public recognition had been about a month before this, so to speak transcendental, manifestation of himself to me in the mist. Everyone had been summoned to the house library to listen to complaints that Parkinson, captain of games, wanted to make on the subject of general slackness. Parkinson, rather a feeble figure who blushed easily, had ended his little speech with the words: 'It is a pity that some of you are not as keen as Widmerpool.' There had been loud laughter at this. Parkinson himself grinned sheepishly, and, as usual, went red, as if he had said something that might be considered, even in his own eyes, more than a little indecent:

lightly touching, as his habit was, a constellation of spots accumulated on one of his cheekbones.

Widmerpool himself had not smiled, though he could hardly have failed to notice the laughter. He had stared seriously at his boots with their thick rubber reinforcements, apparently trying to avoid any imputation of priggishness. While he did this, his fingers twitched. His hands were small and gnarled, with nails worn short and cracked, as if he spent his spare time digging with them deep down into the soil. Stringham had said that the nails of the saint who had hollowed his own grave without tools might fairly have competed against Widmerpool's in a manicure contest. If Widmerpool had not developed boils soon after this crumb of praise had been let fall, he would, by the end of the season, have scraped into the house football team. This achievement, however, was not to be; though from the moment that his ailment began to abate he was training again as hard as ever. Some more popular figure was made twelfth man.

Still pondering on this vision of Widmerpool, I entered the house, encountering in the hall its familiar exhalation of carbolic soap, airing blankets, and cold Irish stew—almost welcoming after the fog outside—and mounted the staircase towards tea. A thick black stripe of paint divided the upper, and yellow, half of the wall from the magenta dado beneath. Above this black line was another, mottled and undulating, where passers-by, up and down the stairs, rested arm or shoulder, discolouring the distemper in a slanting band of grey. Two or three boys were as usual standing in front of the notice-board on the first floor, their eyes fixed on the half-sheets of paper attached by drawing-pins to the green baize, gazing at the scrawled lists and regulations as if intent on a tape-machine liable at any moment to announce the winner. There was nothing more recent than one of the recurrent injunctions emanating from Le Bas, our housemaster, requiring that all boots should be scraped on the scraper, and then once more scoured on the door-mat on entering the hall, to avoid dispersion of mud throughout the house. On the corner of this grubby fiat Stringham, some days before, had drawn a face in red pencil. Several pairs of eyes were now resting glassily on that outward protest against the voice of authority.

Since the beginning of the term I had messed with Stringham and Templer; and I was already learning a lot from them. Both were a shade older than myself, Stringham by about a year. The arrangement was in part a matter of convenience, dictated by the domestic economy of the house: in this case the distribution of teas. I liked and admired Stringham: Templer I was not yet sure about. The latter's boast that he had never read a book for pleasure in his life did not predispose me in his favour: though he knew far more than I of the things about which books are written. He was also an adept at breaking rules, or diverting them to ends not intended by those who had framed them. Having obtained permission, ostensibly at his parents' request, to consult an oculist, Templer was spending that day in London. It was unlikely that he would cut this visit short enough to enable him to be back in time for tea, a meal taken in Stringham's room.

When I came in, Stringham was kneeling in front of the fire, employing a paper-knife shaped like a scimitar as a toasting-fork. Without looking up, he said: 'There is a jam crisis.'

He was tall and dark, and looked a little like one of those stiff, sad young men in ruffs, whose long legs take up so much room in sixteenth-century portraits: or perhaps a younger—and far slighter—version of Veronese's Alexander receiving the children of Darius after the Battle of Issus:

with the same high forehead and suggestion of hair thinning a bit at the temples. His features certainly seemed to belong to that epoch of painting: the faces in Elizabethan miniatures, lively, obstinate, generous, not very happy, and quite relentless. He was an excellent mimic, and, although he suffered from prolonged fits of melancholy, he talked a lot when one of these splenetic fits was not upon him: and ragged with extraordinary violence when excited. He played cricket well enough to rub along: football he took every opportunity of avoiding. I accepted the piece of toast he held out towards me.

'I bought some sausages.'

'Borrow the frying-pan again. We can do them over the fire.'

The room contained two late eighteenth-century coloured prints of racehorses (Trimalchio and The Pharisee, with blue-chinned jockeys) which hung above a picture, cut out of one of the illustrated weeklies and framed in passe-partout, of Stringham's sister at her wedding: the bridegroom in khaki uniform with one sleeve pinned to his tunic. Over the fireplace was a large, and distinctly florid, photograph of Stringham's mother, with whom he lived, a beauty, and an heiress, who had remarried the previous year after parting from Stringham's father She was a South African. Stuck in the corner of the frame was a snapshot of the elder Stringham, an agreeable-looking man in an open shirt, smoking a pipe with the sun in his eyes. He, too, had remarried, and taken his second, and younger, wife, a Frenchwoman, to Kenya. Stringham did not often talk about his home, and in those days that was all I knew about his family; though Templer had once remarked that 'in that direction there was a good deal of money available', adding that Stringham's parents moved in circles that lived 'at a fairly rapid pace'.

I had been so struck by the conception of Widmerpool, disclosed almost as a new incarnation, shortly before on the road in front of the house, that I described, while the sausages cooked, the manner in which he had materialised in a series of jerks out of the shadows, bearing with him such tokens of despondency. Stringham listened, perforating each of the sausages with the scimitar. He said slowly: 'Widmerpool suffers—or suffered—from contortions of the bottom. Dickinson told me that, in the days when the fags used to parade in the library at tea-time, they were all standing by the wall one evening when suddenly there were inarticulate cries. Owing to this infirmity of his, Widmerpool's legs had unexpectedly given way beneath him.'

'Did he fall?'

'He clung to the moulding of the wall, his feet completely off the ground.'

'What next?'

'He was carted off.'

'I see. Have we any mustard?'

'Now I'll tell you what I saw happen last summer,' Stringham went on, smiling to himself, and continuing to pierce the sausages. 'Peter Templer and I had—for an unaccountable reason—been watching the tail-end of some cricket, and had stopped for a drink on the way back. We found Widmerpool standing by himself with a glass of lemonade in front of him. Some of the Eleven were talking and ragging at the far end of the counter and a skinned banana was thrown. This missed its target and hit Widmerpool. It was a bull's-eye. The banana was over-ripe and it burst all over his face, knocking his spectacles sideways. His cap came off and he spilt most of the lemonade down the front of his clothes.'

'Characteristic of the Eleven's throwing-in.'

'Budd himself was responsible. Widmerpool took out his handkerchief and began to clean up the mess. Budd came down the shop, still laughing, and said: "Sorry, Widmerpool. That banana wasn't intended for you." Widmerpool was obviously astonished to hear himself addressed by name, and so politely, by no less a person than the Captain of the Eleven—who could only have known what Widmerpool was called on account of the famous overcoat. Budd stood there smiling, showing a lot of those film-star teeth of his, and looking more than ever like the hero of an adventure story for boys.'

'That noble brow.'

'It doesn't seem to help him to pile up runs,' said Stringham, 'any more than do those fine cutting shots of his which photograph so well.'

He paused and shook his head, apparently in sadness at the thought of Budd's deficiencies as a cricketer; and then continued: 'Anyway, Budd—exuding charm at every pore—said: "I'm afraid I've made you in a bit of a mess, Widmerpool," and he stood there inspecting the havoc he had just caused. Do you know an absolutely *slavish* look came into Widmerpool's face. "I don't mind," he said, "I don't mind at all, Budd. It doesn't matter in the least." '

Stringham's dexterity at imitating the manner in which Widmerpool talked was remarkable. He stopped the narrative to put some bread into the fat in which the sausages were frying, and, when this was done, said: 'It was as if Widmerpool had experienced some secret and awful pleasure. He had taken off his spectacles and was wiping them, screwing up his eyes, round which there were still traces of banana. He began to blow on the glasses and to rub them with a great show of good cheer. The effect was not at all what might have been hoped. In fact all this heartiness threw the most appalling gloom over the shop.

Budd went back to his friends and finished whatever he was eating, or drinking, in deathly silence. The other members of the Eleven—or whoever they were—stopped laughing and began to mutter self-consciously to themselves about future fixtures. All the kick had gone out of them. I have never seen anything like it. Then Budd picked up his bat and pads and gloves and other belongings, and said: "I must be getting along now. I've got the Musical Society tonight," and there was the usual business of "Good-night, Bill, good-night——" '

' "Good-night, Guy . . . good-night, Stephen . . . good-night, John . . . good-night, Ronnie . . . good-night, George . . ." '

'Exactly,' said Stringham. ' "Good-night, Eddie . . . good-night, Simon . . . good-night, Robin . . ." and so on and so forth until they had all said good-night to each other collectively and individually, and shuffled off together, arm-in-arm. Templer wanted to move because he had to go down-town before lock-up; so we left Widmerpool to himself. He had put on his spectacles again, and straightened his cap, and as we went through the door he was rubbing his gritty little knuckles together, still smiling at his great encounter with Budd.'

The account of this incident, illustrating another of Widmerpool's aspects, did not at that moment make any deep impression on me. It was like a number of other anecdotes on the subject that circulated from time to time, differing only in the proficiency with which Stringham told his stories. My own renewed awareness of Widmerpool's personality seemed to me closer and more real. Stringham, however, had not finished with the matter. He said: 'As we walked past the fives courts, Templer remarked: "I'm glad that ass Widmerpool fielded a banana with his face." I asked why he did not like him—for after all there is little harm in the poor old boy—and it turned out that it was Widmerpool who got Akworth sacked.'

Stringham paused to allow this statement to sink in, while he arranged the sausages in a new pattern. I could not recall at all clearly what Akworth's story had been: though I remembered that he had left the school under a cloud soon after my arrival there, and that various rumours regarding his misdoings had been current at the time.

'Akworth tried to set fire to his room, didn't he? Or did he steal everything that was not nailed down?'

'He well may have done both,' said Stringham; 'but he was principally shot out for sending a note to Peter Templer. Widmerpool intercepted the note and showed it to Le Bas. I must admit that it was news to me when Peter told me.'

'And that was why Peter had taken against Widmerpool?'

'Not only that but Widmerpool got hold of Peter and gave him a tremendous jaw on morals.'

'That must have been very good for him.'

'The jaw went on for so long, and Widmerpool came so close, that Templer said that he thought Widmerpool was going to start something himself.'

'Peter always thinks that about everybody.'

'I agree his conceit is invincible,' said Stringham, turning the sausages thoughtfully, as if contemplating Templer's vanity.

'Did Widmerpool start anything?' I asked.

'It is a grim thought, isn't it?'

'What is the answer?'

Stringham laughed. He said: 'Peter made an absolutely typical Templer remark when I asked him the same question. He said: "No, thank God, but he moved about the room breathing heavily like my sister's white pekinese. Did you see how pleased he was just now to be noticed by Budd? He looked as if he had just been kissed under the mistletoe. Bloody fool. He's so wet you could shoot snipe off him." Can you imagine a more exquisitely Templer phrase? Anyhow, that is how poor old Widmerpool looks to our little room-mate.'

'But what is he like really?'

'If you are not sure what Widmerpool is like,' said Stringham, 'you can't do better than have another look at him. You will have an opportunity at prayers tonight. These sausages are done.'

He stopped speaking, and, picking up the paper-knife again, held it upright, raising his eyebrows, because at that moment there had been a kind of scuffling outside, followed by a knock on the door: in itself a surprising sound. A second later a wavering, infinitely sad voice from beyond said: 'May I come in?'

Obviously this was no boy: the approach sounded unlike a master's. The hinge creaked, and, as the door began to open, a face, deprecatory and enquiring, peered through the narrow space released between the door and the wall. There was an impression of a slight moustache, grey or very fair, and a well-worn, rather sporting tweed suit. I realised all at once, not without apprehension, that my Uncle Giles was attempting to enter the room.

I had not seen my uncle since the end of the war, when he had been wearing some sort of uniform, though not one of an easily recognisable service. This sudden appearance in Stringham's room was an unprecedented incursion: the first time that he had found his way here. He delayed entry for a brief period, pressing the edge of the door against his head, the other side of which touched the wall: rigid, as if imprisoned in a cruel trap specially designed to catch him and his like: some ingenious snare, savage in mechanism, though at the same time calculated to preserve from injury the skin of such rare creatures. Uncle Giles's skin was, in point of fact, not easily injured, though experience of years had made him cautious of assuming as a matter of course that his company would be welcome anywhere—anywhere, at least, where other members of his family might be gathered together. At first, therefore, he did not venture to advance farther into the room, meekly conscious that his unexpected arrival might, not unreasonably, be regarded by the occupants as creating a pivot for potential embarrassment.

'I was just passing through on the way to Reading,' he said. 'Thought I might look you up.'

He stood by the door and appeared a little dazed, perhaps overcome by the rich smell of sausages that permeated the atmosphere of the room: possibly reminding him of what might easily have been a scanty luncheon eaten earlier in the day. Why he should be going to Reading was unguessable. If he had come from London, this could hardly be termed 'on the way'; but it might well be that Uncle Giles had not come from London. His locations were not, as a rule, made public. Stringham stood up and pushed the sausages on to a plate.

'This is my uncle—Captain Jenkins.'

Checking the sausages with the paper-knife, Stringham said: 'I'll get another cup. You'll have tea with us, won't you?'

'Thank you, I never take tea,' said Uncle Giles. 'People who eat tea waste half the afternoon. Never wanted to form the habit.' He added: 'Of course, I'm not speaking of *your* sort of tea.'

He looked round at us, as if for sympathy, a bit uncertain as to whether or not this declaration expressed a justifiable attitude towards tea; unsure—and with good reason—if an assertion that he made efforts, however small, to avoid waste of time would prove easily credible, even in the company in which he now found himself. We borrowed a hard chair from next door, and he sat down, blowing his nose into a bandana handkerchief in a series of little grunts.

'Don't let me keep you fellows from your sausages,' he said. 'They will be getting cold. They look damned good to me.'

Neat, and still slightly military in appearance—though he had not held a commission for at least twenty years and 'captain' was probably a more or less honorary rank, gazetted to him by himself and the better disposed of his relations—my father's brother was now about fifty. His arrival that night made it clear that he had not emigrated: a suggestion put forward at one moment to explain his disappearance for a longer period than usual from public view. There had also been some rather uneasy family jokes regarding the possibility of his having overstepped the limits set by the law in the transaction of everyday business, some slip in financial dealings that might account for an involuntary absence from the scene; for Uncle Giles had been relegated by most of the people who knew him at all well to that limbo where nothing is expected of a person, and where more than usually outrageous actions are approached, at least conversationally, as if they constituted a series of practical jokes, more or less enjoyable, according to where responsibility for clearing up matters might fall. The curious thing about persons regarding whom society has taken this largely self-defensive measure is that the existence of the individual himself reaches a pitch when nothing he does can ever be accepted as serious. If he commits suicide, or murder, only thc grotesque aspects of the event dominate the circumstances: on the whole, avoidance of such major issues being an integral part of such a condition. My uncle was a good example of the action of this law; though naturally I did not in those days see him with anything like this clearness of vision. If Reading were his destination, there could be no hint of immediate intention to leave the country: and, unless on ticket-of-leave, he was evidently under no sort of legal restraint. He finished blowing his nose, pushed the handkerchief back up his sleeve, and, using without facetious implication a then popular catchword. said: 'How's your father?'

'All right.'

'And your mother?'

'Very well.'

'Good,' said Uncle Giles, as if it were a relief to him personally that my parents were well, even when the rest of the world might feel differently on the same matter.

There was a pause. I asked how his own health had been, at which he laughed scornfully.

'Oh, me,' he said, 'I've been about the same. Not growing any younger. Trouble with the old duodenal. I rather wanted to get hold of your father about signing some papers. Is he still in Paris? I suppose so.'

'That bit of the Conference is finished.'

'Where is he?'

'London.'

'On leave?'

'Yes.'

'The War Office haven't decided where they are going to send him?'

'No.'

My uncle looked put out at this piece of news. It was most unlikely, hardly conceivable, that he really intended to impose his company on my father, who had for many years discouraged close association with his brother, except when possessed with an occasional and uncontrollable desire to tell Uncle Giles to his face what he thought of him, a mood that rarely lasted more than thirty-six hours; by the end of which period of time the foredoomed inefficacy of any such contact made itself clear.

'In London, is he?' said Uncle Giles, wrinkling the dry, reddish skin at the sides of his nostrils, under which a web of small grey veins etched on his nose seemed to imply preliminary outlines for a game of noughts-and-crosses. He brought out a leather cigarette-case and—before I could prevent him—lighted a cigarette.

'Visitors are not really supposed to smoke here.'

'Oh, aren't they?' said Uncle Giles. He looked very surprised. 'Why not?'

'Well, if the place smells of smoke, you can't tell if someone else smokes too.'

'Of course you can't,' said Uncle Giles readily, blowing outward a long jet of smoke. He seemed puzzled.

'Le Bas might think a boy had been smoking.'

'Who is Le Bas?'

'Our housemaster.'

How he had managed to find the house if he were ignorant of Le Bas's identity was mysterious: even inexplicable. It was, however, in keeping with the way my uncle conducted his life that he should reach his destination without knowing the name of the goal. He continued to take small puffs at his cigarette.

'I see,' he said.

'Boys aren't allowed to smoke.'

'Quite right. Stunts the growth. It is a great mistake to smoke before you are twenty-one.'

Uncle Giles straightened his back and squared his shoulders. One had the impression that he was well aware that young people of the day could scarcely attempt to compete with the rigorous standards that had governed his own youth. He shook his head and flicked some ash on to one of the dirty plates.

'It is a hundred to one Le Bas won't come in,' said Stringham. 'I should take a chance on it.'

'Take a chance on what?' Uncle Giles asked.

'On smoking.'

'You mean I really ought to put this out?'

'Don't bother.'

'Most certainly I shall bother,' said Uncle Giles. 'I should not dream of breaking a rule of that sort. Rules are made to be obeyed, however foolish they may sometimes seem. The question is where had I best put this, now that the regulation has been broken?'

By the time my uncle had decided to extinguish the cigarette on the sole of his shoe, and throw the butt into the fire, there was not much left of it. Stringham collected the ash, which had by now found its way into several receptacles, brushing all of this also into the cinders. For the rest of tea, Uncle Giles, who, for the time being at least, had evidently dismissed from his mind the question of discussing arrangements for meeting my father, discoursed, not very lucidly, on the possibility of a moratorium in connexion with German reparations and the fall of the mark. Uncle Giles's sympathies were with the Germans. 'They work hard,' he said. 'Therefore they have my respect.' Why he had suddenly turned up in the manner was not yet clear. When tea came to an end he muttered about wanting to discuss family matters, and, after saying good-bye—for my uncle, almost effusively—to Stringham, he followed me along the passage.

'Who was that?' he asked, when we were alone together.

As a rule Uncle Giles took not the slightest interest in

anyone or anything except himself and his own affairs—indeed was by this time all but incapable of absorbing even the smallest particle of information about others, unless such information had some immediate bearing on his own case. I was therefore surprised when he listened with a show of comparative attention to what I could tell him about Stringham's family. When I had finished, he remarked:

'I used to meet his grandfather in Cape Town.'

'What was he doing there?'

'His mother's father, that was. He made a huge fortune. Not a bad fellow. Knew all the right people, of course.'

'Diamonds?'

I was familiar with detective stories in which South African millionaires had made their money in diamonds.

'Gold,' said Uncle Giles, narrowing his eyes.

My uncle's period in South Africa was one of the several stretches of his career not too closely examined by other members of his family—or, if examined, not discussed—and I hoped that he might be about to give some account of experiences I had always been warned not to enquire into. However, he said no more than: 'I saw your friend's mother once when she was married to Lord Warrington and a very good-looking woman she was.'

'Who was Lord Warrington?'

'Much older than she was. He died. Never a good life, Warrington's. And so you always have tea with young Stringham?'

'And another boy called Templer.'

'Where was Templer?' asked Uncle Giles, rather suspiciously, as if he supposed that someone might have been spying on him unawares, or that he had been swindled out of something.

'In London, having his eyes seen to.'

'What is wrong with his eyes?'

'They ache when he works.'

My uncle thought over this statement, which conveyed in Templer's own words his personal diagnosis of this ocular complaint. Uncle Giles was evidently struck by some similarity of experience, because he was silent for several seconds. I spoke more about Stringham, but Uncle Giles had come to the end of his faculty for absorbing statements regarding other people. He began to tap with his knuckles on the window-pane, continuing this tattoo until I had given up attempting, so far as I knew it, to describe Stringham's background.

'It is about the Trust,' said Uncle Giles, coming abruptly to the end of his drumming, and adopting a manner at once accusing and seasoned with humility.

The Trust, therefore, was at the bottom of this visitation. The Trust explained this arrival by night in winter. If I had thought harder, such an explanation might have occurred to me earlier; but at that age I cannot pretend that I felt greatly interested in the Trust, a subject so often ventilated in my hearing. Perhaps the enormous amount of time and ingenuity that had been devoted by other members of my family to examining the Trust from its innumerable aspects had even decreased for me its intrinsic attraction. In fact the topic bored me. Looking back, I can understand the fascination that the Trust possessed for my relations: especially for those, like Uncle Giles, who benefited from it to a greater or lesser degree. In those days the keenness of their interest seemed something akin to madness.

The money came from a great-aunt, who had tied it up in such a way as to raise what were, I believe, some quite interesting questions of legal definition. In addition to this, one of my father's other brothers, Uncle Martin, also a beneficiary, a bachelor, killed at the second battle of the Marne, had greatly complicated matters, although there was not a great deal of money to divide, by leaving a will of his own devising, which still further secured the capital without making it absolutely clear who should enjoy the interest. My father and Uncle Giles had accordingly come to a 'gentleman's agreement' on the subject of their respective shares (which brought in about one hundred and eighty-five pounds annually, or possibly nearly two hundred in a good year); but Uncle Giles had never been satisfied that he was receiving the full amount to which he was by right entitled: so that when times were hard—which happened about every eighteen months—he used to apply pressure with a view to squeezing out a few pounds more than his agreed portion. The repetition of these tactics, forgotten for a time and then breaking out again like one of Uncle Giles's duodenal ulcers, had the effect of making my father exceedingly angry; and, taken in conjunction with the rest of my uncle's manner of life, they had resulted in an almost complete severance of relations between the two brothers.

'As you probably know,' said Uncle Giles, 'I owe your father a small sum of money. Nothing much. Decent of him to have given me the use of it, all the same. Some brothers wouldn't have done as much. I just wanted to tell him that I proposed to let him have the sum in question back.'

This proposal certainly suggested an act to which, on the face of it, there appeared no valid objection; but my uncle, perhaps from force of habit, continued to approach the matter circumspectly. 'It is just a question of the trustees,' he said once or twice; and he proceeded to embark on explanations that seemed to indicate that he had some idea of presenting through myself the latest case for the adjustment of his revenue: tacking on repayment of an ancient debt as a piece of live bait. Any reason that might have been advanced earlier for my becoming the medium in these negotiations, on the grounds that my father was still out of England, had been utterly demolished by the information that he was to be found in London. However, tenacity in certain directions—notably that of the Trust—was one of Uncle Giles's characteristics. He was also habitually unwilling to believe that altered circumstances might affect any matter upon which he had already made up his mind. He therefore entered now upon a comprehensive account of the terms of the Trust, his own pecuniary embarrassment, the forbearance he had shown in the past—both to his relations and the world at large—and the reforms he suggested for the future.

'I'm not a great business expert,' he said, 'I don't claim to be a master brain of finance or anything of that sort. The only training I ever had was to be a soldier. We know how much use that is. All the same, I've had a bit of experience in my day. I've knocked about the world and roughed it. Perhaps I'm not quite so green as I look.'

Uncle Giles became almost truculent for a man with normally so quiet a manner when he said this; as if he expected that I was prepared to argue that he was indeed 'green', or, through some other similar failing, unsuited to run his own affairs. I felt, on the contrary, that in some ways it had to be admitted that he was unusually well equipped for looking after himself: in any case a subject I should not have taken upon myself to dispute with him. There was, therefore, nothing to do but agree to pass on anything he had to say. His mastery of the hard-luck story was of a kind never achieved by persons not wholly concentrated on themselves.

'Quand même,' he said at the end of a tremendous parade

of facts and figures, 'I suppose there is such a thing as family feeling?'

I mumbled.

'After all there was the Jenkins they fought the War of Jenkins's Ear about.'

'Yes.'

'We are all descended from him.'

'Not directly.'

'Collaterally then.'

'It has never been proved, has it?'

'What I mean is that he was a relation and that should keep us together.'

'Well, our ancestor, Hannibal Jenkins, of Cwm Shenkin, paid the Hearth Tax in 1674——'

Perhaps justifiably, Uncle Giles made a gesture as if to dismiss pedantry—and especially genealogical pedantry—in all its protean shapes: at the same time picking up his hat. He said: 'All I mean is that just because I am a bit of a radical, it doesn't mean that I believe tradition counts for nothing.'

'Of course not.'

'Don't think that for a moment.'

'Not a bit.'

'Then you will put it to your father?'

'All right.'

'Can you get leave to walk with me as far as the station?'

'No.'

We set off together down the stairs, Uncle Giles continually stopping on the way to elaborate points omitted in his earlier argument. This was embarrassing, as other boys were hanging about the passages, and I tried, without success, to hurry him along. The front door was locked, and Cattle, the porter, had to be found to obtain the key. For a time we wandered about in a kind of no-man's-land of laundry baskets and coke, until Cattle, more or less asleep, was at last discovered in the boot-room. A lumbering, disagreeable character, he unlocked the door under protest, letting into the house a cloud of fog. Uncle Giles reached the threshold and plunged his hand deep into his trouser pocket as if in search of a coin: stood for what seemed an age sunk in reverie: thought better of an earlier impulse: and stepped briskly out into the mist with a curt 'Good-night to you'. He was instantly swallowed up in the gloom, and I was left standing on the steps with Cattle, whose grousing, silenced for the passage of time during which there had seemed hope of money changing hands, now began to rumble again like the buzz of distant traffic. As I returned slowly up the stairs, this sound of complaint sank to a low growling, punctuated with sharp clangs as the door was once more laboriously locked, bolted, and chained.

On the whole it could not be said that one felt better for Uncle Giles's visit. He brought with him some fleeting suggestion, always welcome at school, of an outside world: though against this had to be weighed the disturbing impact of home-life in school surroundings: even home-life in its diminished and undomestic embodiment represented by my uncle. He was a relation: a being who had in him perhaps some of the same essence that went towards forming oneself as a separate entity. Would one's adult days be spent in worrying about the Trust? What was he going to do at Reading? Did he manage to have quite a lot of fun, or did he live in perpetual hell? These were things to be considered. Some apology for his sudden appearance seemed owed to Stringham: after that, I might try to do some work to be dealt with over the week-end.

When I reached the door I heard a complaining voice raised inside the room. Listening for a moment, I recognised the tone as Le Bas's. He was not best pleased. I went in. Le Bas had come to find Templer, and was now making a fuss about the cigarette smoke.

'Here is Jenkins, sir,' said Stringham. 'He has just been seeing his uncle out of the house.'

He glanced across at me, putting on an expression to indicate that the ball was now at my foot. The room certainly smelt abominably of smoke when entered from the passage. Le Bas was evidently pretty angry.

He was a tall, untidy man, clean-shaven and bald with large rimless spectacles that gave him a curiously Teutonic appearance: like a German priest. Whenever he removed these spectacles he used to rub his eyes vigorously with the back of his hand, and, perhaps as a result of this habit, his eyelids looked chronically red and sore. On some occasions, especially when vexed, he had the habit of getting into unusual positions, stretching his legs far apart and putting his hands on his hips; or standing at attention with heels together and feet turned outwards so far that is seemed impossible that he should not overbalance and fall flat on his face. Alternatively, especially when in a good humour, he would balance on the fender, with each foot pointing in the same direction. These postures gave him the air of belonging to some highly conventionalised form of graphic art: an oriental god, or knave of playing cards. He found difficulty with the letter 'R', and spoke—like Widmerpool—rather as if he were holding an object about the size of a nut in his mouth. To overcome this slight impediment he was careful to make his utterance always slow and very distinct. He was unmarried.

'Stringham appears to think that you can explain, Jenkins, why this room is full of smoke.'

'I am afraid my uncle came to see me, sir. He lit a cigarette without thinking.'

'Where is your uncle?'

'I have just been getting Cattle to let him out of the house.'

'How did he get in?'

'I think he came in at the front door, sir. I am not sure.'

I watched Stringham, from where he stood behind Le Bas, make a movement as of one climbing a rope, following these gestures with motions of his elbows to represent the beating of wings, both dumb-shows no doubt intended to demonstrate alternative methods of ingress possibly employed by Uncle Giles.

'But the door is locked.'

'I suppose he must have come in before Cattle shut the door, sir.'

'You both of you—' he turned towards Stringham to include him in the indictment '—know perfectly well that visitors are *not allowed to smoke in the house.*'

He certainly made it sound a most horrible offence. Quite apart from all the bother that this was going to cause, I felt a twinge of regret that I had not managed to control Uncle Giles more effectively: insomuch that I had been brought up to regard any form of allowing him his head as a display of weakness on the part of his own family.

'Of course as soon as he was told, sir . . .'

'But why is there this *smell?*'

Le Bas spoke as if smoking were bad enough in all conscience: but that, if people must smoke, they might at least be expected to do so without the propagation of perceptible fumes. Stringham said: 'I think the stub—the fag-end, sir—may have smouldered. It might have been a *Turkish* cigarette. I believe they have a rather stronger scent than Virginian.'

He looked round the room, and lifted a cushion from one of the chairs, shaking his head and sniffing. This was not the sort of conduct to improve a bad situation. Le Bas, although he disliked Templer, had never showed any special animus against Stringham or myself. Indeed Stringham was rather a favourite of his, because he was quick at knowing the sources of the quotations that Le Bas, when in a good temper, liked to make. However, like most schoolmasters, he was inclined to feel suspicious of all boys in his house as they grew older; not because he was in any sense an unfriendly man, though abrupt and reserved, but simply on account of the increased difficulty in handling the daily affairs of creatures who tended less and less to fit into a convenient and formalised framework: or, at least, a framework that was convenient to Le Bas because he himself had formalised it. That was how Le Bas's attitude of mind appeared to me in later years. At the time of his complaint about Uncle Giles's cigarette, he merely seemed to Stringham and myself a dangerous lunatic, to be humoured and outwitted.

'How am I to know that neither of you smoked too?' he said, sweeping aside the persistent denials that both of us immediately offered. 'How can I possibly tell?'

He sounded at the same time angry and despairing. He said: 'You must write a letter to your uncle, Jenkins, and ask him to *give his word* that neither of you smoked.'

'But I don't know his address, sir. All I know was that he was on his way to Reading.'

'By car?'

'By train, I think, sir.'

'Nonsense, nonsense,' said Le Bas. 'Not know your own uncle's address? Get it from your parents if necessary. I shall make myself very objectionable to you both until I see that letter.'

He raised his hands from his sides a little way, and clenched his fists, as if he were about to leap high into the air like an athlete, or ballet dancer; and in this taut attitude he seemed to be considering how best to carry out his threat, while he breathed heavily inward as if to imbibe the full savour of sausages and tobacco smoke that still hung about the room. At that moment there was a sound of talking, and some laughter, in the passage. The door was suddenly flung open, and Templer burst into the room. He was brought up short by the sight of Le Bas: in whom Templer immediately called up a new train of thought.

'Ah, Templer, there you are. You went to London, didn't you? What time did your train get in this evening?'

'It was late, sir,' said Templer, who seemed more than usually pleased with himself, though aware that there might be trouble ahead: he dropped his voice a little: 'I couldn't afford a cab, sir, so I walked.'

He had a thin face and light blue eyes that gave out a perpetual and quite mechanical sparkle: at first engaging: then irritating: and finally a normal and inevitable aspect of his features that one no longer noticed. His hair came down in a sharp angle on the forehead and his large pointed ears were like those attributed to satyrs, 'a race amongst whom Templer would have found some interests in common', as Stringham had said, when Templer's ears had been dignified by someone with this classical comparison. His eyes flashed and twinkled now like the lamps of a lighthouse as he fixed them on Le Bas, while both settled down to a duel about the railway time-table. Although Templer fenced with skill, it seemed pretty clear that he would be forced, in due course, to admit that he had taken a train later than that prescribed by regulations. But Le Bas, who not uncommonly forgot entirely about the matter in hand, suddenly seemed to lose interest in Templer's train and its time of arrival (just as he had for the moment abandoned the subject of Uncle Giles's cigarette); and he hurried away, muttering something about Greek unseens. For the moment we were free of him. Templer sat down in the armchair.

'Did he come in when you were having a gasper?' he said. 'The room reeks as if camels had been stabled in it.'

'You don't suppose we should be such fools as to smoke in the house,' said Stringham. 'It was Jenkins's uncle. But my dear Peter, why do you always go about dressed as if you were going to dance up and down a row of naked ladies singing "Dapper Dan was a very handy man", or something equally lyrical? You get more like an advertisement for gents' tailoring every day.'

'I think it is rather a good get-up for London,' said Templer, examining a handful of his suit. 'Every item chosen with thought, I can assure you.'

Stringham said: 'If you're not careful you will suffer the awful fate of the man who always knows the right clothes to wear and the right shop to buy them at.'

Templer laughed. He had a kind of natural jauntiness that seemed to require to be helped out by more than ordinary attention to what he wore: a quality that might in the last resort save him from Stringham's warning picture of the dangers of dressing too well. As a matter of fact, although he used to make fun of him to his face, Stringham was stimulated, perhaps a little impressed, by Templer; however often he might repeat that: 'Peter Templer's affectation that he has to find time to smoke at least one pipe a day bores me to death: nor did it cut any ice with me when he pointed out the empty half-bottle of whisky he had deposited behind the conservatory in Le Bas's garden.' The previous summer, Stringham and Templer had managed to attend a race-meeting together one half-holiday afternoon without being caught. Such adventures I felt to be a bit above my head, though I enjoyed hearing about them. I was, as I have said, not yet sure that I really liked Templer. His chief subjects of conversation were clothes, girls, and the persecutions of Le Bas, who, always sensitive to the possibility of being ragged, tended to make himself unnecessarily disagreeable in any quarter that might reasonably be thought to arouse special apprehension. Besides this, Templer could not possibly be looked upon as a credit to the house. He was not much of a hand at the sort of games that are played at school (though his build made him good at tennis and golf), so that he was in a weak position, being fairly lazy at work, to withstand prolonged aggression from a housemaster. Consequently Templer was involved in a continuous series of minor rows. The question of the train was evidently to become the current point for Le Bas's attack.

'Well, that all seems to have blown over for the moment,' Stringham said. 'You ought to keep your uncles in better order, Jenkins.'

I explained that Uncle Giles was known for being impossible to keep in order, and that he always left trouble in his wake. Templer said: 'I suppose Le Bas will go on pestering about that train. You know, I used to be a great pet of his. Now his only object seems to be to get me sacked.'

'He ought to be able to bring that off sooner or later with your help,' said Stringham. 'After all he is not an absolute fool: though pretty near it.'

'I believe he was quite an oar in his youth,' said Templer. 'At least he won the Diamond Sculls. Still, past successes at Henley don't make him any more tolerable to deal with as a housemaster.'

'He started life as a poet,' Stringham said. 'Did you know that? Years ago, after coming back from a holiday in Greece, he wrote some things that he thought were frightfully good. He showed them to someone or other who pointed out that, as a matter of fact, they were frightfully bad. Le Bas never got over it.'

'I can't imagine anything more appalling than a poem by Le Bas,' said Templer, 'though I'm surprised he doesn't make his pupils learn them.'

'Who did he show them to?' I asked.

'Oh, I don't know,' said Stringham. 'Henry James, or Robert Louis Stevenson, or someone like that.'

'Who on earth told you?'

'An elderly character who came to lunch. I believe he is an ambassador somewhere; or was. He used to run round with the same gang as Le Bas. He said Le Bas used to be tremendously promising as a young man. He was good at everything.'

'I can't imagine he was ever much good with the girls,' said Templer.

'Maybe not,' said Stringham. 'Not everyone has your singleness of aim. As a matter of fact do you think Le Bas has any sex life?'

'I don't know about Le Bas,' said Templer, who had evidently been waiting since his arrival back from London for the right moment to make some important announcement about himself, 'but I have. The reason I took the later train was because I was with a girl.'

'You devil.'

'I was a devil, I can assure you.'

'I suppose we shall have to hear about it,' said Stringham. 'Don't spare my feelings. Did you hold hands at the cinema? Where did you meet?'

'In the street.'

'Do you mean you picked her up?'

'Yes.'

'Fair or dark?'

'Fair.'

'And how was the introduction effected?'

'She smiled at me.'

'A tart, in other words.'

'I suppose she was, in a kind of way,' said Templer, 'but quite young.'

'You know, Peter, you are just exactly the sort of boy my parents warned me against.'

'I went back to her flat.'

'How did you acquit yourself?'

'It was rather a success; except that the scent she used was absolutely asphyxiating. I was a bit afraid Le Bas might notice it on my clothes.'

'Not after the cigarette smoked by Jenkins's uncle. Was it a well appointed apartment?'

'I admit the accommodation was a bit on the squalid side,' said Templer. 'You can't have everything for a quid.'

'That wasn't very munificent, was it?'

'All I had. That was why I had to walk from the station.'

'You seem to have been what Le Bas would call "a very unwise young man".'

'I see no reason why Le Bas should be worried by the matter, if he didn't notice the scent.'

'What an indescribably sordid incident,' said Stringham. 'However, let's hear full details.'

'Not if you don't want to be told them.'

'We do.'

Templer was supplying further particulars when Le Bas appeared in the room again. He seemed increasingly agitated, and said: 'Templer, I want you to come and show me in the time-table which train you took. I have telephoned to the station and have been told that the one you should have travelled on was *not* late—and Jenkins, don't forget that I shall expect to see that letter from your uncle by the end of the week. You had better keep him up to it, Stringham, as it is just as much in your interests as his that the matter should be cleared up.'

He tore off up the passage with Templer following behind at a slower pace. Stringham said: 'Peter is crazy. He really will get shot out sooner or later.'

Although incomplete, the story of Templer's London adventure—to be recapitulated on countless future occasions—had sufficiently amplified the incident for its significance to be inescapably clear to Stringham and myself. This was a glimpse through that mysterious door, once shut, that now seemed to stand ajar. It was as if sounds of far-off conflict, or the muffled din of music and shouting, dimly heard in the past, had now come closer than ever before. Stringham smiled to himself and whistled. I think he felt a little uneasy in the awareness that Templer was one up on him now. He did not discuss the matter further: I too had no comment to make before thinking things over. After a time Templer returned to the room. He said: 'What an infernal nuisance that man Le Bas is. I think he is going to write to my father. I particularly do not want trouble at this moment.'

'He seems to have developed a mania for letters flying in all directions,' said Stringham. 'However, I feel competent to deal with his puny onslaughts. Meanwhile, I should like to hear more of this unfortunate incident which you were in the course of describing with such a wealth of colour. Begin at the beginning, please.'

The episode that Stringham continued to call 'Templer's unfortunate incident', not startlingly interesting in itself, somehow crystallised my impression of Templer's character: rather in the same way that seeing Widmerpool coming home from his 'run' had established a picture of him in my mind, not different from the earlier perception held there, but one set in a clearer focus. Templer's adventure indicated the lengths to which he was prepared to go, and behaviour that had previously seemed to me needless—and even rather tiresome—bravado on his part harmonised with a changing and widening experience. I found that I suddenly liked him better. His personality seemed to have fallen into place. There could be no doubt that he himself felt a milestone to have been passed; and, probably for this reason, became in some ways a quieter, more agreeable, friend. In due course, though not before the end of the term had been reached, Le Bas agreed to some sort of a compromise about the train: Templer admitting that he had been wrong in not returning earlier, at the same time producing evidence to show that alterations in the time-table might reasonably be supposed to have misled him. This saved Le Bas's face, and the matter was allowed to drop at the expense of some minor penalty. The question of Uncle Giles's cigarette was, however, pursued with extraordinary relentlessness into the New Year. My uncle's lapse seemed in some manner to have brought home to Le Bas the suspicion that Stringham and I might have developed a tendency, no less pernicious than Templer's, to break rules; and he managed in a number of small ways to make himself, as he had promised, decidedly obnoxious to both of us. I wrote twice to Uncle Giles, though without much hope of hearing from him. Months later, the second letter arrived back from his last address marked 'Gone Away': just as if—as Stringham had remarked—my uncle had been a fox. This envelope finally satisfied Le Bas; but in future he was never quite the same either to Stringham or myself, the deterioration of his relations with Stringham leading ultimately to the incident of 'Braddock alias Thorne', an occasion which illustrated, curiously enough, another aspect of Widmerpool, though in it he played an entirely subordinate part.

This rather absurd affair, which did no one great credit, took place the following summer. Stringham, Templer and I were still messing together; and by then both of them had become so much part of my existence at school that it seemed strange to me that I had ever had doubts about either as a companion: though Stringham remained the one with whom I had most in common. Even now it seems to me that I spent a large proportion of my life in their close company, although the time that we were all three together was less than eighteen months. Their behaviour exemplified two different sides of life, in spite of some outward similarity in their tastes. For Templer, there was no truth except in tangible things: though he was not ambitious. Stringham, as I now see him, was romantic, and would perhaps have liked to play a somewhat different rôle from that which varying moods, and love of eccentricity, entailed upon him. Personally, I was aware of no particular drift to my life at that time. The days passed, and only later could their inexorable comment be recorded; and, pointless in some respects as was the Braddock alias Thorne episode, it retains a place, though not a specially admirable one, in my recollections of Stringham especially.

The three of us had gone for a walk one Sunday afternoon and were wandering about, rather aimlessly, in the heat; Stringham and Templer having wished to proceed in opposite directions. Passing the police-station, which we had finally reached without yet deciding on a line of march, Stringham had paused to read the posters pasted up outside: where, among a collection of notices referring to lost dogs, stolen jewellery, and foot-and-mouth disease, was reproduced the likeness of a man wanted for fraud. He was called 'Braddock alias Thorne', and his portrait showed one of those blurred, nondescript countenances, familiar in advertisements depicting persons who testify that patent medicine has banished their uric acid, or that application of some more efficacious remedy has enabled them to dispense with the use of a truss. The writing under the picture said that Braddock alias Thorne (who seemed to have committed an unusually large number of petty offences) was a man of respectable appearance, probably dressed in a black suit. The description was hardly borne out by what could be resolved from the photograph, which showed a bald, middle-aged criminal in spectacles, who looked capable of any enormity. Stringham remarked that the picture resembled President Woodrow Wilson. Templer said: 'It is much more like Le Bas.'

'More of a poet,' said Stringham, who loved to emphasise this side of Le Bas's personality; and had indeed built up a picture of his housemaster as a man whose every spare moment was spent in scribbling verses with the help of a rhyming dictionary. He said: 'There is a touch of distinction about Braddock alias Thorne, and absolutely none about Le Bas.'

'Must we spend the whole afternoon reading this stuff?' said Templer. 'It is about as interesting as the house notice-board. Let's go somewhere where I can have my pipe. There is no point in trudging about the town on Sunday.'

And so we turned about towards the fields, passing the house again, and entering an area of dusty cow-parsley and parched meadows. While still on the road the figure of Widmerpool appeared in front of us. He was tramping along in the sunlight, swinging arms and legs like an automaton of which the mechanism might be slightly out of order. We walked behind him for a time, Stringham doing an imitation of the way Widmerpool put his feet to the ground. From an unreasoning fear of the embarrassment that would be caused me if Widmerpool should look back and himself observe Stringham's agitated pantomime, I persuaded him to stop this improvisation. I had remained in some odd manner interested in Widmerpool since that night in the fog; and, although Stringham's imitation was ludicrously exact, to think that Widmerpool might see it was for some reason painful to me; though I was almost sorry when the time came to turn off the road and leave Widmerpool to disappear in a distant cloud of dust.

'I don't know what I should do without Widmerpool,' Stringham said. 'He keeps me young.'

'I sometimes wonder whether he is a human being at all,' Templer said. 'He certainly doesn't move like one.'

We passed beyond the railway line to pasture, where Templer lit up his horrible, stubby pipe, and argued as we walked along about the age of the Dolly Sisters, one of whom Stringham held to be the mother of the other. The sun was too hot to make our way straight across the grass, so that we moved along by hedges, where there was some little shade. Templer was still vigorously contesting Stringham's theory of relationship, when we came through some trees and faced a low bank, covered with undergrowth, which stood between us and the next field. The road was by this time fairly far away. Stringham and Templer now ceased to discuss the Dolly Sisters, and both took a run at this obstacle. Stringham got over first, disappearing down the far side: from which a sort of cry, or exclamation, sounded. As Templer came to the top of the mound of grass, I noticed him snatch his pipe from his mouth and jump. I came up the slope at my leisure, behind the other two, and, reaching the crest, saw them at the foot of the bank. There was an unexpectedly deep drop to the ground. In the field below, Stringham and Templer were talking to Le Bas, who was reclining on the ground, leaning on one elbow.

Stringham was bending forward a little, talking hard. Templer had managed to get his pipe back into his pocket, or was concealing it in his hand, because, when I reached the level of the field, it had disappeared: although the rank, musty odour of the shag which he was affecting at that period swept from time to time through the warm air, indicating that the tobacco was still alight in the neighbourhood. Le Bas had in his hand a small blue book. It was open. I saw from the type face that it contained verse. His hat hung from the top of his walking stick, which he had thrust into the ground, and his bald head was sweating a bit on top. He crouched there in the manner of a large animal—some beast alien to the English countryside, a yak or sea-lion—taking its ease: marring, as Stringham said later, the beauty of the summer afternoon. However, Le Bas appeared to be in a moderately good humour. He was saying to Stringham: 'I don't know why I should tolerate this invasion of my favourite spot. Cannot you all understand that I come here to get away from people like you and Jenkins and Templer? I want peace and quiet for once: not to be surrounded by my pupils.'

'It is a nice place, sir,' said Stringham, smiling, though not in the least committing himself by too much friendliness all at once.

Le Bas turned without warning to his book, and, picking it up from the ground, began to read aloud in his guttural, controlled voice:

'"Ah! leave the smoke, the wealth, the roar
Of London, and the bustling street,
For still, by the Sicilian shore,
The murmur of the Muse is sweet,

Still, still, the suns of summer greet
The mountain-grave of Helikê,
And shepherds still their songs repeat,
Where breaks the blue Sicilian sea.

' "Theocritus! thou canst restore
The pleasant years, and over-fleet;
With thee we live as men of yore,
We rest where running waters meet:
And then we turn unwilling feet
And seek the world—so must it be—
We may not linger in the heat
Where breaks the blue Sicilian sea!" '

He shut the book with a snap, and said: 'Now can any one of you tell me who wrote that?'

We made various suggestions—Templer characteristically opting for Shakespeare—and then Stringham said: 'Matthew Arnold.'

'Not a bad shot,' said Le Bas. 'It is Andrew Lang as a matter of fact. Fine lines, you know.'

Another fetid whiff of Templer's shag puffed its way through the ether. It seemed impossible that Le Bas should remain much longer unaware that a pipe was smoking somewhere near him. However, he seemed to be getting into his stride on the subject of poetry. He said: 'There are descriptive verses by Arnold somewhat similar in metre that may have run in your head, Stringham. Things like:

' "The clouds are on the Oberland,
The Jungfrau's snows look faint and far;
But bright are those green fields at hand,
And through those fields comes down the Aar."

'Rather a different geographical situation, it is true, but the same mood of invoking melancholy by graphic description of natural features of the landscape.'

Stringham said: 'The Andrew Lang made me think of:

' "O singer of Persephone!
In the dim meadows desolate
Dost thou remember Sicily?"

'Do you know that, sir? I don't know how it goes on, but the lines keep on repeating.'

Le Bas looked a little uneasy at this. It was evident that Stringham had displeased him in some way. He said rather gruffly: 'It is a villanelle. I believe Oscar Wilde wrote it, didn't he? Not a very distinguished versifier.'

Quickly abandoning what had apparently been taken as a hostile standpoint, Stringham went on: 'And then Heraclitus——'

The words had an instantaneous effect. Le Bas's face cleared at once, and he broke in with more reverberance even than before:

' "Still are thy pleasant voices, thy nightingales awake,
For Death he taketh all away, but them he cannot take."

'I think you are right, Stringham. Good. Very good. In fact, alpha plus. It all has the same note of nineteenth-century nostalgia for a classical past largely of their own imagining.'

Le Bas sighed, and, removing his spectacles, began in his accustomed manner to massage his eyelids, which appeared to be a trifle less inflamed than normally.

'I looked up Heraclitus in the classical dictionary, sir,' said Stringham, 'and was rather surprised to find that he fed mostly on grass and made his house on a dung-hill. I can quite understand his wanting to be a guest if that is how he lived at home, but I shouldn't have thought that he would have been a very welcome one. Though it is true that one would probably remember him afterwards.'

Le Bas was absolutely delighted at this remark. He laughed aloud, a rare thing with him. 'Splendid, Stringham, splendid,' he said. 'You have confused the friend of Callimachus with a philosopher who lived probably a couple of centuries earlier. But I quite agree that if the other Heraclitus's habits had been those you describe, he would not have been any encouragement to hospitality.'

He laughed a lot, and this would have been the moment to leave him, and go on our way. We should probably have escaped without further trouble if Templer—feeling no doubt that Stringham had been occupying too much of the stage—had not begun to shoot out radiations towards Le Bas, long and short, like an ocular Morse code, saying at the same time in his naturally rather harsh voice: 'I am afraid we very nearly jumped on you, sir.'

Le Bas at once looked less friendly. In any case it was an unwise remark to make and Templer managed to imply a kind of threat in the tone, probably the consequence in some degree of his perpetual war with Le Bas. As a result of this observation, Le Bas at once launched into a long, and wholly irrelevant, speech on the topic of his new scheme for the prevention of the theft of books from the slab in the hall: a favourite subject of his for wearing down resistance in members of his house. It was accordingly some time before we were at last able to escape from the field, and from Le Bas: who returned to his book of verse. Fortunately the pipe seemed to have extinguished itself during the latter period of Le Bas's harangue; or perhaps its smell was absorbed by that of the gas-works, which, absent in the earlier afternoon, had now become apparent.

Behind the next hedge Templer took the pipe from his pocket and tapped it out against his heel.

'That was a near one,' he said. 'I burnt my hand on that bloody pipe. Why on earth did you want to go on like that about poetry?'

'How Le Bas failed to notice the appalling stink from your pipe will always be a mystery,' Stringham said. 'His olfactory sense must be deficient—probably adenoids. Why, therefore, did he make so much fuss about Jenkins's uncle's cigarette? It is an interesting question.'

'But Heraclitus, or whoever it was,' said Templer. 'It was all so utterly unnecessary.'

'Heraclitus put him in a good temper,' said Stringham. 'It was your threatening to jump on him that made the trouble.'

'It was your talking about Oscar Wilde.'

'Nonsense.'

'Anyway,' said Templer, 'Le Bas has thoroughly spoiled my afternoon. Let's go back.'

Stringham agreed, and we pursued a grassy path bordered with turnip fields. A short distance farther on, this track narrowed, and traversed a locality made up of allotments, dotted here and there with huts, or potting-sheds. Climbing a gate, we came out on to the road. There was a garage opposite with a shack beside it, in front of which stood some battered iron tables and chairs. A notice offered 'Tea and Minerals'. It was a desolate spot. Stringham said: 'We might just drop in here for a cooling drink.'

Templer and I at once protested against entering this uninviting booth, which had nothing whatever to recommend it outwardly. All shops were out-of-bounds on

Sunday, and there was no apparent reason for running the risk of being caught in such a place; especially since Le Bas might easily decide to return to the house along this road. However, Stringham was so pressing that in the end we were persuaded to accompany him into the shack. The front room was empty. A girl in a grubby apron with untidy bobbed hair came in from the back, where a gramophone was playing:

> Everything is buzz-buzz now,
> Everything is buzz, somehow:
> You ring up on your buzzer,
> And buzz with one anozzer,
> Or, in other words, pow-wow.

The girl moved towards us with reluctance. Stringham ordered ginger-beer. Templer said: 'This place is too awful. Anyway, I loathe sweet drinks.'

We sat down at one of the iron tables, covered with a cloth marked with jagged brown stains. The record stopped: the needle continuing to scratch round and round its centre, revolving slower and slower, until at last the mechanism unwound itself and ceased to operate. Stringham asked the girl if there was a telephone. She made some enquiries from an unseen person, still farther off than the gramophone, and an older woman's voice joined in discussion of the matter. Then the girl came back and told Stringham he could use the telephone in the office of the garage, if he liked to come with her to the back of the building. Stringham disappeared with the girl. Templer said: 'What on earth is happening? He can't be trying to get off with that female.'

We drank our ginger-beer.

'What the hell is he up to?' said Templer again, after

some minutes had passed. 'I hope we don't run into Le Bas coming out of here.'

We finished our drinks, and Templer tried, without success, to engage the girl in conversation, when she came to clear plates and glasses from another table. At last Stringham reappeared, rather hurriedly, his usually pale face slightly flushed. He drank off his ginger-beer at a gulp and said: 'We might be getting along now. I will pay for this.'

Out on the road again, Templer said: 'First we are rushed into this horrible place: then we are rushed out again. What is supposed to be on?"

Stringham said: 'I've just had a word with the police.'

'What about?'

'On the subject of Braddock alias Thorne.'

'Who's that?'

'The chap they wanted for fraud.'

'What about him?'

'Just to inform them of his whereabouts.'

'Is this a joke?'

'Yes.'

'Where did you tell them to look?'

'In a field beyond the railway line.'

'Why?'

'Set your mind to it.'

'Le Bas?'

'Neat, wasn't it?'

'What did they say?'

'I rang up in the character of Le Bas himself,' Stringham said. 'I told them that a man "described as looking rather like me" had been piling up bills at various shops in the town where I had accounts: that I had positive information that the man in question had been only a few minutes earlier at the place I described.'

'Did the police swallow that?'

'They asked me to come to the station. I pretended to get angry at the delay, and—in a really magnificent Le Bas outburst—I said that I had an urgent appointment to address the confirmation candidates (although, as far as I can remember, it is the wrong time of year to be confirmed): that I was late already and must set off at once: and that, if the man were not arrested, I should hold the local police responsible.'

'I foresee the hell of a row,' said Templer. 'Still, one must admit that it was a good idea. Meanwhile, the sooner we get back to the house and supply a few alibis, the better.'

We walked at a fairly smart pace down the road Widmerpool had traversed when I had seen him returning from his run at the end of the previous year: the tar now soft under foot from the heat of the summer sun. Inside, the house was quiet and comparatively cool. Templer, who had recently relaxed his rule of never reading for pleasure, took up *Sanders of the River,* while Stringham and I discussed the probable course that events would take if the police decided to act as a result of the telephone message. We sat about until the bell began to ring for evening chapel.

'Come on,' said Stringham. 'Let's see if there is any news.'

At the foot of the stairs, we met Widmerpool in the hall. He had just come in from outside, and he seemed unusually excited about something. As we passed—contrary in my experience to all precedent so far as his normal behaviour was concerned—he addressed himself to Stringham, in point of age the nearest to him, saying in his shrillest voice: 'I say, do you know Le Bas has been *arrested?*'

He stood there in the shadowy space by the slab in a setting of brown-paper parcels, dog-eared school books, and crumbs—a precinct of which the moral and physical cleansing provoked endless activity in the mind of Le Bas—and stood with his feet apart and eyes expanded, his panting, as Templer had justly described it, like that of an elderly lap-dog: his appearance suggesting rather some unusual creature actually bred in those depths by the slab, amphibious perhaps, though largely belonging to this land-world of blankets and carbolic: scents which attained their maximum density at this point, where they met and mingled with the Irish stew, which, coming from the territories of laundry baskets and coke, reached its most potent force on the first step of the stairs.

Stringham turned to Widmerpool. 'I am not surprised,' he said coldly. 'How did it happen?'

'I was coming back from my walk,' said Widmerpool, in spite of his excitement lowering his voice a little, as though touching on a very sacred subject in thus referring to his personal habits, 'I was coming back from my walk,' he repeated, dwelling on the words, 'and, as I strolled across one of the fields by the railway line, I saw Le Bas lying on the ground reading a book.'

'I hope you weren't smoking, Widmerpool,' said Templer.

Widmerpool ignored this interpolation, and went on: 'Then I noticed that there was a policeman making across the field towards Le Bas. When the policeman—a big, fat fellow—reached Le Bas he seemed to begin reading something from a notebook. Anyway, Le Bas looked very surprised at first. Then he began to get up. I suppose he must have caught his foot in something, because he stumbled. Evidently the policeman thought he was going to try and escape.'

'What happened when he stumbled?' asked Stringham.

'The policeman took his arm.'

'Did he handcuff him?'

'No; but he grabbed him rather roughly.'

'What did Le Bas say?'

'I couldn't hear. It looked as if he were making an awful

fuss. You know the way he stutters when he is angry.'

'And so the policeman led him off?'

'What *could* he have done?' said Widmerpool, who seemed utterly overwhelmed at the idea that his housemaster should have been arrested.

Stringham asked: 'Did anyone else see this?'

'A soldier and a girl appeared from a ditch and watched them go off together.'

'Did Le Bas notice you?'

'I kept behind the hedge. I didn't want to get mixed up with anything awkward.'

'That was wise of you, Widmerpool,' said Stringham. 'Have you told anyone what you saw?'

'Only F. F. Fletcher and Calthorpe Major. I met them on the way back. What can Le Bas have done?'

'Do you mean to tell me you don't know?' said Stringham.

Widmerpool looked taken aback. His breathing had become less heavy while he unburdened himself of his story. Now once more it began to sound like an engine warming up.

'What do you mean?' he asked.

"I don't *mean* anything,' said Stringham, 'except that I am not particularly surprised.'

'But tell me what you think it is.'

Widmerpool spoke almost beseechingly.

'Now look here, Widmerpool,' said Stringham, 'I am awfully sorry. If you have never noticed for yourself anything about our housemaster, it is hardly my place to tell you. You are higher up in the house than I am. You have to shoulder a certain amount of additional responsibility on that account. It is not for me to spread scandals in advance. I fear that we shall all be reading about Le Bas quite soon enough in the papers.'

We left Widmerpool on the steps of the house: to all intents and purposes, a fish recently hauled from the water, making powerful though failing efforts at respiration.

'That boy will be the death of me,' said Stringham, as we walked quickly together up the road.

Most of the crowd who paced up and down by the chapel, passing backwards and forwards over the cobbles, while masters tried to herd them into the building, already knew something of Le Bas's arrest: though only Calthorpe Major, armed with advanced information from Widmerpool, seemed yet to have had time to write home on the subject. 'I sat straight down and sent off a letter to my people about Le Bas having been removed to prison at last,' Calthorpe Major was saying. 'They never liked him. He got his Leander the same time as my father. I've promised to let them know further details as soon as I can get them.' He moved on, repeating the story to friends who had not yet heard the news. Stringham, too, pushed his way through the mob of boys, collecting versions of the scene that had taken place. These were many in number. The bell quickened its ring and stopped with a kind of explosion of sound as the clock began to strike the hour. We were swept up the steps. Stringham said: 'I am afraid it was all in rather doubtful taste. In some ways I regret having been concerned in it. One is such a creature of impulse.'

Although the air under the high vault struck almost chill after the warmth outside in the yard, the evening sun streamed through the windows of the chapel. Rows of boys, fidgeting but silent, provoked, as always, an atmosphere of expectancy before the service began. The voluntary droned quietly for a time, gradually swelling into a bellow: then stopped with a jerk, and began again more gently: remaining for a time at this muted level of sound. Emotional intensity seemed to meet and mingle with an air of indifference, even of cruelty within these ancient walls. Youth and Time here had made, as it were, some compromise. Le Bas came in late, just before the choir, and strode unsteadily towards his stall under the high neo-gothic canopy of carved wood. He looked discomposed. The surface of his skull was red and shining, and, more than once, he seemed to mutter to himself.

Cobberton, another housemaster, and a parson, through gold-rimmed spectacles looked across from the far side of the aisle, lips tightly caught together and eyebrows raised. He and Le Bas had chronically strained relations with one another, and, as it turned out, by one of those happy, or unhappy, chances, Cobberton had finally been the man to establish Le Bas's identity with the police. This fact was subsequently revealed by Cobberton, who also disclosed generally that the policeman who had taken down Stringham's telephone message on the subject of Braddock alias Thorne had remarked to Le Bas, after the matter had been cleared up: 'He'd fair got your manner of speech to a T, sir, whoever he was.'

The congregation rose to sing a hymn. I looked round the packed seats, and lines of faces arranged in tiers. Stringham was opposite, standing with his arms folded, not singing. His cheeks had lost the flush they had taken on during the excitement of all that had followed his telephoning the police-station and had now returned to their usual pallor. He looked grave, lost in thought, almost seraphic: a carved figure symbolising some virtue Resignation or Self-sacrifice. Templer I could not see, because he sat on the same side of the aisle as myself and was too far distant to be visible from my place. On the other side, away to the left, Widmerpool was holding a book in front of him, singing hard: his mouth opening and shutting sharply, more than ever like some uncommon specimen of marine life. He turned his eyes from time to time towards the rafters and high spaces of the roof. I could see his lips forming the syllables. The words of the verse seemed especially applicable to his case, since he was leaving at the end of the term; and I wondered whether the same thought was passing through his own mind:

> As o'er each continent and island
> The dawn leads on another day,
> The voice of prayer is never silent
> Nor dies the strain of praise away.

Somehow I felt rather moved as the hymn rolled on. A group of boys sitting behind me began to chant a descant of their own; making a good deal of noise, not entirely disagreeable. Cobberton noticed the sound, and frowned. Widmerpool also stopped singing for a second and he too glanced across reprovingly. That was my last memory of him at school, because he left, for good, a few weeks later; although owing to some misunderstanding—perhaps Le Bas's mind was more confused than usual on account of the trick played on him—Widmerpool's name continued to appear in the house-list of the following September: a final assertion of the will to remain and strive further for unattainable laurels.

2.

It is not easy—perhaps not even desirable—to judge other people by a consistent standard. Conduct obnoxious, even unbearable, in one person may be readily tolerated in another; apparently indispensable principles of behaviour are in practice relaxed—not always with impunity—in the interests of those whose nature seems to demand an exceptional measure. That is one of the difficulties of committing human action to paper, a perplexity that really justifies the alternations of comedy with tragedy in Shakespearian drama: because some characters and some deeds (Uncle Giles's, as I have mentioned) may be thought of only in terms appropriate to themselves, irrespective of their consequence. On the stage, however, masks are assumed with some regard to procedure: in everyday life, the participants act their parts without consideration either for suitability of scene or for the words spoken by the rest of the cast: the result is a general tendency for things to be brought to the level of farce even when the theme is serious enough. This disregard for the unities is something that cannot be circumvented in human life; though there are times when close observation reveals, one way or another, that matters may not have been so irreconcilable at the close of the performance as they may have appeared in the First Act.

For example, in the course of having tea for nine months of the year with Stringham and Templer, the divergent nature of their respective points of view became increasingly clear to me, though compared with some remote figure like

Widmerpool (who, at that time, seemed scarcely to belong to the same species as the other two) they must have appeared, say to Parkinson, as identical in mould: simply on account of their common indifference to a side of life—notably football—in which Parkinson himself showed every sign of finding absorbing interest. As I came gradually to know them better, I saw that, in reality, Stringham and Templer provided, in their respective methods of approaching life, patterns of two very distinguishable forms of existence, each of which deserved consideration in the light of its own special peculiarities: both, at the same time, demanding adjustment of a scale of values that was slowly taking coherent shape so far as my own canons of behaviour were concerned. This contrast was in the main a matter of temperament. In due course I had opportunities to recognise how much their unlikeness to each other might also be attributed to dissimilar background.

The autumn of the year of Le Bas's arrest turned to winter. Stringham was leaving at Christmas. Before going up to the university, he was to stay for some months with his father in Kenya, a trip for which he showed little enthusiasm, his periods of gloom becoming, if anything, of longer duration and more intense. As the time drew near, he used to give prolonged imitations of his father's probable demeanour in handling the natives of his new African home, in the course of which the elder Stringham—reputed to drink too much, though noted for elaborately good manners—employed circumlocutions a little in the manner of Lord Chesterfield to faithful coloured retainers envisaged in terms of Man Friday or Uncle Tom. 'I imagine everyone in Kenya will be terribly hearty and wear shorts and drink sun-downers and all that sort of thing,' Stringham used to say. 'However, it will be nice to leave school and be on one's own at last, even though it is to be one's own in darkest Africa in those great open spaces where men are men.' It was arranged that I should lunch at his mother's house on my way through London on the first day of the holidays. The weather, from being wet and mild, had changed to frost and bright sun; and we travelled up together through white and sparkling fields.

'You will probably meet Buster at lunch,' Stringham said.

'Who is Buster?'

'My mother's current husband.'

I knew nothing of this figure except that he was called Lieutenant-Commander Foxe, and that Stringham had once described him as 'a polo-playing sailor'. When asked what Buster was like, Stringham had replied that he preferred naval officers who were 'not so frightfully grand'. He had not elaborated this description, which did not at that time convey much to me, most of the naval officers I had come across being accustomed to speak of themselves as far from grand and chronically hard-up; though he added in amplification—as if the presence of a husband in his mother's house was in itself odd enough in all conscience—that Buster was 'always about the place'.

'Doesn't he ever go to sea?'

'At present he is at the Admiralty; and, I believe, starting some leave at any moment. However, I suppose it is better to have him living in the house than arriving there at all hours of the day and night disturbing the servants.'

This sketch of Buster evoked an impression of behaviour decidedly unsatisfactory; and for the rest of the journey I was curious to meet someone of mature years and such apparently irregular habits. When we arrived in London, Stringham explained that he wanted to buy some tropical clothes; and, as this proved an amusing occupation, we did not reach the house again until late in the morning; having delivered the luggage there on our arrival. It was a rather gloomy double-fronted façade in a small street near Berkeley Square: the pillars of the entrance flanked on either side with hollow cones for the linkmen to extinguish their torches.

'Come up to the library,' Stringham said. 'We shall probably find Buster there.'

I followed up the stairs into a room on the first floor, generally crimson in effect, containing a couple of large Regency bookcases. A female portrait, by appearance a Romney, hung over the fireplace, and there was a malachite urn of immense size on a marble-topped table by the window: presented, I learnt later, by the Tsar to one of the Warringtons who had headed some diplomatic mission to Russia at the beginning of the nineteenth century. Buster was standing beside this urn, cleaning a cigarette-holder with the end of a match-stick. He was tall, and at once struck me as surprisingly young; with the slightly drawn expression that one recognises in later life as the face of a man who does himself pretty well, while not ceasing to take plenty of exercise. His turn-out was emphatically excellent, and he diffused waves of personality, strong, chilling gusts of icy air, a protective element that threatened to freeze into rigidity all who came through the door, before they could approach him nearer.

'Hullo, you fellows,' he said, without looking up from his cigarette-holder, at which he appeared to be sneering, as if this object were not nearly valuable enough to presume to belong to him.

'Hullo.'

Stringham took a step forward, and, without moving farther into the room, stood for a moment looking more than ever like Veronese's Alexander. Then he introduced me. Buster slipped his cigarette-holder into his pocket, and nodded. He had a way of making one feel remarkably ill at ease. He said: 'It's a blow, but I have to leave you.'

'Aren't you lunching here?' said Stringham.

'I am trying to buy a Bentley from a man awfully cheap. I've got to keep him sweet.'

'Did you sell the Isotta?'

'I had to.'

Buster smiled a little sadly, as if in half public acknowledgment that he himself had long since seen through any illusions once possessed regarding the extent of his wife's fortune; but indicating by the same smile that he had learnt how to bear disappointment. Stringham said: 'Where are you taking him?'

'Claridge's.'

'Will you ply him with drink?'

'Hock, I think. That is what I am feeling like myself. Are you coming to the Russian Ballet tonight?'

'I didn't know I was asked,' Stringham said. 'I'd like to.'

'Do.'

'Anyone for lunch?'

'Only Tuffy. She will be glad to see you.'

'Then we will wish you good luck with your deal.'

I was conscious that some sort of a duel had been taking place, and that Stringham had somehow gained an advantage by, as it were, ordering Buster from the room. Buster himself began to smile, perhaps recognising momentary defeat, to be disregarded from assurance of ultimate victory. Like a man effortlessly winning a walking-race, he crossed the carpet with long, easy strides: at the same time separating from himself some of the eddies of cold air that surrounded him, and bequeathing them to the atmosphere of the room after he had left it. I was relieved at his departure. Stringham moved across to the window.

He said: 'He gets himself up rather like Peter Templer, doesn't he?'

'Have they ever met?'

To my surprise, Stringham laughed aloud.

'Good Lord, no,' he said.

'Wouldn't they like each other?'

'It is an interesting question.'

'Why not try it?'

'I am devoted to Peter,' Stringham said, 'but really I'm not sure one could have him in the house, could one?'

'Oh?'

'Well, I don't really mean that,' said Stringham. 'Not literally, of course. But you must admit that Peter doesn't exactly fit in with home life.'

'I suppose not.'

'You agree?'

'I see what you mean.'

I certainly saw what Stringham meant; even though the sort of home life that included Buster provided a picture rather different from that which the phrase ordinarily suggested to me from my own experience. At the moment, however, I was chiefly conscious of a new balance of relationship between Stringham and Templer. Although their association together possessed a curiously unrelenting quality, like the union of partners in a business rather than the intimacy of friends, I had always thought of Templer as a far closer and more established crony of Stringham's than was I myself; and it had never crossed my mind that Stringham might share at all the want of confidence that, at least in the earlier stages of our acquaintance, I had sometimes felt towards Templer. Templer certainly did not appear to be designed for domestic life: though for that matter the same might be said of Stringham. Before I could ponder the question further, someone descending the stairs passed in through the door left ajar by Buster. Catching sight of this person, Stringham called out: 'Tuffy, how are you?'

The woman who came into the room was about thirty or thirty-five, I suppose, though at the time she impressed me as older. Dressed in black, she was dark and not bad-looking, with a beaky nose. 'Charles,' she said; and, as she smiled at him, she seemed so positively delighted that her face took on a sudden look of intensity, almost of anxiety, the look that women's faces sometimes show at a moment of supreme pleasure.

That quick, avid glance disappeared immediately, though she continued to smile towards him.

'This is Miss Weedon,' said Stringham, laughing in a friendly way, as he took her left hand in his right. 'How have you been, Tuffy?'

Though less glacial than Buster, Miss Weedon was not overwhelmingly affable when she gave me a palm that felt cool and brittle. She said in an aside: 'You know they nearly forgot to take a ticket for you for the Russian Ballet tonight.'

'Good gracious,' said Stringham. 'What next?'

However, he did not show any sign of being specially put out by this lapse on the part of his family.

'I saw to it that they got an extra one.'

'Thank you, Tuffy.'

She had perhaps hoped for something more exuberant in the way of gratitude, because her face hardened a little, while she continued to fix him with her smile.

'We have just been talking to Buster,' Stringham said, plainly dismissing the subject of the tickets.

She put her head a little on one side and remarked: 'I am sure that he was as charming as ever.'

'If possible, even more so.'

'Buster has been behaving *very* well,' she said.

'I am glad to hear it.'

'Now I must rush off and do some things for your mother before luncheon.'

She was gone in a flash. Stringham yawned. I asked about Miss Weedon. Stringham said: 'Tuffy? Oh, she used to be my sister's governess. She stays here a lot of the time. She does all my mother's odd jobs—especially the Hospital.'

He laughed, as if at the thought of the preposterous amount of work that Miss Weedon had to undertake. I was not very clear as to what 'the Hospital' might be; but accepted it as an activity natural enough for Mrs. Foxe.

'Tuffy is a great supporter of mine,' Stringham added: as if in explanation of something that needed explaining.

He did not extend this statement. A moment or two later his mother appeared. I thought her tremendously beautiful: though smaller than the photograph in Stringham's room had suggested. Still wearing a hat, she had just come into the house. She kissed him, and said: 'Everything is in a terrible muddle. I really can't decide whether or not I want to go to Glimber for Christmas. I feel one ought to; but it is so frightfully cold.'

'Come to Kenya with me, instead,' said Stringham. 'Glimber is much too draughty in the winter. Anyway, it would probably kill Buster, who is used to snug cabins.'

'It would be rather fun to spend Christmas on the boat.'

'Too jolly for words,' said Stringham.

'Buster had to lunch out. Did you see him?'

'I hear he is buying a new car.'

'He really did need one,' she said.

This could hardly have been meant for an apology, but her voice sounded a little apprehensive. Changing the subject, she turned to me and said: 'I think poor Mr. Le

Bas must be so glad that Charles has left at last. He used to write the most pathetic letters about him. Still, you weren't expelled, darling. That was clever of you.'

'It took some doing,' Stringham said.

In view of their relationship, this manner of talking was quite unlike anything I had been used to; though, in a general way, fitting the rough outline pieced together from scraps of information regarding his home, or stories about his mother, that Stringham had from time to time let fall. He had, for example, once remarked that she liked interfering in political matters, and I wondered whether some startling intrigue with a member, or members, of the Cabinet would be revealed during luncheon, which was announced a minute or two later. Miss Weedon came down the stairs after us, and, before following into the dining-room, had some sort of a consultation with the footman, to whom she handed a sheaf of papers. As we sat down, Stringham said: 'I hear we are going to the Russian Ballet tonight.'

'It was Buster's idea. He thought you would like it.'

'That was kind of him.'

'I expect you boys—can I still call you boys?—are going to a matinée this afternoon.'

I told her that I had, unfortunately, to catch a train to the country.

'Oh, but that is too sad,' she said, seeming quite cast down. 'Where are you making for?'

I explained that the journey was to the west of England, where my father was on the staff of a Corps Headquarters. Thinking that the exigencies of army life might in all likelihood be unfamiliar to her, I added something about often finding myself in a place different from that in which I had spent previous holidays.

'I know all about the army,' she said. 'My first husband

was a soldier. That was ages ago, of course. Even apart from that we had a house on the Curragh, because he used to train his horses there—so that nothing about soldiering is a mystery to me.'

There was something curiously overpowering about her. Now she seemed to have attached the army to herself, like a piece of property rediscovered after lying for long years forgotten. Lord Warrington had, it appeared, commanded a cavalry brigade before he retired. She told stories of the Duke of Cambridge, and talked of Kitchener and his collection of china.

'Are you going to be a soldier too?' she asked.

'No.'

'I think Charles ought. Anyway for a time. But he doesn't seem awfully keen.'

'No,' said Stringham, 'he doesn't.'

'But your father liked his time in the Grenadiers,' she insisted. 'He always said it did him a lot of good.'

She looked so beseeching when she said this that Stringham burst out laughing; and I laughed too. Even Miss Weedon smiled at the notion that anything so transitory as service with the Grenadiers could ever have done Stringham's father good. Stringham himself had seemed to be on the edge of one of his fits of depression; but now he cheered up for a time: though his mother seemed to exhaust his energies and subdue him. This was not surprising, considering the force of her personality, which perhaps explained some of Buster's need for an elaborate mechanism of self-defence. Except this force, which had something unrestrained, almost alien, about it, she showed no sign whatever of her South African origin. It is true that I did not know what to expect as outward marks of such antecedents; though I had perhaps supposed that in some manner she would be less assimilated into the world in which she now lived. She said: 'This is the last time you will see Charles until he comes back from Kenya.'

'We meet in the autumn.'

'I wish I wasn't going,' Stringham said. 'It really is the most desperate bore. Can't I get out of it?'

'But, darling, you are sailing in two days' time. I thought you wanted to go. And your father would be so disappointed.'

'Would he?'

His mother sighed. Stringham's despondency, briefly postponed, was now once more in the ascendant. Miss Weedon said with emphasis: 'But you will be back soon.'

Stringham did not answer; but he shot her a look almost of hatred. She was evidently used to rough treatment from him, because she appeared not at all put out by this, and rattled on about the letters she had been writing that morning. The look of disappointment she had shown earlier was to be attributed, perhaps, to her being still unaccustomed to having him at home again, with the kindnesses and cruelties his presence entailed for her. The meal proceeded. Miss Weedon and Mrs. Foxe became involved in a discussion as to whether or not the head-gardener at Glimber was selling the fruit for his own profit. Stringham and I talked of school affairs. The luncheon party—the whole house—was in an obscure way depressing. I had looked forward to coming there, but was quite glad when it was time to go.

'Write and tell me anything that may happen,' said Stringham, at the door. 'Especially anything funny that Peter may do.'

I promised to report any of Templer's outstanding adventures, and we arranged to meet in nine or ten months' time.

'I shall long to come back to England,' Stringham said. 'Not that I specially favour the idea of universities. Undergraduates all look so wizened, and suède shoes appear to be compulsory.'

Berkeley Square, as I drove through it, was cold and bright and remote: like Buster's manner. I wondered how it would be to return to school with only the company of Templer for the following year; because there was no one else with any claim to take Stringham's place, so that Templer and I would be left alone together. Stringham's removal was going to alter the orientation of everyday life. I found a place in a crowded compartment, next to the engine, beside an elderly man wearing a check suit, who, for the whole journey, quarrelled quietly with a clergyman on the subject of opening the window, kept on taking down a dispatch-case from the rack and rummaging through it for papers that never seemed to be there, and in a general manner reminded me of the goings-on of Uncle Giles.

Uncle Giles's affairs had, in fact, moved recently towards something like a climax. After nearly two years of silence—since the moment when he had disappeared into the fog, supposedly on his way to Reading—nothing had been heard of him; until one day a letter had arrived, headed with the address of an hotel in the Isle of Man, the contents of which implied, though did not state, that he intended to get married. In anticipation of this contingency, my uncle advocated a thorough overhaul of the conditions of the Trust; and expressed, not for the first time, the difficulties that lay in the path of a man without influence.

This news caused my parents some anxiety; for, although Uncle Giles's doings during the passage of time that had taken place were unknown in detail, his connection with

Reading had been established, with fair certainty, to be the result of an association with a lady who lived there: some said a manicurist: others the widow of a garage-proprietor. There was, indeed, no reason why she should not have sustained both rôles. The topic was approached in the family circle with even more gloom, and horrified curiosity, than Uncle Giles's activities usually aroused: misgiving being not entirely groundless, since Uncle Giles was known to be almost as indiscriminate in dealings with the opposite sex as he was unreliable in business negotiation. His first serious misadventure, when stationed in Egypt as a young man, had, indeed, centred upon a love affair.

It was one of Uncle Giles's chief complaints that he had been 'put' into the army—for which he possessed neither Mrs. Foxe's romantic admiration nor her hard-headed grasp of military realities—instead of entering some unspecified profession in which his gifts would have been properly valued. He had begun his soldiering in a line regiment: later, with a view to being slightly better paid, exchanging into the Army Service Corps. I used to imagine him wearing a pill-box cap on the side of his head, making assignations under a sub-tropical sun with a beautiful lady dressed in a bustle and sitting in an open carriage driven by a coloured coachman; though such attire, as a matter of fact, belonged to a somewhat earlier period; and, even if circumstances resembled this picture in other respects, the chances were, on the whole, that assignations would be made, and kept, 'in mufti'.

There had been, in fact, two separate rows, which somehow became entangled together: somebody's wife, and somebody else's money: to say nothing of debts. At one stage, so some of his relations alleged, there had even been question of court-martial: not so much to incriminate my unfortunate uncle as to clear his name of some of the rumours in circulation. The court-martial, perhaps fortunately, was never convened, but the necessity for Uncle Giles to send in his papers was unquestioned. He travelled home by South Africa, arriving in Cape Town a short time before the outbreak of hostilities with the Boers. In that town he made undesirable friends—no doubt also encountering at this period Mrs. Foxe's father—and engaged in unwise transactions regarding the marketing of diamonds: happily not involving on his part any handling of the stones themselves. This venture ended almost disastrously; and, owing to the attitude taken up by the local authorities, he was unable to settle in Port Elizabeth, where he had once thought of earning a living. However, like most untrustworthy persons, Uncle Giles had the gift of inspiring confidence in a great many people with whom he came in contact. Even those who, to their cost, had known him for years, sometimes found difficulty in estimating the lengths to which he could carry his lack of reliability—and indeed sheer incapacity—in matters of business. When he returned to England he was therefore seldom out of a job, though usually, in his own words, 'starting at the bottom' on an ascent from which great things were to be expected.

In 1914 he had tried to get back into the army, but his services were declined for medical reasons by the War Office. Not long after the sinking of the Lusitania he obtained a post in the Ministry of Munitions; later transferring himself to the Ministry of Food, from which he eventually resigned without scandal. When the United States entered the war he contrived to find some sort of a job in the provinces at a depot formed for supplying 'comforts' to American troops. He had let it be known that he had made business connexions on the other side of the Atlantic, as a result of this employment. That was why there had been a suggestion—in which wish may have been father to thought in the minds of his relations—that he might take up a commercial post in Philadelphia. The letter from the Isle of Man, with its hint of impending marriage, seemed to indicate that any idea of emigration, if ever in existence, had been abandoned; whilst references throughout its several pages to 'lack of influence' brought matters back to an earlier, and more fundamental, stage in my uncle's presentation of his affairs.

This business of 'influence' was one that played a great part in Uncle Giles's philosophy of life. It was an article of faith with him that all material advancement in the world was the result of influence, a mysterious attribute with which he invested, to a greater or lesser degree, every human being on earth except himself. That the rich and nobly born automatically enjoyed an easy time of it through influence was, of course, axiomatic; and—as society moved from an older order—anybody who might have claims to be considered, at least outwardly, of the poor and lowly was also included by him among those dowered with this almost magic appanage. In cases such as that of the window-cleaner, or the man who came to read the gas-meter, the advantage enjoyed was accounted to less obvious—but, in fact, superior—opportunity for bettering position in an increasingly egalitarian world. '*That* door was banged-to for me at birth,' Uncle Giles used to say (in a phrase that I found, much later, he had lifted from a novel by John Galsworthy) when some plum was mentioned, conceived by him available only to those above, or below, him in the social scale.

It might be imagined that people of the middle sort—people, in other words, like Uncle Giles himself—though he would have been unwilling to admit his attachment to any recognisable social group, could be regarded by him as substantially in the same boat. Nothing could be farther from the truth. Such persons belonged to the class, above all others, surveyed with misgiving by him, because members of it possessed, almost without exception, either powerful relations who helped them on in an underhand way, or business associations, often formed through less affluent relations, which enabled them—or so he suspected—to buy things cheap. Any mention of the City, or, worse still, the Stock Exchange, drove him to hard words. Moreover, the circumstances of people of this kind were often declared by him to be such that they did not have to 'keep up the same standards' in the community as those that tradition imposed upon Uncle Giles himself; and, having thus secured an unfair advantage, they were one and all abhorrent to him.

As a result of this creed he was unconquerably opposed to all established institutions on the grounds that they were entirely—and therefore incapably—administered by persons whose sole claim to consideration was that they could command influence. His own phrase for describing briefly this approach to all social, political and economic questions was 'being a bit of a radical': a standpoint he was at pains to make abundantly clear to all with whom he came in contact. As it happened, he always seemed to find people who would put up with him; and, usually, people who would employ him. In fact, at his own level, he must have had more 'influence' than most persons. He did not, however, answer the enquiries, and counter-proposals, put forward in a reply to his letter sent to the address in the Isle of Man; and, for the time being, no more was heard of his marriage, or any other of his activities.

Settling down with Templer at school was easier than I had expected. Without Stringham, he was more expansive, and I began to hear something of his life at home. His father and uncle (the latter of whom—for public services somewhat vaguely specified—had accepted a baronetcy at the hands of Lloyd George, one of the few subjects upon which Templer showed himself at all sensitive) had made their money in cement. Mr. Templer had retired from business fairly recently, after what his son called 'an appalling bloomer over steel.' There were two sisters: Babs, the eldest of the family, who towards the end of the war had left a husband in one of the dragoon regiments in favour of a racing motorist; and Jean, slightly younger than her brother. Their mother had died some years before I came across Templer, who displayed no photographs of his family, so that I knew nothing of their appearance. Although not colossally rich, they were certainly not poor; and whatever lack of appreciation Peter's father may at one moment have shown regarding predictable fluctuations of his own holdings in the steel industry, he still took a friendly interest in the market; and, by Peter's account, seemed quite often to guess right. I also knew that they lived in a house by the sea.

'Personally I wouldn't mind having a look at Kenya,' said Templer, when I described the luncheon with Stringham and his mother.

'Stringham didn't seem to care for the idea.'

'My elder sister had a beau who lived in the Happy Valley. He shot himself after having a lot of drinks at the club.'

'Perhaps it won't be so bad then.'

'Did you lunch with them in London or the country?'

'London.'

'Stringham says Glimber is pretty, but too big.'

'Will he come into it?'

'Good Lord, no,' said Templer. 'It is only his mother's

for life. He will come into precious little if she goes on spending money at her present rate.'

I was not sure how much of this was to be believed; but, thinking the subject of interest, enquired further. Templer sketched in a somewhat lurid picture of Mrs. Foxe and her set. I was rather surprised to find that he himself had no ambition to become a member of that world, the pleasures of which sounded of a kind particularly to appeal to him.

'Too much of a good thing,' he said. 'I have simpler tastes.'

I was reminded of Stringham's disparagement of Buster on the ground that he was 'too grand'; and also of the reservations he had expressed regarding Templer himself. Clearly some complicated process of sorting-out was in progress among those who surrounded me: though only years later did I become aware how early such voluntary segregations begin to develop; and of how they continue throughout life. I asked more questions about Templer's objection to house-parties at Glimber. He said: 'Well, I imagine it was all rather pompous even at lunch, wasn't it?'

'Buster seemed rather an ass. His mother was awfully nice.'

Even at the time I felt that the phrase was not a very adequate way of describing Mrs. Foxe's forceful, even dazzling, characteristics.

'Oh, she is all right, I have no doubt,' said Templer. 'And damned good-looking still. She gave Stringham's sister absolute hell, though, until she married the first chap that came along.'

'Who was he?'

'I can't remember his name. A well-known criminal with one arm.'

'Stringham certainly seemed in bad form when she was there.'

'She led his father a dance, too.'

'Still, he need not join in all that if he doesn't want to.'

'He will want to,' said Templer. 'Take my word for it, he will soon disappear from sight so far as we are concerned.'

Armed, as I have said, with the knowledge of Stringham's admission regarding his own views on Templer, I recognised that there must be some truth in this judgment of Stringham's character; though some of its implications—notably with regard to myself—I failed, rather naturally, to grasp at that period. That was the only occasion when I ever heard Templer speak seriously about Stringham, though he often used to refer to escapades in which they had shared, especially the incident of Le Bas's arrest.

So far as Templer and I were concerned, nothing further had taken place regarding this affair; though Templer's relations with Le Bas continued to be strained. Although so little involved personally in the episode, I found myself often thinking of it. Why, for example, should Stringham, singularly good-natured, have chosen to persecute Le Bas in this manner? Was it a matter for regret or congratulation: had it, indeed, any meaning at all? The circumstances revealed at once Stringham's potential assurance, and the inadequacy of Le Bas's defences. If Stringham had been brutal, Le Bas had been futile. In spite of his advocacy of the poem, Le Bas had not learnt its lesson:

> 'And then we turn unwilling feet
> And seek the world—so must it be—
> *We* may not linger in the heat
> Where breaks the blue Sicilian sea!'

He was known for a long time after as 'Braddock alias Thorne', especially among his colleagues, whose theory was that the hoaxer had recently left the school, and, while passing through the town, probably in a car, had decided to tease Le Bas. Certainly Stringham would never have been thought capable of such an enormity by any master who had ever come in contact with him. Not unnaturally, however, Le Bas's tendency to feel that the world was against him was accentuated by an experience in many ways humiliating enough; and he persecuted Templer—or, at least, his activities in this direction were represented by Templer as persecution—more energetically than ever.

Finally Templer's habitual carelessness gave Le Bas an opportunity to close the account. This conclusion was the result of Templer leaving his tobacco pouch—on which, characteristically, he had inscribed his initials—lying on the trunk of a tree somewhere among the fields where we had happened on Le Bas. Cobberton, scouting round that neighbourhood, had found the pouch, and passed it on to Le Bas. Nothing definite could be proved against Templer: not even the ownership of a half-filled tobacco pouch, though no one doubted it was his. However, Le Bas moved heaven and earth to be rid of Templer, eventually persuading the headmaster to the view that life would be easier for both of them if Templer left the school. In consequence, Peter's father was persuaded to remove him a term earlier than previously intended. This pleased Templer himself, and did not unduly ruffle his father; who was reported to take the view that schools and universities were, in any case, waste of time and money: on the principle that an office was the place in which to learn the realities of life. And so I was left, as it seemed to me, alone.

Templer was not a great hand at letter-writing after his departure; though an occasional picture post-card used to arrive, stating his score at the local golf tournament, or saying that he was going to Holland to learn business methods.

Before he left school, he had suggested several times that I should visit his home, always qualifying his account of the amusements there offered by a somewhat menacing picture of his father's habitually cantankerous behaviour. I did not take these warnings about his father too seriously because of Templer's tendency to impute bad temper to anyone placed in a position of authority in relation to himself. At the same time, I had the impression that Mr. Templer might be a difficult man to live with; I even thought it possible that Peter's dealings with Le Bas might derive from experience of similar skirmishes with his father. Peter's chief complaint, so far as his father was concerned, seemed directed not towards any violent disagreement between them in tastes, or way of life, so much as to the fact that his father, in control of so much more money than himself, showed in his son's eyes on the whole so little capacity for putting this favourable situation to a suitable advantage. 'Wait till you see the car we have to use for station work,' Peter used to say. 'Then you will understand what sort of a man my father is.'

The invitation arrived just when the mechanical accessories of leaving school were in full swing. Later in the summer it had been arranged that, before going up to the university, I should spend a period in France; partly with a view to learning the language: partly as a solution to that urgent problem—inviting one's own as much as other people's attention—of the disposal of the body of one of those uneasy, stranded beings, no longer a boy and hardly yet a man. The Templer visit could be fitted in before the French trip took place.

Stringham's letters from Kenya reported that he liked the place better than he had expected. They contained drawings of people met there, and of a horse he sometimes rode. He could not really draw at all, but used a convention of blobs and spidery lines, effective in expressing the appearance of persons and things. One of these was of Buster selling a car; another of Buster playing polo. I used to think sometimes of the glimpse I had seen of Stringham's life at home; and—although this did not occur to me at once—I came in time to regard his circumstances as having something in common with those of Hamlet. His father had, of course, been shipped off to Kenya rather than murdered; but Buster and his mother were well adapted to play the parts of Claudius and Gertrude. I did not manage to get far beyond this, except to wonder if Miss Weedon was a kind of female Polonius, working on Hamlet's side. I could well imagine Stringham stabbing her through the arras. At present there was no Ophelia. Stringham himself had a decided resemblance to the Prince of Denmark; or, as Templer would have said: 'It was the kind of part the old boy would fancy himself in.'

At first sight the Templers' house seemed to be an enormously swollen villa, red and gabled, facing the sea from a small park of Scotch firs: a residence torn by some occult power from more appropriate suburban setting, and, at the same time, much magnified. It must have been built about twenty or thirty years before, and, as we came along the road, I saw that it stood on a piece of sloping ground set about a quarter of a mile from the cliff's edge. The clouded horizon and olive-green waves lapping against the stones made it a place of mystery in spite of this outwardly banal appearance: a sea-palace for a version of one of those embarkation scenes of Claude Lorraine—the Queen of Sheba, St. Ursula, or perhaps The Enchanted Castle—where any adventure might be expected.

There were a pair of white gates at the entrance to the drive, and a steep, sandy ascent between laurels. At the summit, the green doors of a row of garages faced a cement platform. As we drove across this open space a girl of about sixteen or seventeen, evidently Peter's unmarried sister, Jean, was closing one of the sliding doors. Fair, not strikingly pretty, with long legs and short untidy hair, she remained without moving, intently watching us, as Peter shut off the engine, and we got out of the car. Like her legs, her face was thin and attenuated, the whole appearance given the effect of a much simplified—and somewhat self-conscious—arrangement of lines and planes, such as might be found in an Old Master drawing, Flemish or German perhaps, depicting some young and virginal saint; the racquet, held awkwardly at an angle to her body, suggesting at the same time an obscure implement associated with martyrdom. The expression of her face, although sad and a trifle ironical, was not altogether in keeping with this air of belonging to another and better world. I felt suddenly uneasy, and also interested: a desire to be with her, and at the same time, an almost paralysing disquiet at her presence. However, any hopes or fears orientated in her direction were quickly dissolved, because she hardly spoke when Peter introduced us, except to say in a voice unexpectedly deep, and almost as harsh as her brother's: 'The hard court needs re-surfacing.'

Then she walked slowly towards the house, humming to herself, and swinging her racquet at the grass borders. Peter shouted after her: 'Has Sunny arrived yet?'

'He turned up just after you left.'

She made this answer without turning her head. It conveyed no implication of disapproval; no enthusiasm either. I watched her disappear from sight.

'Leave your stuff here,' said Peter. 'Someone is bound to collect it. Let's have some tea. What bloody bad manners my sisters have.'

Wearing a soft felt hat squashed down in the shape of a pork-pie, he already showed signs of having freed himself from whatever remaining restraints school had imposed. He had spent a month or two in Amsterdam, where his father had business interests. Mr. Templer's notion was that Peter should gain in this way some smattering of commercial life before going into the City; as all further idea of educating or improving his son had now been abandoned by him. Peter could give no very coherent account of Dutch life, except to say that the canals smelt bad, and that there were two night-clubs which were much better than the others in that city. Apart from such slightly increased emphasis on characteristics already in evidence, he was quite unchanged.

'Who is Sunny?'

'He is called Sunny Farebrother, a friend of my father's. He was staying in the neighbourhood for a funeral and has come over to talk business.'

'Your father's contemporary?'

'Oh, no,' said Peter. 'Much younger. Thirty or thirty-five. He is supposed to have done well in the war. At least I believe he got rather a good D.S.O.'

The name 'Sunny Farebrother' struck me as almost redundant in its suggestion of clear-cut, straightforward masculinity. It seemed hardly necessary for Peter to add that someone with a name like that had 'done well' in the war, so unambiguous was the portrait conjured up by the syllables. I imagined a kind of super-Buster, in whom qualities of intrepidity and simplicity of heart had been added to those of dash and glitter.

'Why is he called Sunny?' I asked, expecting some confirmation of this imaginary personality with which I had invested Mr. Farebrother.

'Because his Christian name is Sunderland,' said Peter. 'I

expect we shall have to listen to a lot of pretty boring conversation between the two of them.'

We entered the house at a side door. The walls of the greater part of the ground floor were faced with panelling, coloured and grained like a cigar-box. At the end of a large hall two men were sitting on a sofa by a tea-table at which Jean was pouring out cups of tea. The elder of this couple, a wiry, grim little fellow, almost entirely bald, and smoking a pipe, was obviously Peter's father. His identity was emphasised by the existence of a portrait of himself hanging on the wall above him—the only picture in the room—representing its subject in a blue suit and hard white collar. The canvas, from the hand of Isbister, the R.A., had been tackled in a style of decidedly painful realism, the aggressive nature of the pigment intensified by the fact that each feature had been made to appear a little larger than life.

'Hullo, Jenkins,' said Mr. Templer, raising his hand. 'Have some tea. Pour him out some tea, Jean. Well, go on, Farebrother—but try and stick to the point this time.'

He turned again to the tall, dark man sitting beside him. This person, Sunny Farebrother presumably, had shaken hands warmly, and given a genial smile when I approached the table. At Mr. Templer's interpellation, this smile faded from his face in a flash, being replaced by a look of almost devotional intensity; and, letting drop my hand with startling suddenness, he returned to what seemed to be a specification of the terms and bearings of a foreign loan—apparently Hungarian—which he and Mr. Templer had evidently been discussing before our arrival. Jean handed me the plate of buttered toast, and, addressing herself to Peter, spoke once more of the hard tennis court.

During tea I had an opportunity of examining Sunny Farebrother more closely. His regular features and ascetic, serious manner did remind me in some way of Buster, curiously enough: though scarcely for the reasons I had expected. In spite of neatness and general air of being well-dressed, Farebrother had none of Buster's consciously reckless manner of facing the world; while, so far from dispensing anything that might be interpreted as an attitude of indirect hostility, his demeanour—even allowing for the demands of a proper respect for a man older than himself and at the same time his host—appeared to be almost unnecessarily ingratiating. I was not exactly disappointed with the reality of someone whose outward appearance I had, rather absurdly, settled already in my mind on such slender grounds; but I was surprised, continuing to feel that I should like to know more of Sunny Farebrother.

The train of thought engendered by this association with Buster took me on, fairly logically, to Miss Weedon; and, for a second, it even occurred to me that some trait possessed in common by Buster and Miss Weedon linked both of them with Sunny Farebrother; the two latter being the most alike, ridiculous as it might sound, of the three. This was certainly not on account of any suggestion, open or inadequately concealed, that Farebrother's temperament was feminine in any abnormal manner, either physically or emotionally; on the contrary; though Miss Weedon for her part might perhaps lay claim to some remotely masculine air. It was rather that both had in common some smoothness, an acceptance that their mission in life was to iron out the difficulties of others: a recognition that, for them, power was won by self-abasement.

Sunny Farebrother's suit, though well cut, was worn and a trifle dilapidated in places. The elbows of the coat were shiny, and, indeed, his whole manner suggested that he might be in distinctly straitened circumstances. I imagined him a cavalryman—something about his long legs and narrow trousers suggested horses—unable to support the expenses of his regiment, unwillingly become a stockbroker, or agent for some firm in the City, in an attempt to make two ends meet; though I learnt later that he had never been a regular soldier. With folded hands and head bent, he was listening, attentively, humbly—almost as if his life depended on it—to the words that Mr. Templer was speaking.

Years later, when I came to know Sunny Farebrother pretty well, he always retained for me something of this first picture of him; a vision—like Jean's—that suggested an almost saintly figure, ill-used by a coarse-grained world: some vague and uncertain parallel with Colonel Newcome came to mind, in the colonel's latter days in the Greyfriars almshouses, and it was easy to imagine Mr. Farebrother answering his name in such a setting, the last rays of sunset falling across his, by then, whitened hair. Everything about him supported claims to such a rôle: from the frayed ends of the evening tie that he wore later at dinner, to the immensely battered leather hat-box that was carried through the hall with the rest of his luggage while we sat at tea. He seemed to feel some explanation for the existence of this last object was required, saying that it contained the top-hat he had recently worn at his great-uncle's funeral, adding that it was the headgear that normally hung on a hook in his office for use as part of the uniform of his calling in the City.

'It cost me a tidy sum in lost business to pay that last tribute,' he said. 'But there aren't many of that grand old fellow's sort left these days. I felt I ought to do it.'

Mr. Templer, his hands deep in his trousers pockets, took scarcely any notice of such asides. He discoursed instead, in a rasping undertone, of redemption dates and capital requirements. Jean finished what she had to say to Peter regarding the hard tennis court, then scarcely spoke at all. Later she went off on her own.

This introduction to the Templer household was fairly representative of its prevailing circumstances for the next few days. Mr. Templer was gruff, and talked business most of the time to Sunny Farebrother: Jean kept to herself: Peter and I bathed, or lounged away the day. I discovered that Peter's account of his lack of accord with his father had been much exaggerated. In reality, they understood each other well, and had, indeed, a great deal in common. Mr. Templer possessed a few simple ideas upon which he had organised his life; and, on the whole, these ideas had served him well, largely because they fitted in with each other, and were of sufficiently general application to be correct perhaps nine times out of ten. He was very keen on keeping fit, and liked to describe in detail exercises he was in the habit of performing when he first rose from his bed in the morning. He was always up and about the house long before anyone else was awake, and he certainly looked healthy, though not young for his age, which was somewhere in the sixties. Sunny Farebrother continued to impress me as unusually agreeable; and I could not help wondering why he was treated by the Templers with so little consideration. I do not mean that, in fact, I gave much thought to this matter; but I noticed from time to time that he seemed almost to enjoy being contradicted by Mr. Templer, or ignored by Jean, whom he used to survey rather hungrily, and attempt, without much success, to engage in conversation. In this, as other respects, Jean remained in her somewhat separate world. Peter used to tease her about this air of existing remote from everything that went on round her. I continued to experience a sense of being at once drawn to her, and yet cut off from her utterly.

The party was increased a few days after my arrival by

the addition of the Striplings—that is to say Peter's married sister, Babs, and her husband, the racing motorist—who brought with them a friend called Lady McReith. These new guests radically altered the tone of the house. Babs was good-looking, with reddish fair hair, and she talked a lot, and rather loudly. She was taller than Jean, without her sister's mysterious, even melancholy, presence. Sitting next to her at dinner there was none of the difficulty that I used to experience in getting some scraps of conversation from Jean. Babs seemed very attached to Peter and asked many questions about his life at school. Her husband, Jimmy Stripling, was tall and burly. He wore his hair rather long and parted in the middle. Like his father-in-law he was gruff in manner, and always looked beyond, rather than at, the person he was talking to. Uncle Giles was, at that period, the only grumbler I had ever met at all comparable in volume: though Stripling, well-equipped financially for his pursuit of motor-racing, had little else in common with my uncle.

It is not unusual for people who look exceptionally robust, and who indulge in hobbies of a comparatively dangerous kind, to suffer from poor health. Stripling belonged to this category. On that account he had been unable to take an active part in the war; unless—as Peter had remarked—persuading Babs to run away with him while her husband was at the front might be regarded as Jimmy having 'done his bit'. This was no doubt an unkind way of referring to what had happened; and, if Peter's own account of Babs's early married life was to be relied upon, there was at least something to be said on her side, as her first husband, whatever his merits as a soldier, had been a far from ideal husband. It was, however, unfortunate from Stripling's point of view that his forerunner's conduct had been undeniably gallant; and this fact had left him with a consuming hatred for all who had served in the armed forces. Indeed, anyone who mentioned, even casually, any matter that reminded him that a war had taken place was liable to be treated by him in a most peremptory manner; although, at the same time, all his topics of conversation seemed, sooner or later, to lead to this subject. His state of mind was perhaps the outcome of too many persons like Peter having made the joke about 'doing his bit'. In consequence of this attitude he gave an impression of marked hostility towards Sunny Farebrother.

In spite of the circumstances of their marriage, outward relations between the Striplings were cool, almost formal; and the link which seemed most firmly to bind them together was, in some curious manner, vested in the person of their friend Lady McReith, known as 'Gwen', a figure whose origins and demeanour suggested enigmas that I could not, in those days, even attempt to fathom. In the first place I could form no idea of her age. When she came into the room on their arrival, I thought she was a contemporary of Jean's: this was only for a few seconds, and immediately after I supposed her to be nine or ten years older; but one afternoon, strolling across the lawn from tennis, when the air had turned suddenly cold and a chilly breeze from the sea had swept across the grass, she had shivered and changed colour, her face becoming grey and mottled, almost as if it were an old woman's. She was tall, though slightly built, with dark hair over a fair skin, beneath which the veins showed: her lips always bright red. Something about her perhaps hinted vaguely of the stage, or at least what I imagined theatrical people to be like. This fair skin with the blue veins running across had a look of extraordinary softness.

'She was married to a partner of my father's,' Peter said, when questioned. 'He had a stroke and died ten days after he was knighted—a remarkable instance of delayed shock.'

Although appearing to accept her as in some manner necessary for the well-being of their household, Jimmy Stripling seemed less devoted than his wife to Lady McReith. There was a certain amount of ragging between them, and Stripling liked scoring off her in conversation: though, for that matter, he liked scoring off anyone. Babs, on the other hand, seemed never tired of walking about the lawn, or through the rose garden, arm in arm with Lady McReith; and demonstrative kissing took place between them at the slightest provocation.

Lady McReith was also on excellent terms with the Templer family, especially Peter. Even Mr. Templer himself sometimes took her arm, and led her into dinner, or towards the drink tray in the evening. Sunny Farebrother, however, evidently regarded her without approval, though he was always scrupulously polite: so much so that Lady McReith was often unable to do more than go off into peals of uncontrollable laughter when addressed by him: the habit of giggling being one of her most pronounced characteristics. Personally, I found her rather alarming, chiefly because she talked, when she spoke at all, of people and things I had never heard of. The Striplings were always laughing noisily at apparently pointless remarks made by her on the subject of acquaintances possessed by them in common. Apart from this banter, she had little or nothing to say for herself; and, unlike Jean, her silences suggested to me no hidden depths. Mr. Templer used to say: 'Come on, Gwen, try and behave for once as if you were grown-up,' a request always followed by such immoderate fits of laughter from Lady McReith that she was left almost helpless. At dinner there would be exchanges between herself and Peter:

'Why aren't you wearing a clean shirt tonight, Peter?'

'I thought this one would be clean enough for you.'

'You ought to keep your little brother up to the mark, Babs.'

'He is always very grubby, isn't he?'

'What about those decomposing lip-sticks Gwen is always leaving about the house? They make the place look like the ladies' cloak-room in a third-rate night-club.'

'Do you spend much of your time in the ladies' cloak-rooms of third-rate night-clubs, Peter? What a funny boy you must be.'

Sunny Farebrother gave the impression of being not at all at his ease in the midst of this rough-and-tumble, in which he was to some degree forced to participate. Mr. Templer fell from time to time into fits of moroseness which made his small-talk at best monosyllabic: at worst, drying up all conversation. He treated his son-in-law with as little ceremony as he did Farebrother; evidently regarding the discussion of serious matters with Stripling as waste of time. He was, however, prepared to listen to Farebrother's views—apparently sensible enough—on how best to handle the difficulties of French reoccupation of the Ruhr (which had taken place earlier in the year), especially in relation to the general question of the shortage of pig-iron on the world market. When on one occasion Farebrother ventured to change the subject and give his opinion regarding professional boxing, Mr. Templer went so far as to say: 'Farebrother, you are talking through your hat. When you have watched boxing for forty years, as I have, it will be quite soon enough to start criticising the stewards of the National Sporting.'

Sunny Farebrother showed no sign of resenting this capricious treatment. He would simply nod his head, and chuckle to himself, as if in complete agreement; after a while giving up any attempt to soothe his host, and trying to join in whatever was happening at the other end of the table. It was at such moments that he sometimes became involved in cross-fire between Peter, Lady McReith, and the Striplings. I was not sure how often the Striplings had met Sunny Farebrother in the past. Each seemed to know a good deal about the other, though they remained on distant terms, Stripling making hardly an effort to conceal his dislike. They would sometimes talk about City matters, in which Stripling took an interest that was probably of a rather amateurish sort; for it was clear that Farebrother rarely agreed with his judgment, even when he outwardly concurred. After these mild contradictions, Stripling would raise his eyebrows and make faces at Farebrother behind his back. Farebrother showed no more sign of being troubled by this kind of behaviour than by Mr. Templer's gruffness; but he sometimes adopted a manner of exaggerated good-fellowship towards Stripling, beginning sentences addressed to him with the words: 'Now then, Jimmy——': and sometimes making a sweeping dive with his fist towards Stripling's diaphragm, as if in a playful effort to disembowel him. It was not Stripling so much as Lady McReith, and, to a lesser degree, Babs, who seemed to make Farebrother uncomfortable. I decided—as it turned out, correctly—that this was a kind of moral disapproval, and that some puritan strain in Farebrother rebelled against Lady McReith especially.

One evening, when Mr. Templer had come suddenly out of one of his gloomy reveries, and nodded curtly to Babs to withdraw the women from the dining-room, Sunny Farebrother jumped up to open the door, and, in the regrouping of seats that took place when we sat down again, placed himself next to me. The Templers, father and son, had begun to discuss with Stripling the jamming of his car's accelerator. Farebrother shifted the port in my direction, without pouring himself out a second glass. He said: 'Did I understand that your father was at the Peace Conference?'

'For a time.'

'I wonder if he and I were ever in the same show.'

I described to the best of my ability how my father had been wounded in Mesopotamia; and, after a spell of duty in Cairo, had been sent to Paris at the end of the war: adding that I was not very certain of the nature of his work. Farebrother seemed disappointed that no details were available on this subject; but he continued to chat quietly of the Conference, and of the people he had run across when he had worked there himself.

'Wonderfully *interesting* people, he said. 'After a time one thought nothing of lunching with, for example, a former Finance Minister of Rumania, as a matter of fact we reached the stage of my calling him "Hilarion" and he calling me "Sunny". I met Monsieur Venizelos with him on several occasions.'

I expressed the respect that I certainly felt for an appointment that brought opportunity to enjoy such encounters.

'It was a different world,' said Sunny Farebrother.

He spoke with more vehemence than usual; and I supposed that he intended to imply that hobnobbing with foreign statesmen was greatly preferable to touting for business from Peter's father. I asked if the work was difficult.

'When they were kind enough to present me with an O.B.E. at the end of it,' said Farebrother, 'I told them I should have to wear it on my backside because it was the only medal I had ever won by sitting in a chair.'

I did not know whether it was quite my place either to approve or to deprecate this unconventional hypothesis, daring in its disregard for authority (if 'they' were superiors immediately responsible for the conferment of the award) and, at the same time, modest in its assessment of its expositor's personal merits. Sunny Farebrother had the happy gift of suggesting by his manner that one had known him for a long time; and I began to wonder whether I had not, after all, been right in supposing that his nickname had been acquired from something more than having been named 'Sunderland'. There was a suggestion of boyishness—the word 'sunny' would certainly be applicable—about his frank manner; but, in spite of this manifest desire to get along with everyone on their own terms, there was also something lonely and inaccessible about him. It seemed to me, equally, that I had not been so greatly mistaken in the high-flown estimate of his qualities that I had formed on first hearing his name, and of his distinguished record. However, before any pronouncement became necessary on the subject of the most appropriate region on which to distribute what I imagined to be his many decorations, his voice took on a more serious note, and he went on: 'The Conference was, of course, a great change from the previous three and a half years, fighting backwards and forwards over the Somme and God knows where else—and fighting damned hard, too.'

Jimmy Stripling caught the word 'Somme', because his mouth twitched slightly, and he began chopping at a piece of pine-apple rind on his plate: though continuing to listen to his father-in-law's diagnosis of the internal troubles of the Mercedes.

'Going up to the university?' Farebrother asked.

'In October.'

'Take my advice,' he said. 'Look about for a good business opening. Don't be afraid of hard work. That was what I said to myself when the war was over—and here we are.'

He laughed; and I laughed too, though without knowing quite why anything should have been said to cause amusement. Farebrother had the knack, so it seemed to me, of making others feel that they were in some conspiracy with him; though clearly that was not how he was regarded by the Striplings. When Peter had asked the day before: 'What do you think of old Sunny?' I had admitted that Farebrother had made a good impression as a man-of-the-world who was at the same time mild and well disposed: though I had not phrased my opinion quite in that way to Peter, in any case never greatly interested in the details of what people thought about each other. Peter had laughed even at the guarded amount of enthusiasm I had revealed.

'He is a downy old bird,' Peter said.

'Is he very hard up?'

'I suppose he is doing just about as nicely in the City as anyone could reasonably expect.'

'I thought he looked a bit down at heel?'

'That is all part of Sunny's line. You need not worry about him. I may be going into the same firm. He is a sort of distant relation, you know, through my mother's family.'

'He and Jimmy Stripling don't care for each other much, do they?'

'To tell the truth, we all pull Sunny's leg when he comes down here,' said Peter. 'He'll stand anything because he likes picking my father's brains, such as they are.'

This picture of Sunny Farebrother did not at all agree with that which I had formed in my own mind; and I should probably have been more shocked at the idea of teasing him if I had entirely believed all Peter had been saying. The fact that I was not prepared fully to accept his commentary was partly because I knew by experience that he was in the habit of exaggerating about such matters: and, even more, because at that age (although one may be prepared to swallow all kinds of nonsense of this sort or that) personal assessment of individuals made by oneself is hard to shake: even when offered by those in a favourable position to know what they are talking about. Besides, I could hardly credit the statement that Peter himself—even abetted by Jimmy Stripling—would have the temerity to rag someone who looked like Sunny Farebrother, and had his war record. However, later on in the same evening on which we had talked together about the Peace Conference, I was given further insight into the methods by which the Stripling-Farebrother conflict was carried on.

Mr. Templer always retired early. That night he went upstairs soon after we had left the dining-room. Jean had complained of a headache, and she also slipped off to bed. Jimmy Stripling was lying in an armchair with his legs stretched out in front of him. He was an inch or two over six foot, already getting a bit fleshy, always giving the impression of taking up more than his fair share of room, wherever he might be standing or sitting. Farebrother was reading *The Times,* giving the sports page that special rapt attention that he applied to everything he did. Babs and Lady McReith were sitting on the sofa, looking at the same illustrated paper. Farebrother came to the end of the column, and before putting aside the paper shook down the sheets with his accustomed tidiness of habit to make a level edge. He strolled across the room to where Peter was looking through some gramophone records, and I heard him say: 'When you come to work in London, Peter, I should strongly recommend you to get hold of a little gadget I make use of. It turns your collars, and reduces laundry bills by fifty per cent.'

I did not catch Peter's reply; but, although Farebrother had spoken quietly, Stripling had noticed this recommendation. Rolling round in his chair, he said: 'What is that about cutting down your laundry bill, Sunny?'

'Nothing to interest a gentleman of leisure like yourself, Jimmy,' said Farebrother, 'but we poor City blokes find it comes pretty hard on white collars. They have now invented a little patent device for turning them. As a matter of fact a small company has been formed to put it on the market.'

'And I suppose you are one of the directors,' said Stripling.

'As a matter of fact I am,' said Farebrother. 'There are one or two other little odds and ends as well; but the collar-turner is going to be the winner in my opinion.'

'You thought you could plant one on Peter?'

'If Peter has got any sense he'll get one.'

'Why not tackle someone of your own size?'

'I'll plant one on you, Jimmy, once you see it work.'

'I bet you don't.'

'You get some collars then.'

The end of it was that both of them went off to their respective rooms, Stripling returning with a round leather collar-box; Farebrother with a machine that looked like a pair of horse-clippers made from wood. All this was accompanied with a great deal of jocularity on Stripling's part. He came downstairs again first, and assured us that 'Old Sunny's leg was going to be well and truly pulled'. Babs and Lady McReith now began to show some interest in what was going on. They threw aside *The Tatler* and each put up her feet on the sofa. Farebrother stood in the centre of the room holding the wooden clippers. He said: 'Now you give me one of your collars, Jimmy.'

The round leather box was opened, and a collar was inserted into the jaws of the machine. Farebrother closed the contraption forward along the edge of the collar. After proceeding about two inches, there was a ripping sound, and the collar tore. It was extracted with difficulty. Everyone roared with laughter.

'What did I say?' said Stripling.

'Sorry, Jimmy,' said Farebrother. 'That collar must have been washed too often.'

'But it was practically new,' said Stripling. 'You did it the wrong way.'

Stripling chose a collar, and himself ran the clippers along it. They slipped from his grip half-way down, so that the collar was caused to fold more or less diagonally.

'Your collars are a different shape from mine,' Farebrother said. 'They don't seem to have the same "give" in them.'

Farebrother had another try, with results rather similar to his first attempt; and, after that, everyone insisted on making the experiment. The difficulty consisted in holding the instrument tight and, at the same time, running it straight. Babs and Lady McReith both crumpled their collars: Peter and I tore ours on the last inch or so of the run. Then Farebrother tried again, bringing off a perfect turn.

'There you are,' he said. 'What could be better than that?'

However, as three collars were ruined and had to be thrown into the waste-paper basket, and three more had to be sent to the laundry, Stripling was not very pleased. Although the utility of Farebrother's collar-turner had certainly been called into question, he evidently felt that to some extent the joke had been turned against him.

'It is something about your collars, old boy,' Farebrother repeated. 'It is not at all easy to make the thing work on them. It might pay you in the long run to get a more expensive kind.'

'They are damned expensive as it is,' said Stripling. 'Anyway, quite expensive enough to have been made hay of like this.'

However, everyone, including his wife, had laughed a

great deal throughout the various efforts to make the machine work, so that, angry as he was, Stripling had to let the matter rest there. Farebrother, I think, felt that he had not provided a demonstration very satisfactory from the commercial point of view, so that his victory over Stripling was less complete on this account than it might otherwise have seemed. Soon after this he went upstairs, carrying the collar-turner with him, and saying that he had 'work to do', a remark that was received with a certain amount of facetious comment, which he answered by saying: 'Ah, Jimmy, I'm not a rich man like you. I have to toil for my daily bread.'

Stripling was, no doubt, glad to see him go. He probably wanted time to recover from what he evidently looked upon as a serious defeat over the collars. Peter turned on the gramophone, and Stripling retired to the corner of the room with him, where while Stripling's temper cooled they played some game with matches. It was soon after this that I made a decidedly interesting discovery about Lady McReith, who had begun to discuss dance steps with Babs, while I looked through some of the records that Peter had been arranging in piles. In order to illustrate some point she wanted to make about fox-trotting, Lady McReith suddenly jumped from the sofa, took my arm and, sliding it round her waist, danced a few steps. 'Like this?' she said, turning her face towards Babs; and then, as she continued to cling to me, tracing the steps back again in the other direction: 'Or like that?' The transaction took place so swiftly, and, so far as Lady McReith was concerned, so unselfconsciously, that Peter and Stripling did not look up from their game; but—although employed merely as a mechanical dummy—I had become aware, with colossal impact, that Lady McReith's footing in life was established in a world of physical action of which at present I knew little or nothing. Up to that moment I had found her almost embarrassingly difficult to deal with as a fellow guest: now the extraordinary smoothness with which she glided across the polished boards, the sensation that we were holding each other close, and yet, in spite of such proximity, she remained at the same time aloof and separate, the pervading scent with which she drenched herself, and, above all, the feeling that all this offered something further, some additional and violent assertion of the will, was—almost literally—intoxicating. The revelation was something far more universal in implication than a mere sense of physical attraction towards Lady McReith. It was realisation, in a moment of time, not only of her own possibilities, far from inconsiderable ones, but also of other possibilities that life might hold; and my chief emotion was surprise.

This incident was, of course, of interest to myself alone, as its importance existed only in my own consciousness. It would never have occurred to me to discuss it with Peter, certainly not in the light in which it appeared to myself, because to him the inferences would—I now realised—have appeared already so self-evident that he would have been staggered by my own earlier obtuseness: an obtuseness which he would certainly have disparaged in his own forceful terms. Keen awareness of Peter's point of view on the subject followed logically on a better apprehension of the elements that went towards forming Lady McReith as a personality: a personality now so changed in my eyes. However, all that happened was that we danced together until the record came to an end, when she whirled finally round and threw herself down again on the sofa, where Babs still lay: and a second later put her arm round Babs's neck. Stripling came across the room and poured out for himself another whisky. He said: 'We must find some way of ragging old Sunny. He is getting too pleased with himself by half.'

Lady McReith went off into such peals of laughter at this, wriggling and squeezing, that Babs, freeing herself, turned and shook her until she lay quiet, still laughing, at last managing to gasp out: 'Do think of something really funny this time, Jimmy.' I asked what had happened on earlier occasions when Sunny Farebrother had been ragged. Peter outlined some rather mild practical jokes, none of which, in retrospect, sounded strikingly amusing. Various suggestions were made, but nothing came of them at the moment; though the discussion might be said to have laid the foundation for a scene of an odd kind enacted on the last night of my stay.

Looking back at the Horabins' dance that took place on that last night, the ball itself seemed merely a prelude to the events that followed. At the time, the Horabins' party itself was important enough, not only on account of the various sequels enacted on our return to the Templers' house—fields in which at that time I felt myself less personally concerned, and, therefore, less interested—but because of the behaviour of Jean Templer at the dance, conduct which to some extent crystallised in my own mind my feelings towards her; at the same time precipitating acquaintance with a whole series of emotions and apprehensions, the earliest of numberless similar ones in due course to be undergone. The Horabins for long after were, indeed, momentous to me simply for that reason. As it happens, I cannot even remember the specific incident that clarified, in some quite uncompromising manner, the positive recognition that Jean might prefer someone else's company to my own; nor, rather unjustly, did the face of this superlatively lucky man —as he then seemed—remain in my mind a year or two later. I have, however, little doubt that the whole matter was something to do with cutting a dance; and that the partner she chose, in preference to myself, persisted dimly in my mind as a figure certainly older, and perhaps with a fair moustache and reddish face. Even if these circumstances are described accurately, it would undoubtedly be true to say that nothing could be less interesting than the manner in which Jean's choice was brought home to me. There was not the smallest reason to infer from anything that had taken place in the course of my visit that I possessed any sort of prescriptive rights over her: and it may well be that the man with the moustache had an excellent claim. Such an argument did not strike me at the time; nor were the disappointment and annoyance, of which I suddenly became aware in an acute degree, tempered by the realisation, which came much later, that such feelings—like those experienced during the incident with Lady McReith—marked development in transmutation from one stage of life to another.

One of the effects of this powerful, and in some ways unexpected, concentration on the subject of Jean at the dance was to distract my attention from everything not immediately connected with her; so that, by the time we were travelling home, several matters that must have been blowing up in the course of the evening had entirely escaped my notice. I was in the back of a chauffeur-driven car, Peter by the far window, and Lady McReith between us. I was conscious that for the first part of the drive these two were carrying on some sort of mutual conflict under the heavy motoring rug that covered the three of us; but I had not noticed how or why she had become separated from the Striplings. Probably the arrangement had something to do with transport to their homes of some other guests who had dined at the Templers' house for the ball. Whatever the reason, one of the consequences of the allotment of seats had been that Jean and Sunny Farebrother had been carried in the Striplings' Mercedes. We rolled along under the brilliant stars, even Peter and Lady McReith at last silent, perhaps dozing: though like electric shocks I could feel the almost ceaseless vibration of her arm next to mine, quivering as if her body, in spite of sleep, knew no calm.

I did not feel at all anxious to retire to bed when we arrived at the house. On the following day I was to travel to London. Farebrother was going on the same train. We were making a late start in order to rest on a little into the morning after the exertions of the ball. Peter, for once, seemed ready for bed, saying good-night and going straight upstairs. The Striplings had arrived before us, and were shifting about restlessly, talking of 'raiding the kitchen', bacon and eggs, more drink, and, in general, showing unwillingness to bring the party to an end. Lady McReith asserted that she was worn out. Sunny Farebrother, too, was evidently anxious to get some sleep as soon as possible. They went off together up the stairs. Finally Babs found her way to the kitchen, and returned with some odds and ends of food: that would for the time postpone the need to bring the night's entertainment to a close. Her husband walked up and down, working himself up into one of his rages against Sunny Farebrother, who had, it appeared, particularly annoyed him on the drive home. Jean had at first gone up to her room; but on hearing voices below came downstairs again, and joined the picnic that was taking place.

'Did you hear what he said about the car on the way back?' Stripling asked. 'Like his ruddy cheek to offer advice about the acceleration. He himself is too mean to have anything but an old broken-down Ford that you couldn't sell for scrap-iron; and he doesn't even take that round with him, but prefers to cadge lifts.'

'Have you seen Mr. Farebrother's luggage?' said Jean. 'It is all piled up outside his room ready to go down to the station first thing in the morning. It looks as if he were going big-game hunting.'

I wondered afterwards whether she said this with any intention of malice. There was not any sign on her part of a desire to instigate trouble; but it is not impossible that she was the true cause of the events that followed. Certainly this remark was responsible for her sister saying: 'Let's go and have a look at it. Jimmy might get an idea for one of his jokes. Anyway, I'm beginning to feel it's time for bed.'

There was, undeniably, a remarkable load of baggage outside Farebrother's bedroom door: several suitcases; a fishing rod and landing net; a cricket bat and pads; a tennis racket in a press; a gun case; and a black tin box of the kind in which deeds are stored, marked in white paint: 'Exors: Amos Farebrother, Esquire'. On the top of this edifice of objects, on the whole ancient, stood the leather hat-box, said by its owner to contain the hat required by tradition for City ritual. Babs pointed to this. Her husband said: 'Yes—and have you seen it? A Jewish old clothes man would think twice about wearing it.'

Stripling tiptoed to the hat-box, and, releasing the catch, opened the lid, taking from within a silk hat that would have looked noticeably dilapidated on an undertaker. Stripling inspected the hat for several seconds, returned it to the box, and closed the lid; though without snapping the fastening. Lowering his voice, he said: 'Get out of sight where you can all watch. I am going to arrange for old Sunny to have a surprise when he arrives at the office.'

My room was next to Peter's at one end of the passage: Farebrother's half-way down: the Striplings slept round the corner beyond. Jean was somewhere farther on still. Stripling said: 'It is a pity Gwen and Peter won't be able to see this. They will enjoy hearing about it. Find a place to squint from.'

He nodded to me, and I moved to my room, from where I regarded the passage through a chink in the door. Stripling, Babs and Jean passed on out of sight; and I suppose the two women remained in the intersecting passage, in a place from which they could command a view of Farebrother's luggage. I waited for at least five minutes, peering through the crack of the barely open door. It was daylight outside, and the passages were splashed with patches of vivid colour, where the morning sun streamed through translucent blinds. I continued to watch for what seemed an age. I had begun to feel very sleepy, and the time at last appeared so long that I was almost inclined to shut the door and make for bed. And then, all at once, Jimmy Stripling came into sight again. He was stepping softly, and carried in his hand a small green chamber-pot.

As he advanced once more along the passage, I realised with a start that Stripling proposed to substitute this object for the top-hat in Farebrother's leather hat-box. My immediate thought was that relative size might prevent this plan from being put successfully into execution; though I had not examined the inside of the hat-box, obviously itself larger than normal (no doubt built to house more commodious hats of an earlier generation), the cardboard interior of which might have been removed to make room for odds and ends. Such economy of space would not have been out of keeping with the character of its owner. In any case it was a point upon which Stripling had evidently satisfied himself, because the slight smile on his face indicated that he was absolutely certain of his ground. No doubt to make an even more entertaining spectacle of what he was about to do, he shifted the china receptacle from the handle by which he was carrying it, placing it between his two hands, holding it high in front of him, as if it were a sacrificial urn. Seeing it in this position, I changed my mind about its volume, deciding that it could indeed be contained in the hat-box. However, before this question of size and shape could be settled one way or the other, something happened that materially altered the course that events seemed to be taking; because Farebrother's door suddenly swung open, and Farebrother himself appeared, still wearing his stiff shirt and evening trousers, but without a collar. It occurred to me that perhaps he knew of some mysterious process by which butterfly collars, too, could be revived, as well as those of an up-and-down sort, and that he was already engaged in metamorphosing the evening collar he had worn at the Horabins'.

Stripling was taken completely by surprise. He stopped dead: though without changing the position of his hands, or the burden that they carried. Then, no doubt grasping that scarcely any other action was open to him, he walked sharply on down the passage, passing my door and disappearing into the far wing of the house, where Mr. Templer's room was situated. Sunny Farebrother watched him go, but did not speak a word. If he were surprised, he did not show it beyond raising his eyebrows a little, in any case a fairly frequent facial movement of his. Stripling, on the other hand, had contorted his features in such a manner that he looked not so much angry, or thwarted, as in actual physical pain. When he strode past me, I could see the sweat shining on his forehead, and at the roots of his rather curly hair. For a moment Farebrother continued to gaze after him down the passage, as if he expected Stripling's return. Then, with an air of being hurt, or worried, he shut his door very quietly. I closed mine too, for I had begun to feel uncommonly tired.

Peter was in the garden, knocking about a golf ball with his mashie, when I found him the following day. Although late on in the morning, no one else had yet appeared from their rooms. I was looking forward to describing the scene Peter had missed between Farebrother and Stripling. As I approached he flicked his club at the ball, which he sent in among the fir trees of the park. While we walked towards the place where it fell, I gave some account of what had happened after he had retired upstairs on returning from the dance. We found the ball in some bracken, and Peter scooped it back into the centre of the lawn, where it lay by the sundial. To my surprise he seemed scarcely at all interested in what had seemed to me one of the most remarkable incidents I had ever witnessed. I thought this attitude might perhaps be due to the fact that he felt a march had been stolen on him for once; though it would have been unlike him to display disappointment in quite that manner.

'I suppose I really ought to have slipped into your room and warned you that something was on.'

'You might not have found me,' he said.

'Why not?'

'I might not have been there.'

His eyes began their monotonous, tinny glistening. I saw that he was very satisfied with himself about something: what was this secret cause for complacency, I did not immediately grasp. I made no effort to solve the enigma posed by him. We talked about when we should meet again, and the possibility of having a party in London with Stringham at Christmas.

'Don't spoil the French girls,' said Peter.

It was only by the merest chance that a further aspect of the previous evening's transactions was brought to my notice: one which explained Peter's evident air of self-satisfaction. The time had come for us to catch our train. Neither the Striplings nor Lady McReith had yet appeared, but Peter's father was pottering about and said: 'I trust you've enjoyed yourself, Jenkins, and that it hasn't been too quiet for you. Peter complains there is never anything to do here.'

Jean said good-bye.

'I hope we meet again.'

'Oh, yes,' she said, 'we *must*.'

Just as I was getting into the car, I remembered that I had left a book in the morning-room.

'I'll get it,' said Peter. 'I know where it is.'

He went off into the house, and I followed him, because I had an idea that its whereabouts was probably behind one of the cushions of the armchair in which I had been sitting. As I came through the door, he was standing on the far side of the morning-room, looking about among some books and papers on a table. He was not far from another door on the opposite side of the room, and, as I reached the threshold, this farther door was opened by Lady McReith. She did not see me, and stood for a second smiling at Peter, but without speaking. Then suddenly she said: 'Catch,' and impelled through the air towards him some small object. Peter brought his right hand down sharply and caught, within the palm, whatever had been thrown towards him. He said: 'Thanks, Gwen. I'll remember next time.'

I saw now that he was putting on his wrist-watch. By this time I was in the room, and making for the book—*If Winter Comes*—which lay on one of the window-seats. I said good-bye to Lady McReith, who responded with much laughter, and Peter returned with me to the car, saying: 'Gwen is quite mad.' Sunny Farebrother was still engaged in some final business arrangement with Mr. Templer, which he brought to a close with profuse thanks. We set out together on the journey to the station.

The manner of Lady McReith's return of Peter's watch was the outward and visible sign to me of his whereabouts after we had returned from the Horabins'. The fact that an incisive step of one sort or another had been taken by him in relation to Lady McReith was almost equally well revealed by something in the air when they spoke to each other: some definite affirmation which made matters, in any case, explicit enough. The propulsion of the watch was merely a physical manifestation of the same thing. In the light of Peter's earlier remark on the subject of absence from his room during the attempted ragging of Sunny Farebrother, this discovery did not perhaps represent anything very remarkable in the way of intuitive knowledge: especially in view of Lady McReith's general demeanour and conversational approach to the behaviour of her friends. At the same time—as in another and earlier of Peter's adventures of this kind—his enterprise was displayed, confirming my conception of him as a kind of pioneer in this increasingly familiar, though as yet still largely unexplored country. It was about this time that I began to think of him as really a more forceful character than Stringham, a possibility that would never have presented itself in earlier days of my acquaintance with both of them.

These thoughts were cut short by Sunny Farebrother, who whispered to me (though two sheets of glass divided us from the chauffeur): 'Were you going to give this chap anything?' Rather surprised at his curiosity on this point, I admitted that two shillings was the sum I had had in mind. I hoped he would not think that I ought to have suggested half a crown. However, he nodded gravely, as if in complete approval, and said: 'So was I; but I've only got a bob in change. Here it is. You add it to your florin and say it's from both of us.'

When the moment came, I forgot to do more than hand the coins to the chauffeur, who, perhaps retaining memories of earlier visits, did not appear to be unduly disappointed.

In spite of the accumulation of luggage, extraordinary exertions on Farebrother's part made it possible to dispense with the assistance of a porter.

'Got to look after the pennies, you know,' he said, as we waited for the train. 'I hope you don't travel First Class, or we shall have to part company.'

As no such difficulty arose, we found a Third Class compartment to ourselves, and stacked the various items of Farebrother's belongings on the racks. They almost filled the carriage.

'Got to be prepared for everything,' he said, as he lifted the bat and pads. 'Do you play this game?'

'Not any longer.'

'I'm not all that keen on it nowadays myself,' he said. 'But a cricketer always makes a good impression.'

For about three-quarters of an hour he read *The Times*. Then we began to talk about the Templers, a subject Farebrother introduced by a strong commendation of Peter's good qualities. This favourable opinion came as something of a surprise to me; because I was accustomed to hear older persons speak of Peter in terms that almost always suggested improvement was absolutely necessary, if he were to come to any good in life at all. This was not at all the view held by Farebrother, who appeared to regard Peter as one of the most promising young men he had ever run across. Much as I liked Peter by that time, I was quite unable to see why anything in his character should appeal so strongly to Farebrother, whose own personality was becoming increasingly mysterious to me.

'Peter should do well,' Farebrother said. 'He is a bit wild. No harm in that. He knows his way about. He's alive. Don't you agree?'

This manner of asking one's opinion I had already noticed, and found it flattering to be treated without question as being no longer a schoolboy.

'Of course his father is a fine old man,' Farebrother went on. 'A very fine old man. A hard man, but a fine one.'

I wondered what had been the result of their business negotiations together, in which so much hardness and fineness must have been in operation. Farebrother had perhaps begun to think of this subject too, for he fell into silence for a time, and sighed once or twice; at last remarking: 'Still, I believe I got the best of him this time.'

As that was obviously a matter between him and his host, I did not attempt to comment. A moment later, he said: 'What did you think of Stripling?'

Again I was flattered at having my opinion asked upon such a subject; though I had to admit to myself that on the previous night I had been equally pleased when Stripling had, as it were, associated me with his projected baiting of Farebrother. Indeed, I could not help feeling, although the joke had missed fire, that I was not entirely absolved from the imputation of being in some degree guilty of having acted in collusion with Stripling on that occasion. I was conscious, therefore, unless I was to appear in my own eyes hopelessly double-dealing, that some evasive answer was required. Accordingly, although I had not much liked Stripling, I replied in vague terms, adding some questions about the relative success of his motor-racing.

'I don't really understand the fellow,' Farebrother said. 'I quite see he has his points. He has plenty of money. He quite often wins those races of his. But he always seems to me a bit too pleased with himself.'

'What was Babs's first husband like?'

'Quite a different type,' said Farebrother, though without particularising.

He lowered his voice, just as he had done in the car,

though we were still alone in the compartment.

'A rather curious thing happened when we got in from that dance last night,' he said. 'As you know, I went straight up to my room. I started to undress, and then I thought I would just cast my eye over an article in *The Economist* that I had brought with me. I find my brain seems a bit clearer for that kind of thing late at night.'

He paused for a moment, and shook his head, suggesting much burning of midnight oil. Then he went on: 'I thought I heard a good deal of passing backwards and forwards and what sounded like whispering in the passage. Well, one year when I stayed with the Templers they made me an apple-pie bed, and I thought something like that might be in the wind. I opened the door. Do you know what I saw?'

At this stage of the story I could not possibly admit that I knew what he had seen, so there was no alternative to denial, which I made by shaking my head, rather in Farebrother's own manner. I had begun to feel a little uncomfortable.

'There was Stripling, marching down the passage holding *a jerry* in front of him as if he were taking part in some ceremony.'

I shook my head again; this time as if in plain disbelief. Farebrother was not prepared to let the subject drop. He said: 'What could he have been doing?'

'I can't imagine.'

'He was obviously very put out at my seeing him. I mean, what the hell could he have been doing?'

Farebrother leant forward, his elbows on his knees, confronting me with this question, as if he were an eminent counsel, and I in the witness box.

'Was it a joke?'

'That was what I thought at first; but he looked quite

serious. Of course we are always hearing that his health is not good.'

I tried to make some non-committal suggestions that might throw light on what had happened.

'Coupled with the rest of his way of going on,' said Farebrother, 'it made a bad impression.'

We journied on towards London. When we parted company Sunny Farebrother gave me one of his very open smiles, and said: 'You must come and lunch with me one of these days. No good my offering you a lift as I'm heading Citywards.' He piled his luggage, bit by bit, on to a taxi; and passed out of my life for some twenty years.

3.

Being in love is a complicated matter; although anyone who is prepared to pretend that love is a simple, straightforward business is always in a strong position for making conquests. In general, things are apt to turn out unsatisfactorily for at least one of the parties concerned; and in due course only its most determined devotees remain unwilling to admit that an intimate and affectionate relationship is not necessarily a simple one: while such persistent enthusiasts have usually brought their own meaning of the word to something far different from what it conveys to most people in early life. At that period love's manifestations are less easily explicable than they become later: often they do not bear that complexion of being a kind of game, or contest, which, at a later stage, they may assume. Accordingly, when I used to consider the case of Jean Templer, with whom I had decided I was in love, analysis of the situation brought no relief from uneasy, almost obsessive thoughts that filled my mind after leaving the Templers' house. Most of all I thought of her while the train travelled across France towards Touraine.

The journey was being undertaken in fiery sunshine. Although not my first visit to France, this was the first time I had travelled alone there. As the day wore on, the nap on the covering of the seats of the French State Railways took on the texture of the coarse skin of an over-heated animal: writhing and undulating as if in an effort to find relief from the torturing glow. I lunched in the restaurant car, and drank some red *vin ordinaire* that tasted unexpectedly sour. The carriage felt hotter than ever on my return: and the train more crowded. An elderly man with a straw hat, black gloves, and Assyrian beard had taken my seat. I decided that it would be less trouble, and perhaps cooler, to stand for a time in the corridor. I wedged myself in by the window between a girl of about fifteen with a look of intense concentration on her pale, angular features, who pressed her face against the glass, and a young soldier with a spectacled, thin countenance, who was angrily explaining some political matter to an enormously fat priest in charge of several small boys. After a while the corridor became fuller than might have been thought possible. I was gradually forced away from the door of the compartment, and found myself unstrategically placed with a leg on either side of a wicker trunk, secured by a strap, the buckle of which ran into my ankle, as the train jolted its way along the line. All around were an immense number of old women in black, one of whom was carrying a feather mattress as part of her luggage.

At first the wine had a stimulating effect; but this sense of exhilaration began to change after a time to one of heaviness and despair. My head buzzed. The soldier and the priest were definitely having words. The girl forced her nose against the window, making a small circle of steam in front of her face. At last the throbbings in my head became so intense that I made up my mind to eject the man with the beard. After a short preliminary argument in which I pointed out that the seat was a reserved one, and, in general, put my case as well as circumstances and my command of the language would allow, he said briefly: '*Monsieur, vous avez gagné*,' and accepted dislodgment with resignation and some dignity. In the corridor, he moved skilfully past the priest and his boys; and, with uncommon agility for his age and size, climbed on to the wicker trunk, which he reduced almost immediately to a state of complete dissolution: squatting on its ruins reading *Le Figaro.* He seemed to know the girl, perhaps his daughter, because once he leaned across and pinched the back of her leg and made some remark to her; but she continued to gaze irritably out at the passing landscape, amongst the trees of which an occasional white château stood glittering like a huge birthday cake left out in the woods after a picnic. By the time I reached my destination there could be no doubt whatever that I was feeling more than a little sick.

The French family with whom I was to stay was that of a retired infantry officer, Commandant Leroy, who had known my father in Paris at the end of the war. I had never met him, though his description, as a quiet little man dominated by a masterful wife, was already familiar to me; so that I hoped there would be no difficulty in recognising Madame Leroy on the platform. There was, indeed, small doubt as to her identity as soon as I set eyes on her. Tall and stately, she was dressed in the deepest black. A female companion of mature age accompanied her, wearing a cone-shaped hat trimmed with luxuriant artificial flowers. No doubt I was myself equally unmistakable, because, even before descending passengers had cleared away, she made towards me with eyebrows raised, and a smile that made me welcome not only to her own house, but to the whole of France. I shook hands with both of them, and Madame Leroy made a gesture, if not of prevention and admonition, at least of a somewhat deprecatory nature, as I took the hand of the satellite, evidently a retainer of some sort, who removed her fingers swiftly, and shrank away from my grasp, as if at once offended and fearful. After this practical repudiation of responsibility for my arrival, Rosalie, as she turned out to be called, occupied herself immediately in some unfriendly verbal exchange with the porter, a sickly-looking young man Madame Leroy had brought with her, who seemed entirely under the thumb of these two females, emasculated by them of all aggressive traits possessed by his kind.

After various altercations with station officials, all more or less trifling, and carried off victoriously by Madame Leroy, we climbed into a time-worn taxi, driven by an ancient whose moustache and peaked cap gave him the air of a Napoleonic grenadier, an elderly *grognard,* fallen on evil days during the Restoration, depicted in some academic canvas of patriotic intention. Even when stationary, his taxi was afflicted with a kind of vehicular counterpart of St. Vitus's dance, and its quaverings and seismic disturbances must have threatened nausea to its occupants at the best of times. On that afternoon something far less convulsive would have affected me adversely; for the weather outside the railway station seemed warmer even than on the train. The drive began, therefore, in unfavourable circumstances so far as my health was concerned: nor could I remember for my own use any single word of French: though happily retaining some measure of comprehension when remarks were addressed to me.

Madame Leroy had evidently been a handsome proposition in her youth. At sixty, or thereabouts, she retained a classical simplicity of style: her dimensions comprehensive, though well proportioned: her eye ironical, but not merciless. She seemed infinitely prepared for any depths of poverty in the French language, keeping up a brisk line of talk, scarcely seeming to expect an answer to questions concerning the health of my parents, the extent of my familiarity with Paris, the heat of the summer in England, and whether crossing the Channel had spoiled a season's hunting. Rosalie was the same age, perhaps a little older, with a pile of grey hair done up on the top of her head in the shape of a farmhouse loaf, her cheeks cross-hatched with lines and wrinkles like those on the side of Uncle Giles's nose: though traced out here on a larger scale. From time to time she muttered distractedly to herself: especially when clouds of white dust from the road blew in at the window, covering us with blinding, smarting powder, at the same time obscuring even more thoroughly the cracked and scarred windscreen, which seemed to have had several bullets put through it in the past: perhaps during the retreat from Moscow. With much stress, and grunting of oaths on the part of the veteran, the car began to climb a steep hill: on one of the corners of which it seemed impossible that the engine would have the power to proceed farther. By some means, however, the summit was achieved, and the taxi stopped, with a final paroxysm of vibration, in front of a door in a whitewashed wall. This wall, along the top of which dark green creeper hung, ran for about fifty yards along the road, joining the house, also white, at a right-angle.

'*Voilà*,' said Madame Leroy. 'La Grenadière.'

Below the hill, in the middle distance, flowed the river, upon which the sun beat down in stripes of blue and gold. Along its banks minute figures of a few fishermen could just be seen. White dust covered all surrounding vegetation; and from a more solid and durable form of this same white material the house itself seemed to have been constructed. The taxi still throbbed and groaned and smelt very vile. To vacate it for the road brought some relief. Madame Leroy led the way through the door in the wall in the manner of a sorceress introducing a neophyte into the land of faërie: a parallel which the oddness of the scene revealed by her went some way to substantiate.

We entered a garden of grass lawns and untidy shrubs,

amongst the stony paths of which a few rusty iron seats were dotted about. In one corner of this pleasure ground stood a summer-house, covered with the same creeper that hung over the outer wall, and hemmed in by untended flower beds. At first sight there seemed to be a whole army of people, including children, wandering about, or sitting on the seats, reading, writing, and talking. Madame Leroy, like Circe, moved forward through this enchanted garden, ignoring the inhabitants of her kingdom as if they were invisible, and we passed into the house, through a glass-panelled door. The hall was as black as night, and I fell over a dog asleep there, which took the accident in bad part, and was the object of much vituperation from Rosalie. Mounting several flights of stairs, Madame Leroy still leading the way, we at last entered a room on the top floor, a garret containing a bed, a chair, and a basin, with its accessories, in blue tin, set on a tripod. A view of the distant river appeared once more, through a port-hole in this austere apartment, one wall of which was decorated with a picture, in cheerful colours, of St. Laurence and his grid-iron; intended perhaps in jocular allusion to the springs of the bed. Rosalie, who had followed us up the stairs bearing a small jug, now poured a few drops of lukewarm water, lightly tinted by some deposit, into the basin on the tripod: intoning a brief incantation as she did this. Madame Leroy stood by, waiting apparently for this final ministration: and, satisfied no doubt that I had become irrevocably subject to her occult powers, she now glided towards the door, having indicated that we might meet again in the garden in due course. As she retired, she said something about *'l'autre monsieur anglais'* having the bedroom next door. At that moment I could scarcely have felt less interest in a compatriot.

When the door shut, I lay for a time on the bed. Something had gone wrong, badly wrong, as a result of luncheon on the train. At first I attributed this recurrent feeling of malaise to the wine: then I remembered that some sort of fish in the hors d'œuvres had possessed an equivocal flavour. Perhaps heat and excitement were the true cause of my feeling unwell. There was a slight improvement after a lapse of about twenty minutes, at the end of which time I rose and peered through the port-hole on to a landscape through which the river ran as straight as a canal, among trees, and white houses similar in size and shape to La Grenadière. I washed my hands in the tin basin, and set off, rather gingerly, down the stairs.

As I reached the hall, the door on the left opened suddenly, and Madame Leroy reappeared. She smiled meaningly, as if to give assurance of her satisfaction in accepting a new catachumen; and pointed to the garden, evidently with a view to undertaking further preliminaries of initiation. We stepped out into the evening sunshine, and, side by side, moved towards the groups gathered together in knots at different points on the grass: from one of which her husband, Commandant Leroy, at once detached himself and came towards us. He was a small man, several inches shorter than his wife, with dark blue glasses and a really colossal moustache. Speaking good English (I remembered he had been an interpreter) he enquired about the journey, explaining that he had been unable to come to the station because his health was not good: he had been gassed, though not seriously, he added, at one of the German attacks on Ypres early in the war, and he was suffering at present from pains in various parts of his body. Madame Leroy heard him with impatience: at length telling him sharply to go and lie down. He shook hands again, and pottered off towards the house. Madame Leroy inclined her head, apparently to express regret that control over her husband even after these many years, was still incomplete. She told me that she had one son, Emile, whom they saw occasionally because he was an instructor at the Cavalry School at Saumur: another, Marcel, serving in Morocco with the Chasseurs d'Afrique: and a daughter, Victorine, married to an army doctor in Saigon.

'Une vraie famille de soldats.'

'Une vraie famille d'officiers,' corrected Madame Leroy, though not unkindly.

We cruised about the garden. The persons assembled there, a trifle less numerous than had at first appeared, were of different classification: some guests, some members of the family. The next introduction was to Berthe, one of the Leroy nieces, a plump brunette, sitting on one of the seats, watching life through sly, greenish eyes set far apart in a face of fawn-coloured rubber. She was engaged, Madame Leroy explained, to the son of the Chef de Cabinet of the Sous-Secrétaire de Marine. Her aunt took this opportunity of speaking a few improving words on the subject of marriage in general, received by Berthe with a tightly compressed smirk; and we passed on to Suzette, another niece, who was writing letters in mauve ink at one of the iron tables. Suzette was small and fair, not a beauty, but dispensing instantaneously, and generously, emotional forces that at once aroused in me recollections of Jean Templer; causing an abrupt renewal—so powerful that it seemed almost that Jean had insinuated herself into the garden—of that restless sense of something desired that had become an increasing burden upon both day and night. Suzette shook hands and smiled in such a manner as to put beyond doubt, were the metaphor to be used, any question of butter melting in the mouth. Then she sat down again and continued her letter, evidently a composition that demanded her closest attention.

Two boys, perhaps great-nephews, followed, somewhere between nine and twelve years of age, with strongly marked features, broadly ironical like Madame Leroy's, to whose side of the family they belonged. Heavy black eyebrows were grafted on to white faces, as if to offset the pattern of dark blue socks against sallow, skinny legs. Both were hard at work with lexicons and notebooks; and, after shaking hands very formally, they returned to work, without looking up again as we passed on from their table. Their names were Paul-Marie and Jean-Népomucène.

Leaving these ramifications of the Leroy household, we approached the outskirts of a Scandinavian pocket in the local community, first represented in the person of a tall young man—in size about six foot three or four—wearing a black suit, light grey cap, and white canvas shoes, who was reading *Les Misérables* with the help of a dictionary. This figure, explained Madame Leroy, as I escaped from his iron grip, was Monsieur Örn—so, at least, after many changes of mind, I decided his name, variously pronounced by his fellow boarders, must be spelt, for during the whole of my stay at La Grenadière I never saw it written down—who was a Norwegian, now learning French, though in principle studying in his own country to be an engineer. From Monsieur Örn's vacant blue eyes a perplexed tangle of marked reactions seemed to signal uncertainly for a second or two, and then die down. I had seen a provincial company perform *The Doll's House* not many months before, and felt, with what I now see to have been quite inadmissible complacency, that I knew all about Ibsen's countrymen.

As Monsieur Örn seemed to be at a loss for words, we proceeded to Monsieur Lundquist, a Swede in dark grey knickerbockers, mending a bicycle. Monsieur Lundquist, although formality itself—he was almost as formal as Paul-

Marie and Jean-Népomucène had been—was much more forthcoming than Monsieur Örn. He repeated several times: *'Enchanté, Monsieur Yenkins,'* putting his heels together, and holding his bicycle-pump as if it were a sword and he were about to march past in review, while he smiled and took Madame Leroy's hand in his after he had let go of my own. His dark curly hair and round chubby face gleamed in the sun, seeming to express outwardly Monsieur Lundquist's complete confidence in his own powers of pleasing.

As we strolled on towards the summer-house, built with its entrance facing obliquely from the centre of the lawn—if the central part of the garden could really be so called—Madame Leroy explained that within this precinct would be found Monsieur and Madame Dubuisson, who had been married only a short time. Having called this fact to mind, she tapped loudly on one of the supports of the arbour before venturing to escort me through its arch. After taking this precaution, she advanced in front of me, and peeped through one of the embrasures in the wall, pausing for a moment, then beckoning me on, until at last we entered the heart of the retreat in which the Dubuissons were sitting side by side.

Afterwards I discovered that Monsieur Dubuisson was only about forty. At first sight he struck me as much older, since the skin of his face fell in diamond-shaped pouches which appeared quite bloodless. Like Monsieur Örn, he wore a cap, a very flat, very large, check cap, with a long peak, like that in which *apaches* used to be portrayed in French comic papers or on the stage. Under this headgear, rank and greying, almost lavender-coloured hair bunched out. He held a book on his knee, but was not reading. Instead he sat gazing with a look of immense and ineradicable scepticism on his face, towards what could be seen of the garden. His long upper lip and general carriage made me think of a French version of the Mad Hatter. His bride, a stocky little woman, younger than her husband, was dressed in white from head to foot: looking as if she had prepared herself for an afternoon's shopping in Paris, but had decided instead to spend her time knitting in the summer-house. This very domestic occupation seemed scarcely to harmonise with the suggestion—conveyed in some manner by her face, even more than her clothes—that she was not, temperamentally, a domestic person: not, at any rate, in the usual meaning of that term. As Stringham had said of Peter Templer, she did not appear to be intended by nature for 'home life'. Whatever domesticity she might possess seemed superimposed on other, and perhaps more predatory, characteristics.

Though still feeling decidedly bilious, I had done my best to make myself agreeable to each of the persons in turn produced by Madame Leroy; and, such is the extraordinary power of sentiment at that age, the impact of Suzette's personality, with its reminder of Jean, had made me forget for a while the consequences of the hors d'œuvres. However, when Monsieur Dubuisson held out to me the book lying on his knee, and said dryly, in excellent English: 'I should be interested to hear your opinion on this rendering,' my head began to go round again. The title on the cover, *Simples Contes des Collines,* for the moment conveyed nothing to me. Fortunately Monsieur Dubuisson did not consider it necessary to receive an answer to his question, because, almost immediately, he went on to remark: 'I read the stories in French merely as—as a matter of interest. For you see I find no—no difficulty at all in expressing myself in the language of the writer.'

The pauses were evidently to emphasise the ease with which he spoke English, and his desire to use the absolutely appropriate word, rather than on account of ignorance of phrasing. He went on: 'I like Kipling. That is, I like him up to a point. Naturally one finds annoying this—this stress on nationalism. Almost blatant nationalism, I should say.'

All this conversation was now becoming a little overwhelming. Madame Leroy, engaged with Madame Dubuisson on some debate regarding *en pension* terms, would in any case, I think, have cut short the development of a serious literary discussion, because she was already showing indications of restlessness at Monsieur Dubuisson's continued demonstration of his command of English. However, a new—and for me almost startling—element at that moment altered the temper of the party. There was the sound of a step behind us, and an additional personage came under the rustic arch of the entrance, refocusing everyone's attention. I turned, prepared for yet another introduction, and found myself face to face with Widmerpool.

Monsieur Dubuisson, quite shrewd in his way, as I learnt later, must have realised at once that he would have to wait for another occasion to make his speech about Kipling, because he stopped short and joined his wife in her investigation of the *en pension* terms. Possibly he may even have felt that his support was required in order that the case for a reduction might be adequately presented. It was evidently a matter that had been discussed between the three of them on a number of earlier occasions, and, so soon as Madame Leroy had spoken of the surprise and pleasure that she felt on finding that Widmerpool and I were already acquainted, she returned vigorously to her contest with the Dubuissons.

Widmerpool said in his thick, flat voice: 'I thought it might be you, Jenkins. Only yours is such a common name that I could not be sure.'

We shook hands, rather awkwardly. Widmerpool had tidied himself up a little since leaving school, though there was still a kind of exotic drabness about his appearance that seemed to mark him out from the rest of mankind. At a later stage of our sojourn at La Grenadière, he confided to me that he had purchased several ties during an afternoon spent in Blois. He was wearing one of these cravats of the country when he came into the summer-house, and its embroidered stripes insinuated that he might not be English, without adding to his appearance the least suggestion of French origins. His familiar air of uneasiness remained with him, and he still spoke as if holding a piece of india-rubber against the roof of his mouth. He also retained his accusing manner, which seemed to suggest that he suspected people of trying to worm out of him important information which he was not, on the whole, prepared to divulge at so cheap a price as that offered. All this uncomfortable side of him came into my mind, and I could think of nothing to say. Madame Leroy was now deeply involved with the Dubuissons regarding the subject of some proposed financial readjustment, and it looked as if the matter was going to come to a head, one way or the other. At last the three of them went off together, talking hard. I was left alone with Widmerpool. He did not speak.

'How long have you been here?' I asked.

He stared hard at me from the solid glass windows through which he observed the world; frowning as if some important canon of decency had already been violated by my ineptitude: and that this solecism, whatever it was, grieved rather than surprised him. Then he said: 'You know we are supposed to talk *French* here, Jenkins.'

It was hard to guess how best to reply to this admonition. To say: '*Oui,* Widmerpool,' would sound silly, even a trifle flippant; on the other hand, to answer in English would be to aggravate my incorrect employment of the language; and might at the same time give the appearance of trying to increase the temptation for Widmerpool to relapse into his native tongue, with which my arrival now threatened to compromise him. In spite of his insignificance at school, I still felt that he might possess claims to that kind of outward deference one would pay to the opinion of a boy higher up in the house, even when there was no other reason specially to respect his views. In any case the sensation of nausea from which I had once more begun to suffer seemed to be increasing in volume, adding to the difficulty of taking quick decisions in so complicated a question of the use of language. After a long pause, during which he appeared to be thinking things over, Widmerpool spoke again.

'It would probably be simpler,' he said, 'if I showed you round first of all *in English*. Then we can talk French for the rest of the time you are here.'

'All right.'

'But tell me in the first place how you knew of La Grenadière?'

I explained about Commandant Leroy and my father. Widmerpool seemed disappointed at this answer. I added that my parents had thought the terms very reasonable. Widmerpool said: 'My mother has always loved Touraine since she visited this country as a girl. And, of course, as you know, the best French is spoken in this part of France.'

I said I had heard a Frenchman question that opinion; but Widmerpool swept this doubt aside, and continued: 'My mother was always determined that I should perfect my French among the châteaux of the Loire. She made enquiries and decided that Madame Leroy's house was far the best of the several establishments for paying-guests that exist in the neighbourhood. Far the best.'

Widmerpool sounded quite challenging; and I agreed that I had always heard well of the Leroys and their house. However, he would not allow that there was much to be said for the Commandant: Madame, on the other hand, he much admired. He said: 'I will take you round the garden first, and introduce you.'

'No, for Heaven's sake—Madame Leroy has already done that.'

Widmerpool looked offended at this speech, and seemed uncertain what should be the next move. He temporised by asking: 'What sort of a journey did you have?'

'Hot.'

'You look a bit green.'

'Let's go into the house.'

'Did you have a change,' he said. 'I came straight through by a clever piece of railway management on my part.'

'Where can I be sick?'

'What do you mean?'

'Where can I be sick?'

At length he understood; and soon after this, with many expressions of sympathy from Madame Leroy, and some practical help from Rosalie, who unbent considerably now that I was established as a member of the household—and an indisposed one—I retired to bed: lying for a long time in a state of coma, thinking about Widmerpool and the other people in the garden. The images of Jean Templer and Suzette hovered in the shadows of the room, until they merged into one person as sleep descended.

How all the inhabitants of La Grenadière were accommodated in a house of that size was a social and mathematical problem, so far as I was concerned, never satisfactorily elucidated during my stay there. I could only assume that there were more bedrooms than passage doors on the upper storeys, and that these rooms led one from another. The dining-room was on the left of the main entrance: the kitchen on the right. In the sunless and fetid segment between these two rooms, Rosalie presided during meals, eating her own portion from a console table that stood on one side of the hall, facing a massive buhl cabinet on the other: the glass doors of this cabinet revealed the ragged spines of a collection of paper-backed novels. This segregation in the hall symbolised Rosalie's footing in the house, by imposing physical separation from her employers on the one hand, and, on the other, from Marthe, a girl of eighteen, showing signs of suffering from goitre, who did the cooking: and did it uncommonly well.

Two dogs—Charley and Bum—shared with Rosalie her pitchy vestibule: a state of perpetual war existing between the three of them. Charley was so named on account of the really astonishing presumption that he looked like an English dog: whereas his unnaturally long brown body, short black legs, and white curly tail, made it almost questionable whether he was indeed a dog at all, and not a survival of a low, and now forgotten, form of prehistoric life. Bum, a more conventional animal, was a white wire-haired terrier. He carried his name engraved on a wide leather collar studded with brass hob-nails. Every Monday he was placed on a table in the garden, and Madame Leroy would bathe him, until his crisp coat looked as if it were woven from a glistening thread of white pipe-cleaners. Charley was never washed, and resenting this attention to his fellow, would on this account pick a quarrel with Bum every seven days. Rosalie was for ever tripping over the dogs in the passage, and cursing them: the dogs squabbling with each other and with Rosalie: at times even stealing food from her plate when she was handing on the next course into the dining-room: where we all sat at a large round table that nearly filled the room.

Most of the talking at meals was done by Madame Dubuisson, Berthe and Paul-Marie, the last of whom was said, by almost everyone who referred to him, to be unusually full of *esprit* for his age: though I was also warned that his remarks were sometimes judged to be *'un peu shocking'*. When he spoke, his black eyebrows used to arch, and then shoot together, and a stream of words would pour out, sending Madame Dubuisson and Berthe, especially, into fits of laughter at his sallies. These sometimes caused Madame Leroy to shake her head in mild reproval: though Madame Leroy herself would often smile admiringly at the ease with which Paul-Marie succeeded in hitting off life's paradoxical situations: especially those connected with the relations of the sexes. For my own part I understood only a small proportion of Paul-Marie's jokes on account of the speed with which he spat out his sentences, and also because of his colloquial manner of expressing himself; but I gathered their general import, which was to the effect that women, owing to their cunning ways, were to be approached with caution. Whether or not they were good jokes I am now in no position to say. I imagine that they belonged, on the whole, to that immense aggregation of synthetic humour on this subject that serves the French pretty well, being adapted to most cases that arise. Indeed, Paul-Marie's synthetic jokes might perhaps be compared with Uncle Giles's synthetic scepticism, both employable for many common situations. Jean-Népomucène was much quieter. With heavy-lidded eyes, he used to watch his brother, and give a short, very grown-up laugh at appropriate moments. Most of the time at table Jean-Népomucène's manner was absent, suggesting that his mind was engaged on preoccupations of his own, perhaps of a similar order to his brother's reflections, but more gravely considered. Berthe and Madame Dubuisson would sometimes try and tease him about his silences, saying: '*Ah, Jean-Népomucène, il est bavard, lui,*' in this way provoking a verbal attack from Paul-Marie, which usually required their combined forces to beat off.

Commandant Leroy rarely spoke. His wife kept him on a diet, and he sat, almost hidden, behind a colossal bottle of Contrexeville water, that always stood in front of him, from which, after every meal, he took a few drops, mixed with grey powder, in a spoon. Monsieur Dubuisson also conversed little at meals, no doubt because he felt his conversation wasted in the intellectual surroundings available at La Grenadière. He would, however, occasionally read aloud some item of news from the papers (his only extravagance seemed to be buying newspapers), after which he would laugh satirically as he qualified these quotations by supplying details of the individual, country, or political group, that provided funds for the journal in question. He used to listen to Paul-Marie's chatter with a look of infinite sourness on his face.

The position of the Dubuissons at La Grenadière always remained something of a mystery. It was evident that they had come there merely to enjoy a cheap holiday, and that Monsieur Dubuisson considered that life owed him something superior to the accommodation to be found with the Leroys. Berthe and Suzette used to have some joke together about Madame Dubuisson, who was apparently held to own a past not to be too closely scrutinised. They were talking the matter over, in whispers, one day, when sitting behind me on the way back from an expedition to Loches. They seemed to have no very definite information, but their conclusions—as I rather dimly understood them—

seemed to be that Madame Dubuisson had been her husband's mistress for a number of years: having at last induced him to marry her. At that time such a subject, illustrated by the practical circumstances of a couple who seemed to me to be so lacking in romance as the Dubuissons, appeared to be of only the most academic interest: to have little or nothing to do with the practical problems of life. At a later date I should have been more curious regarding their story. Madame Dubuisson used to giggle, and behave generally in a fairly free manner, especially when her husband was not present; and I felt that—if an analogy could be drawn between two such different households—she represented at La Grenadière something comparable to Lady McReith's position when staying at the Templers'. Madame Dubuisson was, for example, the guest whom Commandant Leroy undoubtedly liked best, and the boys, too, seemed to get on with her well. I never discovered her husband's occupation. It appeared that—like Sunny Farebrother—he had distinguished himself during the war: or, at least, he mentioned this fact to me on one or two occasions; and at one period he seemed to have taught, or lectured, at some provincial university. He said that at present he was in business, but without specifying its nature.

'I am a very busy man, building up for my corporation, and trying to materialise along the same lines a few ideas regarding the financing of certain needs which actually are most difficult to meet,' he remarked to me soon after my arrival.

He must have suspected that I required further enlightenment before I could answer, because he added: 'I might even come to London, when, and if, certain—certain negotiations pending with British houses mature.'

I asked if he knew London well.

'Probably better than yourself,' he replied; 'being nearly at the head of a finance corporation, I am trying to assure a certain percentage of the insolvency risk which might arise when I guarantee credits by endorsing bills.'

'I see.'

'You must not think,' Monsieur Dubuisson continued, smiling and showing a barrier of somewhat discoloured teeth, 'that I am merely—merely a commercial gent. I am also developing my activity as a newspaperman, and publish weekly one, or a couple, of articles. I hope to be circulated in England soon.'

'Do you write in English?'

'Of course.'

I inquired about the subjects on which he wrote. Monsieur Dubuisson said: 'I sent lately to the *National Review* a longish article entitled "Cash Payments; or Productive Guarantees?" speaking my views on the actual and future relations of France, Great Britain, and Germany. I have had no answer yet, but I have a manuscript copy I can lend you to read.'

He paused; and I thanked him for this offer.

'As a matter of fact I write along three very different lines,' Monsieur Dubuisson went on. 'First as a financial expert: second, summaries of big problems looked upon from an independent threefold point of view—political, military, economic: finally in consideration of the growth of the social idea in English literature.'

All this left me little, if at all, wiser on the subject of the Dubuisson background, but there could be no doubt that Monsieur Dubuisson had plenty of confidence in his own qualifications. Outwardly, he never showed much interest in his wife, though they spent a good deal of their time together: since neither of them took any part in the collective recreations of La Grenadière, such as the excursions to places of interest in the neighbourhood. This lack of public attention from her husband did not appear to worry Madame Dubuisson at all. She chattered away all the time to anyone who happened to find themselves next to her; and without any regard for the question of whether or not her listener understood what she was talking about: a habit perhaps acquired from her husband.

The two Scandinavians did not 'get on' with each other. Both Berthe and Suzette warned me of this, in diplomatic terms, soon after I came to La Grenadière. According to the girls, Monsieur Örn complained that Monsieur Lundquist was 'too proud'; while Monsieur Lundquist had actually stated openly that he considered Monsieur Örn to be lacking in *chic*. Monsieur Örn, like Monsieur Dubuisson, rarely spoke, spending most of his time writing lists of French words in a notebook. Berthe said that Monsieur Örn had confided to her that all Swedes were proud, often for no reason at all; Monsieur Lundquist especially so, for no better cause than that his father happened to be an official at the Law Courts. Monsieur Lundquist himself was going to become a journalist, and Monsieur Örn had told Berthe that Monsieur Lundquist was much inclined to exaggerate the social position that this calling would bring him. Although Monsieur Örn did not talk a great deal, he would sometimes look sternly across the table at Monsieur Lundquist, the whole of his craggy face slowly setting into a gloomy, hostile state: *'comme un Viking'*, Berthe used to call this specially organised physiogonomy. As a matter of fact Berthe had a weak spot for Monsieur Örn, because he was so good at tennis. If she happened to be cutting the melon at luncheon, she would always give him the largest slice, or help him generously to *pot-au-feu*.

Apart from his regret that Monsieur Örn was so hopelessly ill-equipped so far as *chic* was concerned—an opinion of which, I found, he made no secret, expounding the view freely to everyone in the house—Monsieur Lundquist seemed quite unaware of the vigour of Monsieur Örn's disapproval of his own attitude towards the world, which both of them agreed to be characteristically Swedish; nor was he prepared to accept Monsieur Örn's repeated assertions that he did not understand the Swedish language. Monsieur Lundquist, transgressing the rule of La Grenadière, whenever he found his French inadequate to make his meaning clear, would often make use of Swedish. Monsieur Örn would then listen, adjusting his firm features in such a way as to indicate utter failure to comprehend that such outlandish—or, perhaps it was, such affected—sounds could possibly have any meaning at all: even for Swedes. Monsieur Örn would finally make some remark in his notably individual French, evidently wholly irrelevant to the matter raised by Monsieur Lundquist. On such occasions Monsieur Lundquist would only smile, and shake this head, unable to credit Monsieur Örn's unvarying and oppressive lack of *chic*.

In this circle, Widmerpool had made himself an accepted, if not specially popular, figure. There was no question here of his being looked upon by the rest of the community as the oddity he had been regarded at school. In the weeks that followed I came to know him pretty well. We talked French to each other at meals, and kept up some show of using French during expeditions: alone together—usually late in the evening, when the others had gone to their rooms, to devote themselves to study, or to rest—we used to speak English; although Widmerpool rarely did so without making some reference to the reluctance with which he diverged from the rule of the house. He used to work hard at the language all the rest of the time. In spite of inherent difficulty in making words sound like French, he had acquired a large vocabulary, and could carry on a conversation adequately, provided he could think of something to say; for I found that he had no interest in anything that could not be labelled as in some way important or improving, an approach to conversation that naturally limited its scope. His determination to learn French set an example from which I fell lamentably short. In his rigid application to the purpose for which he came to France, he was undoubtedly the most satisfactory of Madame Leroy's boarders, even including the industrious Monsieur Örn, who never could get his genders right.

Like Monsieur Dubuisson, Widmerpool showed no enthusiasm for Paul-Marie's jokes.

'That boy has a corrupt mind,' he said, not many days after I had been in the house. 'Extraordinary for a child of that age. I cannot imagine what would happen to him at an English school.'

'He's like Stringham as a small French boy.'

I said this without thinking at all deeply about the accuracy of the comparison. I did not, in fact, find in Paul-Marie any startling resemblance to Stringham, though some faint affinity must have existed between them, in so much that more than once I had thought of Stringham, when Paul-Marie had been engaged in one of his torrential outbursts of conversation. However, Widmerpool showed sudden interest in the identification of their two characters.

'You were rather a friend of Stringham's, weren't you?' he asked. 'Of course I was a bit senior to know him. I liked the look of him on the whole. I should say he was an amusing fellow.'

For Widmerpool to imply that it was merely a matter of

age that had prevented him from being on easy terms with Stringham struck me, at that time, as showing quite unjustifiable complacency regarding his own place in life. I still looked upon him as an ineffective person, rather a freak, who had no claim to consider himself as the equal of someone like Stringham who, obviously prepared to live dangerously, was not to be inhibited by the narrow bounds to which Widmerpool seemed by nature committed. It was partly for this reason that I said: 'Do you remember the time when you saw Le Bas arrested?'

'An appalling thing to happen,' said Widmerpool. 'I left soon after the incident. Was it ever cleared up how the mistake arose?'

'Stringham rang up the police and told them that Le Bas was the man they wanted to arrest.'

'What do you mean?'

'The criminal they were after looked rather like Le Bas. We had seen a picture of him outside the police-station.'

'But why——'

'As a hoax.'

'Stringham?'

'On the telephone—he said he was Le Bas himself.'

'I never heard anything like it,' said Widmerpool. 'What an extraordinary thing to have done.'

He sounded so furious that I felt that some sort of apology was called for—in retrospect the episode certainly seemed less patently a matter for laughter, now that one was older and had left school—and I said: 'Well, Le Bas was rather an ass.'

'I certainly did not approve of Le Bas, or of his methods of running a house,' said Widmerpool: and I remembered that Le Bas had particularly disliked him. 'But to do a thing like that to his own housemaster . . . And the risk he ran. He might have been expelled. Were you concerned in this too, Jenkins?'

Widmerpool spoke so sternly that for a moment I thought he intended to sit down, there and then, and, in a belated effort to have justice done, report the whole matter in writing to Le Bas or the headmaster. I explained that personally I had had no share in the hoax, beyond having been out walking with Stringham at the time. Widmerpool said, with what I thought to be extraordinary fierceness: 'Of course Stringham was thoroughly undisciplined. It came from having too much money.'

'I never noticed much money lying about.'

'Stringham may not have been given an abnormal amount himself,' said Widmerpool, irritably, 'but his family are immensely wealthy. Glimber is a huge place. My mother and I went over it once on visiting day.'

'But he is not coming in to Glimber.'

I felt glad that I had been supplied by Templer with this piece of information.

'Of course he isn't,' said Widmerpool, as if my reply had been little short of insulting. 'But there are all his mother's South African gold holdings. That divorce of hers was a very unfortunate affair for someone so well known.'

I should have liked to hear more of this last matter, but, Stringham being a friend of mine, I felt that it would be beneath my dignity to discuss his family affairs with someone who, like Widmerpool, knew of them only through hearsay. Later in life, I learnt that many things one may require have to be weighed against one's dignity, which can be an insuperable barrier against advancement in almost any direction. However, in those days, choice between dignity and unsatisfied curiosity was less clear to me as a cruel decision that had to be made.

'And that thin, rather good-looking boy,' Widmerpool

continued, 'who used to be about a lot with you and Stringham?'

'Peter Templer.'

'Was he in the Le Bas affair too?'

'He was out for a walk with us on the same afternoon.'

'He did not have too good a reputation, did he?'

'Not too good.'

'That was my impression,' said Widmerpool. 'That he was not a good influence in the house.'

'You and he were mixed up in the Akworth row, weren't you?' I asked, not from malice, or with a view to keeping him in order on the subject of my friends, so much as for the reason that I was inquisitive to know more of that affair: and, considering the way that Widmerpool had been talking, I felt no particular delicacy about making the enquiry.

Widmerpool went brick-red. He said: 'I would rather not speak of that, if you don't mind.'

'Don't let's, then.'

'I suppose Templer got sacked in the end?' Widmerpool went on: no doubt conscious that he might have sounded over-emphatic, and evidently trying to bring some jocularity into his tone.

'More or less asked to leave.'

'How badly used he really to behave?'

He moistened his lips, though scarcely perceptibly. I thought his mixture of secretiveness and curiosity quite intolerable.

'He had a woman before he left.'

If Widmerpool had been upset by the news that Stringham had played the Braddock alias Thorne trick on Le Bas, and more personally embarrassed by reference to the Akworth scandal, this piece of information, regarding Templer's crowning exploit, threw him almost entirely off his balance. He made a strange sound, half-way between a low laugh and a clearing of the throat, simultaneously swallowing hard. He also went, if possible, redder than ever. Took off his spectacles and began to polish them, as he usually did when his nerves were on edge. I did not feel entirely at ease with the subject myself. To help out the situation, I added: 'I have just been staying with the Templers as a matter of fact.'

Widmerpool clearly welcomed this shift of interest in our conversation, enquiring almost eagerly about the Templers' house, and the manner in which they lived. We talked about the Templers for a time, and I found to my surprise that Widmerpool knew Sunny Farebrother by name, though they had never met. He said: 'A very sharp fellow, they tell me.'

'I liked him.'

'Naturally you did,' said Widmerpool. 'He can make himself very agreeable.'

I found Widmerpool's remarks in this vein so tiresome that I was almost inclined to try and shock him further by describing in detail the various incidents that had taken place while I was staying at the Templers'. In the end I decided that those happenings needed too much explanation before they could be appreciated, anyway by Widmerpool, that there was nothing to be gained by trying to impress him, or attempting to modify his point of view. I told him that Peter was going straight into business, without spending any time at the university. Rather unexpectedly, Widmerpool approved this decision, almost in Sunny Farebrother's own phrase.

'Much better get down to work right away,' he said. 'There was not much money when my father died, so I talked things over with my mother—she has a wonderful grasp of business matters—and we decided we would do the same thing, and cut out Oxford or Cambridge.'

By using the first person plural, he made the words sound as if there had been some question of his mother going up to the university with him. He said: 'This effort to polish up my French is merely in the nature of a holiday.'

'A holiday from what?'

'I am articled to a firm of solicitors.'

'Oh, yes.'

'I do not necessarily propose to remain a solicitor all my life,' said Widmerpool. 'I look to wider horizons.'

'What sort?'

'Business. Politics.'

This all seemed to me such rubbish that I changed the subject, asking where he lived. He replied, rather stiffly, that his mother had a flat in Victoria. It was convenient, he said; but without explaining the advantages. I enquired what life was like in London.

'That depends what you do,' said Widmerpool, guardedly.

'So I suppose.'

'What profession are you going to follow?'

'I don't know.'

It seemed almost impossible to make any remark without in one manner or another disturbing Widmerpool's equanimity. He was almost as shocked at hearing that I had no ready-made plans for a career as he had been scandalised a few minutes earlier at the information regarding the precocious dissipation of Templer's life.

'But surely you have some bent?' he said. 'An ambition to do well at something?'

This ideal conception—that one should have an aim in life—had, indeed, only too often occurred to me as an unsolved problem; but I was still far from deciding what form my endeavours should ultimately take. Being at that moment unprepared for an *a priori* discussion as to what the future should hold, I made several rather lame remarks to the effect that I wanted one day 'to write': an assertion that had not even the merit of being true, as it was an idea that had scarcely crossed my mind until that moment.

'To write?' said Widmerpool. 'But that is hardly a profession. Unless you mean you want to be a journalist—like Lundquist.'

'I suppose I might do that.'

'It is precarious,' said Widmerpool. 'And—although we laugh, of course, at Örn for saying so, right out—there is certainly not much social position attached: unless, for example, you become editor of *The Times*, or something of that sort. I should think it over very carefully before you commit yourself.'

'I am not absolutely determined to become a journalist.'

'You are wise. What are your other interests?'

Feeling that the conversation had taken a turn that delivered me over to a kind of cross-examination, I admitted that I liked reading.

'You can't earn your living by reading,' said Widmerpool, severely.

'I never said you could.'

'It doesn't do to read too much,' Widmerpool said. 'You get to look at life with a false perspective. By all means have some familiarity with the standard authors. I should never raise any objection to that. But it is no good clogging your mind with a lot of trash from modern novels.'

'That was what Le Bas used to say.'

'And he was quite right. I disagreed in many ways with Le Bas. In that one, I see eye to eye with him.'

There was not much for me to say in reply. I had a novel—*If Winter Comes*, which I had now nearly finished

—under my arm, and it was impossible to deny that I had been reading this book. Widmerpool must have noticed this, because he continued in a more kindly tone: 'You must meet my mother. She is one of those rare middle-aged women who have retained their youthful interest in matters of the mind. If you like books—and you tell me you do—you would thoroughly enjoy a chat with her about them.'

'That would be nice.'

'I shall arrange it,' said Widmerpool. *'Et maintenant, il faut se coucher, parce-que je compte de me reveiller de bonne heure le matin.'*

In the course of subsequent conversations between us he talked a good deal about his mother. On the subject of his father he was more reticent. Sometimes I had even the impression that Widmerpool *père* had earned a living in some manner of which his son—an only child—preferred not to speak: though, one evening, in a burst of confidence, he mentioned that his paternal grandfather had been a Scotch business man called Geddes, who had taken the name of Widmerpool after marrying a wife of that name, who was—so Widmerpool indicated in his characteristic manner—of rather higher standing than himself. There seemed to have been some kind of financial crisis when Widmerpool's father had died, either on account of debts, or because the family's income had been thereby much reduced. Life with his mother appeared to be very quiet and to consist of working all day and studying law after dinner most nights; though Widmerpool took care to explain to me that he deliberately took part in a certain amount of what he called 'social life'. He said, with one of his rare smiles: 'Brains and hard work are of very little avail, Jenkins, unless you know the right people.'

I told him that I had an uncle who was fond of saying

the same thing; and I asked what form his relaxations generally took.

'I go to dances,' said Widmerpool; adding, rather grandly: 'in the Season, that is.'

'Do you get a lot of invitations?' I asked, divided between feeling rather impressed by this attitude towards the subject in hand and, at the same time, finding difficulty in believing that he could be overwhelmed by persons wishing to share his company.

Widmerpool was evasive on this point, and muttered something about invitations being 'just a question of getting on a list'. As he seemed unwilling to amplify this statement, I did not press him further, having myself a somewhat indistinct comprehension of what he meant: and appreciating that the relative extent of his invitations, as for anyone, might be, perhaps, a delicate matter.

'I don't get much time for games now,' he said. 'Though once in a way I make a point of going down to Barnes, and driving a ball into a net.'

I was, for some reason, conscious of an odd sense of relief that he should no longer consider himself compelled to undergo those protracted and gruelling trials of endurance against himself for which he still remained chiefly notable in my mind. Driving a golf ball into a net presented an innocuous, immensely less tortured, picture to the mind than that offered by those penitential exertions with which I had formed the habit of associating his hours of recreation. This mitigated strain became even more apparent to me later on, when we used to play tennis, though his old enthusiasm was still quite strong enough.

Tennis at La Grenadière—or rather in the grounds of a ruined nineteenth-century mansion in Renaissance style situated about a mile and a half away on the outskirts of the town—was certainly of a kind to give small opportunity for a parade of that feverish keenness which had made the sight of Widmerpool playing games at school so uncomfortable to watch: although, so far as possible, he always insisted upon a high standard of athletic formality being observed whenever we played. The tennis-court was, however, the stage for him to reveal to me quite another side of his character: an unsuspected strength of personality and power of negotiation. This was in connexion with the rupture of relations between Monsieur Örn and Monsieur Lundquist, both of whom, as it turned out, took their game with seriousness at least equal to Widmerpool's; in spite of the comparatively unprofessional circumstances in which these contests were held.

The several hard tennis courts in this garden, which had been taken over as a park by the municipality, had never been properly kept up since becoming public property; so that in the course of time the soil had receded from the metal bars that formed the lines of demarcation, leaving solid boundaries that protruded so far above the ground that it was easy to catch one's foot in them when running about the court. If the ball hit one of these projecting strips of metal, it might become wedged beneath, or fly off at an unexpected angle; accordingly counting as a 'let'. Both of these types of 'let' took place with fair frequency, somewhat slowing up the cadence of the game, and making it hard to play with the concentration with which Widmerpool liked to approach all forms of sport. In addition to this local impediment to rapid play, neither Berthe nor Suzette were very proficient at the game; and they—with Paul-Marie and Jean-Népomucène, also beginners—always had to be worked into the fours.

Being no great performer myself, I rather enjoyed tennis played in these leisurely, at times undoubtedly eccentric, conditions; but Widmerpool was perpetually grumbling about 'the game not being taken seriously', a complaint that was, from his point of view, fully justified: although he was himself in no sense a good player. If he could possibly manage to do so, he would try to arrange a 'men's four', which usually resulted in one of us partnering a Scandinavian; and it soon became clear that, however much Monsieur Örn and Monsieur Lundquist might be able to cloak their mutual antipathy in the common intercourse of everyday life, their hatred for each other on the tennis court was a passion far less easily curbed. As it happened, a 'men's four' was not so simple for Widmerpool to contrive as might be supposed, because Berthe and Suzette were inclined to resent having to play in a four with Paul-Marie and Jean-Népomucène—another instance of excessive insistence on dignity defeating its own ends, for in that manner the girls would have gained practice which they greatly needed—and also, a more potent reason, because there were at best only four tennis balls; one of which had a gash in its outer covering which adversely affected the bounce. These balls not uncommonly became mislaid in the thickets of the garden; and, although Paul-Marie and Jean-Népomucène were themselves not above playing a single with only one ball (provided this were not the damaged one), the rest of the party looked upon a couple of sound balls as a minimum; and preferred, if possible, to have the use of all available. Sometimes either Berthe or Suzette was *'souffrante'*, and wanted to sit out for a set or two. This rarely occurred to both of them on the same day, so that, as it happened, competition between Monsieur Örn and Monsieur Lundquist, although each occasionally played against the other partnering one of the girls, took on its most violent aspect when both were engaged in a 'men's four': a 'single' between them being, naturally, unthinkable.

If a 'single' had ever taken place, it would undoubtedly have been won by Monsieur Örn, a better player than Monsieur Lundquist, taller and quicker in movement. There was, however, another element that entered into these games, especially when four were playing. This was knowledge of the peculiarities of the court, and their uses in winning a set, of which Monsieur Lundquist had a far keener grasp than Monsieur Örn. Monsieur Lundquist was also accustomed to practice a trick which had for some reason the effect of making Monsieur Örn abandon his normal state of vague, silent acceptance of the hardships of life and become decidedly irritable. This stratagem was for Monsieur Lundquist suddenly to change the style of his service, from a fairly brisk delivery that sent the grit flying about the court, to a gentle lob that only just cleared the net: a stroke which, quite unaccountably, always took Monsieur Örn by surprise, invariably causing him to lose the point.

Monsieur Lundquist never employed this device more than once in the course of an afternoon: often not at all. However, on one unusually hot day, after I had been at La Grenadière for several weeks, he did it twice in the same set, catching out Monsieur Örn on both occasions. It so happened that earlier in the same afternoon a ball lodged itself four or five times under the back line, a particularly annoying circumstance for the player—in every case Monsieur Örn—who certainly would otherwise have won the point. After the last of these 'lets', Monsieur Lundquist served his second lob—an unheard-of thing—catching Monsieur Örn unawares for the second time, with—so far as I was concerned—entirely unexpected effect on the Norwegian's temper.

The actual word, or words, employed by Monsieur Örn never came publicly to light, even after the whole matter had been closed: nor was it ever established whether the epithet, or designation, had been expressed in Swedish, Norwegian, or in some opprobrious term, or phrase, common to both languages. Whatever was said, Monsieur Örn spoke quietly, with closed lips, almost muttering to himself; although in a manner apparently audible to Monsieur Lundquist, who lost all at once his look of enormous self-satisfaction, went red in the face, and walked quickly round to the other side of the net. Widmerpool, his partner, shouted: *'Mais qu'est-ce que vous faites, Monsieur Lundquist? J'en ai ici deux balles. C'est assez?'*

Monsieur Lundquist took no notice of him. It was at least clear to me that, whatever else he might want, he had not crossed the court in search of tennis balls. He went straight up to Monsieur Örn and—I suppose—demanded an apology. 'I thought those northern races did not get hysterical,' Widmerpool said to me afterwards, when we were discussing the distressing scene that followed; which ended with Monsieur Lundquist marching away from the rest of us, jumping on his bicycle, and riding at breakneck speed over the dusty pot-holes that punctuated the drive's steep descent. At one moment, as he rounded the corner, I felt sure that he was going to come off; but he recovered his balance, and passing rapidly through the open gates of wrought iron that led to the road, he disappeared from sight. I agreed with Widmerpool that if he had supposed that hysteria formed no part of the Scandinavian temperament, he had—to use a favourite phrase of his own—based his opinion on insufficient data.

This scene, though in itself a violent one, did not take long to play out. Before its close, Berthe and Suzette had both risen from the seat upon which they had been resting, and done their best to join in. They were only partially successful in this, though they contrived to add appreciably to the hubbub. Finally, we were all left standing in the centre of the court beside Monsieur Örn, who had limited himself throughout the commotion almost entirely to monosyllables. He now began to speak in a deep, strident voice, which after a minute or two showed signs of shaking with emotion. At first Widmerpool and I were unable to grasp the root of the trouble, partly because Monsieur Lundquist's lobbing technique was sufficiently common for none of the rest of us specially to have noticed it that afternoon: partly because at that age I was not yet old enough to be aware of the immense rage that can be secreted in the human heart by cumulative minor irritation. However, the subject of the dispute began to reveal itself in due course after Monsieur Lundquist had left the gardens. In fact Monsieur Örn at length demonstrated the origin of his annoyance by himself tapping a ball—the gashed one—lightly over the net in Monsieur Lundquist's manner, where it fell flat, like a stone, on the reddish dust. '*Jamais*,' said Monsieur Örn, now very quietly, after performing this action several times. '*Jamais—jamais*.' Whether his words were intended to convey that no one should ever practice tricks of that sort, or whether he was expressing an intention never again to play tennis with Monsieur Lundquist was not certain.

The result of all this was a breach between Monsieur Örn and Monsieur Lundquist which there seemed no possibility of closing. By the time we reached the house, I had satisfactorily reconstructed the situation in my own mind; and I imagined—as it turned out, quite incorrectly—that I had grasped its intricacies more thoroughly than Widmerpool. It is doubtful whether the two girls ever understood the true source of the disturbance, though neither of them was backward in explaining what had gone wrong, and how it should be put right. There is no knowing what sort of an account Madame Leroy was given of the trouble, because she heard the first version from Berthe and Suzette as soon as we arrived back at La Grenadière.

Whatever was said was, in any case, sufficient to prepare her for a trying time at dinner that evening, during which meal Monsieur Örn and Monsieur Lundquist spoke no word to each other and very little to anyone else: projecting between them across the table a cloud of hatred that seemed to embarrass even Madame Leroy, not easily disconcerted in her own house. Her husband, it is true, did not show any concern whatever, or, indeed, awareness that something might be amiss; and Paul-Marie and Jean-Népomucène, at first greatly delighted by the grown-up quarrel, soon forgot the Scandinavians in some elaborate and secret diversion of their own. Berthe, Suzette, and Madame Dubuisson were in a state of acute excitement, shooting each other glances intended to be full of meaning; while they conversed in a kind of hissing undertone. Widmerpool, also, was plainly agitated. The only person whole-heartedly amused, and pleased, by what had happened was Monsieur Dubuisson, who talked more than was his custom throughout the meal, amplifying a little the *exposé* he had given on the previous day of one of his favourite subjects, the development of water-power in Morocco. So far as I was concerned myself, these circumstances made me feel very uneasy, and I could see no way for matters to right themselves; nor for normal life to be carried on, except by the hand-to-mouth method symbolised by passing to Monsieur Örn or Monsieur Lundquist whatever food or drink each was likely to need, for which neither would ask the other. This state of affairs lasted throughout the following day, and the next; until there seemed no solution to the problem of how to restore the relationship between Monsieur Örn and Monsieur Lundquist to its old footing, imperfect as this may have been.

To my great surprise, Monsieur Dubuisson began to discuss this situation with me one evening, when we found ourselves alone together in the garden. It had been another bakingly hot day, and the white dust lay thick on the leaves of the shrubs, and over the battered seat upon which I was sitting. I was reading *Bel-Ami,* discovered among the books —on the whole not a very exciting collection—kept in the glass cabinet in the hall. Monsieur Dubuisson had been walking up and down one of the paths, studying a newspaper. Now he came across the withered grass, and sat down beside me, at the same time taking from the pocket of his black alpaca coat his pipe, of which—like Peter Templer—he was, for some reason, immensely proud. As usual he cleared his throat several times before speaking, and then, leaning backwards, spat sideways over the seat. In his slow, disapproving voice he said: 'I think it would be a—a little absurd if I talked French to you in view of our —our relative mastery of each other's tongue. Do you agree, Jenkins, yes?'

'Absolutely.'

One had to admit that he spoke English remarkably well, in spite of the hesitations made necessary by the subtlety of his processes of thought. There could be no doubt that every sentence was intended to knock you down by its penetrative brilliance. Smiling quietly to himself, as if at some essentially witty conception that he was inwardly playing with, and withheld only because its discernment was not for everybody, he began slowly to fill his pipe with tobacco —again like Peter's—that smelt peculiarly abominable.

'There seems to be a regular falling-out between our good friends from the north,' he said.

I agreed.

'You and I,' said Monsieur Dubuisson, 'belong to nations

who have solved their different problems in different ways.'

I admitted that this assertion was undeniable.

'Our countries have even, as you would say, agreed to differ. You lean on tradition: we on logic.'

I was not then aware how many times I was to be informed of this contrast in national character on future occasions by Frenchmen whose paths I might happen to cross; and again I concurred.

'As I understand the affair,' went on Monsieur Dubuisson, 'as I understand the circumstances of the matter, it would be difficult to achieve something in the nature of a reconciliation.'

'Very difficult, I——'

'It would be difficult, because it would be hard to determine whether an appeal should be made, on the one hand, to your congenital leaning towards tradition: or, on the other, to our characteristic preference for logic. Do you agree? The way may even lie near some Scandinavian fusion of these two ideas. You read Strindberg?'

'I have heard of him.'

'I think our Swedish friend, Lundquist, is quite pleased with himself,' said Monsieur Dubuisson, allowing me no opportunity to interrupt his train of thought: at the same time nodding and smiling, as a speaker personally familiar with the exquisite sensations that being pleased with oneself could impart to the whole being. 'Örn, on the other hand, always seems to have the blues. During the war I knew some of your countrymen of that type. Always down at the mouth.'

'Did you see a lot of the British Army?'

'Towards the end, quite a lot. It was obvious, speaking English as I do. For three months I was second-in-command to a battalion. I was wounded twice and have four citations.'

I asked if he had ever come across my father in Paris; but, although Monsieur Dubuisson was unwilling to admit that they had never met—and assured me that he had heard Commandant Leroy speak of my father in the highest terms—it seemed probable that the two of them had never run across one another. On the other hand, Monsieur Dubuisson remarked: 'Much of my work was done with Captain Farebrother, whom you have perhaps met in England. He was called Sunny Farebrother by his comrades in the army.'

'But how astonishing—I have met him.'

As a matter of fact, I had thought of Farebrother almost as soon as Monsieur Dubuisson had mentioned his own war record, because it had immediately occurred to me how much Jimmy Stripling would have loathed Monsieur Dubuisson, with his wounds and citations. Besides, Monsieur Dubuisson's treatment of the circumstances of his war career made Farebrother's references to his own military past seem infinitely fastidious.

'But why should you think it astonishing?' asked Monsieur Dubuisson, with one of his withering smiles, which spread over the whole of his face, crinkling the features into the shape of a formal mask of comedy, crowned with greyish-mauve locks. 'Captain Farebrother is a man I know to go about a great deal in society. What could be more natural than that you should have met him?'

I did not know in those days that it was impossible to convince egoists of Monsieur Dubuisson's calibre that everyone does not look on the world as if it were arranged with them—in this case Monsieur Dubuisson—at its centre; and, not realising that, in his eyes, the only possible justification for my turning up at La Grenadière would be the fact that I had once met someone already known to him, I tried to explain that this acquaintanceship with Farebrother seemed to me an extraordinary coincidence. In addition to this, if I had been old enough to have experienced something of the world of conferences and semi-political affairs, in effect a comparatively small one, it would have seemed less unexpected that their meeting had taken place.

'He was a good fellow,' said Monsieur Dubuisson. 'There was, as a matter of fact, a small question in which Captain Farebrother had shown himself interested, and of which I later heard nothing. Perhaps you know his address?'

'I am afraid not.'

'It is of no consequence,' said Monsieur Dubuisson. 'I can easily trace him.'

All the same he cleared his throat again, rather crossly. I felt that all this talk about the war, by reviving old memories, had put him out of his stride. He pulled at his pipe for a time, and then returned to the subject of Monsieur Örn and Monsieur Lundquist.

'Now you were present when this falling-out took place,' he said. 'Can you recite to me the pertinent facts?'

I told him how matters had looked to me as a witness of them. He listened carefully to the story, which sounded—I had to admit to myself—fairly silly when told in cold blood. When I came to the end he knocked out his pipe against the leg of the seat, and, turning towards me, said quite tolerantly: 'Now look here, Jenkins, you know you and I cannot believe eyewash of that sort. Grown-up men do not quarrel about such things.'

'What were they quarrelling about, then?'

Monsieur Dubuisson gave his slow, sceptical smile. He shook his head several times.

'You are no longer a child, Jenkins,' he said. 'I know that in England such matters are not—not stressed. But you have no doubt noticed at La Grenadière the presence of two charming young ladies. You have?'

I conceded this.

'Very good,' said Monsieur Dubuisson. 'Very good.'

He rose from the seat, and stood looking down at me, holding his hands behind his back. I felt rather embarrassed, thinking that he had perhaps guessed my own feelings for Suzette.

'Then what is there to be done about it?' I asked, to break the silence.

'Ah, *mon vieux*,' said Monsieur Dubuisson. 'Well may you ask what is to be done about it. To me—troubled as I am with a mind that leaps to political parallels—the affairs seems to me as the problems of Europe in miniature. Two young girls—two gentlemen. Which gentleman is to have which young girl? Your Government wishes mine to devalue the franc. We say the solution lies in your own policy of export.'

He shrugged his shoulders.

'I shrug my shoulders,' he said, 'like a Frenchman on the London stage.'

I was entirely at a loss to know how to reply to his presentation of this political and international allegory in relation to the matter in hand: and I found myself unable to grasp the implications of the parallel he drew with sufficient assurance to enable me to express either agreement or disagreement. However, Monsieur Dubuisson, as usual, appeared to expect no reply. He said: 'I appreciate, Jenkins, that you have come here to study. At the same time you may need something—what shall I say?—something more stimulating than the conversation which your somewhat limited fluency in the French language at present allows you to enjoy. Do not hesitate to talk with me when we are alone together on any subject that may happen to interest you.'

He smiled once again; and, while I thanked him, added: 'I am conversant with most subjects.'

As he strolled back across the lawn towards the house, he stowed away his pipe, which he seemed to use as a kind of emblem of common sense, in the pocket of his black alpaca jacket, which he wore over fawn tussore trousers.

I remained on the seat, thinking over his remarks, which required some classification before judgment could be passed on them. I could not accept his theory that jealousy about the girls, at least jealousy in any straightforward form, was at the bottom of the quarrel; because, in so much as the Scandinavians were to be thought of in connexion with Berthe and Suzette, each had paired off—if such an expression could be used of so amorphous a relationship—with a different girl: and everyone seemed perfectly happy with this arrangement. Berthe, as I have said, undoubtedly possessed a slight weakness for Monsieur Örn, which he recognised by markedly chivalrous behaviour towards her, when any such questions arose as the pumping-up of tyres of her bicycle, or carrying parcels back from the village when she did the shopping. Like Berthe, Monsieur Örn, too, was engaged; and he had, indeed, once handed round a small, somewhat faded, snapshot of himself sitting in ski-ing costume in the snow with his fiancée, who came from Trondhjem. Monsieur Lundquist, on the other hand, although interest in himself allowed him to show no more than moderate preference towards girls, or anyone else, seemed distinctly inclined towards Suzette. In so much as this allocation could be regarded as in any way part of a system, it also appeared to be absolutely satisfactory to everyone concerned. Indeed, the only person I knew of who might be said to have suffered from emotions that fell within the range of those suggested by Monsieur Dubuisson was myself; because, although the episode of the tennis court represented the more dramatic side of life at La Grenadière, the image of Suzette played in fact a far more preponderant part in my thoughts than the affairs of the Scandinavians, however unrestrained their behaviour.

I sometimes tried to sort out these feelings that had developed towards Suzette, which had certainly aroused from time to time a sensation of annoyance that Monsieur Lundquist should be talking animatedly to her, or helping her down the spiral staircase of some medieval building that we might be visiting. These were, I was aware, responses to be compared with those aroused by Jean Templer, with whom, as I have said, I now thought of myself as being 'in love'; and I was somewhat put out to find that recurrent projections in the mind of the images of either of them, Jean or Suzette, did not in the least exclude that of the other. That was when I began to suspect that being in love might be a complicated affair.

Naturally these reflections linked themselves with the general question of 'girls', discussed so often in my presence by Stringham and Templer. The curious thing was that, although quite aware that a sentiment of attraction towards Suzette was merely part of an instinct that had occasioned Peter's 'unfortunate incident'—towards which I was conscious of no sense of disapproval—my absorption in the emotional disturbance produced by Jean and Suzette seemed hardly at all connected with the taking of what had been, even in Templer's case, a fairly violent decision. I did not view his conduct on that London afternoon either as a contrast to my own inability to tackle the problem posed by these girls; nor even, for that matter, as an extension—or cruder and more aggravated version—of the same motive. My own position in the matter seemed, even to myself, to be misty: half-pleasant, half-melancholy. I was, however, struck by the reflection that undoubted inconvenience was threatened if this apparently recurrent malady of the heart was to repeat itself throughout life, with the almost dizzy reiteration that had now begun to seem unavoidable.

Suzette herself remained, so far as I was concerned, almost as enigmatic as Jean. Sometimes I thought she liked me to sit beside her at meals, or play as her partner at the strange games of auction bridge that sometimes took place in the evening, bearing the same relation to ordinary card playing that our tennis bore to ordinary tennis; and once there seemed a chance that her preference was shown even a little more definitely. This happened one Monday afternoon, when Bum was having his bath on the table in the garden, and, Madame Leroy suffering from migraine, Suzette was conducting this ceremony.

She had asked me to hold the dog, while he was being soaped all over. Bum usually enjoyed his bath, standing quietly with legs apart, until it was time for him to be dried with a rough towel; then he would run off, wagging his tail. That day, however, he stood on the table peacefully until the soap-suds reached half-way down his back, when, at that point, he suddenly escaped from my hands, and jumped on to the ground. Shaking himself excitedly, he set off across the garden, having decided, evidently, that he had had enough of this bath. At that moment Charley appeared from the front door. I have mentioned that Charley was never bathed, and resented this attention paid to Bum's handsome coat. Charley began to growl, and the two dogs ran round the paths, snarling, though fairly amicably, at each other, chased by Suzette and myself. At last Charley disappeared into the bushes, and we headed Bum into the summer-house. As we came in there after him, he jumped on to the seat, and out of the window. Suzette sat down, rather breathless, shaking her head to show that she proposed to pursue him no farther. I sat down beside her, and found my hand resting on hers. She continued to laugh, and did not remove her fingers from under mine. Whether or not this fortuitous preliminary might have developed along more positive lines is hard to say. I had no plan of campaign in mind, though I knew this to be a moment that would commit us one way or the other. Suzette probably—indeed, certainly—knew far better what it was all about. However, there was no time for the situation to develop because, at that moment, Widmerpool appeared in the summer-house; just as he had done on the day of my arrival.

'*Mais qu'est-ce que c'est que ce bruit effroyable?*' he said. '*On doit penser que tout le monde a devenu fou.*'

'*Tout le monde est fou,*' Sudette said. '*Naturellement, tout le monde est fou.*'

Our hands had separated as Widmerpool came through the door. He sat down between us and began to talk of *Les Misérables,* which he had borrowed from Monsieur Örn. Suzette resumed her well-behaved, well-informed exterior, with which I was by now so familiar, and for a time she discoursed, almost as boringly as Widmerpool himself, on the subject of Victor Hugo. The occasion was past; but in the days that followed I thought often about that moment in the summer-house when our hands had been together, regretting that I had not managed to turn that chance to some account.

The words just spoken by Monsieur Dubuisson while sitting by me on the seat had, therefore, a peculiarly powerful effect in confirming, not only the overwhelming impact of this new, perhaps rather alarming, ascendancy of the emotions; but also my consciousness of the respect which Monsieur Dubuisson obviously paid to these forces, as coming first when any human relationship was to be analysed. I did not feel that I could discuss such things with Widmerpool; and it never occurred to me that he himself might feel equally attracted towards Berthe or Suzette. I still saw him only in the crude, and inadequate, terms with which I had accepted him at school.

If I had decided to discuss Suzette with Widmerpool, I should have had an opportunity that evening, because he mentioned in his more formal manner, after dinner, that he would like to have a word with me alone, before I went off to bed. He showed every sign of being particularly pleased about something, when he spoke to me, and he was rubbing together his 'gritty little knuckles', as Peter Templer had called them. Except at meals, I had seen nothing of him all day. I imagined that he had been working in his bedroom, where he would sometimes disappear for hours on end, while he translated the French classics, or otherwise studied the language.

Everyone, except Commandant Leroy, went off to their rooms early that night; probably because the atmosphere of disquiet spread by Monsieur Örn and Monsieur Lundquist, although perhaps a shade less crushing than on the previous day, was still discouraging to general conversation. After the rest of the household had gone upstairs, Widmerpool, pursing his lips and blowing out his cheeks, kept on looking in the commandant's direction, evidently longing to get rid of him; but the old man sat on, turning over the tattered pages of a long out-of-date copy of *L'Illustration*, and speaking, disjointedly, of the circumstances in which he had been gassed. I liked Commandant Leroy. The fact that he was bullied by his wife had not prevented him from enjoying a life of his own; and, within the scope of his world of patent medicines and pottering about the garden, he had evolved a philosophy of detachment that made his presence restful rather than the reverse. Widmerpool despised him, however, chiefly, so far as I could gather, on the grounds that the commandant had failed to reach a higher rank in the army. Madame Leroy, on the other hand, was respected by Widmerpool. 'She has many of the good qualities of my own mother,' he used to say; and I think he was even a trifle afraid of her.

Commandant Leroy sat describing in scrupulous detail how his unit had been ordered to move into the support line along a network of roads that were being shelled, according to his account, owing to some error committed by the directing staff. He had gone forward to inspect the ground himself, and so on, and so forth. The story came to an end at last, when he found himself in the hands of the army doctors, of whom he spoke with great detestation. Widmerpool stood up. There was another long delay while Bum was let out of the room into the garden: and, after Bum's return, Commandant Leroy shook hands with both of us, and shuffled off to bed. Widmerpool shut the door after him, and sat down in the commandant's chair.

'I have settled the matter between Örn and Lundquist,' he said.

'What on earth do you mean?'

Widmerpool made that gobbling sound, not unlike an engine getting up steam, which meant that he was excited, or put out, about something: in this case unusually satisfied. He said: 'I have had conversations with each of them—separately—and I think I can confidently predict that I am not far from persuading them to make things up.'

'What?'

'In fact I have reason to suppose that within, say, twenty-four hours I shall have achieved that object.'

'Did you tell them not to be such bloody fools?'

This was quite the wrong comment to have made.

Widmerpool, who had previously shown signs of being in a far more complacent mood than was usual in his conversations with me, immediately altered his expression, and, indeed, his whole manner. He said: 'Jenkins, do you mind home truths?'

'I don't think so.'

'First,' said Widmerpool, 'you are a great deal too fond of criticising other people: secondly, when a man's self-esteem has been injured he is to be commiserated with—not blamed. You will find it a help in life to remember those two points.'

'But they have both of them been behaving in the most pompous way imaginable, making life impossible for everyone else. I quite see that Lundquist should not have sent sneaks over the net like that, but Örn ought to be used to them by now. Anyway, if Örn did rap out something a bit stiff, he could easily have said he was sorry. What do you think the word meant?'

'I have no idea what the word meant,' said Widmerpool, 'nor am I in the least interested to learn. I agree with you that Lundquist's play from a certain aspect—I repeat from a *certain* aspect—might be said to leave something to be desired; that is to say from the purest, and, to my mind, somewhat high-flown, sportsmanship. On the other hand there was no question of *cheating*.'

'It is a pretty feeble way of winning a service.'

'Games,' said Widmerpool, 'are played to be won, whatever people may say and write to the contrary. Lundquist has never found that service to fail. Can he, therefore, be blamed for using it?'

He folded his arms and stared fixedly past me, as if he were looking out into the night in search of further dialectical ammunition, if I were to remain unconvinced by his argument.

'But you wouldn't use that service yourself?'

'Everyone has his own standards of conduct,' said Widmerpool. 'I trust mine are no lower than other people's.'

'Anyhow,' I said, as I was getting tired of the subject, 'what did you do to bring them together?'

'First of all I went to Lundquist,' said Widmerpool, relaxing a little the stringency of his manner; 'I explained to him that we all understood that Örn should not have spoken as he did.'

'But we don't know what Örn said.'

Widmerpool made a nervous movement with his hands to show his irritation. He seemed half-inclined to break off his narrative, but changed his mind, and went on: 'I told him that we all knew Örn was a bit of a rough diamond, as Lundquist himself understood, as much—or even more—than the rest of us. It was therefore no good expecting anything very courtly from Örn in the way of behaviour.'

'How did Lundquist take that?'

'He fully agreed. But he emphasised that such defects, attributed by him to inherent weaknesses in the Norwegian system of education, did not alter the fact that his, Lundquist's, honour had been insulted.'

Widmerpool stopped speaking at this point, and looked at me rather threateningly, as if he was prepared for such a statement on Lundquist's part to arouse comment. As I remained silent, he continued: 'That argument was hard to answer. I asked him, accordingly, if I had his permission to speak to Örn on the same subject.'

'What did he say to that?'

'He bowed.'

'It all sounds very formal.'

'It *was* very formal,' said Widmerpool. 'Why should it have been otherwise?'

Not knowing the answer, I did not take up this challenge; thinking that perhaps he was right.

'I went straight to Örn,' said Widmerpool, 'and told him that we all understood his most justifiable annoyance at Lundquist's service; but that he, Örn, must realise, as the rest of us did, that Lundquist is a proud man. No one could be in a better position to appreciate that fact than Örn himself, I said. I pointed out that it could not fail to be painful to Lundquist's *amour-propre* to lose so frequently—even though he were losing to a better tennis-player.'

'Did all this go on in French?'

Widmerpool took no notice of this question; which, both Scandinavians knowing some English, seemed to me of interest.

'Örn was more obstinate than Lundquist,' said Widmerpool. 'Örn kept on repeating that, if Lundquist wished to play pat-ball with the girls—or little boys, he added—there was plenty of opportunity for him to do so. He, Örn, liked to play with men—*hommes*—he shouted the word rather loud. He said that, in his own eyes, *hommes* might be stretched to include Paul-Marie and Jean-Népomucène, but did not include Lundquist.'

Widmerpool paused.

'And he stuck to that?' I asked.

Widmerpool shook his head slowly from side to side, allowing his lips to form a faint smile. He said: 'Örn took a lot of persuading.'

'Then he agreed?'

'He agreed that I should come again tomorrow to renew the discussion.'

'You are certainly taking a lot of trouble about them.'

'These things are worth trouble,' said Widmerpool. 'You may learn that in time, Jenkins.'

I followed him up the stairs, more than a little impressed.

There was something about the obstinacy with which he pursued his aims that could not be disregarded, or merely ridiculed. Even then I did not recognise the quest for power.

The consequence of Widmerpool's efforts was to be seen a couple of nights later, when Monsieur Örn and Monsieur Lundquist sat together, after dinner, at one of the tables in the garden, finishing off between them a bottle of Cognac: after giving a glass to Madame Leroy, Madame Dubuisson, and myself, and two glasses to Monsieur Dubuisson: everyone else, for one reason or another, refusing the offer. Long after I was in bed and asleep that night, I was woken by the sound of the Scandinavians stumbling up to their room, now apparently on the best of terms. It had been a triumph of diplomacy on Widmerpool's part. The enterprise he had shown in the matter displayed a side of his character the existence of which I had never suspected. I had to admit to myself that, in bringing Monsieur Örn and Monsieur Lundquist together again, he had achieved a feat that I should never have ventured even to attempt.

The sense of tension that had prevailed during the period of the row was now replaced by one of perhaps rather strained amiability, in which all but Monsieur Dubuisson joined. Monsieur Dubuisson accepted the brandy as the outward and visible sign of reconciliation, but he showed no vestige of surprise at the changed situation certainly none of satisfaction. Madame Leroy was, of course, delighted; though I do not think that she ever had any idea of how concord had once more been brought about: attributing it entirely to a change of heart on the part of the couple concerned. For the rest of us, there could be no doubt of the improvement. The latter part of my stay at La Grenadière was passed, on the whole, in an atmosphere of good will on all sides: with the exception of a comparatively minor incident which involved Widmerpool only. There was undoubtedly a suggestion of nervous relaxation when Monsieur Lundquist moved, a few days later, to Bonn, where he was to continue his studies. Monsieur Örn shook him very heartily by the hand, and they agreed to meet when Monsieur Örn visited Stockholm, as he assured Monsieur Lundquist he had always intended to do sooner or later; but I do not think there was any doubt that Monsieur Örn was as heartily glad to see the Swede's back as Monsieur Lundquist to escape from Monsieur Örn.

Curiously enough, Widmerpool, although the sole author of the reconciliation, received little or no credit for his achievement. During the few days left to them after they had made things up, Monsieur Örn and Monsieur Lundquist used sometimes to walk up and down in the garden together, when Widmerpool would occasionally try to join them; but I noticed that they would always stroll away from him, or refuse to speak English, or French, which debarred him from conversation. It was hard to say whether or not he noticed this; his last week at La Grenadière being, in any case, blighted by another matter, in its way, sufficiently provoking for him. This was the appearance on the wall of the *cabinet de toilette* of a crude, though not unaccomplished, representation of himself—somewhat in the style of the prehistoric drawings of the caves in the Dordogue—in this case scratched on the plaster with a sharp instrument.

Two things about this composition seemed to me certain: first, that it was intended as a portrait of Widmerpool: secondly, that the artist was French. Beyond these external facts, that seemed to admit of no critical doubt, I was completely at sea as to where responsibility might lie; nor could I be sure of the moment when the design was completed. At the time when I first became aware of its existence, Widmerpool had been out of temper all the previous day; so that his eye had probably fallen on the picture some twenty-four hours or more before it came to my own notice. I could not help wondering whether he would mention the subject.

That evening he remarked: 'I really think something should be done about those two French boys.'

'What have they been up to now?'

'Haven't you noticed a drawing on one of the walls?'

'A sort of scrawl?' I asked, rather dishonestly.

'I don't know what it is meant to be,' said Widmerpool. 'And although it is not exactly indecent, it is suggestive, which is worse. I hardly like to mention it to Madame Leroy, though I certainly think it should be removed.'

'How would you remove it?'

'Well, paint over it, or something like that. It is Paul-Marie, I suppose.'

He said no more about the picture; but I knew that its existence embittered his remaining days at La Grenadière. I felt some curiosity myself as to the identity of the draughtsman, and was not at all sure that Widmerpool was right in recognising the work of Paul-Marie. If one of the boys was to be suspected, I should have put my money on Jean-Népomucène, who might easily have felt a sudden need to express himself in some graphic medium, in order to compete with the conversational gifts in which his elder brother excelled. However, there was no reason to suppose that he was good at drawing, and, especially on account of the facility displayed, the possibility that neither of the boys was responsible could not be disregarded.

I thought in turn of the other persons in the house. On the whole it was hardly likely to be attributable to Madame Leroy, or her husband. Berthe, it was true, had sometimes boasted of her sketches in water-colour: though this would have been an oblique and perverse manner of advertising her talent. I could not even bear to consider that the hand might have been Suzette's, dismissing all consideration of such a thing from my mind. Rosalie worked too hard all day to have had time to make the deep incisions in the wall: she was also short-sighted. Marthe was invariably in the kitchen, and she could hardly ever have had the opportunity to observe Widmerpool's appearance with sufficient thoroughness to have achieved so striking a likeness. It was doubtful whether Madame Dubuisson possessed the creative imagination: though there could be no question that the drawing must have appealed, especially, to her own brand of humour. Monsieur Dubuisson sometimes cleaned out his pipe with a sharp, stiletto-like instrument that could have been used as an etching-point.

There remained the contingency that Widmerpool might have derived some obscure gratification in the production of a self-portrait in such inappropriate circumstances: though here, as an objection, one came up against the essential Frenchness of the design. If Widmerpool himself had indeed been the artist, his display of annoyance had been a superb piece of acting: and it was not credible to me that anything so improbable was at the root of the mystery. Perplexity was increased a day or two later by the addition to the picture of certain extraneous details, in pencil, which, personally, I should have been prepared to swear belonged in spirit to a school of drawing other than that of the originator. However, these appendages may not have been attributable to any single individual. They were mannered, and less sure of touch. This business was never referred to in my presence by anyone except Widmerpool, and then only on that single occasion; though I had reason to suppose that Paul-Marie and Jean-Népomucène used to joke with each other privately on the subject.

When Widmerpool left for England, soon after this, the riddle remained unsolved. He was by then full of a project he had in mind for rearranging his legal books and papers; and, although he muttered that he hoped we might meet again, if I ever came to London, he was preoccupied, evidently thinking of more important matters. It was as if he had already dismissed from his mind the frivolities of Touraine, and peculiarities of the inhabitants of La Grenadière, even before he climbed into the *grognard's* taxi: which had not yet begun its habitual panting and heaving, as its owner was accustomed to coast downhill for the first part of the journey, with a view to saving petrol.

The space left at La Grenadière by the withdrawal of Monsieur Lundquist was filled by Dr. Szczepanowski, a quiet Pole, with gold pince-nez, who wore the rosette of the Légion d'Honneur in his button-hole. Monsieur Dubuisson used to take him for walks, during which, no doubt, he explained some of his theories, including the Moroccan hydraulic scheme. The morning after Widmerpool's departure, another visitor arrived, though for a few days only. This was the father of Paul-Marie and Jean-Népomucène, who was the double of the Frenchman with the Assyrian beard who had occupied my seat in the train on the journey from Paris. Perhaps it was even the man himself: if so, he made no reference to the incident. His presence had a sedative effect on his two sons. Monsieur Dubuisson did not approve of his handling of the French language; warning me not to imitate their father's construction of his sentences, especially in connexion with his use of the preterite. Madame Leroy, on the other hand, greatly admired her relative.

'Quel brave Papa,' she used to say, gazing at him, as he

used to set off down the hill in his straw hat and black gloves.

I never discovered precisely what relation each was to the other, but Madame Leroy's glance seemed to imply that life might have had more compensations if she had married some bearded, titanic figure of this kind, rather than Commandant Leroy. Familiarity with her had not dispelled my impression that she was a kind of sorceress. Life at La Grenadière was not altogether like life in the outer world. Its usage suggested a stage in some clandestine order's ritual of initiation. For a time the presence of Widmerpool had prolonged the illusion that he and I were still connected by belonging to the community of school: and that all that had happened since I had seen him last was that each of us was a year or two older. As the weeks passed at La Grenadière, the changes that had clearly taken place in Widmerpool since he had ceased to be a schoolboy emphasised the metamorphosis that had happened within myself. Now that he had moved on, his absence from La Grenadière made amputation from that earlier stage of life complete; and one day, when Suzette asked me something or other about the way lessons were taught in England, I was surprised to find forgotten the details of what had been for so long a daily routine.

It was, I suppose, an awareness of this change in circumstance that made me increasingly conscious, as the close of my stay in France approached, of the necessity to adopt an attitude towards life, in a general way, more enterprising. This aim owed something to remarks Widmerpool had addressed to me at one time or another; but it was directed particularly towards the project of taking some active step—exactly what step remained undecided—in solving the problem of Suzette: who had established herself as a dominating preoccupation, to which any recollection of

Jean Templer was now, on the whole, subordinate. In spite of prolonged thought devoted to this subject, I managed to devise no more resolute plan than a decision to make some sort of declaration to her when the day came to leave the house: a course of action which, although not remarkable for its daring, would at any rate mark some advance from a state of chronic inaction in such matters from which escape seemed so difficult. The question was: how best to arrange this approach?

Having seen other guests depart from La Grenadière, I knew that the entire household was accustomed to gather round, saying good-bye, and waiting to watch the taxi slide precipitously down the hill. If the question were to arise, for example, of kissing anyone good-bye, it was clear that there might be imminent risk of having to kiss—if such a hypothetical case as kissing were to be considered at all—the whole of the rest of the party gathered together at the door in the wall. Certainly, it might be safely assumed that nothing of the sort would be expected by anyone so anglicised as Monsieur Dubuisson: but I was not at all sure what French etiquette might prescribe in the case of guest and host: though suspecting that anything of the sort was, in general, limited to investitures. It was equally possible that any such comparatively intimate gesture might be regarded as far more compromising in France than in England; and, quite apart from any embarrassing, or unacceptable, situations that might be precipitated if kissing were to become general at my departure from La Grenadière, any hope of making a special impression on Suzette would undoubtedly be lost by collective recourse to this manner of saying good-bye: however pleasant in Suzette's individual case such a leave-taking might be. Some plan was, therefore, required if a hasty decision was to be avoided.

Accordingly, I finished packing early upon the day I was to return to England, and went downstairs to survey the house and garden. The hot weather had continued throughout my stay, and the sun was already beating down on the lawn, where no one except Dr. Szczepanowski was to be seen. I noticed that Suzette's big straw sun-bonnet was gone from the hall, where she was accustomed to leave it on the console table. Bum had once found it there, carrying the hat into the garden and gnawing away some of the brim. Dr. Szczepanowski was writing letters, and he smiled in a friendly manner. Jean-Népomucène at one of the tables appeared a moment later, and requested help in mending an electric torch, as Dr. Szczepanowski was skilled in such matters. Both of them retired to the house to find suitable implements to employ in making the repairs. There was just a chance that Suzette might be sitting in the summer-house, where she occasionally spent some of the morning reading.

I crossed the grass quickly, and went under the arch, preparing to withdraw if Monsieur Dubuisson should turn out to be settled there with his pipe. The excitement of seeing Suzette's straw bonnet was out of all proportion to the undecided nature of my project. She was sitting half-turned from the entrance, and, judging that, if I lost time in talk, I might be manœuvred into a position of formality which could impose insuperable restraint, I muttered that I had come to say good-bye, and took her hand, which, because her arm was stretched along the back of the seat, lay near me. As she turned, I immediately realised that the hand was, in fact, Madame Dubuisson's, who, as she left the house, must have taken up Suzette's straw hat to shield her eyes while she crossed the garden.

It was now too late to retreat. I had prepared a few sentences to express my feelings, and I was already half-way through one of them. Having made the mistake, there was nothing for it but to behave as if it were indeed Madame Dubuisson who had made my visit to La Grenadière seem so romantic. Taking her other hand, I quickly used up the remaining phrases that I had rehearsed so often for Suzette.

The only redeeming feature of the whole business was that Madame Dubuisson herself gave not the smallest sign of being in the least surprised. I cannot remember in what words she answered my halting assurance that her presence at La Grenadière would remain for me by far its sweetest memory; but I know that her reply was entirely adequate: indeed so well rounded that it seemed to have been made use of on a number of earlier occasions when she must have found herself in somewhat similar circumstances. She was small and round and, I decided, really not at all bad-looking. Her contribution to the situation I had induced was, at least from my own point of view, absolutely suitable. She may even have allowed me to kiss her on the cheek, though I could not swear to this. She asked me to send her a picture of Buckingham Palace when I returned to England.

This scene, although taking up only a few minutes, exhausted a good deal of nervous energy. I recognised that there could now be no question of repeating anything of the same sort with Suzette herself, even if opportunity were to present itself in the short time left to me. That particular card had been played, and the curious thing was that its effect had been to provide some genuine form of emotional release. It was almost as if Madame Dubuisson had, indeed, been the focus of my interest while I had been at La Grenadière. I began to feel quite warmly towards her, largely on the strength of the sentiments I had, as it were, automatically expressed. When the time came to say goodbye, hands were shaken all round. Suzette gave mine a little extra squeeze, after relaxing the first grip. I felt that this small attention was perhaps more than I deserved. The passage with Madame Dubuisson seemed at any rate a slight advance in the right direction when I thought things over in the train. It was nearly Christmas before I found the postcard of Buckingham Palace, which perhaps never reached her, as the Dubuissons must, by then, have moved on from La Grenadière.

4.

Prolonged, lugubrious stretches of Sunday afternoon in a university town could be mitigated by attending Sillery's tea-parties, to which anyone might drop in after half-past three. Action of some law of averages always regulated numbers at these gatherings to something between four and eight persons, mostly undergraduates, though an occasional don was not unknown. Towards the middle of my first term I was introduced to them by Short, who was at Sillery's college, a mild second-year man, with political interests. Short explained that Sillery's parties had for years played an established rôle in the life of the university; and that the staleness of the rock-buns, which formed a cardinal element of these at-homes, had become so hackneyed a subject for academical humour that even Sillery himself would sometimes refer to the perennially unpalatable essence of these fossils salvaged from some forgotten cake-world. At such moments Sillery would remind his guests of waggish or whimsical remarks passed on the topic of the rock-buns by an earlier generation of young men who had taken tea with him in bygone days: quoting in especial the galaxy of former undergraduate acquaintances who had risen to some eminence in later life, a class he held in unconcealed esteem.

Loitering about the college in aged sack-like clothes and Turkish slippers, his snow white hair worn longer than that of most of his colleagues, Sillery could lay claim to a venerable appearance: though his ragged, Old Bill moustache (which, he used laughingly to mention, had once been compared with Nietszche's) was still dark. He was, indeed, no more than entering into his middle fifties: merely happening to find convenient a façade of comparative senility. At the beginning of the century he had published a book called *City State and State of City* which had achieved some slight success at a time when works popularising political science and economic theory were beginning to sell; but he was not ambitious to make his mark as an author. In fact one or two of his pupils used to complain that they did not receive even adequate tuition to get them through the schools at anything but the lowest level. This was probably an unjust charge, because Sillery was not a man to put himself easily in the wrong. In any case, circumstances had equipped him with such dazzling opportunity for pursuing his preponderant activity of interfering in other people's business that only those who failed to grasp the extent of his potentiality in his own chosen sphere would expect—or desire—him to concentrate on a pedestrian round of tutorial duties.

Before my first visit, Short described some of this background with care; and he seemed to feel certain qualms of conscience regarding what he termed 'Sillers's *snobisme*'. He explained that it was natural enough that Sillery should enjoy emphasising the fact that he numbered among his friends and former pupils a great many successful people; and I fully accepted this plea. Short, however, was unwilling to encounter too ready agreement on this point, and he insisted that 'all the same' Sillery would have been 'a sounder man'—sounder, at any rate, politically—if he had made a greater effort to resist, or at least conceal, this temptation to admire worldly success overmuch. Short himself was devoted to politics, a subject in which I took little or no interest, and his keenest ambition was to become a Member of Parliament. Like a number of young men of that period, he was a Liberal, though to which of the various brands of Liberalism, then rent by schism, he belonged, I can no longer remember. It was this Liberal enthusiasm which had first linked him with Sillery, who had been on terms with Asquith, and who liked to keep an eye on a political party in which he had perhaps once himself placed hopes of advancement. Short also informed me that Sillery was a keen propagandist for the League of Nations, Czechoslovakia, and Mr. Gandhi, and that he had been somewhat diverted from earlier Gladstonian enthusiasms by the success of the Russian Revolution of 1917.

Short had taken me to Sillery's two or three times before I found myself—almost against my own inclination—dropping in there on Sunday afternoon. At first I was disposed to look on Sillery merely as a kind of glorified schoolmaster—a more easy going and amenable Le Bas—who took out the boys in turn to explore their individual characteristics to know better how to instruct them. This was a manner of regarding Sillery's entertaining so crude as to be positively misleading. He certainly wanted to find out what the boys were like: but not because he was a glorified schoolmaster. His understanding of human nature, coarse, though immensely serviceable, and his unusual ingenuity of mind were both employed ceaselessly in discovering undergraduate connexions which might be of use to him; so that from what he liked to call 'my backwater'—the untidy room, furnished, as he would remark, like a boarding-house parlour—he sometimes found himself able to exercise a respectable modicum of influence in a larger world. That, at least, was how things must have appeared to Sillery himself, and in such activities his spirit was concentrated.

Clay, for example, was the son of a consul in the Levant. Sillery arranged a little affair through Clay which caused inconvenience, minor but of a most irritating kind, to Brightman, a fellow don unsympathetic to him, at that time engaged in archæological digging on a site in the Near East. Lakin, outwardly a dull, even unattractive young man, was revealed as being related through his mother to an important Trade Union official. Sillery discovered this relative—a find that showed something like genius—and managed to pull unexpected, though probably not greatly important, strings when the General Strike came in 1926. Rajagopalaswami's uncle, noted for the violence of his anti-British sentiments, was in a position to control the appointment of a tutor to one of the Ruling Princes; Sillery's nominee got the place. Dwight Wideman's aunt was a powerful influence in the women's clubs in America: a successful campaign was inaugurated to ban the American edition of a novel by an author Sillery disliked. Flannigan-Fitzgerald's brother was a papal chamberlain: the Derwentwater annulment went through without a hitch. These, at least, were the things that people said; and the list of accessories could be prolonged with almost endless instances. All were swept into Sillery's net, and the undergraduate had to be obscure indeed to find no place there. Young peers and heirs to fortune were not, of course, unwelcome; though such specimens as these—for whose friendship competition was already keen—were usually brought into the circle through the offices of secondary agents rather than by the direct approach of Sillery himself, who was aware that in a society showing signs of transition it was essential to keep an eye on the changing focus of power. All the same, if he was known to incline, on the whole, to the Right socially, politically he veered increasingly to the Left.

In the course of time I found that much difference of opinion existed as to the practical outcome of Sillery's scheming, and I have merely presented the picture as first displayed to me through the eyes of Short. To Short, Sillery was a mysterious, politically-minded cardinal of the academical world, 'never taking his tea without an intrigue' (that was the phrase Short quoted); for ever plotting behind the arras. Others, of course, thought differently, some saying that the Sillery legend was based on a kind of kaleidoscope of muddled information, collected in Sillery's almost crazed brain, that his boasted powers had no basis whatever in reality: others again said that Sillery certainly knew a great number of people and passed round a lot of gossip, which in itself gave him some claim to consideration as a comparatively influential person, though only a subordinate one. Sillery had his enemies, naturally, always anxious to denigrate his life's work, and assert that he was nothing more than a figure of fun; and there was probably something to be said at least for the contention that Sillery himself somewhat exaggerated the effectiveness of his own activities. In short, Sillery's standing remained largely a matter of opinion; though there could be no doubt about his turning out to be an important factor in shaping Stringham's career at the university.

Stringham had been due to come into residence the same term as myself, but he was thrown from a horse a day or two before his intended return to England, and consequently laid up for several months. As a result of this accident, he did not appear at his college until the summer, when he took against the place at once. He could scarcely be persuaded to visit other undergraduates, except one or two that he had known at school, and he used to spend hours together sitting in his room, reading detective stories, and complaining that he was bored. He had been given a small car by his mother and we would sometimes drive round the country together, looking at churches or visiting pubs.

On the whole he had enjoyed Kenya. When I told him about Peter Templer and Gwen McReith—an anecdote that seemed to me of outstanding significance—he said: 'Oh, well, that sort of thing is not as difficult as all that,' and he proceeded to describe a somewhat similar incident, in which, after a party, he had spent the night with the divorced wife of a coffee planter in Nairobi. In spite of Madame Dubuisson, this story made me feel very inexperienced. I described Suzette to him, but did not mention Jean Templer.

'There is absolutely nothing in it,' Stringham said. 'It is just a question of keeping one's head.'

He was more interested in what I had to report about Widmerpool, laughing a lot over Widmerpool's horror on hearing the whole truth of Le Bas's arrest. The narrative of the Scandinavians' quarrel struck him only on account of the oddness of the tennis-court on which we had been playing the set. This surprised me, because the incident had seemed of the kind to appeal to him. He had, however, changed a little in the year or more that had passed since I had seen him; and, although the artificial categories of school life were now removed, I felt for the first time that the few months between us made him appreciably older than myself. There was also the question of money—perhaps suggested by Widmerpool's talk on that subject—that mysterious entity, of which one had heard so much and so often without grasping more than that its ownership was desirable and its lack inconvenient: heard of, certainly, without appreciating that its possession can become as much part of someone as the nose on the face. Even Uncle Giles's untiring contortions before the altar of the Trust, when considered in this light, now began to appear less grotesque than formerly; and I realised at last, with great clearness, that a sum like one hundred and eighty pounds a year might indeed be worth the pains of prolonged and acrimonious negotiation. Stringham was, in fact, not substantially richer than most undergraduates of his sort, and, being decidedly free with his money, was usually hard-up, but from the foothills of his background was, now and then, wafted the disturbing, aromatic perfume of gold, the scent which, even at this early stage in our lives, could sometimes be observed to act intoxicatingly on chance acquaintances; whose unexpected perseverance, and determination not to take offence, were a reminder that Stringham's mother was what Widmerpool had described as 'immensely wealthy'.

Peter Templer, as I have said, rarely wrote letters, so that we had, to some extent, lost touch with him. Left to himself there could be little doubt that he would, in Stringham's phrase, 'relapse into primeval barbarism'. Stringham often spoke of him, and used to talk, almost with regret, of the adventures they had shared at school: already, as it were, beginning to live in the past. Some inward metamorphosis was no doubt the cause of Stringham's melancholia, because his attacks of gloom, although qualified by fairly frequent outbursts of high spirits, could almost be given that name. There was never a moment when he became reconciled to the life going on round him. 'The buildings are nice,' he used to say. 'But not the undergraduates.'

'What do you expect undergraduates to be like?'

'Keep bull-pups and drink brandies-and-soda. They won't do as they are.'

'Your sort sound even worse.'

'Anyway, what can one do here? I am seriously thinking of running away and joining the Foreign Legion or the

North-West Mounted Police—whichever work the shorter hours.'

'It is the climate.'

'One feels awful if one drinks, and worse if one's sober. I knew Buster's picture of the jolly old varsity was not to be trusted. After all he never tried it himself.'

'How is he?'

'Doing his best to persuade my mother to let Glimber to an Armenian,' said Stringham, and speaking with perhaps slightly more seriousness: 'You know, Tuffy was very much against my coming up.'

'What on earth did it have to do with her?'

'She takes a friendly interest in me,' said Stringham, laughing. 'She behaved rather well when I was in Kenya as a matter of fact. Used to send me books, and odds and ends of gossip, and all that sort of thing. One appreciates that in the wide open spaces. She is not a bad old girl. Many worse.'

He was always a trifle on the defensive about Miss Weedon. I had begun to understand that his life at home was subject to exterior forces like Buster's disapproval, or Miss Weedon's regard, which brought elements of uncertainty and discord into his family life, not only accepted by him, but almost enjoyed. He went on: 'There has been talk of my staying here only a couple of years and going into the Foot Guards. You know there is some sort of arrangement now for entering the army through the university. That was really my mother's idea.'

'What does Miss Weedon think?'

'She favours coming to London and having a good time. I am rather with her there. The Household Cavalry has been suggested, too. One is said—for some reason—to "have a good time in The Tins".'

'And Buster's view?'

'He would like me to remain here as long as possible—four years, post-graduate course, research fellowship, anything so long as I stay away—since I shattered his dream that I might settle in Kenya.'

It was after one of these conversations in which he had complained of the uneventfulness of his day that I suggested that we should drop in on Sillery.

'What is Sillery?'

I repeated some of Short's description of Sillery, adding a few comments of my own.

'Oh, yes,' said Stringham. 'I remember about him now. Well, I suppose one can try everything once.'

We were, as it happened, first to arrive at that particular party. Sillery, who had just finished writing a pile of letters, the top one of which, I could not avoid seeing, was addressed to a Cabinet Minister, was evidently delighted to have an opportunity to work over Stringham, whom he recognised immediately on hearing the name.

'How is your mother?' he said. 'Do you know, I have not seen her since the private view of the Royal Academy in 1914. No, I believe we met later at a party given by Mrs. Hwfa Williams, if my memory serves me.'

He continued with a stream of questions, and for once Stringham, who had shown little interest in coming to the party, seemed quite taken aback by Sillery's apparent familiarity with his circumstances.

'And your father?' said Sillery, grinning, as if in spite of himself, under his huge moustache.

'Pretty well.'

'You were staying with him in Kenya?'

'For a few months.'

'The climate suits him all right?'

'I think so.'

'That height above sea-level is hard on the blood-pressure,'

Sillery said; 'but your father is unexpectedly strong in spite of his light build. Does that shrapnel wound of his ever give trouble?'

'He feels it in thundery weather.'

'He must take care of it,' said Sillery. 'Or he will find himself on his back for a time, as he did after that spill on the Cresta. Has he run across Dicky Umfraville yet?'

'They see a good deal of each other.'

'Well, well,' said Sillery. 'He must take care about that, too. But I must attend to my other guests, and not talk all the time about old friends.'

I had the impression that Sillery regarded Stringham's father as a falling market, so far as business was concerned; and, although he did not mention Buster, he was evidently far more interested in Mrs. Foxe's household than that of her former husband. However, the room was now filling up, and Sillery began introducing some of the new arrivals to each other and to Stringham and myself. There was a sad Finn called—as nearly as I could catch—Vaalkiipaa: Honthorst, an American Rhodes Scholar, of millionaire stock on both sides of his family: one of Sillery's pupils, a small nervous young man who never spoke, addressed as 'Paul', whose surname I did not discover: and Mark Members, of some standing among the freshmen of my year, on account of a poem published in *Public School Verse* and favourably noticed by Edmund Gosse. Up to that afternoon I had only seen Members hurrying about the streets, shaking from his round, somewhat pasty face a brownish, uneven fringe that grew low on his forehead and made him look rather like a rag doll, or marionette: an air augmented by brown eyes like beads, and a sprinkling of freckles. His tie, a broad, loose knot, left the collar of his shirt a little open. I admired this lack of self-consciousness regarding what I then—rather priggishly—looked on as eccentricity of dress. He appeared to have known Sillery all his life, calling him 'Sillers', a form of address which, in spite of several tea-parties attended, I had not yet summoned courage to employ. The American, Honthorst's, hair was almost as uncontrolled as that of Members. It stood up on the top of his head like the comb, or crest, of a hoopoe, or cassowary; this bird-like appearance being increased by a long, bare neck, ending in a white collar cut drastically low. Honthorst had a good-natured, dazed countenance, and it was hard to know what to say to him. Vaalkiipaa was older than the rest of the undergraduates present. He had a round, sallow face with high cheekbones, and, although anxious to be agreeable, he could not understand why he was not allowed to talk about his work, a subject always vetoed by Sillery.

Conversation was now mostly between Sillery and Members; with the awkward long silences which always characterised the teas. During one of these pauses, Sillery, pottering about the room with the plate of rock-buns, remarked: 'There is a freshman named Quiggin who said he would take a dish of tea with me this afternoon. He comes from a modest home, and is, I think, a little sensitive about it, so I hope you will all be specially understanding with him. He is at one of the smaller colleges—I cannot for the moment remember which—and he has collected unto himself sundry scholarships and exhibitions, which is—I think you will all agree—much to his credit.'

This was a fairly typical thumb-nail sketch of the kind commonly dispensed by Sillery, in anticipation of an introduction: true as far as it went, though giving little or no clue to the real Quiggin: even less to the reason why he had been asked to tea. Indeed, at that period, I did not even grasp that there was always a reason for Sillery's invitations, though the cause might be merely to give opportunity for preliminary investigation: sometimes not worth a follow-up.

No one, of course, made any comment after this speech about Quiggin, because there was really no suitable comment to make. The mention of scholarships once more started off Vaalkiipaa on the subject of his difficulties in obtaining useful instruction from attendance at lectures; while Honthorst, almost equally anxious to discuss educational matters in a serious manner, joined in on the question of gaps in the college library and—as he alleged—out-of-date methods of indexing. Honthorst persisted in addressing Sillery as 'sir', in spite of repeated requests from his host that he should discard this solecism. Sillery was deftly circumventing combined Finnish-American attack, by steering the conversation toward New England gossip by way of hunting in Maine—while at the same time extracting from Vaalkiipaa apparently unpalatable facts about the anti-Swedish movement in Finland—when Quiggin himself arrived: making his presence known by flinging open the door suddenly to its fullest extent, so that it banged against one of the bookcases, knocking over a photograph in a silver frame of three young men in top-hats standing in a row, arm-in-arm.

'Come in,' said Sillery, picking up the picture, and setting it back in its place. 'Come in, Quiggin. Don't be shy. We shan't eat you. This is Liberty Hall. Let me introduce you to some of my young friends. Here is Mr. Cheston Honthorst, who has travelled all the way from America to be a member of my college: and this is Mr. Jenkins, reading history like yourself: and Mr. Stringham, who has been to East Africa, though his home is that beautiful house, Glimber: and Mr. Vaalkiipaa—rather a difficult name, which we shall soon find that we have all got so used to that we shan't be able to understand how we ever found it difficult—and Paul, here, you probably know from Brightman's lectures, which he tells me he loyally attends just as you do; and I nearly forgot Mr. Mark Members, whose name will be familiar to you if you like modern verse—and I am sure you do—so make a place on the sofa, Mark, and Quiggin can sit next to you.'

At first sight, Quiggin seemed to be everything suggested by Sillery's description. He looked older than the rest of us: older, even, than Vaalkiipaa. Squat, and already going bald, his high forehead gave him the profile of a professor in a comic paper. His neck was encircled with a starched and grubby collar, his trousers kept up by a belt which he constantly adjusted. For the first time since coming up I felt that I was at last getting into touch with the submerged element of the university, which, I had sometimes suspected, might have more to offer than was to be found in conventional undergraduate circles. Mark Members was evidently impressed by a similar—though in his case unsympathetic—sense of something unusual so far as Quiggin was concerned; because he drew away his legs, hitherto stretched the length of the sofa, and brought his knees right up to his chin, clasping his hands round them in the position shown in a picture (that used to hang in the nursery of a furnished house we had once inhabited at Colchester) called The Boyhood of Raleigh; while he regarded Quiggin with misgiving.

'Couldn't find the way up here for a long time,' said Quiggin.

He sat down on the sofa, and, speaking in a small, hard voice with a North Country inflexion, addressed himself to Members: seeming to be neither embarrassed by the company, nor by Sillery's sledge-hammer phrases, aimed, supposedly, at putting him at his ease. He went on: 'It's difficult when you're new to a place. I've been suffering a bit here'—indicating his left ear which was stuffed with yellowish cotton-wool—'so that I may not catch all you say too clearly.'

Members offered the ghost of a smile; but there could be no doubt of his uneasiness, as he tried to catch Sillery's eye. However, Sillery, determined that his eye was not to be caught by Members, said: 'The first year is a great period of discovery—and of self-discovery, too. What do you say, Vaalkiipaa? Can you find your way about yet?"

'I make progress,' said Vaalkiipaa, unsmiling: to whom it was perhaps not clear whether Sillery's question referred to discovery in the topographical sense or the more intimate interior examination with which Sillery had linked it. There was a silence, at the end of which Members put in, rather at random: 'Sillers, it is too clever of you to buy a suit the same colour as your loose covers.'

Quiggin sat sourly on the extreme edge of the sofa, glancing round the room like a fierce little animal, trapped by naturalists. He had accepted a rock-bun from Sillery, and for some minutes this occupied most of his attention. Honthorst said: 'They tell me the prospects for the college boat are pretty good, Professor Sillery.'

'Good,' said Sillery, making a deprecatory gesture in our direction to suggest his own unworthiness of this style of address. 'Good. Very good.'

He said this with emphasis, though without in any way committing his opinion on the subject of current aquatics. It was evident that at present Quiggin was the guest who chiefly interested him. Stringham he must have regarded as already in his power because, although he smiled towards him in a friendly manner from time to time, he made no further effort to talk to him individually. Quiggin finished his rock-bun, closely watched by Sillery, picked some crumbs from his trousers, and from the carpet round him:

afterwards throwing these carefully into the grate. Just as Quiggin had dealt with the last crumb, Members rose suddenly from the sofa and cast himself, with a startling bump, almost full length on the floor in front of the fireplace: exchanging in this manner his Boyhood-of-Raleigh posture for that of the Dying Gladiator. Sillery, whose back was turned, started violently, and Members pleaded: 'You don't mind, Sillers? I always lie on the floor.'

'I like my guests to feel at home, Mark,' said Sillery, recovering himself immediately, and playfully pinching the nape of Members's neck between his finger and thumb, so that Members hunched his shoulders and squeaked shrilly. 'And you, Quiggin, are you happy?' Sillery asked.

Quiggin shook his head at the rock-buns, held out towards him once more; and, apparently taking the question to have a more general application than as a mere enquiry as to whether or not he wanted another cup of tea, or was comfortable sitting, as he was, at the springless end of the sofa, said in reply: 'No, I'm not.'

Sillery was enchanted with this answer.

'Not happy?' he said, as if he could not believe his ears.

'Never seem to get enough peace to get any work done,' said Quiggin. 'Always somebody or other butting in.'

Sillery beamed, proffering the plate once more round the room, though without success. Quiggin, as if something had been released within him, now began to enlarge on the matter of his own exasperation. He said: 'All anyone here seems interested in is in messing about with some game or other, or joining some society or club, or sitting up all night drinking too much. I thought people came to the university to study, not to booze and gas all the time.'

'Very good, Quiggin, very good,' said Sillery. 'You find we all fall woefully short of your own exacting standards—formed, no doubt, in a more austere tradition.'

He smiled and rubbed his hands, entranced. It even seemed that he might have been waiting for some such outburst on Quiggin's part: and Quiggin himself somehow gave the air of having made the same speech on other occasions.

'What an extraordinary person,' said Members, under his breath, a remark probably audible only to myself, owing to the fact that the extreme lowness of the armchair in which I was sitting brought my ear almost level with Members's mouth, as he rested with his elbow on the floor. Sillery said: 'What do you think, Mark? Do you find that we are too frivolous?'

Members began to say: 'My dear Sillers——' but, before he could speak the phrase, Sillery cut him short by adding: 'I thought you might be in agreement with Quiggin as your homes are so close, Mark.'

After he had said this, Sillery stood back a bit, as if to watch the effect of his words, still holding the plate of rock-buns in his hand. If he had hoped to strike dismay into the hearts of his listeners, he could hardly have expected a more successful result so far as Quiggin and Members were concerned. Members, thoroughly put out, went pink in the face; Quiggin's expression became distinctly sourer than before, though he did not change colour. 'I had a suspicion that neither of you was aware of this,' said Sillery. 'But you must live *practically* in the same street.'

He nodded his head several times, and changed the subject; or, at least, varied it by asking if I had ever read *Jude the Obscure*. I realised, without achieving any true comprehension of what Sillery was about, that the object of revealing publicly that Members and Quiggin lived close to each other during the vacation was intended in some manner to bring both to heel: in any case I did not know enough of either at the time to appreciate that each might prefer that any details regarding his home life should be doled out by himself alone.

Sillery abandoned the subject after this demonstration of strength on his part, so that the rest of his guests were left in ignorance even of the name of the town Members and Quiggin inhabited. The American and the Finn slipped away soon after this, on the plea that they must work; in spite of protests from Sillery that no one could, or should, work on Sunday evening. As they were leaving, another visitor could be heard coming up the stairs. He must have stood aside for them to pass him, because a moment later, speaking in a resonant, musical voice, like an actor's or practised after-dinner speaker's, he said, as he came through the door: 'Hullo, Sillers, I hoped I might catch you at home.'

This new arrival I recognised as Bill Truscott, who had gone down two or three years before. I had never previously met him, but I had seen him and knew his name well, because he was one of those persons who, from their earliest years, are marked down to do great things; and who so often remain a legend at school, or university, for a period of time after leaving the one or the other: sometimes long after any hope remains, among the world at large, that promise of earlier years will be fulfilled. Sillery was known to be deeply attached to Bill Truscott, though to what extent he inwardly accepted the claims put forward for Truscott's brilliant future, it was not easy to say. Outwardly, of course, he was a strong promoter of these claims; and, in some respects, Truscott could be described as the most characteristic specimen available of what Sillery liked his friends to be; that is to say he was not only successful and ambitious, but was also quite well off for a bachelor (a state he showed no sign of relinquishing), as his father, a Harley Street specialist, recently deceased, had left him a respectable capital. He had gained a good degree, though only by the skin of his teeth, it was rumoured, and, since academical honours represented a good deal of his stock-in-trade, this close shave regarding his 'first' was sometimes spoken of as an ominous sign. However, the chief question seemed still to be how best his brilliance should be employed. To say that he could not make up his mind whether to become in due course Prime Minister, or a great poet, might sound exaggerated (though Short had so described Truscott's dilemma), but in general he was at any rate sufficiently highly regarded in the university, by those who had heard of him, to make him appear a fascinating, and almost alarming, figure.

After sitting down beside Sillery, Truscott at first hardly spoke at all; but at the same time his amused smile acted as a sort of charm on the rest of the company, so that no one could possibly have accused him, on the grounds of this silence, of behaving in an ungracious manner. He was tall and dark, with regular features, caught rather too close together, and the most complete self-assurance that can be imagined. His clothes and hair, even his face, seemed to give out a kind of glossiness, and sense of prosperity, rather like Monsieur Lundquist's. He was already going a little grey, and this added to his air of distinction, preventing him from looking too young and inexperienced. I addressed a remark to him which he acknowledged simply by closing and opening his eyes, making me feel that, the next time I spoke, I ought to make an attempt to find something a trifle less banal to say: though his smile at the same time absolved me from the slightest blame in falling so patently short of his accustomed standards. I was not conscious of being at all offended by this demeanour: on the contrary, Truscott's comportment seemed a kind of spur to encourage all who came to win his esteem; although

—and perhaps because—he was obviously prepared to offer nothing in return.

If Bill Truscott's arrival in the room made a fairly notable impression on myself, chiefly on account of the glowing picture Short had drawn of his charm and brilliance, the rest of Sillery's party treated Truscott, if possible, with even closer attention. Members moved unobtrusively from the floor to a chair, and Quiggin, one of the legs of whose trousers had rucked up, revealing long hirsute pants of grey material, pulled the end of his trouser down towards a black sock, and sat more upright on the sofa. Both he and Members evidently felt that the opportunity had now arrived for Sillery's disclosure regarding the adjacency of their respective homes to be forgotten in discussion of more important matters. Stringham turned out to know Truscott already. He said: 'Hullo, Bill,' and for a minute or two they spoke of some party in London where they had met a month or two before.

'You must tell us about the polite world, Bill," said Sillery, perching on the side of Truscott's chair and slipping an arm round his shoulder. 'Fancy the hostesses allowing you to steal away from their clutches and drop in to visit us here.'

Sillery made this remark gently, through his teeth, so that it was not easy to say whether he intended a compliment, an enquiry, or even an expression of disparagement of the fact that Truscott could spare time for dons and undergraduates at this stage of the Season; when a career had still to be carved out. Truscott certainly accepted the words as tribute to his popularity, and he threw his head back with a hearty laugh to express how great a relief it was for him to escape, even for a short period, from the world of hostesses thus somewhat terrifyingly pictured by Sillery: though he was, at the same time, no doubt aware that a more detailed explanation was required of him to show conclusively that his appearance in the university was due to nothing so ominous as lacking something better to do.

'I have really come on business, Sillers,' he said.

'Indeed?'

'I saw no reason why I should not combine business with pleasure, Eillers. As you know, Pleasure before Business has always been my motto.'

'Pleasure can be so exhausting,' put in Members, fixing Truscott with a winning smile, and thrusting his face forward a little.

However, he seemed a little uncertain, apart from his smile, how best to captivate someone of Truscott's eminence; though clearly determined to make an impression before the opportunity was past. Truscott, for his part, glanced attentively at Members: an appraisal that seemed to result in the decision that, although outwardly Members had not much to offer that was to Truscott's taste, there might be elements not to be despised intellectually. Sillery watched their impact with evident interest. He said: 'I expect you read *Iron Aspidistra,* Bill.'

Truscott nodded; but without producing any keen sense of conviction.

'Mark's poem,' said Sillery. 'It received quite a favourable reception.'

'Surrounded as usual by a brilliant circle of young men, Sillers,' said Truscott, laughing loudly again. 'To tell you the truth, Sillers, I have come up to look for a young man myself.'

Sillery chuckled, pricking up his ears. Truscott stretched out his legs languidly. There was a pause, and muted laughter from the rest of the guests. Truscott looked round, archly.

'For my boss as a matter of fact,' he said.

He laughed quietly to himself this time, as if that were a good joke. Quiggin, who had been silent all the while, though not unattentive, spoke unexpectedly in his grating voice: 'Who is "your boss"?' he asked.

I could not help admiring the cool way in which Truscott turned slowly towards Quiggin, and said, without the slightest suggestion of protest at Quiggin's tone: 'He is called Sir Magnus Donners.'

'The M.P.?'

'I fear that, at the moment, he cannot be so described.'

'But you work for him?' insisted Quiggin.

'Sir Magnus is kind enough to remunerate me as if I worked for him,' said Truscott. 'But you know, really, I scarcely like to describe myself as doing anything that suggests such violent exertions undertaken on his behalf. He is, in any case, the kindest of masters.'

He cocked an eyebrow at Quiggin, apparently not at all displeased by this rather aggressive inquisition. As Truscott had not witnessed Quiggin's arrival and earlier behaviour at the tea-party, I decided that he must find him less odd than he appeared to the rest of us: the thought that perhaps he classed all undergraduate opinion together, as inchoate substance, not to be handled too closely, occurring to me only several years later, after I had come down from the university. Sillery said: 'I don't expect "your master", as you call him, would have much difficulty in returning to the House at any by-election, would he, Bill?"

'His industrial interests take up so much time these days,' said Truscott. 'And really one must admit that ability of his sort is rather wasted in the House of Commons.'

'Isn't he going to get a peerage?' said Stringham, unexpectedly.

Truscott smiled.

'Always a possibility,' he said; and Sillery grinned widely, rubbing his hands together, and nodding quickly several times.

'It's a mortal shame that a big concern like his should be in the hands of a private individual,' said Quiggin, increasing the volume of his North Country accent, and speaking as if he were delivering the opening words of a sermon or address.

'Do you think so?' said Truscott. 'Some people do. Of course, Sir Magnus himself has very progressive ideas, you know.'

'I think you would be surprised, Quiggin, if you ever met Sir Magnus,' said Sillery. 'He has even surprised me at times.'

Quiggin looked as if there was nothing he would like better than to have an opportunity to meet Sir Magnus; but Sillery, who probably feared that conversation might decline from the handling of practical matters, like the disposal of jobs, to one of those nebulous discussions of economic right and wrong, of which he approved in general but obviously considered inopportune at that moment, brought back the subject of Truscott's opening statement by saying: 'And so Sir Magnus wants a man, does he?'

However, Truscott was not disposed to say more of that for the time being. He may even have thought that he had already given away too much. His manner became perceptibly less frivolous, and he said: 'I'll tell you about it later, Sillers.'

Sillery concurred. It was probable that he, too, would prefer the details to be given in private. However, he evidently regarded the acquisition of further information on this matter to be of prime importance; because a minute or two later his impatience got the better of him, and, rising from the arm of Truscott's chair, he announced: 'Bill and I are a pair of very old friends who haven't seen each other for many a long day, so that now I am going to drive you all out into the wind and rain in order that Bill and I can have a chat about matters that would no doubt appear to you all as very tedious.'

He put his head a little on one side. Neither Members nor Quiggin seemed very satisfied by this pronouncement: not at all convinced that they would find any such conversation tedious. Members tried to make some sort of protest by saying: 'Now, Sillers, that is really too bad of you, because you promised that you were going to show me your Gerard Manley Hopkins letter the next time I came to see you.'

'And I wanted to borrow *Fabian Essays,* if it wasn't troubling you,' said Quiggin, very sulky.

'Another time, Mark, another time,' said Sillery. 'And you will find your book in that shelf, Quiggin, with the other Webbs. Take great care of it, because it's a first edition with an inscription.'

Sillery was not at all discomposed, indeed he seemed rather flattered, by these efforts on the part of Members and Quiggin to stay and make themselves better known to Truscott; but he was none the less determined that they should not stand between him and the particulars of why Sir Magnus Donners wanted a young man; and what sort of a young man Sir Magnus Donners wanted. He made a sweeping movement with his hands, as if driving chickens before him in a farmyard, at the same time remarking to Stringham: 'You must come here again soon. There are things I should like to discuss interesting to ourselves.'

He turned quickly, to prevent Quiggin from taking too many of his books, and, at the same time, to say something to the depressed undergraduate called Paul. Stringham and I went down the stairs, followed by Mark Members, who, having failed to prolong his visit, seemed now chiefly interested in escaping from Sillery's without having the company of Quiggin thrust upon him. All three of us left the college through an arched doorway that led to the street. Rain had been falling while we were at tea, but the pavements were now drying under a woolly sky.

'What very Monet weather it has been lately,' said Members, almost to himself. 'I think I must hurry ahead now as I am meeting a friend.'

He disappeared into a side street, his yellow tie caught up over his shoulder, his hands in his pockets and elbows pressed to his sides. In a moment he was lost to sight.

'That must be a lie,' said Stringham. 'He couldn't possibly have a friend.'

'What was Truscott after?'

'He is rather a hanger-on of my mother's,' said Stringham. 'Said to be very bright. He certainly gets about.'

'And Sir Magnus Donners?'

'He was in the Government during the war.'

'What else?'

'He is always trying to get in with my mother, too.'

I had the impression that Stringham was himself quite interested in Bill Truscott, who certainly suggested the existence of an exciting world from which one was at present excluded. We strolled on through the empty streets towards Stringham's college. The air was damp and warm. At the top of the stairs, the sound of voices came from the sitting-room. Stringham paused at the door.

'Somebody has got in,' he said. 'I hope it is not the Boys' Club man again.'

He stood for a moment and listened; then he opened the door. There was a general impression of very light grey flannel suits and striped ties, which resolved itself into three figures, sitting smoking, one of whom was Peter Templer.

'Peter.'

'Bob Duport and Jimmy Brent,' said Peter, nodding towards the other two. 'We thought we would pay a call, to see how your education was getting along.'

He was looking well: perhaps a shade fatter in the face than when I had last seen him; and, having now reached the age for which Nature had, as it were, intended him, he was beginning to lose the look of a schoolboy dressed as a grown man. I should have known Duport and Brent anywhere as acquaintances of Peter's. They had that indefinable air of being up to no good that always characterised Peter himself. Both were a few years older than he; and I vaguely remembered some story of Duport having been involved in a motor accident, notorious for some reason or other. That affair, whatever it was, had taken place soon after he had left school: during my own first year there. He was built on similar lines to Peter, thin and tall, with sandy hair, dressed in the same uncompromising manner, though on the whole less successfully. Brent was big and fat, with spectacles that seemed to have been made with abnormally small circles of glass. Both, it turned out, were business friends, working in the City. They accepted some of Stringham's sherry, and Brent, whose manners seemed on the whole better than Duport's, said: 'What do they rush you for this poison?'

The sum was not revealed, because, almost at the same moment, Duport, who was examining The Pharisee's rider, in one of the pictures that had followed Stringham to this room, remarked: 'I've never seen a jock on land, or sea, sit a horse like that.'

'Put your shirt on him when you do, Bob,' said Peter. 'You may recoup a bit on some of those brilliant speculations of yours that are always going to beat the book.'

'How long are you staying?' asked Stringham, before Duport had time to defend his racing luck.

'Going back to London after dinner.'

I saw that any change that I might have suspected of taking place in the relationship between Templer and Stringham had by now crystallised. It was not that they no longer liked one another, or even that they had ceased to take pleasure in each other's company, so much as the fact that each had grown out of the other's habit of mind: and, in consequence, manner of talking. Stringham had become quieter than he had been at school; though he was, at the same time, more than ever anxious for something new to happen at comparatively short intervals, in order that his attention should be occupied, and depression kept at arm's length. Peter had changed less: merely confirming his earlier attitude towards life. I did not know to what extent, if at all, he was aware of any difference in Stringham. He knew Stringham well, and I could imagine him describing—and laughing over—the warming-up process that seemed to be required that evening: a warming-up that never took place so far as Stringham was concerned. I could, equally, imagine Stringham laughing at the way in which Peter was already shaping along the lines that Stringham had himself so accurately foretold.

'We might all have dinner together,' Stringham said.

'That was the idea.'

In the restaurant, Stringham and I talked to Peter, rather fragmentarily: mainly on the subject of Stringham's stay in Kenya. Duport and Brent grunted to each other from time to time, or, occasionally, to Peter: no sense of fusion quickening the party. Peter told us about his car, recently bought second-hand, and considered a bargain.

'I must take you for a proper run in her,' he said, 'before we go back.'

'Don't forget I want to look in at the Cabaret Club before we hit the hay,' said Brent.

Duport said: 'He's got a girl there who owes him some money.'

'I wish she did,' said Brent: but without elucidating further that cryptic aspiration.

The Vauxhall was, in fact, clearly the foundation of this unpremeditated visit. Peter wanted to try the vehicle out. He continued to assure us how cheap the price had been, inviting admiration of its many good points. This car was adapted for speed, having had the windscreen removed; but it had all the appearance of having passed through a good many hands since the days of its first owner. It certainly put Stringham's two-seater in the shade, and perhaps slightly irritated Stringham on this account. Peter was immensely pleased with the Vauxhall, the purchase of which seemed in some way to have involved Brent. As the evening wore on, Brent's personality became in other respects more determinable. For example, he talked incessantly of women. Peter and Duport treated this preoccupation as something not to be taken at all seriously, making no attempt to hide their concurrent opinion that Brent's attempts to make himself agreeable to girls were entirely unsuccessful: all of which Brent took in fairly good part. His voice managed to be at once deep and squeaky; and he spoke repeatedly of a woman called Flora, who appeared in some manner to have behaved badly to him. On the whole he was undoubtedly preferable to Duport, whose demeanour was aggressive and contradictious. I was not surprised when Duport announced: 'Couldn't stand my place at all. Got sent down my first term. Still it looks worse here.'

I enquired about Jean.

'She's all right,' Peter said. 'In love with a married man twice her age.'

'Is that the sister I'm after?' asked Duport.

'That's the one.'

Towards the end of the meal, things improved a little; though Stringham and I seemed now to know Templer on an entirely different footing from that of the past. Finally, I felt even glad that Duport and Brent had increased the numbers of the party, because their presence alleviated, if it did not conceal, the change that had taken place. Peter was still anxious that we should see how fast the car would travel on a piece of open road, and he promised to deliver us back by midnight; so, after dinner was finished, we agreed to go with him. Stringham and I climbed into the back of the Vauxhall with Duport, not through choice, but because there was more room for everyone if Brent occupied the seat beside the driver. We moved off sharply in the direction of unfrequented roads. I lay back, wishing the seat had been roomy enough to allow sleep. Duport smoked sullenly: Stringham, on the other side of me, was silent: Brent had returned to the subject of Flora, though without receiving much outward sympathy from Peter. We had reached the outskirts of the town, and the car was gathering speed, when—without clearly taking in the meaning of the words—I heard Brent say: 'Let's pick up those two pieces.'

I was scarcely aware that Peter had slowed down, when we stopped with a jerk by the kerb, where, beside a pillar-box at the corner of a side road, two girls were standing. They were wearing flowered dresses, blue and pink respectively, with hats of the same material. Their faces were those of a couple of Dutch dolls. Brent, from the front seat, twisted himself round towards them.

'Would you like to come for half an hour's drive?' he asked, in his unattractive voice, high and oily.

The girls raised no difficulty whatever about falling in with this suggestion. There was not even any giggling to speak of. They jumped in immediately, one of them sitting in front, on Brent's knee; the other joining the three of us at the back, where there was already little enough room to spare. They answered to the names of Pauline and Ena. Ena sat sideways, mainly on Duport, but with her legs stretched across my own knees: her feet, in tight high-heeled shoes, on Stringham's lap. This was a situation similar to many I had heard described, though never previously experienced. In spite of its comparative discomfort, I could not help feeling interest—and some slight excitement—to see how matters would develop. Stringham was obviously not very pleased by the additional company, which left him without the doubtful advantage of any substantial share in either of the girls; but he made the best of things, even attempting some show of pinching Ena's ankles. Neither of the girls had much conversation. However, they began to squeal a little when the car arrived on a more open piece of road, and the engine gathered speed.

'You must admit it was a good buy,' shouted Peter, as we did about seventy-five or eighty.

'All the same we might be returning soon,' said Stringham. 'My physician is insistent that I should not stay up late after my riding accident—especially with anyone, or part of anyone, on my knee.'

'We ought to be getting back, too,' said Duport, freeing himself, apparently dissatisfied, from Ena's long embrace. 'Otherwise it will be tomorrow before we get to London.'

'All right,' said Peter, 'we will turn at the next crossroads.'

It was on the homeward journey, after making this turn, that the mishap occurred. Peter was not driving specially fast, but the road, which was slippery from rain fallen earlier in the evening, took two hairpin bends; and, as we reached the second of these, some kind of upheaval took place within the car. No one afterwards could explain exactly what happened, though the accepted supposition was that Brent, engaged in kissing Pauline, had disturbed her susceptibilities in some manner, so that she had drawn herself unexpectedly away from him; and, in his effort to maintain their equilibrium, Brent had thrust her against Peter's elbow, in such a way that her head obscured the view. That, at least, was one of the main theories afterwards propounded. Whatever the root of the trouble, the memorable consequence was that Peter—in order to avoid a large elm tree—drove into the ditch: where the car stopped abruptly, making a really horrible sound like a dying monster; remaining stuck at an angle of forty-five degrees to the road.

This was an unpleasant surprise for everyone. The girls could not have made more noise if they had been having their throats cut. Brent, too, swore loudly, in his almost falsetto voice, natural, or assumed to meet the conditions of the moment; though, as it happened, he and Pauline, perhaps owing to their extreme proximity to each other, were the only two members of the party who, when we had at last all succeeded in making our way out of the Vauxhall, turned out to be quite unhurt. Stringham was kicked in the face by Ena, who also managed to give Duport a black-eye by concussion between the back of her head and his forehead. Peter bruised his knuckles against the handle of the door. Ena complained of a broken arm from the violence with which Duport had seized her as the car went over the edge. My own injuries were no worse than a sharp blow on the nose from Ena's knee. However, we were all shaken up more than a little; and, as one of the wheels had buckled, the car clearly could not be driven back that night. There had been some difficulty in getting out of the ditch, and, as I stepped up on to the road, I felt the first drop of rain. Now it began to pour.

This was an exceedingly inconvenient occurrence from

everyone's point of view. Probably Stringham and I were in the most awkward position, as there seemed no prospect of either of us reaching college by the required hour; and it would not be easy to convince the authorities that nothing of which they might disapprove had taken place to make us late: or even to keep us out all night, if things should turn out so badly. The girls were, presumably, accustomed to late hours if they were in the habit of accepting lifts at that time of night; but for them, too, this was an uncomfortable situation. Such recrimination that took place was about equally divided between Peter's two friends and Ena and Pauline: although I knew that, in fact, Stringham was far the angriest person present. Rain now began to fall in sheets. We moved in a body towards the elm tree.

'Of all the bloody silly things to do,' said Brent. 'You might have killed the lot of us.'

'I might easily,' said Peter, who was always well equipped for dealing with friends of Brent's kind. 'I wonder I didn't with a lout like you in the boat. Haven't you ever had a girl sitting on your knee before, that you have to heave her right across the car, just because there is a slight bump in the road?'

'What did you want to get a lot of girls in the car for, anyway?' asked Duport, who was holding a rolled-up handkerchief to his eye. 'If you weren't capable of steering?'

'I didn't ask for them.'

'You ought to have some driving lessons.'

Peter replied with a reference to the time when Duport was alleged to have collided with a lamp-post at Henley; and they both went on like this for some minutes. Pauline and Ena, the former of whom was crying, also made a good deal of noise, while they lamented the difficulty of getting home, certainly an insoluble problem as matters stood.

'How far out are we?' Stringham asked, 'and what is the time?'

The hour was a quarter-past eleven; the general view, that we had come about a dozen miles. There was a chance that a car might pass, but we were a large party to be accommodated. In any case, there was no sign of a car. Stringham said: 'We had better make plans for camping out. Brent, you look good at manual labour—will you set to work and construct a palisade?'

'You didn't ought to have brought us here,' said Pauline.

Ena, still complaining of a torn stocking, and bruises on her arm, cried into her handbag. Peter and Duport moved round the car, pulling and pushing its outer surface, or opening the bonnet to inspect the engine. Brent sat panting to himself on the bank.

Peter said: 'The rain seems to be stopping. We may as well walk in the right direction. There is no point in staying here.'

There was not much enthusiasm for this suggestion; and, when attempted, the heel came off one of Ena's shoes, in any case not adapted to a twelve-mile march.

'Can't we change the wheel?' said Duport.

We struggled with the problem of the wheel from different angles of approach. It was impossible to wind the jack into position under the axle. We only managed to embed the car more firmly than ever in the side of the ditch. While we were engaged in these labours, rain began to fall again, a steady, soaking downpour. Once more we retired to the tree, and waited for the shower to clear.

'What a bloody silly thing to do,' said Duport.

'Almost as brilliant as the time you fell into the orchestra on Boat-Race Night.'

Stringham said: 'For my part, I am now in a perfect condition to be received into one of those oriental religions whose only tenet is complete submission to Fate.'

He joined Brent on the bank, and sat with his head in his hands. A minute or two after this, the miracle happened. There was a grinding noise farther up the road, and the glare of powerful headlights appeared. It was a bus. Brent, with surprising agility for so fat a man, jumped up from where he was sitting, and ran out into the centre of the road, holding his arms wide apart as if in supplication. He was followed by Duport, apparently shaking his fist. I felt little interest in possible danger of their being run over: only a great relief that the bus must in any case come to a standstill, whether they were killed or not.

Stringham said: 'What did I foretell? Kismet. It is the Wheel.'

The bus stopped some yards short of Brent. We all clambered up the steps. Inside, the seats were almost empty, and no one seemed to realise from what untold trouble we had all been rescued. The girls now recovered quickly, and were even anxious to make an assignation for another night. They were, however, both set down (with no more than a promise from Brent that he would look them up if again in that neighbourhood) at a point not far from the pillar-box from which they had embarked on that unlucky drive. We reached the centre of the town: Templer, Brent, and Duport still quarrelling among themselves about which hotel they should patronise, and arguing as to whether or not it was worth ringing up a garage that night to arrange for the repair of the Vauxhall. This discussion was still in progress when we left the bus. Stringham and I said good-night to them.

'I'm sorry to have landed you in all this,' Peter said.

'You must come for a drive with us sometime,' said Stringham. 'Anyway, we'll meet soon.'

But I knew that they would not meet soon; and that this was a final parting. Peter, I think, knew this too. A crescent moon came from behind clouds. The others disappeared from sight. Stringham said: 'What a jolly evening, and what nice friends Peter makes.' The clocks were striking midnight at different places all over the town as I stepped through the door of my college. The rain had cleared. Moonlight gave the grass and towers an air of unreality, as if all would be removed in the morning to make way for another scene. My coat hung on me, shapeless and soggy, the damp working down through the cloth to my shoulders.

This incident with Templer's car had two results, so far as Stringham was concerned: it brought an end to his friendship with Peter, and it immensely strengthened his desire to go down as soon as possible from the university. In fact, he was now unwilling even to consider the possibility of staying in residence long enough to take a degree. It was one of those partings of the ways that happen throughout life: in this case, foretold by Peter himself. No doubt Peter, too, had guessed that something had ended, and that his prophecy had come true, while the rain dripped down on all of us, through the branches of that big elm, while we stood in the shadows of the ditch regarding the stranded Vauxhall.

When I say that their friendship came to an end, I do not mean that Stringham no longer spoke of Templer; nor that, when he talked of him, it was with dislike: nor even, in a sense, with disapproval. On the contrary, he used to refer to Peter as frequently as he had done in the past; and the story of the drive, the crash, Ena and Pauline, Brent and Duport, was embroidered by him until it became a kind of epic of discomfort and embarrassment: at the same time, something immensely funny in the light of Peter's chosen manner of life. Nevertheless, there could be no doubt whatever that metamorphosis had taken place; and, sometimes, it was almost as if Stringham were speaking of a friend who had died, or gone beyond the sea to a place from which he would never return. Once he said: 'How appalling Peter will be in fifteen years' time'; and he never spoke, as formerly he had done, of arranging a meeting between the three of us in London.

I was even aware that, in an infinitely lesser degree, I could not avoid being unfavourably included by Stringham in this reorientation; which, almost necessarily, affected anyone who was at once a friend of Peter's and a fellow undergraduate, fated to remain up for at least three years: both characteristics reminding Stringham of sides of life from which he was determined to cut away. Besides, for my own part I shared none of this sense of having seen the last of Peter; though even I had to admit that I did not care for the idea of spending much of my time with his present acquaintances, if Brent and Duport were typical representatives of his London circle. The extent to which Stringham had resolved to settle his own career was brought home to me one morning, through the unexpected agency of Quiggin, next to whom I found myself sitting, when attending one of Brightman's lectures, at which I had not been appearing so regularly as perhaps I should.

On this occasion Quiggin walked back with me towards my college, though without relaxing the harsh exterior he had displayed when we had first met at Sillery's. He seemed chiefly concerned to find out more about Mark Members.

'Where does his stuff appear?' he asked.

'What stuff?'

'His poems have been published, haven't they?'

'The one I read was in *Public School Verse.*'

'Why *"Public"?'* said Quiggin. 'Why *"Public" School Verse?* Why not just *"School Verse"?'*

I was unable to answer that one; and suggested that such a title must for some reason have appealed to the editors, or publisher, of the volume.

'It is not as if they were "public" schools,' said Quiggin. 'They could not be less "public".'

I had heard this objection voiced before, and could only reply that such schools had to have a name of some sort. Quiggin stopped, stuck his hands into his pockets (he was still wearing his black suit) and poked his head forward. He looked thin and unhealthy: undernourished, perhaps.

'Have you got a copy?' he asked.

'Yes.'

'Can I borrow it?'

'All right.'

'Now?'

'If you like to come with me.'

We undertook the rest of the journey to my rooms in silence. Arrived there, Quiggin glanced round at the furnishings, as if he did not rate very highly the value of the objects provided by the college to sit, or lie, upon. They were, indeed, shabby enough. Standing by the bookcase, he took out the copy of *Public School Verse,* which he had lighted upon immediately, and began to run rapidly through the rest of the books.

'Do you know Members well?' he asked.

'I've met him once, since we were at Sillery's.'

This encounter with Members had been at a luncheon party given by Short, where Members had much annoyed and mortified his host by eating nearly all the strawberries before the meal began. In addition, he had not spoken at all during luncheon, leaving before coffee was served, on the grounds that he had to play the gramophone to himself for half an hour every afternoon; and that, unless he withdrew at once, he would not have time for his music owing to a later engagement. Short, for a mild man, had been quite cross.

'I understand that Members is a coming poet,' said Quiggin.

I agreed that *Iron Aspidistra* showed considerable promise. Quiggin gloomily turned the pages of the collection. He said: 'I'd be glad to meet Members again.'

It was on the tip of my tongue to answer that he was almost certain to do this, sooner or later, if their homes were so close; but, as Quiggin evidently meant there and then, rather than in the vacation, I thought it wiser to leave the remark unmade. I promised to let him know if a suitable occasion should arise, such as Members visiting my rooms, though that seemed improbable after his behaviour at Short's luncheon party.

'Can I take *The Green Hat* too?' asked Quiggin.

'Don't lose it.'

'It is all about fashionable life, isn't it?'

'Well, yes.'

I had myself not yet fully digested the subject matter of *The Green Hat*, a novel that I felt painted, on the whole, a sympathetic picture of what London had to offer: though much of the life it described was still obscure to me. I was surprised at Quiggin asking for it. He went on: 'In that case I do not expect that I shall like it. I hate anything superficial. But I will take the book and look at it, and tell you what I think of the writing.'

'Do.'

'I suppose that it depicts the kind of world that your friend Stringham will enter when he joins Donners-Brebner,' said Quiggin, as he continued to inspect the bookshelf.

'How do you mean?'

'Well you must have heard that he has taken the job that Truscott was talking about at Sillery's. Surely he has told you that?'

'What, with Sir Magnus Donners?'

It was no use pretending that I knew something of this already. I was, indeed, so surprised that only after Quiggin had gone did I begin to feel annoyance.

'I should have thought he would have told you,' said Quiggin.

'Where did you hear this?'

'At Sillery's, of course. Sillery says Stringham is just the man.'

'He probably is.'

'Of course,' said Quiggin, 'I knew at once there would be no chance of Truscott thinking of *me*. Not good enough, by any manner of means, I suppose.'

'Would you have liked the job?'

I did not know what else to say: the idea of Quiggin being the sort of man Truscott was looking for seeming to me so grotesque.

Quiggin did not bother to reply to this question. He merely repeated, with a sniff: 'Not good enough by a long chalk,' adding: 'You might come and see me some time in my college, if you can find the way to it. You won't get any priceless port, or anything like that.'

I said that I was not particularly fond of port; and began to give an account of my likes and dislikes in the matter of wine, which Quiggin, with what I now see as excusable impatience, cut short by saying: 'I live very quietly. I can't afford to do otherwise.'

'Neither can I.'

Quiggin did not answer. He gave me a look of great contempt; as I supposed, for venturing, even by implication, to draw a parallel between a lack of affluence that might, literally, affect my purchase of rare vintages, and a figure of speech intended delicately to convey his own dire want for the bare necessities of life. He remained silent for several seconds, as if trying to make up his mind whether he could ever bring himself to speak to me again; and then said gruffly: 'I've got to go now.'

As he went off, all hunched up on one side with *Public School Verse* and *The Green Hat* under his arm, I felt rather ashamed of myself for having made such a thoughtless remark. However, I soon forgot about this, at the time, in recalling the news I had learnt about Stringham, which I wanted to verify as soon as possible. In general, however, I continued to feel an interest in Quiggin, and the way he lived. He had something of the angry solitude of spirit that held my attention in Widmerpool.

Stringham, when I next saw him, seemed surprised at the importance with which I invested his decision.

'I thought I'd told you,' he said. 'As a matter of fact it isn't finally fixed yet. What awful cheek of your friend Quiggin, if I may say so.'

'What do you think of him?'

'The man is a closed book to me,' Stringham said. 'And one that I confess I have little temptation to open. Bill Truscott, on the other hand, was rather impressed.'

'With Quiggin?'

'Curiously enough.'

'Will you work with Truscott?'

'I shall be the other personal secretary.'

'Did Sillery put up the suggestion?'

'He is very keen on it. He agrees one's family will have to be consulted.'

'Will your family raise difficulties?'

'For once,' said Stringham, 'I don't think they will. My

mother will at last see hopes of getting me settled in life. Buster—most mistakenly—will suppose this to be the first step on the stair to a seat on the Donners-Brebner Board. My father will be filled with frank astonishment that I should be proving myself capable of earning a living in any capacity whatsoever.'

'What about a degree?'

'Bill Truscott reports Sir Magnus as demanding who the hell wants a degree these days; and saying all he needs is men who know the world, and can act and think quickly.'

'Strong stuff.'

'I suppose I can take lessons from Bill.'

'Then you won't come up next term?'

'Not if I can avoid it.'

Sillery's part in this matter was certainly of interest. He might have been expected—as Stringham himself agreed—to encourage as many undergraduates as possible to remain, for as long as possible, within his immediate range. Later on, however, I began to understand something of his reasons for recommending this course. If Stringham remained at the university, it was probable that he would fall under influences other than—and alien to—Sillery's. Even if he remained Sillery's man, he was obviously a person who might easily get involved in some scrape for which Sillery (if too insistent on taking Stringham under his wing) might be held in some degree answerable. Placed in a key position in Donners-Brebner—largely due to Sillery's own recommendation—Stringham could not only supply news of that large concern, but could also keep an eye on Sillery's other man, Truscott. In due course Sillery would no doubt find himself in a position to renew acquaintance in most satisfactory conditions. In short, power without responsibility could hardly be offered to Sillery, within this limited sphere, upon cheaper terms. Such a series of crude images would scarcely have suggested themselves in quite this manner to Sillery's mind—still less did I see them myself in any such clarity—but the apparent paradox of why Sillery threw in his weight on the side of Stringham's going-down became in due course comparatively plain to me.

'Anyway,' said Stringham, 'you'll be in London yourself soon.'

'I suppose so.'

'Then we'll have some fun.'

Somehow, I felt doubts about this. Life no longer seemed to present quite the same uncomplicated façade as at a time when dodging Le Bas and shirking football had been cardinal requirements to make the day tolerable. Although I might not feel, with Stringham, that Peter Templer was gone for good, Peter certainly seemed now to inhabit a world that offered limited attractions. The sphere towards which Stringham seemed to be heading, little as I knew of it, was scarcely more tempting to me. Perhaps Widmerpool had been right in advocating a more serious attitude of mind towards the problem of the future. I thought over some of the remarks he had made on this subject while we had both been staying at La Grenadière.

As it turned out, Mrs. Foxe did not show the complacence Stringham had expected in agreeing, at once, that he should cease to be a member of the university. On the contrary, she wrote to say that she thought him too young to spend all his time in London; even going so far as to add that she had no desire for him to turn into 'something like Bill Truscott': of whom she had always been supposed to approve. However, this was an obstacle not entirely unforeseen; in spite of Stringham's earlier hope that his mother might decide on the spur of the moment that a job was the best possible thing for him.

'Of course that's Buster,' he said, when he spoke of the letter.

I was not sure that he was right. The tone of his mother's remarks did not at all suggest arguments put forward at second-hand. They sounded much more like her own opinions. Stringham reasserted his case. The end of it was that she decided to come and talk things over.

'Really rather good of her,' said Stringham. 'You can imagine how busy she must be at this time of year.'

'Do you think you will persuade her?'

'I'm going to rope in Sillery.'

'Take her to see him?'

'Have him to lunch. Will you come and play for my side?'

'I can't play for your side, if I don't want you to go down.'

'Well, just keep the ring then.'

This was about the stage when I began to become dimly conscious of what Short was trying to convey when he spoke of Sillery's influence, and his intrigues; although, as far as it went, a parent's discussion of her son's future with a don still seemed natural enough. Sillery, I thought, was like Tiresias: for, although predominantly male, for example, in outward appearance, he seemed to have the seer's power of assuming female character if required. With Truscott, for instance, he would behave like an affectionate aunt; while his perennial quarrel with Brightman—to take another instance of his activities—was often conducted with a mixture of bluntness and self-control that certainly could not be thought at all like a woman's row with a man: or even with another woman; though, at the same time, it was a dispute that admittedly transcended somehow a difference of opinion between two men. Certainly Sillery had no dislike for the company of women in the way of ordinary social life, provided they made no personal demands on him. I was anxious to see how he would deal with Mrs. Foxe.

Meanwhile, I continued occasionally to see something of Quiggin, although I came no nearer to deciding which of the various views held about him were true. He was like Widmerpool, as I have said, in his complete absorption in his own activities, and also in his ambition. Unlike Widmerpool, he made no parade of his aspirations, on the contrary, keeping as secret as possible his appetite for getting on in life, so that even when I became aware of the purposeful way in which he set about obtaining what he wanted, I could never be sure where precisely his desires lay. He used to complain of the standard of tutoring, or how few useful lectures were available, and at times he liked to discuss his work in great detail. In fact I thought, at first, that he worked far harder than most of the men I knew. Later I came to doubt this, finding that Quiggin's work was something to be discussed rather than tackled, and that what he really enjoyed was drinking cups of coffee at odd times of day. He had another characteristic with which I became in due course familiar: he was keen on meeting people he considered important, and surprisingly successful in impressing persons—as he seemed to have impressed Truscott—who might have been reasonably expected to take amiss his manner and appearance.

The subject of Quiggin came up at one those luncheons that Short, who had a comfortable allowance, gave periodically. Mark Members, in spite of his behaviour on the earlier occasion, was again of the party (because Short regarded him as intellectually 'sound'); though Brightman was the guest of honour this time. Two undergraduates, called respectively Smethwyck and Humble, were there, and perhaps others. Short was inclined to become sentimental after he had eaten and drunk a fairly large amount in the middle of the day, and he had remarked: 'Quiggin must find it hard to make two ends meet up here. He told me his father used to work on the railway line outside some Midland town.'

'Not a word of truth,' said Brightman, who was the only don present. 'Quiggin is in my college. I went into the whole question of his financial position when he came up. He has certainly no less money than the average—probably more with his scholarships.'

'What *does* his father do then, Harold?' asked Short, who was quite used to being contradicted by Brightman; and, indeed, by almost everyone else in the university.

'Deceased.'

'But what did he do?'

'A builder—keen on municipal politics. So keen, he nearly landed in jail. He got off on appeal.'

Brightman could not help smiling to himself at the ease with which he could dispose of Short.

'But he may have worked on the railway line all the same.'

'The only work Quiggin the Elder ever did on the railway line,' said Brightman, becoming more assertive at encountering argument, 'was probably to travel without a ticket.'

'But that doesn't prove that his son has got any money,' said Humble, who did not care for Brightman.

'He was left a competence,' Brightman said. 'Quiggin lives with his mother, who is a town councillor. Isn't that true, Mark?'

A more vindictive man than Short might have been suspected of having raised the subject of Quiggin primarily to punish Members for his former attack on the strawberries; but Short was far too good-natured ever to have thought of such a revenge. Besides, he would never have considered baiting anyone whom he admired on intellectual grounds.

Brightman, on the other hand, had no such scruples, and he went on to say: 'Come on, Mark. Let's hear your account of Quiggin. You are neighbours, according to Sillers.'

Members must have seen that there was no way of avoiding the subject. Shaking his hair out of his eyes, he said: 'There is a disused railway-siding that was turned into allotments. He probably worked there. It adjoins one of the residential suburbs.'

There was a general laugh at this answer, which was certainly a neat way of settling the questions of both Quiggin and Brightman himself, so far as Members was concerned. Smethwyck began to talk of a play he had seen in London, and conversation took a new course. However, the feelings of self-reproach that contact with Quiggin, or discussions about him, commonly aroused in me were not entirely set at rest by this description of his circumstances. Brightman's information was notoriously unreliable: and Members's words had clearly been actuated by personal dislike. The work on the railway line might certainly have been of a comparatively recreational nature: that had to be admitted in the light of Mark Members's knowledge of the locality; but, even were this delineation of the background true, that would not prevent Quiggin from finding in his life some element chronically painful to him. Even though he might exaggerate to himself, and to others, his lack of means in relation to the financial circumstances of his contemporaries, this in itself pointed to a need for other—and deeply felt—discontents. It was possible that, in the eyes of Quiggin, money represented some element in which he knew himself deficient: rather in the same way that Widmerpool, when he wanted to criticise Stringham, said that he had too much money: no doubt in truth envying the possession of assets that were, in fact, not material ones. It was some similar course of speculation that seemed to give shape to Quiggin's character and outward behaviour.

Short's luncheon took place the day before I was to meet Mrs. Foxe again, and I thought over the question of Quiggin on my way to Stringham's rooms.

'This may be rather a ghastly meal,' Stringham said, while we waited for his mother, and Sillery, to arrive.

Sillery appeared first. He had cleaned himself up a little for the occasion, trimmed his moustache at the corners, and exchanged his usual blue bow for a black silk tie with white spots. Stringham offered him sherry, which was refused. Like many persons more interested in power than sensual enjoyment, Sillery touched no strong drink. Prowling about the room for a minute or two, he glanced at the invitations on the mantelpiece: a London dance or two, and some undergraduate parties. He found nothing there that appeared to interest him, because he turned, and, stepping between Stringham and myself, took each of us by an arm, resting his weight slightly.

'I hear you have been seeing something of Brother Quiggin,' he said to me.

'We met at one of Brightman's lectures, Sillers.'

'You both go to Brightman's lectures, do you?' said Sillery. 'I hope they are being decently attended.'

'Moderate.'

'Mostly women, I fear.'

'A sprinkling of men.'

'I heard they were getting quite painfully empty. It's a pity, because Brightman is such an able fellow. He won golden opinions as a young man,' said Sillery. 'But tell me, how do you find Brother Quiggin?'

I hardly knew what to say. However, Sillery seemed to require no answer. He said: 'Brother Quiggin is an able young man, too. We must not forget that.'

Stringham did not seem much in the mood for Sillery.

He moved away towards the window. A gramophone was playing in the rooms above. Outside, the weather was hot and rather stuffy.

'I hope my mother is not going to be really desperately late,' he said.

We waited. Sillery began to describe a walking tour he had once taken in Sicily with two friends, one of whom had risen to be Postmaster-General: the other, dead in his twenties, having shown promise of even higher things. He was in the middle of an anecdote about an amusing experience they had had with a German professor in a church at Syracuse, when there was a step on the stairs outside. Stringham went to the door, and out on to the landing. I heard him say: 'Why, hullo, Tuffy. Only you?'

Miss Weedon's reply was not audible within the room. She came in a moment later, looking much the same as when I had seen her in London. Stringham followed. 'My mother is awfully sorry, Sillers, but she could not get away at the last moment,' he said. 'Miss Weedon very sweetly motored all the way here, in order that we should not have a vacant place at the table.'

Sillery did not take this news at all well. There could be no doubt that he was deeply disappointed at Mrs. Foxe's defection; and that he did not feel Miss Weedon to be, in any way, an adequate substitute for Stringham's mother. We settled down to a meal that showed no outward prospect of being particularly enjoyable. Stringham himself did not appear in the least surprised at this miscarriage of plans. He was evidently pleased to see Miss Weedon, who, of the two of them, seemed the more worried that a discussion regarding Stringham's future would have to be postponed. Sillery decided that the first step was to establish his own position in Miss Weedon's eyes before, as he no doubt intended, exploring her own possibilities for exploitation.

'Salmon,' he remarked. 'Always makes me think of Mr. Gladstone.'

'Have some, all the same,' said Stringham. 'I hope it's fresh.'

'Did you arrange all this lunch yourself?' asked Miss Weedon, before Sillery could proceed further with his story. 'How wonderful of you. You know your mother was really distressed that she couldn't come.'

'The boys were at choir-practice when I passed this way,' said Sillery, determined that he should enter the conversation on his own terms. 'They were trying over that bit from *The Messiah*'—he hummed distantly, and beat time with his fork—'you know, those children's voices made me mighty sad.'

'Charles used to have a nice voice, didn't you?' said Miss Weedon: plainly more as a tribute to Stringham's completeness of personality, rather than because the matter could be thought to be of any great musical interest.

'I really might have earned my living that way, if it hadn't broken,' said Stringham. 'I should especially have enjoyed singing in the street. Perhaps I shall come to it yet.'

'There's been a terrible to-do about the way you earn your living,' said Miss Weedon. 'Buster doesn't at all like the idea of your living in London.'

Sillery showed interest in this remark, in spite of his evident dissatisfaction at the manner in which Miss Weedon treated him. He seemed unable to decide upon her precise status in the household: which was, indeed, one not easy to assess. It was equally hard to guess what she knew, or thought, of Sillery; whether she appreciated the extent of his experience in such situations as that which had arisen in regard to Stringham. Sitting opposite him, she seemed to have become firmer and more masculine; while Sillery himself, more than ever, took the shape of a wizard or shaman, equipped to resist either man or woman from a bisexual vantage.

This ineffective situation might have continued throughout Miss Weedon's visit, if Moffet—about whom a word should be said—had not handed Stringham a telegram, when he brought the next course. Moffet, a tall, gloomy man, on account of his general demeanour, which was certainly oppressive enough, had in some degree contributed to Stringham's dislike for university life. Stringham used to call Moffet 'the murderer', not on account of anything outwardly disreputable in his appearance, which might have been that of some ecclesiastical dignitary, but because of what Stringham named 'the cold cruelty of Moffet's eye'. If Moffet decided, for one reason or another, that an undergraduate on his staircase was worth cultivating, there was something sacerdotal about the precision with which he never left him free from attentions; as if the victim must be converted, come what may, to Moffet's doctrines. Moffet had at first sight made up his mind that Stringham was one to be brought under his sway.

One of Moffet's tenets was in connexion with the manner in which Stringham arranged several ivory elephants along the top of his mantelpiece. Stringham liked the elephants to follow each other in column: Moffet preferred them to face the room in line. I had been present, on one occasion, when Moffet, having just finished 'doing the room', had disappeared from it. Stringham walked over to the fireplace, where the elephants stood with their trunks in line, and turned them sideways. As he completed this rearrangement, Moffet came in once more through the door. Stringham had the last elephant in his hand. Moffet stared across at him forbiddingly.

'I am afraid I do not arrange ornaments very well, sir,' said Moffet.

'Just a whim of mine regarding elephants.'

'I will try to remember, sir,' said Moffet. 'They take a powerful lot of dusting.'

He retired again, adding: 'Thank you, sir,' as he closed the door. The incident disturbed Stringham. 'Now I shall have to go down,' he said.

However, Moffet was in an excellent mood at having an opportunity to wait on Sillery, of whom, for some reason, he approved more than of most dons. He brought in the telegram with a flourish. The message was from Stringham's mother: she would be arriving, after all: Buster was driving her down. At this, Sillery cheered up at once; and Miss Weedon, too, saw hope that negotiations might now take place. Stringham himself seemed as indifferent as before.

'If Buster is coming,' he said, 'he will certainly queer the pitch.'

'I am looking forward to meeting Buster,' said Sillery, smiling straight across the table to Miss Weedon. 'I think I shall persuade him to our point of view.'

He put the tips of his fingers together. Miss Weedon looked a little surprised at this whole-hearted way in which Sillery offered himself as an ally. She had perhaps assumed that, as a don, he would inevitably attempt to prevent Stringham from going down. She said: 'Commander Foxe's great regret is that he never went to the university.'

I did not know whether this remark was intended to excuse Buster, or to suggest to Sillery a line of attack.

'No doubt he acquired a very useful education in a different sphere,' said Sillery. 'I have made enquiries, and find that we have many friends in common. Bill Truscott, for example.'

Miss Weedon did not feel equally enthusiastic about Bill Truscott. I wondered if they had crossed swords.

'Mr. Truscott has been in the house a lot lately,' she said, guardedly.

'Bill knows the situation perfectly,' said Sillery. 'It would be a great advantage to work in harness with him.'

All Miss Weedon was prepared to admit was the statement that 'Mr. Truscott is always very kind'. However, Sillery's changed mood much improved the atmosphere; luncheon continuing with less sense of strain.

Mrs. Foxe and Buster arrived just as Moffet was clearing the table. They brought with them a hamper; caviare, grapes, a bottle of champagne. The effect of their entrance was immediate. Sillery and Miss Weedon at once abjured a great proportion of the hermaphroditic humours assumed by each of them for the purpose of more convenient association with the other: Miss Weedon relapsing into her normal rôle of attendance on Mrs. Foxe: Sillery steering himself more decidedly towards the part of eccentric professor, and away from the comparatively straightforward manner in which he had been discussing Stringham's affairs. This was the first time I had seen Mrs. Foxe and Buster together. They made an unusual couple. This was not due to the fact that she was a few years the elder of the two, which was scarcely noticeable, because Buster, though he had lost some of his look of anxiety, was distinctly fatter, and less juvenile in appearance, than he had seemed in London a year or more before. He was still dressed with care, and appeared in a more amenable temper than at our earlier meeting.

'We brought some grub down,' he said to Stringham, putting the hamper on a chair; and, turning to me, he remarked: 'I think one can always use caviare, don't you?'

It was clear that he accepted the fact that in the presence of his wife he was a subordinate figure, wherever he might rank away from her. Mrs. Foxe's ownership of

Buster seemed complete when they were in a room together. From time to time she would glance at him as if to make sure that he were behaving himself; but her look was one of absolute assurance that a word from her would be sufficient to quell even the smallest outbreak of conduct of a kind which she might disapprove. I found out, much later, that the circumstances of their marriage had been, so far as they went, respectable enough; and that nothing could have been farther from the truth than Widmerpool's suggestion that her divorce had been a particularly scandalous one. At that time, however, I had not heard any of the story; and I was still curious to know where she and Buster had met, and what romantic climax had been the cause of their going off together.

Sillery now showed great activity. He moved quickly forward to Mrs. Foxe, for a moment or two engaging her in conversation that took up the threads of their acquaintanceship of years before. Then he made for Buster, on whom he evidently intended to concentrate his forces, manœuvring him to the far end of the room; and, after a short while, taking his arm. Moffet had come in to ask if more coffee was required. He was in his element in this somewhat confused scene. Mrs. Foxe and Buster, not yet having lunched, some sort of a picnic was now organised among the remnants of the meal just consumed.

Sillery must have made his point, whatever it was, with Buster almost immediately, because soon he led him back to the food, assuring us that it was extraordinary that, during his war work with the Y.M.C.A., they had never met, though how this meeting could possibly have happened he did not explain. Whatever they had found in common was satisfactory to Buster, too, since he laughed and talked with Sillery as if he had known him for years. I have sometimes wondered whether Sillery made some specific offer on that occasion: a useful business introduction, for example, might have been dangled before Buster, then, as I knew from Stringham, contemplating retirement from the Navy. On the whole it is probable that nothing more concrete took place than that the two of them were aware, as soon as they set eyes on one another, of mutual sympathy: Sillery confining himself to flattery, and perhaps allowing Buster to hear the names of some of the more impressive specimens in his collection. Whatever the reason, Stringham's fate was settled in these first few minutes, because it was then that Buster must have decided to withdraw opposition. How serious this opposition was likely to be, if Sillery had not stepped in, is another question hard to answer. Buster might be in comparative subjection to his wife, but he was not necessarily without influence with her on that account. On the contrary, his subjection was no doubt a source of power to him in such matters. It was not surprising that he was against Stringham going down; his change of heart was much less to be expected. However, by the time Mrs. Foxe decided to leave, after scarcely any discussion over the caviare, champagne and grapes (the last of which Sillery consented to share), it was agreed that Stringham should go down at the end of the term. When he said good-bye, Sillery assured Mrs. Foxe that he was always at her service: when he took Buster's hand he put his own left hand over their combined grip, as if to seal it: to Miss Weedon he was polite and friendly, though less demonstrative. Moffet was waiting on the stairs. Something in the dignity of his bow must have moved Buster, because a coin changed hands.

Although a letter from Uncle Giles was by no means unknown, he did not write often; and only when he wanted something done for him: requiring details of an address he had lost, for example, or transmitting an account of some project in which he was commercially interested at that moment and wished recommended to all persons his relations might come across. He possessed a neat, stiff, old-fashioned handwriting, not at all suggestive of vagaries of character. There was usually a card from him at Christmas, undecorated, and very small in size: sent out in plenty of time. When, towards the end of the Michaelmas term, an envelope arrived addressed in his angular hand, I supposed at first that he had now taken to dispatching these Christmas greetings more than a month in advance. 'I am staying in London for some weeks,' he wrote, 'and I should like to see you one evening. After all, I have only three nephews. I dine every night at the Trouville Restaurant. Just drop in. It is very simple, of course, but you get good value for your money. We must take care of the pennies, these days. Any night will do.' Sunny Farebrother, I remembered, had made the same remark about the pennies. The fact that I might not be in a position to 'drop in' to a restaurant in London 'any night' did not appear to have struck my uncle, never very good at grasping principles that might govern other people's lives and movements. His letter was written from Harrods, so that there was no means of sending an answer; and I made up my mind that, even if I were to visit London—as I was doing, so it happened, the following day, to dine with Stringham—I should not spend the evening at the Trouville Restaurant. Uncle Giles did not state the reason for his wish to meet me, which may have sprung from completely disinterested affection for a member of his family not seen for some time. I suspected, perhaps unjustly, that such was not the motive; and, since at that age behaviour of older people seems, more often than not, entirely meaningless, I dismissed Uncle Giles's letter from my mind, as I now think, rather inexcusably. I had not seen Stringham since the summer, and had heard very little from him on the subject of his job. For one reason or another arrangements to meet had fallen through, and I felt, instinctively, that he was passing into an orbit where we should from now on see less of each other. I was thinking about this subject that afternoon, feeling disinclined for work, watching the towers of the neighbouring college, with the leaden sky beyond, when there was a knock on the door.

'Come in.'

It was Le Bas.

'I've been lunching with your Dean,' he said. 'He mentioned your name. I thought I would look you up.'

For some reason I felt enormously surprised to see him standing there. He had passed so utterly from daily life. This surprise was certainly not due to Le Bas having altered in appearance. On the contrary, he looked the same in all respects: except that he seemed to have shrunk slightly in size, and to have developed a kind of deadness I had not remembered in the texture of his skin. He stood by the door, as if he had just glanced in to make sure that no misbehaviour was in progress, and would proceed immediately on his way to other rooms in the college, to see that there, too, all was well. I asked him to sit down. He came farther into the room, but appeared unwilling to seat himself; standing in one of his characteristic poses, holding up both his hands, one a little above the other, like an Egyptian god, or figure from the Bayeux tapestry.

'How are you getting on, Jenkins?' he asked, at last agreeing, though with apparent reluctance, to occupy an armchair. 'You have a nice view from here, I see.'

He rose again, and stared out of the window for a minute or two, at the place where clouds had begun to darken the sky. The sound of undergraduate voices came up from below. Le Bas turned his gaze down on the passers-by.

'I expect you know the story of Calverley throwing pebbles at the Master of Balliol's window,' he said. 'Just to make him look out for the benefit of some visitors. Parkinson was some sort of a connexion of Calverley's, I believe. I saw Parkinson the other day. In fact I rowed in a Duffers' Eight with him. Parkinson was in your time, wasn't he? Or am I confusing dates?'

'Yes, he was. He only went down from here last year.'

'He missed his "blue", didn't he?'

'I think he was only tried out a couple of times.'

'Who else is there from my house?'

'Stringham went down last term.'

'Went down, did he? Was he sent down?'

'No, he——'

'Of course I remember Stringham,' said Le Bas. 'Wrote a shocking hand. Never saw such a fist. What was he sent down for?'

'He wasn't sent down. He got a job with Donners-Brebner. I am going to see him tomorrow.'

'Who else?' insisted Le Bas, who had evidently never heard of Donners-Brebner.

'I saw Templer not long ago. He is in the City now.'

'Templer?' said Le Bas. 'Oh, yes, Templer. In the City, is he? Did he go up to the university?'

'No.'

'Probably just as well,' said Le Bas. 'Still it might have toned him down a bit. I suppose as it is he will spend the rest of his life wearing those startling socks. It was Templer, wasn't it, who always wore those dreadful socks?'

'Yes—it was.'

'Still, he may grow out of it,' said Le Bas.

'Or them,' I said; and, since Le Bas did not smile, added: 'I stayed in the same French family as Widmerpool, the summer after I left.'

'Ah yes, Widmerpool.'

Le Bas thought for a long time. He climbed up on to the fender, and began to lift himself by the edge of the mantelpiece. I thought for a moment that he might be going to hoist himself right on to the shelf; perhaps lie there.

'I was never quite happy about Widmerpool,' he admitted at last.

This statement did not seem to require an answer.

'As you probably know,' said Le Bas, 'there were jokes about an overcoat in the early days.'

'I remember being told something about it.'

'Plenty of keenness, but somehow——'

'He used to train hard.'

'And a strong—well——' Le Bas seemed rather at a loss, ending somewhat abruptly with the words: 'Certain moral qualities, admirable so far as they went, but——'

I supposed he was thinking of the Akworth affair, which must have caused him a good deal of trouble.

'He seemed to be getting on all right when I saw him in France.'

This statement seemed in the main true.

'I am glad to hear it,' said Le Bas. 'Very glad. I hope he will find his level in life. Which college did you say?'

'He didn't go to the university.'

'What is he going to be?'

'A solicitor.'

'Do none of my pupils consider a degree an advantage in life? I hope you will work hard for yours.'

Facetiously, I held up a copy of Stubbs's *Charters* that happened to be lying at hand on the table.

'Do you know Sillery?' I asked.

'Sillery? Sillery? Oh, yes, of course I know Sillery,' Le Bas said; but he did not rise to this bait.

There was a pause.

'Well, I have enjoyed our talk,' Le Bas said. 'I expect I shall see you on Old Boy Day.'

He got up from the chair, and stood for a few seconds, as if undecided whether or not to bring his visit to an end.

'Friendships have to be kept up,' he said, unexpectedly.

I suppose that his presence had recalled—though unconsciously—the day of Braddock alias Thorne; because for some reason, inexplicable to myself, I said: 'Like Heraclitus.'

Le Bas looked surprised.

'You know the poem, do you?' he said. 'Yes, I remember you were rather keen on English.'

Then he turned and made for the door, still apparently pondering the questions that this reference to Heraclitus had aroused in his mind. Having reached the door, he stopped. There was evidently some affirmation he found difficulty in getting out. After several false starts, he said: 'You know, Jenkins, do always try to remember one thing—it takes all sorts to make a world.'

I said that I would try to remember that.

'Good,' said Le Bas. 'You will find it a help.'

I watched him from the window. He walked quickly in the direction of the main entrance of the college: suddenly he turned on his heel and came back, very slowly, towards my staircase, at the foot of which he stopped for about a minute: then he moved off again at a moderate pace in another quarter: finally disappearing from sight, without leaving any impression of decision as to his next port of call. The episode of Braddock alias Thorne, called up by Le Bas's visit, took on a more grotesque aspect than ever, when thought of now. I wondered whether Le Bas had himself truly accepted his own last proposition. Nothing in his behaviour had ever suggested that his chosen principles were built up on a deep appreciation of the diversity of human character. On the contrary, he had always demanded of his pupils certain easily recognisable conventions of conduct: though, at the same time, it occurred to me that the habit of making just such analyses of motive as this was precisely what Le Bas had a moment before so delicately deprecated in myself.

There are certain people who seem inextricably linked in life; so that meeting one acquaintance in the street means that a letter, without fail, will arrive in a day or two from an associate involuntarily harnessed to him, or her, in time. Le Bas's appearance was one of those odd preludes that take place, and give, as it were, dramatic form to occurrences that have more than ordinary significance. It is as if the tempo altered gradually, so that too violent a change of sensation should not take place; in this case, that some of the atmosphere of school should be reconstructed, although only in a haphazard fashion, as if for an amateur performance, in order that I should not meet Stringham in his new surroundings without a reminder of the circumstances in which we had first known one another.

For some reason, during the following day in London, I found myself thinking all the time of Le Bas's visit; although it was long before I came to look upon such transcendental manipulation of surrounding figures almost as a matter of routine. The weather was bad. When the time came, I was glad to find myself in the Donners-Brebner building, although the innate dejection of spirit of that part of London was augmented by regarding its landscape from this huge and shapeless edifice, recently built in a style as wholly without ostensible order as if it were some vast prehistoric cromlech. Stringham's office was on one of the upper storeys, looking north over the river. It was dark now outside, and lights were reflected in the water, from the oppressive and cheerless, as well as beautiful, riverside. Stringham looked well: better than I had seen him for a long time.

'Let's get out of here,' he said.

'I'm a bit late.'

'We'll have a drink.'

'Where shall we make for?'

For a brief second, for an inexpressibly curtailed efflux of time, so short that its duration could be appreciated only in recollection, being immediately engulfed at the moment of birth, I was conscious of a sensation I had never before encountered: an awareness that Stringham was perhaps a trifle embarrassed. He took a step forward, and made as if to pat my head, as one who makes much of an animal.

'There, there,' he said. 'Good dog. Don't growl. The fact is I am cutting your date. Cutting it in slow motion before your eyes.'

'Well?'

'It is an absolutely inexcusable thing to do. I've been asked to rather a good party at short notice—and have to dine and go to a play first. As the party can hardly fail to be rather fun, I thought you wouldn't mind.'

'Of course not.'

'An intolerable act, I admit.'

'Not if it's a good party.'

'I thought the thing to do would be for you to come back and talk while I changed. Then I could drop you wherever you are going to dine.'

'Let's do that.'

I could pretend to Stringham that I did not mind: within, I was exceedingly annoyed. This was quite unlike him. A rearrangement of plans would now be necessary. His car was parked outside. We drove northward.

'How are things at the old coll.?'

'Le Bas visited me yesterday.'

'Our former housemaster?'

'Braddock alias Thorne.'

'Good heavens, I had forgotten all about that.'

'I wonder if he has.'

'Did you tell him how it happened?'

'No.'

'How extraordinary for him to swim to the surface.'

'He asked about you.'

'No?'

Stringham was not interested. Le Bas was scarcely a memory. I began to realise that considerable changes had indeed been taking place.

'What is it like in London?'

'I'm rather enjoying myself. You must come and live here soon.'

'I suppose I shall in due course.'

'Can't you get sent down? No one could stand three years of university life.'

We arrived at the house, and, passing between the pillars of the doorway, collected drinks in the dining-room. Then we went upstairs. The place seemed less gloomy than on my earlier visit. Stringham's bedroom was a rather comfortless apartment, looking out on to the roofs of another row of large houses.

'Who are you dining with?'

'The Bridgnorths.'

'Haven't I seen pictures of a rather captivating daughter called Lady Peggy Stepney?'

'The last photograph was taken at Newmarket. I've been wondering whether it wasn't time for her to get married and settle down,' said Stringham. 'I seem to have been a bachelor an awfully long time.'

'What does Lady Peggy think about it?'

'There are indications that she does not actively dislike me.'

'Why not, then?'

We talked in a desultory way, Stringham walking to and fro, wearing only a stiff shirt, and some black silk socks, while he washed his hands, and brushed his hair. I did not know how serious he might be with regard to the Bridgnorths' daughter. The idea of one of my friends getting married had scarcely occurred to me, even as a possibility. I saw now that such a thing was not absolutely out of the question. From time to time a footman appeared, offering different collars, because Stringham could find none he liked.

'I suppose this must be one of Buster's,' he said, at last accepting a collar that satisfied him. 'I shall sell the rest of mine off cheap to the clergy to wear back-to-front.'

He slipped on his tail-coat, pulling at the cuffs of his shirt.

'Come on,' he said; 'we'll have another drink on the way out.'

'Where is your dinner-party?'

'Grosvenor Square. Where shall I drop you?'

'Grosvenor Square will do for me.'

'But what will you do?'

'Dine with an uncle of mine.'

'Does he live there?'

'No—but he isn't expecting me just yet.'

'He was expecting you then?'

'A standing invitation.'

'So I really haven't left you too high and dry?'

'Not in the least.'

'You are jolly lucky to have relations you can drop in on at any time,' said Stringham. 'My own are much too occupied with their own affairs to care for that.'

'You met Uncle Giles once. He suddenly arrived one night when we were having tea. It was the day of Peter's "unfortunate incident".'

Stringham laughed. He said: 'I remember about Peter, but not about your uncle.'

We reached the car again, and drove for a time in silence. 'We'll meet soon,' Stringham said. 'I suppose you are going back tonight—otherwise we might have lunched tomorrow.'

'I'll be up in a week or two.'

'We will get together then.'

We had reached Grosvenor Square, and he slowed up.

'Now where?'

'I'll climb down here.'

'I expect it will be a really frightful party, and Peggy will have decided not to turn up.'

He waved, and I waved, as the car went on to the far side of the square.

The evening was decidedly cool, and rain was half-heartedly falling. I knew now that this parting was one of those final things that happen, recurrently, as time passes: until at last they may be recognised fairly easily as the close of a period. This was the last I should see of Stringham for a long time. The path had suddenly forked. With regret, I accepted the inevitability of circumstance. Human relationships flourish and decay, quickly and silently, so that those concerned scarcely know how brittle, or how inflexible, the ties that bind them have become. Lady Bridgnorth, by her invitation that night, had effortlessly snapped one of the links—for practical purposes the main one—between Stringham and myself; just as the accident in Templer's car, in a rather different manner, had removed Templer from Stringham's course. A new epoch was opening: in a sense this night was the final remnant of life at school.

I was glad to have remembered Uncle Giles. It was, I suppose, justification of the family as a social group that, upon such an occasion, my uncle's company seemed to offer a restorative in the accidental nature of our relationship and the purely formal regard paid by him to the fact that I was his nephew. Finding a telephone box, I looked up the address of the Trouville Restaurant, which turned out to be in Soho. It was fairly early in the evening. Passing slowly through a network of narrow streets, and travelling some distance, I came at last to the Trouville. The outside was not inviting. The restaurant's façade was boarded up with dull, reddish shutters. At the door hung a table d'hôte menu, slipped into a brass frame that advertised Schweppes' mineral waters—Blanchailles—Potage Solférino—Sole Bercy—Côtelettes d'Agneau Reform—Glace Néapolitaine—Café. The advertised charge seemed very reasonable. The immense depression of this soiled, claret-coloured exterior certainly seemed to meet the case; for there is always something solemn about change, even when accepted.

Within, the room was narrow, and unnaturally long, with a table each side, one after another, stretching in perspective into shadows that hid the service lift: which was set among palms rising from ornate brass pots. The emptiness, dim light, silence—and, to some extent, the smell—created a faintly ecclesiastical atmosphere; so that the track between the tables might have been an aisle, leading, perhaps, to a hidden choir. Uncle Giles himself, sitting alone at the far end of this place, bent over a book, had the air of a sleepy worshipper, waiting for the next service to begin. He did not look specially pleased to see me, and not at all surprised.

'You're a bit late,' he said. 'So I started.'

It had not occurred to him that I should do otherwise than come straight up to London, so soon as informed that there was an opportunity to see him again. He put his book face-downwards on the tablecloth. I saw that it was called *Some Things That Matter*. We discussed the Trust until it was time to catch my train.

A Buyer's Market

For Osbert and Karen

1.

THE last time I saw any examples of Mr. Deacon's work was at a sale, held obscurely in the neighbourhood of Euston Road, many years after his death. The canvases were none of them familiar, but they recalled especially, with all kind of other things, dinner at the Walpole-Wilsons', reviving with a jerk that phase of early life. They made me think of long-forgotten conflicts and compromises between the imagination and the will, reason and feeling, power and sensuality; together with many more specifically personal sensations, experienced in the past, of pleasure and of pain. Outside, the spring weather was cool and sunny: Mr. Deacon's favourite season of the year. Within doors, propped against three sides of a washstand, the oil-paintings seemed, for some reason, appropriate to those surroundings, dusty, though not displeasing; even suggesting, in their way, the kind of home Mr. Deacon favoured for himself and his belongings: the sitting-room over the shop, for example, informal, not too permanent, more than a trifle decayed. His haunts, I remembered, had bordered on these northern confines of London.

Accumulations of unrelated objects brought together for auction acquire, in their haphazard manner, a certain dignity of their own: items not to be tolerated in any inhabited dwelling finding each its own level in these expansive, anonymous caverns, where, making no claim to individual merit, odds and ends harmonise quietly with each other, and with the general sobriety of background.

Such precincts have something of museums about them, the roving crowd on the whole examining the assembled relics with an expert, unselfconscious intensity, not entirely commercial or acquisitive.

On these particular premises almost every man-made thing seemed represented. Comparatively new mowing machines: scabbardless and rusty cavalry sabres: ebony fragments of African fetish: a nineteenth-century typewriter, poised uncertainly on metal stilts in the midst of a tea-set in Liverpool ware, the black-and-white landscapes of its design irreparably chipped. Several pillows and bolsters covered with the Union Jack gave a disturbing hint that, somewhere beneath, a corpse awaited burial with military honours. Farther off, high rolls of linoleum, coloured blue, green and pink, were ranged against the wall like pillars, a Minoan colonnade from which wicker arm-chairs and much-used pieces of luggage formed a semicircle. Within this open space, placed rather like an emblem arranged for worship, stood the washstand round which the pictures were grouped. On its marble top rested an empty bird-cage, two men-at-arms in lead, probably German, and a dog-eared pile of waltz music. In front of a strip of Axminster carpet, displayed like faded tapestry from the side of a near-by wardrobe in pitch pine, a fourth painting stood upside down.

All four canvases belonged to the same school of large, untidy, exclusively male figure compositions, light in tone and mythological in subject: Pre-Raphaelite in influence without being precisely Pre-Raphaelite in spirit: a compromise between, say, Burne-Jones and Alma-Tadema, with perhaps a touch of Watts in method of applying the paint. One of them—ripping away from its stretcher at the top—was dated 1903. A decided weakness of drawing was emphasised by that certitude—which overtakes, after all, some of the greatest artists—that none of Mr. Deacon's pictures could possibly have been painted at any epoch other than its own: this hallmark of Time being specially attributable to the painter's inclination towards large, blank expanses of colour, often recklessly laid on. Yet, in spite of obvious imperfections, the pictures, as I have said, were not utterly unsympathetic in that situation. Even the forest of inverted legs, moving furiously towards their goal in what appeared to be one of the running events of the Olympic Games, were manifested to what might easily have been greater advantage in that reversed position, conveying, as they did, an immense sense of nervous urgency, the flesh tints of the athletes' straining limbs contrasting strangely with pink and yellow contours of three cupids in debased Dresden who tripped alongside on top of a pedestal cupboard.

In due course two bucolic figures in cloth caps, shirt-sleeves, and green baize aprons held up Mr. Deacon's pictures, one by one, for examination by a small knot of dealers: a depressed gang of men, looking as if they had strayed into that place between more congenial interludes on the race-course. I was not sure how this display might strike other people, and was glad, when exposure took place, that no unfriendly comment was aroused. The prodigious size of the scenes depicted might in itself reasonably have provoked laughter; and, although by that time I knew enough of Mr. Deacon to regard his painting as nothing more serious than one of a number of other warring elements within him, open ridicule of his work would have been distressing. However, all four elevations were received, one after another, in apathetic silence; although the 'lot' was finally knocked down for a few pounds only, bidding was reasonably brisk: possibly on account of the frames, which were made of some black substance, ornamented with gold in a floral pattern, conceivably of the painter's own design.

Mr. Deacon must have visited the house at least half a dozen times when I was a child, occasions when, by some unlikely chance, I had seen and spoken with him more than once; though I do not know why our paths should have crossed in this manner, because he was always reported 'not to like children', so that our meetings, such as they were, would not have been deliberately arranged on the part of my parents. My father, amused by his conversation, was in the habit of referring to Mr. Deacon's painting without enthusiasm; and when, as he sometimes did, Mr. Deacon used to assert that he preferred to keep—rather than sell—his own works, the remark usually aroused mildly ironical comment at home after he was gone. It would not be fair, however, to suggest that, professionally, Mr. Deacon was unable to find a market for his classical subjects. On the contrary, he could always name several faithful patrons, mostly business people from the Midlands. One of these, especially, spoken of as a 'big iron man'—whom I used to envisage as physically constructed of the metal from which he derived his income—would, for example, come down from Lancashire once a year: always returning northward in possession of an oil sketch of Antinous, or sheaf of charcoal studies of Spartan youth at exercise. According to Mr. Deacon, one of these minor works had even found its way into the ironmaster's local art gallery, a fulfilment which evidently gave great satisfaction to the painter; although Mr. Deacon would mention the matter in a deprecatory sort of way, because he disapproved of what he called 'official art', and used to speak with great bitterness of the Royal Academy. When I met him in later life I discovered that he disliked the Impressionists and Post-Impressionists almost equally; and was, naturally, even more opposed to later trends like Cubism, or the works of the Surrealists. In fact Puvis de Chavannes and Simeon Solomon, the last of whom I think he regarded as his master, were the only painters I ever heard him speak of with unqualified approval. Nature had no doubt intended him to be in some manner an adjunct to the art movement of the Eighteen-Nineties; but somehow Mr. Deacon had missed that spirit in his youth, a moral separateness that perhaps accounted for a later lack of integration.

He was not rich, although his income, in those days, allowed the preservation of a fairly independent attitude towards the more material side of being an artist. He had once, for example, turned down the opportunity to decorate the interior of a fish restaurant in Brighton—where he lived—on grounds that the sum offered was incommensurate with the demeaning nature of the work demanded. His means had also enabled him to assemble what was said to be an excellent little collection of hour-glasses, silhouettes, and bric-à-brac of various kinds. At the same time he liked to describe how, from time to time, in order to avoid the expense and responsibility of domestic staff, he deliberately underwent long periods of undertaking his own cooking. 'I could always earn my living as a chef,' he used to say; adding, in joke, that he would look 'enormously ornamental' in a white cap. When travelling on the Continent he commonly went on foot with a haversack on his back, rather than by trains, which he found 'stuffy and infinitely filled with tedious persons'. He was careful, even rather fussy, about his health, especially in relation to personal cleanliness and good sanitation; so that some of the more sordid aspects of these allegedly *terre-à-terre* excursions abroad must at times have been a trial to him. Perhaps his Continental visits were, in fact, more painful for managers of hotels and restaurants frequented by him; for he was a great believer in insisting absolutely upon the minute observance by others of his own wishes. Such habits of travelling, in so much as they were indeed voluntary and not to some degree enforced by financial consideration, were no doubt also connected in his mind with his own special approach to social behaviour, in which he was guided by an aversion, often expressed, for conduct that might be looked upon either as conventional or conservative.

In this last respect Mr. Deacon went further than my Uncle Giles, whose creed of being 'a bit of a radical' was also well publicised within his own family circle; or, indeed, wherever he might find himself. My uncle, however, dealt in substance he knew and, although he would never have admitted as much, even to some extent revered, merely desiring most aspects of that familiar world to be more nicely adjusted to his own taste. Mr. Deacon, on the other hand, was in favour of abolishing, or ignoring, the existing world entirely, with a view to experimenting with one of an entirely different order. He was a student of Esperanto (or, possibly, one of the lesser-known artificial languages), intermittently vegetarian, and an advocate of decimal coinage. At the same time he was strongly opposed to the introduction of 'spelling reform' for the English language (on grounds that for him such changes would mar *Paradise Lost*), and I can remember it said that he hated 'suffragettes'.

These preferences, with the possible exception of decimal coinage, would have been regarded as mere quirks in my uncle; but, as they were presented in what was almost always a moderately entertaining manner, they were tolerated by my parents to a far greater degree than were similar prejudices disseminated by Uncle Giles, whose heartily deplored opinions were naturally associated in the minds of most of his relatives with threat of imminent financial worry for themselves, not to mention potential scandal within the family. In any case, aggressive personal opinions, whatever their kind, might justly be regarded as uncalled for, or at best allowed only slight weight, when voiced by a man whose career had been so uniformly unsuccessful as had that of my uncle. Mr. Deacon's persuasions, on the other hand, could be regarded with tolerance as part of the stock-in-trade of a professional artist, by no means a failure in life, and to be accepted, however unwillingly, as the inevitable adjunct of a Bohemian profession: even valuable in their way as illustrating another side of human experience.

At the same time, although no doubt they rather enjoyed his occasional visits, my parents legitimately considered Mr. Deacon an eccentric, who, unless watched carefully, might develop into a bore, and it would not be precisely true to say that they liked him; although I believe that, in his way, Mr. Deacon liked both of them. The circumstances of their first meeting were unrecorded. An introduction may have taken place at one of the concerts held at the Pavilion, which they sometimes attended when my father was stationed near Brighton in the years before the war. During that period a call was certainly paid on Mr. Deacon in his studio: several small rooms converted to that use at the top of a house in one of the quiet squares remote from 'the front'. He had chosen this retired position because the sight of the sea disturbed him at his work: a prejudice for which psychological explanation would now certainly be available.

I never saw the studio myself, but often heard it spoken of as well stocked with curiosities of one kind or another. We moved from that neighbourhood before the war came in 1914, and, I suppose, lost touch with Mr. Deacon; but for a long time I remembered the impression of height he gave when, one day after tea, he presented me with a wooden paint-box—the pigments contained in tubes—the heavy scent of the tobacco he smoked hanging round the pleats and belt of his Norfolk jacket, a garment already beginning to look a little old-fashioned, and the sound of his voice, deep and earnest, while he explained the range of colours to be found within the box, and spoke of the principles of light and shade: principles—I could not help reflecting as I examined the canvases in the sale-room—which his brush must have so often and so violently abused.

By the stage of life when I happened on these four pictures, I had, of course, during our brief latter-day acquaintance, had opportunity to observe Mr. Deacon in surroundings rather different from my parents' domestic interior, where I had first heard his peculiarities discussed; and I had also, by the time I found myself in the auction-room, talked over his character with persons like Barnby, who knew him at closer range than I myself ever experienced. All the same, I could not help pondering once again the discrepancy that existed between a style of painting that must have been unfashionable, and at best aridly academic, even in his early days; and its contrast with the revolutionary principles that he preached and—in spheres other than æsthetic—to some considerable extent practised. I wondered once again whether this apparent inconsistency of approach, that had once disconcerted me, symbolised antipathetic sides of his nature; or whether his life and work and judgment at some point coalesced with each other, resulting in a standpoint that was really all of a piece—as he himself would have said—that 'made a work of art'.

Certainly I could not decide that question there and then in the auction-room among the furniture and linoleum, to the sound of bidding and taps of the hammer, even in the light of later circumstances in which I had known him, and I have never really succeeded in coming to a positive conclusion on the subject. Undoubtedly his painting, in its own direction, represented the farthest extremity of Mr. Deacon's romanticism, and I suppose it could be argued that upon such debris of classical imagery the foundations of at least certain specific elements of twentieth-century art came to be built. At the same time lack of almost all imaginative quality in Mr. Deacon's painting resulted, finally, in a product that suggested not 'romance'—far less 'classicism'—as some immensely humdrum pattern of every-day life: the Greek and Roman episodes in which he dealt belonging involuntarily to a world of cosy bar-parlours and 'nice cups of tea'—'At least when thought of,' as Barnby used to say, 'in terms of pictorial reproduction in, say, photo-gravure'—even though Barnby himself, in some moods, would attempt a defence at least of certain aspects of Mr. Deacon's art. In short, the pictures recalled something given away with a Christmas Number, rather than the glories of Sunium's marbled steep, or that blue Sicilian sea that had provided a back-cloth for the Victorian Hellenism propagated at school by my housemaster, Le Bas. Mr. Deacon's painting might, indeed, have been compared, though at a greatly inferior level of the imagination's facul-ties, with Le Bas's day-dreams of Hellas; and perhaps, in the last resort, Mr. Deacon, too, would have been wiser to have chosen teaching as a career. Undeniably there was something didactic about his manner, although, as a child, I had naturally never speculated on his idiosyncrasies, of which I knew only by hearing them particularised by my parents or the servants.

This touch of pedantry had been apparent at a later date, when we ran across Mr. Deacon in the Louvre, during summer holidays taken soon after the termination of the war, when my father was still on duty in Paris. That afternoon, although I did not immediately recognise him, I had already wondered who might be the tall, lean, rather bent figure, moving restlessly about at the far end of the gallery; and his name, spoken again after so many years, at once identified him in my mind. When we had come up with him he was inspecting with close attention Perugino's St. Sebastian, for the better examination of which, stooping slightly, he had just produced a small magnifying-glass with a gold rim. He wore a thickish pepper-and-salt suit—no longer cut with belt and side-pleats—and he carried in his hand a hat, broad-brimmed and furry, the general effect of the whole outfit being, perhaps intentionally, a trifle down-at-heel: together with the additionally disturbing suggestion that his slightly curved torso might be enclosed within some form of imperfectly fitting corset. His grey hair, which needed cutting, was brushed straight back, showing off a profile distinguished rather than otherwise: a little like that of an actor made up to play the part of Prospero, the face heavily lined and grave, without conveying any sense of dejection.

He recognised my parents at once, greeting them with an odd, stilted formality, again like an old-fashioned actor's. My father—who was not in uniform—began to explain that he was attached to the staff of the Conference. Mr. Deacon, listening with an absorbed expression, failed or, perhaps it would be truer to say, pretended for reasons of his own to misunderstand the nature of this employment. In his resonant, faintly ironical voice, he asked: 'And what might you be conferring about?'

At that period Paris was full of missions and delegates, emissaries and plenipotentiaries of one kind and another, brought there by the traffic of the Peace Treaty; and probably my father could not imagine why Mr. Deacon should appear to want further details about his job (which had, I believe, something to do with disarmament), a matter which could, after all, at least in its details, be only of professional interest. He certainly did not guess that Mr. Deacon must have decided for the moment to close his eyes to the Conference, together with much—if not all—that had led to its existence; or, at least, preferred, anyway at that juncture, to ignore all its current circumstances. My father's reply, no doubt intentionally discreet, was therefore worded in general terms; and the explanation, so far as could be seen, took Mr. Deacon no farther in discovering why we were at that hour in the Louvre.

'In connexion with those *expositions* the French love so much?' he suggested. 'So you are no longer *militaire?*'

'As a matter of fact, they have not given nearly so much trouble as you might expect,' said my father, who must have taken this query to be a whimsical manner of referring to some supposed form of intransigence over negotiation on the part of the French staff-officer constituting his 'opposite number'.

'I don't know much about these things,' Mr. Deacon admitted.

The matter rested there, foundations of conversation changing to the delineation of St. Sebastian: Mr. Deacon suddenly showing an unexpected grasp of military hierarchy —at least of a somewhat obsolete order—by pointing out that the Saint, holding as he did the rank of centurion—and being, therefore, a comparatively senior non-commissioned or warrant officer—probably possessed a less youthful and altogether more rugged appearance than that attributed to him by Perugino: and, indeed, commonly, by most other painters of hagiographical subjects. Going on to speak more generally of the Peruginos to be found throughout the rest of the gallery, Mr. Deacon alleged that more than one was labelled 'Raphael'. We did not dispute this assertion. Questioned as to how long he had himself been living in Paris, Mr. Deacon was vague; nor was it clear how he had occupied himself during the war, the course of which he seemed scarcely to have noticed. He implied that he had 'settled abroad' more or less permanently; anyway, for a long time.

'There really are moments when one feels one has more in common with the French than with one's own countrymen,' he said. 'Their practical way of looking at things appeals to a certain side of me—though perhaps not the best side. If you want something here, the question is: Have you got the money to pay for it? If the answer is "yes", all is well; if "no", you have to go without. Besides, there is a freer atmosphere. That is something that revolutions do. There is really nowhere else in the world like Paris.'

He was living, he told us, 'in a little place off the Boul' Mich'.'

'I'm afraid I can't possibly ask you there in its present state,' he added. 'Moving in always takes an age. And I have so many treasures.'

He shook his head after an enquiry regarding his painting.

'Much more interested in my collections now,' he said. 'One of the reasons I am over here is that I have been doing a little buying for friends as well as for myself.'

'But I expect you keep your own work up now and then.'

'After all, why should one go on adding to the detritus in this transitory world?' asked Mr. Deacon, raising his shoulders and smiling. 'Still I sometimes take a sketch-book to a café—preferably some little estaminet in one of the working-class quarters. One gets a good head here, and a vigorous pose there. I collect heads—and necks—as you may remember.'

He excused himself politely, though quite definitely, from an invitation to luncheon at the Interallié, a club of which he had, apparently, never heard; though he complained that Paris was more expensive than formerly, expressing at the same time regret at the 'Americanisation' of the Latin Quarter.

'I sometimes think of moving up to Montmartre, like an artist of Whistler's time,' he said.

Conversation waned after this. He asked how long we were staying in France, seeming, if anything, relieved to hear that we should all of us be back in England soon. On parting, there was perhaps a suggestion that the encounter had been, for no obvious reason, a shade uncomfortable; in this respect not necessarily worse than such meetings are apt to turn out between persons possessing little in common who run across each other after a long separation, and have to rely on common interests, by then half-forgotten. This faint sense of tension may also have owed something to Mr. Deacon's apparent unwillingness to go even so far in comparing autobiographical notes as might have been thought allowably free from the smallest suggestion of an undue display of egotism; especially when conversation was limited chiefly because one side lacked any idea of what the other had been doing for a number of years.

'I was glad to see Deacon again,' my father said afterwards, when, that afternoon, we were on our way to tea at the Walpole-Wilsons' flat in Passy. 'He looked a lot older.'

That must have been almost the last time that I heard either of my parents refer to Mr. Deacon or his affairs.

However, the meeting at the Louvre, among other experiences of going abroad for the first time, remained in my mind as something rather important. Mr. Deacon's reappearance at that season seemed not only to indicate divorce of maturity from childhood, but also to emphasise the dependence of those two states one upon the other. 'Grown-up' in the 'old days', Mr. Deacon was grown-up still: I myself, on the other hand, had changed. There was still distance to travel, but I was on the way to drawing level with Mr. Deacon, as a fellow grown-up, himself no longer a figment of memory from childhood, but visible proof that life had existed in much the same way before I had begun to any serious extent to take part; and would, without doubt, continue to prevail long after he and I had ceased to participate. In addition to this appreciation of his status as a kind of milestone on the winding and dusty road of existence, I found something interesting—though not entirely comfortable—about Mr. Deacon's personality. He had given me a long, appraising glance when we shook hands, an action in itself, for some reason, rather unexpected, and later he had asked which were my favourite pictures in the gallery, and elsewhere, in the same deep, grave voice with which he had formerly explained his views on tone values: listening to the reply as if the information there contained might possess considerable importance for himself.

This apparent deference to what was necessarily unformed opinion seemed so flattering that I remembered him clearly long after our return to England; and, six or seven years later, when I saw the signature 'E. Bosworth Deacon' in the corner of an oil-painting that hung high on the wall of the innermost part of the hall in the Walpole-Wilsons' house in Eaton Square, the atmosphere of that occasion in the Louvre, the talk about the Conference and St. Sebastian, the feeling of constraint—of embarrassment, almost—the visit, later in the day, to the Walpole-Wilsons themselves, came back all at once very clearly: even the illusion of universal relief that belonged to that historical period: of war being, surprisingly, at an end: of the imminence of 'a good time': of all that odd sense of intellectual emancipation that belonged, or, at least, seemed, perhaps rather spuriously, to belong, to the art of that epoch: its excitement and its melancholy mingling with kaleidoscopic impressions of a first sight of Paris. All these thoughts briefly and speedily suggested themselves, when, taking off my overcoat on my first visit to the house in Eaton Square—after I had come to live in London—I observed Mr. Deacon's picture. The canvas, comparatively small for a 'Deacon', evidently not much considered by its owners, had been placed beyond the staircase above a Victorian barometer in a polished mahogany case. The subject was in a similar vein to those other scenes lying in the sale-room: the gold tablet at the foot of the frame baldly stating, without mentioning the artist's name, *'Boyhood of Cyrus'*. This was, in fact, the first 'Deacon' I had ever set eyes upon.

The importance that *Boyhood of Cyrus* eventually assumed had, however, nothing to do with the painter, or the merits, such as they were, of the picture itself: its significance being attained simply and solely as symbol of the probable physical proximity of Barbara Goring, Lady Walpole-Wilson's niece. This association of ideas was, in deed, so powerful that even years after I had ceased to be a guest at the Walpole-Wilson table I could not hear the name 'Cyrus' mentioned—fortunately, in the circumstances, a fairly rare occurrence in everyday life—without being reminded of the pains of early love; while at the time of which I write almost any oil-painting illustrative of a remotely classical scene (such as one sees occasionally in the windows of dealers round St. James's normally specialising in *genre* pictures) would be liable to recall the fact, if by some unlikely chance forgotten, that I had not seen Barbara for a longer or shorter period.

I must have been about twenty-one or twenty-two at the time, and held then many rather wild ideas on the subject of women: conceptions largely the result of having read a good deal without simultaneous opportunity to modify by personal experience the recorded judgment of others upon that matter: estimates often excellent in their conclusions if correctly interpreted, though requiring practical knowledge to be appreciated at their full value.

At school I had known Tom Goring, who had later gone into the Sixtieth, and, although we had never had much to do with each other, I remembered some story of Stringham's of how both of them had put up money to buy a crib for Horace—or another Latin author whose works they were required to render into English—and of trouble that ensued from the translation supplied having contained passages omitted in the official educational text-book. This fact of her elder brother having been my contemporary—the younger son, David, was still at school—may perhaps have had something to do with finding myself, immediately after our first meeting, on good terms with Barbara; though the matter of getting on well with young men in no circumstances presented serious difficulty to her.

'Do be quick, if you are going to ask me for a dance,' she had said, when her cousin, Eleanor Walpole-Wilson, had first introduced us. 'I can't wait all night while you make up your mind.'

I was, I must admit, enchanted on the spot by this comportment, which I found far from discouraging. On some earlier occasion a dowager had referred to Barbara in my presence as 'that rather noisy little Goring girl', and the description was a just one. She was small and dark, with hair cut in a square 'bob', which—other girls used to complain—was always hopelessly untidy. Her restlessness was of that deceptive kind that usually indicates a fundamental deficiency, rather than surplus of energy, though I cannot claim, either in principle, or with particular reference to Barbara herself, to have speculated on this diagnosis until many years later. I remember, however, that when we met fortuitously in Hyde Park one Sunday afternoon quite a long time later (as it seemed to me), I still retained some sense of proportion about her, although we had by then seen a good deal of each other. She was walking in the Park that afternoon with Eleanor Walpole-Wilson, fated apparently to be witness of the various stages of our relationship. I had not managed to get away from London that week-end, and to fall in by chance with these two seemed a wonderful piece of luck. That was the last day for many months that I woke up in the morning without immediately thinking of Barbara.

'Oh, what fun to meet like this,' she had said.

I felt immediately a sense of extraordinary exhilaration at this harmless remark. It was June, and there had been rain the day before, so that the grass smelt fresh and luxuriant. The weather, though warm, was not disagreeably hot. The precise location of our meeting was a spot not far from the Achilles statue. We strolled, all three, towards Kensington Gardens. The Row was empty. Sparkles of light radiated this way and that from the clusters of white statuary and nodular gilt pinnacles of the Albert Memorial, towards which we were steadily moving. Eleanor Walpole-Wilson, a square, broad-shouldered girl, rather above the average in height, wore her hair plaited in a bun at the back, which always looked as if it were about to come down at any moment: and did sometimes, in fact, descend piecemeal. She had brought with her Sultan, a labrador, and was trying to train this dog by blasts on a whistle, which she accompanied with harsh, monosyllabic shouting. That enterprise, the training of Sultan, was in keeping with Eleanor's habit of behaviour, as she was always accustomed to act, in principle, as if London were the country, an exercise of will she rarely relaxed.

We ascended the steps of the Albert Memorial and inspected the figures of the Arts and Sciences loitering in high relief round the central mass of that monument. Eleanor, still blowing her whistle fitfully, made some comment regarding the muscles of the bearded male figure belonging to the group called 'Manufactures' which caused Barbara to burst out laughing. This happened on the way down the steps at the south-east corner, approaching the statues symbolising Asia, where, beside the kneeling elephant, the Bedouin forever rests on his haunches in hopeless contemplation of Kensington Gardens' trees and thickets, the blackened sockets of his eyes ranging endlessly over the rich foliage of these oases of the mirage.

For some reason Eleanor's words seemed immensely funny at that moment. Barbara stumbled, and, for a brief second, took my arm. It was then, perhaps, that a force was released, no less powerful for its action proving somewhat delayed; for emotions of that kind are not always immediately grasped. We sat on chairs for a time, and then walked to the north side of the park, in the direction of the Budds' house in Sussex Square, where the girls were invited to tea. When I said good-bye at the gates I experienced a sense of unaccountable loss, similar in its suddenness to that earlier exhilaration of our meeting. The rest of the day dragged, that feeling of anxiety—which haunts youth so much more than maturity—descending, coupled with almost unbearable nervous fatigue. I dined alone, and retired early to bed.

My parents' acquaintance—not a very close one—with the Walpole-Wilsons dated from that same period of the Peace Conference during which we had run across Mr. Deacon in the Louvre, a time when Sir Gavin Walpole-Wilson had also been working in Paris. He had by then already left the Diplomatic Service, and was associated with some voluntary organisation—of dubious practical importance, so my father used to hint—devoted to the assistance of certain specialised categories of refugee; for Sir Gavin's career had been brought to a close soon after receiving his K.C.M.G., as Minister to a South American republic. There had been trouble connected with the dispatch of a telegram; His Majesty's Government, so it subsequently appeared, having already recognised the Leader of the Opposition as Head of the State in place of the Junta that had enjoyed power for some years previously. It was generally agreed that Sir Gavin, whatever the misdemeanour, had been guilty of nothing worse than a perfectly correct effort to 'keep in' with both sides: coupled, possibly, with a certain denseness of comprehension regarding potential fallibility of Foreign Secretaries, and changes recently observable in the political stature of General Gomez; but he had taken the matter to heart, and resigned. Pressure from above may have made this course involuntary, a point upon which opinion varied.

Although not at all inclined to under-estimate the personal part he had played in the Councils of Europe, or, indeed, of the World, Sir Gavin was apt to give the impression that he was always anxious, even in the smallest matters, to justify himself; so that an air of supposing life to have treated him less generously than his talents deserved made him, although a far more forceful personality, sometimes seem to resemble Uncle Giles. He was, for example, also fond of proclaiming that he set little store by rank—rank, at least, when contrasted with ability—a taste which he shared with my uncle. It was possible that in days before his marriage Sir Gavin may have suffered similar financial anxieties, for I believe his own family had been far from rich, with difficulty scraping together the money then required for entering the Diplomatic Service. After retirement—I had, of course, not known him before—he wore his hair rather long, and favoured loose, shaggy suits. A firm belief that things were more likely than not to go wrong was another characteristic of Sir Gavin's approach to life, induced no doubt by his own regrets. Indeed, he could not be entirely absolved from suspicion of rather enjoying the worst when it happened: at times almost of engineering disaster of a purely social kind.

'For lust of knowing what we should not know,' he was fond of intoning, 'we take the Golden Road to Samarkand.'

This quotation may have offered to his mind some explanation of human adversity, though scarcely applicable in his own case, as he was a man singularly lacking in intellectual curiosity, and it was generally supposed that the inopportune step in his career had been the result of too much caution rather than any disposition to experiment in that exploration, moral or actual, to which the lines seem to refer. That trait, as it happened, was more noticeable in his wife. She was one of the two daughters of Lord Aberavon, a shipping magnate, now deceased, to whom, as I had discovered in due course, *Boyhood of Cyrus* had once belonged; Mr. Deacon's picture, for some inexplicable reason, being almost the sole residue from wholesale disposal on the collector's death of an accumulation of paintings unsympathetic to the taste of a later generation. Lady Walpole-Wilson suffered from 'nerves', though less oppressively than her sister, Barbara's mother, who even regarded herself as a semi-invalid on that account. Indeed, I had scarcely ever seen Lady Goring, or her husband: for, like his niece, Eleanor, Lord Goring shunned London whenever possible. He was said to be an expert on scientific methods of cultivation, and possessed an experimental fruit farm that was, I believe, rather famous for daring methods.

Uncle Giles was fond of calling people richer or in a general way more advantageously placed than himself, against whom he could at the same time level no specifically disparaging charge, 'well connected enough, I don't doubt', a descriptive phrase which he would sometimes indiscriminately apply; but I suppose that the Gorings might truthfully have been so labelled. They used to take a house in Upper Berkeley Street for the first part of the summer, though dinner-parties were rare there, and not as a rule convivial. Most of the responsibility for Barbara's 'season' fell on her aunt, who probably regarded her niece's lively character as an alleviation of difficulties posed by her own daughter, rather than any additional burden on the household.

Lady Walpole-Wilson, for whom I felt a decided affection, was a tall, dark, distinguished looking woman, with doe-like eyes, to whose appearance some vice-regal or ambassadorial marriage seemed appropriate. Her comparative incapacity to control her own dinner-parties, at which she was almost always especially discomposed, seemed to me a kind of mute personal protest against circumstances—in the shape of her husband's retirement—having deprived her of the splendours, such as they were, of that position in life owed to her statuesque presence; for in those days I took a highly romantic view, not only of love, but also of such things as politics and government: supposing, for example, that eccentricity and ineptitude were unknown in circles where they might, in fact, be regarded—at least so far as the official entertaining of all countries is concerned—almost as the rule rather than the exception. I can now see that Lady Walpole-Wilson's past experience may have made her aware of this tendency on the part of wives of distinguished public figures to be unable, or unwilling, to make suitable hostesses: a knowledge, coupled with her natural diffidence, that caused her to give an impression sometimes that at all costs she would like to escape from her own house: not because dispensation of hospitality was in itself in the least disagreeable to her as much as on account of accumulated memories from the past of wounded feelings when matters had 'gone wrong'.

To these sentiments was no doubt added the self-inflicted embarrassment implicit in the paraphernalia of launching a daughter—and, if it could be remarked without unkindness, 'what a daughter'—on to an obdurate world; not to mention grappling with purely hypothetical questions, such as the enigma, universally insoluble, of what other mothers would think of the manner in which she herself, as a mother, was sustaining this load of care. In this last affliction Sir Gavin's attitude was often of no great help, and it is hard to say whether either of them really believed that Eleanor, who had always been more or less of a 'problem'—there were endless stories of nose-bleeds and headaches—would ever find a husband. Eleanor had always disliked feminine pursuits. When we had met in Paris before either of us had grown up, she had told me that she would at that moment much prefer to be staying with her cousins in Oxfordshire: an attitude of mind that had culminated in detestation of dances. This resentment, since I had known her in those early days, did not seem as strange to me as to many of the young men who encountered her for the first time at the dinner-table, where she could be both abrupt and sulky. Barbara used to say: 'Eleanor should never have been removed from the country. It is cruelty to animals.' She was also fond of remarking: 'Eleanor is not a bad old girl when you get to know her,' a statement unquestionably true; but, since human life is lived largely at surface level, that encouraging possibility, true or false, did not appreciably lighten the burden of Eleanor's partners.

The Walpole-Wilsons, accordingly, provided not only the foundation, but frequently the immediate locality, also, for my association with Barbara, whom I used to meet fairly often at dances, after our walk together in the park. Sometimes we even saw a film together, or went to a matinée. That was in the summer. When she came to London for a few weeks before Christmas, we met again. By the opening of the following May I was beginning to wonder how the situation was to be resolved. Such scuffles as had, once in a way, taken place between us, on the comparatively rare occasions when we found ourselves alone together, were not exactly encouraged by her; in fact she seemed only to like an intermittent attack for the pleasure of repulsing it. Certainly such aggression carried neither of us any farther. She liked ragging; but ragging—and nothing more—these rough-and-tumbles remained. 'Don't get sentimental,' she used to say; and, so far as it went, avoidance of sentiment—as much as avoidance of sentimentality—appeared, on her side, a genuine inclination.

This affair with Barbara, although taking up less than a year, seemed already to have occupied a substantial proportion of my life; because nothing establishes the timelessness of Time like those episodes of early experience seen, on re-examination at a later period, to have been crowded together with such unbelievable closeness in the course of a few years; yet equally giving the illusion of being so infinitely extended during the months when actually taking place.

My frame of mind—perhaps I should say the state of my heart—remained unchanged, and dances seemed pointless unless Barbara was present. During that summer *Boyhood of Cyrus* developed its mystic significance, representing on my arrival in front of it a two-to-one chance of seeing Barbara at dinner. If we both ate at the Walpole-Wilsons', she was at least under my eye. She herself was always quite unaware of the sentimental meaning thus attached to Mr. Deacon's picture. When first asked about it, she could not for a long time make out what picture I spoke of; and once, when we were both in the hall at the same time and I drew her attention to where it hung, she assured me that she had never before noticed its existence. Eleanor was equally vague on the subject.

'Are they going bathing?' she had asked. 'I don't care for it.'

This matter of being able to establish Barbara's whereabouts for a specific number of hours brought at least limited relief from agonies of ignorance as to what her movements might be, with consequent inability to exercise control over her in however slight a degree; for love of that sort—the sort where the sensual element has been reduced to a minimum—must after all, largely if not entirely, resolve itself to the exercise of power: a fact of which Barbara was, of course, more aware than I.

These torments, as I have said, continued for a number of months, sometimes with great severity; and then one afternoon, when I was correcting proofs in the office, Barbara rang up and asked if I would dine at Eaton Square that evening for the Huntercombes' dance. I decided immediately that I would put off Short (my former undergraduate acquaintance, now become a civil servant), with whom, earlier in the week, I had arranged to have a meal, and at once agreed to come. I had experienced the usual feeling of excitement while talking with her on the telephone; but suddenly as I hung up the receiver—thinking that perhaps I was leaving Short rather ruthlessly in the lurch so far as his evening was concerned—I found myself wondering whether I was still in love. Barbara's voice had sounded so peremptory, and it was clear that someone else had failed her at the last moment. In that there was, of course, nothing to be taken reasonably amiss. Obviously I could not expect to sit next to her at dinner every night of our lives—unless I married her; perhaps not even then. And yet my heart seemed a shade lighter. Was the fever passing? I was myself still barely conscious of its declension. I had not at that time met Barnby, nor had opportunity to digest one of his favourite maxims: 'A woman always overplays her hand.'

I had, naturally, given a good deal of thought at one time or another to the question of love. Barbara did not represent the first attack. There had been, for example, Peter Templer's sister, Jean, and Madame Leroy's niece, Suzette; but Jean and Suzette now seemed dim, if desirable, memories; and I felt, for no particular reason, more sure now of the maturity of my approach. At the same time there was certainly little to boast about in my handling of the problem of Barbara. I could not even make up my mind—should anything of the sort have been practicable—whether or not I really wanted to marry her. Marriage appeared something remote and forbidding, with which desire for Barbara had little or no connexion. She seemed to exist merely to disturb my rest: to be possessed neither by lawful nor unlawful means: made of dreams, yet to be captured only by reality. Such, at least, were the terms in which I thought of her as I approached the Walpole-Wilsons' that evening.

Taxis were drawing up in the late sunshine before several

of the houses in the square, and young men in tails and girls in evening dress, looking rather selfconscious in the bright daylight, were paying fares or ringing front-door bells. It was that stagnant London weather without a breath of air. One might almost have been in the Tropics. Even Archie Gilbert, who had immediately preceded me in the hall—he had never been known to be late for dinner—looked that night as if he might be feeling the heat a little. His almost invisibly fair moustache suggested the same piqué material as the surface of his stiff shirt; and, as usual, he shed about him an effect of such unnatural cleanliness that some secret chemical process seemed to have been applied, in preparation for the party, both to himself and his clothes: making body and its dazzling integument, sable and argent rather than merely black and white, proof against smuts and dust. Shirt, collar, tie, waistcoat, handkerchief, and gloves were like snow: all these trappings, as always, apparently assumed for the first time: even though he himself looked a shade pinker than usual in the face owing to the oppressive climatic conditions.

His whole life seemed so irrevocably concentrated on 'débutante dances' that it was impossible to imagine Archie Gilbert finding any tolerable existence outside a tail-coat. I could never remember attending any London dance that could possibly be considered to fall within the category named, at which he had not also been present for at least a few minutes; and, if two or three balls were held on the same evening, it always turned out that he had managed to look in at each one of them. During the day he was said to 'do something in the City'—the phrase 'non-ferrous metals' had once been hesitantly mentioned in my presence as applicable, in some probably remote manner to his daily employment. He himself never referred to any such subordination, and I used sometimes to wonder whether this putative job was not, in reality, a polite fiction, invented on his own part out of genuine modesty, of which I am sure he possessed a great deal, in order to make himself appear a less remarkable person than in truth he was: even a kind of superhuman ordinariness being undesirable, perhaps, for true perfection in this rôle of absolute normality which he had chosen to play with such *éclat*. He was unthinkable in everyday clothes; and he must, in any case, have required that rest and sleep during the hours of light which his nocturnal duties could rarely, if ever, have allowed him. He seemed to prefer no one woman—débutante or chaperone—to another; and, although not indulging in much conversation, as such, he always gave the impression of being at ease with, or without, words; and of having danced at least once with every one of the three or four hundred girls who constituted, in the last resort, the final cause, and only possible justification, of that social organism. He appeared also to be known by name, and approved, by the mother of each of these girls: in a general way, as I have said, getting on equally well with mothers and daughters.

Even Eleanor's consistently severe manner with young men was modified appreciably for Archie Gilbert, and we had hardly arrived in the drawing-room before she was asking him to help her in the forcible return of Sultan to the huge wicker hutch, occupying one complete corner of the room, in which the labrador had his being. Together Archie Gilbert and Eleanor dragged back the dog, while Sultan thumped his tail noisily on the carpet, and Lady Walpole-Wilson protested a little that the struggle would mar the beauty of Archie Gilbert's clothes.

Her own eagerness of manner always suggested that Lady Walpole-Wilson would have enjoyed asking congenial people to her parties if only she could have found people who were, indeed, congenial to her; and she was, of course, not the only hostess who must, from time to time, have suffered a twinge of misgiving on account of more than one of the young men who formed the shifting male population of the London ballrooms. Supposing most other people to live a more amusing life than herself, her humility in this respect was combined with a trust, never entirely relinquished, that with a different collection of guests in the house things might take a turn for the better. This inward condition, in which hope and despair constantly gave place to one another, undeniably contributed to a lack of ease in her drawing-room.

Sir Gavin was moving about dramatically, even rather tragically, in the background. He was, as I have suggested, inclined to affect a few mild eccentricities of dress. That evening, for example, he was wearing an old-fashioned straight-ended white tie like a butler's: his large, almost square horn-rimmed spectacles, tanned complexion, and moustache, bristling, but at the same time silky, giving him a rather fierce expression, like that of an angry rajah. Although deeper-chested and more weather-beaten, he certainly recalled Uncle Giles. Walking, as he did at times, with a slight limp, the cause of which was unknown to me—possibly it was assumed to indicate a certain state of mind—he took my arm almost fiercely, rather as if acting in an amateur production of Shakespeare; and, no doubt because he prided himself on putting young men at their ease, drew my attention to another guest, already arrived in the room before Archie Gilbert and myself. This person was standing under Lavery's portrait of Lady Walpole-Wilson, painted at the time of her marriage, in a white dress and blue sash, a picture he was examining with the air of one trying to fill in the seconds before introductions begin to take place, rather than on account of a deep interest in art.

'Have you met Mr. Widmerpool?' asked Sir Gavin, disconsolately, suddenly dropping his energetic demeanour, as if suffering all at once from unaccountable foreboding about the whole party.

Widmerpool's advent in Eaton Square that night did not strike me at the time as anything more than a matter of chance. He had cropped up in my life before, and, if I considered him at all as a recurrent factor, I should have been prepared to admit that he might crop up again. I did not, however, as yet see him as one of those symbolic figures, of whom most people possess at least one example, if not more, round whom the past and the future have a way of assembling. We had not met for years; since the summer after I had left school, when both of us had been trying to learn French staying with the Leroys in Touraine—the place, in fact, where I had supposed myself in love with Suzette. I had hardly thought of him since the moment when he had climbed ponderously into the *grognard's* taxi, and coasted in a cloud of white dust down the hill from La Grenadière. Now he had exchanged his metal-edged glasses for spectacles with a tortoise-shell frame, similar, though of lesser proportions, to those worn by his host, and in general smartened up his personal appearance. True to the old form, there was still something indefinably odd about the cut of his white waistcoat; while he retained that curiously piscine cast of countenance, projecting the impression that he swam, rather than walked, through the rooms he haunted.

Just as the first sight of *Boyhood of Cyrus*, by its association with Mr. Deacon and life before the war, had brought back memories of childhood, the sight of Widmerpool called up in a similar manner—almost like some parallel scene from Mr. Deacon's brush entitled *Boyhood of Widmerpool*—all kind of recollections of days at school. I remembered the interest once aroused in me by Widmerpool's determination to become a success in life, and the brilliance with which Stringham used to mimic his movements and manner of speech. Indeed, Widmerpool's presence in the flesh seemed even now less real than Stringham's former imitations of him: a thought that had often struck me before, now renewed unexpectedly in the Walpole-Wilsons' drawing-room. Widmerpool still represented to my mind a kind of embodiment of thankless labour and unsatisfied ambition. When we had met at La Grenadière, he had talked of his activities in London, but somehow I had never been able to picture his life as an adult; idly fancying him, if thought of at all, forever floundering towards the tape in races never won. Certainly it had not once occurred to me that I should meet him at a dinner-party given for a dance, although I recalled now that he had talked of dances; and, when I came to consider the matter, there was not the smallest reason why he should not turn up upon an occasion such as this—at the Walpole-Wilsons' house or anywhere else. That had to be admitted without question. He seemed in the best of spirits. We were immediately left together by Sir Gavin, who wandered off muttering to himself in a dissatisfied undertone about some impenetrable concerns of his own.

'Good gracious, Jenkins,' said Widmerpool, in that thick voice of his which remained quite unchanged, 'I had no idea that you were a dancing man.'

'I had formed the same wrong impression about yourself.'

'But I have never seen you anywhere before.' He sounded rather aggrieved.

'We must be asked to different parties.'

This reply, made on the spur of the moment without any suggestion of seriousness—certainly not intended to discredit the dances frequented by Widmerpool—must, for some reason, have sounded caustic to his ears. Perhaps I had inadequately concealed surprise felt on learning from his manner that he evidently regarded himself as a kind of standard 'spare man': in short something closely akin to Archie Gilbert. Whatever the cause, the words had obviously given offence. He went red in the face, and made one of those awkward jerks of the body which Stringham used to imitate so deftly.

'As a matter of fact, I have been about very little this summer,' he said, frowning. 'I found I had been working a shade too hard, and had to—well—give myself a bit of a rest.'

I remembered the interest he had always taken, even while still a schoolboy, in his own health and its diurnal changes. In France it had been the same. A whole afternoon had been spent in Tours trying to find the right medicine to adjust the effect on him of the local wine, of which the Leroys' vintage, drunk the night before, had been of disastrously recent growth.

'Then, the year before, I got jaundice in the middle of the season.'

'Are you fit again now?'

'I am better.'

He spoke with gravity.

'But I intend to take care of myself,' he added. 'My mother often tells me I go at things too hard. Besides, I don't really get enough air and exercise—without which one can never be truly robust.'

'Do you still go down to Barnes and drive golf-balls into a net?'

'Whenever feasible.'

He made not the smallest acknowledgment of the feat of memory on my part—with which, personally, I felt rather satisfied—that had called to mind this detail (given years before at the Leroys') of his athletic exercises in outer London. The illusion that egoists will be pleased, or flattered, by interest taken in their habits persists throughout life; whereas, in fact, persons like Widmerpool, in complete subjection to the ego, are, by the nature of that infirmity, prevented from supposing that the minds of others could possibly be occupied by any subject far distant from the egoist's own affairs.

'Actually, one can spend too much time on sport if one is really going to get on,' said Widmerpool. 'And then I have my Territorials.'

'You were going to be a solicitor when we last met.'

'That would hardly preclude me from holding a Territorial officer's commission,' said Widmerpool, smiling as broadly as his small mouth would allow, as if this were a repartee of quite unusual neatness.

'Of course it wouldn't.'

His remark seemed to me immensely silly.

'I am with a firm of solicitors—Turnbull, Welford and Puckering, to be exact,' he said. 'But you may be sure that I have other interests too. Some of them not unimportant, I might add.'

He smiled with some self-satisfaction, but clearly did not wish to be questioned further, at least there and then, regarding his professional activities. That was reasonable enough in the circumstances. However, his next words surprised me. Giving a short intake of breath, he said in a lower voice, with one of those unexpected outbursts of candour that I remembered from La Grenadière: 'Do you know our host and hostess well? I have been on excellent terms with the family for a number of years, but this is the first time I have been asked to dinner. Of course I really know the Gorings better.'

This admission regarding his invitation to dine at Eaton Square was apparently intended to convey some hint, or confession, of past failure; although at the same time Widmerpool seemed half inclined by his tone to impart the news of his better acquaintance with the Gorings equally as a matter for congratulation. Indeed, he was evidently unable to decide in his own mind whether this allegedly long familiarity with the Walpole-Wilsons was—in the light of this being his first appearance in the house—something to boast of, or conceal.

Our conversation, taking place intermittently, while people continually arrived in the room, was several times broken off when one or other of us was introduced to, or spoke with, another guest. Two of the girls present I had not met before. The taller, Lady Anne Stepney, wore an evening dress that had seen better days: which looked, indeed, rather like an old nightdress furbished up for the occasion. She seemed quite unconcerned about her decidedly untidy appearance, her bearing in some respects resembling Eleanor's, though she was much prettier than Eleanor, with large dark eyes and reddish hair. Her name was familiar to me, for what reason I could not at first recall. The lively, gleaming little Jewess in a scarlet frock, who came into the room on the heels of Lady Anne, was announced as 'Miss Manasch', and addressed by the Walpole-Wilsons as 'Rosie'. Both girls were immediately, and simultaneously, engaged by Archie Gilbert, who happened to be free at their moment of entering the room.

Over by the window, Margaret Budd, a beauty, was talking to Pardoe, a Grenadier; and laughing while he demonstrated with a small shovel taken from the fireplace a scooping shot, successful or the reverse, that he, or someone known to him, had recently performed on the links. When she laughed, Margaret looked like an immensely—almost ludicrously—pretty child. She was, as it were, the female equivalent of Archie Gilbert: present at every dance, always lovely, always fresh, and yet somehow quite unreal. She scarcely spoke at all, and might have been one of those huge dolls which, when inclined backwards, say 'Ma-ma' or 'Pa-pa': though impossible to imagine in any position so undignified as that required for the mechanism to produce these syllables: equally hard to conceive her dishevelled, or bad-tempered, or, indeed, capable of physical passion—though appearances may be deceptive in no sphere so much as the last. Never without a partner, usually booked up six or seven dances ahead, this was her third or fourth season—so Barbara had once pointed out—and there had, as yet, been no sign of her getting engaged. 'Margaret is rather a Guardee's girl,' Barbara had added, evidently intending the label to imply no great compliment in her own eyes.

Widmerpool's presence reminded me that Margaret was cousin of the Budd who had been Captain of the Eleven one year at school; and I remembered the story Stringham had told me, years before, of Widmerpool's pleased acceptance—delight almost—on being struck in the face with a banana thrown by that comparatively notable cricketer. I could not help toying with the fantasy that some atavistic strain, deep-seated in the Budd family, might cause Margaret to assail Widmerpool in similar manner; perhaps later in the evening when dessert, tempting as a missile, appeared at the Walpole-Wilsons' table. Such a vision was improbable to an almost infinite degree, because Margaret was the kindest, quietest creature imaginable; really, I think, almost wholly unaware, in gentle concentration on herself, of the presence of most of the people moving about her. Even her laughter was rare, and its audible provocation before dinner that evening by his strokes in the air with the shovel did Pardoe credit.

From a girl's point of view, there was no doubt something to be said for considering Pardoe the most interesting person present that evening. He had recently inherited a house on the Welsh Border (Jacobean in architecture, though with more ancient historical associations going back to the Wars of the Roses), together with enough money, so it was said, to 'keep up' the estate. He was an agreeable, pink-faced ensign, very short, square, and broad-shouldered, with a huge black moustache, brushed out so forcibly that it seemed to be false and assumed for a joke. Such affluent young men were known to have a tendency to abandon dances and frequent night-clubs. Pardoe, however, was still available, so it appeared; no one could tell for how long. Unlike Archie Gilbert, he had a great deal to say for himself though his newly acquired possessions made small-talk scarcely necessary—and, as he modestly treated his own appearance as a matter for laughter, the moustache was a considerable asset in his anecdotes. He had at last abandoned the shovel, and, mildly interested in music, had become engaged in some operatic argument with Miss Manasch. To this discussion Sir Gavin, from the background where he had been hovering, his moustache bristling more than ever, now cut in with the emphatic words:

'No one could sing it like Slezak.'

'Did you ever hear him in *Lohengrin*?' demanded Pardoe, taking the ends of his own moustache with both hands, as if about to tear it off and reveal himself in a new identity.

'Many a time and oft,' said Sir Gavin, defiantly. 'But what was that you were saying about *Idomeneo*?'

All three of them embarked clamorously on a new

musical dispute. The rest of us chatted in a desultory way. Barbara arrived late. She was wearing her gold dress that I knew of old did not suit her; and that spirit of contradiction that especially governs matters of the heart caused the fact that she was not looking her best to provoke in me a stab of affection. Even so, I was still able to wonder whether the situation between us—between myself and her, would perhaps be more accurate—remained quite unchanged; and, as I let go of her small cluster of fingers—each one of which I was conscious of as a single entity while I held her hand—I thought that perhaps that night I should not, as in past months, experience the same recurrent torments as she danced with other men. As soon as she had come into the room, Widmerpool skirted the sofa and made towards her, leaving me with the impression that I might in some manner have appeared unfriendly to him after our comparative intimacy in France. I decided to try to correct this apprehension, should it exist, later in the evening when suitable opportunity might arise.

The minutes passed: conversation flagged. The Louis Seize clock standing on a wall-bracket gave out a threatening tick-tock. One of the male guests had still not yet turned up. In those days, at that sort of party, there were no drinks before dinner; and, while Eleanor told me about her Girl Guides, the evening sun deflected huge golden squares of phosphorescent colour (spread rather in the manner advocated by Mr. Deacon, giving formal juxtaposition to light and shade) against the peacock-green shot-silk shadows of the sofa cushions. Outside, the detonation of loudly-slammed taxi doors, suggesting the opening of a cannonade, had died down. In place of those sounds some cats were quarrelling, or making love, in the gardens running the length of the square. I began to long for the meal to begin. After total silence had fallen on the room for the second time, Lady Walpole-Wilson, apparently with an effort, for her lips faltered slightly when she spoke, came to a decision to await the late-comer no further.

'Let's go down in a troop,' she said, 'and—as Mr. Tompsitt is so unpunctual—not bother about "taking in". I really do not think we can delay dinner any longer.'

In speaking to each other the Walpole-Wilsons were inclined to give an impression that they were comparative strangers, who had met for the first time only a week or two before, but at this remark her husband, no doubt wanting food as much as—perhaps even more than—the rest of those present, replied rather gruffly: 'Of course, Daisy, of course.'

He added, without any suggestion of complaint—on the contrary, if anything, with approbation: 'Young Tompsitt is always late.'

The news that Tompsitt had been invited would once have filled me with dismay. Even at that moment, sudden mention of his name caused an instinctive hope that his absence was due to illness or accident, something that might prevent him from putting in any appearance at all, preferably grave enough to exclude him from dances for many months: perhaps for ever. He was one of various young men moving within Barbara's orbit whose relationship with her, though impossible to estimate at all precisely, was yet in a general way disturbing for someone who might have claims of his own to put forward in that quarter. In that respect Tompsitt's connexion was of a particularly distasteful kind in that Barbara evidently found him not unattractive; while his approach to her, or so it seemed to me, was conditioned entirely by the ebb and flow of his own vanity: no inconsiderable element when gauged at any given moment, though laying a course hard for an unsympathetic observer to chart. That is to say he was obviously flattered by the fact that Barbara found him, apparently, prepossessing enough; and, at the same time, not sufficiently stirred within himself to spend more than comparatively brief spells in her company, especially when there were other girls about, who might be supposed, for one reason or another, to represent in his eyes potentially superior assets.

That was what I used, perhaps unjustly, to reflect; at the same time having to admit to myself that Tompsitt's attitude towards Barbara posed, from my own point of view, a dilemma as to what, short of his own bodily removal, would constitute a change for the better. His relative lack of enthusiasm, though acceptable only with all kinds of unpalatable reservations, had, in its way, to be approved; while apprehension that his feelings towards Barbara might suddenly undergo some violent emotional stimulation was—or had certainly been until that evening—an ever present anxiety. At last, however, I felt, anyway on second thoughts, fairly indifferent as to whether or not Tompsitt turned up. Inwardly I was becoming increasingly convinced of this, and I might even have looked forward to Tompsitt's entry if there had been serious threat of dinner being further delayed on his account.

In the dining-room I found myself sitting at the oval-ended table between Barbara and Anne Stepney, the second of whom was on Sir Gavin's right. The Walpole-Wilsons defied prevailing mode by still employing a table-cloth, a preference of Sir Gavin's, who prided himself on combining in his own home tastes of 'the old school' with a progressive point of view in worldly matters. The scented geranium leaf usually to be found floating in the finger-bowls could be attributed to his wife's leaning towards a more exotic way of life. Beyond Barbara was Archie Gilbert, probably placed on Lady Walpole-Wilson's left to make up for having Tompsitt—or rather an empty chair, where in due course he would sit, if he had not forgotten the invitation—on her right. Tompsitt, a protégé of Sir Gavin's, was not greatly liked either by Eleanor or her mother.

This chasm left by Tompsitt divided Margaret Budd, who had Widmerpool on her other side, from her hostess. Widmerpool's precise channel of invitation to the house was still obscure, and the fact that he himself seemed on the whole surprised to find himself dining there made his presence even more a matter for speculation. He had been placed next to Eleanor, who had presumably been consulted on the subject of seating accommodation at the dinner table, though he seemed by his manner towards her to know her only slightly; while she herself showed signs, familiar to me from observing her behaviour on past occasions, of indifference, if not dislike, for his company. Barbara had been the only member of the party greeted by him as an old acquaintance; though she had done no more than wring him rather warmly by the hand when she arrived, quickly passing on to someone else, at which he had looked discouraged. Pardoe sat between Eleanor and Miss Manasch who brought the party round once more to Sir Gavin. The table had perhaps not been easy to arrange. Its complications of seating must have posed problems that accounted for Lady Walpole-Wilson's more than usually agitated state.

'There does not seem any substantial agreement yet on the subject of the Haig statue,' said Widmerpool, as he unfolded his napkin. 'Did you read St. John Clarke's letter?'

He spoke to Eleanor, though he had glanced round the table as if hoping for a larger audience to hear his views on the matter. The subject, as it happened, was one upon which I knew Eleanor to hold decided opinions, and was therefore a question to be avoided, unless driven to conversational extremities, as she much preferred statement to discussion. The fact of broaching it was yet another indication that Widmerpool could not have seen a great deal of her at all recently.

'Surely they can find someone to carve a horse that looks like a horse.'

She spoke with truculence even at the outset.

'The question, to my mind,' said Widmerpool, 'is whether a statue is, in reality, an appropriate form of recognition for public services in modern times.'

'Don't you think great men ought to be honoured?' Eleaner asked, rather tensely. 'I do.'

She clenched her lips tightly together as if prepared to contest the point to the death—with Widmerpool or anyone else.

'Nobody—least of all myself—denies the desirability of honouring great men,' he said in return, rather sharply, 'but some people think the traffic problem—already severe enough in all conscience—might be adversely effected if any more space is taken up by monuments in busy thoroughfares.'

'I can't see why they can't make a model of a real horse,' said Barbara. 'Couldn't they do it in plaster of Paris or something. Don't you think?'

This last question, propitiatory in tone, and addressed in a fairly low voice to myself, could still make me feel, for reasons quite subjective in origin, that there might be something to be said for this unconventional method of solving what had become almost the chief enigma of contemporary æsthetic.

'Need there be a horse?' asked Lady Walpole-Wilson, putting a brave face on the discussion, though evidently well aware, even apart from Eleanor's potential pronouncements on the subject, of its manifold dangers.

'You can't very well have him sitting at his desk,' said Sir Gavin, bluffly, 'though I expect that was where he spent a good deal of his time. When I saw him in Paris at the time of the Conference——'

'Why shouldn't he be on a horse?' demanded Eleanor, angrily. 'He used to ride one, didn't he?'

'We all agree that he used to ride one,' said Widmerpool, indulgently this time. 'And that, if commemoration is to take the form proposed, the Field-Marshal should certainly be represented mounted on his charger. I should have supposed there was no doubt upon that point.'

'Oh, I don't know,' said Pardoe, shooting out his moustache once more. 'Why not put him in a staff-car? You could have the real thing, with his flag flying at the bonnet.'

'Of course if you want to make a joke of it . . .' said Eleanor, casting a look of great contempt in Pardoe's direction.

Archie Gilbert and Margaret Budd appeared to hold no strong convictions regarding the statue. Miss Manasch made the practical suggestion that they should pay off the sculptor of the work under discussion, if—as it certainly appeared—this had not met with general approval, and make a fresh start with another candidate who might provide something of a more popular nature.

'I think they ought to have got Mestroviç in the first place,' said Lady Anne, coldly, during the silence that followed Miss Manasch's proposal.

This unexpected opinion was plainly issued as a challenge; but controversy regarding the memorial was now cut short by the sudden arrival in the dining-room of Tompsitt.

After somewhat perfunctory apology for his lateness, he sat down between Lady Walpole-Wilson and Margaret Budd, though without taking a great deal of notice of either of them. Lady Walpole-Wilson shot him a look to suggest her collusion in his apparent inclination to assume that the time for regrets and excuses was now long past; though her glance was also no doubt intended to urge—even to plead with—him to make amends best by showing himself agreeable to his neighbour, since Eleanor had relapsed into further argument that demanded Widmerpool's close attention, leaving Margaret Budd, for all her beauty, high and dry so far as personal attention was concerned.

However, now that he had arrived, formal conversation seemed the last thing to which Tompsitt was at all disposed. He smiled across the table to Barbara, who had crooked her finger at him as he entered the room. Then, picking up the menu, he studied it carefully. The card was inscribed for some reason—probably because she had looked in at tea-time and Eleanor hated the job—in Barbara's own scratchy, laborious hand that I knew so well; not because I had ever received many letters from her in the course of our relationship, but on account of the fact that such scrawled notes as I possessed used to live for months in my pocket, seeming to retain in their paper and ink some atom of Barbara herself to be preserved and secreted until our next meeting. I wondered whether that schoolgirl script breathed any such message to Tompsitt, as it broke the news that he was about to eat the identical meal he must have consumed at every dinner-party—if given specifically for a London dance—that he had ever attended.

He was a large, fair young man, with unbrushed hair and a grey smudge on the left-hand side of his shirt-front: cramming for—perhaps by then even admitted to—the Foreign Office. Sir Gavin held strong views on 'broadening the basis' of the selection of candidates for governmental service, and he took an interest in Tompsitt as prototype of a newer and less constricted vehicle for handling foreign affairs. Certainly Tompsitt's appearance was calculated to dispose effectually of the myth, dear to the public mind, of the 'faultlessly dressed diplomat', and he had been educated—the details were elusive—in some manner not absolutely conventional: though his air of incivility that so delighted Sir Gavin could no doubt have been inculcated with at least equal success at any public school. It was perhaps fair to regard him a young man rather different from those normally recruited for the purpose, and, in return for this patronage, Tompsitt, supercilious in his manner to most people, accorded a deep respect to Sir Gavin's utterances; although, a posture not uncommon in such dual relationships, this deference sometimes took the more flattering form of apparent disagreement. They had met a year or two before at a gathering of some local branch of the League of Nations Union, where Sir Gavin had given a talk on 'Collective Security'.

All the time he was reading the menu, Tompsitt smiled to himself, as if exceedingly content to exist in a world from which most, if not all, surrounding distractions had been effectively eliminated. It had to be agreed that there was some forcefulness in his complete disregard for the rest of the party. Lady Walpole-Wilson began to look rather despairing. Widmerpool, on the other hand, seemed to share, as if by instinct, Sir Gavin's approbation for Tompsitt, or at least felt distinct interest in his personality, because after a time he ceased to give his views on the Horse in Sculpture, and cast several searching glances down the table. Sir Gavin, whose conversation was habitually diversified by a murmur of 'm'm . . . m'm . . . m'm . . .' repeated under his breath while his interlocutor was speaking—a technique designed to discourage over-long disquisitions on the other side—did no more than nod approvingly at Tompsitt. For the first few minutes of dinner Sir Gavin had contrived to monopolise the conversation of the girls he sat between. Now, however, he concentrated more particularly on Miss Manasch, from whom, with much laughter and by-play on his part, he appeared to be attempting to extract certain concrete opinions supposedly held by her father regarding the expansion of the Donners-Brebner Company in the Balkans. His attitude suggested that he also found Miss Manasch rather unusually attractive physically.

Now that the small, though appreciable, disturbance caused by Tompsitt's entry had finally settled down, the moment had come for some sort of conversational skirmish to begin between Lady Anne Stepney and myself. Ever since we had been introduced, I had been wondering why her name suggested some episode in the past: an incident vaguely unsatisfactory or disturbing. The mention of Donners-Brebner now reminded me that, the uneasy recollections were in connexion with this girl's sister, Peggy, whom Stringham on that night years before at the Donners-Brebner building had spoken, perhaps not very seriously, of marrying. In fact, I remembered now that he had been on his way to dinner with their parents, the Bridgnorths. That was the last time I had seen Stringham; it must have been—I tried to remember—four or five years before. The link seemed to provide a suitable topic to broach.

'Have you ever come across someone called Charles Stringham? I think he knows your sister.'

'Oh, yes,' she said, 'one of Peggy's pompous friends, isn't he?'

I found this a staggering judgment. There were all kinds of things to be said against Stringham's conduct—he could be offhand, even thoroughly bad-mannered—but 'pompous' was the last adjective in the world I ever expected to hear applied to him. It occurred to me, a second later, that she used the word with specialised meaning; or perhaps—this was most probable—merely intended to imply that her sister and Stringham were asked to grander parties than herself. Possibly she became aware that her remark had surprised me, because she added: 'I hope he isn't a great friend of yours.'

I was about to reply that Stringham was, indeed, a 'great friend' of mine, when I remembered that by now this description could scarcely be held to be true, since I had not seen nor heard of him for so long that I had little or no idea what he was doing with himself; and, for all I knew, he might almost have forgotten my existence. I had to admit to myself that, for my own part, I had not thought much about him either, since we had last met; though this sudden realisation that we now barely knew one another was, for a moment, oddly painful. In any event, nothing seemed to have come out of his talk of wanting to marry Peggy Stepney, and mention of his name had been, in the circumstances, perhaps tactless.

'I haven't seen him for three or four years.'

'Oh, I thought you might know him well.'

'I used to.'

'As a matter of fact, Peggy hasn't spoken of Charles Stringham for ages,' she said.

She did not actually toss her head—as girls are sometimes said to do in books—but that would have been the gesture appropriate to the tone in which she made this comment. It was evident that the subject of Stringham could supply no basis for discussion between us. I searched my mind for other themes. Lady Anne herself showed no sign of making any immediate contribution. She left the remains of her clear soup, and fixed her eyes on Miss Manasch; whether to satisfy herself about technical detail regarding the red dress, or to observe how well she was standing up to Sir Gavin's interrogation, which hovered between flirtation and apprisement how best to handle his investments, I was unable to decide. Whatever the question, it was settled fairly quickly in her mind during the brief period in which soup plates were removed and fried sole presented.

'What do you do?' she asked. 'I think men always enjoy talking about their work.'

I had the disturbing impression that she was preparing for some sort of a war between the sexes—as represented by herself and me—to break out at any moment. What vehement rôle she saw herself as playing in the life that surrounded us was problematical; some deep-felt resentment, comparable to Eleanor's and yet widely differing from hers, clearly existed within her: her clothes, no doubt outward and visible sign of this rebellion against circumstance. I told her my firm specialised in art books, and attempted to steer a line from Mestroviç, with unsuccessful results. We talked for a time of Botticelli, the only painter in whom she appeared to feel any keen interest, a subject which led to the books of St. John Clarke, one of which was a story of Renaissance Italy. This was the author mentioned by Widmerpool as writing to *The Times* regarding the Haig statue.

'And then there was one about the French Revolution.'

'I was on the side of the People,' she said, resolutely.

This assertion opened the road to discussion deeper, and altogether more searching, than I felt prepared to pursue at that stage of dinner. As it happened, there were by then signs all round the table of conversation becoming moribund. Lady Walpole-Wilson must have noticed this falling off, because she remarked at large that there were two dances being given that evening.

'And both in Belgrave Square,' said Archie Gilbert.

He sounded relieved that for once at least his self-imposed duties would not keep him travelling all over London; his worst nights being no doubt those experienced—as must happen once in a way—on occasions when a party was given in some big house at Richmond or Roehampton, while there was also, on the same night, perhaps more than one ball to be attended in the heart of London.

'The Spaniards are having some sort of a reception there, too,' said Tompsitt, who, having satisfied his immediate hunger, seemed disposed to show himself more genial than earlier. 'At their new Embassy.'

'I'm rather glad we don't have to attend those big official crushes any more as a duty,' said Lady Walpole-Wilson, with a sigh. 'We had to turn out in honour of Prince Theodoric the other night, and, really, it was too exhausting. Now that one is rather out of touch with that world one does so much prefer just to see one's own friends.'

'Is Prince Theodoric over for long?' asked Widmerpool, assuming an air of importance. 'I understand he is here largely for economic reasons—I believe Donners-Brebner are considering big expansions in his country.'

'Base metals, for one thing,' said Tompsitt, with at least equal *empressement*. 'There has also been talk of installing a railway to the coast. Am I right, Sir Gavin?'

At the phrase 'base metals' there had passed over Archie Gilbert's face perhaps the most imperceptible flicker of professional interest, that died down almost immediately as he turned once more to speak with Barbara of dance bands.

'No doubt about it,' said Sir Gavin. 'I used to see a lot of Theodoric's father when I was chargé d'affaires there. We often went fishing together.'

'Gavin was a great favourite with the old King,' said Lady Walpole-Wilson, as if it were a matter of mild surprise to her that her husband could be a favourite with anyone. 'I am afraid Prince Theodoric's brother is quite a different sort of person from their father. Do you remember that awkward incident when Janet was staying with us and how nice the King was?'

Sir Gavin glanced across the table at his wife, possibly apprehensive for a moment that she seemed inclined to particularise more precisely than might be desirable at the dinner table this contrast between father and son. Perhaps he did not wish to bring up the episode, whatever it had been, in which 'Janet'—his sister—had been involved.

'Theodoric, on the other hand, is a serious young man,' he said. 'A pity, really, that he is not King. The party given for him at their Legation was certainly dull enough—though personally I enjoy such jollifications as, for example, the court ball when our own King and Queen visited Berlin in 1913.'

'For the wedding of the Kaiser's daughter?' Tompsitt asked, briskly.

'Princess Victoria Louise,' said Sir Gavin, nodding with approval at this scoring of a point by his satellite. 'I went quite by chance, in place of Saltonstall, who——'

'Though, of course, it makes one feel quite ill to think of dancing with a German now,' said Lady Walpole-Wilson, anxiously.

She had taken the war hard.

'Do you really think so, Lady Walpole-Wilson?' said Widmerpool. 'Now, you know, I can feel no prejudice against the Germans. None whatever. French policy, on the other hand, I regard at the moment as very mistaken. Positively disastrous, in fact.'

'They did the Torch Dance,' said Sir Gavin, not to be put off nostalgic reminiscences so easily. 'The King and the Tsar danced, with the bride between them. A splendid sight. Ah, well, little we thought . . .'

'I loved the Swiss Guard when we were in Rome last

winter,' said Miss Manasch. 'And the Noble Guard were divine, too. We saw them at our audience.'

'But what a demoralising life for a young man,' said Lady Walpole-Wilson. 'I am sure many of them must make unsuitable marriages.'

'I can just imagine myself checking a Papal Guardsman's arms and equipment,' said Pardoe. 'Sergeant-Major, this halbert is filthy.'

'I'd love to see you in those red and yellow and blue stripes, Johnny,' said Miss Manasch, with perhaps a touch of unfriendliness. 'They'd suit you.'

Discussion as to whether or not ceremony was desirable lasted throughout the cutlets and ice. Lady Anne and Tompsitt were against pomp and circumstance; Eleanor and Widmerpool now found themselves on the same side in defending a reasonable degree of outward show. Tompsitt was rather pleased at the general agreement that he would go to pieces in the Tropics as a result of not changing for dinner, and certainly, so far as his evening clothes were concerned, he put his principles into practice.

'You should cart our Regimental Colour round,' said Pardoe. 'Then you'd all know what heavy ceremonial means. It's like a Salvation Army banner.'

'I'm always trying to get a decent Colour for the Guides,' said Eleanor, 'and not have to carry about a thing like a child's Union Jack. Not that anyone cares.'

'You won't be too long, Gavin, will you?' said Lady Walpole-Wilson at this, hastily rising from the table.

By then I had only exchanged a word or two with Barbara, though this, in a way, was a mark of intimacy rather than because she had been unwilling to talk, or because any change had already consciously taken place in our relationship. Most of dinner she had spent telling Archie Gilbert rather a long story about some dance. Now she turned towards me, just before she went through the door, and gave one of those half-smiles that I associated with moments—infrequent moments—when she was not quite sure of herself: smiles which I found particularly hard to resist, because they seemed to show a less familiar, more mysterious side of her that noisiness and ragging were partly designed to conceal. On that occasion her look seemed to be intended perhaps to reconcile the fact that throughout the meal she had allowed me so little of her attention. Sir Gavin assured his wife that we would 'not be long' in further occupation of the dining-room; and, when the door was closed, he moved the port in the direction of Pardoe.

'I hear you're letting your shooting,' he remarked.

'Got to cut down somewhere,' said Pardoe. 'That seemed as good a place as anywhere to begin.'

'Outgoings very heavy?'

'A lot of things to be brought up to date.'

The two of them settled down to discuss Shropshire coverts, with which Sir Gavin had some familiarity since his father-in-law, Lord Aberavon, had settled on the borders of that county during the latter part of his life; though the house had been sold at his death. Archie Gilbert, having successfully undertaken the operation of releasing the ladies from the room, returned to the chair next to mine. I asked who was giving the other dance that night.

'Mrs. Samson.'

'What will it be like?'

'Probably better than the Huntercombes'. Mrs. Samson has got Ambrose—though of course the band is not everything.'

'Are you going to Mrs. Samson's.'

He gave the ghost of a smile at what he must have regarded as a question needlessly asked.

'I expect I shall look in.'

'Is it for Daphne?'

'For Cynthia, the youngest girl,' he said, with gentle reproof at the thoughtlessness once more shown in putting this enquiry, which betrayed an altogether insufficiently serious approach to the world of dances. 'Daphne has been out for ages.'

On the other side of the table Widmerpool seemed, for some reason, determined to make a good impression on Tompsitt. Together they had begun to talk over the question of the Far East; Tompsitt treating Widmerpool's views on that subject with more respect than I should have expected him to show.

'I see the Chinese marshals have announced their victory to the spirit of the late Dr. Sun Yat-sen,' Widmerpool was saying.

He spoke rather as if he had himself expected an invitation to the ceremony, but was prepared to overlook its omission on this occasion. Tompsitt, pursing his lips, rather in Widmerpool's own manner, concurred that such solemn rites had indeed taken place.

'And the Nationalists have got to Pekin,' Widmerpool pursued.

'But who are the Nationalists?' asked Tompsitt, in a measured voice, gazing round the table with an air of quiet aggression. 'Can anyone tell me that?'

Neither Archie Gilbert nor I ventured any attempt to clarify the confused situation in China; and not even Widmerpool seemed disposed to hazard any immediate interpretation of conflicting political aims there. There was a pause, at the end of which he said: 'I dare say we shall have to consider tariff autonomy—with reservations, of course.'

Tompsitt nodded, biting his lip a trifle. Widmerpool's face assumed a dramatic expression that made him look rather like a large fish moving swiftly through opaque water to devour a smaller one. Sir Gavin had begun to grow restive as scraps of this stimulating dialogue were wafted across to him, and he now abandoned the subject of Salopian pheasants in favour of trenchant examination of Celestial affairs.

'To speak of treaty-revision before China has put her house in order,' he announced rather slowly, between puffs of his cigarette, 'is thought by some—having regard to the *status quo*—substantially to put the cart before the horse. The War-Lords——'

'A cousin of mine in the Coldstream went out last year,' Pardoe interrupted. 'He said it wasn't too bad.'

'Was that at Kowloon?' asked Widmerpool, speaking somewhat deferentially. 'I hear, by the way, they are sending the Welsh Guards to Egypt instead of a Line regiment.'

'You spoke of treaty revision, Sir Gavin,' said Tompsitt, ignoring Widmerpool's adumbrations on the incidence of the trooping season. 'Now it seems to me that we should strike when the iron is hot. The iron has never been hotter than at this moment. There are certain facts we have got to face. For example——'

'Some of them were under canvas on the race-course,' said Pardoe. 'Not that there were any starters, I should imagine.' And, presumably with a view to disposing finally of the Chinese question and turning to subjects of more local interest, he added: 'You know, legalising the tote is going to make a big difference to racing.'

Sir Gavin looked dissatisfied with the turn taken by—or rather forced on—the conversation; possibly, in fact certainly, possessing further views on the international situation in the East which he was not unwilling to express. However, he must have decided that time did not allow any return to these matters, for he made, as it were, a mystic circle before himself in the air with the decanter, as if to show that the fate of China—and of racing, too for that matter—was in the lap of the gods.

'Nobody having any port,' he stated, rather than asked. 'Then I suppose we shall be getting into trouble if we don't make a move. Anyone for along the passage?'

'Yes,' said Tompsitt, setting off impatiently.

While we waited for him, Sir Gavin expatiated to Pardoe whom he seemed, for some reason, particularly to enjoy lecturing, on the advantages to be gained for the country by mustering young men of Tompsitt's kind.

'Had the smooth type too long,' he remarked, shaking his head a number of times.

'Need something crisper these days, do we?' enquired Pardoe, who, standing on tiptoe, was straightening his white tie reflected in the glass of the barometer hanging under *Boyhood of Cyrus*.

'All very well a century ago to have a fellow who could do the polite to the local potentate,' explained Sir Gavin. 'Something a bit more realistic required these days.'

'A chap who knows the man-in-the-street?'

Sir Gavin screwed his face into an expression calculated to convey that such was the answer.

'Where does he come from?' asked Pardoe, who did not seem absolutely convinced by these arguments, and still fiddled with his tie.

Sir Gavin seemed rather pleased by this question, which gave him further opportunity for stating uncompromisingly his confidence in Tompsitt's almost congenital *bona fides*.

'Goodness knows where he comes from,' he affirmed vigorously. 'Why should you or I be concerned with that—or any of us, for that matter? What we need is a man who can do the job.'

'I quite agree with you, sir,' said Widmerpool, breaking

unexpectedly into this investigation. 'Professionalism in diplomacy is bad enough, in all conscience, without restricting the range of the country's diplomatic representation to a clique of prize pupils from a small group of older public schools.'

Sir Gavin looked rather taken aback, as I was myself, at such a sudden assertion of considered opinion regarding the matter in hand—and also at being called 'sir'—even though Widmerpool's views seemed so closely identified with his own. However, Widmerpool did not attempt to amplify his proposition, and circumstances, represented by the return of Tompsitt, prevented a more exhaustive examination of the problem.

In his distrust of 'smoothness' and hankering for 'realism', Sir Gavin once more reminded me of Uncle Giles, but such reflections were interrupted by the necessity of making a decision regarding means of transport to the Huntercombes' house. The Walpole-Wilsons' cars were both, for some reason, out of commission—Eleanor had driven one of them against the mounting-block in the stable yard at Hinton Hoo—and Pardoe's sports-model two-seater was not specially convenient for a girl in a ball dress; although I could imagine Barbara wishing to travel in it if she had a chance. As it happened, Pardoe's general offer of 'a lift' was immediately accepted by Tompsitt, which settled the matter so far as the rest of the party were concerned: this residue being divided between two taxis. I found myself in Lady Walpole-Wilson's vehicle, with Barbara, Miss Manasch, and Archie Gilbert; Eleanor, Anne Stepney, Margaret Budd, and Widmerpool accompanying Sir Gavin. We all packed ourselves in, Archie Gilbert and I occupying the tip-up seats. The butler slammed the taxi door as if glad to be rid of us.

'I hope the others will be all right,' said Lady Walpole-Wilson, as our conveyance moved off uncertainly, though I could not guess what her fears might be for potential ill that could befall the group under the command of her husband.

'Aren't we going to be too early, Aunt Daisy?' Barbara said. 'It is so awful when you are the first to arrive. We did it at the Cecils.'

I thought I could feel her foot against mine, but, a moment later, found the shoe in question to belong to Miss Manasch, who immediately removed her own foot; whether because aware of a pressure that had certainly been quite involuntary, if, indeed, it had taken place at all, or merely by chance, I was unable to tell.

'I do hope Eleanor will not insist on going home as soon as we arrive,' said Lady Walpole-Wilson, more to herself than to the rest of the company in the taxi.

As we covered the short distance to Belgrave Square, she dropped her bag on the floor, recovering it before anyone else could help, opened the clasp, and began to rummage in its depths. There she found whatever she had been seeking. Archie Gilbert was sitting next to the door by which we should descend, and now she made as if to offer him some object concealed in her hand, the thing, no doubt a coin, for which she had been searching in the bag. However, he strenuously denied acceptance of this.

'Please,' said Lady Walpole-Wilson. 'You must.'

'On the contrary.'

'I insist.'

'No, no, absurd.'

'Mr. Gilbert!'

'Really.'

'I shall be very cross.'

'Not possibly.'

During the several seconds that elapsed before we finally drew up, delayed for a time by private cars and other taxis waiting in a queue in front of our own, the contest continued between them; so that by the moment when the taxi had at last stopped dead in front of the Huntercombes' house, and Archie Gilbert, flinging open the door, had reached the pavement, I was still doubtful whether or not he had capitulated. Certainly he had ejected himself with great rapidity, and unhesitatingly paid the taxi-driver, brushing aside a proffered contribution.

There seemed no reason to suppose, as Barbara had suggested, that we might have come too early. On the contrary, we went up the carpeted steps into a hall full of people, where Sir Gavin, whose taxi had arrived before our own, was already waiting impatiently for the rest of his party. His reason for personal attendance at a dance which he would not have normally frequented was presumably because the Huntercombes lived near the Walpole-Wilsons in the country. In fact there could be no doubt that a good many country neighbours had been asked, for, even on the way up the stairs, densely packed with girls and young men, some of them already rather hot and flushed, there was that faint though perceptible flavour of the hunt ball to be observed about some of the guests. While putting away our hats, curiosity had overcome me, and I asked Archie Gilbert whether he had, in fact, refused or accepted Lady Walpole-Wilson's money. At the coarseness of the question his smile had been once again somewhat reproving.

'Oh, I took it,' he said. 'Why not? It wasn't enough. It never is.'

These words made me wonder if, after all, some faint trace of dissatisfaction was concealed deep down under that armour of black-and-white steel that encased him; and, for a moment, the terrible suspicion even suggested itself that, night after night, he danced his life away through the ballrooms of London in the unshakable conviction that the whole thing was a sham. Was he merely stoical like the Spartan boy—clad this time in a white tie—with the fox of bitterness gnawing, through stiff shirt, at his vitals. It was a thought in its horror to be dismissed without further examination. Such cynicism could hardly be possible. His remark, however, had for some reason recalled the occasion when I had been leaving the Templers' house and Mr. Farebrother had added his shilling to the chauffeur's tip.

'Have you ever come across someone called Sunny Farebrother?' I asked.

'Of course I've met him. Quite interested in the metal market, isn't he? He is rather well known in the City for his charm.'

I saw that I had been right in supposing that the pair of them had something in common. Archie Gilbert had, indeed, sounded surprised that I should ever have been in doubt about his knowing Farebrother. Meanwhile, we had proceeded almost to the top of the stairs and were about to reach the first-floor landing, where a big man-servant with a huge bottle nose was bawling out the names of the guests in a contemptuous, raucous voice that well suggested his own keen enjoyment of the duty.

'. . . Sir Gavin and Lady Walpole-Wilson . . . Miss Walpole-Wilson . . . Captain Hackforth . . . Mr. Cavendish . . . Lady Anne Stepney . . . Miss Budd . . . Miss Manners . . . Mr. Pardon . . . Mr. Tompsey . . . Lady Augusta Cutts . . . Miss Cutts . . . Lord Erridge . . . Miss Mercy Cutts . . . Lord and Lady Edward Wentworth . . . Mr. Winterpool . . .'

It was a fearful struggle to get through the door into the ballroom. Even the bottle-nosed man, familiar with such tumult as he must have been, had to pause and smile broadly to himself once or twice; but whether amused at the confusion of the crowd, or at the hash he was himself making of their individual names, it was impossible to guess. The whining of the band seemed only to encourage the appalling tussle taking place on stairs and landing.

'I took one look at you—
That's all I meant to do—
And then my heart—stood still . . .'

Hanging at the far end of the ballroom was a Van Dyck—the only picture of any interest the Huntercombes kept in London—representing Prince Rupert conversing with a herald, the latter being, I believe, the personage from whom the surviving branch of the family was directly descended. The translucent crystals of the chandeliers oscillated faintly as the dancers below thumped by. A knot of girls were standing not far from the door, among them Eleanor, who, in a purposeful manner, was pulling on a pair of long white gloves. These gloves, always affected by her, were evidently a kind of symbol assumed in connexion with her own attitude towards dances; at once intended to keep her partners physically farther from her, at the same time creaking ominously, as if voicing the audible disapproval of their wearer, whenever she moved her arms. We took the floor together. Eleanor danced well, though implacably. I asked how long she had known Widmerpool, mentioning that we had been at school together.

'Uncle George used to get his liquid manure from Mr. Widmerpool's father when he was alive,' said Eleanor curtly. 'We tried some at home, but it was a failure. Different soil, I suppose.'

Widmerpool's old acquaintance with Barbara's family, and his own presence that night at the Walpole-Wilsons', were now both satisfactorily explained. There could be no doubt that the fertiliser mentioned by Eleanor was the basic cause of the secrecy with which he had always been inclined to veil his father's business activities; for, although there was, of course, nothing in the faintest degree derogatory about agricultural science—Lord Goring himself was, after all, evidence of that fact—I had been associated with Widmerpool long enough to know that he could not bear to be connected personally with anyone, or anything, that might be made, however remotely, the subject of ridicule which could recoil even in a small degree upon himself. He was, for example, as I discovered much later, almost physically incapable of making himself agreeable to a woman whom he regarded as neither good-looking nor, for some other reason, worth cultivating: a trait vested, perhaps, in a kind of natural timidity, and a nature that required a sense of support from the desirable qualities of company in which he found himself. This characteristic of his, I can now see, was an effort to obtain a kind of vicarious acquisition of power from others. Accordingly, any sense of failure or inadequacy in his surroundings made him uncomfortable. The mere phrase 'artificial manure' told the whole story.

However, when it became clear that Eleanor did not much like him, I found myself, I hardly knew why, assuring her that Widmerpool, at school and in France, had always been quite an amiable eccentric; though I could not explain, then or now, why I felt his defence a duty; still less why I should have arbitrarily attributed to him what was, after all, an almost wholly imaginary personality, in fact one in many respects far from accurate. At that time I still had very little idea of Widmerpool's true character: neither its qualities nor defects.

'They had a small house on the Pembringham estate while experimenting with the manure,' said Eleanor. 'Aunt Constance is frightfully kind, when she isn't feeling too ill, you know, and used to ask them over quite often. That was where I first met him. Now his mother has taken a cottage near *us* at Hinton. Barbara doesn't mind Mr. Widmerpool. Of course, she has often met him. I don't really care for him very much. We were absolutely at our wits' end for a man tonight, so he had to come. Have you ever seen his mother?'

I did not hear Eleanor's views on Mrs. Widmerpool, because at that moment the music ceased; and, after clapping had died down and couples round us dispersed, the subject of Widmerpool and his family was quickly forgotten.

The ball took its course: dance-tune following dance-tune: partner following partner. From time to time, throughout the course of the evening, I saw Widmerpool ploughing his way round the room, as if rowing a dinghy in rough water, while he talked energetically to girls more often than not unknown to me; though chosen, no doubt, with the care devoted by him to any principle in which he was interested. He did not, as it happened, appear to be dancing much with any member of the Walpole-Wilson dinner-party, perhaps regarding them, when considered as individuals, as unlikely to lead to much that he could personally turn to profit. Later on in the evening, while sitting out with Miss Manasch, I was suddenly made aware of him again when he stumbled over her foot on his way upstairs.

'I know who he is!' she said, when he had apologised and disappeared from sight with his partner. 'He is the Frog Footman. He ought to be in livery. Has he danced with Anne yet?'

'Anne Stepney?'

'They would be so funny together.'

'Is she a friend of yours?'

'We were at the same finishing school in Paris.'

'They didn't do much finishing on her, surely?'

'She is so determined to take a different line from that very glamorous sister of hers.'

'Is Peggy Stepney glamorous?'

'You must have seen pictures of her.'

'A friend of mine called Charles Stringham used to talk about her.'

'Oh, yes—Charles Stringham,' said Miss Manasch. '*That* has been over a long time. I think he is rather a fast young man, isn't he? I seem to have heard.'

She laughed, and rolled her beady little eyes, straightening her frock over plump, well-shaped little legs. She looked quite out of place in this setting; intended by nature to dance veiled, or, perhaps, unveiled, before the throne of some Oriental potentate—possibly one of those exacting rulers to whom Sir Gavin's well-mannered diplomatists of the past might have appealed—or occupying herself behind the scenes in all the appetising labyrinth of harem intrigue. There existed the faintest suspicion of blue hairs upon her upper lip, giving her the look of a beauty of the Byronic era.

'Anne Stepney said he was pompous. As a matter of fact, I haven't seen him for ages.'

'Anne thinks Charles Stringham pompous, does she?' said Miss Manasch, laughing again quietly to herself.

'What do you think?'

'I don't know him. At least only by reputation. I have met his mother, who is, of course, too wonderful. They say she is getting rather tired of Commander Foxe and thinking of having another divorce. Charles was more or less engaged to Anne's sister, Peggy, at one stage, as I suppose you know. That's off now, as I said. I hear about Peggy occasionally from a cousin of mine, Jimmy Klein, who has a great passion for her.'

'Is Charles about to marry anyone at the moment?'

'I don't think so.'

I had the impression that she knew more about Stringham than she was prepared to divulge, because her face assumed an expression that made her features appear more Oriental than ever. It was evident that she possessed affiliations with circles additional to—perhaps widely different from—those to be associated with Walpole-Wilsons, Gorings, or Huntercombes. Only superficially invested with the characteristics of girls moving within that world, she was at once coarser in texture and at the same time more subtle. Up to that moment she had been full of animation, but now all at once she became melancholy and silent.

'I think I shall leave.'

'Have you had enough?'

'Going home seems the only alternative to sitting among the coats,' she said.

'Whatever for?'

'I comb my hair there.'

'But does it need combing?'

'And while I tug at it, I cry.'

'Surely not necessary tonight?'

'Perhaps not,' she said.

She began to laugh softly to herself once more; and, a minute or two later, went off with some partner who appeared satisfied that the moment had come to claim her. I set about looking for Barbara, with whom at the beginning of the evening I had danced only once. She was in one of the rooms downstairs, talking excitedly to a couple of young men, but she seemed not unwilling to leave their company.

'Let's sit this one out,' she said.

We made our way outside and to the garden of the square. Guests like Archie Gilbert, who had been asked to both dances, and no doubt also a few who had not enjoyed that privilege—were passing backwards and forwards from one party to another. The reception at the Spanish Embassy, mentioned by Tompsitt, was still in full swing, so far as could be seen. Now and then a breath of air lightened the heavy night, once even causing the shrubs to sway in what was almost a breeze. The windows of both ballrooms stood open, music from the rival bands playing sometimes in conflict, sometimes appearing to belong to a system of massed orchestras designed to perform in unison.

'We'll have a—Blue Room a——
New room for—two room——
Where we will raise a family . . .
Not like a—ballroom a——
Small room a—hall room . . .'

An equally insistent murmur came from the other side of the square:

'In the mountain greenery——
Where God makes the scenery . . .
Ta-rum . . . Ta-roo . . .'

'Why are you so glum?' said Barbara, picking up some pebbles and throwing them into the bushes. 'I must tell you what happened at Ranelagh last week.'

In the face of recent good resolutions, I tried to take her hand. She snatched it away, laughing, and as usual in such circumstances said: 'Oh, don't get sentimental.'

This tremendous escape, quite undeserved, sobered me. We walked round the lawns. Barbara talked of Scotland, where she was going to stay later in the summer.

'Why not come up there?' she said. 'Surely you can find someone to put you up?'

'Got to work.'

'Of course they don't need you all the time at the office.'

'They do.'

'Have you ever danced reels? Johnny Pardoe is going to be there. He says he'll teach me.'

She began to execute capers on the lawn. Stopping at last she examined her arm, holding it out, and saying: 'How blue my hand looks in the moonlight.'

I found myself wondering whether, so far from loving her, I did not actually hate her. Another tune began and we strolled back through the garden. At the gate Tompsitt came up from somewhere among the shadows.

'This is ours, I think.'

In his manner of speaking, so it seemed to me, he contrived to be at once uncivil and pedantic. Barbara began to jump about on the path as if leaping over imaginary puddles, while almost at the top of her small, though shrill, voice she said: 'I can't, really I can't. I must have made a muddle. I am dancing with Mr. Widmerpool. I have put him off till now, and I really must.'

'Cut him,' said Tompsitt.

He sounded as if taking Barbara away from her rightful partner would give him even more pleasure than that to be derived from dancing with her himself. I wondered if she had called Widmerpool 'Mister' because her acquaintance with him had never been brought to a closer degree of intimacy, or if she spoke facetiously. From what Eleanor had said, the latter seemed more probable. It suddenly struck me that after all these years of knowing him I still had no idea of Widmerpool's Christian name.

'Shall I?' said Barbara. 'He would be terribly angry.'

Suddenly she took each of us by the hand, and began to charge along the pavement. In this unusual manner we reached the door of the Huntercombes' house. By the time we had ceased running even Tompsitt seemed, in the last resort, rather taken aback; the combined movement of the three of us—rather like that of horses in a troika—being probably as unexpected for him as for myself. Barbara, for her part, was delighted with her own violent display of high spirits. She broke free and rushed up the steps in front of us.

In the hall, although the hour was not yet late, a few people were already making preparations to leave. As it happened, Widmerpool was standing by the staircase, looking, I thought, a little uneasy, and fingering a tattered pair of white gloves. I had seen him with just that expression on his face, waiting for the start of one of the races for which he used so unaccountably to enter: finishing, almost without exception, last or last but one. When he saw Barbara, he brightened a little, and moved towards us.

'The Merry Widow Waltz,' he said. 'I always like that, don't you? I wish I had known Vienna in the old days before the war.'

Barbara once more seized Tompsitt and myself by whichever arm was nearest to her. She said to Widmerpool: 'My dear, I have made a muddle again. I have told all sorts of people that I will dance this one with them, but—as I can't possibly dance with all three of you—let's all go and have some supper instead.'

'But I've already had supper——' began Widmerpool.

'So have I,' said Barbara. 'Of course we have all had supper. We will have some more.'

'*I* haven't had supper,' said Tompsitt.

Widmerpool did not look at all pleased at Barbara's proposal; nor, for that matter, did Tompsitt, who must have realised now that instead of carrying Barbara gloriously away from a dashing rival—he had probably failed to catch Widmerpool's name at the dinner-party—he was himself to be involved in some little game played by Barbara for her own amusement. Perhaps for that reason he had felt it more dignified to deny a previous supper; for I was fairly sure that I had seen him leaving the supper-room earlier that night. I could not help feeling pleased that Barbara had insisted on my joining them, although I was at the same time aware that even this pleasure was a sign that I was by now myself less seriously concerned with her; for a few weeks before I should have endured all kind of vexation at this situation. Widmerpool, on the other hand, was by no means prepared to give in at once, though his struggles to keep Barbara to himself were feeble enough, and quite ineffectual.

'But look here,' he said. 'You promised——'

'Not another word.'

'But——'

'Come along—all of you.'

Almost dragging Widmerpool with her, she turned, and set off towards the door of the supper-room; bumped heavily into two dowagers on their way out, and said: 'Oh, sorry', but did not pause. As I passed these ladies, I caught the words 'Constance Goring's girl,' spoken by the dowager who had suffered least from the impact. She was evidently attempting to explain, if not excuse, this impetuosity on some hereditary ground connected with Barbara's grandfather. Her more elderly and bedraggled companion, who seemed to have been badly shaken, did not appear to find much solace in this historical, or quasi-scientific, approach to Barbara's indifferent manners. They went off together up the stairs, the elder one still muttering angrily, while Tompsitt and I followed Barbara and Widmerpool to one of many tables decorated with blue hydrangeas in gilt baskets.

The room was still fairly full of people, but we found a

place in the corner underneath a picture of Murillo's school in which peasant boys played with a calf. A large supper-party, making a good deal of noise, were seated at the next table, among them Pardoe, who was telling a complicated story about something that had happened to him—or possibly a brother officer—when 'on guard' at the Bank of England.

'The first thing is to get some lemonade,' said Barbara, who never touched any strong drink, in spite of behaviour that often suggested the contrary.

Clearly Widmerpool had been outraged by the loss of his dance. This annoyance, on the face of it, seemed scarcely reasonable, because by that stage of the evening several 'extras' had been played, causing the numbers of dances to become confused, so that there had been plenty of excuse for an unimpeachable mistake to have been made; and obviously Barbara was the kind of girl, at best, to be expected to be in a chronic state of tangle about her partners. However, such considerations seemed to carry no weight whatever with Widmerpool, who sat in silence, refusing food and drink, while he gloomily crumbled a roll of bread. Barbara, who possessed a healthy appetite at all times of day or night, ordered lobster salad. Tompsitt drank—in which I joined him—a glass of what he called 'The Widow'. The wine had the effect of making him discourse on racing, a subject regarding which I was myself unfortunately too ignorant to dispose as summarily as I should have wished of the almost certainly erroneous opinions he put forward. Barbara embarked upon an account of her own experiences at Ascot, of no great interest in themselves, though at the same time hardly justifying the splenetic stare which Widmerpool fixed on her, while she unfolded a narrative based on the matter of starting prices for runners in the Gold Cup, associated at the same time with the question whether or not she had been finally swindled by her bookmaker.

She was, as usual, talking at the top of her voice, so that people at surrounding tables could hear most of what she said. Owing to this very general audibility of her remarks, she became in some way drawn into an argument with Pardoe, who had apparently been a member of the same Ascot party as herself. Although Barbara's voice was not without a penetrating quality, and Pardoe, who spoke, as it were, in a series of powerful squeaks, could no doubt make the welkin ring across the parade-grounds of Wellington Barracks or Caterham, they did not, for some reason, contrive to reach any mutual understanding in their attempts to make their respective points of view plain to each other; so that at last Barbara jumped up from her seat, saying: 'I'm going across to tell him just what did happen.'

There was a vacant chair next to the place where Pardoe sat. If Barbara ever reached that place, there could be little doubt that she would spend the rest of her time in the supper-room—perhaps the remainder of her time at the dance—discussing with Pardoe bets, past, present, and future; because he had abandoned any effort to talk to the girl next to him, who was, in fact, amusing herself happily enough with two or three other young men in the neighbourhood. The consequence of these various circumstances was for a decidedly odd incident to take place, with Widmerpool for its central figure: an incident that brought back to me once more expressive memories of Widmerpool as he had been at school. This crisis, as it might reasonably be called, came about because Widmerpool himself must have grasped immediately that, if Barbara abandoned our table at that moment, she would be lost to him for the rest of the time both of them were under the Huntercombes' roof. That, at least, seemed the only possible explanation of the action he now took, when—just as Barbara stood up, in preparation to leave us—he snatched her wrist.

'Look here, Barbara,' he said—and he sounded in actual pain. 'You can't leave me like this.'

Certain actions take place outside the normal course of things so unexpectedly that they seem to paralyse ordinary capacity for feeling surprise; and I watched Widmerpool seize hold of Barbara in this way—by force—without at the precisely operative moment experiencing that amazement with which his conduct on this occasion afterwards, on reconsideration, finally struck me. To begin with, his act was a vigorous and instantaneous assertion of the will, quite out of keeping with the picture then existing in my mind of his character; for although, as I have said before, I no longer thought of him exactly as that uneasy, irrelevant figure he had seemed when we were both schoolboys, his behaviour in France, even when latent power of one kind or another had been unquestionably perceptible in him, had equally suggested a far more plodding manner of getting what he wanted.

In any case, he had been always inclined to shrink from physical contact. I remembered well how, one day at La Grenadière, Madame Leroy's niece, Berthe, standing in the garden and pointing to the river, which shone distantly in a golden glow of evening light, had remarked: 'Quel paysage féerique', and touched his arm. Widmerpool, at that instant, had started violently, almost as if Berthe's plump fingers were red-hot, or her pointed nails had sharply entered his flesh. That had been several years before, and there was no reason why he should not have changed in this, as in certain outward respects. All the same, it was wholly unexpected—and perhaps a little irritating, even in the light of comparative emancipation from regarding Barbara as my own especial concern—to watch him snatch at her with those blunt, gnarled fingers. Tompsitt, at that critical moment attempting to get hold of more champagne, did not notice this gesture of Widmerpool's. The grabbing movement had, indeed, taken only a fraction of a second, Widmerpool having released Barbara's wrist almost as soon as his fingers had closed upon it.

If she had been in a calmer mood, Barbara would probably, in the light of subsequent information supplied on the subject, have paid more attention to the strength, and apparent seriousness, of Widmerpool's feelings at that moment. As it was, she merely said: 'Why are you so sour tonight? You need some sweetening.'

She turned to the sideboard that stood by our table, upon which plates, dishes, decanters, and bottles had been placed out of the way before removal. Among this residue stood an enormous sugar castor topped with a heavy silver nozzle. Barbara must suddenly have conceived the idea of sprinkling a few grains of this sugar over Widmerpool, as if in literal application of her theory that he 'needed sweetening', because she picked up this receptacle and shook it over him. For some reason, perhaps because it was so full, no sugar at first sprayed out. Barbara now tipped the castor so that it was poised vertically over Widmerpool's head, holding it there like the sword of Damocles above the tyrant. However, unlike the merely minatory quiescence of that normally inactive weapon, a state of dispensation was not in this case maintained, and suddenly, without the slightest warning, the massive silver apex of the castor dropped from its base, as if severed by the slash of some invisible machinery, and crashed heavily to the floor: the sugar pouring out on to Widmerpool's head in a dense and overwhelming cascade.

More from surprise than because she wished additionally to torment him, Barbara did not remove her hand before the whole contents of the vessel—which voided itself in an instant of time—had descended upon his head and shoulders, covering him with sugar more completely than might have been thought possible in so brief a space. Widmerpool's rather sparse hair had been liberally greased with a dressing—the sweetish smell of which I remembered as somewhat disagreeable when applied in France—this lubricant retaining the grains of sugar, which, as they adhered thickly to his skull, gave him the appearance of having turned white with shock at a single stroke; which, judging by what could be seen of his expression, he might very well in reality have done underneath the glittering incrustations that enveloped his head and shoulders. He had writhed sideways to avoid the downpour, and a cataract of sugar had entered the space between neck and collar; yet another jet streaming between eyes and spectacles.

Barbara was, without doubt, dismayed by the consequences of what she had done; not, I think, because she cared in the least about covering Widmerpool with sugar, an occurrence, however deplorable, that was hard to regard, with the best will in the world, as anything other than funny at that moment. This was the kind of incident, however, to get a girl a bad name; a reputation for horseplay having, naturally, a detrimental effect on invitations. So far as everyone else, among those sitting near us, were concerned, there was a great deal of laughter. Even if some of the people who laughed may also have felt sorry for Widmerpool in his predicament, there was no escape from the fact that he looked beyond words grotesque. The sugar sparkled on him like hoar-frost, and, when he moved, there was a faint rustle as of snow falling gently from leaves of a tree in some wintry forest.

It was a hard situation for anyone to carry off with dignity and good temper. Widmerpool did not exactly attempt to conform to either of these two ideal standards; though in a rather specialised sense—to the eye of an attentive observer—he displayed elements of both qualities. His reaction to circumstances was, in its way, peculiarly characteristic of his nature. He stood up, shook himself like an animal, sending out specks of sugar over many persons in the immediate vicinity, and, smiling slightly, almost apologetically, to himself, took off his spectacles and began to rub their lenses with his handkerchief.

For the second time that night I recalled Stringham's story of Budd and the banana. It must have been, I could now appreciate, just such a moment as this one. I remembered Stringham's exact phrase: 'Do you know, an absolutely *slavish* look came into Widmerpool's face.' There could have been no better description of his countenance as he shook off the sugar on to the carpet beneath him. Once again the same situation had arisen; parallel acceptance of public humiliation; almost the identically explicit satisfaction derived from grovelling before someone he admired; for this last element seemed to show itself unmistakably—though only for a flash—when he glanced reproachfully towards Barbara: and then looked away. This self-immolation, if indeed to be recorded as such, was displayed for so curtailed a second that any substance possessed by that almost immediately shifting mood was to be appreciated only by someone, like myself, cognisant already of the banana incident; so that when Widmerpool pushed his way between the chairs, disappearing a minute later through the doors of the supper-room, he seemed to the world at large, perhaps correctly, to be merely a man in a towering rage.

However, reaction took place so soon as he was gone. There fell all at once a general public dejection similar in every respect, as recorded by Stringham, to that evoked by

Widmerpool's former supposedly glad acceptance of the jolt from Budd's over-ripe fruit. This frightful despondency appeared to affect everyone near enough the scene of action to share a sense of being more or less closely concerned in the affair. For my own part, oddly enough, I was able to identify this sudden sensation of discomfort, comparable to being dowsed with icy water, as instantaneous realisation—simultaneously and most emphatically conveyed in so objective a form—that I had made an egregious mistake in falling in love with Barbara. Up to that moment the situation between us had seemed to be on the way to resolving itself, on my side at least, rather sadly, perhaps not irretrievably, with excusably romantic melancholy. Now I felt quite certain that Barbara, if capable of an act of this sort, was not—and had never been—for me. This may have been a priggish or cowardly decision. Certainly I had had plenty of opportunity to draw similar conclusions from less dramatic occasions. It was, however, final. The note struck by that conclusion was a disagreeable one; totally unlike the comparatively acceptable sentiments of which it took the place.

Barbara herself at first made no serious effort to repair, morally or physically, any of the damage she had caused. Indeed, it was not easy to see what she could do. Now she went so far as to pick up the top of the sugar-castor, and, before she sat down again, returned, in their separate states, the upper and lower halves of this object to the sideboard.

'It really wasn't my fault,' she said. 'How on earth was I to know that the top of the wretched thing would fall off like that? People ought to screw everything of that sort on tight before they give a party.'

She abandoned her project of going to sit with Pardoe, who was still very red in the face from laughter, changing her topic of conversation from racing to that of good works of some kind or other, with which she was, as I already knew, irregularly occupied in Bermondsey. There was no reason whatever to doubt the truth of her own account of the generous proportion of her time spent at the girls' club, or some similar institution, situated there; nor her popularity with those thereby brought within her orbit. All the same, this did not seem to be the ideal moment to hear about her philanthropic activities. Barbara herself may have felt this transition of mood to have been effected with too much suddenness, because quite soon she said: 'I'm going to rescue Aunt Daisy now. It isn't fair to keep her up all night. Besides, Eleanor must have been longing to go home for hours. No—no—don't dream of coming too. Good-night to both of you. See you soon.'

She ran off before either Tompsitt or I could even rise or say good-night. We sat for a minute or two together, finishing our wine: Tompsitt smiling rather acidly to himself, as if aware of the answer to a great many questions, some of them important questions at that.

'Do you know the chap Barbara poured sugar on?' he asked, at last.

'I was at school with him.'

'What was he like?'

'Rather the kind of man people pour sugar on.'

Tompsitt looked disapproving and rather contemptuous. I thought at the time that his glance had reference to Widmerpool. I can now see that it was directed, almost certainly, towards my own remark, which he must have regarded, in some respects justly, as an answer inadequate to his question. Looking back on this exchange, I have no doubt that Tompsitt had already recognised as existing in Widmerpool some potential to which I was myself still almost totally blind; and, although he may neither have liked nor admired Widmerpool, he was at the same time aware of a shared approach to life which supplied a kind of bond between them. My own feeling that it would have been unjustifiable to mention the story of the banana, because I felt myself out of sympathy with Tompsitt, and, although often irritated by his behaviour, was conscious of a kind of uncertain loyalty, even mild liking, for Widmerpool, probably represented a far less instinctive and more artificial or unreal understanding between two individuals.

It would, indeed, be hard to over-estimate the extent to which persons with similar tastes can often, in fact almost always, observe these responses in others: women: money: power: whatever it is they seek; while this awareness remains a mystery to those in whom such tendencies are less highly, or not at all, developed. Accordingly, Tompsitt's acceptance of Widmerpool, and indifference, even rudeness, to many other persons of apparently greater outward consideration—in so much as I reflected on it—seemed to me odd; but this merely because, at that time, I did not understand the foundations required to win Tompsitt's approval. In any case, I saw no advantage in enquiring further into the matter at that hour, having myself already decided to go home to bed as soon as possible. Tompsitt, too, had no doubt had enough of the *tête-à-tête*. He rose, as a matter of fact, before I did, and we walked out together, separating as soon as we had passed through the door, Tompsitt strolling upstairs again towards the ballroom, while I made for the cloak-room. Eleanor was crossing the hall.

'Off to get my bonnet and shawl,' she remarked, delighted that for her, at least, another dance was at an end.

I handed in the ticket, and was waiting while they looked for my hat, when Widmerpool himself appeared from the back regions of the house. He, and no doubt others too, had engaged in a thorough scouring of his person and clothes, most of the sugar having been by now removed, though a few grains still glistened round the button-hole of his silk lapel. He appeared also to have recovered his normal self-possession, such as it was. One of the servants handed him an opera hat, which he opened with a sharp crepitation, placing it on his head at a tilt as we went down the steps together. The night was a little cooler, though still mild enough.

'Which way do you go?' he asked.

'Piccadilly.'

'Are you taxi-ing?'

'I thought I might walk.'

'It sounds as if you lived in a rather expensive area,' said Widmerpool, assuming that judicial air which I remembered from France.

'Shepherd's Market. Quite cheap, but rather noisy.'

'A flat?'

'Rooms—just beside an all-night garage and opposite a block of flats inhabited almost exclusively by tarts.'

'How convenient,' said Widmerpool; rather insincerely, I suspected.

'One of them threw a lamp out of her window the other night.'

'I go towards Victoria,' said Widmerpool.

He had evidently heard enough of a subject that might reasonably be regarded as an unpleasant one, because the local prostitutes were rowdy and aggressive: quite unlike the sad sisterhood of innumerable novels, whose members, by speaking of the days of their innocence, bring peace to lonely men, themselves compromised only to unburden their hearts. My neighbours quarrelled and shouted all night long; and, when business was bad, were not above tapping on the ground-floor window in the small hours.

'My mother's flat is near the Roman Catholic Cathedral,' Widmerpool added. 'We usually let it for a month or two later on in the summer, if we can find a tenant, and take a cottage in the country. Last year we went quite near the Walpole-Wilsons at Hinton Hoo. We are going to do the same next month. I take my holiday then, and, if working, come up every day.'

We strolled towards Grosvenor Place. I hardly knew whether or not to condole with him on the sugar incident. Widmerpool marched along, breathing heavily, rather as if he were taking part in some contest.

'Are you going to the Whitneys' on Thursday?' he asked suddenly.

'No.'

'Neither am I.'

He spoke with resignation; perhaps with slight relief that he had met another who remained uninvited to the Whitneys' dance.

'What about Mrs. Soundness?'

'I can't think why, but I haven't been asked to Mrs. Soundness's,' said Widmerpool, almost petulantly. 'I was taken to dinner there not so long ago—at rather short notice, I agree. But I expect I shall see you at Bertha, Lady Drum's and Mrs. Arthur Clinton's.'

'Probably.'

'I am dining with Lady Augusta Cutts for the Drum Clinton dance,' said Widmerpool. 'One eats well at Lady Augusta's. But I feel annoyed—even a little hurt—about Mrs. Soundness. I don't think I could possibly have done or said anything at dinner to which exception might have been taken.'

'The card may have gone astray in the post.'

'As a matter of fact,' said Widmerpool, 'one gets very tired of these dances.'

Everyone used to say that dances bored them; especially those young men—with the honourable exception of Archie Gilbert—who never failed to respond to an invitation, and stayed, night after night, to the bitter end. Such complaints were made rather in the spirit of people who grumble at the inconvenience they suffer from others falling in love with them. There was, of course, nothing out of the way in Widmerpool, who had apparently been attending dances for several years, showing by that time signs of disillusionment, especially in the light of his experience at the Huntercombes'; although the way he was talking suggested that he was still keen enough to receive invitations. This projection of himself as a 'dancing man', to use his own phrase, was an intimation—many more were necessary before the lesson was learnt—of how inadequate, as a rule, is one's own grasp of another's assessment of his particular rôle in life. Widmerpool's presence at the Walpole-Wilsons' had at first struck me, rather inexcusably perhaps, as just another proof of the insurmountable difficulties experienced by hostesses in their untiring search for young men at almost any price. It had never occurred to me, when at La Grenadière he had spoken of London dances, that Widmerpool regarded himself as belonging to the backbone of the system.

'You must come and lunch with me in the City,' he said. 'Have you an office in that part of the world?'

Thinking it unlikely that he would ring up, I gave him the telephone number, explaining that my work did not take place in the City. He made some formal enquiries about the firm, and seemed rather disapproving of the nature of the business.

'Who exactly buys "art books"?'

His questions became more searching when I tried to give an account of that side of publishing, and of my own part in it. After further explanations, he said: 'It doesn't sound to me a very serious job.'

'Why not?'

'I can't see it leading to much.'

'What ought it to lead to?'

'You should look for something more promising. From what you say, you do not even seem to keep very regular hours.'

'That's its great advantage.'

Widmerpool shook his head, and was silent for a time. I supposed him to be pondering my affairs—trying to find a way in which my daily occupation could be directed into more ambitious avenues—and I felt grateful, indeed rather touched, at any such interest. However, it turned out that he had either dismissed my future momentarily from his mind when he spoke again, or the train of thought must somehow have led him back to his own problems, because his words were quite unexpected.

'To tell the truth,' he said, 'I was upset—very upset—by what happened tonight.'

'It was silly of Barbara.'

'It was more than silly,' said Widmerpool, speaking with unusual intensity, his voice rising in tone. 'It was a cruel thing to do. I shall stop seeing her.'

'I shouldn't take it all too seriously.'

'I shall certainly take it seriously. You are probably not aware of the situation.'

'What situation?'

'As I think I told you before dinner, Barbara and I used to live near each other in the country. She knows well what my feelings are for her, even though I may not have expressed them in so many words. Of course I see now that it was wrong to take hold of her as I did.'

This disclosure was more than a little embarrassing, both

for its unexpectedness and also in the light of my own sentiments, or at least former sentiments, on the subject of Barbara. At that stage of life all sorts of things were going on round about that only later took on any meaning or pattern. Thus some people enjoyed distinctly public love affairs, often quickly forgotten, while others fell in love without anyone, perhaps even including the object of their love, knowing or caring anything about these covert affections. Only years later, if at all, could the consequences of such bottled-up emotions sometimes be estimated: more often, of course, they remained entirely unknown. In Widmerpool's case, for example, I had no idea, and could, I suppose, have had no idea, that he had been in love with Barbara all the time that I myself had adored her. Moreover, in those days, as I have already indicated, I used to think that people who looked and behaved like Widmerpool had really no right to fall in love at all, far less have any success with girls—least of all a girl like Barbara—a point of view that in due course had, generally speaking, to be revised: sometimes in mortifying circumstances. This failure to recognise Widmerpool's passion had, of course, restricted any understanding of his conduct, when at the supper table he had appeared so irritable from the mere consequence of the loss of a dance. I could now guess that, while we sat there, he had been burning in the fires of hell.

'Of course I appreciate that the Gorings are a family of a certain distinction,' said Widmerpool. 'But without the Gwatkin money they would never be able to keep up Pembringham Woodhouse as they do.'

'What was the Gwatkin money?'

'Gwatkin was Lord Aberavon's family name. The peerage was one of the last created by Queen Victoria. As a matter of fact the Gwatkins were perfectly respectable landed stock, I believe. And, of course, the Gorings have not produced a statesman of the first rank since their eighteenth-century ancestor—and he is entirely forgotten. As you probably know, they have no connexion whatever with the baronets of the same name.'

He produced these expository facts as if the history of the Gorings and the Gwatkins offered in some manner a key to his problem.

'What about Barbara's father?'

'As a young man he was thought to show promise of a future in the House of Lords,' said Widmerpool. 'But promise in that Chamber has become of late years increasingly difficult to develop to any satisfactory end. He performed, I have been told, a lot of useful work in committee, but he never held office, and sank into political obscurity. As I heard Sir Horrocks Rusby, K.C., remark at dinner the other night: "It's no good being useful if you don't achieve recognition." Sir Horrocks added that this maxim was a natural corollary of the appearance of sin being as bad as sin itself. On the other hand the farming at Pembringham is some of the most up-to-date in the country, and that is well known.'

'Were you going to propose to Barbara?'

'You don't suppose I have the money to marry, do you?' he said violently. 'That is why I am telling you all this.'

He spoke as if everyone ought already to be familiar with his emotional predicament; indeed, as if it were not only unobservant, but also rather heartless on my part, to have failed to comprehend the implications of his earlier ill-humour. By some curious manipulation of our respective positions—a trick of his I remembered from our time together at the Leroys'—his manner contrived also to suggest that I was being at once callous and at the same time unnecessarily inquisitive about his private affairs.

Such aspects of this sudden revelation about himself and Barbara occurred to me only after I had thought things over the following day. At that moment I was not even particularly struck by the surprising fact that Widmerpool should suddenly decide to unburden himself on the subject of a love affair to someone whose relationship to him was neither that of an intimate friend, nor yet sufficiently remote to justify the man-to-man methods of imparting confidences employed by the total stranger who unfolds his life story in a railway carriage or bar. However, I was impressed at that point chiefly by the fact that Widmerpool had described so closely my own recently passed dilemma: a problem formerly seeming to admit of no solution, from which I had now, however, been freed as abruptly and absolutely as its heavy obligation had so mysteriously arisen in the months before.

By this time we had come to Grosvenor Place, in sight of the triumphal arch, across the summit of which, like a vast paper-weight or capital ornament of an Empire clock, the Quadriga's horses, against a sky of indigo and silver, pranced desperately towards the abyss. Here our ways divided. It was on the tip of my tongue to say something of my own position regarding Barbara; for it is always difficult to hear anyone lay claim to having endured the agonies of love without putting forward pretensions to similar experience: especially when the same woman is in question. Whether or not some such reciprocal confidence, advisable or the contrary, would finally have passed between us is hard to say. Probably any material I could have contributed to the subject would have proved all but meaningless, or at best merely irritating, to Widmerpool in his current mood. That is my opinion in face of subsequent dealings with him. However, at that stage in the walk one of those curious changes took place in circumstances of mutual intercourse that might almost be compared, scientifically speaking, with the addition in the laboratory of one chemical to another, by which the whole nature of the experiment is altered: perhaps even an explosion brought about.

For a minute or two we had been standing by the edge of the pavement. Widmerpool was no doubt preparing to say good-night, because he took a sudden step backward. Like so many of his movements, this one was effected awkwardly, so that he managed to precipitate himself into the path of two persons proceeding, side by side, in the direction of Hyde Park Corner. There was, in fact, a minor collision of some force, in which the other parties were at once established as a comparatively elderly man, unusually tall, and a small woman, or girl. Upon the last of these Widmerpool had apparently trodden heavily, because she exclaimed in a raucous voice: 'Hi, you, why the bloody hell can't you go where you're looking!'

So aggressive was the manner in which this question was put that at first I thought the pair of them were probably drunk: a state which, in addition, the discrepancy between their respective heights for some reason quite illogically helped to suggest. Widmerpool began to apologise, and the man now answered at once in a deep tone: 'No, no. Of course it was an accident. Gypsy, I have told you before that you must control yourself when you are out with me. I will not tolerate gratuitous rudeness.'

There was something strangely familiar about these words. He was grey-haired and hatless, carrying a fairly bulky parcel of newspapers, or so they appeared, under his left arm. His voice bore with it memories of time long past. Its tone was, indeed, laden with forgotten associations of childhood; those curious, rather fearful responses weighted with a sense of restriction and misgiving. Even so, there was also something about the stranger that seemed to belong to the immediate present; something that made me feel that a matter which had to do with him, even on that very evening, had already been brought to my notice. Yet his presence conveyed, too, an instant and vertiginous sense of being 'abroad', this last impression suddenly taking shape as that of a far-off visit to Paris. The same scattered records of sight and sound that *Boyhood of Cyrus* had suggested when first seen at the Walpole-Wilsons'. I had another look at the whitening hairs, and saw that they were Mr. Deacon's, last surveyed, years before, on that day in the Louvre among the Peruginos.

He looked much the same, except that there was now something wilder—even a trifle sinister—in his aspect; a representation of Lear on the heath, or Peter the Hermit, in some nineteenth-century historical picture, preaching a crusade. Sandals worn over black socks gave an authentically medieval air to his extremities. The former rôle was additionally suggested by the undeniably boyish exterior of his companion, whose hair was cut short: barbered, in fact, in a most rough-and-ready fashion in the style then known as an 'Eton crop'. This young woman might, so far as outward appearances were concerned, have passed easily on the stage for the aged king's retainer, for, although her manner was more actively combative than the Fool's, the shortness of her skirt, and bare knees, made her seem to be clad in a smock, or tunic, of the kind in which the part is sometimes played.

When I think of that encounter in Grosvenor Place, my attempt to reintroduce myself to Mr. Deacon in such circumstances seems to me strange, foolhardy even, and the fact still more extraordinary that he should almost immediately have succeeded in grasping my own identity. It was an occasion that undoubtedly did more credit to

Mr. Deacon's social adroitness than to my own, because I was still young enough to be only dimly aware that there are moments when mutual acquaintance may be allowed more wisely to pass unrecognised. For example, to find a white-haired gentleman wandering about the streets in the small hours in the company of a young woman wearing an ample smear of lipstick across her face, and with stockings rolled to the knee, might easily prove a juncture when former meetings in irreproachable surroundings could, without offence, have been tactfully disregarded; although, as it turned out, there was not the smallest breath of scandal at that moment encompassing either of them.

'I had dinner at a house where one of your pictures hangs,' I told him, when enquiries about my family had been made and answered.

'Good gracious,' said Mr. Deacon. 'Which one?'

'Boyhood of Cyrus.'

'Was that Aberavon's? I thought he was dead these twenty years.'

'One of his daughters became Lady Walpole-Wilson. The picture is at her house in Eaton Square.'

'Well, I'm glad to know its whereabouts,' said Mr. Deacon. 'I always make bold to consider it rather a successful achievement of mine, within the limits of the size of the canvas. It is unusual for people of that sort to have much taste in art. Aberavon was the exception. He was a man with vision. I expect his descendants have hung it in some quite incongruous place.'

I thought it wiser to supply no further details on the subject of the hanging of *Boyhood of Cyrus*. 'Skyed' in the hall was a position even the most modest of painters could hardly regard as complimentary; though I was impressed by Mr. Deacon's perspicacity in guessing this fate.

It is, indeed, strange how often persons, living in other respects quite unobjectively, can suddenly become acutely objective about some specific concern of their own. However, no answer was required, because at that moment Widmerpool suddenly stepped in.

At first, after making some sort of an apology for his earlier clumsiness, he had stood staring at Mr. Deacon and the girl as if exhibits at a freak show—which it would hardly be going too far to say they somewhat resembled—but now he seemed disposed to dispute certain matters raised by Mr. Deacon's remarks. I had felt, immediately after making this plunge of recognition, that Widmerpool, especially in his existing mood, would scarcely be inclined to relish this company. In fact, I could not understand why he did not at once make for home, leaving us in peace to wind up the reunion, a duty that my own eagerness, perhaps misplaced, had imposed mutually upon Mr. Deacon and myself. Now to my surprise Widmerpool suddenly said: 'I think, if you meet her, you will find Lady Walpole-Wilson most appreciative of art. She was talking to me about the Academy only this evening—in connexion with the question of the Haig statue—and her comments were illuminating.'

Mr. Deacon was delighted by this frank expression of opinion. There was, naturally, no reason why he should possess any knowledge of Widmerpool, whom I discovered in due course to be—in Mr. Deacon's pre-determined view and own words—'a typical empty-headed young fellow with more money than is good for him' who was now preparing to tell an older man, and an artist, 'what was what in the field of painting'. This was, indeed, the kind of situation in which Mr. Deacon had all his life taken pleasure, and such eminence as he had, in fact, achieved he owed largely to making a habit of speaking in an overbearing and sarcastic, sometimes almost insulting, manner to the race thus generically described as having 'more money than was good for them'. He looked upon himself as the appointed scourge of all such persons, amongst whom he had immediately classed Widmerpool. The mistake was perhaps inevitable in the circumstances. In fairness to Mr. Deacon it should be added that these onslaughts were almost without exception accepted by the victims themselves—a fact born out by Barnby—as in some eclectic manner complimentary, so that no harm was done; even good, if the sale of Mr. Deacon's pictures could be so regarded.

'Should I ever have the honour of meeting her Ladyship,' said Mr. Deacon, with the suggestion of a flourish, 'I shall much look forward to a discussion on the subject of that *interesting* institution, the Royal Academy. When in need of mirth, I should be lost without it. I expect Isbister, R.A., is one of her special favourites.'

'I have not heard her mention his name,' said Widmerpool, forgoing none of his seriousness. 'But, for my own part, I was not displeased with Isbister's portrait of Cardinal Whelan at Burlington House last year. I preferred it to—was it the wife of the Solicitor-General—that was so much praised?'

It showed a rather remarkable effort of will on the part of Widmerpool, whose interest in such matters was not profound, to have been able to quote these examples on the spur of the moment; and there is no knowing into what inextricable tangle this subject would not have led them both, if their conversation had not been mercifully interrupted by the girl, who now said: 'Are we going to stand here all night? My feet hurt.'

'But how shameful,' said Mr. Deacon, with all his earlier formality. 'I have not introduced you yet. This is Miss

Gypsy Jones. Perhaps you have already met, She goes about a great deal.'

I mentioned Widmerpool's name in return, and Miss Jones nodded to us, without showing much sign of friendliness, Her face was pale, and she possessed an almost absurdly impudent expression, in part natural outcome of her cast of features, but also, as almost immediately became apparent, in an even greater degree product of her temperament. She looked like a thoroughly ill-conditioned errand-boy. Her forehead had acquired a smudge of coal-dust or lamp-black, darker and denser than, though otherwise comparable to, the smudge on Tompsitt's shirt-front. It seemed to have been put there deliberately to offset her crimson mouth. Like Mr. Deacon, she too clutched a pile of papers under her arm, somehow suggesting in doing so the appearance of one of those insects who carry burdens as large, or even larger, than their own puny frame.

'You must wonder why we are on our way home at this late hour,' said Mr. Deacon. 'We have been attempting in our poor way to aid the cause of disarmament at Victoria Station.'

Mr. Deacon's purpose had not, in fact, occurred to me—it is later in life that one begins to wonder about other people's activities—nor was it immediately made clear by Gypsy Jones extracting a kind of broadsheet from the sheaf under her arm, and holding it towards Widmerpool.

'Penny, *War Never Pays!*' she said.

Widmerpool, almost counterfeiting the secretive gesture of Lady Walpole-Wilson pressing money on Archie Gilbert in the taxi, fumbled in his trouser pocket, and in due course passed across a coin to her. In return she gave him the sheet, which, folding it without examination, he transferred to an inner pocket on his hip or in his tails. Scarcely knowing how to comment on the dealings in which Mr.

Deacon and his companion were engaged, I enquired whether night-time was the best season to dispose of this publication.

'There is the depot,' said Mr. Deacon. 'And then some of the late trains from the Continent. It's not too bad a pitch, you know.'

'And now you are going home?'

'We decided to have a cup of coffee at the stall by Hyde Park Corner,' said Mr. Deacon, adding with what could only be described as a deep giggle: 'I felt I could venture there chaperoned by Gypsy. Coffee can be very grateful at this hour. Why not join us in a cup?'

While he was speaking a taxi cruised near the kerb on the far side of the road. Widmerpool was still staring rather wildly at Gypsy Jones, apparently regarding her much as a doctor, suspecting a malignant growth, might examine a diseased organism under the microscope; although I found later that any such diagnosis of his attitude was far from the true one. Thinking that physical removal might put him out of his supposed misery, I asked if he wanted to hail the passing cab. He glanced uncertainly across the street. For a second he seemed seriously to contemplate the taxi; and then, finally, to come to a decision important to himself.

'I'll join you in some coffee, if I may,' he said. 'On thinking things over, coffee is just what I need myself.'

This resolution was unexpected, to say the least. However, if he wanted to prolong the night in such company, I felt that determination to be his own affair. So far as I was myself concerned, I was not unwilling to discover more of someone like Mr. Deacon who had loomed as a mysterious figure in my mind in the manner of all persons discussed by grown-ups in the presence of a child.

We set oft up the hill together, four abreast: Widmerpool and Gypsy Jones on the flanks. Across the road the coffee-stall came into sight, a spot of light round which the scarlet tunics and white equipment of one or two Guardsmen still flickered like the bright wings of moths attracted from nocturnal shadows by a flame. From the park rose the heavy scent of London on a summer night. Here, too, bands could be heard distantly throbbing. We crossed the road at the island and joined a knot of people round the stall, at the side of which, as if killing time while he waited for a friend late in arrival, an elderly person in a dinner-jacket was very slowly practising the Charleston, swaying his weight from one side of his patent leather shoes to the other, while he kept the tips of his fingers delicately in his coat pockets. Mr. Deacon glanced at him with disapproval, but acknowledged, though without warmth, the smirk proffered by a young man in a bright green suit, the uncomfortable colour of which was emphasised by auburn hair, erratically dyed. This was perhaps not a spot one might have chosen to soothe Widmerpool after his unfortunate experience with Barbara and the sugar. All the same, at the far end of the stall's little counter, he seemed already to have found something to discuss with Gypsy Jones—aspects of the question of the Haig statue, possibly, or the merits of Isbister's portrait-painting—and both of them seemed fairly happy. Mr. Deacon began to explain to me how contemporary Paris had become 'altogether too rackety' for his taste.

'The Left Bank was all right when I met you in the Louvre with your family,' he said. 'Wasn't the Peace Conference in progress then? I didn't take much interest in such things in those days. Now I know better. The truth is one gets too intimate with too many people if one stays in Montparnasse too long. I have come back to England for a little quiet. Besides, the French can be very interfering in their own particular way.'

Purveying *War Never Pays!* at midnight in the company of Gypsy Jones seemed, on the face of it, a capricious manner of seeking tranquillity; but—as I knew nothing of the life abandoned by Mr. Deacon to which such an undertaking was alternative—the extent of its potentially less tempting contrasts was impossible to gauge. Regarded from a conventional standpoint, Mr. Deacon gave the impression of having gone down-hill since the days when he had been accustomed to visit my parents, to whom he made little or no reference beyond expression of pious hopes that both of them enjoyed good health. It appeared that he was himself now running a curiosity-shop in the neighbourhood of Charlotte Street. He pressed me to 'look him up' there at the earliest opportunity, writing the address on the back of an envelope. In spite of his air of being set apart from worldly things, Mr. Deacon discoursed with what at least sounded like a good deal of practical common sense regarding the antique business, hours spent in the shop, time given to buying, closing arrangements, and such material points. I did not know what his financial position might be, but the shop was evidently providing, for the time being, an adequate livelihood.

'There are still a few people who are prepared to pay for nice things,' he remarked.

When given coffee, he had handed back his cup, after examination, in objection to the alleged existence on the rim of the china of cracks and chips 'in which poison might collect'.

'I am always worried as to whether or not the crockery is properly washed up in places like this,' he said.

Reflectively, he turned in his hand the cup that had replaced the earlier one, and continued to digress on the general inadequacy of sanitary precautions in shops and restaurants.

'It's just as bad in London as in Paris cafés—worse in some ways,' he said.

He had just returned the second cup as equally unsatisfactory, when someone at my elbow asked: 'Can one get matches here?' I was standing half-turned away from the counter, listening to Mr. Deacon, and did not see this new arrival. For some reason the voice made me glance towards Widmerpool; not because its tone bore any resemblance to his own thick utterance, but because the words suggested, oddly enough, Widmerpool's almost perpetual presence as an unvaried component of everyday life rather than as an unexpected element of an evening like this one. A moment later someone touched my arm, and the same voice said: 'Where are you off to, may I ask, in all those fine clothes?' A tall, pale young man, also in evening dress, though without a hat, was standing beside me.

At first sight Stringham looked just the same; indeed, the fact that on the former occasion, as now, he had been wearing a white tie somehow conveyed the illusion that he had been in a tail-coat for all the years since we had last met. He looked tired, perhaps rather irritable, though evidently pleased to fall in like this with someone known to him. I was conscious of that peculiar feeling of restraint in meeting someone, of whom I had once seen so much, now dropped altogether from everyday life: an extension—and refinement, perhaps—of the sensation no doubt mutually experienced between my parents and Mr. Deacon on that day in the Louvre: more acute, because I had been far more closely associated with Stringham than ever they with Mr. Deacon. The presence of Widmerpool at the stall added a touch of fantasy to Stringham's appearance at that spot; for it was as if Widmerpool's own antics had now called his mimic into being as inexorable accessory to any real existence to which Widmerpool himself might aspire. I introduced Mr. Deacon and Gypsy Jones.

'Why, hullo, Stringham,' said Widmerpool, putting down his coffee-cup with a clatter and puffing out his cheeks in a great demonstration of heartiness. 'We haven't met since we were at Le Bas's.'

He thought, no doubt—if he thought of the matter at all—that Stringham and I were friends who continued to see each other often, inevitably unaware that this was, in fact, our first meeting for so long. Stringham, on his side, clearly supposed that all four of us—Widmerpool, Mr. Deacon, Gypsy Jones, and myself—had been spending an evening together; though it was obvious that he could determine no easy explanation for finding me in Widmerpool's company, and judged our companionship immensely funny. He laughed a lot when I explained that Widmerpool and I had been to the Huntercombes' dance.

'Well, well,' he said. 'It's a long time since I went to a dance. How my poor mother used to hate them when my sister was first issued to an ungrateful public. Was it agony?'

'May one enquire why you should suppose a splendid society ball to have been agony?' asked Mr. Deacon, rather archly.

There could be no doubt that, at first sight, he had taken a great fancy to Stringham. He spoke in his ironically humorous voice from deep down in his throat.

'In the first place,' said Stringham, 'I rather dislike being crowded and uncomfortable—though, heaven knows, dances are not the only places where that happens. A more serious criticism I put forward is that one is expected, when attending them, to keep at least moderately sober.'

When he said this, it struck me that Stringham had

already, perhaps, consumed a few drinks before meeting us.

'And otherwise behave with comparative rectitude?' said Mr. Deacon, charmed by this answer. 'I believe I understand you perfectly.'

'Exactly,' said Stringham. 'For that reason I am now on my way—as I expect you are too—to Milly Andriadis's. I expect that will be crowded and uncomfortable too, but at least one can behave as one wishes there.'

'Is that woman still extorting her toll from life?' asked Mr. Deacon.

'Giving a party in Hill Street this very night. I assumed you were all going there.'

'This coffee tastes of glue,' said Gypsy Jones, in her small, rasping, though not entirely unattractive voice.

She was dissatisfied, no doubt, with the lack of attention paid to her; though possibly also stimulated by the way events were shaping.

'One heard a lot of Mrs. Andriadis in Paris,' said Mr. Deacon, taking no notice of this interruption. 'In fact, I went to a party of hers once—at least I think she was joint hostess with one of the Murats. A deplorable influence she is, if one may say so.'

'One certainly may,' said Stringham. 'She couldn't be worse. As a matter of fact, my name is rather intimately linked with hers at the moment—though naturally we are unfaithful to each other in our fashion, when opportunity arises, which in my case, I have to confess, is not any too often.'

I really had no very clear idea what all this talk was about, and I had never heard of Mrs. Andriadis. I was also uncertain whether Stringham truly supposed that we might all be on our way to this party, or if he were talking completely at random. Mr. Deacon, however, seemed to grasp the situation perfectly, continuing to laugh out a series of deep chuckles.

'Where do you come from now?' I asked.

'I've a flat just round the corner,' said Stringham. 'At first I couldn't make up my mind whether I was in the vein for a party, and thought a short walk would help me decide. To tell the truth, I have only just risen from my couch. There had, for one reason and another, been a number of rather late nights last week, and, as I didn't want to miss poor Milly's party in case she felt hurt—she is too touchy for words—I went straight home to bed this afternoon so that I might be in tolerable form for the festivities—instead of the limp rag one feels most of the time. It seemed about the hour to stroll across. Why not come, all of you? Milly would be delighted.'

'Is it near?'

'Just past those Sassoon houses. Do come. That is, if none of you mind low parties.'

2.

Uncle Giles's standard of values was, in most matters, ill-adapted to employment by anyone except himself. At the same time, I can now perceive that by unhesitating contempt for all human conduct but his own—judged among his immediate relatives as far from irreproachable—he held up a mirror to emphasise latent imperfections of almost any situation that momentary enthusiasm might, in the first instance, have overlooked. His views, in fact, provided a kind of yardstick to the proportions of which no earthly yard could possibly measure up. This unquestioning condemnation of everyone, and everything, had no doubt supplied armour against some of the disappointments of life; although any philosophical satisfaction derived from reliance on these sentiments had certainly not at all diminished my uncle's capacity for grumbling, in and out of season, at anomalies of social behaviour to be found, especially since the war, on all sides. To look at things through Uncle Giles's eyes would never have occurred to me; but—simply as an exceptional expedient for attempting to preserve a sense of proportion, a state of mind, for that matter, neither always acceptable nor immediately advantageous—there may have been something to be said for borrowing, once in a way, something from Uncle Giles's method of approach. This concept of regarding one's own affairs through the medium of a friend or relative is not, of course, a specially profound one; but, in the case of my uncle, the field of vision surveyed was always likely to be so individual to himself that almost any scene contemplated from this point of vantage required, on the part of another observer, more than ordinarily drastic refocusing.

He would, for example, have dismissed the Huntercombes' dance as one of those formal occasions that he himself, as it were by definition, found wholly unsympathetic. Uncle Giles disapproved on principle of anyone who could afford to live in Belgrave Square (for he echoed almost the identical words of Mr. Deacon regarding people 'with more money than was good for them'), especially when they were, in addition, bearers of what he called 'handles to their names'; though he would sometimes, in this same connexion, refer with conversational familiarity, more in sorrow than anger, to a few members of his own generation, known to him in a greater or lesser degree in years gone by, who had been brought by inheritance to this unhappy condition. He had, for some reason, nothing like so strong an aversion for recently acquired wealth—from holders of which, it is true, he had from time to time even profited to a small degree—provided the money had been amassed by owners safely to be despised, at least in private, by himself or anyone else; and by methods commonly acknowledged to be indefensible. It was to any form of long-established affluence that he took the gravest exception, particularly if the ownership of land was combined with any suggestion of public service, even when such exertions were performed in some quite unspectacular, and apparently harmless, manner, like sitting on a borough council, or helping at a school-treat. 'Interfering beggars,' he used to remark of those concerned.

My uncle's dislike for the incidence of Mrs. Andriadis's party—equally, as a matter of course, overwhelming—would have required, in order to avoid involving himself as an auxiliary of more than negative kind in some warring faction, the selection of a more careful approach on his part than that adopted to display potential disapproval of the Huntercombes; for, by taking sides too actively, he might easily find himself in the position of defending one or another of the systems of conducting human existence which he was normally to be found attacking in another sector of the battlefield. At the same time, it would hardly be true to say that Uncle Giles was deeply concerned with the question of consistency in argument. On the contrary, inconsistency in his own line of thought worried him scarcely at all. As a matter of fact, if absolutely compelled to make a pronouncement on the subject, he—or, so far as that went, anyone else investigating the matter—might have taken a fairly firm stand on the fact that immediate impressions at Mrs. Andriadis's were not, after all, greatly different from those conveyed on first arrival at Belgrave Square.

The house, which had the air of being rented furnished only for a month or two, was bare; somewhat unattractively decorated in an anonymous style which, at least in the upholstery, combined touches of the Italian Renaissance with stripped panelling and furniture of 'modernistic' design, these square, metallic pieces on the whole suggesting Berlin rather than Paris. Although smaller than the Huntercombes', my uncle would have detected there a decided suggestion of wealth, and also—something to which his objection was, if possible, even more deeply ingrained—an atmosphere of frivolity. Like many people whose days are passed largely in a state of inanition, when not of crisis, Uncle Giles prided himself on his serious approach to life, deprecating nothing so much as what he called 'trying to laugh things off'; and it was true that a lifetime of laughter would scarcely have sufficed to exorcise some of his own fiascos.

On the whole, Mrs. Andriadis's guests belonged to a

generation older than that attending the dance, and their voices swelled more loudly throughout the rooms. The men were in white ties and the ladies' dresses were carried in general with a greater flourish than at the Huntercombes': some of the wearers distinctly to be classed as 'beauties'. A minute sprinkling of persons from both sexes still in day clothes absolved Mr. Deacon and Gypsy Jones from looking quite so out of place as might otherwise have been apprehended; and, during the course of that night, I was surprised to notice how easily these two (who had deposited their unsold copies of *War Never Pays!* in the hall, under a high-backed crimson-and-gold chair, designed in an uneasy compromise between *avant garde* motifs and seventeenth-century Spanish tradition) faded unobtrusively into the general background of the party. There were, indeed, many girls present not at all dissimilar in face and figure to Gypsy Jones; while Mr. Deacon, too, could have found several prototypes of himself among a contingent of sardonic, moderately distinguished, grey-haired men, some of whom smelt of bath-salts, dispersed here and there throughout the gathering. The comparative formality of the scene to be observed on our arrival had cast a certain blight on my own—it now seemed too ready—acceptance of Stringham's assurance that invitation was wholly unnecessary; for the note of 'frivolity', to which Uncle Giles might so undeniably have taken exception, was, so I could not help feeling, infused with an undercurrent of extreme coolness, a chilly consciousness of conflicting egoisms, far more intimidating than anything normally to be met with at Walpole-Wilsons', Huntercombes', or, indeed, anywhere else of 'that sort'.

However, as the eye separated individuals from the mass, marks of a certain exoticism were here revealed, notably absent from the scene at Belgrave Square: such deviations from a more conventional standard alleviating, so far as they went, earlier implications of stiffness; although these intermittent patches of singularity—if they were to be regarded as singular—were, on the whole, not necessarily predisposed to put an uninvited newcomer any more at his ease; except perhaps in the sense that one act of informality in such surroundings might, roughly speaking, be held tacitly to excuse another.

For example, an elderly gentleman with a neat white moustache and eye-glass, evidently come from some official assemblage—perhaps the reception at the Spanish Embassy—because he wore miniatures, and the cross of some order in white enamel and gold under the points of his collar, was conversing with a negro, almost tawny in pigmentation, rigged out in an elaborately waisted and square-shouldered tail-coat with exaggeratedly pointed lapels. It was really this couple that had made me think of Uncle Giles, who, in spite of advocacy of the urgent dissolution of the British Empire on grounds of its despotic treatment of backward races, did not greatly care for coloured people, whatever their origin; and, unless some quite exceptional circumstance sanctioned the admixture, he would certainly not have approved of guests of African descent being invited to a party to which he himself had been bidden. In this particular case, however, he would undoubtedly have directed the earlier momentum of his disparagement against the man with the eye-glass, since my uncle could not abide the wearing of medals. 'Won 'em in Piccadilly, I shouldn't wonder,' he was always accustomed to comment, when his eye fell on these outward and visible awards, whoever the recipient, and whatever the occasion.

Not far from the two persons just described existed further material no less vulnerable to my uncle's censure for a heavily-built man, with a greying beard and the air of a person of consequence, was unsuccessfully striving, to the accompaniment of much laughter on both sides, to wrest a magnum of champagne from the hands of an ancient dame, black-browed, and wearing a tiara, or jewelled head-dress of some sort, who was struggling manfully to retain possession of the bottle. Here, therefore, were assembled in a single group—as it were of baroque sculpture come all at once to life—three classes of object all equally abhorrent to Uncle Giles; that is to say, champagne, beards, and tiaras: each in its different way representing sides of life for which he could find no good to say; beards implying to him Bohemianism's avoidance of those practical responsibilities with which he always felt himself burdened: tiaras and champagne unavoidably conjuring up images of guilty opulence of a kind naturally inimical to 'radical' principles.

Although these relatively exotic embellishments to the scene occurred within a framework on the whole commonplace enough, the shifting groups of the party created, as a spectacle, illusion of moving within the actual confines of a picture or tapestry, into the depths of which the personality of each new arrival had to be automatically amalgamated; even in the case of apparently unassimilable material such as Mr. Deacon or Gypsy Jones, both of whom, as I have said, were immediately absorbed, at least to the eye, almost as soon as they had crossed the threshold of Mrs. Andriadis.

'Who is this extraordinary old puss you have in tow?' Stringham had asked, while he and I had walked a little ahead of the other three, after we had left the coffee-stall.

'A friend of my parents.'

'Mine know the oddest people too—especially my father. And Miss Jones? Also a friend—or a cousin?'

He only laughed when I attempted to describe the circumstances that had led to my finding myself with Mr. Deacon, who certainly seemed to require some explanation at the stage of life, and of behaviour, that he had now reached. Stringham pretended to think—or was at least unwilling to disbelieve—that Gypsy Jones was my own chosen companion, rather than Mr. Deacon's. However, he had shown no sign of regarding either of them as noticeably more strange than anyone else, encountered on a summer night, who might seem eligible to be asked to a party given by a friend. It was, indeed, clear to me that strangeness was what Stringham now expected, indeed, demanded from life: a need already become hard to satisfy. The detachment he had always seemed to possess was now more marked than ever before. At the same time he had become in some manner different from the person I had known at school, so that, in spite of the air almost of relief that he had shown at falling in with us, I began to feel uncertain whether, in fact, Anne Stepney had not used the term 'pompous' in the usual, and not some specialised, sense. Peter Templer, too, I remembered, had employed the same word years before at school when he had enquired about Stringham's family. 'Well, I imagine it was all rather pompous even at lunch, wasn't it?' he had asked. At that time I associated pomposity with Le Bas, or even with Widmerpool, both of whom habitually indulged in mannerisms unthinkable in Stringham. Yet there could be no doubt that he now possessed a personal remoteness, a kind of preoccupation with his own affairs, that gave at least some *prima facie* excuse for using the epithet. All the rather elaborate friendliness, and apparent gratitude for the meeting—almost as if it might offer means of escape from some burdensome commitment—was unquestionably part of a barrier set up against the rest of the world. Trying to disregard the gap, of which I felt so well aware, as it yawned between us, I asked about his family.

'My father sits in Kenya, quarrelling with his French wife.'

'And your mother?'

'Similarly occupied with Buster over here.'

'At Glimber?'

'Glimber—as arranged by Buster—is let to an Armenian. They now live in a house of more reasonable proportions at Sunningdale. You must come there one day—if only to see dawn breaking over the rock garden. I once arrived there in the small hours and had that unforgettable experience.'

'Is Buster still in the Navy?'

'Not he.'

'A gentleman of leisure?'

'But much humbled. No longer expects one to remember every individual stroke he made during the polo season.'

'So you both rub along all right?'

'Like a house on fire,' said Stringham. 'All the same, you know parents—especially step-parents—are sometimes a bit of a disappointment to their children. They don't fulfil the promise of their early years. As a matter of fact, Buster may come to the party if he can get away.'

'And Miss Weedon?'

'Tuffy has left. I see her sometimes. She came into a little money. My mother changes her secretary every week now. She can't get along with anyone since Tuffy resigned.'

'What about Peggy Stepney?'

'What, indeed!'

'I sat next to her sister, Anne, at dinner tonight.'

'Poor Anne, I hope you were kind to her.'

He gave no hint as to whether or not he was still involved with Peggy Stepney. I presumed that there was at least no longer any question of an engagement.

'Are you still secretary to Sir Magnus Donners?'

'Still to be seen passing from time to time through the Donners-Brebner Building,' said Stringham, laughing again. 'It might be hard to establish my precise status there.'

'Nice work if you can get it!'

' "A transient and embarrassed spectre", as Le Bas used to say, when one tried to slip past him in the passage without attracting undue attention. As a matter of fact I saw Le Bas not so long ago. He turned up at Cowes last year. Not my favourite place at the best of times, but Buster seems to like the life.'

'Was Le Bas sailing?'

'Got up rather like a park-keeper. It is extraordinary how schoolmasters never get any older. In early life they settle on a cruising speed and just stick to it. Le Bas confused me with a Kenya friend of my father's called Dicky Umfraville—you probably know the name as a gentleman-rider—who left the school—sacked as a matter of fact—some fifteen or twenty years earlier than myself.'

It was true that Le Bas, like most of his profession, was accustomed to behave as if never particularly clear as to the actual decade in which he might, at any given moment, be existing; but, once assuming that recognition had not been immediate, his supposition that Stringham was something more than twenty-three or twenty-four—whatever his age at their meeting at Cowes—was not altogether surprising, because he looked, so it seemed to me by then, at least ten years older than when we had last seen each other. At the same time, it was no doubt unreasonable to mistake Stringham for Dicky Umfraville, of whose activities in Kenya I remember Sillery speaking a word of warning towards the end of my first year at the university. However, *tête-à-tête* conversation between Stringham and myself had now to come to an end, because by this time we had been admitted to the house, and the presence of a surrounding crowd of people put a stop to that kind of talk.

In one room the carpet had been rolled back, and a hunchback wearing a velvet smoking-jacket was playing an accordion, writhing backwards and forwards as he attacked his instrument with demiurgic frenzy.

'I took one look at you——
That's all I meant to do——
And then my heart—stood still . . .'

To this music, cheek to cheek, two or three couples were dancing. Elsewhere the party, again resembling the Huntercombes', had spread over the entire building, its density as thick on landings and in passages as among the rooms. There were people everywhere, and voices sounded from the upper levels of bedroom floors. Stringham pushed his way through this swarming herd, the rest of us following. There was a buffet in the drawing-room, where hired butlers were serving drinks. Moving through the closely packed mob, from which a powerful aroma of tobacco, alcohol, and cosmetics arose, like the scent of plants and flowers in some monstrous garden, we came suddenly upon Mrs. Andriadis herself, when a further, and enormous, field of speculation was immediately projected into being. Stringham took her hand.

'Milly . . .'

'Darling . . .' she said, throwing an arm round his neck and kissing him energetically. 'Why so disgustingly late?'

'Overslept.'

'Milly ought to have been there.'

'Why wasn't she?'

'Milly thought this was going to be a horrible party and she was going to hate it.'

'Not now?'

'Couldn't be.'

I did not remember exactly what outward appearance I had planned before arrival for Mrs. Andriadis. A suspicion may not have been altogether suppressed that she might turn out to resemble, in physiognomy and dress, one of those formalised classical figures from bronze or ceramic art, posed as Le Bas would sometimes contort himself; but my invention, though perhaps in one aspect ancient Greek, was certainly modern Greek in another. However, the shape any imaginary portrait may have taken was quite unlike this small woman with powder-grey hair, whose faint touch of a Cockney accent, like her coiffure, was evidently retained deliberately as a considered attraction. She was certainly pretty, though the effect was obtained in some indirect and unobtrusive manner. Her dark eyebrows were strongly marked.

She stood clinging to Stringham's arm, while, as if dancing, she twitched her body this way and that. Her eyes were brown and very bright, and the jewels she wore, in rather defiant profusion, looked as if they might have cost a good deal of money. She could have been about thirty-five; perhaps a year or two more. At first it seemed to me that she must have been a great beauty ten or fifteen years earlier; but I discovered, in due course, from those who had known Mrs. Andriadis for a long time, that, on the contrary, the epoch of this party represented perhaps the peak of her good looks—that is, if her looks (or anyone else's) could be admitted as open to objective judgment by some purely hypothetical standard; for, as Barnby used to say: 'It's no good being a beauty alone on a desert island.' Barnby himself adhered to the theory that Mrs. Andriadis's appearance had been greatly improved after her hair had turned grey: being accustomed to add to this opinion the statement that the change of shade had taken place 'After her first night with The Royal Personage, as Edgar always calls him.' I was strongly reminded by her appearance—so it seemed to me—of another woman; though of whom I could not decide.

'I brought some friends along, Milly,' said Stringham. 'You don't mind?'

'You darlings,' said Mrs. Andriadis. 'It is going to be a lovely party now. All arranged on the spur of the moment. Come with me, Charles. We are making Deauville plans.'

Although obviously in the habit of having her own way in most matters, she showed no surprise at all at the sight of Widmerpool, Mr. Deacon, Gypsy Jones, and myself. Indeed, it seemed probable that, as newly-arrived entities, she took cognisance, so far as our self-contained group was concerned, of no more than Mr. Deacon and me, since Widmerpool and Gypsy Jones, threading their way across the room, had been left some little way behind the rest of us. Even Mr. Deacon, in spite of strenuous efforts on his own part, scarcely managed to shake hands with Mrs. Andriadis, although, as he bent almost double, the tips of their fingers may have touched. It was at that instant of tenuous contact that Mr. Deacon attempted to explain the matter, mentioned already by him at the coffee-stall, to the effect that he thought they had met once before 'in Paris with the Murats'. An assertion of which Mrs. Andriadis herself took no notice whatsoever.

As it turned out, neither Widmerpool nor Gypsy Jones ever reached her at that—nor, as far as I know, any other—stage of the party, because, evidently deciding to spend no more time on her welcome of such miscellaneous guests, she took Stringham by the arm, and bore him away. Widmerpool, with a set expression on his face, passed obliquely through the crowd, still filled, as I supposed, with an unquenchable determination, even stronger, if possible, than Mr. Deacon's, to make himself at all costs known to his hostess. Gypsy Jones also disappeared from sight at the same moment, though not, it might be presumed, with the same aim. Their effacement was effected rather to my relief, because I had feared from Widmerpool a stream of comment of a kind for which I felt not at all in the mood; while at the same time, rather snobbishly, I did not wish to appear too closely responsible for being the cause, however indirect, of having brought Mr. Deacon and Gypsy Jones to the house. This was the moment when the surrounding tableaux formed by the guests began to take coherent shape in my eyes, when viewed from the corner by the grand piano, where I had been left beside Mr. Deacon, who now accepted, with a somewhat roguish glance, a beaker of champagne from the tray of one of the men-servants.

'I cannot say I altogether like these parties,' he said. 'A great many of them seem to be given these days. Paris was just the same. I really should not have accepted your nice-looking friend's invitation if we had not had such a very indifferent evening with *War Never Pays!* As it was, I felt some recreation was deserved—though I fear I shall not find much here. Not, at least, in any form likely to appeal to my present mood. By the way, I don't know whether you would ever care to lend a hand with *War Never Pays!*, a penny, one of these days? We are always glad to enlist new helpers.'

I excused myself decisively from any such undertaking on grounds of lacking aptitude for any kind of salesmanship.

'Not everyone feels it a bounden duty,' said Mr. Deacon. 'I need not tell you that Gypsy is scarcely a colleague I should choose, if I were a free agent, but she is so keen I cannot very well raise objection. Her political motives are not identical with my own, but Pacifism is ally of all who desire this country's disarmament. Do you know, I even put her up at my place? After all, you can't expect her to get all the way back to Hendon Central at this time of night. It wouldn't be right.'

He spoke almost with unction at the nobiltiy of such self-sacrifice, and, finishing his champagne at a gulp, wiped the corners of his mouth carefully with a silk handkerchief. On the wall opposite us, one of the panels of the room had been replaced—possibly with the object of increasing the rather 'daring' effect at which decoration of the house evidently aimed—with squares of looking-glass, in the reflections of which could be observed the changing pattern made by the occupants of the room.

The lady with the tiara had at last reluctantly abandoned the magnum to her bearded opponent (now accommodated with a younger, though less conspicuous, woman), and, apparently much flattered by the attention, she was accepting a cigarette from the negro's long case, which he was holding out towards her, the metal seeming delicately matched in tone with the skin of its owner's hand, also the tint of old gold. Beyond this couple, the gentleman with the eye-glass and medals was now talking to a figure whose back-view—for some reason familiar—showed an immensely time-worn suit of evening clothes, the crumpled tails of which hung down almost to its wearer's heels, giving him the appearance of a musical-hall comedian, or conjuror of burlesque, whose baggy Charlie Chaplin trousers, threatening descent to the ground at any moment, would probably reveal red flannel, grotesquely spotted, or some otherwise traditionally comic, underclothes, or lack of them, beneath. Matted white hair protruded over the back of this person's collar, and he was alternately rubbing together his hands and replacing them in the pockets of these elephantine trousers, while he stood nodding his head, and sagging slightly at the knees. I suddenly became aware, with some surprise, that the man with the medals was Colonel Budd—Margaret Budd's father—who held some minor appointment at Court. He had also perhaps, 'come on' from the Huntercombes'.

'She reposes herself at the back of the shop,' said Mr. Deacon, pursuing the topic of his connexion with Gypsy Jones. 'I make up the bed—a divan—myself, with some rather fine Cashmere shawls a former patron of mine left me in his will. However, I don't expect she will need them on a warm night like this. Just as well, if they are not to be worn to shreds. As a matter of fact they are going for a mere song if you happen to know anyone interested in Oriental textiles. I can always find something else to put over Gypsy. Of course Barnby doesn't much like her being there.'

I did not at that time know who Barnby might be, though I felt sure that I had heard of him; connecting the name—as it turned out, correctly—with painting.

'I see his point,' said Mr. Deacon, 'even though I know little of such things. Gypsy's attitude naturally—perhaps Barnby would prefer me to say "unnaturally"—offends his *amour propre*. In some ways he is not an ideal tenant himself. I don't want women running up and down stairs all day long—and all night long too, for that matter—just because I have to put up with Gypsy in a good cause.'

He spoke complainingly, and paused for breath, coughing throatily, as if he might be suffering from asthma. Both of us helped ourselves to another drink. Meanwhile, seen in the looking-glass, Colonel Budd and the wearer of the Charlie Chaplin trousers now began to edge their way round the wall to where a plump youth with a hooked nose and black curly hair, perhaps an Oriental, was talking to a couple of strikingly pretty girls. For a minute or two I had already been conscious of something capable of recognition about the old clothes and assured carriage of the baggy-trousered personage, whose face, until that moment, had been hidden from me. When he turned towards the room, I found that the features were Sillery's, not seen since I had come down from the university.

To happen upon Sillery in London at that season of the year was surprising. Usually, by the time the first few weeks of the Long Vacation had passed, he was already abroad, in Austria or Italy, with a reading party of picked undergraduates: or even a fellow don or two, chosen with equal care, always twenty or thirty years younger than himself. Sillery, probably with wisdom, always considered himself at a disadvantage outside his own academical strongholds. He was accordingly accustomed, on the whole, to emphasise the corruption of metropolitan life as such, in spite of almost febrile interest in the affairs of those who found themselves habitually engaged in London's social activities; but, on the other hand, if passing through on his way to the Continent, he would naturally welcome opportunity to be present, as if by accident, at a party of this kind, when luck put such a chance in his way. The accumulated gossip there obtainable could be secreted, and eked out for weeks and months—even years—at his own tea-parties; or injected in judiciously homeopathic doses to rebut and subdue refractory colleagues at High Table. Possibly, with a view to enjoying such potential benefits, he might even have delayed departure to the lakes and mountains where his summers were chiefly spent; but if he had come to London specially to be present, there could be no doubt that it was to pursue here some negotiation judged by himself to be of first-rate importance.

As they skirted the wall, Sillery and his companion, by contrast remarkably spruce, had almost the appearance of a pair of desperadoes on their way to commit an act of violence, and, on reaching the place where the dark young man was standing, the Colonel certainly seemed to get rid of the women without much ceremony, treating them almost as a policeman might peremptorily 'move on' from the corner of the street female loiterers of dubious complexion. The taller of the two girls was largely built, with china-blue eyes and yellow hair, holding herself in a somewhat conventionally languorous style: the other, dark, with small, pointed breasts and a neat, supple figure. The combined effect of their beauty was irresistible, causing a kind of involuntary pang, as if for a split-second I loved both of them passionately; though a further survey convinced me that nothing so disturbing had taken place. The girls composedly allowed themselves to be dislodged by Colonel Budd and Sillery: at the same time remaining on guard in a strategic position at a short distance, talking and laughing with each other, and with people in the immediate neighbourhood: evidently unwilling to abandon entirely their original stations *vis-à-vis* the young man.

The Colonel, imperceptibly inclining his neck in an abrupt gesture suggesting almost the sudden suppression of an unexpected eructation, presented Sillery, not without deference to this rather mysterious figure, regarding whom I had begun to feel a decided curiosity. The young man, smiling graciously, though rather shyly, held out a hand. Sillery, grinning broadly in return, made a deep bow that seemed, by its mixture of farce and formality, to accord perfectly with the cut of his evening clothes, in their implication of pantomime or charade. However, fearing that absorption in this scene, as reflected in the looking-glass, might have made me seem inattentive to Mr. Deacon's exposition of difficulties experienced in contending with his household, I made further enquiries regarding Barnby's status as a painter. Mr. Deacon did not warm to this subject. I found when I knew him better that this lukewarm attitude was not to be attributed entirely to jealousy he might feel towards Barnby's success, but rather because, finding his own views on the subject so opposed to contemporary opinion as to be in practice untenable, he preferred to close his eyes to the existence of modern painting, just as formerly he had closed his eyes to politics and war. Accordingly, I asked about the nature of Barnby's objections to Gypsy Jones.

'When Gypsy and I were first acquainted,' said Mr. Deacon, lowering his voice, 'I was given to understand—well, hasn't Swinburne got some lines about "wandering watery sighs where the sea sobs round Lesbian promontories"? In fact restriction to such a coastline was almost a condition of our association.'

'Did Barnby object?'

'I think he undoubtedly felt resentment,' said Mr. Deacon. 'But, as a very dear friend of mine once remarked when I was a young man—for I was a young man once, whatever you may think to the contrary—"Gothic manners don't mix with Greek morals." Gypsy would never learn that.'

Mr. Deacon stopped speaking. He seemed to be deliberating within himself whether or not to ask some question, in the wording of which he found perhaps a certain embarrassment. After a few seconds he said: 'As a matter of fact I am rather worried about Gypsy. I suppose you don't happen to know the address of any medicos—I don't mean the usual general practitioner with the restricted views of his profession—no, I didn't for a moment suppose that you did. And of course one does not wish to get mixed up. I feel just the same as yourself. But you were enquiring about Barnby. I really must arrange for you to meet. I think you would like each other.'

When such scraps of gossip are committed to paper, the words bear a heavier weight than when the same information is imparted huskily between draughts of champagne, in the noise of a crowded room; besides which, my thoughts hovering still on the two girls who had been displaced by Sillery and Colonel Budd, I had not been giving very full attention to what Mr. Deacon had been saying. However, if I had at that moment considered Gypsy Jones's difficulties with any seriousness, I should probably have decided, rightly or wrongly, that she was well able to look after herself. Even in the quietest forms of life the untoward is rarely far from the surface, and in the intemperate circles to which she seemed to belong nothing was surprising. I felt at the time absolutely no inclination to pursue the matter further. Mr. Deacon himself became temporarily lost in thought.

Our attention was at that moment violently reorientated by the return to the room of Mrs. Andriadis, who now shouted—a less forcible word would have been inadequate to describe her manner of announcing the news—that 'darling Max' was going to sing: a statement creating a small upheaval in our immediate surroundings, owing to the proximity of the piano, upon which a bottle of champagne was now placed. A mild-looking young man in spectacles was thrust through the crowd, who seating himself on the music-stool, protested: 'Must I really tickle the dominoes?' A number of voices at once encouraged him to embark upon his musical activity, and, after winding round the seat once or twice, apparently more as a ritual than for practical reasons, he struck a few chords.

'Really,' said Mr. Deacon, as if entitled to feel honest disgust at this development, 'Mrs. Andriadis does not seem to care in the least whom she makes friends with.'

'Who is he?'

'Max Pilgrim—a public performer of some sort.'

The young man now began to sing in a tremulous, quavering voice, like that of an immensely ancient lady, though at the same time the words filled the room with a considerable volume of sound:

> 'I'm Tess of Le Touquet,
> My morals are flukey,
> Tossed on the foam, I couldn't be busier;
> Permanent waves
> Splash me into the caves;
> Everyone loves me as much as Delysia.
> When it's wet on the Links, I know where to
>   have a beau
> Down in the club-house—next door to the
>   lavabo.'

There was muffled laughter and some fragmentary applause, though a hum of conversation continued to be heard round about us.

'I don't care for this at all,' said Mr. Deacon. 'To begin with, I do not entirely understand the meaning of the words—if they have any meaning—and, in the second place, the singer once behaved to me in what I consider an objectionable manner. I can't think how Mrs. Andriadis can have him in the house. It can't do her reputation any good.'

The appearance of Max Pilgrim at the piano had thoroughly put out Mr. Deacon. In an attempt to relieve the gloom that had fallen on him I enquired about Mrs. Andriadis's past.

'Barnby knows more about her than I do,' he said, rather resentfully. 'She is said to have been mistress of a Royal Personage for a time. Personally I am not greatly stimulated by such revelations.'

'Is she still kept?'

'My dear boy, you have the crudest way of putting things,' said Mr. Deacon, smiling at this, and showing signs of cheering up a little. 'No—so far as I am aware—our hostess is no longer "kept", as you are pleased to term the former state of life to which she was called by Providence. A client of mine told me that her present husband—there have been several—possessed comprehensive business interests in Manchester, or that region. My friend's description suggested at least a sufficient competence on the latest husband's part for the condition of dependence you mention to be, financially speaking, no longer necessary for his lady—even, perhaps, undesirable. Apart from this, I know little of Mr. Andriadis, though I imagine him to be a man of almost infinite tolerance. You are, I expect, familiar, with Barnby's story of the necklace?'

'What necklace?'

'Milly,' said Mr. Deacon, pronouncing Mrs. Andriadis's name with affected delicacy, 'Milly saw a diamond-and-emerald necklace in Cartier's. It cost, shall we say, two million francs. She approached the Royal Personage, who happened to be staying at the Crillon at that moment, and asked for the money to buy herself the necklace as a birthday present. The Royal Personage handed her the bank-notes—which he was no doubt accustomed to keep in his pocket—and Milly curtsied her way out. She went round the corner to the apartment of a well-known French industrialist—I cannot remember which, but you would know the name—who was also interested in her welfare, and requested him to drive there and then to Cartier's and buy the necklace on the spot. This the industrialist was obliging enough to do. Milly was, therefore, two million francs to the good, and could, at the same time, give pleasure to both her protectors by wearing the necklace in the company of either. Simple—like all great ideas.'

Mr. Deacon paused. He seemed all at once to regret this sudden, and uncharacteristic, outburst of sophistication on so mundane a subject. The anecdote had certainly been told in a manner entirely foreign to his accustomed tone in dealing with worldly matters; discussed by him in general, at least publicly—as I found at a later date, as if all practical transactions were wrapped in mystery impenetrable for one of his simple outlook. Such an approach had been, indeed, habitual with him at all times, and, even so far back as the days when my parents used to speak of him, I could recall banter about Mr. Deacon's repeatedly expressed ignorance of the world. This attitude did not, of course, repudiate on his part a certain insistence on his own knowingness in minor, and more 'human', affairs, such as the running of his shop, described so precisely by him a short time earlier at the coffee-stall. The story of the necklace was, I thought, in some way vaguely familiar to me. It had possibly figured in the repertoire of Peter Templer at school, the heroine of Templer's anecdote, so I believed, represented as a well-known actress rather than Mrs. Andriadis herself.

'Not that I know anything of such gallivanting,' said Mr. Deacon, as if by now ashamed of his momentary abandonment of the unassailable position vouchsafed to him by reliance, in all circumstances, on an artist's traditional innocence of heart. 'Personally I should be delighted for kings, priests, armament manufacturers, *poules de luxe*, and *hoc genus omne* to be swept into the dust-bin—and I might add all the nonsense we find about us tonight.'

As he stopped speaking, the words of the song, which had been proceeding through a number of verses, now became once more audible:

> 'Even the fairies
> Say how sweet my hair is;
> They mess my mascara and pinch the peroxide.
> I know a coward
> Would be overpowered,
> When they all offer to be orthodox. I'd
> Like to be kind, but say: "Some other day, dears;
> Pansies for thoughts remains still the best way,
> dears." '

This verse gave great offence to Mr. Deacon. Indeed, its effect was almost electric in the suddenness of the ferment it caused within him. He brushed away a lock of grey hair fallen over his forehead, and clenched his fist until the knuckles were white. He was evidently very angry. 'Insufferable!' he said. 'And from such a person.'

He had gone quite pale with irritation. The negro, too, perhaps himself a vocalist, or performer upon some instrument, had also been watching Max Pilgrim with a look of mounting, though silent, hatred that had contracted the whole of his face into a scowl of self-righteous rage. This look seemed by then to have dramatised his bearing into the character of Othello. But the pianist, taking occasional nips at his champagne, showed no sign of observing any of the odium aroused by him in these or other quarters. Mr. Deacon sighed. There was a moment when I thought he might, there and then, have decided to leave the house. His chest heaved. However, he evidently made up his mind to dismiss unpleasant reflections.

'Your young friend appears to hold the place of honour here,' he said, in a more restrained voice. 'Is he rich? Who are his parents—if I am not being inquisitive?'

'They are divorced. His father married a Frenchwoman and lives in Kenya. His mother was a South African, also remarried—to a sailor called Foxe.'

'Buster Foxe?'

'Yes.'

'Rather a chic sailor,' said Mr. Deacon. 'If I mistake not, I used to hear about him in Paris. And she started life as wife of some belted earl or other.'

He was again showing recklessness in giving voice to these spasmodic outbursts of worldly knowledge. The champagne perhaps caused this intermittent pulling aside of the curtain that concealed some, apparently considerable, volume of practical information about unlikely people: a little storehouse, the existence of which he was normally unwilling to admit, yet preserved safely at the back of his mind in case of need.

'What was the name?' he went on. 'She is a very handsome woman—or was.'

'Warrington.'

'The Beautiful Lady Warrington!' said Mr. Deacon. 'I remember seeing a photograph of her in *The Queen*. There was some nonsense there, too, about a fancy-dress ball she had given. When will people learn better? And Warrington himself was much older than she, and died soon after their marriage. He probably drank.'

'So far as I know, he was a respectable brigadier-general. It is Charles Stringham's father who likes the bottle.'

'They are all the same,' said Mr. Deacon, decisively.

Whether this condemnation was aimed at all husbands

of Stringham's mother, or, more probably, intended, in principle, to embrace members of the entire social stratum from which these husbands had, up to date, been drawn, was not made clear. Once more he fell into silence, as if thinking things over. Max Pilgrim continued to hammer and strum and take gulps of champagne, while against an ever-increasing buzz of conversation, he chanted his song continuously, as if it were a narrative poem or saga recording the heroic, legendary deeds of some primitive race:

'I do hope Tallulah
Now feels a shade cooler,
But why does she pout, as she wanders so far off
From Monsieur Citröen,
Who says something knowin'
To Lady Cunard and Sir Basil Zaharoff?
Has someone guessed who was having a beano
At Milly's last party behind the Casino?'

This verse turned out to be the climax. Max Pilgrim, removing his spectacles, rose and bowed. Since the beginning of the song, many people, among them Mrs. Andriadis herself, had drifted away, and the room was now half empty, though a small group of enthusiasts still hovered round the piano. This residuum now clapped and applauded heartily. Pilgrim was almost immediately led away by two ladies, neither of them young. What remained of the crowd began to shift and rearrange its component parts, so that in the movement following the song's termination Mr. Deacon was swept away from his corner. I watched him betake himself by easy stages to the door, no doubt with the object of further exploration. While I was looking, someone grasped my arm, and I found that Sillery was standing beside me.

By employment of a successful disengaging movement, the dark young man had by then managed to extract himself from the encirclement that had cut him off from the two girls, to whom he had now successfully returned; an operation made easier by the fact that the girls themselves had remained conveniently near, chattering and tittering together. At this development Sillery, who seemed to be enjoying himself hugely, must have pottered away from Colonel Budd, with whom his association was no doubt on a purely business footing. He had paused by me, as if to take breath, apparently unable to decide where best to make his next important descent, puffing out his still dark walrus moustache, and leaning forward, as he swayed slightly. This faint oscillation was not, of course, due to drink, which he touched in no circumstances, but sustained himself through hour after hour of social adventure on a cup or two of *café au lait,* with perhaps an occasional sandwich or biscuit. His white tie was knotted so loosely that it formed a kind of four-in-hand under the huge wings of his collar, itself limp from want of starch.

'Why so thoughtful?' he asked, grinning widely. 'Did Charles Stringham bring you here? Such a friend of our hostess is Charles, isn't he? I heard that you and Charles had not been seeing so much of each other as you used in the old days when you were both undergraduates.'

He was obviously well aware that Stringham's life had changed greatly from the period of which he spoke, and he probably knew, too, as his words implied, that Stringham and I had not met for years. On such stray pieces of information, the cumulative effect not to be despised, Sillery's intelligence system was built up. As to the effectiveness of this system, opinion, as I have said before, differed greatly. At any rate, Sillery himself believed implicitly in his own powers, ceaselessly collecting, sorting, and collating small items in connexion with the personal relationships of the people he knew; or, at least, knew about. No doubt a few of these units of information turned out to be of value in prosecuting schemes in which, for one reason or another, he might himself become suddenly interested.

I admitted that I had not seen Stringham for some little time before that evening, but I did not feel it necessary to reveal in detail to Sillery the circumstances that had brought me to the house of Mrs. Andriadis.

'You stayed too long in the company of that gentleman with the equivocal reputation,' said Sillery, giving my arm a pinch. 'People have to be careful about such things. They do, indeed. Can't think how he got to this very respectable party—but don't let's talk about such matters. I have just been having a most enlightening chat with Prince Theodoric.'

'The Levantine young man?'

'A dark young prince with curly hair,' said Sillery, chuckling. 'That's quite a Tennysonian line, isn't it? Handsome, if it were not for that rather too obtrusive nose. One would never guess him descended from Queen Victoria. Perhaps he isn't. But we mustn't be scandalous. A very clever family, his Royal House—and well connected, too.'

I remembered that there had been some talk of Prince Theodoric at the Walpole-Wilsons'. Although aware that his visit was in progress, I could not recall much about the Prince himself, nor the problems that he was called upon to discuss. Remarks made by Widmerpool and Tompsitt on the subject earlier that evening had become somewhat confused in my mind with the substance of an article in one of the 'weeklies', skimmed through recently in a club, in which the writer associated 'the question of industrial development of base metals'—the phrase that had caught

Archie Gilbert's ear at dinner—with 'a final settlement in Macedonia'. The same periodical, in its editorial notes, had spoken, rather slightingly, of 'the part Prince Theodoric might be hoped to play on the Balkan chess-board', adding that 'informed circles in Belgrade, Bucharest, and Athens are watching this young man's movements closely; while scarcely less interest has been evoked in Sofia and Tirana, in spite of a certain parade of aloofness in the latter capital. Only in Ankara is scepticism freely expressed as to the likelihood of the links of an acceptable solution being welded upon the, by now happily obsolescent, anvil of throne-room diplomacy'. Sillery's description of the Prince as 'well connected' made me think again, involuntarily, of Uncle Giles, who would no doubt, within the same reference, also have commented on Prince Theodoric's employment of 'influence' in the advancement of his own or his country's interests.

'Mrs. Andriadis must be at least a tiny bit flattered to find H.R.H. here tonight,' said Sillery. 'Although, of course, our hostess, as you are probably aware, is no stranger to Royalty in its lighter moments. I expect it is the first time, too, that the good Theodoric has been at the same party as one of our coloured cousins. However, he is broad-minded. It is that touch of Coburgh blood.'

'Is he over here for long?'

'Perhaps a month or two. Is it aluminium? Something like that. Hope we are paying a fair price. Some of us try and organise public opinion, but there are always people who think we should have our own way, no matter what, aren't there? However, I expect all that is safe in the hands of such a great and good man as Sir Magnus Donners—with two such great and good assistants as Charles Stringham and Bill Truscott.'

He chuckled again heartily at his last comment.

'Was Prince Theodoric educated over here?'

Sillery shook his head and sighed.

'Tried to get him,' he said. 'But it couldn't be did. All the same, I think we may be going to have something almost as good.'

'Another brother?'

'Better than that. Theodoric is interested in the proposed Donners-Brebner Fellowships. Picked students to come to the university at the Donners-Brebner Company's expense. After all, we have to do something for them, if we take away their metal, don't we?'

'Will you organise the Fellowships, Sillers?'

'The Prince was good enough to ask my advice on certain academical points.'

'And you told him how it should be done?'

'Said I would help him as much as he liked, if he promised not to give me one of those great gawdy decorations that I hate so much, because I never know how to put them on right when I have to go out all dressed up to grand parties.'

'Did he agree to that?'

'Also said a few words 'bout de political sitchivashun,' remarked Sillery, ignoring the question and grinning more broadly than ever. 'Dull things for de poor Prince, I'm 'fraid. 'Spect he's 'joying hisself more now.'

He gave no explanation of this sudden metamorphosis into confused memories of Uncle Remus and the diction of the old plantations, aroused perhaps at that moment by sight of the negro, who passed by, now in friendly conversation with Pilgrim. Possibly the impersonation was merely some Dickensian old fogey. It was impossible to say with certainty. Probably the act had, in truth, no meaning at all. These sudden character parts were a recognised element in Sillery's technique of attacking life. There could be no doubt that he was delighted with the result of his recent conversation, whatever the ground covered; though he was probably correct in his suggestion that the Prince was more happily occupied at that moment with the girls than in earlier discussion of economic or diplomatic problems.

However, apart from the fact that he had presumably initiated the counter-move that had finally displaced Sillery, Prince Theodoric, as it happened, was showing little, if any, outward sign of this presumed partiality. He was gravely watching the two young women between whom he stood, as if attempting to make up his mind which of this couple had more to offer. I could not help feeling some envy at his monopoly of the companionship of such an attractive pair, each in her contrasted looks seeming to personify a style of beauty both exquisite and notably fashionable at that moment: the latter perhaps a minor, even irrelevant, consideration, but one hard to resist. I enquired the names of these friends of Prince Theodoric.

'Well-known nymphs,' said Sillery, sniggering. 'The smaller one is Mrs. Wentworth—quite a famous person in her way—sister of Jack Vowchurch. Mixed up in the divorce of Charles's sister. I seem to remember her name was also mentioned in the Derwentwater case, though not culpably. The tall and statuesque is Lady Ardglass. She was, I believe, a mannequin before her marriage.'

He began to move off, nodding, and rubbing his hands together, deriving too much pleasure from the party to waste any more valuable time from the necessarily limited period of its prolongation. I should have liked to make the acquaintance of one or both ladies, or at least to hear more of them, but I could tell from Sillery's manner that he knew neither personally, or was, at best, far from being at ease with them, so that to apply for an introduction—should they ever leave Prince Theodoric's side—would, therefore, be quite useless. Mrs. Wentworth was, outwardly, the more remarkable of the pair, on account of the conspicuous force of her personality: a characteristic accentuated by the simplicity of her dress, short curly hair, and look of infinite slyness. Lady Ardglass was more like a caryatid, or ship's figurehead, though for that reason no less superb. Seeing no immediate prospect of achieving a meeting with either, I found my way to another room, where I suddenly came upon Gypsy Jones, who appeared to have taken a good deal to drink since her arrival.

'What's happened to Edgar?' she asked clamorously.

She was more untidy than ever, and appeared to be in a great state of excitement: even near to tears.

'Who is Edgar?'

'Thought you said you'd known him since you were a kid!'

'Do you mean Mr. Deacon?'

She began to laugh uproariously at this question.

'And your other friend,' she said. 'Where did you pick that up?'

Laughter was at that moment modified by a slight, and quickly mastered, attack of hiccups. Her demeanour was becoming more noticeably hysterical. The state she was in might easily lead to an awkward incident. I was so accustomed to the general principle of people finding Widmerpool odd that I could hardly regard her question as even hypercritical. It was, in any case, no more arbitrary an enquiry, so far as it went, than Stringham's on the subject of Mr. Deacon; although long-standing friendship made Stringham's form of words more permissible. However, Gypsy Jones's comment, when thought of later, brought home the impossibility of explaining Widmerpool's personality at all briefly, even to a sympathetic audience. His case was not, of course, unique. He was merely one single instance, among many, of the fact that certain acquaintances remain firmly fixed within this or that person's particular orbit; a law which seems to lead inexorably to the conclusion that the often repeated saying that people can 'choose their friends' is true only in a most strictly limited degree.

However, Gypsy Jones was the last person to be expected to relish discussion upon so hypothetical a subject, even if the proposition had then occurred to me, or she been in a fit state to argue its points. Although she seemed to be enjoying the party, even to the extent of being in sight of hysteria, she had evidently also reached the stage when moving to another spot had become an absolute necessity to her; not because she was in any way dissatisfied with the surroundings in which she found herself, but on account of the coercive dictation of her own nerves, not to be denied in their insistence that a change of scene must take place. I was familiar with a similar spirit of unrest that sometimes haunted Barbara.

'I want to find Edgar and go to The Merry Thought.'

She clung on to me desperately, whether as an affectionate gesture, a means of encouraging sympathy, or merely to maintain her balance, I was uncertain. The condition of excitement which she had reached to some extent communicated itself to me, for her flushed face rather improved her appearance, and she had lost all her earlier ill-humour.

'Why don't you come to The Merry Thought?' she said. 'I got a bit worked up a moment ago. I'm feeling better now.'

Just for a second I wondered whether I would not fall in with this suggestion, but the implications seemed so many, and so varied, that I decided against accompanying her. I felt also that there might be yet more to experience in Mrs.

Andriadis's house; and I was not uninfluenced by the fact that I had, so far as I could remember, only a pound on me.

'Well, if Edgar can't be found, I shall go without him,' said Gypsy Jones, speaking as if such a deplorable lack of gallantry was unexpected in Mr. Deacon.

She seemed to have recovered her composure. While she proceeded down the stairs, somewhat unsteadily, I called after her, over the banisters, a reminder that her copies of *War Never Pays!* should preferably not be allowed to lie forgotten under the chair in the hall, as I had no wish to share, even to a small degree, any responsibility for having imported that publication into Mrs. Andriadis's establishment. Gypsy Jones disappeared from sight. It was doubtful whether she had heard this admonition. I felt, perhaps rather ignobly, that she were better out of the house.

Returning through one of the doorways a minute or two later, I collided with Widmerpool, also red in the face, and with hair, from which customary grease had perhaps been dried out by sugar, ruffled into a kind of cone at the top of his head. He, too, seemed to have drunk more than he was accustomed.

'Have you seen Miss Jones?' he asked, in his most breathless manner.

Even though I had been speaking with her so recently, I could not immediately grasp, under this style, the identity of the person sought.

'The girl we came in with,' he muttered impatiently.

'She has just gone off to a night-club.'

'Is someone taking her there?'

'Not that I know of.'

'Do you mean she has gone by herself?'

'That was what she said.'

Widmerpool seemed more fussed than ever. I could not understand his concern.

'I don't feel she should have set off like that alone,' he said. 'She had had rather a lot to drink—more than she is used to, I should imagine—and she is in some sort of difficulty, too. She was telling me about it.'

There could now be no doubt at all that Widmerpool himself had been equally indiscreet in taking more champagne than usual.

'We were having rather an intimate talk together,' he went on. 'And then I saw a man I had been wanting to speak to for weeks. Of course, I could have rung him up, but I preferred to wait for a chance meeting. One can often achieve so much more at such moments than at an interview. I crossed the room to have a word with him—explaining to her, as I supposed quite clearly, that I was going to return after a short business discussion—and when I came back she had vanished.'

'Too bad.'

'That was very foolish of me,' said Widmerpool, in a tone almost as if he were apologising abjectly for some grave error of taste. 'Rather bad-mannered, too. . . .'

He paused, seeming thoroughly upset: much as he had looked—I called to mind—on the day when he had witnessed Le Bas's arrest when we had been at school together. At the moment when he spoke those words, if I could have laid claim to a more discerning state of mind, I might have taken greater notice of the overwhelming change that had momentarily come over him. As it was, I attributed his excitement simply to drink: an entirely superficial view that even brief reflection could have corrected. For example—to illustrate how little excuse there was for my own lack of grasp—I had never before, so far as I can now recollect, heard Widmerpool suggest that anything he had ever done could be classed as foolish, or bad-mannered; and even then, on that evening, I suppose I ought to have been dimly aware that Gypsy Jones must have aroused his interest fairly keenly, as it were 'on the rebound' from having sugar poured over his head by Barbara.

'There really are moments when one should forget about business,' said Widmerpool. 'After all, getting on isn't everything.'

This precept, so far as I was myself concerned in those days, was one that required no specially vigorous inculcation.

'Pleasure before Business has always been my motto,' I remembered Bill Truscott stating at one of Sillery's tea-parties when I was an undergraduate; and, although it would have been misleading to suppose that, for Truscott himself, any such label was in the least—in the smallest degree—applicable, the maxim seemed to me such a truism at the moment when I heard it quoted that I could not imagine why Truscott should seem to consider the phrase, on his part, something of an epigram or paradox. Pleasure still seemed to me a natural enough aim in life; and I certainly did not, on that night in Hill Street, appreciate at all how unusually disturbed Widmerpool must have been to have uttered aloud so profane a repudiation of his own deep-rooted system of opinion. However, he was prevented from further particularising of the factors that had impelled him to this revolutionary conclusion, by the arrival beside us of the man whose practical importance had seemed sufficient to cause abandonment of emotional preoccupations. That person had, so it appeared, additional dealings to negotiate. I was interested to discover the identity of this figure who had proved, in the circumstances, so powerful a counter-attraction to the matter in hand. The disclosure was, in a quiet way, sufficiently dramatic. The 'man' turned out to be Bill Truscott himself, who seemed, through another's pursuance of his own loudly proclaimed precept, to have been, at least to some degree, temporarily victimised.

When I had last seen him, earlier in the year, at a Rothschild dance chatting with the chaperones, there could be no doubt that Truscott was still a general favourite: a 'spare man' treated by everyone with respect and in quite a different, and distinctly higher, category in the hierarchy of male guests from, say, Archie Gilbert. It was, indeed, impossible to deny Truscott's good looks, and the dignity of his wavy, youthfully grey hair and broad shoulders. All the same, the final form of his great career remained still, so far as I knew, undecided. It was not that he was showing signs of turning out less capable—certainly not less reliable—than his elders had supposed; nor, as had been evident on the night when I had seen him, was he growing any less popular with dowagers. On the contrary, many persons, if not all, continued to speak of Truscott's brilliance almost as a matter of course, and it was generally agreed that he was contriving most successfully to retain the delicate balance required to remain a promising young man who still survived in exactly the same place—and a very good place, too—that he had taken on coming down from the university; rather than preferring to make his mark as an innovator in breaking new, and possibly unfruitful, ground in forwarding ambitions that seemed, whatever they were, fated to remain long masked from friends and admirers. At least outwardly, he had neither improved nor worsened his position, so it was said, at least, by Short, who, upon such subjects, could be relied upon to take the entirely unimaginative view of the world in general. In fact, Truscott might still be expected to make name and fortune before he was thirty, though the new decade must be perilously near, and he would have to be quick about it. The promised volume of poems (or possibly *belles lettres*) had never appeared; though there were still those who firmly declared that Truscott would 'write something' one day. Meanwhile he was on excellent terms with most people, especially, for some reason, elderly bankers, both married and unmarried, with whom he was, almost without exception, a great favourite.

On that earlier occasion when I had seen him at the dance, Truscott, although he might excusably have forgotten our two or three meetings with Sillery in days past, had dispensed one of those exhausted, engaging smiles for which he was noted; while his eyes wandered round the ballroom 'ear-marking duchesses', as Stringham—years later—once called that wistful, haunted intensity that Truscott's eyes took on, from time to time, among any large concourse of people that might include individuals of either sex potentially important to an ambitious young man's career. As he came through the door at that moment, he gave his weary smile again, to show that he still remembered me, saying at the same time to Widmerpool: 'You went away so quickly that I had no time to tell you that the Chief will very likely be here tonight. He is an old friend of Milly's. Besides, I happen to know that he told Baby Wentworth he would look in—so it's a virtual certainty.'

Truscott was still, so far as I knew, one of the secretaries of Sir Magnus Donners, to whom it was to be presumed he referred as 'the Chief'. Stringham's vagueness in speaking of his own employment had left me uncertain whether or not he and Truscott remained such close colleagues as formerly, though Sillery's remarks certainly suggested that they were still working together.

'Well, of course, that would be splendid,' said Widmerpool slowly.

But, although unquestionably interested in the information just given him, he spoke rather forlornly. His mind seemed to be on other things: unable to concentrate fully on the comings and goings even of so portentous a figure as Sir Magnus Donners.

'He could meet you,' Truscott said dryly. 'And then we could talk things over next week.'

Widmerpool, trying to collect himself, seemed still uncertain in his own mind. He smoothed down his hair, the disarrangement of which he must have observed in the mural looking-glass in front of us.

'The Chief is the most unconventional man in the world,' said Truscott, more encouragingly. 'He loves informality.'

He stood there, smiling down at Widmerpool, for, although not more than an inch or two taller, he managed to give an impression of height. His thick and glossy hair had grown perceptibly more grey round the ears. I wondered how Truscott and Widmerpool had been brought together, since it was clear that arrangements projected for that night must have been the result of earlier, possibly even laborious, negotiation between them. There could be no doubt, whatever my own opinion of Widmerpool's natural endowments, that he managed to make a decidedly good impression on people primarily interested in 'getting on'. For example, neither Tompsitt nor Truscott had much in common except concentration on 'the main chance', and yet both had apparently been struck—in Tompsitt's case, almost immediately—by some inner belief in Widmerpool's fundamental ability. This matter of making headway in life was one to which I felt perhaps I, too, ought to devote greater consideration in future, if I were myself not to remain inextricably fixed in a monotonous, even sometimes dreary, groove.

'You don't think I had better ring you up in the morning?' said Widmerpool, rather anxiously. 'My brain is a bit confused tonight. I don't want to make a poor impression on Sir Magnus. To tell the truth, I was thinking of going home. I don't usually stay up as late as this.'

'All right,' said Truscott, not attempting to repress a polite smile at the idea of anyone being so weak in spirit as to limit their chances of advancement by reluctance to keep late hours. 'Perhaps that might be best. Donners-Brebner, Extension 5, any time after ten o'clock.'

'I don't expect it would be much use looking for my hostess to say good-bye,' said Widmerpool, gazing about him wildly as if by now tired out. 'You know, I haven't managed to meet her properly the whole time I have been here.'

'Not the slightest use,' said Truscott, smiling again at such naïveté.

He regarded Widmerpool as if he thought—now that a decision to retire to bed had been finally taken—that the sooner Widmerpool embarked upon a good night's rest, the better, if he were to be fit for the plans Truscott had in store for him in the near future.

'Then I'll bid you good-night,' said Widmerpool, turning to me and speaking in a voice of great exhaustion.

'Sweet dreams.'

'Tell Stringham I was sorry not to see him before I left the party.'

'I will.'

'Thank him for bringing us. It was kind. He must lunch with me in the City.'

He made his way from the room. I wondered whether or not it had indeed been kind of Stringham to bring him to the party. Kind or the reverse, I felt pretty sure that Stringham would not lunch with Widmerpool in the City. Truscott showed more surprise at Widmerpool's mention of Stringham than he usually allowed himself, at least in public.

'Does he know Charles, then?' he asked, as Widmerpool disappeared through the door.

'We were all at the same house at school.'

'Indeed?'

'Widmerpool was a shade senior.'

'He really might be quite useful in our new politico-legal branch,' said Truscott. 'Not necessarily full time—anyway at first—and the Chief always insists on hand-picking everyone himself. He'll grow out of that rather unfortunate manner, of course.'

I thought it improbable that Widmerpool would ever change his manner at the mandate of Sir Magnus Donners, Truscott, Stringham, or anyone else, though the projected employment—an aspect of those rather mysterious business activities, so different from those of my own small firm—sounded normal enough. In fact the job, as such, did not at the time make any strong impression on me. I felt more interest in trying to learn something of Stringham's life. This seemed an opportunity to make some enquiries.

'Oh, yes,' said Truscott, almost with enthusiasm. 'Of course Charles is still with us. He can really be quite an asset at times. Such charm, you know. But I see my Chief has arrived. If you will forgive me . . .'

He was gone instantaneously, stepping quickly across the floor to meet, and intercept, a tallish man, who, with Mrs. Wentworth at his side, had just entered the room. At first I was uncertain whether this outwardly unemphatic figure could indeed be Sir Magnus Donners, the person addressed by Truscott being so unlike my pre-conceived idea of what might be expected from the exterior of a public character of that particular kind. Hesitation on this point was justifiable. The name of Sir Magnus Donners, both in capacity of well-known industrialist and former member of the Government (in which he had never reached Cabinet rank) attached to the imagination, almost automatically, one of those paraphrases—on the whole uncomplimentary—presented by the cartoonist; representations that serve, more or less effectually, to supply the mind on easy terms with the supposedly salient traits, personal, social, or political, of individuals or types: such delineations being naturally concerned for the most part with men, or categories of men, to be thought of as important in exercising power in one form or another.

In the first place, it was unexpected that Sir Magnus Donners should look at least ten years younger than might reasonably have been supposed; so that, although well into his middle fifties—where he stood beneath an unsatisfying picture executed in the manner of Derain—he seemed scarcely middle-aged. Clean-shaven, good-looking rather than the reverse, possibly there was something odd, even a trifle disturbing, about the set of his mouth. Something that perhaps conveyed interior ferment kept in severe repression. Apart from that his features had been reduced, no doubt by laborious mental discipline, to a state of almost unnatural ordinariness. He possessed, however, a suggestion about him that was decidedly parsonic: a lay-reader, or clerical headmaster: even some distinguished athlete, of almost uncomfortably rigid moral convictions, of whose good work at the boys' club in some East End settlement his own close friends were quite unaware. The complexion was of a man whose life appeared to have been lived, on the whole, out of doors. He seemed, indeed, too used to the open air to be altogether at ease in evening clothes, which were carelessly worn, as if only assumed under protest, though he shared that appearance of almost chemical cleanliness characteristic, in another form, of Archie Gilbert. At the same time, in spite of these intimations of higher things, the heavy, purposeful walk implied the professional politician. A touch of sadness about his face was not unprepossessing.

That ponderous tread was also the only faint hint of the side expressed by common gossip, for example, at Sillery's—where Bill Truscott's connexion with Donners-Brebner made Sir Magnus's name a relatively familiar one in the twilight world of undergraduate conversation—that is to say, of a kind of stage 'profiteer' or 'tycoon': a man of Big Business and professionally strong will. Such, indeed, I had previously pictured him. Now the matter, like so many others, had to be reconsidered. Equally, he showed still less of that aspect called up by the remark once let fall by Stringham: 'He is always trying to get in with my mother.' Everything about Sir Magnus seemed far too quiet and correct for any of his elements even to insinuate that there could be in his conduct, or nature, anything that might urge him to push his way into a world where welcome admission might be questionable—even deliberately withheld. Indeed, much later, when I came to hear more about him, there could be no doubt that whatever efforts Sir Magnus may have made to ingratiate himself with Mrs. Foxe, through her son, or otherwise—and there was reason to suppose such efforts had in truth been made—must have been accountable to one of those whims to which men of his sort are particularly subject; that is to say, desire to cut a figure somewhere outside the circle familiar to themselves; because Sir Magnus was, after all, in a position, so far as that went, to 'go' pretty well anywhere he might happen to wish. The social process he elected to follow was rather like that of mountaineers who chose deliberately the sheer ascent of the cliff face; for it was true I found particular difficulty in associating him with Stringham, or, so far as I knew of them, with Stringham's family. Widmerpool, on the other hand, though this was by the way, was a victim easily imaginable; no doubt, as I guessed, fated to be captivated irrevocably at his pending interview by that colourless, respectable, dominating exterior of 'the Chief'.

What part Mrs. Wentworth played in Sir Magnus's life was, of course, a question that at once suggested itself. He was not married. Truscott's words: 'He told Baby Wentworth he would look in—so it's a virtual certainty', seemed to imply a fairly firm influence, or attachment, of one kind or another, probably temporary. However, as Sir Magnus and Mrs. Wentworth came through the door, side by side, there was nothing in their outward appearance to denote pleasure in each other's company. On the contrary, they had entered the room together, both of them, with an almost hang-dog air, and Mrs. Wentworth's features had lost all the gaiety and animation assumed earlier to charm Prince Theodoric. She now appeared sulky, and, if the word could be used at all of someone so self-possessed, and of such pleasing face and figure, almost awkward. It was rather as if they were walking away together from some excessively embarrassing scene in which they had been taking joint part: some incident for which the two of them felt both equally to blame, and heartily ashamed. I could not help thinking of one of those pictures—neither traditional, nor in Mr. Deacon's vernacular, but in 'modern dress' a pictorial method of treating Biblical subjects then somewhat in vogue—of Adam and Eve leaving the Garden of Eden after the Fall: this impression being so vivid that I almost expected them to be followed through the door by a well-tailored angel, pointing in their direction a flaming sword.

Any such view of them was not only entirely fanciful, but perhaps also without any foundation in fact, because Truscott seemed to regard their bearing as perfectly normal. He came up to them buoyantly, and talked for a minute or two in his accustomed easy style. Mrs. Wentworth lit a cigarette, and, without smiling, watched him, her eyebrows slightly raised. Then she spoke to Sir Magnus, at which he nodded his head heavily several times. Perhaps arrangements were being made for sending her home in his car, because he looked at his watch before saying good-night, and asked Truscott some questions. Then Mrs. Wentworth, after giving Sir Magnus little more than a nod, went off with Truscott; who returned a minute or two later, and settled down with his employer on the sofa. They began to talk gravely, looking rather like father and son, though, strangely enough, it might have been Truscott who was playing the paternal rôle.

By now the crowd had thinned considerably, and the music of the hunchback's accordion had ceased. I was beginning to feel more than a little exhausted, yet, unable to make up my mind to go home, I wandered rather aimlessly round the house, throughout which the remaining guests were now sitting about in pairs, or larger groups. Chronological sequence of events pertaining to this interlude of the party became afterwards somewhat confused in my head. I can recall a brief conversation with a woman—not pretty, though possessing excellent legs—on the subject of cheese, which she alleged to be unprocurable at the buffet. Prince Theodoric and Sillery had disappeared, and already there was the impression, given by most parties, sooner or later, that the residue still assembled under Mrs. Andriadis's roof was gradually, inexorably, sinking to a small band of those hard cases who can never tear themselves away from what still remains, for an hour or so longer, if not of gaiety, then at least some sort of mellow companionship, and protection from the austerities of the outer world.

Two young men strolled by, and I heard one of them

say: 'Poor Milly really got together quite an elegant crowd tonight.'

The other, who wore an orchid in his button-hole, replied: 'I felt that Sillery imparted a faintly bourgeois note —and there were one or two extraordinary figures from the lofts of Chelsea.'

He added that, personally, he proposed to have 'one more drink' before leaving, while the other murmured something about an invitation to 'bacon and eggs at the Kit-Cat'. They parted company at this, and when the young man with the orchid returned from the bar, he set down his glass near me, and without further introduction, began to discuss, at large, the house's style of decoration, of which he appeared strongly to disapprove.

'Of course it must have cost a fortune to have had all those carpets cut right up to the walls,' he said. 'But why go and spoil everything by these appalling Italianate fittings—and the pictures—my God, the pictures.'

I asked if the house belonged to Mrs. Andriadis.

'Good heavens, no,' he said. 'Milly has only taken it for a few months from a man named Duport.'

'Bob Duport?'

'Not an intimate friend of yours, I hope?'

'On the contrary.'

'Because his manners don't attract me.'

'Nor me.'

'Not that I ever see him these days, but we were at the same college—before he was sent down.'

I commented to the effect that, however unsatisfactory its decoration might be, I found the house an unexpectedly sumptuous place for Duport to inhabit. The young man with the orchid immediately assured me that Duport was not short of money.

'He came into quite a bit,' he said. 'And then he is one

of those men money likes. He is in the Balkans at the moment—doing well there, too, I have no doubt. He is, I regret to say, that sort of man.'

He sighed.

'Is he married?'

'Rather a nice wife.'

Although I scarcely knew Bob Duport, he had always remained in my mind on account of his having been one of the company when Peter Templer, in a recently purchased car, had driven Stringham and myself into the ditch, together with a couple of shop-girls and another unprepossessing friend of Templer's called Brent. That episode had been during the single term that Stringham had remained in residence at the university. The incident seemed absurd enough when looked back upon, but I had not greatly liked Duport. Now I felt, for some reason, inexplicably annoyed that he should own a house like this one, however ineptly decorated, and also be the possessor of a wife whom my informant—whose manner suggested absolute infallibility on such matters—regarded as attractive; while I myself, at the same time, lived a comparative hand-to-mouth existence in rooms, and was no longer in love with Barbara—a girl to whom, in my own case, there had never been any serious prospect of getting married. This seemed, on examination, a contrast from which I came out rather poorly.

Since living in London, I had seen Peter Templer several times, but, in the course of an interminable chain of anecdotes about his ever-changing circle of cronies, I could not remember the name of Duport figuring, so that I did not know whether or not the two of them continued to see each other. Peter himself had taken to the City like a duck to water. He now talked unendingly of 'cleaning up a packet' and 'making a killing'; money, with its multifarious imagery and restrictive mystique, holding a place in his mind only seriously rivalled by preoccupation with the pursuit of women: the latter interest having proportionately increased with opportunity to experiment in a wider field than formerly.

When we had lunched or dined together, the occasions had been enjoyable, although there had hardly been any renewal of the friendship that had existed between us at school. Peter did not frequent the world of dances because —like Stringham—he was bored by their unduly respectable environment.

'At least,' he said once, when discussing the matter, 'I don't go as a habit to the sort of dance you see reported in *The Morning Post* or *The Times*. I don't say I have never attended similar entertainments in some huge and gloomy house in Bayswater or Holland Park—probably Jewish—if I happened to take a fancy to a girl who moves in those circles. There is more fun to be found amongst all that mahogany furniture and Moorish brasswork than you might think.'

In business, at least in a small way, he had begun to 'make a bit' on his own, and there seemed no reason to disbelieve his account of himself as looked upon in his firm as a promising young man. In fact, it appeared that Peter, so far from becoming the outcast from society prophesied by our housemaster, Le Bas, now showed every sign of being about to prove himself a notable success in life: an outcome that seemed to demand another of those revisions of opinion, made every day more necessary, in relation to such an enormous amount of material, accepted as incontrovertible at an earlier period of practical experience.

Thinking that if the young man with the orchid knew Duport, he might also know Peter, whom I had not by then seen for about a year, I asked if the two of them had ever met.

'I've never run across Templer,' he said. 'But I've heard tell of him. As a matter of fact, I believe Duport married Templer's sister, didn't he? What was her name?'

'Jean.'

'That was it. A thin girl with blue eyes. I think they got married abroad—South America or somewhere, was it?'

The sudden awareness of displeasure felt a second earlier at the apparent prosperity of Duport's general state was nothing to the pang I suffered on hearing this piece of news: the former sense of grievance caused, perhaps, by premonition that worse was to come. I had not, it was true, thought much of Jean Templer for years, having relegated any question of being, as I had once supposed, 'in love' with her to a comparatively humble position in memory; indeed, regarding the incident as dating from a time when any such feelings were, in my own eyes, hopelessly immature, in comparison, for example, with sentiments felt for Barbara. However, I now found, rather to my own surprise, deep vexation in the discovery that Jean was the wife of someone so unsympathetic as Bob Duport.

Such emotions, sudden bursts of sexual jealousy that pursue us through life, sometimes without the smallest justification that memory or affection might provide, are like wounds, unknown and quiescent, that suddenly break out to give pain, or at least irritation, at a later season of the year, or in an unfamiliar climate. The party, and the young man with the orchid, supplied perfect setting for an attack of that kind. I was about to return to the subject of Duport, with a view to relieving this sense of annoyance by further unfavourable comment regarding his personality (as it had appeared to me in the past) in the hope that my views would find ready agreement, when I became suddenly aware that Stringham and Mrs. Andriadis were together engaged in vehement argument just beside the place we sat.

'But, sweetie,' Mrs. Andriadis was saying, 'you can't possibly want to go to the Embassy *now*.'

'But the odd thing is,' said Stringham, speaking slowly and deliberately, 'the odd thing is that is just what I do want to do. I want to go to the Embassy *at once*. Without further delay.'

'But it will be closed.'

'I am rather glad to hear that. I never really liked the Embassy. I shall go somewhere else.'

'But you said it was just the Embassy you wanted to go to.'

'I can't think why. I really want to go somewhere quite different.'

'You really are being too boring for words, Charles.'

'I quite agree,' said Stringham, suddenly changing his tone. 'The fact is I am much too boring to stay at a party. That is exactly how I feel myself. Especially one of your parties, Milly—one of your charming, gay, exquisite, unrivalled parties. I cast a gloom over the merry scene. "Who is that corpse at the feast?" people ask, and the reply is "Poor old Stringham".'

'But you wouldn't feel any better at the Embassy, darling, even if it were open.'

'You are probably right. In fact, I should certainly feel no better at the Embassy. I should feel worse. That is why I am going somewhere much lower than that. Somewhere really frightful.'

'You are being very silly.'

'The Forty-Three would be too stuffy—in all senses—for my present mood.'

'You can't want to go to the Forty-Three.'

'I repeat that I do not want to go to the Forty-Three. I am at the moment looking into my soul to examine the interesting question of where exactly I do want to go.'

'Wherever it is, I shall come too.'

'As you wish, Milly. As you wish. As a matter of fact I was turning over the possibilities of a visit to Mrs. Fitz.'

'Charles, you are impossible.'

I suppose he had had a good deal to drink, though this was, in a way, beside the point, for I knew from past experience that he could be just as perverse in his behaviour when there had been no question of drinking. If he were a little drunk, apart from making a slight bow, he showed no physical sign of such a condition. Mrs. Andriadis, who was evidently determined to master the situation—and who still, in her own particular style, managed to remain rather dazzling, in spite of being obviously put out by this altercation—turned to one of the men-servants who happened to be passing at that moment, carrying a tray laden with glasses, and said: 'Go and get my coat—and be quick about it.'

The man, an old fellow with a blotched face, who had perhaps taken the opportunity to sample the champagne himself more freely than had been wise, stared at her, and, setting down the tray, ambled slowly off. Stringham caught sight of us sitting near-by. He took a step towards me.

'At least I can rely on you, Nick, as an old friend,' he said, 'to accompany me to a haunt of vice. Somewhere where the stains on the table-cloth make the flesh creep—some cellar far below the level of the street, where ageing harlots caper cheerlessly to the discordant strains of jazz.'

Mrs. Andriadis grasped at once that we had known each other for a long time, because she smiled with one of those looks of captivating and whole-hearted sincerity that must have contributed in no small degree to her adventurous career. I was conscious that heavy artillery was now ranged upon my position. At the same time she managed to present herself—as it were, stood before me—in her weakness, threatened by Stringham's behaviour certainly aggravating enough, remarking softly: 'Do tell him not to be such an ass.'

Stringham, too, perfectly took in the situation, evidently deciding immediately, and probably correctly, that if any kind of discussion were allowed to develop between the three of us, Mrs. Andriadis would, in some manner, bring him to heel. There had been, presumably, some collision of wills between them in the course of the evening; probably the consequence of mutual irritation extending over weeks, or even months. Perhaps he had deliberately intended to provoke a quarrel when he had arrived at the house that evening. The situation had rather the appearance of something of the sort. It was equally possible that he was suffering merely from the same kind of restlessness that had earlier afflicted Gypsy Jones. I did not know. In any case, though no business of mine, a break between them might be for the best. However, no time remained to weigh such question in the balance, because Stringham did not wait. He laughed loudly, and went off through the door. Mrs. Andriadis took my arm.

'Will you persuade him to stay!' she said, with that trace of Cockney which—as Barnby would have remarked—had once 'come near to breaking a royal heart.'

At that moment the young man with the orchid, who had risen with dignity from the sofa where he had been silently contemplating the world, came towards us, breaking into the conversation with the words: 'My dear Milly, I simply must tell you the story about Theodoric and the Prince of Wales . . .'

'Another time, darling.'

Mrs. Andriadis gave him a slight push with her left hand, so that he collapsed quietly, and apparently quite happily, into an easy-chair. Almost simultaneously an enormous, purple-faced man with a decided air of authority about him, whose features were for some reason familiar to me, accompanied by a small woman, much younger than himself, came up, mumbling and faintly swaying, as he attempted to thank Mrs. Andriadis for entertaining them. She brushed him aside, clearly to his immense, rather intoxicated surprise, with the same ruthlessness she had shown to the young man with the orchid: at the same time saying to another servant, whom I took, this time, to be her own butler: 'I told one of those bloody hired men to fetch my coat. Go and see where he's got to.'

All these minor incidents inevitably caused delay, giving Stringham a start on the journey down the stairs, towards which we now set off, Mrs. Andriadis still grasping my arm, along which, from second to second, she convulsively altered the grip of her hand. As we reached the foot of the last flight together, the front door slammed. Three or four people were chatting, or putting on wraps, in the hall, in preparation to leave. The elderly lady with the black eyebrows and tiara was sitting on one of the crimson and gold high-backed chairs, beneath which I could see a pile of *War Never Pays!*: Mr. Deacon's, or those forgotten by Gypsy Jones. She had removed her right shoe and was examining the heel intently, to observe if it were still intact. Mrs. Andriadis let go my arm, and ran swiftly towards the door, which she wrenched open violently, just in time to see a taxi drive away from the front of the house. She made use of an expletive that I had never before—in those distant days—heard a woman employ. The phrase left no doubt in the mind that she was extremely provoked. The door swung on its hinge. In silence Mrs. Andriadis watched it shut with a bang. It was hard to know what comment, if any, was required. At that moment the butler arrived with her coat.

'Will you wear it, madam?'

'Take the damned thing away,' she said. 'Are you and the rest of them a lot of bloody cripples? Do I have to wait half an hour every time I want to go out just because I haven't a rag to put round me?'

The butler, accustomed no doubt to such reproaches as all in the day's work—and possibly remunerated on a scale to allow a generous margin for hard words—seemed entirely undisturbed by these strictures on his own agility, and that of his fellows. He agreed at once that his temporary colleague 'did not appear to have his wits about him at all'. In the second's pause during which Mrs. Andriadis seemed to consider this statement, I prepared to say good-bye, partly from conviction that the occasion for doing so, once missed, might not easily recur; even more, because immediate farewell would be a convenient method of bringing to an end the distressing period of tension that had come into existence ever since Stringham's departure, while Mrs. Andriadis contemplated her next move. However, before there was time, on my own part, to take any step in the direction of leave-taking, a loud noise from the stairs behind distracted my attention. Mrs. Andriadis, too, was brought by this sudden disturbance out of the state of suspended animation into which she appeared momentarily to have fallen.

The cause of the commotion now became manifest. Mr. Deacon and the singer, Max Pilgrim, followed by the negro, were descending the stairs rapidly, side by side, jerking down from step to step in the tumult of a frantic quarrel. At first I supposed, improbable as such a thing would be, that some kind of practical joke or 'rag' was taking place in which all three were engaged; but looking closer, it became plain that Mr. Deacon was angry with Pilgrim, while the negro was more or less a spectator, not greatly involved except by his obvious enjoyment of the row. The loose lock of Mr. Deacon's hair had once more fallen across his forehead: his voice had taken on a deep and mordant note. Pilgrim was red in the face and sweating, though keeping his temper with difficulty, and attempting to steer the dispute, whatever its subject, into channels more facetious than polemical.

'There are always leering eyes on the look-out,' Mr. Deacon was saying. 'Besides, your song puts a weapon in the hands of the puritans.'

'I don't expect there were many puritans present——' began Pilgrim.

Mr. Deacon cut him short.

'It is a matter of *principle,*' he said. 'If you have any.'

'What do you know about my principles?' said Pilgrim. 'I don't expect your own principles bear much examination when the lights are out.'

'I can give you an assurance that *you* have no cause to worry about *my* principles,' Mr. Deacon almost screamed. 'Such a situation could never arise—I can assure you of that. This is not the first time, to my knowledge, that you have presumed on such a thing.'

This comment seemed to annoy Pilgrim a great deal, so that he now became scarcely less enraged than Mr. Deacon himself. His quavering voice rose in protest, while Mr. Deacon's sank to a scathing growl: the most offensive tone I have ever heard him employ.

'You person,' he said.

Turning fiercely away from Pilgrim, he strode across the hall in the direction of the chair under which he had stored away *War Never Pays!* Together with his own copies, he gathered up those brought by Gypsy Jones—forgotten by her, as I had foreseen—and, tucking a sheaf under each arm, he made towards the front door. He ignored the figure of Mrs. Andriadis, of whose presence he was no doubt, in his rage, entirely unaware. The catch of the door must have jammed, for that, or some other cause, prevented the hinge from opening freely. Mr. Deacon's first intention was evidently to hold all the papers, his own and those belonging to Gypsy Jones, under his left arm for the brief second during which he opened the door with his right hand to sweep for ever from the obnoxious presence of Max Pilgrim. However, the two combined packets of *War Never Pays!* made quite a considerable bundle, and he must have found himself compelled to bring his left hand also into play, while he hugged most of the copies of the publication—by then rather crumpled—by pressure from his left elbow against his side. The door swung open suddenly. Mr. Deacon was taken by surprise. All at once there was a sound as of the rending of silk, and the papers, like a waterfall—or sugar on Widmerpool's head—began to tumble, one after another, to the ground from under Mr. Deacon's arm. He made a violent effort to check their descent, contriving only to increase the area over which they were freely shed; an unexpected current of air blowing through the open door at that moment into the house helped to scatter sheets of *War Never Pays!* far and wide throughout the hall, even up to the threshold of the room beyond. There was a loud, stagey laugh from the stairs in the background. 'Ha! Ha! Ha!'

It was the negro. He was grinning from ear to ear, now more like a nigger minstrel—a coon with bones and tambourine from some old-fashioned show on the pier at a seaside resort of the Victorian era—than his former dignified, well-groomed self. The sound of his wild, African laughter must have caused Mrs. Andriadis to emerge unequivocally from her coma. She turned on Mr. Deacon.

'You awful old creature,' she said, 'get out of my house.'

He stared at her, and then burst into a fearful fit of coughing, clutching at his chest. My hat stood on a table not far away. While Mrs. Andriadis was still turned from me, I took it up without further delay, and passed through the open door. Mr. Deacon had proved himself a graver responsibility than I, for one, by then felt myself prepared to sustain. They could, all of them, arrange matters between themselves without my help. It would, indeed, be better so. Whatever solution was, in fact, found to terminate the complexities of that moment, Mr. Deacon's immediate expulsion from the house at the command of Mrs. Andriadis was not one of them; because, when I looked back—after proceeding nearly a hundred yards up the road—there was still no sign of his egress, violent or otherwise, from the house.

It was already quite light in the street, and although the air was fresh, almost breezy, after the atmosphere of the party, there was a hint, even at this early hour, of another sultry day on the way. Narrow streaks of blue were already beginning to appear across the flat surface of a livid sky. The dawn had a kind of heaviness, perhaps of thundery weather in the offing. No one was about, though the hum of an occasional car driving up Park Lane from time to time broke the silence for a few seconds, the sound, mournful as the huntsman's horn echoing in the forest, dying away quickly in the distance. Early morning bears with it a sense of pressure, a kind of threat of what the day will bring forth. I felt unsettled and dissatisfied, though not in the least drunk. On the contrary, my brain seemed to be working all at once with quite unusual clarity. Indeed,

I found myself almost deciding to sit down, as soon as I reached my room, and attempt to compose a series of essays on human life and character in the manner of, say, Montaigne, so icily etched in my mind at that moment appeared the actions and nature of those with whom that night I had been spending my time. However, second thoughts convinced me that any such efforts at composition would be inadvisable at such an hour. The first thing to do on reaching home would be to try and achieve some sleep. In the morning, literary matters might be reconsidered. I was conscious of having travelled a long way since the Walpole-Wilsons' dinner-party. I was, in fact, very tired.

Attempting to sort out and classify the events of the night, as I walked home between the grey Mayfair houses, I found myself unable to enjoy in retrospect the pleasure reasonably to be expected from the sense of having broken fresh ground. Mrs. Andriadis's party had certainly been something new. Its strangeness and fascination had not escaped me. But there appeared now, so far as I could foresee, no prospect of setting foot again within those unaccustomed regions; even temporary connexion with them, tenuously supplied by Stringham in his latest avatar, seeming uncompromisingly removed by the drift of circumstance.

Apart from these reflections, I was also painfully aware that I had, so it appeared to me, prodigally wasted my time at the party. Instead, for example, of finding a girl to take the place of Barbara—she, at least had been finally swept away by Mrs. Andriadis—I had squandered the hours of opportunity with Mr. Deacon, or with Sillery. I thought suddenly of Sunny Farebrother, and the pleasure he had described himself as deriving from meeting 'interesting people' in the course of his work at the Peace Conference. No such 'interesting' contacts, so far as I myself had been concerned that evening, could possibly have been said to have taken place. For a moment I regretted having refused Gypsy Jones's invitation to accompany her to The Merry Thought. From the point of view of either sentiment or snobbery, giving both terms their widest connotation, the night had been an empty one. I had, so it appeared, merely stayed up until the small hours—no doubt relatively incapacitating myself for serious work on the day following—with nothing better to show for it than the certainty, now absolute, that I was no longer in love with Barbara Goring; though this emancipation would include, of course, relief also from such minor irritations as Tompsitt and his fellows. I remembered now, all at once, Widmerpool's apprehensions at what had seemed to him the 'unserious' nature of my employment.

As I reached the outskirts of Shepherd Market, at that period scarcely touched by rebuilding, I regained once more some small sense of exultation, enjoyed whenever crossing the perimeter of that sinister little village, that I lived within an enchanted precinct. Inconvenient, at moments, as a locality: noisy and uncomfortable: stuffy, depressing, unsavoury: yet the ancient houses still retained some vestige of the dignity of another age; while the inhabitants, many of them existing precariously on their bridge earnings, or hire of their bodies, were—as more than one novelist had, even in those days, already remarked—not without their own seedy glory.

Now, touched almost mystically, like another Stonehenge, by the first rays of the morning sun, the spot seemed one of those clusters of tumble-down dwellings depicted by Canaletto or Piranesi, habitations from amongst which arches, obelisks and viaducts, ruined and overgrown with ivy, arise from the mean houses huddled together below them. Here, too, such massive structures might, one felt, at any moment come into existence by some latent sorcery, for the place was scarcely of this world, and anything was to be surmised. As I penetrated farther into the heart of that rookery, in the direction of my own door, there even stood, as if waiting to greet a friend, one of those indeterminate figures that occur so frequently in the pictures of the kind suggested—Hubert Robert or Pannini—in which the architectural subject predominates. This materialisation took clearer shape as a man, middle-aged to elderly, wearing a bowler hat and discreetly horsy overcoat, the collar turned-up round a claret-coloured scarf with white spots. He leant a little to one side on a rolled umbrella, just as those single figures in romantic landscape are apt to pose; as if the painter, in dealing with so much static matter, were determined to emphasise 'movement' in the almost infinitesimal human side of his composition.

'Where are you off to?' this person suddenly called across the street.

The voice, grating on the morning air, was somewhat accusing in tone. I saw, as a kind of instantaneous revelation, that it was Uncle Giles who stood on the corner in front of the public-house. He seemed undecided which road to take. It was plain that, a minute or two earlier, he had emerged from one of the three main centres of nocturnal activity in the immediate neighbourhood, represented by the garage, the sandwich bar, and the block of flats of dubious repute. There was not a shred of evidence pointing to one of these starting points in preference to another, though other alternatives seemed excluded by his position. I crossed the road.

'Just up from the country,' he said, gruffly.

'By car?'

'By car? Yes, of course.'

'Is it a new one?'

'Yes,' said Uncle Giles. 'It's a new one.'

He spoke as if he had only just thought of that aspect of the vehicle, supposedly his property, that was stated to have brought him to London. One of those pauses followed for which my uncle's conversation was noted within the family circle. I explained that I was returning from a dance, a half-truth that seemed to cover whatever information was required, then and there, to define my circumstances in as compact and easily intelligible a form as possible. Uncle Giles was not practised in following any narrative at all involved in its nature. His mind was inclined to stray back to his own affairs if a story's duration was of anything but the briefest. My words proved redundant, however. He was not in the least interested.

'I am here on business,' he said. 'I don't want to waste a lot of time. Never was keen on remaining too long in London. Your hand is never out of your pocket.'

'Where are you staying?'

My uncle thought for a moment.

'Bayswater,' he said, slowly and rather thoughtfully.

I must have looked surprised at finding him so comparatively far afield from his *pied-à-terre,* because Uncle Giles added:

'I mean, of course, that Bayswater is where I am going to stay—at the Ufford, as usual. There is a lot to be said for a place where they know you. Get some civility. At the moment I am on my way to my club, only round the corner.'

'My rooms are just by here.'

'Where?' he asked, suspiciously.

'Opposite.'

'Can't you find anywhere better to live—I mean it's rather a disreputable part of the world, isn't it?'

As if in confirmation of my uncle's misgivings, a prostitute, small, almost a dwarf, with a stumpy umbrella tucked under her arm, came hurrying home, late off her beat—tap-tap-tap-tap-tap-tap-tap-tap—along the pavement, her extravagant heels making a noise like a woodpecker attacking a tree. She wore a kind of felt helmet pulled low over her face, which looked exceedingly bad-tempered. Some instinct must have told her that neither my uncle nor I were to be regarded in the circumstances as potential clients; for altering her expression no more than to bare a fang at the side of her mouth like an angry animal, she sped along the street at a furious pace—tap-tap-tap-tap-tap-tap—and up the steps of the entrance to the flats, when she disappeared from sight. Uncle Giles averted his eyes. He still showed no sign of wishing to move from the spot, almost as if he feared even the smallest change of posture might in some unforeseen manner prejudice the veil of secrecy that so utterly cloaked his immediate point of departure.

'I have been with friends in Surrey,' he said grudgingly, as if the admission were unwillingly drawn from him. 'It's a favourite county of mine. Lovely in the autumn. I'm connected with the paper business now.'

I hoped sincerely that this connexion took, as was probable, remote and esoteric form, and that he was not associated with some normal branch of the industry with which my own firm might be expected to open an account. However, he showed no desire to pursue this matter of his new employment. Instead, he produced from his overcoat pocket a handful of documents, looking like company reports, and glanced swiftly through them. I thought he was going to begin discussing the Trust—by now the Trust remained practically the only unsevered link between himself and his relations—in spite of the earliness of the hour. If his original idea had been to make the Trust subject of comment, he must have changed his mind, finding these memoranda, if such they were, in some way wanting, because he replaced the papers carefully in order and stuffed them back into his coat.

'Tell your father to try and get some San Pedro Warehouses Deferred,' he said, shortly. 'I have had reliable advice about them.'

'I'll say you said so.'

'Do you always stay up as late as this?'

'No—it was a specially good party.'

I could see from my uncle's face that not only did he not accept this as an excuse, but that he had also chosen to consider the words as intended deliberately to disconcert him.

'Take a bit of advice from one who has knocked about the world for a good many years,' he said. 'Don't get in the habit of sitting up till all hours. It never did anyone any good.'

'I'll bear it in mind.'

'Parents well?'

'Very well.'

'I've been having trouble with my teeth.'

'I'm sorry.'

'Well, I must be off. Good-bye to you.'

He made a stiff gesture, rather as if motioning someone away from him, and moved off suddenly in the direction of Hertford Street, striding along very serious, with his umbrella shouldered, as if once more at the head of his troops, drums beating and colour flying, as the column, conceded all honours of war, marched out of the capitulated town. Just as I opened the door of my house, he turned to wave. I raised my hand in return. Within, the bedroom remained unaltered, just as it had appeared when I had set out for the Walpole-Wilsons', the suit I had worn the day before hanging dejectedly over the back of a chair. While I undressed I reflected on the difficulty of believing in the existence of certain human beings, my uncle among them, even in the face of unquestionable evidence—indications sometimes even wanting in the case of persons for some reason more substantial to the mind—that each had dreams and desires like other men. Was it possible to take Uncle Giles seriously? And yet he was, no doubt, serious enough to himself. If a clue to that problem could be found, other mysteries of life might be revealed. I was still pondering Uncle Giles and his ways when I dropped into an uneasy sleep.

3.

I USED to imagine life divided into separate compartments, consisting, for example, of such dual abstractions as pleasure and pain, love and hate, friendship and enmity; and more material classifications like work and play: a profession or calling being, according to that concept—one that seemed, at least on the surface, unequivocally assumed by persons so dissimilar from one another as Widmerpool and Archie Gilbert, something entirely different from 'spare time'. That illusion, as such a point of view was, in due course, to appear—was closely related to another belief: that existence fans out indefinitely into new areas of experience, and that almost every additional acquaintance offers some supplementary world with its own hazards and enchantments. As time goes on, of course, these supposedly different worlds, in fact, draw closer, if not to each other, then to some pattern common to all; so that, at last, diversity between them, if in truth existent, seems to be almost imperceptible except in a few crude and exterior ways: unthinkable, as formerly appeared, any single consummation of cause and effect. In other words, nearly all the inhabitants of these outwardly disconnected empires turn out at last to be tenaciously inter-related; love and hate, friendship and enmity, too, becoming themselves much less clearly defined, more often than not showing signs of possessing characteristics that could claim, to say the least, not a little in common; while work and play merge indistinguishably into a complex tissue of pleasure and tedium.

All the same, although still far from appreciating many of the finer points of Mrs. Andriadis's party—for there were, of course, finer points to be appreciated in retrospect—and, on the whole, no less ignorant of what the elements there present had consisted, I was at the same time more than half aware that such latitudes are entered by a door through which there is, in a sense, no return. The lack of ceremony that had attended our arrival, and the fact of being so much in the dark as to the terms upon which the party was being given, had been both, in themselves, a trifle embarrassing; but, looking back on the occasion, armed with later knowledge of individual affiliations among the guests, there is no reason to suppose that mere awareness of everyone's identity would have been calculated to promote any greater feeling of ease: if anything, rather the reverse. The impact of entertainments given by people like Mrs. Andriadis, as I learnt in due course, depends upon rapidly changing personal relationships; so that to be apprised suddenly of the almost infinite complication of such associations—if any such omniscience could, by some magical means, have been imparted—without being oneself, even at a distance, at all involved, might have been a positive handicap, perhaps a humiliating one, to enjoyment.

To begin with, there was the unanswered question of Stringham's entanglement with Mrs. Andriadis herself. I did not know how long in duration of time the affair had already extended, nor how seriously it was to be regarded. Their connexion, on his part at least, seemed no more than a whim: a fancy for an older woman, of which, for example, in a Latin country nothing whatever would be thought. On the other hand, Mrs. Andriadis herself evidently accepted the fact that, so far as things went, she was fairly deeply concerned. I thought of the casual adventure with the woman in Nairobi that he had described to me, and of the days when he and Peter Templer had been accustomed to discuss 'girls' together at school.

I could now recognise in Stringham's attitude a kind of reticence, never apparent at the time when such talks had taken place. This reticence, when I thought it over, was not in what Stringham said, or did not say, so much as in what, I suppose, he felt; and, when he used to sweep aside objections raised by myself to Templer's often cavalier treatment of the subject, I saw—at this later date—his attitude was assumed to conceal a lack of confidence at least comparable with my own. I did not, of course, come to these conclusions immediately. They were largely the result of similar talks pursued later over a long period with Barnby, of whom Mr. Deacon, congenitally unappreciative in that sphere, used to say: 'I can stand almost anything from Barnby except his untidiness and generalisations about women.' However, personally I used to enjoy Barnby's pronouncements on the subject of feminine psychology, and, when I came to know him well, we used to have endless discussions on that matter.

This—as Barnby himself liked to think—almost scientific approach to the subject of 'women' was in complete contrast to Peter Templer's, and, I think, to Stringham's too, both of whom were incurious regarding questions of theory. Templer, certainly, would have viewed these relatively objective investigations as fearful waste of time. In a different context, this antithesis of approach could be illustrated by quoting a remark of Stringham's made a dozen or more years later, when we met during the war. 'You know, Nick,' he said, 'I used to think all that was necessary to fire a rifle was to get your eye, sights, and target in line, and press the trigger. Now I find the Army have written a whole book about it.' Both he and Templer would have felt a similar superfluity attached to these digressions with Barnby, with whom, as it happened, my first words exchanged led, as if logically, to a preliminary examination of the subject: to be followed, I must admit, by a lifetime of debate on the same theme.

The circumstances of our initial encounter to some extent explain this early emphasis. It had been the end of August, or beginning of September, in days when that desolate season of late summer had fallen like a pall on excavated streets, over which the fumes of tar hung heavy in used-up air, echoing to the sound of electric drills. After two or three weeks away from London, there was nothing to be enjoyed in anticipation except an invitation to spend a week-end at Hinton with the Walpole-Wilsons: a visit arranged months ahead, and still comparatively distant, so it seemed, in point of time. Every soul appeared to be away. A sense of isolation, at least when out of the office, had become oppressive, and I began to feel myself a kind of hermit, threading his way eternally through deserted and sultry streets, never again to know a friend. It was in this state of mind that I found myself wondering whether some alleviation of solitude could be provided by 'looking up' Mr. Deacon, as he had suggested at the coffee-stall; although it had to be admitted that I felt no particular desire to see him after the closing scenes of the party, when his behaviour had struck me as intolerable. However, there appeared to exist no other single acquaintance remaining within a familiar orbit, and the Walpole-Wilson week-end still seemed lost in the future. As a consequence of prolonged, indeed wholly disproportionate, speculation on the matter, I set out one afternoon, after work, for the address Mr. Deacon had scrawled on an envelope.

Charlotte Street, as it stretches northward towards Fitzroy Square, retains a certain unprincipled integrity of character, though its tributaries reach out to the east, where, in Tottenham Court Road, structural anomalies pass all bounds of reason, and west, into a nondescript ocean of bricks and mortar from which hospitals, tenements and warehouses gloomily manifest themselves in shapeless bulk above mean shops. Mr. Deacon's 'place' was situated in a narrow by-street in this westerly direction: an alley-way, not easy to find, of modest eighteenth-century—perhaps even late seventeenth-century—houses, of a kind still to be seen in London, though growing rarer, the fronts of some turned to commercial purposes, others bearing the brass plate of dentist or midwife. Here and there a dusty creeper trailed from window to window. Those that remained private dwellings had three or four bells, one above the other, set beside the door at a height from the ground effectively removed from children's runaway rings. Mr. Deacon's premises stood between a French polisher's and the offices of the Vox Populi Press. It was a sordid spot, though one from which a certain implication of expectancy was to be derived. Indeed, the façade was not unlike that row of shops that form a backcloth for the harlequinade; and, as I approached the window, I was almost prepared for Mr. Deacon, with mask and spangles and magic wand, suddenly to pirouette along the pavement, tapping, with disastrous consequence, all the passers-by.

However, the shop was shut. Through the plate glass, obscured in watery depths, dark green like the interior of an aquarium's compartments, Victorian work-tables, *papier-mâché* trays, Staffordshire figures, and a varnished scrap screen—upon the sombrely coloured *montage* of which could faintly be discerned shiny versions of *Bubbles* and *For He Had Spoken Lightly Of A Woman's Name*—swam gently into further aqueous recesses that eddied back into yet more remote alcoves of the double room: additional subterranean grottoes, hidden from view, in which, like a grubby naiad, Gypsy Jones, as described so vividly by Mr. Deacon, was accustomed, from time to time, to sleep, or at least to recline, beneath the monotonous, conventionalised arabesques of rare, if dilapidated, Oriental draperies. For some reason, the thought roused a faint sense of desire. The exoticism of the place as a bedroom was undeniable. I had to ring the bell of the side door twice before anyone answered the summons. Then, after a long pause, the door was half opened by a young man in shirt-sleeves, carrying a dustpan and brush.

'Yes?' he asked abruptly.

My first estimate of Barnby, whom I immediately guessed this to be, the *raisonneur* so often quoted at the party by Mr. Deacon as inhabiting the top floor of the house, was not wholly favourable; nor, as I learnt later, was his own assessment of myself. He looked about twenty-six or twenty-seven, dark, thick-set, and rather puffed under the eyes. There was the impression of someone who knew how to look after his own interests, though in a balanced and leisurely manner. I explained that I had come to see Mr. Deacon.

'Have you an appointment?'

'No.'

'Business?'

'No.'

'Mr. Deacon is not here.'

'Where is he?'

'Cornwall.'

'For long?'

'No idea.'

This allegedly absolute ignorance of the duration of a landlord's retirement to the country seemed scarcely credible in a tenant whose life, at least as presented in Mr. Deacon's anecdotes, was lived at such close range to the other members of the household. However, the question, put in a somewhat different form, achieved no greater success. Barnby stared hard, and without much friendliness. I saw that I should get no further with him at this rate, and requested that he would inform Mr. Deacon, on his return, of my call.

'What name?'

'Jenkins.'

At this, Barnby became on the spot more accommodating. He opened the door wider and came out on to the step.

'Didn't you take Edgar to Milly Andriadis's party?' he asked, in a different tone.

'In a manner of speaking.'

'He was in an awful state the next day,' Barnby said. 'Worried, too, about losing so many copies of that rag he hawks round. I believe he had to pay for them out of his own pocket. Anyway, Edgar is too old for that kind of thing.'

He spoke this last comment sadly, though without implication of disapproval. I mentioned the unusual circumstances that had brought Mr. Deacon and myself to the party. Barnby listened in a somewhat absent manner, and then made two or three enquiries regarding the names of other guests. He seemed, in fact, more interested in finding out who had attended the party than in hearing a more specific account of how Mr. Deacon had received his invitation, or had behaved while he was there.

'Did you run across a Mrs. Wentworth?' he asked. 'Rather a handsome girl.'

'She was pointed out to me. We didn't meet.'

'Was she with Donners?'

'Later in the evening. She was talking to a Balkan royalty when I first saw her.'

'Theodoric?'

'Yes.'

'Had Theodoric collected anyone else?'

'Lady Ardglass.'

'I thought as much,' said Barnby. 'I wish I'd managed to get there. I've met Mrs. Andriadis—but I can't say I really know her.'

He nodded gravely, more to himself than in further comment to me, seeming to admit by this movement the justice of his own absence from the party. For a moment or two there was silence between us. Then he said: 'Why not come in for a minute? You know, all sorts of people ask for Edgar. He likes some blackmailers admitted, but by no means all of them. One has to be careful.'

I explained that I had not come to blackmail Mr. Deacon.

'Oh, I guessed that almost at once,' said Barnby. 'But I was doing a bit of cleaning when you rang—the studio gets filthy—and the dust must have confused my powers of differentiation.'

All this was evidently intended as some apology for earlier gruffness. As I followed up a narrow staircase, I assured him that I had no difficulty in grasping that caution might be prudent where Mr. Deacon's friends were concerned. In answer to this Barnby expressed himself very plainly regarding the majority of Mr. Deacon's circle of acquaintance. By this time we had reached the top of the house, and entered a fairly large, bare room, with a north light, used as a studio. Barnby pointed to a rickety armchair, and throwing dustpan and brush in the corner by the stove, sat down on a kind of divan that stood against one wall.

'You've known Edgar for a long time?'

'Since I was a child. But the other night was the first time I ever heard him called that.'

'He doesn't let everyone use the name,' said Barnby. 'In fact, he likes to keep it as quiet as he can. As it happens, my father was at the Slade with him.'

'He has given up painting, hasn't he?'

'Entirely.'

'Is that just as well?'

'Some people hold that as a bad painter Edgar carries all before him,' said Barnby. 'I know good judges who think there is literally no worse one. I can't say I care for his work myself—but I'm told Sickert once found a good word to say for some of them, so there may have been something there once.'

'Is he making a success of the antique business?'

'He says people are very kind. He marks the prices up a bit. Still, there always seems someone ready to pay—and I know he is glad to be back in London.'

'But I thought he liked Paris so much.'

'Only for a holiday, I think. He had to retire there for a number of years. There was a bit of trouble in the park, you know.'

This hint of a former contretemps explained many things about Mr. Deacon's demeanour. For example, the reason for his evasive manner in the Louvre was now made plain; and I recalled Sillery's words at Mrs. Andriadis's party. They provided an illustration of the scope and nature of Sillery's stock of gossip. Mr. Deacon's decided air of having 'gone downhill' was now also to be understood. I began to review his circumstances against a more positive perspective.

'What about *War Never Pays!*, and Gypsy Jones?'

'The pacifism came on gradually,' said Barnby. 'I think it followed the period when he used to pretend the war had not taken place at all. Jones's interests are more political—world revolution, at least.'

'Is she in residence at the moment?'

'Returned to the bosom of her family. Her father is a schoolmaster in the neighbourhood of Hendon. But may I ask if you, too, are pursuing her?'

After the remarks, largely incoherent, though apparently pointed enough, made by Mr. Deacon at the party, to the effect that Barnby's disapproval of Gypsy Jones's presence in the house was radically vested in his own lack of success in making himself acceptable to her, I assumed this question to be intended to ascertain whether or not I was myself to be considered a rival in that quarter. I therefore assured him at once that he could set his mind at rest upon that point, explaining that my enquiry had been prompted by the merest curiosity.

The inference on my part may have been a legitimate one in the light of what Mr. Deacon had said, but it proved to be a long way wide of the mark. Barnby appeared much annoyed at the suggestion that his own feelings for Gypsy Jones could be coloured by any sentiment short of the heartiest dislike: stating in the most formidable terms at hand his ineradicable unwillingness for that matter actual physical incapacity, to be inveigled into any situation that might threaten intimacy with her. These protests struck me at the time as perhaps a shade exaggerated, since I had to admit that, for my own part, I had found Gypsy Jones, sluttish though she might be, less obnoxious than the impression of her conveyed by Barnby's words. However, I tried to make amends for the unjust imputation laid upon him, although, owing to their somewhat uncomplimentary nature, I was naturally unable to explain in precise terms the form taken by Mr. Deacon's misleading comments.

'I meant the chap with spectacles,' said Barnby. 'Isn't he

a friend of yours? He always seems to be round here when Jones is about. I thought she might have made a conquest of you as well.'

The second that passed before I was able to grasp that Barnby referred to Widmerpool was to be attributed to that deep-seated reluctance that still remained in my heart, in the face of a volume of evidence to the contrary, to believe Widmerpool capable of possessing a vigorous emotional life of his own. He was a person outwardly unprepossessing, and therefore, according to a totally misleading doctrine, confined to an inescapable predicament that allowed no love affairs: or, at best, love affairs of so obscure and colourless a kind as to be of no possible interest to the world at large. Apart from its many other flaws, this approach was entirely subjective in its assumption that Widmerpool must of necessity appear, even to persons of the opposite sex, as physically unattractive as he seemed to me; though there could probably be counted on my side, in support of this misapprehension, the opinion of most, perhaps all, of our contemporaries at school. On the other hand, I could claim a certain degree of vindication regarding this particular point at issue by insisting, with some justice, that Gypsy Jones, on the face of it, was the last girl on earth who might be expected to occupy Widmerpool's attention; which, on his own comparatively recent showing, seemed so unhesitatingly concentrated on making a success, in the most conventional manner, of his own social life.

At least that was how matters struck me when I was talking to Barnby; though I remembered then how the two of them—Gypsy Jones and Widmerpool—had apparently found each other's company congenial at the party. It was a matter to which I had given no thought at the time. Now I considered some of the facts. Although the theory that, in love, human beings like to choose an 'opposite' may be genetically unsound, there is also, so it seems, a basic validity in such emotional situations as Montague and Capulet, Cavalier and Roundhead. If certain individuals fall in love from motives of convenience, they can be contrasted with plenty of others in whom passion seems principally aroused by the intensity of administrative difficulty in procuring its satisfaction. In fact, history is full of examples of hard-headed personages—to be expected to choose partners in love for reasons helpful to their own career—who were, as often as not, the very people most to embarrass themselves, even to the extent of marriage, in unions that proved subsequently formidable obstacles to advancement.

This digression records, naturally, a later judgment; although even at the time, thinking things over, I could appreciate that there was nothing to be regarded as utterly unexpected in Widmerpool, after the sugar incident, taking a fancy to someone, 'on the rebound', however surprisingly in contrast with Barbara the next girl might be. When I began to weigh the characteristics of Gypsy Jones, in so far as I knew them, I wondered whether, on examination, they made, indeed, so violent an antithesis to Barbara's qualities as might at first sight have appeared. Arguments could unquestionably be brought forward to show that these two girls possessed a good deal in common. Perhaps, after all, Barbara Goring and Gypsy Jones, so far from being irreconcilably different, were in fact notably alike; Barbara's girls' club, or whatever it was, in Bermondsey even pointing to a kind of sociological preoccupation in which there was—at least debatably—some common ground.

These speculations did not, of course, occur to me all at once. Still less did I think of a general law enclosing, even in some slight degree, all who share an interest in the same woman. It was not until years later that the course matters took in this direction became more or less explicable to me along such lines—that is to say, the irresistible pressure in certain emotional affairs of the most positive circumstantial inconvenience to be found at hand. Barnby, satisfied that I was clear regarding his own standpoint, was now prepared to make concessions.

'Jones has her admirers, you know,' he said. 'In fact, Edgar swears that she is the toast of the 1917 Club. It's my belief that in a perverted sort of way he rather fancies her himself—though, of course, he would never admit as much.'

'He talked a lot about her at the party.'

'What did he say?'

'He was deploring that she found herself in rather an awkward spot.'

'You know about that, do you?'

'Mr. Deacon seemed very concerned.'

'You make me laugh when you call Edgar "Mr. Deacon",' said Barnby. 'It certainly makes a new man of him. As a matter of fact, I rather think Jones has solved her problem. You know, she is older than you'd think—too old to get into that sort of difficulty. What do you say to going across the road for a drink?'

On the way out of the studio I asked if one of the unframed portraits standing against the easel could be a likeness of Mrs. Wentworth. Barnby, after scarcely perceptible hesitation, agreed that the picture represented that lady.

'She is rather paintable,' he explained.

'Yes?'

'But tricky at times.'

The subject of Mrs. Wentworth seemed to dispirit him a little, and he remained silent until we were sitting in front of our drinks in the empty saloon bar of the pub on the corner.

'Do you have any dealings with Donners?' he asked at last.

'A friend of mine called Charles Stringham has some sort of a job with him.'

'I've heard Baby speak of Stringham. Wasn't there something about a divorce?'

'His sister's.'

'That was it,' said Barnby. 'But the point is—what is happening about Baby and Donners?'

'How do you mean?'

'They are seen about a lot together. Baby has been appearing with some rather nice diamond clips, and odds and ends of that sort, which seem to be recent acquisitions.'

Barnby screwed up his face in thought.

'Of course,' he said. 'I realise that a poor man competing with a rich one for a woman should be in a relatively strong position if he plays his cards well. Even so, Donners possesses to a superlative degree the advantages of his handicaps—so that one cannot help feeling a bit agitated at times. Especially with Theodoric cutting in, though I don't think he carries many guns.'

'What about Mrs. Wentworth's husband?'

'Divorced,' said Barnby. 'She may even want to marry Donners. The point is, in this—as, I believe, in business matters too—he is rather a man of mystery. From time to time he has a girl hanging about, but he never seems to settle down with anyone. The girls themselves are evasive. They admit to no more than accepting presents and giving nothing in return. That's innocent enough, after all.'

Although he spoke of the matter as if not to be taken too seriously, I suspected that he was, at least for the moment, fairly deeply concerned in the matter of Baby Wentworth; and, when conversation turned to the supposed whims of Sir Magnus, Barnby seemed to take a self-tormenting pleasure in the nature of the hypotheses he put forward. It appeared that the position was additionally complicated by the fact that he had sold a picture to Sir Magnus a month or two before, and that there was even some question of his undertaking a mural in the entrance hall of the Donners-Brebner building.

'Makes the situation rather delicate,' said Barnby.

He was, so I discovered, a figure of the third generation (perhaps the descent, if ascertainable, would have proved even longer) in the world in which he moved: a fact that seemed to give his judgment, based on easy terms of long standing with the problems involved, a scope rather unusual among those who practise the arts, even when they themselves perform with proficiency. His father—though he had died comparatively young, and left no money to speak of—had been, in his day, a fairly successful sculptor of an academic sort; his grandfather, not unknown in the 'sixties and 'seventies, a book illustrator in the Tenniel tradition.

There were those, as I found later, among Barnby's acquaintances who would suggest that his too extensive field of appreciation had to some degree inhibited his own painting. This may have been true. He was himself fond of saying that few painters, writers or musicians had anything but the vaguest idea of what had been thought by their forerunners even a generation or two before; and usually no idea at all, however much they might protest to the contrary, regarding each other's particular branch of æsthetic. His own work diffused that rather deceptive air of emancipation that seemed in those years a kind of neo-classicism, suggesting essentially that same impact brought home to me by Paris in the days when we had met Mr. Deacon in the Louvre: an atmosphere I can still think of as excitingly peculiar to that time.

Sir Magnus's interest in him showed enterprise in a great industrialist, for Barnby was then still comparatively unknown as a painter. In some curious manner his pictures seemed to personify a substantial proportion of that wayward and melancholy, perhaps even rather spurious, content of the self-consciously disillusioned art of that epoch. I mention these general aspects of the period and its moods, not only because they serve to illustrate Barnby, considered, as it were, as a figure symbolic of the contemporary background, but also because our conversation, when later we had dinner together that night, drifted away from personalities into the region of painting and writing; so that, by the time I returned to my rooms, I had almost forgotten his earlier remarks about such individuals as Widmerpool and Gypsy Jones, or Mrs. Wentworth and Sir Magnus Donners.

As it turned out, some of the things Barnby had told me that night threw light, in due course, on matters that would otherwise have been scarcely intelligible; for I certainly did not expect that scattered elements of Mrs. Andriadis's party would recur so comparatively soon in my life; least of all supposing that their new appearance would take place through the medium of the Walpole-Wilsons, who were involved, it is true, only in a somewhat roundabout manner. All the same, their commitment was sufficient to draw attention once again to that extraordinary process that causes certain figures to appear and reappear in the performance of one or another sequence of a ritual dance.

Their summons to the country, although, as an invitation, acceptable to say the least at that time of year, was in itself, unless regarded from a somewhat oblique angle, not specially complimentary. This was because Eleanor herself looked upon house-parties at Hinton Hoo without enthusiasm, indeed with reluctance, classing them as a kind of extension of her 'season', calculated on the whole to hinder her own chosen activities by bringing to her home people who had, in a greater or lesser degree, to be entertained; thereby obstructing what she herself regarded, perhaps with reason, as the natural life of the place. There was no doubt something to be said for this point of view; and her letter, painfully formulated, had made no secret of a sense of resignation, on her own part, to the inevitable, conveying by its spirit, rather than actual words, the hope that at least I, for one, as an old, if not particularly close, friend, might be expected to recognise the realities of the situation, and behave accordingly.

Eleanor's candour in this respect certainly did not preclude gratitude. On the other hand, it had equally to be admitted that some fundamental support sustaining the Walpole-Wilson family life had become at some stage of existence slightly displaced, so that a visit to Hinton, as to all households where something fundamental has gone obscurely wrong, was set against an atmosphere of tensity. Whether this lack of harmony had its roots in Sir Gavin's professional *faux pas* or in some unresolved imperfection in the relationship of husband and wife could only be conjectured. Hard up as I was at that moment for entertainment, I might even have thought twice about staying there—so formidable could this *ambience* sometimes prove—if I had not by then been wholly converted to Barbara's view that 'Eleanor was not a bad old girl when you know her.' I was rather glad to think that Barbara herself was in Scotland, so that there would be no likelihood of meeting her at her uncle's house. I felt that, if we could avoid seeing each other for long enough, any questions of sentiment—

so often deprecated by Barbara herself—could be allowed quietly to subside, and take their place in those niches of memory especially reserved for abortive emotional entanglements of that particular kind.

All the same, this sensation of starting life again, as it were, with a clean sheet, made me regret a little to find on arrival that the assembled house-party consisted only of Sir Gavin's unmarried sister, Miss Janet Walpole-Wilson, Rosie Manasch, and Johnny Pardoe. On the way down in the train I had felt that it would be enjoyable to meet some new girl, even at risk of becoming once more victim to the afflictions from which I had only recently emerged. However, it seemed that no such situation was on this occasion likely to arise. Miss Janet Walpole-Wilson I knew of only by name, though I had heard a great deal about her from time to time when talking to Eleanor, who, possessing a great admiration for her aunt, often described the many adventures for which she was noted within the family.

The other two guests, although in theory a perfectly suitable couple to invite together, were, I thought, not quite sure whether they liked one another. Barnby used to say that a small man was at more of a disadvantage with a small woman than with a big one, and it was certainly true that the short, squat, black figures of Rosie Manasch and Pardoe sometimes looked a little absurd side by side. 'Johnnie is so amusing,' she used to say, and he had been heard to remark: 'Rosie dances beautifully,' but almost any other pair of Eleanor's acquaintances would have liked each other as well, if not better. As a matter of fact, Sir Gavin, hardly concealed a certain *tendresse* for Rosie, which may have accounted for her presence; and he certainly felt strong approval of Pardoe's comfortable income. Eleanor's own indifference to the matter might be held to excuse her parents for asking to the house guests who at least appealed in one way or another to their own tastes.

The red brick Queen Anne manor house stood back from the road in a small park, if such an unpretentious setting of trees and paddocks could be so called. A walled orchard on the far side stretched down to the first few cottages of the village. The general impression of the property was of an estate neat and well superintended, rather than large. The place possessed that quality, perhaps more characteristic of country houses in England than in some other parts Europe, of house and grounds forming an essential part of the landscape. The stables stood round three sides of a courtyard a short way from the main buildings, and there Eleanor was accustomed to spend a good deal of her time, with animals of various kinds, housed about the loose-boxes in hutches and wooden crates.

Within, there existed, rather unexpectedly, that somewhat empty, insistently correct appearance of the private dwellings of those who have spent most of their lives in official residences of one kind or another. A few mementoes of posts abroad were scattered about. For example, an enormous lacquer cabinet in the drawing-room had been brought from Pekin—some said Tokyo—by Sir Gavin, upon the top of which stood several small, equivocal figures carved in wood by the Indians of an obscure South American tribe. The portraits in the dining-room were mostly of Wilson forebears: one of them, an admiral, attributed to Zoffany. There was also a large painting of Lady Walpole-Wilson's father by the Academician, Isbister (spoken of with such horror by Mr. Deacon), whose portrait of Peter Templer's father I remembered as the only picture in the Templer home. This canvas was in the painter's earlier manner, conveying the impression that at any moment Lord Aberavon, depicted in peer's robes, would step from the frame and join the company below him in the room.

The Wilsons had lived in the county for a number of generations, but Sir Gavin had bought Hinton (with which he possessed hereditary connexions through a grandmother) only after retirement. This comparatively recent purchase of the house was a subject upon which Sir Gavin's mind was never wholly at rest; and he was always at pains to explain that its ownership was not to be looked upon as an entirely new departure so far as any hypothetical status might be concerned as a land-owner 'in that part of the world'.

'As a matter of fact, the Wilsons are, if anything, an older family than the Walpoles—well, perhaps not that, but at least as old,' he used to say. 'I expect you have heard of Beau Wilson, a young gentleman who spent a lot of money in the reign of William and Mary, and was killed in a duel. I have reason to suppose he was one of our lot. And then there was a Master of the Mint a bit earlier. The double-barrel, which I greatly regret, and would discard if I could, without putting myself and my own kith and kin to a great deal of inconvenience, was the work of a great-uncle—a most consequential ass, between you and me, and a bit of a snob, I'm afraid—and has really no basis whatever, beyond the surname of a remote ancestor in the female line.'

He was accustomed to terminate this particular speech with a number of 'm'ms', most of them interrogative, and some uneasy laughter. His sister, on this occasion, looked rather disapproving at these excursions into family history. She was a small, defiant woman, some years younger than Sir Gavin, recently returned from a journey in Yugoslavia, where she had been staying with a friend married to a British consul in that country. Although spoken of as 'not well off', Miss Janet Walpole-Wilson was also reported to maintain herself at a respectable level of existence by intermittent odd jobs that varied between acting as secretary, usually in a more or less specialised capacity, to some public figure, often a friend or relative of the family; alternatively, by undertaking, when they travelled abroad, the rôle of governess or duenna to children of relations, some of whom were rather rich.

'Aunt Janet says you must never mind asking,' Eleanor had informed me, when speaking of the ease with which Miss Walpole-Wilson, apparently on account of her freedom from inhibition upon this point, always found employment. Her aunt certainly seemed to have enjoyed throughout her life a wide variety of confidences and experiences. She dressed usually in tones of brown and green, colours that gave her for some reason, possibly because her hats almost always conveyed the impression of being peaked, an air of belonging to some dedicated order of female officials, connected possibly with public service in the woods and forests, and bearing a load of responsibility, the extent of which was difficult for a lay person—even impossible if a male—to appreciate, or wholly to understand. The outlines of her good, though severe, features were emphasised by a somewhat reddish complexion.

Sir Gavin, though no doubt attached to his sister, was sometimes openly irritated by her frequent, and quite uncompromising, pronouncements on subjects that he must have felt himself, as a former diplomatist of some standing, possessing the right, at least in his own house, to speak of with authority. Lady Walpole-Wilson, on the other hand, scarcely made a secret of finding the presence of her sister-in-law something of a strain. A look of sadness would steal over her face when Miss Walpole-Wilson argued with Sir Gavin about ethnological problems in the Sanjak of Novi Bazar, or spoke of times when 'the Ford's big end went in the Banat', or 'officials made themselves so disagreeable at Nish': geographical entities of that kind playing a great part in her conversation. Although seriously concerned with the general welfare of the human race, she sometimes displayed a certain capricious malignity towards individuals, taking, for example, a great dislike to Pardoe, though she showed a guarded friendship towards Rosie Manasch. I was relieved to find her attitude to myself suggested nothing more hostile than complete indifference.

One, perhaps the chief, bone of contention lying between herself and her brother was Miss Walpole-Wilson's contention that the traditions of his service, by their very nature, must have rendered him impervious to anything in the way of new ideas or humanitarian concepts; so that much of Sir Gavin's time was taken up in attempting to demonstrate to his sister that, so far from lagging behind in the propagation of reforms of almost every kind, he was prepared to go, theoretically at least, not only as far as, but even farther than, herself. Both of them knew Sillery, who had recently stayed in the neighbourhood, and for once they were in agreement that he was 'full of understanding'. The subject of Sillery's visit came up at dinner on the night of my arrival.

'It was at Stourwater,' said Lady Walpole-Wilson. 'As a matter of fact we have been asked over there on Sunday. Prince Theodoric is staying there with Sir Magnus Donners.'

I knew the castle by name, and was even aware in a vague kind of way that it had often changed hands during the previous fifty or hundred years; but I had never seen the place, nor had any idea that Sir Magnus Donners lived there.

'And I so much wanted that afternoon to see those two hound puppies Nokes is walking,' said Eleanor. 'Now it turns out we are being forced to go to this ghastly luncheon-party.'

'Got to be civil to one's neighbours, my dear,' said Sir Gavin. 'Besides, Theodoric has particularly asked to see me.'

'I don't know what you call "neighbours",' said Eleanor. 'Stourwater is twenty-five miles, at least.'

'Nonsense,' said Sir Gavin. 'I doubt if it is twenty-three.'

His attitude towards Eleanor varied between almost doting affection and an approach most easily suggested by the phrase 'making the best of a bad job'. There were times when she vexed him. Arguing with her father brought out the resemblance between the two of them, though features that, in Sir Gavin, seemed conventionalised to the point, almost, of stylisation took on a peculiar twist in his daughter. As she sat there at the table, I could recognise no similarity whatever to Barbara—of whom at times I still found myself thinking—except for their shared colouring.

'I explained to Donners that we should be quite a large party,' said Sir Gavin, 'but he would not hear of anyone being left behind. In any case, there is plenty of room there, and the castle itself is well worth seeing.'

'I don't think I shall come after all, Gavin,' said Miss Walpole-Wilson. 'No one will want to see me there—least of all Prince Theodoric. Although I dare say he is too young to remember the misunderstanding that arose, when I stayed with you, regarding that remark about "a travesty of democratic government"—and you know I never care for people with too much money.'

'Oh, come, Janet,' said Sir Gavin. 'Of course they will all want to see you—the Prince especially. He is a very go-ahead fellow, everyone who has met him agrees. As a matter of fact, you know as well as I do, the old King laughed heartily when I explained the circumstance of your remark. He made a rather broad joke about it. I've told you a thousand times. Besides, Donners is not a bad fellow at all.'

'I can't get on with those people—ever.'

'I don't know what you mean by "those people",' said Sir Gavin, a trifle irritably. 'Donners is no different from anyone else, except that he may be a bit richer. He didn't start life barefoot—not that I for one should have the least objection if he had, more power to his elbow—but his father was an eminently solid figure. He was knighted, I believe, for what that's worth. Donners went to some quite decent school. I think the family are of Scandinavian, or North German, extraction. No doubt very worthy people.'

'Oh, I do hope he isn't German,' said Lady Walpole-Wilson. 'I never thought of that.'

'Personally, I have a great admiration for the Germans—I do not, of course, mean the Junkers,' said her sister-in-law. 'They have been hardly treated. No one of liberal opinions could think otherwise. And I certainly do not object to Sir Magnus on snobbish grounds. You know me too well for that, Gavin. I have no doubt, as you say, that he has many good points. All the same, I think I had better stay at home. I can make a start on my article about the Bosnian Moslems for the news-sheet of the Minority Problems League.'

'If Aunt Janet doesn't go, I don't see why I should,' said Eleanor. 'I don't in the least want to meet Prince Theodoric.'

'I do,' said Rosie Manasch. 'I thought he looked too fetching at Goodwood.'

In the laugh that followed this certainly tactful expression of preference, earlier warnings of potential family difference died away. Sir Gavin began to describe, not for the first time, the occasion when, as a young secretary in some Oriental country, he had stained his face with coffee-grounds and, like Haroun-al-Raschid, 'mingled' in the bazaar: with, so it appeared, useful results. The story carried dinner safely to the dessert, a stage when Pardoe brought conversation back once more to Sunday's expedition by asking whether Sir Magnus Donners had purchased Stourwater from the family with whom Barbara was staying in Scotland, for whose house he was himself bound on leaving Hinton.

'He bought it from a relation of mine,' said Rosie Manasch. 'Uncle Leopold always says he sold it—with due respect to you, Eleanor—because the hunting round here wasn't good enough. I think it was really because it cost too much to keep up.'

'It is all very perfect now,' said Sir Gavin. 'Rather too perfect for my taste. In any case, I am no medievalist.'

He looked round the table challengingly after saying this, rather as Uncle Giles was inclined to glare about him after making some more or less tendentious statement, whether because he suspected that one or other of us, in spite of this disavowal, would charge him with covert medievalism, or in momentary hesitation that, in taking so high a line on the subject of an era at once protracted and diversified, he ran risk of exposure to the impeachment of 'missing something' thereby, was uncertain.

'There is the Holbein, too,' said Lady Walpole-Wilson. 'You really must come, Janet. I know you like pictures.'

'The castle belongs, like Bodiam, to the later Middle Ages,' said Sir Gavin, assuming all at once the sing-song tones of a guide or lecturer. 'And, like Bodiam, Stourwater possesses little or no historical interest, as such, while remaining, so far as its exterior is concerned, architecturally one of the most complete, and comparatively unaltered, fortified buildings of its period. For some reason——'

'——for some reason the defences were not dismantled—"sleighted", I think you call it—at the time of the Civil Wars,' cut in Lady Walpole-Wilson, as if answering the responses in church, or completing the quotation of a well-known poem to show appreciation of its aptness. 'Though subsequent owners undertook certain improvements in connexion with the structural fabric of the interior, with a view to increasing Stourwater's convenience as a private residence in more peaceful times.'

'I have already read a great deal of what you have been saying in *Stourwater and Its Story,* a copy of which was kindly placed by my bed,' said Miss Walpole-Wilson. 'I doubt if all the information given there is very accurate.'

For some reason a curious sense of excitement rose within me at prospect of this visit. I could not explain to myself this feeling, almost of suspense, that seemed to hang over the expedition. I was curious to see the castle, certainly, but that hardly explained an anxiety that Eleanor's hound puppies, or Miss Walpole-Wilson's humours, might prevent my going there. That night I lay awake thinking about Stourwater as if it had been the sole motive for my coming to Hinton: fearing all the time that some hitch would occur. However, the day came and we set out, Miss Walpole-Wilson, in spite of her earlier displeasure, finally agreeing to accompany the party, accommodated in two cars, one of them driven by Sir Gavin himself. There was perhaps a tacit suggestion that he would have liked Rosie Manasch to travel with him, but, although as a rule not unwilling to accept his company, and approval, she chose, on this occasion, the car driven by the chauffeur.

When we came to Stourwater that Sunday morning, the first sight was impressive. Set among oaks and beeches in a green hollow of the land, the castle was approached by a causeway crossing the remains of a moat, a broad expanse of water through which, with great deliberation, a pair of black swans, their passage sending ripples through the pond weed, glided between rushes swaying gently in the warm September air. Here was the Middle Age, from the pages of Tennyson, or Scott, at its most elegant: all sordid and painful elements subtly removed. Some such thought must have struck Sir Gavin too, for I heard him murmuring at the wheel:

> '"And sometimes thro' the mirror blue
> The knights come riding two and two . . ."'

There was, in fact, no one about at all; neither knights nor hinds, this absence of human life increasing a sense of unreality, as if we were travelling in a dream. The cars passed under the portcullis, and across a cobbled quadrangle. Beyond this open space, reached by another archway, was a courtyard of even larger dimensions, in the centre of which a sunken lawn had been laid out, with a fountain at the centre, and carved stone flower-pots, shaped like urns, at each of the four corners. The whole effect was not, perhaps, altogether in keeping with the rest of the place. Through a vaulted gateway on one side could be seen the high yew hedges of the garden. Steps led up to the main entrance of the castle's domestic wing, at which the cars drew up.

Mounted effigies in Gothic armour guarded either side of the door by which we entered the Great Hall; and these dramatic figures of man and horse struck a new and somewhat disturbing note; though one at which the sunken garden had already hinted. Such implications of an over-elaborate solicitude were followed up everywhere the eye rested, producing a result altogether different from the cool, detached vision manifested a minute or two earlier by grey walls and towers rising out of the green, static landscape. Something was decidedly amiss. The final consequence of the pains lavished on these halls and galleries was not precisely that of a Hollywood film set, the objects assembled being, in the first place, too genuine, too valuable; there was even a certain sense of fitness, of historical association more or less correctly assessed. The display was discomforting, not contemptible. The impression was of sensations that might precede one of those episodes in a fairy story, when, at a given moment, the appropriate spell is pronounced to cause domes and minarets, fountains and pleasure-gardens, to disappear into thin air; leaving the hero—in this case, Sir Magnus Donners—shivering in rags beneath the blasted oak of a grim forest, or scorched by rays of a blazing sun among the rocks and boulders of some desolate mountain-side. In fact, Sir Gavin's strictures on Stourwater as 'too perfect' were inadequate as a delineation to the extent of being almost beside the point.

I had supposed that, in common with most visits paid on these terms in the country, the Walpole-Wilson group might be left most of the time huddled in a cluster of their own, while the Donners house-party, drawn together as never before by the arrival of strangers, would discourse animatedly together at some distance off, the one faction scarcely mixing at all with the other. This not uncommon predicament could no doubt in a general way have been exemplified soon after we had been received by Sir Magnus—looking more healthily clerical than ever—in the Long Gallery (at the far end of which hung the Holbein, one of the portraits of Erasmus), had not various unforeseen circumstances contributed to modify what might be regarded as a more normal course of events. For example, among a number of faces in the room possessing a somewhat familiar appearance, I suddenly noticed Stringham and Bill Truscott, both of whom were conversing with an unusually pretty girl.

We were presented, one by one, to Prince Theodoric, who wore a grey flannel suit, unreservedly continental in cut, and appeared far more at his ease than at Mrs. Andriadis's party: smiling in a most engaging manner when he shook hands. He spoke that scrupulously correct English, characteristic of certain foreign royalties, that confers on the language a smoothness and flexibility quite alien to the manner in which English people themselves talk. There was a word from him for everyone. Sir Gavin seized his hand as if he were meeting a long lost son, while Prince Theodoric himself seemed, on his side, equally pleased at their reunion. Lady Walpole-Wilson, probably because she remembered Prince Theodoric only as a boy, showed in her eye apparent surprise at finding him so grown-up. Only Eleanor's, and her aunt's, firmly-clasped lips and stiff curtsey suggested entire disapproval.

Further introductions took place. The Huntercombes were there—Lord Huntercombe was Lord Lieutenant of the county—and there were a crowd of persons whose identities, as a whole, I failed to assimilate; though here and there was recognisable an occasional notability like Sir Horrocks Rusby, whose name I remembered Widmerpool mentioning on some occasions, who had not so long before achieved a good deal of prominence in the newspapers as counsel in the Derwentwater divorce case. I also noticed Mrs. Wentworth—whom Sir Horrocks had probably cross-questioned in the witness-box—still looking rather sulky, as she stood in one of the groups about us. When the formalities of these opening moves of the game had been completed, and we had been given cocktails, Stringham strolled across the room. His face was deeply burned by the sun. I wondered whether this was the result of the Deauville trip, of which Mrs. Andriadis had spoken, or if, on the contrary, division between them had been final. He had not wholly lost his appearance of fatigue.

'You must inspect my future wife,' he said at once

This announcement of imminent marriage was a complete surprise. Barnby had said, during the course of the evening we had spent together: 'When people think they are never further from marriage, they are often, in reality, never nearer to it,' but that kind of precept takes time to learn. I had certainly accepted the implication that nothing was more distant than marriage from Stringham's intentions when he had so violently abandoned Mrs. Andriadis's house; although now I even wondered whether he could have decided to repair matters by making Mrs. Andriadis herself his wife. To be able to consider this a possibility showed, I suppose, in its grasp of potentialities, an advance on my own part of which I should have been incapable earlier in the year. However, without further developing the news, he led me to the girl from whose side he had come, who was still talking to Truscott.

'Peggy,' he said, 'this is an old friend of mine.'

Apart from former signs given by Stringham's behaviour, external evidence had been supplied, indirectly by Anne Stepney, and directly by Rosie Manasch, to the effect that anything like an engagement was 'off'. Peggy Stepney, whom I now recognised from pictures I had seen of her, was not unlike her sister, with hair of the same faintly-reddish shade, though here, instead of a suggestion of disorder, the elder sister looked as if she might just have stepped gracefully from the cover of a fashion magazine; 'too perfect', indeed, as Sir Gavin might have said. She was, of course, a 'beauty', and possessed a kind of cold symmetry, very taking, and at the same time a little alarming. However, this exterior was not accompanied by a parallel coolness of manner; on the contrary, she could in the circumstances scarcely have been more agreeable. While we talked, we were joined by Mrs. Wentworth, at whose arrival I was conscious of a slight stiffening in Stringham's bearing, an almost imperceptible acerbity, due possibly—though by no means certainly, I thought—to the part played by Mrs. Wentworth in his sister's divorce. In comparing the looks of the two young women, it was immediately clear that Peggy Stepney was more obviously the beauty; though there was something about Mrs. Wentworth that made the discord she had aroused in so many quarters easily understandable.

'How long have I got to go on sitting next to that equerry of Theodoric's, Bill?' she asked. 'I've been through his favourite dance tunes at dinner last night. I can't stand them at lunch again to-day. I'm not as young as I was.'

'Talk to him about birds and beasts,' said Stringham. 'I've already tried that with great success—the flora and fauna of England and Wales.'

Mrs. Wentworth seemed not greatly amused by this facetiousness. Her demeanour was less friendly than Peggy Stepney's, and she did no more than glance in my direction when we were introduced. I was impressed by Barnby's temerity in tackling so formidable an objective. Luncheon was announced at that moment, so that the four of us temporarily parted company.

The dining-room was hung with sixteenth-century tapestries. I supposed that they might be Gobelin from their general appearance, blue and crimson tints set against lemon yellow. They illustrated the Seven Deadly Sins. I found myself seated opposite *Luxuria,* a failing principally portrayed in terms of a winged and horned female figure, crowned with roses, holding between finger and thumb one of her plump, naked breasts, while she gazed into a looking-glass, supported on one side by Cupid and on the other by a goat of unreliable aspect. The four-footed beast of the Apocalypse, with his seven dragon-heads dragged her triumphal car, which was of great splendour. Hercules, bearing his clubs, stood by, somewhat gloomily watching this procession, his mind filled, no doubt, with disquieting recollections. In the background, the open doors of a pillared house revealed a four-poster bed, with hangings rising to an apex, under the canopy of which a couple lay clenched in a priapic grapple. Among trees, to the right of the composition, further couples and groups, three or four of them at least, were similarly occupied in smaller houses and Oriental tents; or, in one case, simply on the ground.

I had been placed next to Rosie Manasch, who was, at the moment of seating herself, engaged in talk with her neighbour on the far side; and—curious to investigate some of the by-products of indulgence depicted in this sequence of animated, and at times enigmatic, incidents—I found myself fully occupied in examining unobtrusively the scenes spread out on the tapestry. There had been, I was dimly aware, some rearrangement of places on my right-hand side, where a chair had remained empty for a moment or two. Now a girl sat down there, next to me, to whom I had not yet, so far as I knew, been introduced, with some muttered words from Truscott, who had instigated the change of position—possibly to relieve Mrs. Wentworth from further strain of making conversation with Prince Theodoric's equerry.

'I don't think you remember me,' she said, almost at once, in a curiously harsh voice that brought back, in fact, that same sense of past years returning that Stringham's enquiry for matches had caused me at the coffee-stall. 'I used to be called Jean Templer. You are a friend of Peter's, and you came to stay with us years ago.'

It was true that I had not recognised her. I think we might even have exchanged words without my guessing her identity, so little had she been in my thoughts, so unexpected a place was this to find her. That was not because she had changed greatly. On the contrary, she still seemed slim, attenuated, perhaps not—like the two other girls with whom I had been talking, and round whom my thoughts, before the distraction of the tapestry, had been drifting—exactly a 'beauty'; but, all the same, mysterious and absorbing: certainly pretty enough, so far as that went, just as she had seemed when I had visited the Templers after leaving school. There was perhaps a touch of the trim secretary of musical comedy. I saw also, with a kind of relief, that she seemed to express none of the qualities I had liked in Barbara. There was a sense of restraint here, a reserve at present unpredictable. I tried to excuse my bad manners in having failed at once to remember her. She gave one of those quick, almost masculine laughs. I was not at all sure how I felt about her, though conscious suddenly that being in love with Barbara, painful as some of its moments had been, now seemed a rather amateurish affair; just as my feelings for Barbara had once appeared to me so much more mature than those previously possessed for Suzette; or, indeed, for Jean herself.

'You were so deep in the tapestry,' she said.

'I was wondering about the couple in the little house on the hill.'

'They have a special devil—or is he a satyr?—to themselves.'

'He seems to be collaborating, doesn't he?'

'Just lending a hand, I think.'

'A guest, I suppose—or member of the staff?'

'Oh, a friend of the family,' she said. 'All newly-married couples have someone of that sort about. Sometimes several. Didn't you know? I see you can't be married.'

'But how do you know they are newly married?'

'They've got such a smart little house,' she said. 'They must be newly married. And rather well off, too, I should say.'

I was left a trifle breathless by this exchange, not only because it was quite unlike the kind of luncheon-table conversation I had expected to come my way in that particular place, but also on account of its contrast with Jean's former deportment, when we had met at her home. At that moment I hardly considered the difference that age had made, no doubt in both of us. She was, I thought, about a couple of years younger than myself. Feeling unable to maintain this show of detachment towards human—and, in especial, matrimonial—affairs, I asked whether it was not true that she had married Bob Duport. She nodded; not exactly conveying, it seemed to me, that by some happy chance their union had introduced her to an unexpected terrestrial paradise.

'Do you know Bob?'

'I just met him years ago with Peter.'

'Have you seen Peter lately?'

'Not for about a year. He has been doing very well in the City, hasn't he? He always tells me so.'

She laughed.

'Oh, yes,' she said. 'He has been making quite a lot of money, I think. That is always something. But I wish he would settle down, get married, for instance.'

I was aware of an unexpected drift towards intimacy, although this sudden sense of knowing her all at once much better was not simultaneously accompanied by any clear portrayal in my own mind of the kind of person she might really be. Perhaps intimacy of any sort, love or friendship, impedes all exactness of definition. For example, Mr. Deacon's character was plainer to me than Barnby's, although by then I knew Barnby better than I knew Mr.

Deacon. In short, the persons we see most clearly are not necessarily those we know best. In any case, to attempt to describe a woman in the broad terms employable for a man is perhaps irrational.

'I went to a party in your London house given by Mrs. Andriadis.'

'How very grand,' she said. 'What was it like? We let the place almost as soon as we took it, because Bob had to go abroad. It's rather a horrid house, really. I hate it, and everything in it.'

I did not know how to comment on this attitude towards her own home, which—as I had agreed upon that famous night with the young man with the orchid—certainly left, in spite of its expensive air, a good deal to be desired. I said that I wished she had been present at the party.

'Oh, us,' she said laughing again, as if any such eventuality were utterly unthinkable. 'Besides, we were away. Bob was arguing about nickel or aluminium or something for months on end. As a matter of fact, I think we shall have to sue Mrs. Andriadis when he comes back. She has raised absolute hell in the house. Burnt the boiler out and broken a huge looking-glass.'

She reminded me immediately of her brother in this disavowal of being the kind of person asked to Mrs. Andriadis's parties; for the setting in which we found ourselves seemed, on the face of it, to be perfectly conceivable as an extension of Mrs. Andriadis's sort of entertaining. Indeed, it appeared to me, in my inexperience, that almost exactly the same chilly undercurrent of conflict was here perceptible as that permeating the house in Hill Street a month or two before. Dialectical subtleties could no doubt be advanced—as Stringham had first suggested, and remarks at Sillery's had seemed to substantiate—to demolish Sir Magnus's pretensions, hierarchically speaking, to more than the possession of 'a lot of money'; in spite of various testimonials paid to him, at Hinton and elsewhere, on the score of his greatness in other directions. However, even allowing that Sir Magnus might be agreed to occupy a position only within this comparatively modest category of social differentiation, such assets as were his were not commonly disregarded, even in the world of Mrs. Andriadis. Her sphere might be looked upon, perhaps, as a more trenchant and mobile one, though it was doubtful if even this estimate were beyond question.

In fact, I was uncertain whether or not I might have misunderstood Jean, and that she had intended to imply that her existence was at a higher, rather than lower, plane. Some similar thought may have struck her too, because, as if in explanation of a matter that needed straightening out, she said: 'Baby brought me here. She wanted someone to play for her side, and Bob's aluminium fitted in nicely for this week-end, as Theodoric knew Bob—had even met him.'

The concept of 'playing for her side' opened up in the imagination fascinating possibilities in connexion with Mrs. Wentworth's position in the household. I remembered the phrase as one used by Stringham when enlisting my own support in connexion with his project of 'going down' from the university after a single term of residence—the time, in fact, when he had asked his mother to lunch to meet Sillery. However, the status of Mrs. Wentworth at the castle was obviously not a matter to be investigated there and then, while, in addition to any question of diffidence in enquiring about that particular affair, Jean's initial display of vivacity became suddenly exhausted, and she sank back into one of those silences that I remembered so well from the time when we had first met. For the rest of the meal she was occupied in fragmentary conversation with the man on her right, or I was myself talking with Rosie Manasch; so that we hardly spoke to one another again while in the dining-room.

The rest of the members of the luncheon-party, on the whole, appeared to be enjoying themselves. Prince Theodoric, sitting at the other end of the long table between Lady Walpole-Wilson and Lady Huntercombe, was conversing manfully, though he looked a shade cast down. From time to time his eyes wandered, never for more than an instant, in the direction of Mrs. Wentworth, who had cheered up considerably under the stimulus of food and drink, and was looking remarkably pretty. I noticed that she made no effort to return the Prince's glances, in the manner she had employed at Mrs. Andriadis's party. Truscott was clearly doing wonders with Miss Walpole-Wilson, whose wide social contacts he must have regarded as of sufficient importance, possibly as an ancillary factor in publicising Donners-Brebner concerns, to justify, on his own part, slightly more than normal attention. It was even possible, though I thought on the whole improbable, that Miss Walpole-Wilson's rather unaccommodating exterior might, in itself, have been sufficient to put Truscott on his mettle to display, without ulterior motive, his almost unequalled virtuosity in handling intractable material of just the kind Miss Walpole-Wilson's personality provided. In rather another field, I had seen Archie Gilbert, on more than one occasion, do something of that sort; on the part of Truscott, however, such relatively frivolous expenditure of energy would have been unexpected.

Only Eleanor, still no doubt contemplating hound puppies and their diet, or perhaps disapproving in general of the assembled company's formal tone, appeared uncompromisingly bored. Sir Magnus himself did not talk much, save intermittently to express some general opinion. His words, wafted during a comparative silence to the farther end of the table, would have suggested on the lips of a lesser man processes of thought of a banality so painful—of such profound and arid depths, in which neither humour, nor imagination, nor, indeed, any form of human understanding could be thought to play the smallest part—that I almost supposed him to be speaking ironically, or teasing his guests by acting the part of a bore in a drawing-room comedy. I was far from understanding that the capacity of men interested in power is not necessarily expressed in the brilliance of their conversation. Even in daylight he looked young for his age, and immensely, almost unnaturally, healthy.

At the end of the meal, on leaving the dining-room, Sir Gavin, who had one of his favourite schemes to discuss, cornered Lord Huntercombe, and they went off together. Lord Huntercombe, a small man, very exquisite in appearance and possessing a look of ineffable cunning, was trustee of one, if not more, of the public galleries, and Sir Gavin was anxious to interest him in a project, dear to his heart, of which he had spoken at Hinton, regarding the organisation of a special exhibition of pictures to be thought of as of interest in connexion with the history of diplomatic relations between England and the rest of the world. The two of them retired among the yew hedges, Lord Huntercombe's expression presaging little more than sufferance at the prospect of listening to Sir Gavin's plan. The rest of the party broke up into groups. Jean, just as she used to disappear from the scene in her own home, was nowhere to be found on the terrace, to which most of the party now moved. Peggy Stepney, too, seemed to have gone off on her own. Finding myself sitting once more with Stringham and Truscott, I asked when the wedding was to take place.

'Oh, any moment now,' Stringham said. 'I'm not sure it isn't this afternoon. To be precise, the second week in October. My mother can't make up her mind whether to laugh or cry. I think Buster is secretly rather impressed.'

I found it impossible to guess whether he was getting married because he was in love, because he hoped by taking this step to find a more settled life, or because he was curious to experiment with a new set of circumstances. The absurdity of supposing that exact reasons for marriage can ever be assigned had not then struck me; perhaps excusably, since it is a subject regarding which everyone considers, at least where friends are concerned, the assumption of categorical knowledge to be an inalienable right. Peggy Stepney herself looked pleased enough, though the formality of her style was calculated to hide outward responses. There had been an incident—hardly that—while we had been talking before luncheon. She had let her hand rest on a table in such a way that it lay, at least putatively, in Stringham's direction. He had placed his own hand over hers, upon which she had jerked her fingers away, almost angrily, and begun to powder her face. Stringham had shown absolutely no sign of noticing this gesture. His first movement had been made, so it had appeared, almost automatically, not even very specifically as a mark of affection. It was possible that some minor quarrel had just taken place; that she was teasing him; that the action had no meaning at all. Thinking of the difficulties inherent in his situation, I began to turn over once more the meeting with Jean, and asked Stringham if he knew that Peter Templer's sister was one of the guests at Stourwater.

'Didn't even know he had a sister—of course, yes, I remember now—he had two at least. One of them, like my own, was always getting divorced.'

'This is the younger one. She is called Mrs. Duport.'

'What, Baby's friend?'

He did not show the least interest. It was inexplicable to me that he had apparently noticed her scarcely at all; for, although Widmerpool's love for Barbara had seemed an outrageous presumption, Stringham's indifference to Jean was, in the opposite direction, almost equally disconcerting. My own feelings for her might still be uncertain, but his attitude was not of indecision so much as complete unawareness. However, the thought of Mrs. Wentworth evidently raised other questions in his mind.

'What sort of progress is Theodoric making with Baby?' he asked.

Truscott smiled, making a deprecatory movement with his finger to indicate that the matter was better undiscussed: at least while we remained on the terrace.

'Not very well, I think,' Stringham said. 'It will be Bijou Ardglass, after all. I'll have a bet on it.'

'Did the Chief strike you as being a bit off colour at luncheon, Charles?' Truscott asked, ignoring these suppositions.

He spoke casually, though I had the impression he might be more anxious about Sir Magnus's state of temper than he wished outwardly to admit.

'I heard him say once that it took all sorts to make a world,' said Stringham. 'He ought to write some of his aphorisms down so that they are not forgotten. Would it be an occasion for the dungeons?'

He made this last remark in that very level voice of his that I recognised, as of old, he was accustomed to employ when intending to convey covert meaning to some apparently simple statement or question. Truscott pouted, and lowered his head in rather arch reproof. I saw that he was amused about some joke shared in secret between them, and I knew that I had judged correctly in suspecting latent implication in what Stringham had said.

'Baby doesn't like it.'

'Who cares what Baby likes?'

'The Chief is never unwilling,' Truscott said, still smiling. 'It certainly might cheer him up. *You* ask him, Charles.'

Sir Magnus was talking to Lady Huntercombe only a short distance from us. Stringham moved across the terrace towards them. As he came up, Lady Huntercombe, whose features and dress had been designed to recall Gainsborough's Mrs. Siddons, turned, almost as if she had been expecting his arrival, and pointed, with an appropriately dramatic gesture, to the keep of the castle, as if demanding some historical or architectural information. I could see Stringham repress a smile. Her words had perhaps made his enquiry easier to present. Before answering, he inclined towards Sir Magnus, and, with perhaps more deference than had been common to his manner in former days, put some question. Sir Magnus, in reply, raised his eyebrows, and—like Truscott a few minutes earlier, who had perhaps unconsciously imitated one of his employer's mannerisms—made a deprecatory movement with his forefinger; his face at the same time taking on the very faintest suggestion of a deeper colour, as he in turn addressed himself to Lady Huntercombe, apparently requesting her opinion on the point brought to his notice by Stringham. She nodded at once in such a way as to indicate enthusiasm, the rather reckless gaiety of a great actress on holiday, one of the moods, comparatively limited in range, to which her hat and general appearance committed her. Stringham looked up, and caught Truscott's eye.

The result of the consultation was a public announcement by Truscott, as Sir Magnus's mouthpiece, that our host, who had by then spoken a word with Prince Theodoric, would himself undertake a personally conducted tour of the castle, 'including the dungeons'. This was the kind of exordium Truscott could undertake with much adroitness, striking an almost ideal mean between putting a sudden stop to conversation, and, at the same time, running no risk of being ignored by anyone in the immediate neighbourhood. No doubt most of those assembled round about had already made the inspection at least once. Some showed signs of unwillingness to repeat the performance. There was a slight stir as sightseers began to sort themselves out from the rest. The end of the matter was that about a dozen persons decided to make up the company who would undertake the tour. They were collected into into one group and led indoors.

'I'll get the torches,' said Truscott.

He went off, and Stringham returned to my side.

'What is the joke?'

'There isn't one, really,' he said, but his voice showed that he was keeping something dark.

Truscott returned, carrying two electric torches, one of which he handed to Stringham. The party included Prince Theodoric, Lady Huntercombe, Miss Janet Walpole-Wilson, Eleanor, Rosie Manasch, and Pardoe: together with others, unknown to me. Stringham went ahead with Truscott, who acted as principal guide, supplying a conjunction of practical information and historical detail, in every way suitable to the circumstances of the tour. As we moved round, Sir Magnus watched Truscott with approval, but at first took no part himself in the exposition. I felt certain that Sir Magnus was secure in exact knowledge of the market price of every object at Stourwater: that kind of insight that men can develop without possessing any of the æsthete's, or specialist's, cognisance of the particular category, or implication, of the valuable concerned. Barnby used to say that he knew a chartered accountant, scarcely aware even how pictures are produced, who could at the same time enter any gallery and pick out the most expensively priced work there 'from Masaccio to Matisse', simply through the mystic power of his own respect for money.

We passed through room after room, apartments of which the cumulative magnificence seemed only to enhance the earlier fancy that, at some wave of the wand—somewhat in the manner of Peer Gynt—furniture and armour, pictures and hangings, gold and silver, crystal and china, could turn easily and instantaneously into a heap of withered leaves blown about by the wind. From time to time Prince Theodoric made an appreciative comment, or Miss Walpole-Wilson interjected a minor correction of statement; although, in the latter case, it was clear that Truscott's effective handling of the matter of sitting next to her at luncheon had greatly reduced the potential of her critical assault.

We made an end of that part of the interior of the castle to be regarded as 'on show', returning to the ground floor, where we came at length to the head of a spiral staircase, leading down to subterranean depths. Here Sir Magnus was handed one of the torches by Truscott, and from this point he took over the rôle of showman. There was a slight pause. I saw Stringham and Truscott exchange a look.

'We are now descending to the dungeons,' said Sir Magnus, his voice trembling slightly. *'I sometimes think that is where we should put the girls who don't behave.'*

He made this little speech with an air almost of discomfort. A general titter rippled across the surface of the party, and there was a further pause, as of expectancy, perhaps on account of an involuntary curiosity to learn whether he would put this decidedly threatening surmise to practical effect. Truscott smiled gently, rather like a governess, or nanny, of wide experience who knows only too well that 'boys will be boys'. I could see from Stringham's face that he was suppressing a tremendous burst of laughter. It struck me, at this moment, that such occasions, the enjoyment of secret laughter, remained for him the peak of pleasure, for he looked suddenly happier; more buoyant, certainly, than when he had introduced me to Peggy Stepney. What perverse refinements, verbal or otherwise, were actually implied by Sir Magnus's words could only be guessed. It seemed that this remark, as an assertion of opinion, had always to be uttered at this point in the itinerary, and that its unfailing regularity was considered by his secretaries—if Stringham and Truscott could be so called—as an enormous hidden joke.

There was also the point to be remembered that Baby Wentworth, as Truscott had earlier reminded Stringham, 'did not like' these visits to the dungeons. I recalled some of Barnby's speculations regarding the reputed relationship between her and Sir Magnus. While scarcely to be supposed that, in truth, he physically incarcerated Mrs. Wentworth, or his other favourites, in the manner contemplated, frequent repetition of the words no doubt drew attention to sides of his nature that a girl often seen in his company might reasonably prefer to remain unemphasised. Sir Magnus's eyes had, in fact, paused for a second on Rosie Manasch when he had spoken that sentence. Now they ranged quickly over the faces of Lady Huntercombe, Miss Janet Walpole-Wilson, and Eleanor: coming to rest on the ingenuous profile of a little fair girl whose name I did not know. Then, moistening his lips slightly, he beckoned us on. The party began to descend the stairs, Sir Magnus leading the way.

It so happened that at that moment my shoe-lace came unfastened. There was an oak bench by the side of the staircase, and, resting my foot on this, I stooped to retie the lace, which immediately, as is the way, re-knotted itself tightly, delaying progress for a minute or more. The heels of the women echoed on the stones as the people clattered down the stairs, and then the sound of voices grew fainter, until hum of chatter and shuffle of feet became dim, ceasing at last in the distance. As soon as the shoe-lace was tied once more, I started off quickly down the steps, beside which an iron rail had been fixed as a banister. The way was dark, and the steps cut deep, so that I had slowed up by the time I came, only a short way below, to a kind of landing. Beyond this space the stairs continued again. I had passed this stage, and had just begun on the second flight, when a voice—proceeding apparently from out of the walls of the castle—suddenly spoke my name, the sound of which echoed round me, as the footsteps of the party ahead had echoed a short time before.

'Jenkins?'

I have to admit that I was at that moment quite startled by the sound. The tone was thick and interrogative. It seemed to emerge from the surrounding ether, a voice from out of the twilight of the stair, isolated from human agency, for near approach of any speaker, up or down the steps, would have been audible to me before he could have come as close as the sound suggested. A second later I became aware of its place of origin, but instead of relief at the simple explanation of what had at first seemed a mysterious, even terrifying, phenomenon, a yet more nameless apprehension was occasioned by the sight revealed. Just level with my head—as I returned a step or more up the stair—was a narrow barred window, or squint, through the iron grill of which, his face barely distinguishable in the shadows, peered

Widmerpool.

'Where is the Chief?' he asked, in a hoarse voice.

Once in a way, for a brief instant of time, the subconscious fantasies of the mind seem to overflow, so that we make, in our waking moments, assumptions as outrageous and incredible as those thoughts and acts which provide the commonplace of dreams. Perhaps Sir Magnus's allusion to the appropriate treatment of 'girls who don't behave', presumably intended by him at least in a relatively jocular manner, as he had pronounced the sentence, although, it was true, his voice had sounded unnaturally serious, had, for some unaccountable reason, resulted in the conjuration of this spectre, as the image seemed to be, that took form at that moment before my eyes. It was a vision of Widmerpool, imprisoned, to all outward appearance, in an underground cell, from which only a small grating gave access to the outer world: even those wider horizons represented only by the gloom of the spiral staircase. I felt a chill at my heart in the fate that must be his, thus immured, while I racked my brain, for the same brief instant of almost unbearable anxiety, to conjecture what crime, or dereliction of duty, he must have committed to suffer such treatment at the hands of his tyrant.

I record this absurd aberration on my own part only because it had some relation to what followed, for, so soon as anything like rational thought could be brought to bear on the matter, it was clear to me that Widmerpool was merely speaking from an outer passage of the castle, constructed on a lower level than the floor from which, a short time earlier, we had approached the head of the spiral stair. He had, in fact, evidently arrived from the back entrance, or, familiar with the ground plan of the building, had come by some short cut straight to this window.

'Why are you staring like that?' he asked, irritably.

I explained as well as I could the circumstances that caused me to be found in this manner wandering about the castle alone.

'I gathered from one of the servants that a tour was in progress,' said Widmerpool. 'I came over with the draft speech for the Incorporated Metals dinner. I am spending the week-end with my mother, and knew the Chief would like to see the wording as soon as possible—so that I could make a revision when one or two points had been settled. Truscott agreed when I rang up.'

'Truscott is showing the party round.'

'Of course.'

All this demonstrated clearly that arrangements initiated by Truscott at Mrs. Andriadis's party had matured in such a manner as to graft Widmerpool firmly on to the Donners-Brebner organisation, upon the spreading branches of which he seemed to be already positively blossoming. Before I could make further enquiries, on the tip of my tongue, regarding such matters as the precise nature of his job, or the closeness of touch maintained by him with his chief in tasks like the writing of speeches, Widmerpool continued to speak in a lower and more agitated tone, pressing his face between the iron bars, as if attempting to worm his way through their narrow interstices. Now that my eyes had become accustomed to the oddness of his physical position, some of the earlier illusion of forcible confinement dissolved; and, at this later stage, he seemed merely one of those invariably power-conscious beings—a rôle for which his temperament certainly well suited him—who preside over *guichets* from which tickets are dispensed for trains or theatres.

'I am glad to have an opportunity for speaking to you alone for a moment,' he said. 'I have been worried to death lately.'

This statement sent my thoughts back to his confession about Barbara on the night of the Huntercombes' dance, and I supposed that he had been suddenly visited with one of those spasms of frustrated passion that sometimes, like an uncured disease, break out with renewed virulence at a date when treatment seemed no longer necessary. After all, it was only in a fit of anger, however justifiable, that he had sworn he would not see her again. No one can choose, or determine, the duration of such changes of heart. Indeed, the circumstances of his decision to break with her after the sugar incident made such a renewal far from improbable.

'Barbara?'

He tried to shake his head, apparently in vehement negation, but was prevented by the bars from making this movement at all adequately to convey the force of his feelings.

'I was induced to do an almost insanely indiscreet thing about the girl you introduced me to.'

The idea of introducing Widmerpool to any girl was so far from an undertaking I was conscious ever of having contemplated, certainly a girl in relation to whom serious indiscretion on his part was at all probable, that I began to wonder whether success in securing the Donners-Brebner job had been too much for his brain, already obsessed with self-advancement, and that he was, in fact, raving. It then occurred to me that I might have brought him into touch with someone or other at the Huntercombes', although no memory of any introduction remained in my mind. In any case, I could not imagine how such a meeting might have led to a climax so ominous as that suggested by his tone.

'Gypsy,' he said, hesitating a moment over the name, and speaking so low as to be almost inaudible.

'What about her?'

The whole affair was hopelessly tangled in my head. I could remember that Barnby had said something about Widmerpool being involved with Gypsy Jones, but I have already spoken of the way of looking at life to which, in those days, I subscribed—the conception that sets individuals and ideas in hermetically sealed receptacles—and the world in which such things could happen at which Widmerpool seemed to hint appeared infinitely removed, I cannot now think why, from Stourwater and its surroundings. However, it was at last plain that Widmerpool had, in some manner, seriously compromised himself with Gypsy Jones. A flood of possible misadventures that could have played an unhappy part in causing his distress now invaded my imagination.

'A doctor was found,' said Widmerpool.

He spoke in a voice hollow with desperation, and this news did not allay the suspicion that whatever was amiss must be fairly serious; though for some reason the exact cause of his anxiety still remained uncertain in my mind.

'I believe everything is all right now,' he said. 'But it cost a lot of money. More than I could afford. You know, I've never even committed a technical offence before—like using the untransferable half of somebody else's return ticket, or driving a borrowed car insured only in the owner's name.'

Giving expression to his dismay seemed to have done him good: at least to have calmed him.

'I felt I could mention matters to you as you were already familiar with the situation,' he said. 'That fellow Barnby told me you knew. I don't much care for him.'

Now, at last, I remembered the gist of what Mr. Deacon had told me, and, incredible as I should have supposed their course to be, the sequence of events began to become at least dimly visible: though much remained obscure. I have spoken before of the difficulties involved in judging other people's behaviour by a consistent standard—for, after all, one must judge them, even at the price of being judged oneself—and, had I been told of some similar indiscretion on the part, say, of Peter Templer I should have been particularly disturbed. There is, or, at least, should be, a fitness in the follies each individual pursues, and uniformity of pattern is, on the whole, rightly preserved in human behaviour. Such unwritten regulations seemed now to have been disregarded wholesale.

In point of fact Templer was, so far as I knew, capable of conducting his affairs without recourse to such extremities; and a crisis of this kind appeared to me so foreign to Widmerpool's nature—indeed, to what might almost be called his station in life—that there was something distinctly shocking, almost personally worrying, in finding him entangled with a woman in such circumstances. I could not help wondering whether or not there had been, or would be, material compensation for these mental, and financial, sufferings. Having regarded him, before hearing of his feelings for Barbara, as existing almost in a vacuum so far as the emotion of love was concerned, an effort on my own part was required to accept the fact that he had been engaged upon so improbable, indeed, so sinister, a liaison. If I had been annoyed to find, a month or two earlier, that he considered himself to possess claims of at least some tenuous sort on Barbara, I was also more than a trifle put out to discover that Widmerpool, so generally regarded by his contemporaries as a dull dog, had been, in fact, however much he might now regret it, in this way, at a moment's notice, prepared to live comparatively dangerously.

'I will tell you more some other time. Naturally my mother was distressed by the knowledge that I have had something on my mind. You will, of course, breathe a word to no one. Now I must find the Chief. I think I will go to the other end of this passage and cut the party off there. It is almost as quick as coming round to where you are.'

His voice had now lost some of its funereal note, returning to a more normal tone of impatience. The outline of his face disappeared as suddenly as it had become visible a minute or two before. I found myself alone on the spiral staircase, and now hurried on once more down the steep steps, trying to digest some of the information just conveyed. The facts, such as they were, certainly appeared surprising enough. I reached the foot of the stair without contriving to set them in any very coherent order.

Other matters now intervened. The sound of voices and laughter provided an indication of the path to follow, leading along a passage, pitch-dark and smelling of damp, at the end of which light flashed from time to time. I found the rest of the party standing about in a fairly large vaulted chamber, lit by the torches held by Sir Magnus and Truscott. Attention seemed recently to have been directed to certain iron staples, set at irregular intervals in the walls a short way from the paved floor.

'Where on earth did you get to?' asked Stringham, in an undertone. 'You missed an ineffably funny scene.'

Still laughing quietly to himself, he went on to explain that some kind of horse-play had been taking place, in the course of which Pardoe had borrowed the dog-chain that was almost an integral part of Eleanor's normal equipment, and, with this tackle, had attempted by force to fasten Rosie Manasch to one of the staples. In exactly what manner this had been done I was unable to gather, but he seemed to have slipped the chain round her waist, producing in this manner an imitation of a captive maiden, passable enough to delight Sir Magnus. Rosie Manasch herself, her bosom heaving slightly, seemed half cross, half flattered by this attention on Pardoe's part. Sir Magnus stood by, smiling very genially, at the same time losing none of his accustomed air of asceticism. Truscott was smiling, too, although he looked as if the situation had been allowed to get farther out of control than was entirely comfortable for one of his own cautious temperament. Eleanor, who had recovered her chain, which she had doubled in her hand and was swinging about, was perhaps not dissatisfied to see Rosie, sometimes a little patronising in her tone, reduced to a state of fluster, for she appeared to be enjoying herself for the first time since our arrival at the castle. It was perhaps a pity that her father had missed the tour. Only Miss Janet Walpole-Wilson stood sourly in the shadows, explaining that the supposed dungeon was almost certainly a kind of cellar, granary, or storehouse; and that the iron rings, so far from being designed to shackle, or even torture, unfortunate prisoners, were intended to support and secure casks or trestles. However, no one took any notice of her, even to the extent of bothering to contradict.

'The Chief was in ecstasies,' said Stringham. 'Baby will be furious when she hears of this.'

This description of Sir Magnus's bearing seemed a little exaggerated, because nothing could have been more matter-of-fact than the voice in which he enquired of Prince Theodoric: 'What do you think of my private prison, sir?'

The Prince's features had resumed to some extent that somewhat embarrassed fixity of countenance worn when I had seen him at Mrs. Andriadis's; an expression perhaps evoked a second or two earlier by Pardoe's performance, the essentially schoolboy nature of which Prince Theodoric, as a foreigner, might have legitimately failed to grasp. He seemed at first to be at a loss to know exactly how to reply to this question, in spite of its evident jocularity, raising his eyebrows and stroking his dark chin.

'I can only answer, Sir Magnus,' he said at last, 'that you should see the interior of one of our own new model prisons. They might surprise you. For a poor country we have some excellent prisons. In some ways, I can assure you, they compare very favourably, so far as modern convenience is concerned, with the accommodation in which my own family is housed—certainly during the season of the year when we are obliged to inhabit the Old Palace.'

This reply was received with suitable amusement; and, as the tour was now at an end—at least the serious part of it—we moved back once more along the passage. Our host, in his good-humour, had by then indisputably lost interest in the few minor points of architectural consideration that remained to be displayed by Truscott on the ascent of the farther staircase. Half-way up these stairs, we encountered Widmerpool, making his way down. He retired before the oncoming crowd, waiting at the top of the stairway for Sir Magnus, who was the last to climb the steps. The two of them remained in conference together, while the rest of us returned to the terrace overlooking the garden, where Sir Gavin and Lord Huntercombe were standing, both, by that time, showing unmistakable signs of having enjoyed enough of each other's company. Peggy Stepney had also reappeared.

'Being engaged really takes up all one's time,' said Stringham, after he had described to her the incidents of the tour. 'Weren't you talking of Peter? Do you ever see him these days? I never meet anyone or hear any gossip.'

'His sister tells me he ought to get married.'

'It comes to us all sooner or later. I expect it's hanging over you, too. Don't you, Peggy? He'll have to submit.'

'Of course,' she said, laughing.

They seemed now very much like any other engaged couple, and I decided that there could have been no significance in the withdrawal of her hand from his. In fact, everything about the situation seemed normal. There was not even a sense of the engagement being 'on' again, after its period of abeyance, presumably covered by the interlude with Mrs. Andriadis. I wondered what the Bridgnorths thought about it all. I did not exactly expect Stringham to mention the Andriadis party, indeed, it would have been surprising had he done so; but, at the same time, he was so entirely free from any suggestion of having 'turned over a new leaf', or anything that could possibly be equated with that state of mind, that I felt curious to know what the stages had been of his return to a more conventional form of life. We talked of Templer for a moment or two.

'I believe you have designs on that very strange girl you came over here with,' he said. 'Admit it yourself.'

'Eleanor Walpole-Wilson?'

'The one who produced the chain in the dungeon. How delighted the Chief was. Why not marry her?'

'I think Baby will be rather angry,' said Peggy Stepney, laughing again and blushing exquisitely.

'The Chief likes his few whims,' said Stringham. 'I don't think they really amount to much. Still, people tease Baby sometimes. The situation between Baby and myself is always rather delicate in view of the fact that she broke up my sister's married life, such as it was. Still, one mustn't let a little thing like that prejudice one. Here she is, anyway.'

If Mrs. Wentworth, as she came up, heard these last remarks, which could have been perfectly audible to her, she made no sign of having done so. She was looking, it was true, not best pleased, so that it was to be assumed that someone had already taken the trouble to inform her of the dungeon tour. At the same time she carried herself, as ever, with complete composure, and her air of dissatisfaction may have been no more than outward expression of a fashionable indifference to life. I was anxious to escape from the group and look for Jean, because I thought it probable that we should not stay for tea, and all chance of seeing her again would be lost. I had already forgotten about Widmerpool's troubles, and did not give a thought to the trying time he might be experiencing, talking business while overwhelmed with private worry, though it could at least have been said in alleviation that Sir Magnus, gratified by Pardoe's antics, was probably in a receptive mood. This occurred to me later when I considered Widmerpool's predicament with a good deal of interest; but at the time the people round about, the beauty of the castle, the sunlight striking the grass and water of the moat, made such decidedly sordid difficulties appear infinitely far away.

Even to myself I could not explain precisely why I wanted to find Jean. Various interpretations were, of course, readily available, of which the two simplest were, on the one hand, that—as I had at least imagined myself to be when I had stayed with the Templers—I was once more 'in love' with her; or, on the other, that she was an unquestionably attractive girl, whom any man, without necessarily ulterior motive, might quite reasonably hope to see more of. However, neither of these definitions completely fitted the case. I had brought myself to think of earlier feelings for her as juvenile, even insipid, in the approach, while, at the same time, I was certainly not disinterested enough to be able honestly to claim the second footing. The truth was that I had become once more aware of that odd sense of uneasiness which had assailed me when we had first met, while no longer able to claim the purely romantic conceptions of that earlier impact; yet so far was this feeling remote from a simple desire to see more of her that I almost equally hoped that I might fail to find her again before we left Stourwater, while a simultaneous anxiety to search for her also tormented me.

Certainly I know that there was, at that stage, no coherent plan in my mind to make love to her; if for no other reason, because, rather naïvely, I thought of her as married to someone else, and therefore removed automatically from any such sphere of interest. I was even young enough to think of married women as belonging, generically, to a somewhat older group than my own. All this must be admitted to be an altogether unapprehending state of mind; but its existence helps to interpret the strange, disconcerting fascination that I now felt: if anything, more divorced from physical desire than those nights lying in bed in the hot little attic room at La Grenadière, when I used to think of Jean—or Suzette, and other girls remembered from the past or seen in the course of the day.

Perhaps a consciousness of future connexion was thrown forward like a deep shadow in the manner in which such perceptions are sometimes projected: a process that may well explain what is called 'love at first sight': that knowledge that someone who has just entered the room is going to play a part in our life. Analysis at that moment was in any case out of reach, because I realised that I had been left, at that moment, standing silently by Mrs. Wentworth, to whom I now explained, *à propos de bottes*, that I knew Barnby. This information appeared, on the whole, to please her, and her manner became less disdainful.

'Oh, yes, how is Ralph?' she said. 'I didn't manage to see him before leaving London. Is he having lots of lovely love affairs?'

A sudden move on the part of the Walpole-Wilsons,

made with a view to undertaking preparations for return to Hinton, exempted me then and there from need to answer this question; rather to my relief, because it seemed by its nature to obstruct any effort to present Barnby, as I supposed he would wish, in the condition of a man who thought exclusively of Mrs. Wentworth herself. The decision to leave was probably attributable in the main to Miss Janet Walpole-Wilson, evidently becoming restless in these surroundings, admittedly unsympathetic to her. She had been standing in isolation for some time at the far end of the terrace, looking rather like a governess waiting to bring her charges home after an unusually ill-behaved children's party. Sir Gavin, too, showed signs of depression, after his talk with Lord Huntercombe. Even Prince Theodoric's friendliness, when we took leave of him did not succeed in lifting the cloud of his sense of failure in forwarding a favourite scheme.

'Getting on in life now, sir,' he said, in answer to some remark made by the Prince. 'Got to make way for younger men.'

'Nonsense, Sir Gavin, nonsense.'

Prince Theodoric insisted on coming to the door to say a final good-bye. A number of other guests, with Sir Magnus, followed to the place in the courtyard where the cars were waiting. Among this crowd of people I suddenly noticed Jean had reappeared.

'Bob is returning next month,' she said, when I approached her. 'Come to dinner, or something. Where do you live?'

I told her my address, feeling at the same time that dinner with the Duports was not exactly the answer to my problem. I suddenly began to wonder whether or not I liked her at all. It now seemed to me that there was something awkward and irritating about the manner in which she had suggested this invitation. At the same time she reminded me of some picture. Was it Rubens and *Le Chapeau de Paille*: his second wife or her sister? There was that same suggestion, though only for an instant, of shyness and submission. Perhaps it was the painter's first wife that Jean resembled, though slighter in build. After all, they were aunt and niece. Jean's grey-blue eyes were slanting and perhaps not so large as theirs. Some trivial remarks passed between us, and we said good-bye.

Turning from this interlude, I noticed a somewhat peculiar scene taking place, in which Widmerpool was playing a leading part. This was in process of enactment in front of the steps. He must have completed his business with Sir Magnus and decided to slip quietly away, because he was sitting in an ancient Morris which now resolutely refused to start. Probably on account of age, and hard use suffered in the past, the engine of this vehicle would roar for a second or two, when the car would give a series of jerks; and then, after fearful, thunderous shaking, the noise would die down and cease altogether. Widmerpool, red in the face, could be seen through the thick grime of the almost opaque windscreen, now pressing the self-starter, now accelerating, now shifting the gears. The car seemed hopelessly immobilised. Sir Magnus, the ground crunching under his tread, stepped heavily across towards the spot.

'Is anything wrong?' he asked, mildly.

The question was no doubt intended as purely rhetorical, because it must have been clear to anyone, even of far less practical grasp of such matters than Sir Magnus, that something was very wrong indeed. However, obeying that law that requires most people to minimise to a superior a misfortune which, to an inferior, they would magnify, Widmerpool thrust his head through the open window of the car, and, smiling reverentially, gave an assurance that all was well.

'It's quite all right, sir, quite all right,' he said. 'She'll fire in a moment. I think I left her too long in the sun.'

For a time, while we all watched, the starter screeched again without taking effect; the sound was decreasing and this time it stopped finally. It was clear that the battery had run out.

'We'll give you a push,' said Pardoe. 'Come on, boys.'

Several of the men went over to help, and Widmerpool, in his two-seater, was trundled, like Juggernaut, round and round the open space. At first these efforts were fruitless, but suddenly the engine began to hum, this sound occurring at a moment when, facing a wall, the car was so placed to make immediate progress forward impossible. Widmerpool therefore applied the brake, 'warming up' for several seconds. I could see, when once more he advanced his head through the window, that he was greatly agitated. He shouted to Sir Magnus: 'I must apologise for this, sir, I really must. It is too bad.'

Sir Magnus inclined his head indulgently. He evidently retained his excellent humour. It was then, just as the Walpole-Wilson party were settled in their two cars, that the accident happened. My attention had been momentarily distracted from the scene in which Widmerpool was playing the main rôle by manœuvres on the part of Sir Gavin to steer Rosie Manasch, this time successfully, into the seat beside him; with the unforeseen result that Miss Janet Walpole-Wilson, as if by irresistible instinct, immediately seated herself in the back of the same car. While these dispositions were taking place, Widmerpool, making up his mind to move, must have released the brake and pressed the accelerator too hard. Perhaps he was unaware that his gear was still in 'reverse'. Whatever the reason, the Morris suddenly shot backward with terrific force for so small a body, running precipitately into one of the stone urns where it stood, crowned with geraniums, at the corner of the sunken lawn. For a moment it looked as if Widmerpool and his car would follow the flower-pot and its heavy base, as they crashed down on to the grass, striking against each other with so much force that portions of decorative moulding broke from off the urn. Either the impact, or some sudden, and quite unexpected, re-establishment of control on Widmerpool's part, prevented his own wholesale descent on to the lower levels of the lawn. The engine of the Morris stopped again, giving as it did so a kind of wail like the departure of an unhappy spirit, and, much dented at the rear, the car rolled forward a yard or two, coming to rest at an angle, not far from the edge of the parapet.

Before this incident was at an end, the Walpole-Wilson chauffeur had already begun to move off, and, looking back, the last I saw of the actors was a glimpse of the absolutely impassive face of Sir Magnus, as he strode with easy steps once more across the gravel to where Widmerpool was climbing out of his car. The sun was still hot. Its rays caught the sweat glistening on Widmerpool's features, and flashed on his spectacles, from which, as from a mirror, the light was reflected. There was just time to see him snatch these glasses from his nose as he groped for a handkerchief. We passed under the arch, reaching the portcullis, and crossing the causeway over the moat, before anyone spoke. Once more the car entered the lanes and byways of that romantic countryside.

'That was a near one,' said Pardoe.

'Ought we to have stopped?' asked Lady Walpole-Wilson, anxiously.

'I wonder who it was,' she continued a moment later.

'Why, didn't you see?' said Eleanor. 'It was Mr. Widmerpool. He arrived at Stourwater some time after luncheon. Is he staying there, do you think?'

This information threw her mother into one of her not uncommon states of confusion, though whether the nervous attack with which Lady Walpole-Wilson was now visited could be attributed to some version, no doubt by that time hopelessly garbled, having come to her ears regarding Barbara and the sugar incident, it was not possible to say. More probably she merely looked upon Widmerpool and his mother as creators of a social problem with which she was consciously unwilling to contend. Possibly she had hoped that, in subsequent summers, the Widmerpools would find somewhere else in England to rent a cottage; or, at least, that after a single invitation to dinner the whole matter of Widmerpool's existence might be forgotten once and for all. Certainly she would not wish, over and above such strands as already existed, to be additionally linked to his mother. That was certain. Nor could there be any doubt that she would not greatly care for the idea of Widmerpool himself being in love with her niece. At the same time, nothing could be more positive than the supposition that Lady Walpole-Wilson would, if necessary, have shown the Widmerpools, mother and son, all the kindness and consideration that their presence in the locality—regarded, of course, in relation to his father's former agricultural connexion with her brother-in-law—might, in the circumstances, justly demand.

'Oh, I hardly think Mr. Widmerpool would be staying at Stourwater,' she said; adding almost immediately: 'Though I don't in the least know why I should declare that. Anyway . . . he seemed to be driving away from the castle when we last saw him.'

This last sentence was the product of instinctive kindness of heart, or fear that she might have sounded snobbish: the latter state of mind being particularly abhorrent to her at that moment because the attitude, if existent, might seem applied to an establishment which she could not perhaps wholly respect. She looked so despairing at the idea of Widmerpool possessing, as it were, an operational base in extension to the cottage from which he, and his mother, could already potentially molest Hinton, that I felt it my duty to explain with as little delay as possible that Widmerpool had recently taken a job at Donners-Brebner, and had merely come over that afternoon to see Sir Magnus on a matter of business. This statement seemed, for some reason, to put her mind at ease, at least for the moment.

'I was really wondering whether we should ask Mr. Widmerpool and his mother over to tea,' she said, as if the question of how to deal with the Widmerpools had now crystallised in her mind. 'You know Aunt Janet likes an occasional talk with Mrs. Widmerpool—even though they don't always see eye to eye.'

What followed gave me the impression that Lady Walpole-Wilson's sudden relief may have been to some extent attributable to the fact that she had all at once arrived at a method by which the Widmerpools might be evaded, or a meeting with them at least postponed. If this was her plan—and, although in many ways one of the least disingenuous of women, I think she must quickly have devised a scheme on that occasion—the design worked effectively, because, at this suggestion of her mother's, Eleanor at once clenched her teeth in a manner that always indicated disapproval.

'Oh, don't let's have them over when Aunt Janet is here,' she said. 'You know I don't really care for Mr. Widmerpool very much—and Aunt Janet has plenty of opportunity to have her gossips with his mother when they are both in London.'

Lady Walpole-Wilson made a little gesture indicating 'So be it', and there the matter seemed to rest, where, I suppose, she had intended it to rest. Disturbed by mixed feelings set in motion by benevolence and conscience, she had been no doubt momentarily thrown off her guard. Comparative equilibrium was now restored. We drove on; and, by that evening, Widmerpool was forgotten by the rest of the party at Hinton Hoo. However, although nothing further was said about Widmerpool, other aspects of the visit to Stourwater were widely discussed. The day had left Sir Gavin a prey to deep depression. The meeting with Prince Theodoric had provided, naturally enough, a reminder of former grandeurs, and the congenial nature of their reunion, by agreeable memories aroused, had no doubt at the same time equally called to mind the existence of old, unhealed wounds.

'Theodoric is a man of the middle of the road,' he said. 'That, in itself, is sympathetic to me. In my own case, such an attitude has, of course, been to a large extent a professional necessity. All the same it is in men like Károlyi and Sforza that I sense a kind of fundamental reciprocity of thought.'

'He seems a simple young man,' said Miss Walpole-Wilson. 'I find no particular fault in him. No doubt he will have a difficult time with that brother of his.'

'Really, the Prince could not have been more friendly,' said Lady Walpole-Wilson, 'and Sir Magnus, too. He was so kind. I can't think why he has never married. So nice to see the Huntercombes. Pretty little person, Mrs. Wentworth.'

'So your friend Charles Stringham is engaged again,' said Rosie Manasch, rather maliciously. 'I wonder why it hasn't been in the papers. Do you think his mother is holding up the announcement for some reason? Or the Bridgnorths? They sound rather a stuffy pair, so it may be them.'

'How long ought one to wait until one puts an engagement in print?' asked Pardoe.

'Are you secretly engaged, Johnny?' said Rosie. 'I'm sure he is, aren't you?'

'Of course I am,' said Pardoe. 'To half a dozen girls, at least. It's just a question of deciding which is to be the lucky one. Don't want to make a mistake.'

'I've arranged to see the hound puppies on Tuesday,' said Eleanor. 'What a pity you will all be gone by then.'

However, she spoke as if she could survive the disbandment of our party. I pondered some of the events of the day, especially the situations to which, by some inexorable fate, Widmerpool's character seemed to commit him. This last misfortune had been, if anything, worse than the matter of Barbara and the sugar. And yet, like the phœnix, he rose habitually, so I concluded, recalling his other worries, from the ashes of his own humiliation. I could not help admiring the calm manner in which Sir Magnus had accepted damage of the most irritating kind to his property: violation which, to rich or poor, must always represent, to a greater or lesser degree, assault upon themselves and their feelings. From this incident, I began to understand at least one small aspect of Sir Magnus's prescriptive right to have become in life what Uncle Giles would have called 'a person of influence'. The point about Jean that had impressed me most, I thought, was that she was obviously more intelligent than I had previously supposed. In fact she was almost to be regarded as an entirely new person. If the chance arose again, it was in that capacity that she must be approached.

Sir Gavin straightened the photograph of Prince Theodoric's father, wearing hussar uniform, that stood on the piano in a plain silver frame, surmounted by a royal crown.

'His helmet now shall make a hive for bees . . .' he remarked, as he sank heavily into an arm-chair.

4.

A SENSE of maturity, or at least of endured experience, is conveyed, for some reason, in the smell of autumn; so it seemed to me, passing one day, by chance, through Kensington Gardens. The eighteen months or less since that Sunday afternoon on the steps of the Albert Memorial, with the echoing of Eleanor's whistle, and Barbara's fleeting grasp of my arm, had become already measureless as an eternity. Now, like scraps of gilt peeled untidily from the mosaic surface of the neo-Gothic canopy, the leaves, stained dull gold, were blowing about in the wind, while, squatting motionless beside the elephant, the Arab still kept watch on summer's mirage, as, once more, the green foliage faded gradually away before his displeased gaze. Those grave features implied that for him, too, that year, for all its monotony, had also called attention, in different aspects, to the processes of life and death that are always on the move. For my own part, I felt myself peculiarly conscious of these unalterable activities. For example, Stringham, as he had himself foreshadowed, was married to Peggy Stepney in the second week of October; the same day, as it happened, that saw the last of Mr. Deacon.

'Don't miss Buster's present,' Stringham just had time to remark, as the conveyor-belt of wedding guests evolved sluggishly across the carpet of the Bridgnorths' drawing-room in Cavendish Square.

There was opportunity to do no more than take the hand, for a moment, of bride and bridegroom; but Buster's present could hardly have remained invisible: a grandfather clock, gutted, and fitted up with shelves to form a 'cocktail cabinet', fully equipped with glasses, two shakers, and space for bottles. A good deal of money had evidently been spent on this ingenious contrivance. There was even a secret drawer. I could not make up my mind whether the joke was not, in reality, against Stringham. The donor himself, perhaps physically incapacitated by anguish of jealousy, had been unable to attend the church; and, since at least one gossip column had referred to 'popular Commander Foxe's temporary retirement to a nursing home', there seemed no reason to disbelieve in the actuality of Buster's seizure.

Stringham's mother, no less beautiful, so it seemed to me, than when, as a schoolboy, I had first set eyes on her—having at last made up her mind, as her son had put it, 'whether to laugh or cry'—had wept throughout the whole of the service into the corner of a small, flame-coloured handkerchief. By the time of the reception, however, she had made a complete recovery. His sister, Flavia, I saw for the first time. She had married as her second husband an American called Wisebite, and her daughter, Pamela Flitton, a child of six or seven, by the earlier marriage, was one of the bridesmaids. Well dressed, and good-looking, Mrs. Wisebite's ties with Stringham were not known to me. She was a few years older than her brother, who rarely mentioned her. Miss Weedon, rather pale in the face, and more beaky than I remembered, sat in one of the back pews. I recalled the hungry looks she used to dart at Stringham on occasions when I had seen them together years before.

Neither of Peggy Stepney's parents looked specially cheerful, and rumours were current to the effect that objections had been raised to the marriage by both families. It appeared to have been Stringham himself who had insisted upon its taking place. Such opposition as may have existed had been, no doubt, finally overcome by conviction on the Bridgnorths' part that it was high time for their elder daughter to get married, since she could not subsist for ever on the strength of photographs, however charming, in the illustrated papers; and they could well have decided, in the circumstances, that she might easily pick on a husband less presentable than Stringham. Lord Bridgnorth, a stout, red-faced man, wearing a light grey stock and rather tight morning clothes, was notable for having owned a horse that won the Derby at a hundred to seven. His wife—daughter of a Scotch duke, to one of the remote branches of whose house Sir Gavin Walpole-Wilson's mother had belonged—was a powerful figure in the hospital world, where she operated, so I had been informed, in bitter competition with organisations supported by Mrs. Foxe: a rivalry which their new relationship was hardly likely to decrease. The Walpole-Wilsons themselves were not present, but Lady Huntercombe, arrayed more than ever like Mrs. Siddons, was sitting with her daughters on the bride's side of the church, and later disparaged the music.

Weddings are notoriously depressing affairs. It looked as if this one, especially, had been preceded by more than common display of grievance on the part of persons regarding themselves as, in one way or another, fairly closely concerned, and therefore possessing the right to raise difficulties and proffer advice. Only Lady Anne Stepney appeared to be, for once, enjoying herself unreservedly. She was her sister's chief bridesmaid, and, as a kind of public assertion of rebellion against convention of all kind, rather in Mr. Deacon's manner, she was wearing her wreath back to front; a disorder of head-dress that gravely prejudiced the general appearance of the cortège as it passed up the aisle. Little Pamela Flitton, who was holding the bride's train, felt sick at this same moment, and rejoined her nurse at the back of the church.

I returned to my rooms that evening in rather low spirits; and, just as I was retiring to bed, Barnby rang up with the news—quite unexpected, though I had heard of his indisposition—that Mr. Deacon had died as the result of an accident. Barnby's account of how this had come about attested the curious fitness that sometimes attends the manner in which people finally leave this world; for, although Mr. Deacon's end was not exactly dramatic within the ordinary meaning of the term, its circumstances, as he himself would have wished, could not possibly be regarded as commonplace. In many ways the embodiment of bourgeois thought, he could have claimed with some justice that his long struggle against the shackles of convention, sometimes inwardly dear to him, had, in the last resort, come to his aid in releasing him from what he would have considered the shame of a bourgeois death.

Although the demise was not a violent one in the most usual sense of the word, it unquestionably partook at the same time of that spirit of carelessness and informality always so vigorously advocated by Mr Deacon as a precept for pursuing what Sillery liked to call 'The Good Life'. Sillery's ideas upon that subject were, of course, rather different, on the whole, from Mr. Deacon's, in spite of the fact that both of them, even according to their own lights, were adventurers. But, although each looked upon himself as a figure almost Promethean in spirit of independence—godlike, and following ideals of his own, far from the well-worn tracks of fellow men—their chosen roads were also acknowledged by each to be set far apart.

Mr. Deacon and Sillery must, in fact, have been just about the same age. Possibly they had known each other in their troubled youth (for even Sillery had had to carve out a career for himself in his early years), and some intersection of those unrestricted paths to which each adhered no doubt explained at least a proportion of Sillery's disapproval of Mr. Deacon's habits. Any such strictures on Sillery's part were at least equally attributable to prudence: that sense of self-preservation, and desire to 'keep on the safe side', of which Sillery, among the many other qualities to which he could lay claim, possessed more than a fair share.

When, in an effort to complete the picture, I had once asked Mr. Deacon whether, in the course of his life, he had ever run across Sillery, he had replied in his deep voice, accompanied by that sardonic smile: 'My father, a man of modest means, did not send me to the university, I sometimes think—with due respect, my dear Nicholas, to your own *Alma Mater*—that he was right.'

In that sentence he avoided a direct answer, while framing a form of words not specifically denying possibility of the existence of an ancient antagonism; his careful choice of phrase at the same time excusing him from commenting in any manner whatsoever on the person concerned. It was as if he insisted on upon Sillery's status as an essentially academical celebrity: a figure not properly to be discussed by one who had never been—as Mr. Deacon was accustomed to put it in the colloquialism of his own generation—'a 'varsity man'. There was also more than a hint of regret implicit in the deliberately autobiographical nature of this admission, revealing an element to be taken into account in any assessment of Mr. Deacon's own outlook.

At the time of his death, few, if any, of Mr. Deacon's friends knew the jealously guarded secret of his age more exactly than within a year or two; in spite of the fatal accident having taken place on his birthday—or, to be pedantic about chronology, in the small hours of the day following his birthday party. I was myself not present at the latter stages of this celebration, begun at about nine o'clock on the evening before, having preferred, as night was already well advanced, to make for home at a moment when Mr. Deacon, with about half a dozen remaining guests, had decided to move on to a night-club. Mr. Deacon had taken this desertion—my own and that of several other friends, equally weak in spirit—in bad part, quoting: 'Blow, blow, thou winter wind . . .' rather as if enjoyment of his hospitality had put everyone on his honour to accept subjection to the host's will for at least a period of twelve hours on end. However, the dissolution of the party was clearly inevitable. The club that was their goal, newly opened, was expected by those conversant with such matters to survive no more than a week or two, before an impending police raid: a punctual visit being, therefore, regarded as a matter of comparative urgency for any amateur of 'night life'. In that shady place, soon after his arrival there, Mr. Deacon fell down the stairs.

Even in this undignified mishap there had been, as ever, that touch of martyrdom inseparable from the conduct of his life, since he had been on his way, so it was learnt afterwards, to lodge a complaint with the management regarding the club's existing sanitary arrangements: universally agreed to be deplorable enough. It was true that he might have taken a little more to drink than was usual for someone who, after the first glass or two, was relatively abstemious in his habit. His behaviour at Mrs. Andriadis's, occasioned, of course, far more by outraged principles than unaccustomed champagne, had been, so I discovered from Barnby, quite exceptional in its unbridled nature, and had proved, indeed, a source of great worry to Mr. Deacon in the weeks that followed.

As a matter of fact, I had never learnt how the question of his exit from the house in Hill Street had been finally settled. Whether Mr. Deacon had attempted to justify himself with Mrs. Andriadis, or whether she, on her part, compelled him—with, or without, the assistance of men-servants, Max Pilgrim, or the negro—to clear up the litter of papers in the hall, the future never revealed. Mr. Deacon himself, on subsequent occasions, chose to indicate only in the most general terms that he had found Mrs. Andriadis's party unenjoyable. When her name had once cropped up in conversation, he echoed a sentiment often expressed by Uncle Giles, in remarking: 'People's manners have changed a lot since the war—not always for the better.' He did not disclose, even to Barnby, who acted in some respects almost as his conscience, the exact reason for his quarrel with the singer, apart from the fact that he had taken exception to specific phrases in the song, so that the nature of his difference with Pilgrim on some earlier occasion remained a matter for speculation.

However, if undeniable that at Hill Street Mr. Deacon had taken perhaps a glass or two more of champagne than was wise, the luxurious style of the surroundings had no doubt also played their part in stimulating that quixotic desire, never far below the surface in all his conduct, to champion his ideals, wherever he found himself, however unsuitable the occasion. At the night-club he was, of course, in more familiar environment, and it was agreed by everyone present that the fall had been in no way attributable to anything more than a rickety staircase and his own habitual impetuosity. The truth was that, as a man no longer young, he would have been wiser in this, and no doubt in other matters too, to have shown less frenzied haste in attempting to bring about the righting of so many of life's glaring wrongs.

At such an hour, in such a place, nothing much was thought of the fall at the time, neither by Mr. Deacon nor the rest of his party. He had complained, so it was said, only of a bruise on his thigh and a 'shaking up' inside. Indeed, he had insisted on prolonging the festivities, if they could be so called, until four o'clock in the morning: an hour when Barnby, woken at last after repeated knocking, had been roused to admit him, with Gypsy, once more to the house, because the latch-key had by that time been lost or mislaid. Mr. Deacon had gone into hospital a day or two later. He must have sustained some internal injury, for he died within the week.

We had met fairly often in the course of renewed acquaintance, for I had taken to dropping in on Barnby once or twice a week, and we would sometimes descend to the shop, or Mr. Deacon's sitting-room, for a talk, or go across with him to the pub for a drink. Now he was no more. Transition between the states of life and death had been effected with such formidable rapidity that his anniversary seemed scarcely completed before he had been thus silently called away; and, as Barnby remarked some time later, it was 'hard to think of Edgar without being overwhelmed with moralisings of a somewhat banal kind'. I certainly felt sad that I should not see Mr. Deacon again. The milestones provided by him had now come suddenly to an end. The road stretched forward still.

'Edgar's sister is picking up the pieces,' Barnby said. 'She is a clergyman's wife, living in Norfolk, and has already had a shattering row with Jones.'

He had made this remark when informing me by telephone of arrangements made for the funeral, which was to take place on a Saturday: the day, as it happened, upon which I had agreed to have supper with Widmerpool and his mother at their flat. This invitation, arriving in the form of a note from Mrs. Widmerpool, had added that she was looking forward to meeting 'so old a friend' of her son's. I was not sure that this was exactly the light in which I wished, or, indeed, had any right, to appear; although I had to admit to myself that I was curious to learn from Widmerpool's lips, as I had not seen him since Stourwater, an account, told from his own point of view, of the course events had taken in connexion with himself and Gypsy Jones. I had already received one summary from Barnby on my first visit to Mr. Deacon's shop after return from the Walpole-Wilsons'. He had spoken of the subject at once, so that no question of betraying Widmerpool's confidence arose.

'Your friend paid,' Barnby had said. 'And that was all.'

'How do you know?'

'Jones told me.'

'Is she to be believed?'

'No statement on that subject can ever be unreservedly accepted,' said Barnby. 'But he has never turned up here since. Her story is that he left in a rage.'

'I don't wonder.'

Barnby shook his head and laughed. He did not like Gypsy, nor she him, and, so far as he was concerned, that was an end of the matter. I saw his point, though personally I did not share the obduracy of his views. In fact there were moments when Gypsy turned up at the shop and we seemed to get on rather well together. Her egotism was of that entirely unrestrained kind, always hard to resist when accompanied by tolerable looks, a passionate self-absorption of the crudest kind, extending almost far enough to threaten the limits of sanity: with the added attraction of unfamiliar ways and thought. Besides, there was something disarming, almost touching, about her imperfectly concealed respect for 'books', which played a considerable part in her conversation when not talking of 'chalking' and other political activities. However—as Barbara might have said—there was no need to become sentimental. Gypsy usually showed herself, on the whole, more agreeable than on the first night we had met, but she could still be tiresome enough if the mood so took her.

'Jones is an excellent specimen of middle-class female education brought to its logical conclusions,' Barnby used to say. 'She couldn't be more perfect even if she had gone to the university. Her head is stuffed full of all the most pretentious nonsense you can think of, and she is incapable—but literally incapable—of thought. The upper and lower classes can sometimes keep their daughters in order—the middle classes rarely, if ever. I belong to the latter, and I know.'

I felt this judgment unnecessarily severe. Claiming, as she did, some elementary knowledge of typing and shorthand, Gypsy was temporarily employed in some unspecified capacity, next-door to Mr. Deacon's, at the offices of the Vox Populi Press: duties alleged by Barnby to be contingent on 'sleeping with Craggs', managing director of that concern. There seemed no reason either to accept or refute this statement, for, as Mr. Deacon used to remark, not without a touch of pride in his voice: 'Indiscretion is Gypsy's creed.' There could be no doubt that she lived up to this specification, although, as a matter of fact, shared political sympathies might equally well have explained close association with Craggs, since the Press (which was, in truth, merely a small publishing business, and did not, as its name implied, print its own publications) was primarily concerned with producing books and pamphlets of an insurgent tone.

Mr. Deacon had talked a lot about his birthday party before it had taken place, discussing at great length who should, and who should not, be invited. He had determined, for some reason, that it was to be a 'respectable' gathering, though no one, not even Barnby and Gypsy

Jones, knew where—or rather at whom—Mr. Deacon was likely to draw the line. Naturally, these two were themselves to be present, and they were to ask, at Mr. Deacon's suggestion, some of their own friends. However, when the names of prospective candidates for invitation were actually put forward, there had been a good deal of argument on Mr. Deacon's part as to whether or not he could agree to allow some of the postulants 'in the house'—using the phrase I remembered Stringham attaching to Peter Templer years before—because a great many people, often unknown to themselves, had, at one time or another, caused offence to him in a greater or lesser degree. In the end he relented, vetoing only a few of Barnby's female acquaintances: procedure which certainly caused no hard feelings on Barnby's part.

Speaking for myself, I had been prepared for anything at Mr. Deacon's party. I was conscious, as it happened, of a certain sense of disappointment, even of annoyance, in my own life, and weariness of its routine. This was because, not many days before, I had rung up the Duports' house in Hill Street, and a caretaker, or whoever had answered the telephone, had informed me that the Duports had gone abroad again, and were coming back in the spring. This statement was accompanied by various hypotheses and suggestions on the part of the speaker, embedded in a suitable density of hesitation and subterfuge, that made the fact that Jean was, as my informant put it, 'expecting', no longer a secret even before this definitive word itself dropped into our conversation. This eventuality, I realised at once, was something to be inevitably associated with the married state; certainly not to be looked upon as unreasonable, or—as Mr. Deacon would say—'indiscreet'.

All the same, I felt, as I have said, disappointed, although aware that I could hardly claim that anything had taken place to justify even the faintest suspicion of a broken 'romance'. In fact, I could not even explain to myself why it was, for some reason, necessary to make this denial—that a relatively serious hope had been blighted—sufficiently clear in my own mind. In short, the situation encouraged the kind of mood that made the prospect of an entertainment such as Mr. Deacon's party promised to be, acceptable rather than the reverse. The same pervading spirit of being left, emotionally speaking, high and dry on a not specially Elysian coast, had also caused a faint pang, while having my hair cut, at seeing a picture of Prince Theodoric, sitting on the sands of the Lido between Lady Ardglass and a beautiful Brazilian, a reminder of the visit to Stourwater that now seemed so long past, and also of the perennial charm of female companionship in attractive surroundings. On thinking over this photograph, however, I recalled that, even apart from circumstances inherent in our different walks of life, the Prince's own preferred associate had been Mrs. Wentworth, so that he, too, had probably suffered a lack of fulfilment. Barnby had been delighted when his attention had been drawn to this snapshot.

'I knew Baby would ditch Theodoric,' he said. 'I wonder who the Brazilian girl was.'

He had even expressed a hope that he might succeed in bringing Mrs. Wentworth to Mr. Deacon's party.

'Somewhere where she would at least be sure of not meeting Donners,' he had added.

Certainly, Sir Magnus had not turned up at Mr. Deacon's, nor, for that matter, anyone at all like him. The sitting-room had been largely cleared of the many objects overflowed from the shop that were usually contained there. Chairs and sofa had been pushed back to the walls, which were hung on all sides, frame to frame, with his own paintings, making a kind of memorial hall of Mr. Deacon's art. Even this drastic treatment of the furniture did not entirely exempt the place from its habitually old-maidish air, which seemed, as a rule, to be vested in the extraordinary number of knick-knacks, tear-bottles and tiny ornamental cases for needles or toothpicks, that normally littered every available space.

At either end of the mantelpiece stood a small oval frame —the pair of them uniformly ornamented with sea shells— one of which contained a tinted daguerreotype of Mr. Deacon's mother, the other enclosing a bearded figure, the likeness, so it appeared, of Walt Whitman, for whom Mr. Deacon possessed a profound admiration. The late Mrs. Deacon's features so much resembled her son's as for the picture, at first sight, almost to cause the illusion that he had himself posed, as a *jeu d'esprit,* in crinoline and pork-pie hat. Juxtaposition of the two portraits was intended, I suppose, to suggest that the American poet, morally and intellectually speaking, represented the true source of Mr. Deacon's otherwise ignored paternal origins.

The atmosphere of the room had already become rather thick when I arrived upstairs that night, and a good many bottles and glasses were set about on occasional tables. After the meticulous process of selection to which they had been subjected, the first sight of the people assembled there came as something of an anti-climax; and Mr. Deacon's method of choosing was certainly not made at once apparent by a casual glance round the room. A few customers had been invited, picked from the ranks of those specially distinguished in buying expensive 'antiques'. These were mostly married couples, middle-aged to elderly, their position in life hard to define with any certainty. They laughed rather uneasily throughout the evening, in due course leaving early. The rest of the gathering was predominantly made up of young men, some of whom might reasonably have been considered to fall within Mr. Deacon's preferential category of 'respectable', together with others whose claim to good repute was, at least outwardly, less pronounced: in some cases, even widely open to question.

There were, however, two persons present who, as it now seems to me, first revealed themselves at Mr. Deacon's party as linked together in that mysterious manner that circumscribes certain couples, and larger groups of human beings: a subject of which I have already spoken in connexion with Widmerpool and myself. These two were Mark Members and Quiggin; although at that period I was, of course, unable to appreciate that this pair had already begun the course of their long pilgrimage together, regarding them as no more connected with each other than with myself. I had not set eyes upon Quiggin since coming down from the university, although, as it happened, I had already learnt that he was to be invited as the result of a chance remark let fall by Gypsy during discussion of arrangements to be made for the party.

'Don't let Quiggin get left over in the house at the end of the evening,' she had said. 'I don't want him snuffling round downstairs after I have just dropped off to sleep.'

'Really, the ineffable vanity of woman,' Mr. Deacon had answered sharply. 'Quiggin will not molest you. He thinks too much about himself, for one thing, to bother about anyone else. You can set your mind at rest on that point.'

'I'd rather be safe than sorry,' said Gypsy. 'He showed signs of making himself quite a nuisance the other night, you may like to know. I'm just warning you, Edgar.'

Thinking the person named might well be the same Quiggin I had known as an undergraduate, I enquired about his personal appearance.

'Very plain, I'm afraid, poor boy,' said Mr. Deacon. 'With a shocking North-Country accent—though I suppose one should not say such a thing. He is nephew of a client of mine in the Midlands. Rather hard up at the moment, he tells me, so he lends a hand in the shop from time to time. I'm surprised you have never run across him here. It gives him a pittance—and leisure to write. That's where his heart is.'

'He is J. G. Quiggin, you know,' said Gypsy. 'You must have read things by him.'

She may have thought that the importance she had ascribed to Quiggin as a potential source of nocturnal persecution of herself had been under-estimated by me, through ignorance of his relative eminence as a literary figure; and it was certainly true that I was unfamiliar with the name of the magazine mentioned by her as the organ to which he was said most regularly to contribute.

'No doubt about Quiggin's talent,' said Mr. Deacon. 'Though I don't like all his ideas. He's got a rough manner, too. All the same, he made himself very useful disposing of some books of a rather awkward sort—you need not snigger like that, Barnby—that I wanted to get rid of.'

Trying to recall terms of our mutual relationship when we had last seen anything of each other, I could remember only that I had met Quiggin from time to time up to the early part of my second year at the university, when, for some reason, he had passed completely out of my life. In this process of individual drifting apart, there was, where university circles were concerned, of course, nothing out of the way: undergraduate acquaintance flourishing and decaying often within a matter of weeks. I could remember commenting at one of Sillery's tea-parties that Quiggin seemed not to have been about for some time, at which, so far as I could recall, Sillery, through the medium of considerable verbal convolution, had indicated, or at least implied, that Quiggin's scholarship had been withdrawn by his college on grounds of idleness, or some other cause of dissatisfaction to the authorities; and that, not long after this had happened, he had been 'sent down'. That story had been, I thought, more or less substantiated by Brightman, a don at Quiggin's college. Certainly Brightman, at some luncheon party, had referred to 'that path trodden by scholarship boys whose mental equipment has been somewhat over-taxed at an earlier stage of their often injudiciously promoted education', and it was possible that he had used the case of Quiggin as an illustration.

I was rather impressed to hear that in the unfamiliar form of 'J. G. Quiggin' this former acquaintance was already known as a 'writer'; and admired, if only by Gypsy Jones. I also felt a little ashamed, perhaps merely on account of this apparent notoriety of his, to think, after finding in him something that had interested, if not exactly attracted, me, I had so easily forgotten about his existence.

My first sight of him at the party suggested that he had remained remarkably unchanged. He was still wearing his shabby black suit, the frayed trousers of which were maintained insecurely by a heavy leather belt with a brass buckle. His hair had grown a shade sparser round the sides of his dome-like forehead, and he retained that look of an undomesticated animal of doubtful temper. At the same time there was also his doggy, rather pathetic look about the eyes that had reminded me of Widmerpool, and which is a not uncommon feature of those who have decided to live by the force of the will. When we talked, I found that he had abandoned much of the conscious acerbity of manner that had been so much a part of social equipment at the university. It was not that he was milder—on the contrary, he seemed more anxious than ever to approach on his own terms every matter that arose—but he appeared to have come much nearer to perfection of method in his particular method of attacking life, so that for others there was not, as in former days, the same field of conversational pitfalls to be negotiated. No doubt this greater smoothness of intercourse was also to be explained by the fact that we had both 'grown up' in the year or two that had passed. He asked some searching questions, comparable to Widmerpool's, regarding my firm's publications, almost immediately suggesting that he should write a preface for a book to be included in one or other of some series mentioned to him.

It was at that stage we had been joined by Members, rather to my surprise, because, as undergraduates, Members and Quiggin had habitually spoken of each other in a far from friendly manner. Now a change of relationship seemed to have taken place, or, it would perhaps be more exact to say, appeared desired by each of them; for there was no doubt that they were prepared, at least momentarily, to be on the best of terms. The three of us talked together, at first perhaps with a certain lack of ease, and then with greater warmth than I remembered in the past.

I had, in fact, met Members with Short, who was a believer in what he called 'keeping up with interesting people', soon after I had come to live in London. This taste of Short's, with whom I occasionally had dinner or saw a film—as we had planned to do on the night when I had cut him for the Walpole-Wilson dinner-party—resulted in running across various former acquaintances not seen regularly as a matter of course, and Members, by now of some repute as a *litterateur,* was one of these. To find him at Mr. Deacon's was unexpected, however, for I had supposed Members, for some reason, to frequent literary circles of a more sedate kind, though quite why I should have thus regarded him I hardly know.

In contrast with Quiggin, Mark Members had altered considerably since his undergraduate period, when he had been known for the relative flamboyance of his dress. Him too I remembered chiefly from my first year at the university, though this was not because he had left prematurely, but rather on account of his passing into a world of local hostesses of more or less academical complexion, which I did not myself frequent. If I had considered the matter, it was to some similar layer of society in London that I should have pictured him attached: perhaps a reason for supposing him out of place at Mr. Deacon's. Possibly these ladies, most of them hard-headed enough in their own way, had been to some extent responsible for the almost revolutionary changes that had taken place in his appearance; for, even since our meeting with Short, Members had worked hard on his own exterior, in much the same manner that Quiggin had effected the interior modifications to which I have already referred.

There had once, for example, been at least a suggestion of side-whiskers, now wholly disappeared. The Byronic collar and loosely tied tie discarded, Members looked almost as neat round the neck as Archie Gilbert. His hair no longer hung in an uneven fringe, but was brushed severely away from his forehead at an acute angle; while he had also, by some means, ridded himself of most of his freckles, acquiring a sterner expression that might almost have been modelled on Quiggin's. In fact, he looked a rather distinguished young man, evidently belonging to the world of letters, though essentially to the end of that world least well disposed to Bohemianism in its grosser forms. He had been brought—Mr. Deacon had finally declared himself resigned to a certain number of uninvited guests, 'modern manners being what they are'—by a strapping, black-haired model called Mona, a friend of Gypsy's belonging, so Barnby reported, to a stage of Gypsy's life before she was known to Mr. Deacon.

Short had told me that Members did occasional work for one of the 'weeklies'—the periodical, in fact, that had commented rather disparagingly on Prince Theodoric's visit to England—and I had, indeed, read, with decided respect, some of the pieces there written by him. He had, I believed, failed to secure the 'first' expected of him, by Sillery and others, at the end of his university career, but, like Bill Truscott in another sphere, he had never relinquished the reputation of being 'a coming young man'. Speaking of reviews written by Members, Short used to say: 'Mark handles his material with remarkable facility,' and, not without envy, I had to agree with that judgment; for this matter of writing was beginning to occupy an increasing amount of attention in my own mind. I had even toyed with the idea of attempting myself to begin work on a novel: an act that would thereby have brought to pass the assertion made at La Grenadière, merely as a conversational pretext to supply an answer to Widmerpool, to the effect that I possessed literary ambitions.

As I have already said of Mrs. Andriadis's party, such latitudes are entered by a door through which there is rarely if ever a return. In rather the same manner, that night at Mr. Deacon's seemed to crystallise certain matters. Perhaps this crystallisation had something to do with the presence there of Members and Quiggin, though they themselves were in agreement as to the displeasure they both felt in the company assembled.

'You must admit,' said Members, looking round the room, 'it all looks rather like that picture in the Tate of the Sea giving up the Dead that were in It. I can't think why Mona insisted on coming.'

Quiggin concurred in finding Mr. Deacon's guests altogether unacceptable, at the same time paying suitable commendation to the aptness of the pictorial allusion. He looked across the room to where Mona was talking to Barnby, and said: 'It is a very unusual figure, isn't it? Epstein would treat it too sentimentally, don't you think? Something more angular is required, in the manner of Lipchitz or Zadkine.'

'She really *hates* men,' said Members, laughing dryly.

His amusement was no doubt directed at the impracticability of the unspoken desires of Quiggin, who, perhaps with the object of moving to ground more favourable to himself, changed the subject.

'Did I hear that you had become secretary to St. John Clarke?' he asked, in a casual voice.

Members gave his rather high laugh again. This was evidently a matter he wished to be approached delicately. He seemed to have grown taller since coming to London. His slim waist and forceful, interrogative manner rather suggested one of those strong-willed, elegant young salesmen, who lead the customer from the shop only after the intention to buy a few handkerchiefs has been transmuted into a reckless squandering on shirts, socks, and ties, of patterns to be found later fundamentally unsympathetic.

'At first I could not make up my mind whether to take it,' he admitted. 'Now I am glad I decided in favour. St. J. is rather a great man in his way.'

'Of course, one could not exactly call him a very great novelist,' said Quiggin, slowly, as if deliberating the question carefully within himself. 'But he is a *personality*, certainly, and some of his critical writing might be labelled as—well—shall we say "not bad"?'

'They have a certain distinction of thought, of course, in their rather old-fashioned manner.'

Members seemed relieved to concede this. He clearly felt that Quiggin, catching him in a weak position, had let him off lightly. St. John Clarke was the novelist of whom Lady Anne Stepney had spoken with approval. I had read some of his books towards the end of my time at school with great enjoyment; now I felt myself rather superior to his windy, descriptive passages, two-dimensional characterisation, and, so I had come to think, the emptiness of the writing's inner content. I was surprised to find someone I regarded as so impregnable in the intellectual field as I supposed Members to be, saddled with a figure who could only be looked upon by those with literary pretensions of any but the crudest kind as an Old Man of the Sea; although, in one sense, the metaphor should perhaps have been reversed, as it was Members who had, as it were, climbed upon the shoulders of St. John Clarke.

I can now see his defence of St. John Clarke as an interesting example of the power of the will, for his disinclination for St. John Clarke's works must have been at least equal to my own: possibly far in excess. As Members had made up his mind to accept what was probably a reasonable salary—though St. John Clarke was rather well known for being 'difficult' about money—his attitude was undoubtedly a sagacious one; indeed, a great deal more discerning than my own, based upon decidedly romantic premises. The force of this justification certainly removed any question of Quiggin, as I had at first supposed he might, opening up some sort of critical attack on Members, based on the charge that St. John Clarke was a 'bad writer'. On the contrary, Quiggin now seemed almost envious that he had not secured the post for himself.

'Of course, if I had a job like that, I should probably say something one day that wouldn't go down,' he commented, rather bitterly. 'I've never had the opportunity to learn the way successful people like to be treated.'

'St. J. knows your work,' said Members, with quiet emphasis. 'I brought it to his attention.'

He watched Quiggin closely after saying this. Once more I wondered whether there was any truth in Sillery's story, never verified in detail, to the effect that the two of them lived almost next-door in the same Midland town. In spite of Quiggin's uncouth, drab appearance, and the new spruceness of Members, there could be no doubt that they had something in common. As Quiggin's face relaxed at these complimentary words, I could almost have believed that they were cousins. Quiggin did not comment on the subject of this awareness of his own status as a writer now attributed to St. John Clarke, but, in friendly exchange, he began to question Members about his books, in process of being written or already in the press: projected works that appeared to be several in number—at least three, possibly four—consisting of poems, a novel, a critical study, together with something else, more obscure in form, the precise nature of which I have forgotten, as it never appeared.

'And you, J.G.?' asked Members, evidently not wishing to appear grudging.

'I am trying to remain one of the distinguished few who have not written a novel,' said Quiggin, lightly. 'The Vox Populi may be doing a fragment of autobiography of mine in the spring. Otherwise I just keep a few notes—odds and ends I judge of interest. I suppose they will find their way into print in due course. Everything does these days.'

'No streams of consciousness, I hope,' said Members, with a touch of malignity. 'But the Vox Populi isn't much of a publishing house, is it? Will they pay a decent advance?'

'I get so sick of all the "fine" typography you see about,' said Quiggin, dismissing the matter of money. 'I've told

Craggs to send it out to a jobbing printer, just as he would one of his pamphlets—print it on lavatory paper, if he likes. At least Craggs has the right political ideas.'

'I question if there is much of the commodity you mention to be found on the premises of the Vox Populi,' said Members, giving his thin, grating laugh. 'But no doubt that *format* would ensure a certain sale. Don't forget to send me a copy, so that I can try and say something about it somewhere.'

In leaving behind the kind of shell common to all undergraduates, indeed to most young men, they had, in one sense, taken more definite shape by each establishing conspicuously his own individual identity, thereby automatically drawing farther apart from each other. Regarded from another angle, however, Quiggin and Members had come, so it appeared, closer together by their concentration, in spite of differences of approach, upon the same, or at least very similar, aims. They could be thought of, perhaps, as representatives, if not of different cultures, at least of opposed traditions; Quiggin, a kind of abiding prototype of discontent against life, possessing at the same time certain characteristics peculiar to the period: Members, no less dissatisfied than Quiggin, but of more academic derivation, perhaps even sharing some of Mr. Deacon's intellectual origins.

Although he had already benefited from the tenets of what was possibly a dying doctrine, Members was sharp enough to be speedily jettisoning appurtenances, already deteriorated, of an outmoded æstheticism. Quiggin, with his old clothes and astringent manner, showed a similar sense of what the immediate future intimated. This was to be a race neck-and-neck, though whether the competitors themselves were already aware of the invisible ligament binding them together in apparently eternal contrast and comparison, I do not know. Certainly the attitude that was to exist mutually between them—perhaps best described as 'love-hate'—must have taken root long before anything of the sort was noticed by me. At the university their eclectic personalities had possessed, I had thought, a curious magnetism, unconnected with their potential talents. Now I was almost startled by the ease with which both of them appeared able to write books in almost any quantity; for Quiggin's relative abnegation in that field was clearly the result of personal choice, rather than lack of subject matter, or weakness in powers of expression.

Quiggin was showing no public indication of the attempts to ingratiate himself with Gypsy suggested by her earlier remarks. On the contrary, he seemed to be spending most of his time talking business or literary gossip of the kind in which he had indulged with Members. On the whole, he restricted himself to the men present, though once or twice he hovered, apparently rather ill at ease, in the vicinity of the model, Mona, in whom Barnby was also showing a certain interest. Gypsy had taken manifest steps to clean herself up for the party. She was wearing a bright, fussy little frock that emphasised her waif-like appearance. When I noticed her at a later stage of the evening's evolution, sitting on the knee of Howard Craggs, a tall, baldish man, in early middle age, with a voice like a radio announcer's, rich, oily, and precise in its accents, this sight made me think again of her brush with Widmerpool, and wish for a moment that I knew more of its details. Perhaps some processes of thought-transference afforded at that moment an unexpected dispensation from Gypsy herself of further enlightenment to my curiosity.

Craggs had been making fairly free for a considerable time in a manner that certainly suggested some truth in the aspersions put forward by Barnby. However, this perseverance on his part had apparently promoted no very ardent feeling of sympathy between them, there and then, for she was looking sullen enough. Now she suddenly scrambled out of his lap, straightening her skirt, and pushed her way across the room to where I was sitting on the sofa, talking—as I had been for some time—to a bearded man interested in musical-boxes. This person's connexion with Mr. Deacon was maintained purely and simply through their common interest in the musical-box market, a fact the bearded man kept on explaining: possibly fearing that his reputation might otherwise seem cheap in my eyes. At the arrival of Gypsy, probably supposing that the party was getting too rough for a person of quiet tastes, he rose from his seat, remarking that he must be 'finding Gillian and making for Hampstead'. Gypsy took the deserted place. She sat there for a second or two without speaking.

'We don't much like each other, do we?' she said at length.

I replied, rather lamely, that, even supposing some such mutual hostility to exist between us, there was no good reason why anything of the sort should continue; and it was true that I was conscious, that evening, of finding her notably more engaging than upon earlier meetings, comparatively amicable though some of these had been.

'Have you been seeing much of your friend Widmerpool lately?' she asked.

'I've just had a letter from his mother inviting me to dine with them next week.'

She laughed a lot at this news.

'I expect you heard he forked out,' she said.

'I gathered something of the sort.'

'Did he tell you himself?'

'In a manner of speaking.'

'Was he fed up about it?'

'He was, rather.'

She laughed again, though less noisily. I wondered what unthinkable passages had passed between them. It was evident that any interest, emotional or venal, invested by her in Widmerpool was now expended. There was something odious about her that made her, at the same time—I had to face this—an object of desire.

'After all, somebody had to cough up,' she said, rather defensively.

'So I suppose.'

'In the end he went off in a huff.'

This statement seemed explicit enough. There could be little doubt now that she had made a fool of Widmerpool I felt, at that moment, she was correct in assuming that I did not like her. She was at once aware of this disapproval.

'Why are you so stuck up?' she asked, truculently.

'I'm just made that way.'

'You ought to fight it.'

'I can't see why.'

As far as I can remember, she went on to speak of the 'social revolution', a subject that occupied a great deal of her conversation and Craggs's, too, while even Mr. Deacon could hold his own in such discussions, though representing a wilder and less regimented point of view than the other two. I was relieved of the necessity of expressing my own opinions on this rather large question—rivalling in intensity Lady Anne Stepney's challenge to the effect that she was herself 'on the side of the People' in the French Revolution—by the sudden appearance of Howard Craggs himself in the neighbourhood of the sofa upon which we were sitting; or rather, by then, lying, since for some reason she had put up her feet in such a manner as to require, so it seemed at the time, a change of position on my own part.

'I'm going soon, Gypsy,' said Craggs in his horrible voice, as if speaking lines of recitation for some public performance, an illusion additionally suggested by the name itself. 'Should you be requiring a lift?'

'I'm dossing down here,' she said. 'But I've got one or two thing to tell you before you leave.'

'All right, Gypsy, I'll have one more drink.'

He shambled off. We chatted for a time in a desultory manner—and some sort of an embrace may even have taken place. Soon after that she had said that she must find Craggs and tell him whatever information she wished to pass on. The party was by then drawing to close, or at least changing its venue, with such disastrous consequences for its host. I did not see Mr. Deacon again, after saying good-night to him on the pavement: nor Barnby until we met at the cremation.

Most funerals incline, through general atmosphere, to suggest the presence, or at least the more salient characteristics of the deceased; and, in the case of Mr. Deacon, the ceremony's emphasis was on the disorganised, undisciplined aspect of his character, rather than an echo of the shrewdness and precision that certainly made up the opposite side of his nature. Matters had been arranged by his sister, a small, grey-haired woman, whose appearance hardly at all recalled her brother. There had been some question as to what rites would be appropriate, as Mr. Deacon, latterly agnostic, was believed to have been a Catholic convert for some years as a young man. His sister had ruled out the suggestion of an undenominational service in favour of that of the Church of England. Upon this subject, according to Barnby, she had had words with Gypsy Jones; with the result that Gypsy, on anti-religious grounds, had finally refused to attend the funeral. This withdrawal had not worried Mr. Deacon's sister in the least. Indeed, it may have relieved her, since there was reason to suppose that she suspected, perhaps not unreasonably, the propriety of Gypsy's connexion with the shop. However, Barnby was extremely annoyed.

'Just like the little bitch,' he said.

The weather had turned warmer, almost muggy. About a dozen or fifteen people showed up, most of them belonging to that race of shabby, anonymous mourners who form the bulk of the congregation at all obsequies, whether high or low, rich or poor; almost as if the identical band trooped round unceasingly—like Archie Gilbert to his dances—from interment to interment. Among the leaden-coloured garments of these perpetual attendants upon Death, the lightish suit of a tall young man in spectacles stood out. The face was, for some reason, familiar to me. During the responses his high, quavering voice, repeating the words from the row behind, resounded throughout the little chapel. The sound was churchly, yet not of the Church. Then I remembered that this young man was Max Pilgrim, the 'public entertainer'—as Mr. Deacon had called him—with whom the scene had taken place at the end of Mrs. Andriadis's party. At the close of the service, his willowy figure shuddering slightly as he walked, Pilgrim hurried away. The reasons that had brought him there, however commendable, were only to be conjectured, and could be interpreted according to taste.

'That was a desperate affair,' Barnby had said, as we returned to the shop together.

We climbed the stairs to his studio, where, in preparation for tea, he put a kettle on a gas-ring, and, although it was still warm, lighted the fire; then, changing into overalls, began to prepare a canvas. I lay on the divan. We talked of Mr. Deacon for a time, until conversation fell into more general channels, and Barnby began to discourse on the subject of love.

'Most of us would like to be thought of as the kind of man who has a lot of women,' he said. 'But take such fellows as a whole, there are few enough of them one would wish to be at all like.'

'Do you wish to change your identity?'

'Not in the least. Merely to improve my situation in certain specific directions.'

'Which particular Don Juan were you thinking of?'

'Oh, myself, of course,' said Barnby. 'Funerals make one's mind drift in the direction of moral relaxation—though it's unaccountable to me the way intimate relations between the sexes are always spoken of, and written about, as if of necessity enjoyable or humorous. In practice they might much more truly be described as encompassing the whole range of human feeling from the height of bliss to the depths of misery.'

'Is something on your mind?'

Barnby agreed that this diagnosis was correct. He was about to enter into some further explanation, when, as if making a kind of rejoinder to the opinion just expressed, the bell of the telephone began to ring from below. Barnby wiped his hands on a cloth, and went off down the stairs to where the instrument stood on a ledge by the back entrance to the shop. For a time I heard him talking. Then he returned to the room, greatly exhilarated.

'That was Mrs. Wentworth,' he said. 'I was about to tell you when the telephone went that she was, in fact, the matter on my mind.'

'Is she coming round here?'

'Better than that. She wants me to go round and see her right away. Do you mind? Finish your tea, of course, and stay here as long as you like.'

He tore off his overalls, and, without attempting to tidy up the material of his painting, was gone almost immediately. I had never before seen him so agitated. The front door slammed. A sense of emptiness fell on the house.

In the circumstances, I could not possibly blame Barnby for absenting himself so precipitately, experiencing at the same time a distinct feeling of being left in a void, not less so on account of the substance of our conversation that had been in this way terminated so abruptly. I poured out another cup of tea, and thought over some of the things he had been saying. I could not help envying the opportune nature, so far as Barnby himself was concerned, of the telephone call, which seemed an outward indication of the manner in which he had—so it seemed to me in those days—imposed his will on the problem at hand.

His life's unusual variety of form provided a link between what I came, in due course, to recognise as the world of Power, as represented, for example, by the ambitions of Widmerpool and Truscott, and that imaginative life in which a painter's time is of necessity largely spent: the imagination, in such a case, being primarily of a visual kind. In the conquest of Mrs. Wentworth, however, other spheres—as the figures of Sir Magnus Donners and Prince Theodoric alone sufficiently illustrated—had inevitably to be invaded by him. These hinterlands are frequently, even compulsively, crossed at one time or another by almost all who practise the arts, usually in the need to earn a living; but the arts themselves, so it appeared to me as I considered the matter, by their ultimately sensual essence, are, in the long run, inimical to those who pursue power for its own sake. Conversely, the artist who traffics in power does so, if not necessarily disastrously, at least at considerable risk. I was making preparations to occupy my mind with such thoughts until it was time to proceed to the Widmerpools', but the room was warm, and, for a time, I dozed.

Nothing in life can ever be entirely divorced from myriad other incidents; and it is remarkable, though no doubt logical, that action, built up from innumerable causes, each in itself allusive and unnoticed more often than not, is almost always provided with an apparently ideal moment for its final expression. So true is this that what has gone before is often, to all intents and purposes, swallowed up by the aptness of the climax, opportunity appearing, at least on the surface, to be the sole cause of fulfilment. The circumstances that had brought me to Barnby's studio supplied a fair example of this complexity of experience. There was, however, more to come.

When I awoke from these sleepy, barely coherent reflections, I decided that I had had enough of the studio, which merely reminded me of Barnby's apparent successes in a field in which I was then, generally speaking, feeling decidedly unsuccessful. Without any very clear idea of how I would spend my time until dinner, I set off down the stairs, and had just reached the door that led from the back of the shop to the foot of the staircase, when a female voice from the other side shouted: 'Who is that?'

My first thought was that Mr. Deacon's sister had returned to the house. After the cremation, she had announced herself as retiring for the rest of the day to her hotel in Bloomsbury, as she was suffering from a headache. I supposed now that she had changed her mind, and decided to continue the task of sorting her brother's belongings, regarding some of which she had already consulted Barnby, since there were books and papers among Mr. Deacon's property that raised a number of questions of disposal, sometimes of a somewhat delicate kind. She had probably come back to the shop and again sought guidance on some matter. It was to be hoped that the point would not prove an embarrassing one. However, when I said my name, the person beyond the door turned out to be Gypsy.

'Come in for a moment,' she called.

I turned the handle and entered. She was standing behind the screen, in the shadows, at the back of the shop. My first impression was that she had stripped herself stark naked. There was, indeed, good reason for this misapprehension, for a second look showed that she was wearing a kind of bathing-dress, flesh-coloured, and of unusually sparing cut. I must have showed my surprise, because she burst into a paroxysm of laughter.

'I thought you would like to see my dress for the Merry Thought fancy-dress party,' she said. 'I am going as Eve.'

She came closer.

'Where is Barnby?' she asked.

'He went out. Didn't you hear him go? After he spoke on the telephone.'

'I've only just come in,' she said. 'I wanted to try out my costume on both of you.'

She sounded disappointed at having missed such an opportunity to impress Barnby, though I thought the display would have annoyed rather than amused him; which was no doubt her intention.

'Won't you be cold?'

'The place is going to be specially heated. Anyway, the weather is mild enough. Still, shut the door. There's a bit of a draught.'

She sat down on the divan. That part of the shop was shut off from the rest by the screen in such a way as almost to form a cubicle. As Mr. Deacon had described, shawls or draperies of some sort were spread over the surface of this piece of furniture.

'What do you think of the fig leaf?' she asked. 'I made it myself.'

I have already spoken of the common ground shared by conflicting emotions. As Barnby had remarked, the funeral had been 'hard on the nerves', and a consciousness of sudden relief from pressure was stimulating. Gypsy, somewhat altering the manner she had adopted on my first arrival in the shop, now managed to look almost prim. She had the air of waiting for something, of asking a question to which she already knew the answer. There was also something more than a little compelling about the atmosphere of the alcove: the operation perhaps of memories left over as a residue from former states of concupiscence, although so fanciful a condition could hardly be offered in extenuation. I asked myself whether this situation, or something not far from it, was not one often premeditated, and, although I still felt only half awake, not to be lightly passed by.

The lack of demur on her part seemed quite in accordance with the almost somnambulistic force that had brought me into that place, and also with the torpid, dream-like atmosphere of the afternoon. At least such protests as she put forward were of so formal and artificial an order that they increased, rather than diminished, the impression that a long-established rite was to be enacted, among Staffordshire figures and *papier-mâché* trays, with the compelling, detached formality of nightmare. Perhaps some demand, not to be denied in its overpowering force, had occasioned simultaneously both this summons and Mrs. Wentworth's telephone call; each product of that slow process of building up of events, as already mentioned, coming at last to a head. I was conscious of Gypsy changing her individuality, though at the same time retaining her familiar form; this illusion almost conveying the extraordinary impression that there were really three of us—perhaps even four, because I was aware that alteration had taken place within myself too—of whom the pair of active participants had been, as it were, projected from out of our normally unrelated selves.

In spite of the apparently irresistible nature of the circumstances, when regarded through the larger perspectives that seemed, on reflection, to prevail—that is to say of a general subordination to an intricate design of cause and effect—I could not help admitting, in due course, the awareness of a sense of inadequacy. There was no specific suggestion that anything had, as it might be said, 'gone wrong'; it was merely that any wish to remain any longer present in those surroundings had suddenly and violently decreased, if not disappeared entirely. This feeling was, in its way, a shock. Gypsy, for her part, appeared far less impressed than myself by consciousness of anything, even relatively momentous, having occurred. In fact, after the brief interval of extreme animation, her subsequent indifference, which might almost have been called torpid, was, so it seemed to me, remarkable. This imperturbability was inclined to produce an impression that, so far from knowing each other a great deal better, we had progressed scarcely at all in that direction; perhaps, become more than ever, even irretrievably, alienated. Barbara's recurrent injunction to avoid any question of 'getting sentimental' seemed, here in the embodiment of Gypsy, now carried to lengths which might legitimately be looked upon as such a principle's logical conclusion.

This likeness to Barbara was more clearly indicated, however, than by a merely mental comparison of theory, because, while Gypsy lay upon the divan, her hands before her, looking, perhaps rather self-consciously, a little like Goya's *Maja nude*—or possibly it would be nearer the mark to cite that picture's derivative, Manet's *Olympia,* which I had, as it happened, heard her mention on some former occasion—she glanced down, with satisfaction, at her own extremities.

'How brown my leg is,' she said. 'Fancy sunburn lasting that long.'

Were Barbara and Gypsy really the same girl, I asked myself. There was something to be said for the theory; for I had been abruptly reminded of Barbara's remark, uttered under the trees of Belgrave Square earlier in the year: 'How blue my hand is in the moonlight.' Self-admiration apart, there could be no doubt now that they had a great deal in common. It was a concept that made me feel that, in so far as I was personally involved in matters of sentiment, the season was, romantically speaking, autumn indeed, and that the leaves had undeniably fallen from the trees so far as former views on love were concerned: even though such views had been held by me only so short a time before. Here, at least, at the back of Mr. Deacon's shop, some conclusion had been reached, though even that inference, too, might be found open to question. At the same time, I could not help being struck, not only by a kind of wonder that I now found myself, as it were, with Barbara in conditions once pictured as beyond words vain of achievement, but also at that same moment by a sense almost of solemnity at this latest illustration of the pattern that life forms. A new phase in conversation was now initiated by a question from Gypsy.

'What was the funeral like?' she asked, as if making a deliberate return to every-day conditions.

'Short.'

'I think I was right not to go.'

'You didn't miss much.'

'It was a matter of conscience.'

She developed for a time this line of thought, and I agreed that, regarded in the light of her convictions, her absence might be looked upon as excusable, if any such severity of doctrine was indeed insurmountable. I agreed further that Mr. Deacon himself might have appreciated such scruples.

'Max Pilgrim was there.'

'The man who sings the songs?'

'He didn't at the cremation.'

'There comes a moment when you've got to make a stand.'

I presumed that she had returned to the problems of her own conscience rather than to refer to Pilgrim's restraint in having kept himself from breaking into song at the crematorium.

'Where will you stay now that the shop is coming to an end?'

'Howard says he can put me up once in a way at the Vox Populi. They've got a camp-bed there. He's taking me to the party tonight.'

'What's he going as?'

'Adam.'

'Is he arriving here in that guise?'

'We're dining early, and going back to his place to dress up. Only I thought I must try out my costume first. As a matter of fact he is picking me up here fairly soon.'

She looked rather doubtful, and I saw that I must not overstay my welcome. There was nothing to be said for allowing time to slip by long enough for Craggs to arrive. It appeared that Gypsy was going to the country—it was to be presumed with Craggs—in the near future. We said good-bye. Later, as I made my way towards the Widmerpools', association of ideas led inevitably to a reminder, not a specially pleasant one, of Widmerpool himself and his desires; parallel, it appeared, in their duality, with my own, and fated to be defrauded a second time. The fact that I was dining at his flat that evening in no way reduced the accentuation given by events to that sense of design already mentioned. Whatever the imperfections of the situation from which I had just emerged, matters could be considered with justice only in relation to a much larger configuration, the vast composition of which was at present—that at least was clear—by no means even nearly completed.

There is a strong disposition in youth, from which some individuals never escape, to suppose that everyone else is having a more enjoyable time than we are ourselves; and, for some reason, as I moved southwards across London, I was that evening particularly convinced that I had not yet succeeded in striking a satisfactory balance in my manner of conducting life. I could not make up my mind whether the deficiencies that seemed so stridently to exist were attributable to what had already happened that day, or to a growing certainty in my own mind that I should much prefer to be dining elsewhere. The Widmerpools—for I felt that I had already heard so much of Widmerpool's mother that my picture of her could not be far from the truth—were the last persons on earth with whom I wished to share the later part of the evening. I suppose I could have had a meal by myself, thinking of some excuse later to explain my absence, but the will to take so decisive a step seemed to have been taken physically from me.

They lived, as Widmerpool had described, on the top floor of one of the smaller erections of flats in the neighbourhood of Westminster Cathedral. The lift, like an ominously creaking funicular, swung me up to these mountainous regions, and to a landing where light shone through frosted panes of glass. The door was opened by a depressed elderly maid, wearing cap and pince-nez, who showed me into a drawing-room, where Widmerpool was sitting alone, reading *The Times*. I was dimly aware of a picture called *The Omnipresent* hanging on one of the walls, in which three figures in bluish robes stand or kneel on the edge of a precipice. Widmerpool rose, crumpling the paper, as if he were surprised to see me, so that for a painful moment I wondered whether, by some unhappy mistake, I had arrived on the wrong night. However, a second later, he made some remark to show I was expected, and asked me to sit down, explaining that 'in a minute or two' his mother would be ready.

'I am very much looking forward to your meeting my mother,' he said.

He spoke as if introduction to his mother was an experience, rather a vital one, that every serious person had, sooner or later, to undergo. I became all at once aware that this was the first occasion upon which he and I had met anywhere but on neutral ground. I think that Widmerpool, too, realised that a new relationship had immediately risen between us from the moment when I had entered the drawing-room; for he smiled in a rather embarrassed way, after making this remark about his mother, and seemed to make an effort, more conscious than any he had ever shown before, to appear agreeable. In view of the embarrassments he had spoken of when we had last met—and their apparent conclusion so far as he were concerned—I had expected to find him depressed. On the contrary, he was in unusually high spirits.

'Miss Walpole-Wilson is supping with us,' he said.

'Eleanor?'

'Oh, no,' he said, as if such a thing were unthinkable. 'Her aunt. Such a knowledgeable woman.'

Before any comment were possible, Mrs. Widmerpool herself came through the door, upon the threshold of which she paused for a moment, her head a little on one side.

'Why, Mother,' said Widmerpool, speaking with approval, 'you are wearing your bridge-coat.'

We shook hands, and she began to speak at once, before I could take in her appearance.

'And so you were both at Mr. Le Bas's house at school,' she said. 'I never really cared for him as a man. I expect he had his good qualities, but he never quite appreciated Kenneth.'

'He was an odd man in many ways.'

'Kenneth so rarely brings the friends of his school days here.'

I said that we had also stayed together with the same French family in Touraine; for, if I had to be regarded as a close friend of her son's, it was at La Grenadière that I had come to know him best, rather than at school, where he had always seemed a figure almost too grotesque to take seriously.

'At the Leroys'?' she asked, as if amazed at the brilliance of my parents in having hit on the only possible household in the whole of France.

'For six weeks or so.'

She turned to Widmerpool.

'But you never told me that,' she said. 'That was naughty of you!'

'Why should I?' said Widmerpool. 'You didn't know him.'

Mrs. Widmerpool clicked her tongue against the roof of her mouth. Her large features distinctly recalled the lineaments of her son, though she had perhaps been good looking when younger. Even now she seemed no more than in her late forties, though I believe she was, in fact, older than that. However, her well-preserved appearance was in striking contrast with Widmerpool's own somewhat decaying youth, so that the pair of them appeared almost more like contemporaries, even husband and wife, rather than mother and son. Her eyes were brighter than his, and she rolled them, expanding the pupils, in comment to any remark that might be thought at all out of the ordinary. Her double row of firm teeth were set between cheeks of brownish red, which made her a little resemble Miss Walpole-Wilson, with whom she clearly possessed something discernibly in common that explained their friendly connexion. She seemed a person of determination, from whom no doubt her son derived much of his tenacity of purpose. The garment to which he referred was of flowered velvet, with a fringe, and combined many colours in its pattern.

'I hear you know the Gorings,' she said. 'It seems such a pity they have allowed Barbara to run so wild. She used to be such a dear little girl. There really appears to be something a trifle queer about Lord Aberavon's grandchildren.'

'Oh, shut up, Mother,' said Widmerpool, changing his almost amatory manner unexpectedly. 'You don't know anything about it.'

He must have felt, not entirely without reason, that his mother was on delicate ground in bringing up so early, and in such a critical spirit, the subject of Gorings and Walpole-Wilsons. Mrs. Widmerpool seemed not at all put out by the brusque form of address used by her son, continuing to express herself freely on the characteristics, in her eyes, good, bad and indifferent, of Barbara and Eleanor, adding that she understood that neither of the Goring sons were 'very much of a hand at their books'. She felt perhaps that now was the time to unburden herself upon matters hardly to be pursued with the same freedom after the arrival of Miss Janet Walpole-Wilson. From her comments, I supposed that Widmerpool must have given his mother, perhaps involuntarily, some indication that the Gorings were out of favour with him; although it was impossible to guess how accurately she might be informed about her son's former feelings for Barbara: even if she knew of them at all. It was possible that she had attributed the anxiety he had gone through with Gypsy Jones to a later aggravation of his entanglement with Barbara: in fact, the same conclusion to which I had myself first arrived, when, at Stourwater, he had spoken of the troubles that were oppressing him.

'There doesn't seem any sign of Eleanor getting married yet,' said Mrs. Widmerpool, almost dreamily, as if she were decrying in the depths of the gas-fire a vision invisible to the rest of us, revealing the unending cavalcade of Eleanor's potential suitors.

'Perhaps she doesn't want to,' said Widmerpool, in a tone evidently intended to close the subject. 'I expect you two will like a talk on books before the end of the evening.'

'Yes, indeed, for I hear you are in the publishing trade,' said his mother. 'You know, I have always liked books and bookish people. It is one of my regrets that Kenneth is really too serious-minded to enjoy reading for its own sake. I expect you are looking forward to those articles in *The Times* by Thomas Hardy's widow. I know I am.'

While I was making some temporising answer to these reassurances on Mrs. Widmerpool's part regarding her inclination towards literature, Miss Walpole-Wilson was announced, who excused her lateness on the grounds of the chronic irregularity of the bus service from Chelsea, where her flat was situated. She was wearing a mackintosh, of which, for some reason, she had refused to divest herself in the hall; exemplifying in this manner a curious trait common to some persons of wilful nature, whose egotism seems often to make them unwilling, even incapable, of shedding anything of themselves until they can feel that they have safely reached their goal. She now removed this waterproof, folding and establishing it upon a chair—an act watched by her hostess with a fixed smile that might have signified disapproval—revealing that she, too, was wearing a richly-coloured coat. It was made of orange, black, and gold silk: a mandarin's coat, so she explained, that Sir Gavin had given her years before.

The relationship between Mrs. Widmerpool and Miss Walpole-Wilson, in general an amicable one, gave the impression of resting not exactly upon planned alliance so much as community of interest, unavoidable from the nature of the warfare both waged against the rest of the world. Miss Walpole-Wilson was, of course, as she sometimes described herself, 'a woman of wide interests', while Mrs. Widmerpool concerned herself with little that had not some direct reference to the career of her son. At the same time there was an area of common ground where disparagement of other people brought them close together, if only on account of the ammunition with which each was able to provide the other: mutual aid that went far to explain a friendship long established.

Miss Walpole-Wilson's manner that evening seemed intended to notify the possession of some important piece of news to be divulged at a suitable moment. She had, indeed, the same air as Widmerpool: one, that is to say, suggesting that she was unusually pleased with herself. We talked for a time, until the meal was despondently announced by the decrepit house-parlourmaid, who, a minute or two later, after we had sat down to cold food in a neighbouring room, hurried plates and dishes round the table with reckless speed, as if she feared that death—with which the day seemed still associated in my mind—would intervene to terminate her labours. There was a bottle of white wine. I asked Miss Walpole-Wilson whether she had been seeing much of Eleanor.

'Eleanor and I are going for a sea trip together,' she said. 'A banana boat to Guatemala.'

'Rather wise to get her away from her family for a bit,' said Mrs. Widmerpool, making a grimace.

'Her father is full of old-fashioned ideas,' said Miss Walpole-Wilson, 'and he won't be laughed out of them.'

'Eleanor will enjoy the free life of the sea,' Mrs. Widmerpool agreed.

'Of course she will,' said Miss Walpole-Wilson; and, pausing for a brief second to give impetus to her question, added: 'You have heard, I expect, about Barbara?'

It was clear from the way she spoke that she felt safe in assuming that none of us could possibly have heard already whatever her news might be. I thought, though the supposition may have been entirely mistaken, that for an instant she fixed her eyes rather malignantly on Widmerpool; and certainly there was no reason to suggest that she knew anything of his former interest in Barbara. However, if she intended to tease him, she scored a point, for at mention of the name his face at once took on a somewhat guilty expression. Mrs. Widmerpool enquired curtly what had happened. She also seemed to feel that Miss Walpole-Wilson might be trying to provoke her son.

'Barbara is engaged,' said Miss Walpole-Wilson, smiling, though without good-humour.

'Who to?' asked Widmerpool, abruptly.

'I can't remember whether you know him,' she said. 'He is a young man in the Guards. Rich, I think.'

I felt certain, immediately, that she must refer to someone I had never met. Many people can never hear of any engagement without showing envy, and no one can be quite disinterested who has been at one time an implicated party. The thought that the man would turn out to be unknown to me was, therefore, rather a relief.

'But what is the name?' said Widmerpool, insistently.

He was already nettled. There could be no doubt that Miss Walpole-Wilson was deliberately tormenting him, although I could not decide whether this was simply her usual technique in delaying the speed at which she passed on gossip with the object of making it more appetising, or because she knew, either instinctively or from specific information in her possession, that he had been concerned with Barbara. For a moment or two she smiled round the table frostily.

'He is called Pardoe,' she said, at last. 'I think his other name is John.'

'Her parents *must* be pleased,' said Mrs. Widmerpool. 'I always thought that Barbara was becoming—well—almost a problem in a small way. She got so noisy. Such a pity when that happens to a girl.'

I could see from Widmerpool's pursed lips and glassy eyes that he was as astonished as myself. The news went some way to dispel his air of self-satisfaction, that had seemed only momentarily displaced by irritation with Miss Walpole-Wilson before this announcement. I was myself conscious of a faint sense of bitterness, rather indefinite in its application. Among the various men who had, at one time or another, caused me apprehension, just or unjust, in connexion with Barbara, Pardoe had never, at any moment, figured in the smallest degree. Why this immunity from my jealousy should have attached to him, I was now quite unable to understand, when, in the light of the information just imparted, I considered past incidents. Even after deciding that I was no longer in love with Barbara, I could still slightly resent her attitude towards Tompsitt; but objection—like Widmerpool's—to her crossing the supper-room to sit with Pardoe would never have entered my mind.

In fact, Widmerpool's instinct on the matter, if not his action, had, in one sense, been sound, so it now appeared; though it was true that his own emotions were still at that time deeply involved, a condition having a natural tendency to sharpen all perceptions in that particular direction. The manner in which jealousy operates is, indeed, curious enough, having perhaps relatively little bearing on the practical menace offered by a rival. Barnby used to describe a husband and lover known to him, who had both combined against a third—or rather fourth—party, found to be intervening. However, that situation was, of course, poles apart from the one under examination. Widmerpool now made an effort to control his voice.

'When did this happen?' he asked, speaking casually.

'I think they actually became engaged in Scotland,' said Miss Walpole-Wilson, pleased with the impression she had made. 'But it has not been made public yet.'

There was a pause. Widmerpool had failed to rise above the situation. For the moment he had lost all his good-humour. I think he was cross not only at Barbara's engagement, but also at the inability he was experiencing to conceal his own annoyance. I felt a good deal of sympathy for him in what he was going through.

'Rather a ridiculous little man,' he said, after a time. 'Still, the fortune is a large one, and I have been told it is a nice house. I hope she will be very happy.'

'Barbara has great possibilities,' said Miss Walpole-Wilson. 'I don't know how she will like being an officer's wife. Personally, I always find soldiers so dull.'

'Oh, not in the *Guards,* surely?' said Mrs. Widmerpool, baring her teeth, as if in expectation, or memory, of behaviour on the part of Guardsmen infinitely removed from anything that could be regarded as dull, even by the most satiated.

'Of course, one of Barbara's brothers went into the Army,' said Miss Walpole-Wilson, as if that might be calculated to soften the blow.

Discussion of the engagement continued in a desultory manner. Such matters are habitually scrutinised from angles that disregard almost everything that might be truly looked upon as essential in connexion with a couple's married life together; so that, as usual, it was hard to think with even moderate clearness how the marriage would turn out. The issues were already hopelessly confused, not only by Miss Walpole-Wilson and Mrs. Widmerpool, but also by the anarchical litter enveloping the whole subject, more especially in the case of the particular pair concerned: a kind of phantasmagoria taking possession of the mind at the thought of them as husband and wife. The surroundings provided by the Widmerpool flat were such as to encourage, for some reason, the wildest flights of imagination, possibly on account of some inexplicable moral inadequacy in which its inhabitants seemed themselves to exist. Barbara's engagement lasted as a topic throughout the meal.

'Shall we leave the gentlemen to their port?' said Mrs. Widmerpool, when finally the subject had been picked bone-dry.

She mouthed the words 'gentlemen' and 'port' as if they might be facetiously disputable as strictly literal descriptions in either case. Widmerpool shut the door, evidently glad to be rid of both women for the time being. I wondered whether he would begin to speak of Barbara or Gypsy. To my surprise, neither girl turned out to be his reason for his so impatiently desiring a *tête-à-tête* conversation.

'I say, I've had an important move up at Donners-Brebner,' he said. 'That speech at the Incorporated Metals dinner had repercussions. The Chief was pleased about it.'

'Did he forgive you for knocking his garden about?'

Widmerpool laughed aloud at the idea that such a matter should have been brought up against him.

'You know,' he said, 'you sometimes make me feel that you must live completely out of the world. A man like Sir Magnus Donners does not bother about an accident of that sort. He has something more important to worry about. For example, he said to me the other day that he did not give tuppence what degrees a man had. What he wanted was someone who knew the ropes and could think and act quickly.'

'I remember him saying something of the sort when Charles Stringham went into Donners-Brebner.'

'Stringham is leaving us now that he is married. Just as well, in my opinion. I believe Truscott really thinks so too. People talk a great deal about "charm", but something else is required in business, I can assure you. Perhaps Stringham will settle down now. I believe he had some rather undesirable connexions.'

I enquired what Stringham was going to do now that he was departing from Donners-Brebner, but Widmerpool was ignorant on that point. I was unable to gather from him precisely what form his own promotion, with which he was so pleased, would take, though he implied that he would probably go abroad in the near future.

'I think I may be seeing something of Prince Theodoric,' he said. 'I believe you just met him.'

'Sir Gavin Walpole-Wilson could tell you all about Theodoric.'

'I think I may say I have better sources of information at hand than that to be derived from diplomats who have been "unstuck",' said Widmerpool, with complacency. 'I have been brought in touch recently with a man you probably know from your university days, Sillery—"Sillers"—I find him quite a character in his way.'

Feeling in no mood to discuss Sillery with Widmerpool, I asked him what he thought about Barbara and Pardoe.

'I suppose it was only to be expected,' he said, reddening a bit.

'But had you any idea?'

'I really do not devote my mind to such matters.'

In saying this, I had no doubt that he was speaking the truth. He was one of those persons capable of envisaging others only in relation to himself, so that, when in love with Barbara, it had been apparently of no interest to him to consider what other men might stand in the way. Barbara was either in his company, or far from him; the latter state representing a kind of void in which he was uninterested except at such a moment as that at the Huntercombes', when her removal was brought painfully to his notice. Turning things over in my mind, I wondered whether I could be regarded as having proved any more sentient myself. However, I felt now that the time had come to try and satisfy my curiosity about the other business.

'What about the matter you spoke of at Stourwater?'

Widmerpool pushed back his chair. He took off his spectacles and rubbed the lenses. I had the impression that he was about to make some important pronouncement, rather in the manner of the Prime Minister allowing some aspect of governmental policy to be made known at the Lord Mayor's Banquet or Royal Academy Dinner.

'I am glad you asked that,' he said, slowly. 'I wondered if you would. Will you do me a great favour?'

'Of course—if I can.'

'Never mention the subject again.'

'All right.'

'I behaved unwisely, perhaps, but I gained something.'

'You did?'

I had accented the question in the wrong manner. Widmerpool blushed again.

'Possibly we do not mean the same thing,' he said. 'I referred to being brought in touch with a new side of life—even new political opinions.'

'I see.'

'I am going to tell you something else about myself.'

'Go ahead.'

'No woman who takes my mind off my work is ever to play a part in my life in the future.'

'That sounds a wise decision so far as it goes.'

'And another thing . . .'

'Yes?'

'If I were you, Nicholas—I hope, by the way, you will call me Kenneth in future, we know each other well enough by now to use Christian names—I should avoid all that set. Deacon and the whole lot of them. You won't get any good out of it.'

'Deacon is dead.'

'What?'

'I went to the funeral this afternoon. He was cremated.'

'Really,' said Widmerpool.

He demanded no details, so I supplied none. I felt now that we were, in a curious way, fellow-conspirators, even though Widmerpool might be unaware of this, and I was myself not unwilling to connive at his desire to draw a veil over the matter of which we had spoken. For a time we talked of other things, such as the arrangements to be made when he went abroad. After a while we moved into the next room, where Miss Walpole-Wilson was describing experiences in the Far East. When I left, at a comparatively early hour, she was still chronicling the occasion when she had trudged across the face of Asia.

'You must come again soon,' said Mrs. Widmerpool. 'We never managed to have our chat about books.'

During the descent in the lift, still groaning precariously, thinking over Widmerpool and his mother, and their life together, it came to me in a flash who it was Mrs. Andriadis had resembled when I had seen her at the party in Hill Street. She recalled, so I could now see, two persons I had met, and although these two were different enough from each other, their elements, or at least some of them, were combined in her. These two were Stringham's mother and her former secretary, Miss Weedon. I remembered the dialogue that had taken place when Stringham had quarrelled with Mrs. Andriadis at the end of that night. 'As you wish, Milly,' he had said; just as I could imagine him, in his younger days, saying to Miss Weedon: 'As you wish, Tuffy', at the termination of some trivial dispute at his home.

It was a moonlight night. That region has an atmosphere peculiar to itself, separated in spirit as far from the historic gloom of Westminster's more antique streets as from the *louche* seediness and Victorian decay of the wide squares of Pimlico beyond Vauxhall Bridge Road. For some reason, perhaps the height of the tower, or more probably the prodigal inappropriateness to London of the whole structure's architectural style, the area immediately adjacent to the cathedral imparts a sense of vertigo, a dizziness almost alarming in its intensity: lines and curves of red brick appearing to meet in a kind of vortex, rather than to be ranged in normal forms of perspective. I had noticed this before when entering the terrain from the north, and now the buildings seemed that evening almost as if they might swing slowly forward from their bases, and downward into complete prostration.

Certain stages of experience might be compared with the game of Russian billiards, played (as I used to play with Jean, when the time came) on those small green tables, within the secret recesses of which, at the termination of a given passage of time—a quarter of an hour, I think—the hidden gate goes down; after the descent of which, the white balls and the red return no longer to the slot to be replayed; and all scoring is doubled. This is perhaps an image of how we live. For reasons not always at the time explicable, there are specific occasions when events begin suddenly to take on a significance previously unsuspected, so that, before we really know where we are, life seems to have begun in earnest at last, and we ourselves, scarcely aware that any change has taken place, are careering uncontrollably down the slippery avenues of eternity.

The Acceptance World

For Adrian

1.

ONCE in a way, perhaps as often as every eighteen months, an invitation to Sunday afternoon tea at the Ufford would arrive on a postcard addressed in Uncle Giles's neat, constricted handwriting. This private hotel in Bayswater, where he stayed during comparatively rare visits to London, occupied two corner houses in a latent, almost impenetrable region west of the Queen's Road. Not only the battleship-grey colour, but also something at once angular and top-heavy about the block's configuration as a whole, suggested a large vessel moored in the street. Even within, at least on the ground floor, the Ufford conveyed some reminder of life at sea, though certainly of no luxuriously equipped liner; at best one of those superannuated schooners of Conrad's novels, perhaps decorated years before as a rich man's yacht, now tarnished by the years and reduced to ignoble uses like traffic in tourists, pilgrims, or even illegal immigrants; pervaded—to borrow an appropriately Conradian mannerism—with uneasy memories of the strife of men. That was the feeling the Ufford gave, riding at anchor on the sluggish Bayswater tides.

To this last retrospective, and decidedly depressing, aspect of the hotel's character, Uncle Giles himself had no doubt in a small degree contributed. Certainly he had done nothing to release the place from its air of secret, melancholy guilt. The passages seemed catacombs of a hell assigned to the subdued regret of those who had lacked in life the income to which they felt themselves entitled; this suspicion that the two houses were an abode of the dead being increased by the fact that no one was ever to be seen about, even at the reception desk. The floors of the formerly separate buildings, constructed at different levels, were now joined by unexpected steps and narrow, steeply slanting passages. The hall was always wrapped in silence; letters in the green baize board criss-crossed with tape remained yellowing, for ever unclaimed, unread, unchanged.

However, Uncle Giles himself was attached to these quarters. 'The old pub suits me,' I had once heard him mutter thickly under his breath, high commendation from one so sparing of praise; although of course the Ufford, like every other institution with which he came in contact, would fall into disfavour from time to time, usually on account of some 'incivility' offered him by the management or staff. For example, Vera, a waitress, was an old enemy, who would often attempt to exclude him from his favourite table by the door 'where you could get a breath of air'. At least once, in a fit of pique, he had gone to the De Tabley across the road; but sooner or later he was back again, grudgingly admitting that the Ufford, although going downhill from the days when he had first known the establishment, was undoubtedly convenient for the purposes of his aimless, uncomfortable, but in a sense dedicated life.

Dedicated, it might well be asked, to what? The question would not be easy to answer. Dedicated, perhaps, to his own egotism; his determination to be—without adequate moral or intellectual equipment—absolutely different from everybody else. That might offer one explanation of his behaviour. At any rate, he was propelled along from pillar to post by some force that seemed stronger than a mere instinct to keep himself alive; and the Ufford was the nearest thing he recognised as a home. He would leave his luggage there for weeks, months, even years on end; complaining afterwards, when he unpacked, that dinner-jackets were not only creased but also ravaged by moth, or that oil had been allowed to soak through the top of his cane trunk and ruin the tropical clothing within; still worse —though exact proof was always lacking—that the pieces left in the hotel's keeping had actually been reduced in number by at least one canvas valise, leather hat-box, or uniform-case in black tin.

On most of the occasions when I visited the Ufford, halls and reception rooms were so utterly deserted that the interior might almost have been Uncle Giles's private residence. Had he been a rich bachelor, instead of a poor one, he would probably have lived in a house of just that sort: bare: anonymous: old-fashioned: draughty: with heavy mahogany cabinets and sideboards spaced out at intervals in passages and on landings; nothing that could possibly commit him to any specific opinion, beyond general disapproval of the way the world was run.

We always had tea in an apartment called 'the lounge', the back half of a large double drawing-room, the inner doors of which were kept permanently closed, thus detaching 'the lounge' from 'the writing-room', the half overlooking the street. (Perhaps, like the doors of the Temple of Janus, they were closed only in time of Peace; because, years later, when I saw the Ufford in war-time these particular doors had been thrown wide open.) The lace-curtained windows of the lounge gave on to a well; a bleak outlook, casting the gloom of perpetual night, or of a sky for ever dark with rain. Even in summer the electric light had to be switched on during tea.

The wallpaper's intricate floral design in blue, grey and green ran upwards from a cream-coloured lincrusta dado to a cornice also of cream lincrusta. The pattern of flowers, infinitely faded, closely matched the chintz-covered sofa and armchairs, which were roomy and unexpectedly comfortable. A palm in a brass pot with ornamental handles stood in one corner: here and there were small tables of Moorish design upon each of which had been placed a heavy white globular ash-tray, equipped with an attachment upon which to rest a cigar or cigarette. Several circular gilt looking-glasses hung about the walls, but there was only one picture, an engraving placed over the fireplace, of Landseer's *Bolton Abbey in the Olden Time*. Beneath this crowded scene of medieval plenty—presenting a painful contrast with the Ufford's *cuisine*—a clock, so constructed that pendulum and internal works were visible under its glass dome, stood eternally at twenty minutes past five. Two radiators kept the room reasonably warm in winter, and the coal, surrounded in the fireplace with crinkled pink paper, was never alight. No sign of active life was apparent in the room except for several much-thumbed copies of *The Lady* lying in a heap on one of the Moorish tables.

'I think we shall have this place to ourselves,' Uncle Giles used invariably to remark, as if we had come there by chance on a specially lucky day, 'so that we shall be able to talk over our business without disturbance. Nothing I hate more than having some damn'd fellow listening to every word I say.'

Of late years his affairs, in so far as his relations knew anything of them, had become to some extent stabilised, although invitations to tea were inclined to coincide with periodical efforts to extract slightly more than his agreed share from 'the Trust'. Either his path had grown more tranquil than formerly, or crises were at longer intervals and apparently less violent. This change did not imply that he approached life itself in a more conciliatory spirit, or had altered his conviction that worldly success was a matter of 'influence'. The country's abandonment of the Gold Standard at about this time—and the formation of the

National Government—had particularly annoyed him. He propagated contrary, far more revolutionary, economic theories of his own as to how the European monetary situation should be regulated.

He was, however, a shade less abrupt in personal dealings. The anxiety of his relations that he might one day get into a really serious financial tangle, never entirely at rest, had considerably abated in comparison with time past; nor had there been recently any of those once recurrent rumours that he was making preparations for an unsuitable marriage. He still hovered about the Home Counties, seen intermittently at Reading, Aylesbury, Chelmsford, or Dover—and once so far afield as the Channel Islands—his 'work' now connected with the administration of some charitable organisation which paid a small salary and allowed a reasonably high expense account.

I was not sure, however, in the light of an encounter during one of my visits to the Ufford, that Uncle Giles, although by then just about in his sixties, had wholly relinquished all thought of marriage. There were circumstances that suggested a continued interest in such a project, or at least that he still enjoyed playing with the idea of matrimony when in the company of the opposite sex.

On that particular occasion, the three fish paste sandwiches and slice of seed cake finished, talk about money was about to begin. Uncle Giles himself never ate tea, though he would usually remove the lid of the teapot on its arrival and comment: 'A good sergeant-major's brew you've got there,' sometimes sending the tea back to the kitchen if something about the surface of the liquid specially displeased him. He had blown his nose once or twice as a preliminary to financial discussion, when the door of the lounge quietly opened and a lady wearing a large hat and purple dress came silently into the room.

She was between forty and fifty, perhaps nearer fifty, though possibly her full bosom and style of dress, at a period when it was fashionable to be thin, made her seem a year or two older than her age. Dark red hair piled high on her head in what seemed to me an outmoded style, and good, curiously blurred features from which looked out immense, misty, hazel eyes, made her appearance striking. Her movements, too, were unusual. She seemed to glide rather than walk across the carpet, giving the impression almost of a phantom, a being from another world; this illusion no doubt heightened by the mysterious, sombre *ambiance* of the Ufford, and the fact that I had scarcely ever before seen anybody but Uncle Giles himself, or an occasional member of the hotel's staff, inhabit its rooms.

'Why, Myra,' said Uncle Giles, rising hurriedly, and smoothing the worn herring-bone tweed of his trouser leg, 'I thought you said you were going to be out all day.'

He sounded on the whole pleased to see her, although perhaps a trifle put out that she should have turned up just at that moment. He would very occasionally, and with due warning, produce an odd male acquaintance for a minute or two, never longer, usually an elderly man, probably a retired accountant, said to possess 'a very good head for business', but never before had I seen him in the company of a woman not a member of the family. Now as usual his habitual air of hardly suppressed irritation tended to cloak any minor emotion by the strength of its cosmic resentment. All the same, a very rare thing with him, faint patches of colour showed for a moment in his cheeks, disappearing almost immediately, as he fingered his moustache with a withered, skinny hand, as if uncertain how best to approach the situation.

'This is my nephew Nicholas,' he said; and to me: 'I don't think you have met Mrs. Erdleigh.'

He spoke slowly, as if, after much thought, he had chosen me from an immense number of other nephews to show her at least one good example of what he was forced to endure in the way of relations Mrs. Erdleigh gazed at me for a second or two before taking my hand, continuing to encircle its fingers even after I had made a slight effort to relax my own grasp. Her palm felt warm and soft, and seemed to exude a mysterious tremor. Scent, vaguely Oriental in its implications, rolled across from her in great stifling waves. The huge liquid eyes seemed to look deep down into my soul, and far, far beyond towards nameless, unexplored vistas of the infinite.

'But he belongs to another order,' she stated at once.

She spoke without surprise and apparently quite decisively; indeed as if the conclusion had been the logical inference of our hands' prolonged contact. At the same time she turned her head towards Uncle Giles, who made a deprecatory sound in his throat, though without venturing to confirm or deny her hypothesis. It was evident that he and I were placed violently in contrast together in her mind, or rather, I supposed, her inner consciousness. Whether she referred to some indefinable difference of class or bearing, or whether the distinction was in moral standards, was not at all clear. Nor had I any idea whether the comparison was in my uncle's favour or my own. In any case I could not help feeling that the assertion, however true, was untimely as an opening gambit after introduction.

I had half expected Uncle Giles to take offence at the words, but, on the contrary, he seemed not at all annoyed or surprised; even appearing rather more resigned than before to Mrs. Erdleigh's presence. It was almost as if he now knew that the worst was over; that from this moment relations between the three of us would grow easier.

'Shall I ring for some more tea?' he asked, without in any way pressing the proposal by tone of voice.

Mrs. Erdleigh shook her head dreamily. She had taken the place beside me on the sofa.

'I have already had tea,' she said softly, as if that meal had been for her indeed a wonderful experience.

'Are you sure?' asked my uncle, wonderingly; confirming by his manner that such a phenomenon was scarcely credible.

'Truly.'

'Well, I won't, then.'

'No, please, Captain Jenkins.'

I had the impression that the two of them knew each other pretty well; certainly much better than either was prepared at that moment to admit in front of me. After the first surprise of seeing her, Uncle Giles no longer called Mrs. Erdleigh 'Myra', and he now began to utter a disconnected series of conventional remarks, as if to display how formal was in fact their relationship. He explained for the hundredth time how he never took tea as a meal, however much encouraged by those addicted to the habit, commented in desultory phrases on the weather, and sketched in for her information a few of the outward circumstances of my own life and employment.

'Art books, is it?' he said. 'Is that what you told me your firm published?'

'That's it.'

'He sells art books,' said Uncle Giles, as if he were explaining to some visitor the strange habits of the aborigines in the land where he had chosen to settle.

'And other sorts too,' I added, since he made the publication of art books sound so shameful a calling.

In answering, I addressed myself to Mrs. Erdleigh, rather in the way that a witness, cross-questioned by counsel, replies to the judge. She seemed hardly to take in these trivialities, though she smiled all the while, quietly, almost rapturously, rather as if she were enjoying a warm bath after a trying day's shopping. I noticed that she wore no wedding ring, carrying in its place on her third finger a large opal, enclosed by a massive gold serpent swallowing its own tail.

'I see you are wondering about my opal,' she said, suddenly catching my eye.

'I was admiring the ring.'

'Of course I was born in October.'

'Otherwise it would be unlucky?'

'But *not* under the Scales.'

'I am the Archer.'

I had learned that fact a week or two before from the astrological column of a Sunday newspaper. This seemed a good moment to make use of the knowledge. Mrs. Erdleigh was evidently pleased even with this grain of esoteric apprehension. She took my hand once more, and held the open palm towards the light.

'You interest me,' she said.

'What do you see?'

'Many things.'

'Nice ones?'

'Some good, some less good.'

'Tell me about them.'

'Shall I?'

Uncle Giles fidgeted. I thought at first he was bored at being momentarily out of the conversation, because, in his self-contained, unostentatious way, he could never bear to be anything less than the centre of interest; even when that position might possess an unpleasant significance as sometimes happened at family gatherings. However, another matter was on his mind.

'Why not put the cards out?' he broke in all at once with forced cheerfulness. 'That is, if you're in the mood.'

Mrs. Erdleigh did not reply immediately to this suggestion. She continued to smile, and to investigate the lines of my palm.

'Shall I?' she again said softly, almost to herself. 'Shall I ask the cards about you both?'

I added my request to my uncle's. To have one's fortune told gratifies, after all, most of the superficial demands of egotism. There is no mystery about the eternal popularity of divination. All the same, I was surprised that Uncle Giles should countenance such pursuits. I felt sure he would have expressed loud contempt if anyone else had been described to him as indulging in efforts to foretell the future. Mrs. Erdleigh pondered a few seconds, then rose, still smiling, and glided away across the room. When she had shut the door we remained in silence for some minutes. Uncles Giles grunted several times. I suspected he might be feeling rather ashamed of himself for having put this request to her. I made some enquiries about his friend.

'Myra Erdleigh?' he said, as if it were strange to meet anyone unaware of Mrs. Erdleigh's circumstances. 'She's a widow, of course. Husband did something out in the East. Chinese Customs, was it? Burma Police? Something of the sort.'

'And she lives here?'

'A wonderful fortune-teller,' said Uncle Giles, ignoring the last question. 'Really wonderful. I let her tell mine once in a while. It gives her pleasure, you know—and it interests me to see how often she is right. Not that I expect she will have much to promise me at my time of life.'

He sighed; though not, I thought, without a certain self-satisfaction. I wondered how long they had known one another. Long enough, apparently, for the question of fortune-telling to have cropped up between them a number of times.

'Does she tell fortunes professionally?'

'Has done, I believe, in the past,' Uncle Giles admitted. 'But of course there wouldn't be any question of a five guinea consultation fee this evening.'

He gave a short, angry laugh to show that he was joking, adding rather guiltily: 'I don't think anyone is likely to come in. Even if they did, we could always pretend we were taking a hand at cut-throat.'

I wondered if Mrs. Erdleigh used Tarot cards. If so, three-handed bridge might not look very convincing to an intruder; for example, should one of us try to trump 'the drowned Phœnician Sailor' with 'the Hanged Man'. In any case, there seemed no reason why we should not have our fortunes told in the lounge. That would at least be employing the room to some purpose. The manner in which Uncle Giles had spoken made me think he must enjoy 'putting the cards out' more than he cared to acknowledge.

Mrs. Erdleigh did not come back to the room immediately. We awaited her return in an atmosphere of expectancy induced by my uncle's unconcealed excitement. I had never before seen him in this state. He was breathing heavily. Still Mrs. Erdleigh did not appear. She must have remained away at least ten minutes or a quarter of an hour. Uncle Giles began humming to himself. I picked up one of the tattered copies of *The Lady*. At last the door opened once more. Mrs. Erdleigh had removed her hat, renewed the blue make-up under her eyes, and changed into a dress of sage green. She was certainly a conspicuous, perhaps even a faintly sinister figure. The cards she brought with her were grey and greasy with use. They were not a Tarot pack. After a brief discussion it was agreed that Uncle Giles should be the first to look into the future.

'You don't think it has been too short an interval?' he asked, obviously with some last-moment apprehensions.

'Nearly six months,' said Mrs. Erdleigh, in a more matter-of-fact voice than that she had used hitherto; adding, as she began to shuffle the pack: 'Although, of course, one should not question the cards too often, as I have sometimes warned you.'

Uncle Giles slowly rubbed his hands together, watching her closely as if to make certain there was no deception, and to ensure that she did not deliberately slip in a card that would bring him bad luck. The rite had something solemn about it: something infinitely ancient, as if Mrs. Erdleigh had existed long before the gods we knew, even those belonging to the most distant past. I asked if she always used the same pack.

'Always the same dear cards,' she said, smiling; and to my uncle, more seriously: 'Was there anything special?'

'Usually need to look ahead in business,' he said, gruffly. 'That would be Diamonds, I suppose. Or Clubs?'

Mrs. Erdleigh continued to smile without revealing any of her secrets, while she set the cards in various small heaps on one of the Moorish tables. Uncle Giles kept a sharp eye on her, still rubbing his hands, making me almost as nervous as himself at the thought of what the predictions could involve. There might always be grave possibilities to be faced for someone of his erratic excursion through life, however I was naturally much more interested in what she would say about myself. Indeed, I was then so far from grasping the unchanging mould of human nature that I found it even surprising that at his age he could presuppose anything to be called 'a future'. So far as I myself was concerned, on the other hand, there seemed no reason to curb the wildest absurdity of fancy as to what might happen the very next moment.

However, when Uncle Giles's cards were examined, their secrets did not appear to be anything like so ominous as might have been feared. There was a good deal of opposition to his 'plans', perhaps not surprisingly; also, it was true, much gossip, even some calumny surrounded him.

'Don't forget you have Saturn in the Twelfth House,' Mrs. Erdleigh remarked in an aside. 'Secret enemies.'

As against these threatening possibilities, someone was going to give him a present, probably money; a small sum, but acceptable. It looked as if this gift might come from a woman. Uncle Giles, whose cheeks had become furrowed at the thought of all the gossip and calumny, cheered up a little at this. He was told he had a good friend in a woman—possibly the one who was to make him a present—the Queen of Hearts, in fact. This, too, Uncle Giles accepted willingly enough.

'That was the marriage card that turned up, wasn't it?' he asked at one point.

'Could be.'

'Not necessarily?'

'Other influences must be taken into consideration.'

Neither of them commented on this matter, though their words evidently had regard to a question already reconnoitred in the past. For a moment or two there was perhaps a faint sense of additional tension. Then the cards were collected and shuffled again.

'Now let's hear about *him*,' said Uncle Giles.

He spoke more with relief that his own ordeal was over, rather than because he was seriously expressing any burning interest in my own fate.

'I expect *he* wants to hear about *love*,' said Mrs. Erdleigh, beginning to titter to herself again.

Uncle Giles, to show general agreement with this supposition, grunted a disapproving laugh. I attempted some formal denial, although it was perfectly true that the thought was uppermost in my mind. The situation in that quarter was at the moment confused. In fact, so far as 'love' was concerned, I had been living for some years past in a rather makeshift manner. This was not because I felt the matter to be of little interest, like a man who hardly cares what he eats provided hunger is satisfied, or one prepared to discuss painting, should the subject arise, though never tempted to enter a picture gallery. On the contrary, my interest in love was keen enough, but the thing itself seemed not particularly simple to come by. In that direction, other people appeared more easily satisfied than myself. That at least was how it seemed to me. And yet, in spite of some show of picking and choosing, my experiences, on subsequent examination, were certainly no more admirable than those to which neither Templer nor Barnby, for example, would have given a second thought; they were merely fewer in number. I hoped the cards would reveal nothing too humiliating to my own self-esteem.

'There is a link between us,' said Mrs. Erdleigh, as she set out the little heaps. 'At present I cannot see what it is—but there is a link.'

This supposed connexion evidently puzzled her.

'You are musical?'

'No.'

'Then you write—I think you have written a book?'

'Yes.'

'You live between two worlds,' she said. 'Perhaps even more than two worlds. You cannot always surmount your feelings.'

I could think of no possible reply to this indictment.

'You are thought cold, but you possess deep affections,

sometimes for people worthless in themselves. Often you are at odds with those who might help you. You like women, and they like you, but you often find the company of men more amusing. You expect too much, and yet you are also too resigned. You must try to understand life.'

Somewhat awed by this searching, even severe analysis, I promised I would do better in future.

'People can only be themselves,' she said. 'If they possessed the qualities you desire in them, they would be different people.'

'That is what I should like them to be.'

'Sometimes you are too serious, sometimes not serious enough.'

'So I have been told.'

'You must make a greater effort in life.'

'I can see that.'

These strictures certainly seemed just enough; and yet any change of direction would be hard to achieve. Perhaps I was irrevocably transfixed, just as she described, half-way between dissipation and diffidence. While I considered the matter, she passed on to more circumstantial things. It turned out that a fair woman was not very pleased with me; and a dark one almost equally vexed. Like my uncle—perhaps some family failing common to both of us—I was encompassed by gossip.

'They do not signify at all,' said Mrs. Erdleigh, referring thus rather ruthlessly to the women of disparate colouring. 'This is a much more important lady—medium hair, I should say—and I think you have run across her once or twice before, though not recently. But there seems to be another man interested, too. He might even be a husband. You don't like him much. He is tallish, I should guess. Fair, possibly red hair. In business. Often goes abroad.'

I began to turn over in my mind every woman I had ever met.

'There is a small matter in *your* business that is going to cause inconvenience,' she went on. 'It has to do with an elderly man—and two young ones connected with him.'

'Are you sure it is not two elderly men and one young man?'

It had immediately struck me that she might be *en rapport* with my firm's growing difficulties regarding St. John Clarke's introduction to *The Art of Horace Isbister*. The elderly men would be St. John Clarke and Isbister themselves—or perhaps St. John Clarke and one of the partners—and the young man was, of course, St. John Clarke's secretary, Mark Members.

'I see the two young men quite plainly,' she said. 'Rather a troublesome couple, I should say.'

This was all credible enough, including the character sketch, though perhaps not very interesting. Such trivial comment, mixed with a few home truths of a personal nature, provide, I had already learnt, the commonplaces of fortune-telling. Such was all that remained in my mind of what Mrs. Erdleigh prophesied on that occasion. She may have foretold more. If so, her words were forgotten by me. Indeed, I was not greatly struck by the insight she had shown; although she impressed me as a woman of dominant, even oddly attractive personality, in spite of a certain absurdity of demeanour. She herself seemed well pleased with the performance.

At the end of her sitting it was time to go. I was dining that evening with Barnby, picking him up at his studio. I rose to say good-bye, thanking her for the trouble she had taken.

'We shall meet again.'

'I hope so.'

'In about a year from now.'

'Perhaps before.'

'No,' she said, smiling with the complacence of one to whom the secrets of human existence had been long since occultly revealed. 'Not before.'

I did not press the point. Uncle Giles accompanied me to the hall. He had by then returned to the subject of money, the *mystique* of which was at least as absorbing to him as the rites upon which we had been engaged.

'. . . and then one could not foresee that San Pedro Warehouses Deferred would become entirely valueless,' he was saying. 'The expropriations were merely the result of a liberal dictator coming in—got to face these changes. There was one of those quite natural revulsions against foreign capital. . . .'

He broke off. Supposing our meeting now at an end, I turned from him, and made preparations to plunge through the opaque doors into the ocean of streets, in the grey ebb and flow of which the Ufford floated idly upon the swell. Uncle Giles put his hand on my arm.

'By the way,' he said, 'I don't think I should mention to your parents the matter of having your fortune told. I don't want them to blame me for leading you into bad habits, superstitious ones, I mean. Besides, they might not altogether approve of Myra Erdleigh.'

His brown, wrinkled face puckered slightly. He still retained some vestige of good looks, faintly military in character. Perhaps this hint, increased with age, of past regimental distinction in some forgotten garrison town was what Mrs. Erdleigh admired in him. Neither my parents, nor any of the rest of Uncle Giles's relations, were likely to worry about his behaviour if the worst he ever did was to persuade other members of the family to have their fortunes told. However, recognising that silence upon the subject of Mrs. Erdleigh might be a reasonable request, I assured him that I would not speak of our meeting.

I was curious to know what their relationship might be. Possibly they were planning marriage. The 'marriage card' had clearly been of interest to my uncle. There was something vaguely 'improper' about Mrs. Erdleigh, almost deliberately so; but impropriety of an unremembered, Victorian kind: a villa in St. John's Wood, perhaps, and eccentric doings behind locked doors and lace curtains on sultry summer afternoons. Uncle Giles was known to possess a capacity for making himself acceptable to ladies of all sorts, some of whom had even been rumoured to contribute at times a trifle towards his expenses; those many expenses to which he was subject, and never tired of detailing. Mrs. Erdleigh looked not so much 'well off' as eminently capable of pursuing her own interests effectively. Possibly Uncle Giles considered her a good investment. She, on her side, no doubt had her uses for him. Apart from material considerations, he was obviously fascinated by her occult powers, with which he seemed almost religiously preoccupied. Like all such associations, this one probably included a fierce struggle of wills. It would be interesting to see who won the day. On the whole, my money was on Mrs. Erdleigh. I thought about the pair of them for a day or two, and then they both passed from my mind.

As I made my way towards the neighbourhood of Fitzroy Square, experiencing as usual that feeling of release that always followed parting company with Uncle Giles, I returned to the subject of future business difficulties foretold in the cards. These, as I have said, had seemed to refer to St. John Clarke's introduction to *The Art of Horace Isbister,* already a tiresome affair, quite likely to pass from bad to worse. The introduction had been awaited for at least a year now, and we seemed no nearer getting the manuscript. The delay caused inconvenience at the office, since blocks had been made for a series of forty-eight monochrome plates and four three-colour half-tones; to which St. John Clarke was to add four or five thousand words of biographical reminiscence.

Isbister himself had been ill, on and off, for some little time, so that it had not been possible through him to bring pressure to bear on St. John Clarke, although the painter was the novelist's old friend. They may even have been at school together. Isbister had certainly executed several portraits of St. John Clarke, one of them (the sitter in a high, stiff collar and limp spotted bow tie) showing him as quite a young man. The personal legend of each, for publicity purposes, took the form of a country lad who had 'made good', and they would occasionally refer in print to their shared early struggles. St. John Clarke, in the first instance, had positively gone out of his way to arrange that the introduction should be written by himself, rather than by some suitable hack from amongst the Old Guard of the art critics, several of whom were in much more need of the fee, not a very princely one, that my firm was paying for the work.

That a well-known novelist should take on something that seemed to call in at least a small degree for an accredited expert on painting was not so surprising as might at first sight have appeared, because St. John Clarke, although certainly quieter of late years, had in the past often figured in public controversy regarding the arts. He had been active, for example, in the years before the war in supporting the erection of the Peter Pan statue in Kensington Gardens: a dozen years later, vigorously opposing the establishment of Rima in the bird sanctuary of the same neighbourhood. At one of the Walpole-Wilsons' dinner parties I could remember talk of St. John Clarke's intervention in the question of the Haig memorial, then much discussed. These examples suggest a special interest in sculpture, but St. John Clarke often expressed himself with equal force regarding painting and music. He had certainly been associated with opposition to the Post-Impressionists in 1910: also in leading some minor skirmish in operatic circles soon after the Armistice.

I myself could not have denied a taste for St. John Clarke's novels at about the period when leaving school. In fact Le Bas, my housemaster, finding me reading one of them, had taken it from my hand and glanced through the pages.

'Rather morbid stuff, isn't it?' he had remarked.

It was a statement rather than a question, though I doubt whether Le Bas had ever read any of St. John Clarke's novels himself. He merely felt, in one sense correctly, that there was something wrong with them. At the same time he made no attempt to disallow, or confiscate, the volume. However, I had long preferred to forget the days when I had regarded St. John Clarke's work as fairly daring. In fact I had become accustomed to refer to him and his books with the savagery which, when one is a young man, seems—perhaps rightly—the only proper and serious attitude towards anyone, most of all an older person, practising the arts in an inept or outworn manner.

Although a few years younger than the generation of H. G. Wells and J. M. Barrie, St. John Clarke was connected in my mind with those two authors, chiefly because I had once seen a snapshot of the three of them reproduced in the memoirs of an Edwardian hostess. The photograph had probably been taken by the lady herself. The writers were standing in a group on the lawn of a huge, rather gracelessly pinnacled country seat. St. John Clarke was a little to one side of the picture. A tall, cadaverous man, with spectacles and long hair, a panama hat at the back of his head, he leant on a stick, surveying his more diminutive fellow guests with an expression of uneasy interest; rather as if he were an explorer or missionary, who had just coaxed from the jungle these powerful witch-doctors of some neighbouring, and on the whole unfriendly, tribe. He seemed, by his expression, to feel that constant supervision of the other two was necessary to foil misbehaviour or escape. There was something of the priest about his appearance.

The picture had interested me because, although I had already read books by these three writers, all had inspired me with the same sense that theirs was not the kind of writing I liked. Later, as I have said, I came round for a time to St. John Clarke with that avid literary consumption of the immature which cannot precisely be regarded either as enjoyment or the reverse. The flavour of St. John Clarke's novels is hard to describe to those unfamiliar with them, perhaps on account of their own inexactitudes of thought and feeling. Although no longer looked upon as a 'serious' writer, I believe he still has his readers in number not to be disregarded. In his early years he had been treated with respect by most of the eminent critics of his time, and to the day of his death he hoped in vain for the Nobel Prize. Mark Members, his secretary, used to say that once, at least, that award had seemed within his grasp.

We had never met, but I had seen him in Bond Street, walking with Members. Though his hair was by then white and straggling, he still looked remarkably like his picture in the book of memoirs. He was wearing a grey soft hat, rather high in the crown with a band of the same colour, a black suit and buff double-breasted waistcoat. As he strolled along he glanced rather furtively about him, seeming scarcely aware of Members, sauntering by his side. His features bore that somewhat exasperated expression that literary men so often acquire in middle life. For a second I had been reminded of my old acquaintance, Mr. Deacon, but a Mr. Deacon far more capable of coping with the world. Members, in his black homburg, swinging a rolled umbrella, looked quite boyish beside him.

St. John Clarke's reputation as a novelist had been made by the time he was in his thirties. For many years past he had lived the life of a comparatively rich bachelor, able to indulge most of his whims, seeing only the people who suited him, and making his way in what he used to call, 'rather lovingly', so Members said, the '*beau monde*'. Even in those days, critics malicious enough to pull his books to pieces in public were never tired of pointing out that investigations of human conduct, based on assumptions accepted when St. John Clarke was a young man, were hopelessly out of date. However, fortunately his sales did not depend on favourable reviews, although, in spite of this, he was said to be—like so many financially successful writers—painfully sensitive to hostile criticism. It was perhaps partly for the reason that he felt himself no longer properly appreciated that he had announced he would write no more novels. In due course memoirs would appear, though he confessed he was in no hurry to compose them.

His procrastination regarding the introduction had, therefore, nothing to do with pressure of work. Putting the Isbister task in its least idealistic and disinterested light, it would give him a chance to talk about himself, a perfectly legitimate treat he was as a rule unwilling to forgo. Friendship made him a suitable man for the job. Those who enjoy finding landmarks common to different forms of art might even have succeeded in tracing a certain similarity of approach tenuously relating the novels of St. John Clarke with the portrait painting of Isbister. The delay was, indeed, hard to explain.

There had been, however, various rumours recently current regarding changes supposedly taking place in St. John Clarke's point of view. Lately, he had been seen at parties in Bloomsbury, and elsewhere, surrounded by people who were certainly not readers of his books. This was thought to show the influence of Members, who was said to be altering his employer's outlook. Indeed, something suggesting a change of front in that quarter had been brought to my own notice in a very personal manner.

St. John Clarke had contributed an article to a New York paper in which he spoke of the younger writers of that moment. Amongst a rather oddly assorted collection of names, he had commented, at least by implication favourably, upon a novel of my own, published a month or two before—the 'book' to which Mrs. Erdleigh had referred. Latterly, St. John Clarke had rarely occupied himself with occasional journalism, and in print he had certainly never before shown himself well disposed towards a younger generation. His remarks, brief and relatively guarded though they had been, not unnaturally aroused my interest, especially because any recommendation from that quarter was so entirely unexpected. I found myself looking for excuses to cover what still seemed to me his own shortcomings as a novelist.

As I turned over these things in my mind, on the way to Barnby's studio, it struck me that Barnby himself might be able to tell me something of St. John Clarke as a person; for, although unlikely that Barnby had read the novels, the two of them might well have met in the widely different circles Barnby frequented. I began to make enquiries soon after my arrival there.

Barnby rubbed his short, stubby hair, worn *en brosse,* which, with his blue overalls, gave him the look of a *sommelier* at an expensive French restaurant. By then we had known each other for several years. He had moved house more than once since the days when he had lived above Mr. Deacon's antique shop, emigrating for a time as far north as Camden Town. Still unmarried, his many adventures with women were a perpetual topic between us. In terms of literature, Barnby might have found a place among Stendhal's heroes, those power-conscious young men, anxious to achieve success with women without the banal expedient of 'falling in love': a state, of course, necessarily implying, on the part of the competitor, a depletion, if not entire abrogation, of 'the will'. Barnby was, on the whole, more successful than his Stendhalian prototypes, and he was certainly often 'in love'. All the same, he belonged in that group. Like Valmont in *Les Liaisons Dangereuses,* he set store 'upon what terms' he possessed a woman, seeking a relationship in which sensuality merged with power, rather than engaging in their habitual conflict.

Like everyone else, at that moment, Barnby was complaining of 'the slump', although his own reputation as a painter had been rising steadily during the previous two or three years. The murals designed by him for the Donners-Brebner Building had received, one way and another, a great deal of public attention; the patronage of Sir Magnus Donners himself in this project having even survived Barnby's love affair with Baby Wentworth, supposed mistress of Sir Magnus. Indeed, it had been suggested that 'the Great Industrialist', as Barnby used to call him, had been glad to make use of that or some other indiscretion, soon after the completion of the murals, as an excuse for bringing to an end his own association with Mrs. Wentworth. There appeared to be no bad feeling between any of the persons concerned in this triangular adjustment. Sir Magnus was now seen about with a *jolie laide* called Matilda Wilson; although, as formerly in the Baby Wentworth connexion, little or nothing definite was known of this much discussed liaison. Baby herself had married an Italian and was living in Rome.

'You'll never get that introduction now,' Barnby said, after listening to my story. 'St. John Clarke in these days would think poor old Isbister much too *pompier*.'

'But they are still great friends.'

'What does that matter?'

'Besides, St. John Clarke doesn't know a Van Dyck from a Van Dongen.'

'Ah, but he does now,' said Barnby. 'That's where you are wrong. You are out of date. St. John Clarke has undergone a conversion.'

'To what?'

'Modernism.'

'Steel chairs?'

'No doubt they will come.'

'Pictures made of shells and newspaper?'

'At present he is at a slightly earlier stage.'

I asked for further details.

'The outward and visible sign of St. John Clarke's conversion,' said Barnby, portentously, 'is that he has indeed become a collector of modern pictures—though, as I understand it, he still loves them on this side Surrealism. As a matter of fact he bought a picture of mine last week.'

'This conversion explains his friendly notice of my book.'

'It does.'

'I see.'

'You yourself supposed that something unusual in the quality of your writing had touched him?'

'Naturally.'

'I fear it is all part of a much larger design.'

'Just as good for me.'

'Doubtless.'

All the same, I felt slightly less complimented than before. The situation was now clear. The rumours already current about St. John Clarke, less explicit than Barnby's words, had equally suggested some kind of intellectual upheaval. Isbister's portraits of politicians, business men and ecclesiastics, executed with emphatic, almost aggressive disregard for any development of painting that could possibly be called 'modern', would now certainly no longer appeal to his old friend. At the same time the ray of St. John Clarke's approval directed towards myself, until then so phenomenal, was in fact only one minute aspect of the novelist's new desire to ally himself with forces against which, for many years, he had openly warred.

'That secretary of his even suggested Clarke might commission a portrait.'

'It is Members, of course, who has brought this about.'

'Oh, I don't know,' said Barnby. 'This sort of thing often happens to successful people when they begin to get old. They suddenly realise what dull lives they have always led.'

'But St. John Clarke hasn't led a dull life. I should have thought he had done almost everything he wanted—with just sufficient heights still to climb to give continued zest to his efforts.'

'I agree in one sense,' said Barnby. 'But for a man of his comparative intelligence, St. John Clarke has always limited himself to the dullest of dull ideas—in order to make money, of course, a very reasonable aim, thereby avoiding giving offence to his public. Think of the platitudes of his books. True, I have only read a few pages of one of them, but that was sufficient. And then that professional world of bogus artists and bogus writers which he himself frequents. No wonder he wants to escape from it once in a while, and meet an occasional duchess. Men like him always feel they have missed something. You can leave the arts alone, but it is very dangerous to play tricks with them. After all, you yourself tell me he has agreed to write an introduction to the work of Isbister—and then you ask me why I consider St. John Clarke leads a dull life.'

'But will this new move make his life any better?'

'Why not?'

'He must always have been picture-blind.'

'Some of my best patrons are that. Don't be so idealistic.'

'But if you are not really interested in pictures, liking a Bonnard doesn't make you any happier than liking a Bouguereau.'

'The act of conversion does, though.'

'Besides, this will open up a new, much more lively world of social life. One must admit that.'

'Of course.'

'You are probably right.'

Perhaps it was surprising that nothing of the kind had happened earlier, because St. John Clarke had employed a whole dynasty of secretaries before Members. But former secretaries had been expected to work hard in the background, rather than to exist as an important element in the household. Members had built up the post to something far more influential than anything achieved by those who had gone before him. The fact was that, as St. John Clarke grew older, he wrote less, while his desire to cut a social figure gained in volume. He began to require a secretary who was something more than a subordinate to answer the telephone and remember the date of invitations. It was natural enough that St. John Clarke, who was unmarried, should wish to delegate power in his establishment, and rely on someone to help him plan his daily life. He was fortunate in finding a young man so well equipped for the job; for even those who did not much care for Members personally had to admit that his methods, often erratic, were on the whole admirably suited to the life St. John Clarke liked to lead.

'Nothing equivocal about the position of Members in that *ménage,* do you think?' said Barnby.

'Not in the least.'

'I don't think St. John Clarke is interested in either sex,' said Barnby. 'He fell in love with himself at first sight and it is a passion to which he has always remained faithful.'

'Self-love seems so often unrequited.'

'But not in the case of St. John Clarke,' said Barnby. 'He is entirely capable of getting along without what most of the rest of us need.'

I had often heard that particular question discussed. Although his novels not uncommonly dealt with the intricate problems of married life, St. John Clarke did not, in general, greatly care for the society of women, except that of ladies in a position to invite him to agreeable dinners and week-end parties. Such hospitality was, after all, no more than a small and fitting return for the labours of a lifetime, and one that few but the envious would have begrudged him. However, this lack of interest in the opposite sex had from time to time given rise to gossip. Those persons who make a hobby, even a kind of duty, of tracking down malicious whispers to their source were forced to report in the case of St. John Clarke that nothing in the smallest degree reprobate could be confirmed. This did not prevent the circulation of a certain amount of rather spiteful badinage on the subject of his secretary. Members was impervious to any such innuendo, perhaps even encouraging it to screen his own affairs with women. St. John Clarke, indifferent to this indulgence himself, naturally disapproved of an irregular life in others: especially in someone at such close quarters.

'So there he goes,' said Barnby. 'Head-first into the contemporary world.'

He hunched his shoulders, and made a grimace, as if to express the violence, even agony, that had accompanied St. John Clarke's æsthetic metamorphosis. By easy stages we moved off to dinner at Foppa's.

2.

A YEAR or more later Isbister died. He had been in bad health for some little time, and caught pneumonia during a period of convalescence. The question of the introduction, pigeon-holed indefinitely, since St. John Clarke utterly refused to answer letters on the subject, was now brought into the light again by the obituaries. Little or no general news was about at the time, so these notices were fuller than might have been expected. One of them called Isbister 'the British Franz Hals'. There were photographs of him, with his Van Dyck beard and Inverness cape, walking with Mrs. Isbister, a former model, the 'Morwenna' of many of his figure subjects. This was clearly the occasion to make another effort to complete and publish *The Art of Horace Isbister*. Artists, especially academic artists, can pass quickly into the shadows: forgotten as if they had never been.

Almost as a last resort, therefore, it had been arranged that I should meet Mark Members out of office hours, and talk things over 'as man to man'. For this assignation Members had chosen—of all places—the Ritz. Since becoming St. John Clarke's secretary he had acquired a taste for rich surroundings. It was that prolonged, flat, cheerless week that follows Christmas. My own existence seemed infinitely stagnant, relieved only by work on another book. Those interminable latter days of the dying year create an interval, as it were, of moral suspension: one form of life already passed away before another has had time to assert some new, endemic characteristic. Imminent change of direction is for some reason often foreshadowed by such colourless patches of time.

Along Piccadilly a north wind was blowing down the side streets, roaring hoarsely for a minute or two at a time, then dropping suddenly into silence; then again, after a brief pause, beginning to roar once more, as if perpetually raging against the inconsistency of human conduct. The arches of the portico gave some shelter from this hurricane, at the same time forming a sort of ante-chamber leading on one side, through lighted glass, into another, milder country, where struggle against the forces of nature was at least less explicit than on the pavements. Outside was the northern winter; here among the palms the climate was almost tropical.

Although a Saturday evening, the place was crowded. A suggestion of life in warmer cities, far away from London, was increased by the presence of a large party of South Americans camped out not far from where I found a seat at one of the grey marble-topped tables. They were grouped picturesquely beneath the figure of the bronze nymph perched in her grotto of artificial rocks and fresh green ferns, a large family spreading over three or four of the tables while they chatted amicably with one another. There were swarthy young men with blue chins and pretty girls in smart frocks, the latter descending in point of age to mere children with big black eyes and brightly coloured bows in their hair. A bald, neat, elderly man, the rosette of some order in his buttonhole, his grey moustache closely clipped, discoursed gravely with two enormously animated ladies, both getting a shade plump in their black dresses.

Away on her pinnacle, the nymph seemed at once a member of this Latin family party, and yet at the same time morally separate from them: an English girl, perhaps, staying with relations possessing business interests in South

America, herself in love for the first time after a visit to some neighbouring estancia. Now she had strayed away from her hosts to enjoy delicious private thoughts in peace while she examined the grimacing face of the river-god carved in stone on the short surface of wall by the grotto. Pensive, quite unaware of the young tritons violently attempting to waft her away from the fountain by sounding their conches at full blast, she gazed full of wonder that no crystal stream gushed from the water-god's contorted jaws. Perhaps in such a place she expected a torrent of champagne. Although stark naked, the nymph looked immensely respectable; less provocative, indeed, than some of the fully dressed young women seated below her, whose olive skins and silk stockings helped to complete this most unwintry scene.

Waiting for someone in a public place develops a sense of individual loneliness, so that amongst all this pale pink and sage green furniture, under decorations of rich cream and dull gold, I felt myself cut off from the rest of the world. I began to brood on the complexity of writing a novel about English life, a subject difficult enough to handle with authenticity even of a crudely naturalistic sort, even more to convey the inner truth of the things observed. Those South Americans sitting opposite, coming from a Continent I had never visited, regarding which I possessed only the most superficial scraps of information, seemed in some respects easier to conceive in terms of a novel than most of the English people sitting round the room. Intricacies of social life make English habits unyielding to simplification, while understatement and irony—in which all classes of this island converse—upset the normal emphasis of reported speech.

How, I asked myself, could a writer attempt to describe in a novel such a young man as Mark Members, for example, possessing so much in common with myself, yet so different? How could this difference be expressed to that grave middle-aged South American gentleman talking to the plump ladies in black? Viewed from some distance off, Members and I might reasonably be considered almost identical units of the same organism, scarcely to be differentiated even by the sociological expert. We were both about the same age, had been to the same university, and were committed to the same profession of literature; though Members could certainly claim in that sphere a more notable place than myself, having by then published several books of poems and made some name for himself as a critic.

Thinking about Members that evening, I found myself unable to consider him without prejudice. He had been, I now realised, responsible for preventing St. John Clarke from writing the Isbister introduction. That was in itself understandable. However, he had also prevaricated about the matter in a way that showed disregard for the fact that we had known each other for a long time; and had always got along together pretty well. There were undoubtedly difficulties on his side too. Prejudice was to be avoided if—as I had idly pictured him—Members were to form the basis of a character in a novel. Alternatively, prejudice might prove the very element through which to capture and pin down unequivocally the otherwise elusive nature of what was of interest, discarding by its selective power the empty, unprofitable shell making up that side of Members untranslatable into terms of art; concentrating his final essence, his position, as it were, in eternity, into the medium of words.

Any but the most crude indication of my own personality would be, I reflected, equally hard to transcribe; at any rate one that did not sound a little absurd. It was all very well for Mrs. Erdleigh to generalise; far less easy to take an objective view oneself. Even the bare facts had an unreal, almost satirical ring when committed to paper, say in the manner of innumerable Russian stories of the nineteenth century: 'I was born in the city of L——, the son of an infantry officer . . .' To convey much that was relevant to the reader's mind by such phrases was in this country hardly possible. Too many factors had to be taken into consideration. Understatement, too, had its own banality; for, skirting cheap romanticism, it could also encourage evasion of unpalatable facts.

However, these meditations on writing were dispersed by the South Americans, who now rose in a body, and, with a good deal of talking and shrill laughter, trooped down the steps, making for the Arlington Street entrance. Their removal perceptibly thinned the population of the palm court. Among a sea of countenances, stamped like the skin of Renoir's women with that curiously pink, silky surface that seems to come from prolonged sitting about in Ritz hotels, I noticed several familiar faces. Some of these belonged to girls once encountered at dances, now no longer known, probably married; moving at any rate in circles I did not frequent.

Margaret Budd was there, with a lady who looked like an aunt or mother-in-law. In the end this 'beauty' had married a Scotch landowner, a husband rather older than might have been expected for such a lovely girl. He was in the whisky business, said to be hypochondriacal and bad-tempered. Although by then mother of at least two children, Margaret still looked like one of those golden-haired, blue-eyed dolls which say, 'Ma-Ma' and 'Pa-Pa', closing their eyes when tilted backward: unchanged in her possession of that peculiarly English beauty, scarcely to be altered by grey hair or the pallor of age. Not far from her, on one of the sofas, sandwiched between two men, both of whom had the air of being rather rich, sat a tall, blonde young woman I recognised as Lady Ardglass, popularly supposed to have been for a short time mistress of Prince Theodoric. Unlike Margaret Budd—whose married name I could not remember—Bijou Ardglass appeared distinctly older: more than a little ravaged by the demands of her strenuous existence. She had lost some of that gay, energetic air of being ready for anything which she had so abundantly possessed when I had first seen her at Mrs. Andriadis's party. That occasion seemed an eternity ago.

As time passed, people leaving, others arriving, I began increasingly to suspect that Members was not going to show up. That would not be out of character, because cutting appointments was a recognised element in his method of conducting life. This habit—to be in general associated with a strong, sometimes frustrated desire to impose the will—is usually attributed on each specific occasion to the fact that 'something better turned up'. Such defaulters are almost as a matter of course reproached with trying to make a more profitable use of their time. Perhaps, in reality, self-interest in its crudest form plays less part in these deviations than might be supposed. The manœuvre may often be undertaken for its own sake. The person awaited deliberately withholds himself from the person awaiting. Mere absence is in this manner turned into a form of action, even potentially violent in its consequences.

Possibly Members, from an inner compulsion, had suddenly decided to establish ascendancy by such an assertion of the will. On the other hand, the action would in the circumstances represent such an infinitesimal score against life in general that his absence, if deliberate, was probably attributable to some minor move in domestic politics vis-à-vis St. John Clarke. I was thinking over these possibilities, rather gloomily wondering whether or not I would withdraw or stay a few minutes longer, when an immensely familiar head and shoulders became visible for a second through a kind of window, or embrasure, looking out from the palm court on to the lower levels of the passage and rooms beyond. It was Peter Templer. A moment later he strolled up the steps.

For a few seconds Templer gazed thoughtfully round the room, as if contemplating the deterioration of a landscape, known from youth, once famed for its natural beauty, now ruined beyond recall. He was about to turn away, when he caught sight of me and came towards the table. It must have been at least three years since we had met. His sleekly brushed hair and long, rather elegant stride were just the same. His face was perhaps a shade fuller, and his eyes at once began to give out that familiar blue mechanical sparkle that I remembered so well from our schooldays. With a red carnation in the buttonhole of his dark suit, his shirt cuffs cut tightly round the wrist so that somehow his links asserted themselves unduly, Templer's air was distinctly prosperous. But he also looked as if by then he knew what worry was, something certainly unknown to him in the past.

'I suppose you are waiting for someone, Nick,' he said, drawing up a chair. 'Some ripe little piece?'

'You're very wide of the mark.'

'Then a dowager is going to buy your dinner—after which she will make you an offer?'

'No such luck.'

'What then?'

'I'm waiting for a man.'

'I say, old boy, sorry to have been so inquisitive. Things have come to that, have they?'

'You couldn't know.'

'I should have guessed.'

'Have a drink, anyway.'

I remembered reading, some years before, an obituary notice in the *Morning Post,* referring to his father's death. This paragraph, signed 'A.S.F.', was, in fact, a brief personal memoir rather than a bald account of the late Mr. Templer's career. Although the deceased's chairmanship of various companies was mentioned—his financial interests had been chiefly in cement—more emphasis was laid on his delight in sport, especially boxing, his many undisclosed benefactions to charity, the kind heart within him, always cloaked by a deceptively brusque manner. The initials, together with a certain banality of phrasing, suggested the hand of Sunny Farebrother, Mr. Templer's younger City associate I had met at their house. That visit had been the sole occasion when I had seen Templer's father. I had wondered vaguely—to use a favourite expression of his son's—'how much he had cut up for'. Details about money are always of interest; even so, I did not give the matter much thought. Already I had begun to think of Peter Templer as a friend of my schooldays rather than one connected with that more recent period of occasional luncheons together, during the year following my own establishment in London after coming down from the university. When, once in a way, I had attended the annual dinner for members of Le Bas's House, Templer had never been present.

That we had ceased to meet fairly regularly was due no doubt to some extent to Templer's chronic inability—as our housemaster Le Bas would have said—to 'keep up' a friendship. He moved entirely within the orbit of events of the moment, looking neither forward nor backward. If we happened to run across each other, we arranged to do something together; not otherwise. This mutual detachment had been brought about also by the circumstances of my own life. To be circumscribed by people constituting the same professional community as myself was no wish of mine; rather the contrary. However, an inexorable law governs all human existence in that respect, ordaining that sooner or later everyone must appear before the world as he is. Many are not prepared to face this sometimes distasteful principle. Indeed, the illusion that anyone can escape from the marks of his vocation is an aspect of romanticism common to every profession; those occupied with the world of action claiming their true interests to lie in the pleasure of imagination or reflection, while persons principally concerned with reflective or imaginative pursuits are for ever asserting their inalienable right to participation in an active sphere.

Perhaps Templer himself lay somewhere within the range of this definition. If so, he gave little indication of it. In fact, if taxed, there can be no doubt that he would have denied any such thing. The outward sign that seemed to place him within this category was his own unwillingness ever wholly to accept the people amongst whom he had chosen to live. A curious streak of melancholy seemed to link him with a less arid manner of life than that to which he seemed irrevocably committed. At least I supposed something of that sort could still be said of his life; for I knew little or nothing of his daily routine, in or out of the office, though suspecting that neither his activities, nor his friends, were of a kind likely to be very sympathetic to myself.

However, various strands, controlled without much method and then invisible to me, imparted a certain irregular pattern to Templer's personal affairs. For example, he liked his friends to be rich and engrossed in whatever business occupied them. They had to be serious about money, though relatively dissipated in their private lives; to possess no social ambitions whatever, though at the same time to be disfigured by no grave social defects. The women had to be good-looking, the men tolerably proficient at golf and bridge, without making a fetish of those pastimes. Both sexes, when entertained by him, were expected to drink fairly heavily; although, here again, intoxication must not be carried to excess. In fact, broadly speaking, Templer disliked anything that could be labelled 'bohemian', as much as anything with claims to be 'smart'. He did not fancy even that sort of 'smartness' to be found to a limited extent in the City, a form of life which had, after all, so much in common with his own tastes.

'You know, I really rather hate the well-born,' he used to say. 'Not that I see many of them these days.'

Nothing might be thought easier than gratification of these modest requirements among a circle of intimates; and the difficulty Templer found in settling down to any one set of persons limited by these terms of reference, and at the same time satisfactory to himself, was really remarkable. This side of him suggested a kind of 'spoiled intellectual'. There was also the curious sympathy he could extend to such matters as the story of the St. John Clarke introduction, which he now made me outline after I had explained my purpose in the Ritz. The facts could scarcely have been very interesting to him, but he followed their detail as if alteration of the bank rate or fluctuations of the copper market were ultimately concerned. Perhaps this capacity for careful attention to other people's affairs was the basis of his own success in business.

'Of course I know about Isbister, R.A.,' he said. 'He painted that shocking picture of my old man. I tried to pop it when he dropped off the hooks, but there were no takers. I know about St. John Clarke, too. Mona reads his books. Absolutely laps them up, in fact.'

'Who is Mona?'

'Oh, yes, you haven't met her yet, have you? Mona is my wife.'

'But, my dear Peter, I had no idea you were married.'

'Strange, isn't it? Our wedding anniversary, matter of fact. Broke as I am, I thought we could gnaw a cutlet at the Grill to celebrate. Why not join us? Your chap is obviously not going to turn up.'

He began to speak of his own affairs, talking in just the way he did when we used to have tea together at school. Complaining of having lost a lot of money in 'the slump', he explained that he still owned a house in the neighbourhood of Maidenhead.

'More or less camping out there now,' he said. 'With a married couple looking after us. The woman does the cooking. The man can drive a car and service it pretty well, but he hasn't the foggiest idea about looking after my clothes.'

I asked about his marriage.

'We met first at a road-house near Staines. Mona was being entertained there by a somewhat uncouth individual called Snider, an advertising agent. Snider's firm was using her as a photographer's model. You'll know her face when you see her. Laxatives—halitosis—even her closest friend wouldn't tell her—and so on.'

I discovered in due course that Mona's chief appearance on the posters had been to advertise toothpaste; but both she and her husband were inclined to emphasise other more picturesque possibilities.

'She'd already had a fairly adventurous career by then,' Templer said.

He began to enlarge on this last piece of information,

like a man unable to forgo irritating the quiescent nerve of a potentially aching tooth. I had the impression that he was still very much in love with his wife, but that things were perhaps not going as well as he could wish. That would explain a jerkiness of manner that suggested worry. The story itself seemed commonplace enough, yet containing implications of Templer's own recurrent desire to escape from whatever world enclosed him.

'She *says* she's partly Swiss,' he said. 'Her father was an engineer in Birmingham, always being fired for being tight. However, both parents are dead. The only relation she's got is an aunt with a house in Worthing—a boarding-house, I think.'

I saw at once that Mona, whatever else her characteristics, was a wife liberally absolving Templer from additional family ties. That fact, perhaps counting for little compared with deeper considerations, would at the same time seem a great advantage in his eyes. This desire to avoid new relations through marriage was connected with an innate unwillingness to identify himself too closely with any one social group. In that taste, oddly enough, he resembled Uncle Giles, each of them considering himself master of a more sweeping mobility of action by voluntary withdrawal from competition at any given social level of existence.

At the time of narration, I did not inwardly accept all Templer's highly coloured statements about his wife, but I was impressed by the apparent depths of his feeling for Mona. Even when telling the story of how his marriage had come about, he had completely abandoned any claim to have employed those high-handed methods he was accustomed to advocate for controlling girls of her sort. I asked what time she was due at the Ritz.

'When she comes out of the cinema,' he said. 'She was

determined to see *Mädchen in Uniform*. I couldn't face it. After all, one meets quite enough lesbians in real life without going to the pictures to see them.'

'But it isn't a film about lesbians.'

'Oh, isn't it?' said Templer. 'Mona thought it was. She'll be disappointed if you're right. However, I'm sure you're wrong. Jimmy Brent told me about it. He usually knows what's what in matters of that kind. My sister Jean is with Mona. Did you ever meet her? I can't remember. They may be a little late, but I've booked a table. We can have a drink or two while we wait.'

Jean's name recalled the last time I had seen her at that luncheon party at Stourwater where I had been taken by the Walpole-Wilsons. I had not thought of her for ages, though some small residue of inner dissatisfaction, which survives all emotional expenditure come to nothing, now returned.

'Jean's having a spot of trouble with that husband of hers,' said Templer. 'That is why she is staying with us for the moment. She married Bob Duport, you know. He is rather a handful.'

'So I should imagine.'

'You don't know him.'

'We met when you drove us all into the ditch in your famous second-hand Vauxhall.'

'My God,' said Templer, laughing. 'That was a shambles, wasn't it? Fancy your remembering that. It must be nearly ten years ago now. The row those bloody girls made. Old Bob was in poor form that day, I remember. He thought he'd picked up a nail after a binge he'd been on a night or two before. Completely false alarm, of course.'

'As Le Bas once said: "I can't accept ill health as a valid excuse for ill manners."'

'Bob's not much your sort, but he's not a bad chap when

you get to know him. I was surprised you'd ever heard of him. I've had worse brothers-in-law, although, God knows, that's not saying much. But Bob *is* difficult. Bad enough running after every girl he meets, but when he goes and loses nearly all his money on top of that, an awkward situation is immediately created.'

'Are they living apart?'

'Not officially. Jean is looking for a small flat in town for herself and the kid.'

'What sex?'

'Polly, aged three.'

'And Duport?'

'Gone abroad, leaving a trail of girl-friends and bad debts behind him. He is trying to put through some big stuff on the metal market. I think the two of them will make it up in due course. I used to think she was mad about him, but you can never tell with women.'

The news that Polly was to be born was the last I had heard of her mother. Little as I could imagine how Jean had brought herself to marry Duport—far less be 'mad about him'—I had by then learnt that such often inexplicable things must simply be accepted as matters of fact. His sister's matrimonial troubles evidently impressed Templer as vexatious, though in the circumstances probably unavoidable; certainly not a subject for prolonged discussion.

'Talking of divorces and such things,' he said. 'Do you ever see Charles Stringham now?'

There had been little or no scandal connected with the break-up of Stringham's marriage. He and Peggy Stepney had parted company without apparent reason, just as their reason for marrying had been outwardly hard to understand. They had bought a house somewhere north of the Park, but neither ever seemed to have lived there for more than a few weeks at a time, certainly seldom together. The house itself, decorated by the approved decorator of that moment, was well spoken of, but I had never been there. The marriage had simply collapsed, so people said, from inanition. I never heard it suggested that Peggy had taken a lover. Stringham, it was true, was seen about with all kinds of women, though nothing specific was alleged against him either. Soon after the decree had been made absolute, Peggy married a cousin, rather older than herself, and went to live in Yorkshire, where her husband possessed a large house, noted in books of authentically recorded ghost stories for being rather badly haunted.

'That former wife of his—The Lady Peggy—was a good-looking piece,' said Templer. 'But, as you know, such grand life is not for me. I prefer simpler pleasures——

' "Oh, give me a man to whom naught comes amiss,
One horse or another, that country or this. . . ." '

'You know you've always hated hunting and hunting people. Anyway, whose sentiments were those?'

'Ah,' he said, 'chaps like you think I'm not properly educated, in spite of the efforts of Le Bas and others, and that I don't know about beautiful poetry. You find you're wrong. I know all sorts of little snatches. As a matter of fact I was thinking of women, really, rather than horses, and taking 'em as you find 'em. Not being too choosy about it as Charles has always been. Of course they are easier to take than to find, in my experience—though of course it is not gentlemanly to boast of such things. Anyway, as you know, I have given up all that now.'

At school I could remember Templer claiming that he had never read a book for pleasure in his life; and, although an occasional Edgar Wallace was certainly to be seen in his hand during the period of his last few terms, the quotation was surprising. That was a side of him not entirely unexpected, but usually kept hidden. Incidentally, it was a conversational trick acquired—perhaps consciously copied—from Stringham.

'You remember the imitations Charles used to do of Widmerpool?' he said. 'I expect he is much too grand to remember Widmerpool now.'

'I saw Widmerpool not so long ago. He is with Donners-Brebner.'

'But not much longer,' said Templer. 'Widmerpool is joining the Acceptance World.'

'What on earth is that?'

'Well, actually he is going to become a bill-broker,' said Templer, laughing. 'I should have made myself clearer to one not involved in the nefarious ways of the City.'

'What will he do?'

'Make a lot of heavy weather. He'll have to finish his lunch by two o'clock and spend the rest of the day wasting the time of the banks.'

'But what is the Acceptance World?'

'If you have goods you want to sell to a firm in Bolivia, you probably do not touch your money in the ordinary way until the stuff arrives there. Certain houses, therefore, are prepared to 'accept' the debt. They will advance you the money on the strength of your reputation. It is all right when the going is good, but sooner or later you are tempted to plunge. Then there is an alteration in the value of the Bolivian exchange, or a revolution, or perhaps the firm just goes bust—and you find yourself stung. That is, if you guess wrong.'

'I see. But why is he leaving Donners-Brebner? He always told me he was such a success there and that Sir Magnus liked him so much.'

'Widmerpool was doing all right in Donners-Brebner—in fact rather well, as you say,' said Templer. 'But he used to bore the pants off everyone in the combine by his intriguing. In the end he got on the nerves of Donners himself. Did you ever come across a fellow called Truscott? Widmerpool took against him, and worked away until he had got him out. Then Donners regretted it, after Truscott had been sacked, and decided Widmerpool was getting too big for his boots. He must go too. The long and the short of it is that Widmerpool is joining this firm of bill-brokers—on the understanding that a good deal of the Donners-Brebner custom follows him there.'

I had never before heard Templer speak of Widmerpool in this matter-of-fact way. At school he had disliked him, or, at best, treated him as a harmless figure of fun. Now, however, Widmerpool had clearly crystallised in Templer's mind as an ordinary City acquaintance, to be thought of no longer as a subject for laughter, but as a normal vehicle for the transaction of business; perhaps even one particularly useful in that respect on account of former associations.

'I was trying to get Widmerpool to lend a hand with old Bob,' said Templer.

'What would he do?'

'Bob has evolved a scheme for collecting scrap metal from some place in the Balkans and shipping it home. At least that is the simplest way of explaining what he intends. Widmerpool has said he will try to arrange for Bob to have the agency for Donners-Brebner.'

I was more interested in hearing of this development in Widmerpool's career than in examining its probable effect on Duport, whose business worries were no concern of mine. However, my attention was at that moment distracted from such matters by the sudden appearance in the palm court of a short, decidedly unconventional figure who now came haltingly up the steps. This person wore a black leather overcoat. His arrival in the Ritz—in those days—was a remarkable event.

Pausing, with a slight gesture of exhaustion that seemed to imply arduous travel over many miles of arid desert or snowy waste (according to whether the climate within or without the hotel was accepted as prevailing), he looked about the room; gazing as if in amazement at the fountain, the nymph, the palms in their pots of Chinese design: then turning his eyes to the chandeliers and the glass of the roof. His bearing was at once furtive, resentful, sagacious, and full of a kind of confidence in his own powers. He seemed to be surveying the tables as if searching for someone, at the same time unable to believe his eyes, while he did so, at the luxuriance of the oasis in which he found himself. He carried no hat, but retained the belted leather overcoat upon which a few drops of moisture could be seen glistening as he advanced farther into the room, an indication that snow or sleet had begun to fall outside. This black leather garment gave a somewhat official air to his appearance, obscurely suggesting a Wellsian man of the future, hierarchic in rank. Signs of damp could also be seen in patches on his sparse fair hair, a thatch failing to roof in completely the dry, yellowish skin of his scalp.

This young man, although already hard to think of as really young on account of the maturity of his expression, was J. G. Quiggin. I had been reflecting on him only a short time earlier in connexion with Mark Members; for the pair of them—Members and Quiggin—were, for some reason, always associated together in the mind. This was not only because I myself had happened to meet both of them during my first term at the university. Other people, too, were accustomed to link their names together, as if they were a business firm, or, more authentically, a couple whose appearance together in public inevitably invoked the thought of a certain sort of literary life. Besides that, a kind of love-hate indissolubly connected them.

Whether or not the birth of this relationship had in fact taken place at that tea party in Sillery's rooms in college, where we had all met as freshmen, was not easy to say. There at any rate I had first seen Quiggin in his grubby starched collar and subfusc suit. On that occasion Sillery had rather maliciously suggested the acquaintance of Members and Quiggin dated from an earlier incarnation; in fact boyhood together—like Isbister and St. John Clarke—in some Midland town. So far as I knew, that assertion had neither been proved nor disproved. Some swore Quiggin and Members were neighbours at home; others that the story was a pure invention, produced in malice, and based on the fact that Sillery had found the two names in the same provincial telephone directory. Sillery certainly devoted a good deal of his time to the study of such works of reference as telephone books and county directories, from which he managed to extract a modicum of information useful to himself. At the same time there were those who firmly believed Members and Quiggin to be related; even first cousins. The question was largely irrelevant; although the acutely combative nature of their friendship, if it could be so called, certainly possessed all that intense, almost vindictive rivalry of kinship.

Quiggin had quietly disappeared from the university without taking a degree. Now, like Members, he had already made some name for himself, though at a somewhat different literary level. He was a professional reviewer of notable ability, much disliked by some of the older critics for the roughness with which he occasionally handled accepted reputations. One of the smaller publishing houses employed him as 'literary adviser'; a firm of which his friend Howard Craggs (formerly of the Vox Populi Press, now extinct, though partly reincorporated as Boggis & Stone) had recently become a director. A book by Quiggin had been advertised to appear in the spring, but as a rule his works never seemed, at the last moment, to satisfy their author's high standard of self-criticism. Up to then his manuscripts had always been reported as 'burnt', or at best held back for drastic revision.

Quiggin, certainly to himself and his associates, represented a more go-ahead school of thought to that of Members and his circle. Although not himself a poet, he was a great adherent of the new trends of poetry then developing, which deprecated 'Art for Art's sake', a doctrine in a general way propagated by Members. However, Members, too, was moving with the times, his latest volume of verse showing a concern with psychoanalysis; but, although 'modern' in the eyes of a writer of an older generation like St. John Clarke, Members—so Quiggin had once remarked—'drooped too heavily over the past, a crutch with which we younger writers must learn to dispense'. Members, for his part, had been heard complaining that he himself was in sympathy with 'all liberal and progressive movements', but 'J.G. had advanced into a state of mind too political to be understood by civilised people'. In spite of such differences, and reported statements of both of them that they 'rarely saw each other now', they were not uncommonly to be found together, arguing or sulking on the banquettes of the Café Royal.

When Quiggin caught sight of me in the Ritz he immediately made for our table. As he moved across the white marble floor his figure seemed thicker than formerly. From being the spare, hungry personage I had known as an undergraduate he had become solid, almost stout. It was possible that Members, perhaps maliciously, perhaps as a matter of convenience to himself, had arranged for Quiggin to pick him up for dinner at an hour when our business together would be at an end. Supposing this had been planned, I was preparing to explain that Members had not turned up, when all at once Quiggin himself began to speak in his small, hard, grating North Country voice; employing a tone very definitely intended to sweep aside any question of wasting time upon the idle formalities of introduction, or indeed anything else that might postpone, even momentarily, some matter that was his duty to proclaim without delay.

'I could not get away earlier,' he began, peremptorily. 'St. J. is rather seriously ill. It happened quite suddenly. Not only that, but a difficult situation has arisen. I should like to discuss things with you.'

This introductory speech was even less expected than Quiggin's own arrival, although the tense, angry seriousness with which he had invested these words was not uncommon in his way of talking. Once I had thought this abrupt, aggressive manner came from a kind of shyness; later that theory had to be abandoned when it became clear that Quiggin's personality expressed itself naturally in this form. I was surprised to hear him refer to St. John Clarke as 'St. J.', a designation appropriated to himself by Mark Members, and rarely used by others; in fact a nickname almost patented by Members as an outward sign of his own intimacy with his friend and employer.

I could not imagine why Quiggin, on that particular night, should suddenly wish that we should dine *tête-à-tête*. In the past we had occasionally spent an evening together after meeting at some party, always by accident rather than design. We were on quite good terms, but there was no subject involving St. John Clarke likely to require urgent discussion between us. At the university, where he had seemed a lonely, out-of-the-way figure, I had felt an odd interest in Quiggin; but our acquaintance there, such as it was, he now treated almost as a matter to live down. Perhaps that was natural as he came to invest more and more of his personality in his own literary status. At that moment, for example, his manner of speaking implied that any of his friends should be prepared to make sacrifices for an exceptional occasion like this one: a time when opportunity to be alone with him and talk seriously was freely offered.

'Did you come to meet Mark?' I asked. 'He hasn't turned up. It is not very likely he will appear now.'

Quiggin, refusing an invitation to sit down, stood upright by the table, still enveloped in his black, shiny livery. He had unfastened the large buttons of the overcoat, which now flapped open like Bonaparte's, revealing a dark grey jumper that covered all but the knot of a red tie. The shirt was also dark grey. His face wore the set, mask-like expression of an importunate beggar tormenting a pair of tourists seated on the perimeter of a café's *terrasse*. I felt suddenly determined to be no longer a victim of other people's disregard for their social obligations. I introduced Templer out of hand—an operation Quiggin had somehow prevented until that moment—explaining at the same time that I was that evening already irrevocably booked for a meal.

Quiggin showed annoyance at this downright refusal to be dislodged, simultaneously indicating his own awareness that Members had been unable to keep this appointment. It then occurred to me that Members had persuaded Quiggin to make the excuses for his own absence in person. Such an arrangement was unlikely, and would in any case not explain why Quiggin should expect me to dine with him. However, Quiggin shook his head at this suggestion, and gave a laugh expressing scorn rather than amusement. Templer watched us with interest.

'As a matter of fact St. J. has a new secretary,' said Quiggin slowly, through closed lips. 'That is why Mark did not come this evening.'

'What, has Mark been sacked?'

Quiggin was evidently not prepared to reply directly to so uncompromising an enquiry. He laughed a little, though rather more leniently than before.

'Honourably retired, perhaps one might say.'

'On a pension?'

'You are very inquisitive, Nicholas.'

'You have aroused my interest. You should be flattered.'

'Life with St. J. never really gave Mark time for his own work.'

'He always produced a fair amount.'

'Too much, from one point of view,' said Quiggin, savagely; adding in a less severe tone: 'Mark, as you know, always insists on taking on so many things. He could not always give St. J. the attention a man of his standing quite reasonably demands. Of course, the two of them will continue to see each other. I think, in fact, Mark is going to look in once in a way to keep the library in order. After all, they are close friends, first and foremost, quite apart from whether or not Mark is St. J.'s secretary. As you probably know, there have been various difficulties from time to time. Minor ones, of course. Still, one thing leads to another. Mark can be rather querulous when he does not get his own way.'

'Who is taking Mark's place?'

'It is not exactly a question of one person taking another's place. Merely coping with the practical side of the job more —well—conscientiously.'

Quiggin bared his teeth, as if to excuse this descent on his own part to a certain smugness of standpoint.

'Yourself?'

'At first just as an experiment on both sides.'

I saw at once that in this change, if truly reported, all kind of implications were inherent. Stories had circulated in the past of jobs for which Quiggin and Members had been in competition, most of them comparatively unimportant employments in the journalistic field. This was rather larger game; because, apart from other considerations, there was the question of who was to be St. John Clarke's heir. He was apparently alone in the world. It was not a vast fortune, perhaps, but a tidy sum. A devoted secretary might stand in a favourable position for at least a handsome bequest. Although I had never heard hints that Quiggin was anxious to replace Members in the novelist's household, such an ambition was by no means unthinkable. In fact the change was likely to have been brought about by long intrigue rather than sudden caprice. The news was surprising, though of a kind to startle by its essential appropriateness rather than from any sense of incongruity.

Although I did not know St. John Clarke, I could not help feeling a certain pity for him, smitten down among his first editions, press cuttings, dinner invitations, and signed photographs of eminent contemporaries, a sick man of letters, fought over by Members and Quiggin.

'That was why I wanted to have a talk about St. J.'s affairs,' said Quiggin, continuing to speak in his more conciliatory tone. 'There have been certain changes lately in his point of view. You probably knew that. I think you are interested in getting this introduction. I see no reason why he should not write it. But I am of the opinion that he will probably wish to approach Isbister's painting from a rather different angle. The pictures, after all, offer a unique example of what a capitalist society produces where art is concerned. However, I see we shall have to discuss that another time.'

He stared hard at Templer as chief impediment to his plans for the evening. It was at that point that 'the girls' arrived; owing to this conversation, entering the room unobserved by me until they were standing beside us. I was immediately aware that I had seen Templer's wife before. Then I remembered that he had warned me I should recognise the stylised, conventionally smiling countenance, set in blonde curls, that had formerly appeared so often, on the walls of buses and underground trains, advocating a well-known brand of toothpaste. She must have been nearly six foot in height: in spite of a rather coarse complexion, a beautiful girl by any standards.

'It was *too* wonderful,' she said, breathlessly.

She spoke to Templer, but turned almost at once in the direction of Quiggin and myself. At the sight of her, Quiggin went rather red in the face and muttered inaudible phrases conveying that they already knew one another. She replied civilly to these, though evidently without any certainty as to where that supposed meeting had taken place. She was obviously longing to talk about the film, but Quiggin was not prepared for the matter of their earlier encounter to be left vague.

'It was years ago at a party over an antique shop,' he insisted, 'given by an old queen who died soon after. Mark Members introduced us.'

'Oh, yes,' she said, indifferently, 'I haven't seen Mark for ages.'

'Deacon, he was called.'

'I believe I remember.'

'Off Charlotte Street.'

'There were a lot of parties round there,' she agreed. Then I knew that something other than the toothpaste advertisements had caused Mona's face to seem so familiar. I, too, had seen her at Mr. Deacon's birthday party. Since then she had applied peroxide to her naturally dark hair. When Templer had spoken of his wife's former profession I had not connected her with 'Mona', the artist's model of whom Barnby, and others, used sometimes to speak. Barnby had not mentioned her for a long time.

In due course I found that Mona had abandoned that 'artist's' world for commercial employments that were more lucrative. The people she met in these less pretentious circles were also no doubt on the whole more sympathetic to her, although she would never have admitted that. Certainly the impact of her earlier career as a model for painters and sculptors was never erased from her own mind. With the extraordinary adaptability of women, she had managed to alter considerably the lines of her figure, formerly a striking synthesis of projections and concavities that certainly seemed to demand immediate expression in bronze or stone. Now her body had been disciplined into a fashionable, comparatively commonplace mould. She smiled in a friendly way at Quiggin, but made no effort to help him out in his efforts to suggest that they really already knew each other.

Quiggin himself continued to stand for a time resentfully beside us, giving the impression not so much that he wished to join the Templer party, as that he hoped for an invitation to do so, which would at once be curtly refused; though whether, had the chance arisen, he would in fact have withheld his company was, of course, speculative. Mona threw him another smile, her regular rows of teeth neatly displayed between pink lips parted in a cupid's bow: an ensemble invoking more than ever her career on the hoardings. For some reason this glance confirmed Quiggin's intention to depart. After a final word with me to the effect that he would ring up early the following week and arrange a meeting, he nodded in an offended manner to the world in general, and tramped away across the room and down the steps. He held himself tautly upright, as if determined to avoid for ever in future such haunts of luxury and those who frequent them.

Just as he was making this move, Lady Ardglass, followed by her spruce, grey-haired admirers, at heel like a brace of well-groomed, well-bred, obedient sporting dogs, passed us on the way out. A natural blonde, Bijou Ardglass possessed a fleeting facial resemblance to Mona. She was said to have been a mannequin before her marriage. My attention had been caught momentarily by Quiggin's words, but, even while he was speaking, I was aware of this resemblance as Lady Ardglass approached; although her smooth hair and mink made a strong contrast with Mona's camel-hair coat and rather wild appearance. All the same there could be no doubt that the two of them possessed something in common. As the Ardglass cortège came level with us, I saw exchanged between the two of them one of those glances so characteristic of a woman catching sight of another woman who reminds her of herself: glances in which deep hatred and also a kind of passionate love seem to mingle voluptuously together for an instant of time.

Templer, at the same moment, shot out an all-embracing look, which seemed in an equally brief space to absorb Bijou Ardglass in her entirety. He appeared to do this more from force of habit than because she greatly interested him. It was a memorandum for some future date, should the need ever arise, recording qualities and defects, charms and blemishes, certainties and potentialities, both moral and physical. Jean saw Lady Ardglass too. Just as Quiggin was making his final remark to me, I was conscious that she touched her brother's arm and muttered something to him that sounded like 'Bob's girl': words at which Templer raised his eyebrows.

I did not fully take in Jean's appearance until that moment. She was wearing a red dress with a black coat, and some kind of a scarf, folded over like a stock, emphasised the long, graceful curve of her neck. Mona's strident personality occupied the centre of the stage, and, besides, I felt for some reason a desire to postpone our meeting. Now, as she spoke to her brother, her face assumed an expression at once mocking and resigned, which had a sweetness about it that reminded me of the days when I had thought myself in love with her. I could still feel the tension her presence always brought, but without any of that hopeless romantic longing, so characteristic of love's very early encounters: perhaps always imperfectly recaptured in the more realistic love-making of later life. Now, I experienced a kind of resentment at the reserve which enclosed her. It suggested a form of self-love, not altogether attractive. Yet the look of irony and amusement that had come into her face when she whispered the phrase about 'Bob's girl' seemed to add something unexpected and charming to her still mysterious personality.

She was taller than I remembered, and carried herself well. Her face, like her brother's, had become a shade fuller, a change that had coarsened his appearance, while in her the sharp, almost animal look I remembered was now softened. She had not entirely lost her air of being a school-girl; though certainly, it had to be admitted, a very smartly dressed school-girl. I thought to myself, not without complacence, that I was able to appreciate her without in any way losing my head, as I might once have done. There was still a curious fascination about her grey-blue eyes, slanting a little, as it were caught tightly between soft, lazy lids and dark, luxurious lashes. Once she had reminded me of Rubens's *Chapeau de Paille*. Now for some reason—though there was not much physical likeness between them—I thought of the woman smoking the hookah in Delacroix's *Femmes d'Alger dans leur appartement*. Perhaps there was something of the odalisque about Jean, too. She looked pale and rather tired. Any girl might excusably have appeared pale beside Mona, whose naturally high colouring had been increased by her own hand, almost as if for the stage or a cabaret performance.

'Do you remember where we last met?' she said, when Quiggin was gone.

'At Stourwater.'

'What a party.'

'Was it awful?'

'Some of it wasn't very nice. Terrible rows between Baby and our host.'

'But I thought they never had rows in public.'

'They didn't. That was what was so awful. Sir Magnus tremendously bland all the time and Baby absolutely bursting with bad temper.'

'Do you ever hear from Baby Wentworth now?'

'I had a card at Christmas. She is cloudlessly happy with her Italian.'

'What is his profession?'

'I don't think I know you well enough to tell you. Perhaps after dinner.'

This, I remembered, was the way things had been at Stourwater: brisk conversation that led in the end to acres of silence. I made up my mind that this time I would not feel put out by her behaviour, whatever form it took.

'Let's have some food,' said Templer, 'I'm famished. So must you girls be, after your intellectual film.'

Afterwards, I could never recall much about that dinner

in the Grill, except that the meal conveyed an atmosphere of powerful forces at work beneath the conversation. The sight of her husband's mistress had no doubt been disturbing to Jean, who as usual spoke little. It soon became clear that the Templers' mutual relationship was not an easy one. Different couples approach with varied technique the matrimonial vehicle's infinitely complicated machinery. In the case of the Templers, their method made it hard to believe that they were really married at all. Clearly each of them was accustomed to a more temporary arrangement. Their conduct was normal enough, but they remained two entirely separate individuals, giving no indication of a life in common. This was certainly not because Templer showed any lack of interest in his wife. On the contrary, he seemed extravagantly, almost obsessively fond of her, although he teased her from time to time. In the past he had sometimes spoken of his love affairs to me, but I had never before seen him, as it were, in action. I wondered whether he habitually showed this same tremendous outward enthusiasm when pursuing more casual inclinations; or whether Mona had touched off some hitherto unkindled spark.

How far Mona herself reciprocated these feelings was less easy to guess. Possibly she was already rather bored with being a wife, and her surfeit in this respect might explain her husband's conciliatory attitude. She spoke and acted in a manner so affected and absurd that there was something appealing about the artificiality of her gestures and conversation. She was like some savage creature, anxious to keep up appearances before members of a more highly civilised species, although at the same time keenly aware of her own superiority in cunning. There was something hard and untamed about her, probably the force that had attracted Templer and others. She seemed on good terms with Jean, who may have found her sister-in-law's crude, violent presence emphasised to advantage her own quieter, though still undisclosed nature.

Quiggin had made an impression upon Mona, because, almost immediately after we sat down to dinner, she began to make enquiries about him. Possibly, on thinking it over, she felt that his obvious interest in her had deserved greater notice. In answer to her questions, I explained that he was J. G. Quiggin, the literary critic. She at once asserted that she was familiar with his reviews in one of the 'weeklies', mentioning, as it happened, a periodical for which, so far as I knew, he had never written.

'He was a splendid fellow in his old leather overcoat,' said Templer. 'Did you notice his shirt, too? I expect you know lots of people like that, Nick. To think I was rather worried at not having struggled into a dinner-jacket tonight, and he just breezed in wearing the flannel trousers he had been sleeping in for a fortnight, and not caring a damn. I admire that.'

'I couldn't remember a thing about meeting him before,' said Mona. 'I expect I must have been a bit tight that night, otherwise I should have known his name. He said Mark Members introduced us. Have you heard of him? He is a well-known poet.'

She said this with an ineffable silliness that was irresistible.

'I was going to meet him here, as a matter of fact, but he never turned up.'

'Oh, *were* you?'

She was astonished at this; and impressed. I wondered what on earth Members had told her about himself to have won such respect in her eyes. Afterwards, I found that it was his status as 'a poet', rather than his private personality, that made him of such interest to her.

'I never knew Mark well,' she said, rather apologetic at having suggested such ambitious claims.

'He and Quiggin are usually very thick together.'

'I didn't realise Nick was waiting for an old friend of yours, sweetie,' said Templer. 'Is he one of those fascinating people you sometimes tell me about, who wear beards and sandals and have such curious sexual habits?'

Mona began to protest, but Jean interrupted her by saying: 'He's not a bad poet, is he?'

'I think rather good,' I said, feeling a sudden unaccountable desire to encourage in her an interest in poetry. 'He is St. John Clarke's secretary—or, at least, he was.'

I remembered then that, if Quiggin was to be believed, the situation between Members and St. John Clarke was a delicate one.

'I used to like St. John Clarke's novels,' said Jean. 'Now I think they are rather awful. Mona adores them.'

'Oh, but they are *too* wonderful.'

Mona began to detail some of St. John Clarke's plots, a formidable undertaking at the best of times. This expression of Jean's views—that Members was a goodish poet, St. John Clarke a bad novelist—seemed to me to indicate an impressive foothold in literary criticism. I felt now that I wanted to discuss all kind of things with her, but hardly knew where to begin on account of the barrier she seemed to have set up between herself and the rest of the world. I suspected that she might merely be trying to veer away conversation from a period of Mona's life that would carry too many painful implications for Templer as a husband. It could be design, rather than literary interest. However, Mona herself was unwilling to be deflected from the subject.

'Do you run round with all those people?' she went on. 'I used to myself. Then—oh, I don't know—I lost touch with them. Of course Peter doesn't much care for that sort of person, do you, sweetie?'

'Rubbish,' said Templer. 'I've just said how much I liked Mr. J. G. Quiggin. In fact I wish I could meet him again, and find out the name of his tailor.'

Mona frowned at this refusal to take her remark seriously. She turned to me and said: 'You know, you are not much like most of Peter's usual friends yourself.'

That particular matter was all too complicated to explain, even if amenable to explanation, which I was inclined to doubt. I knew, of course, what she meant. Probably there was something to be said for accepting that opinion. The fact that I was not specially like the general run of Templer's friends had certainly been emphasised by the appearance of Quiggin. I was rather displeased that the Templers had seen Quiggin. To deal collectively with them on their own plane would have been preferable to that to which Quiggin had somehow steered us all.

'What was the flick like?' Templer enquired.

'Marvellous,' said Mona. 'The sweetest—no, really—but *the* sweetest little girl you ever saw.'

'She was awfully good,' said Jean.

'But what happened?'

'Well, this little girl—who was called Manuela—was sent to a very posh German school.'

'Posh?' said Templer. 'Sweetie, what an awful word. Please never use it in my presence again.'

Rather to my surprise, Mona accepted this rebuke meekly: even blushing slightly.

'Well, Manuela went to this school, and fell *passionately* in love with one of the mistresses.'

'What did I tell you?' said Templer. 'Nick insisted the film wasn't about lesbians. You see he just poses as a man of the world, and hasn't really the smallest idea what is going on round him.'

'It isn't a bit what *you* mean,' said Mona, now bursting

with indignation. 'It was a really beautiful story. Manuela tried to *kill* herself. I cried and cried and cried.'

'It really was good,' said Jean to me. 'Have you seen it?'

'Yes. I liked it.'

'He's lying,' said Templer. 'If he had seen the film, he would have known it was about lesbians. Look here, Nick, why not come home with us for the week-end? We can run you back to your flat and get a toothbrush. I should like you to see our house, uncomfortable as staying there will be.'

'Yes, *do* come, darling,' said Mona, drawing out the words with her absurd articulation. 'You will find everything quite mad, I'm afraid.'

She had by then drunk rather a lot of champagne.

'You must come,' said Jean, speaking in her matter-of-fact tone, almost as if she were giving an order. 'There are all sorts of things I want to talk about.'

'Of course he'll come,' said Templer. 'But we might have the smallest spot of armagnac first.'

Afterwards, that dinner in the Grill seemed to partake of the nature of a ritual feast, a rite from which the four of us emerged to take up new positions in the formal dance with which human life is concerned. At the time, its charm seemed to reside in a difference from the usual run of things. Certainly the chief attraction of the projected visit would be absence of all previous plan. But, in a sense, nothing in life is planned—or everything is—because in the dance every step is ultimately the corollary of the step before; the consequence of being the kind of person one chances to be.

While we were at dinner heavy snow was descending outside. This downfall had ceased by the time my things were collected, though a few flakes were still blowing about in the clear winter air when we set out at last for the

Templers' house. The wind had suddenly dropped. The night was very cold.

'Had to sell the Buick,' Templer said. 'I'm afraid you won't find much room at the back of this miserable vehicle.'

Mona, now comatose after the wine at dinner, rolled herself up in a rug and took the seat in front. Almost immediately she went to sleep. Jean and I sat at the back of the car. We passed through Hammersmith, and the neighbourhood of Chiswick: then out on to the Great West Road. For a time I made desultory conversation. At last she scarcely answered, and I gave it up. Templer, smoking a cigar in the front, also seemed disinclined to talk now that he was at the wheel. We drove along at a good rate.

On either side of the highway, grotesque buildings, which in daytime resembled the temples of some shoddy, utterly unsympathetic Atlantis, now assumed the appearance of an Arctic city's frontier forts. Veiled in snow, these hideous monuments of a lost world bordered a broad river of black, foaming slush, across the surface of which the car skimmed and jolted with a harsh crackling sound, as if the liquid beneath were scalding hot.

Although not always simultaneous in taking effect, nor necessarily at all equal in voltage, the process of love is rarely unilateral. When the moment comes, a secret attachment is often returned with interest. Some know this by instinct; others learn in a hard school.

The exact spot must have been a few hundred yards beyond the point where the electrically illuminated young lady in a bathing dress dives eternally through the petrol-tainted air; night and day, winter and summer, never reaching the water of the pool to which she endlessly glides. Like some image of arrested development, she returns for ever, voluntarily, to the springboard from which she started her leap. A few seconds after I had seen this bathing belle journeying, as usual, imperturbably through the frozen air, I took Jean in my arms.

Her response, so sudden and passionate, seemed surprising only a minute or two later. All at once everything was changed. Her body felt at the same time hard and yielding, giving a kind of glow as if live current issued from it. I used to wonder afterwards whether, in the last resort, of all the time we spent together, however ecstatic, those first moments on the Great West Road were not the best.

To what extent the sudden movement that brought us together was attributable to sentiment felt years before; to behaviour that was almost an obligation within the Templer orbit; or, finally, to some specific impetus of the car as it covered an unusually bad surface of road, was later impossible to determine with certainty. All I knew was that I had not thought it all out beforehand. This may seem extraordinary in the light of what had gone before; but the behaviour of human beings is, undeniably, extraordinary. The incredible ease with which this evolution took place was almost as if the two of us had previously agreed to embrace at that particular point on the road. The timing had been impeccable.

We had bowled along much farther through the winter night, under cold, glittering stars, when Templer turned the car off the main road. Passing through byways lined with beech trees, we came at last to a narrow lane where snow still lay thick on the ground. At the end of this, the car entered a drive, virginally white. In the clear moonlight the grotesquely gabled house ahead of us, set among firs, seemed almost a replica of that mansion by the sea formerly inhabited by Templer's father. Although smaller in size, the likeness of general outline was uncanny. I almost expected to hear the crash of wintry waves beneath a neighbouring cliff. The trees about the garden were powdered with white. Now and then a muffled thud resounded as snow fell through the branches on to the thickly coated ground. Otherwise, all was deathly silent.

Templer drew up with a jerk in front of the door, the wheels churning up the snow. He climbed quickly from his seat, and went round to the back of the car, to unload from the boot some eatables and wine they had brought from London. At the same moment Mona came out of her sleep or coma. With the rug still wrapped round her, she jumped out of her side of the car, and ran across the Sisley landscape to the front door, which someone had opened from within. As she ran she gave a series of little shrieks of agony at the cold. Her footprints left deep marks on the face of the drive, where the snow lay soft and tender, like the clean, clean sheets of a measureless bed.

'Where shall I find you?'

'Next to you on the left.'

'How soon?'

'Give it half an hour.'

'I'll be there.'

'Don't be too long.'

She laughed softly when she said that, disengaging herself from the rug that covered both of us.

The interior of the house was equally reminiscent of the Templers' former home. Isbister's huge portrait of Mr. Templer still hung in the hall, a reminder of everyday life and unsolved business problems. Such things seemed far removed from this mysterious, snowy world of unreality, where all miracles could occur. There were the same golf clubs and shooting-sticks and tennis racquets; the same barometer, marking the weather on a revolving chart; the same post-box for letters; even the same panelling in light wood that made the place seem like the interior of a vast, extravagant cabinet for cigars.

'What we need,' said Templer, 'is a drink. And then I think we shall all be ready for bed.'

For a second I wondered whether he were aware that something was afoot; but, when he turned to help Mona with the bottles and glasses, I felt sure from their faces that neither had given a thought to any such thing.

3.

EARLY in the morning, snow was still drifting from a darkened sky across the diamond lattices of the window-panes; floating drearily down upon the white lawns and grey muddy paths of a garden flanked by pines and fir trees. Through these coniferous plantations, which arose above thick laurel bushes, appeared at no great distance glimpses of two or three other houses similar in style to the one in which I found myself; the same red brick and gables, the same walls covered with ivy or virginia creeper.

This was, no doubt, a settlement of prosperous business men; a reservation, like those created for indigenous inhabitants, or wild animal life, in some region invaded by alien elements: a kind of refuge for beings unfitted to battle with modern conditions, where they might live their own lives, undisturbed and unexploited by an aggressive outer world. In these confines the species might be saved from extinction. I felt miles away from everything, lying there in that bedroom: almost as if I were abroad. The weather was still exceedingly cold. I thought over a conversation I had once had with Barnby.

'Has any writer ever told the truth about women?' he had asked.

One of Barnby's affectations was that he had read little or nothing, although, as a matter of fact, he knew rather thoroughly a small, curiously miscellaneous collection of books.

'Few in this country have tried.'

'No one would believe it if they did.'

'Possibly. Nor about men either, if it comes to that.'

'I intend no cheap cynicism,' Barnby said. 'It is merely that in print the truth is not credible for those who have not thought deeply of the matter.'

'That is true of almost everything.'

'To some extent. But painting, for example—where women are concerned—is quite different from writing. In painting you can state everything there is to be said on the subject. In other words, the thing is treated purely æsthetically, almost scientifically. Writers always seem to defer to the wishes of the women themselves.'

'So do painters. What about Reynolds or Boucher?'

'Of course, of course,' said Barnby, whose capacity for disregarding points made against him would have supplied the foundation for a dazzling career at the Bar. 'But in writing—perhaps, as you say, chiefly writing in this country—there is no equivalent, say, of Renoir's painting. Renoir did not think that all women's flesh was *literally* a material like pink satin. He used that colour and texture as a convention to express in a simple manner certain pictorial ideas of his own about women. In fact he did so in order to get on with the job in other aspects of his picture. I never find anything like that in a novel.'

'You find plenty of women with flesh like that sitting in the Ritz.'

'Maybe. And I can paint them. But can you write about them?'

'No real tradition of how women behave exists in English writing. In France there is at least a good rough and ready convention, perhaps not always correct—riddled with every form of romanticism—but at least a pattern to which a writer can work. A French novelist may conform with the convention, or depart from it. His readers know, more or less, which he is doing. Here, every female character has to be treated empirically.'

'Well, after all, so does every woman,' said Barnby, another of whose dialectical habits was suddenly to switch round and argue against himself. 'One of the troubles, I think, is that there are too many novelists like St. John Clarke.'

'But novelists of the first rank have not always been attracted to women physically.'

'If of the first rank,' said Barnby, 'they may rise above it. If anything less, homosexual novelists are, I believe, largely responsible for some of the extraordinary ideas that get disseminated about women and their behaviour.'

Barnby's sententious tone had already indicated to me that he was himself entangled in some new adventure. Those utterances, which Mr. Deacon used to call 'Barnby's generalisations about women', were almost always a prelude to a story involving some woman individually. So it had turned out on that occasion.

'When you first make a hit with someone,' he had continued, 'you think everything is going all right with the girl, just because it is all right with you. But when you are more used to things, you are always on your guard—prepared for trouble of one sort or another.'

'Who is it this time?'

'A young woman I met on a train.'

'How promiscuous.'

'She inspired a certain confidence.'

'And things are going wrong?'

'On the contrary, going rather well. That is what makes me suspicious.'

'Have you painted her?'

Barnby rummaged among the brushes, tubes of paint,

newspapers, envelopes and bottles that littered the table; coming at last to a large portfolio from which he took a pencil drawing. The picture was of a girl's head. She looked about twenty. The features, suggested rather than outlined, made her seem uncertain of herself, perhaps on the defensive. Her hair was untidy. There was an air of self-conscious rebellion. Something about the portrait struck me as familiar.

'What is her name?'

'I don't know.'

'Why not?'

'She won't tell me.'

'How very secretive.'

'That's what I think.'

'How often has she been here?'

'Two or three times.'

I examined the drawing again.

'I've met her.'

'Who is she?'

'I'm trying to remember.'

'Have a good think,' said Barnby, sighing. 'I like to clear these matters up.'

But for the moment I was unable to recall the girl's name. I had the impression our acquaintance had been slight, and was of a year or two earlier. There had been something absurd, or laughable, in the background of the occasion when we had met.

'It would be only polite to reveal her identity by now,' Barnby said, returning the drawing to the portfolio and making a grimace.

'How did it start?'

'I was coming back from a week-end with the Manaschs'. She arrived in the compartment about an hour before we reached London. We began to talk about films. For some reason we got on to the French Revolution. She said she was on the side of the People.'

'Dark eyes and reddish hair?'

'The latter unbrushed.'

'Christian name, Anne?'

'There was certainly an "A" on her handkerchief. That was a clue I forgot to tell you.'

'Generally untidy?'

'Decidedly. As to baths, I shouldn't think she overdid them.'

'I think I can place her.'

Don't keep me in suspense.'

'Lady Anne Stepney.'

'A friend of yours?'

'I sat next to her once at dinner years ago. She made the same remark about the French Revolution.'

'Did she, indeed,' said Barnby, perhaps a shade piqued at this apparently correct guess. 'Did you follow up those liberal convictions at the time?'

'On the contrary. I doubt if she would even remember my name. Her sister married Charles Stringham, whom I've sometimes talked of. They are getting a divorce, so I saw in the paper.'

'Oh, yes,' said Barnby. 'I read about it too. Stringham was the Great Industrialist's secretary at one moment, wasn't he? I met him with Baby and liked him. He has that very decorative mother, Mrs. Foxe, whom really I wouldn't——'

He became silent; then returned to the subject of the girl.

'Her parents are called Bridgnorth?'

'That's it.'

'One starts these things,' Barnby said, 'and then the question arises: how is one to continue them? Before you know where you are, you are thoroughly entangled. That is what we all have to remember.'

'We do, indeed.'

Lying in bed in the Templers' house, feeling more than a little unwilling to rise into a chilly world, I thought of these words of Barnby's. There could be no doubt that I was now, as he had said, 'thoroughly entangled'.

Everyone came down late to breakfast that morning. Mona was in a decidedly bad temper. Her irritation was perhaps due to an inner awareness that a love affair was in the air, the precise location of which she was unable to identify; for I was fairly certain that neither of the Templers guessed anything was 'on' between Jean and myself. They seemed, indeed, fully occupied by the discord of their own relationship. As it happened, I found no opportunity to be alone with Jean. She seemed almost deliberately to arrange that we should always be chaperoned by one of the other two. She would once more have appeared as calm, distant, unknown to me, as when first seen, had she not twice smiled submissively, almost shyly, when our eyes met.

Mona's sulkiness cast a gloom over the house. Although obviously lazy and easy-going in her manner of life, she possessed also an energy and egotism that put considerable force behind this display of moodiness. Templer made more than one effort to cheer her up, from time to time becoming annoyed himself at his lack of success; when conciliation would suddenly turn to teasing. However, his continued attempts to fall in with his wife's whims led in due course to an unexpected development in the composition of the party.

We were sitting in a large room of nebulous character, where most of the life of the household was carried on, reading the Sunday papers, talking, and playing the gramophone. The previous night's encounter with Quiggin had enflamed Mona's memories of her career as an artist's model. She began to talk of the 'times' she had had in various studios, and to question me about Mark Members; perhaps regretting that she had allowed this link with her past to be severed so entirely. Professionally, she had never come across such figures as Augustus John, or Epstein, trafficking chiefly with a group of the lesser academic painters; though she had known a few young men, like Members and Barnby, who frequented more 'advanced' circles. She had never even sat for Isbister, so she told me. All the same, that period of her life was now sufficiently far away to be clouded with romance; at least when compared in her own mind with her married circumstances.

When I agreed that both Members and Quiggin were by then, in their different ways, quite well-known 'young writers', she became more than ever enthusiastic about them, insisting that she must meet Quiggin again. In fact conversation seemed to have been deliberately steered by her into these channels with that end in view. Templer, lying in an armchair with his legs stretched out in front of him, listened indifferently to her talk while he idly turned the pages of the *News of the World*. His wife's experiences among 'artists' probably cropped up fairly often as a subject: a regular, almost legitimate method of exciting a little domestic jealousy when life at home seemed flat. Her repeated questions at last caused me to explain the change of secretary made by St. John Clarke.

'But this is all *too* thrilling,' she said. 'I told you St. John Clarke was my favourite author. Can't we get Mr. Quiggin to lunch and ask him what really *has* happened?'

'Well——'

'Look, Pete,' she exclaimed noisily. '*Do* let's ask J. G.

Quiggin to lunch today. He could get a train. Nick would ring him up—you will, won't you, darling?'

Templer threw the *News of the World* on to the carpet, and, turning towards me, raised his eyebrows and nodded his head slowly up and down to indicate the fantastic lengths to which caprice could be carried by a woman.

'But would Mr. Quiggin want to come?' he asked, imitating Mona's declamatory tone. 'Wouldn't he want to finish writing one of his brilliant articles?'

'We could try.'

'By all means, if you like. Half-past eleven on the day of the luncheon invitation is considered a bit late in the best circles, but fortunately we do not move in the best circles. I suppose there will be enough to eat. You remember Jimmy is bringing a girl friend?'

'Jimmy doesn't matter.'

'I agree.'

'What do you think, Nick?' she asked. 'Would Quiggin come?'

One of the charms of staying with the Templers had seemed the promise of brief escape from that routine of the literary world so relentlessly implied by the mere thought of Quiggin. It was the world in which I was thoroughly at home, and certainly did not wish to change for another, only for once to enjoy a week-end away from it. However, to prevent the Templers from asking Quiggin to lunch if they so desired was scarcely justifiable to anyone concerned. Besides, I was myself curious to hear further details regarding St. John Clarke; although I should have preferred by then to have heard Members's side of the story. Apart from all that—indeed quite overriding such considerations—were my own violent feelings about Jean which had to be reduced inwardly to some manageable order.

'Who is "Jimmy"?' I asked.

'Surely you remember Jimmy Stripling when you stayed with us years ago?' said Templer. 'My brother-in-law. At least he was until Babs divorced him. Somehow I've never been able to get him out of my life. Babs can demand her freedom and go her own way. For me there is no legal redress. Jimmy hangs round my neck like a millstone. I can't even get an annulment.'

'Didn't he go in for motor racing?'

'That's the chap.'

'Who disliked Sunny Farebrother so much?'

'Hated his guts. Well, Jimmy is coming to lunch today and bringing some sort of a piece with him—he asked if he could. Not too young, I gather, so your eyes need not brighten up. I can't remember her name. I could not refuse for old times' sake, though he is a terrible bore is poor old Jimmy these days. He had a spill at Brooklands a year or two ago. Being shot out of his car arse-first seems to have affected his brain in some way—though you wouldn't think there was much there to affect.'

'What does he do?'

'An underwriter at Lloyd's. It is not his business capacity so much as his private life that has seized up. He still rakes in a certain amount of dough. But he has taken up astrology and theosophy and numerology and God knows what else. Could your friend Quiggin stand that? Probably love it, wouldn't he? The more the merrier so far as I'm concerned.'

'Quiggin would eat it up.'

'*Do* ring him, then,' said Mona.

'Shall I?'

'Go ahead,' said Templer. 'The telephone is next door.'

There was no reply from Quiggin's Bloomsbury flat, so I rang St. John Clarke's number; on the principle that if a thing is worth doing, it is worth doing well. The bell buzzed for some seconds, and then Quiggin's voice sounded, gratingly, at the other end of the line. As I had supposed, he was already engaged on his new duties. At first he was very suspicious of my seeking him out at that place. These suspicions were not allayed when I explained about the invitation to lunch with the Templers.

'But *today*?' he said, irritably. 'Lunch today? Why, it's nearly lunch-time already.'

I repeated to him Mona's apologies for the undoubted lateness of the invitation.

'But I don't know them,' said Quiggin. 'Are they very rich?'

He still sounded cross, although a certain interest was aroused in him. I referred again to his earlier meeting with Mona.

'So she remembered me at Deacon's party after all?' he asked, rather more hopefully this time.

'She has talked of nothing but that evening.'

'I don't think I ought to leave St. J.'

'Is he bad?'

'Better, as a matter of fact. But there ought to be someone responsible here.'

'Couldn't you get Mark?' I asked, to tease him.

'St. J. does not want to see Mark just at the moment,' said Quiggin, in his flattest voice, ignoring any jocular implications the question might have possessed. 'But I suppose there is really no reason why the maid should not look after him perfectly well if I went out for a few hours.'

This sounded like weakening.

'You could catch the train if you started now.'

He was silent for a moment, evidently anxious to accept, but at the same time trying to find some excuse for making himself so easily available.

'Mona reads your articles.'

'She does?'

'Always quoting them.'

'Intelligently?'

'Come and judge for yourself.'

'Should I like their house?'

'You'll have the time of your life.'

'I think I will,' he said. 'Of course I shall be met at the station?'

'Of course.'

'All right, then.'

He replaced the receiver with a bang, as if closing an acrimonious interchange. I returned to the drawing-room. Templer was sprawling on the sofa, apparently not much interested whether Quiggin turned up or not.

'He's coming.'

'Is he *really*?' said Mona, shrilly. 'How *wonderful*.'

'Mona gets a bit bored with my friends,' said Templer. 'I must say I don't blame her. Now you can sample something of another kind at lunch, sweetie.'

'Well, we never see anybody *interesting*, sweetie,' said Mona, putting on a stage pout. 'He'll at least remind me of the days when I *used* to meet intelligent people.'

'Intelligent people?' said Templer. 'Come, come, darling, you aren't being very polite to Nick. He regards himself as tremendously intelligent.'

'Then we are providing some intelligent company for him,' said Mona. 'Your ex-brother-in-law isn't likely to come out with anything very sparkling in the way of conversation—unless he has changed a lot since we went with him to Wimbledon.'

'What do you expect at Wimbledon?' said Templer. 'To sit in the centre court listening to a flow of epigrams about foot-faults and forehand drives? Still, I see what you mean.'

I remembered Jimmy Stripling chiefly on account of

various practical jokes in which he had been concerned when, as a boy, I had stayed with the Templers. In this horseplay he had usually had the worst of it. He remained in my memory as a big, gruff, bad-tempered fellow, full of guilty feelings about having taken no part in the war. I had not much cared for him. I wondered how he would get on with Quiggin, who could be crushing to people he disliked. However, one of the traits possessed by Quiggin in common with his new employer was a willingness to go almost anywhere where a free meal was on offer; and this realistic approach to social life implied, inevitably, if not toleration of other people, at least a certain rough and ready technique for dealing with all sorts. I could not imagine why Mona was so anxious to see Quiggin again. At that time I failed entirely to grasp the extent to which in her eyes Quiggin represented high romance.

'What happened to Babs when she parted from Jimmy Stripling?'

'Married a lord,' said Templer. 'The family is going up in the world. But I expect she still thinks about Jimmy. After all, you couldn't easily forget a man with breath like his.'

Some interruption changed the subject before I was able to ask the name of Babs's third husband. Mona went to tell the servants that there would be an additional guest. Templer followed her to look for more cigarettes. For a moment Jean and I were left alone together. I slipped my hand under her arm. She pressed down upon it, giving me a sense of being infinitely near to her; an assurance that all would be well. There is always a real and an imaginary person you are in love with; sometimes you love one best, sometimes the other. At that moment it was the real one I loved. We had scarcely time to separate and begin a formal conversation when Mona returned to the room.

There the four of us remained until the sound came of a car churning up snow before the front door. This was Quiggin's arrival. Being, in a way, so largely responsible for his presence at the Templers' house, I was relieved to observe, when he entered the room, that he had cleaned himself up a bit since the previous evening. Now he was wearing a suit of cruelly blue cloth and a green knitted tie. From the start it was evident that he intended to make himself agreeable. His sharp little eyes darted round the walls, taking in the character of his hosts and their house.

'I see you have an Isbister in the hall,' he said, dryly.

The harsh inflexion of his voice made it possible to accept this comment as a compliment, or, alternatively, a shared joke. Templer at once took the words in the latter sense.

'Couldn't get rid of it,' he said. 'I suppose you don't know anybody who would make an offer? An upset price, of course. Now's the moment.'

'I'll look about,' said Quiggin. 'Isbister was a typical artist-business man produced by a decaying society, don't you think? As a matter of fact Nicholas and I have got to have a talk about Isbister in the near future.'

He grinned at me. I hoped he was not going to raise the whole question of St. John Clarke's introduction there and then. His tone might have meant anything or nothing, so far as his offer of help was concerned. Perhaps he really intended to suggest that he would try to sell the picture for Templer; and get a rake-off. His eyes continued to stray over the very indifferent nineteenth-century seascapes that covered the walls; hung together in patches as if put up hurriedly when the place was first occupied. No doubt that was exactly what had happened to them. In the Templers' house by the sea they had hung in the dining-room. Before the Isbister could be discussed further, the two other guests arrived.

The first through the door was a tall, rather overpowering lady, followed closely by Jimmy Stripling himself, looking much older than I had remembered him. The smoothness of the woman's movements, as she advanced towards Mona, almost suggested that Stripling was propelling her in front of him like an automaton on castors. I knew at once that I had seen her before, but could not at first recall the occasion: one so different, as it turned out, from that of the moment.

'How are you, Jimmy?' said Templer.

Stripling took the woman by the arm.

'This is Mrs. Erdleigh,' he said, in a rather strangled voice. 'I have told you so much about her, you know, and here she is.'

Mrs. Erdleigh shook hands graciously all round, much as if she were a visiting royalty. When she came to me, she took my hand in hers and smiled indulgently.

'You see I was right,' she said. 'You did not believe me, did you? It is just a year.'

Once more, suffocating waves of musk-like scent were distilled by her presence. By then, as a matter of fact, a month or two must have passed beyond the year that she had foretold would precede our next meeting. All the same, it was a respectable piece of prognostication. I thought it wiser to leave Uncle Giles unmentioned. If she wished to speak of him, she could always raise the subject herself. I reflected, at the same time, how often this exterior aspect of Uncle Giles's personality must have remained 'unmentioned' throughout his life; especially where his relations were concerned.

However, Mrs. Erdleigh gave the impression of knowing very well what was advisable to 'mention' and what inadvisable. She looked well; younger, if anything, than when I had seen her at the Ufford, and smartly dressed in a style that suggested less than before her inexorably apocalyptic role in life. In fact, her clothes of that former occasion seemed now, in contrast, garments of a semi-professional kind; vestments, as it were, appropriate to the ritual of her vocation. With Stripling under her control—as he certainly was—she could no doubt allow herself frivolously to enjoy the fashion of the moment.

Stripling himself, on the other hand, had changed noticeably for the worse in the ten years or more gone since our former meeting. His bulk still gave the impression that he was taking up more than his fair share of the room, but the body, although big, seemed at the same time shrivelled. His hair, still parted in the middle, was grey and grizzled. Although at that time still perhaps under forty, he looked prematurely old. There was an odd, disconnected stare in his eyes, which started from his head when he spoke at all emphatically. He appeared to be thoroughly under the thumb of Mrs. Erdleigh, whose manner, kindly though firm, implied supervision of a person not wholly responsible for his own actions. Later, it was noticeable how fixedly he watched her, while in conversation he inclined to refer even the most minor matters to her arbitration. In spite of his cowed air, he was far more friendly than when we had met before, an occasion he assured me he remembered perfectly.

'We had a lot of fun that summer with my old pal, Sunny Farebrother, didn't we?' he said in a melancholy voice.

He spoke as if appealing for agreement that the days when fun could be had with Sunny Farebrother, or indeed with anyone else, were now long past.

'Do you remember how we were going to put a po in his hat-box or something?' he went on. 'How we all laughed. Good old Sunny. I never seem to see the old boy now, though I hear he's making quite a bit of money.

It's just the same with so many folks one used to know. They pass by on the other side or join the Great Majority.'

His face had lighted up when, upon entering the room, he had seen Jean, and he had taken both her hands in his and kissed her enthusiastically. She did not seem to regard this act as anything out of the way, nor even specially repugnant to her. I felt a twinge of annoyance at that kiss. I should have liked no one else to kiss her for at least twenty-four hours. However, I reminded myself that such familiarity was reasonable enough in an ex-brother-in-law; in fact, if it came to that, reasonable enough in any old friend; though for that reason no more tolerable to myself. Stripling also held Jean's arm for a few seconds, but, perhaps aware of Mrs. Erdleigh's eye upon him, removed his hand abruptly. Fumbling in his pocket, he produced a long gold cigarette-case and began to fill it from a packet of Players. Although physically dilapidated, he still gave the impression of being rich. The fact that his tweeds were crumpled and the cuffs of his shirt greasy somehow added to this impression of wealth. If there had been any doubt about Stripling's money, his satisfactory financial position could have been estimated from Quiggin's manner towards him, a test like litmus paper where affluence was concerned. Quiggin was evidently anxious—as I was myself—to learn more of this strange couple.

'How's the world, Jimmy?' said Templer, clapping his former brother-in-law on the back, and catching my eye as he handed him an unusually stiff drink.

'Well,' said Stripling, speaking slowly, as if Templer's enquiry deserved very serious consideration before an answer was made, 'well, I don't think the *World* will get much better as long as it clings to material values.'

At this Quiggin laughed in a more aggressive manner than he had adopted hitherto. He was evidently trying to decide whether it would be better to be ingratiating to Stripling or to attack him; either method could be advantageous from its respective point of view.

'*I* think material values are just what want reassessing,' Quiggin said. 'Nor do I see how we can avoid clinging to them, since they are the only values that truly exist. However, they might be linked with a little social justice for a change.'

Stripling disregarded this remark, chiefly, I think, because his mind was engrossed with preoccupations so utterly different that he had not the slightest idea what Quiggin was talking about. Templer's eyes began to brighten as he realised that elements were present that promised an enjoyable clash of opinions. Luncheon was announced. We passed into the dining-room. As I sat down at the table I saw Mrs. Erdleigh's forefinger touch Mona's hand.

'As soon as I set eyes on you, my dear,' she said, gently, 'I knew that you belonged to the Solstice of Summer. When *is* your birthday?'

As usual, her misty gaze seemed to envelop completely whomsoever she addressed. There could be no doubt that her personality had immediately delighted Mona, who had by then already lost all her earlier sulkiness. Indeed, as the meal proceeded, Mrs. Erdleigh showed herself to be just what Mona had required. She provided limitlessly a kind of conversational balm at once maternal and sacerdotal. The two of them settled down to a detailed discussion across the table of horoscopes and their true relation to peculiarities of character. I was for some reason reminded of Sillery dealing with some farouche undergraduate whom he wished especially to enclose within his net. Even Mona's so recently excited interest in Quiggin was forgotten in this torrent of astrological self-examination, systematically controlled, in spite of its urgency of expression, by such a sympathetic informant. Mona seemed now entirely absorbed in Mrs. Erdleigh, whose manner, vigorous, calm, mystical, certainly dominated the luncheon table.

The meal passed off, therefore, with more success than might have been expected from such oddly assorted company. I reflected, not for the first time, how mistaken it is to suppose there exists some 'ordinary' world into which it is possible at will to wander. All human beings, driven as they are at different speeds by the same Furies, are at close range equally extraordinary. This party's singular composition was undoubtedly enhanced by the commonplace nature of its surroundings. At the same time it was evident that the Templers themselves saw nothing in the least out-of-the-way about the guests collected round their table for Sunday luncheon; except possibly the fact that both Quiggin and I were professionally connected with books.

If Quiggin disapproved—and he did undoubtedly disapprove—of the turn taken by Mona's and Mrs. Erdleigh's talk, he made at first no effort to indicate his dissatisfaction. He was in possession of no clue to the fact that he had been arbitrarily deposed from the position of most honoured guest in the house that day. In any case, as a person who himself acted rarely if ever from frivolous or disinterested motives, he would have found it hard, perhaps impossible, to understand the sheer irresponsibility of his invitation. To have been asked simply and solely on account of Mona's whim, if he believed that to be the reason, must have been in itself undeniably flattering to his vanity; but, as Mr. Deacon used sadly to remark, 'those who enjoy the delights of caprice must also accustom themselves to bear caprice's lash'. Even if Quiggin were aware of this harsh law's operation, he had no means of appreciating the ruthless manner in which it had been put into execution that afternoon. Mona's wish to see him had been emphasised by me when I had spoken with him on the telephone. If she continued to ignore him, Quiggin would logically assume that for one reason or another either Templer, or I myself, must have desired his presence. He would suspect some ulterior motive as soon as he began to feel sceptical as to Mona's interest in him being the cause of his invitation. As the meal progressed, this lack of attention on her part undoubtedly renewed earlier suspicions. By the time we were drinking coffee he was already showing signs of becoming less amenable.

I think this quite fortuitous situation brought about by the presence of Mrs. Erdleigh was not without effect on Quiggin's future behaviour towards Mona herself. If Mrs. Erdleigh had not been at the table he would undoubtedly have received the full force of his hostess's admiration. This would naturally have flattered him, but his shrewdness would probably also have assessed her deference as something fairly superficial. As matters turned out, apparent disregard for him keenly renewed his own former interest in her. Perhaps Quiggin thought she was deliberately hiding her true feelings at luncheon. Perhaps he was right in thinking that. With a woman it is impossible to say.

In the early stages of the meal Quiggin had been perfectly agreeable, talking to Jean of changes taking place in contemporary poetry, and of the personalities involved in these much advertised literary experiments. He explained that he considered the work of Mark Members commendable, if more than a trifle old-fashioned.

'Mark has developed smoothly from beginnings legitimately influenced by Browning, paused perhaps too long in byways frequented by the Symbolists, and reached in his own good time a categorically individual style and phraseology. Unfortunately his *œuvre* is at present lacking in any real sense of social significance.'

He glanced at Mona after saying this, perhaps hoping that a former friend of Gypsy Jones might notice the political implications of his words. However he failed to catch her attention, and turned almost immediately to lighter matters, evidently surprising even Templer by sagacious remarks regarding restaurant prices in the South of France, and an unexpected familiarity with the *Barrio chino* quarter in Barcelona. However, in spite of this conversational versatility, I was aware that Quiggin was inwardly turning sour. This could be seen from time to time in his face, especially in the glances of dislike he was beginning to cast in the direction of Stripling. He had probably decided that, rich though Stripling might be, he was not worth cultivating.

Stripling, for his part, did not talk much; when he spoke chiefly addressing himself to Jean. He had shown—perhaps not surprisingly—no interest whatever in Quiggin's admirably lucid exposition of the New School's poetic diction, in which Communist convictions were expressed in unexpected metre and rhyme. On the other hand Stripling did sometimes rouse himself in an attempt to break into the stream of astrological chatter that bubbled between Mrs. Erdleigh and Mona. His mind seemed to wander perpetually through the mystic territories of clairvoyance, a world of the spirit no doubt incarnate to him in Mrs. Erdleigh herself. Although this appearance of permanent preoccupation, coupled with his peculiar, jerky manner, conveyed the impression that he might not be quite sane, Templer seemed to attach more importance to Stripling's City gossip than his father had ever done. Mr. Templer, I remembered, had been very curt with his son-in-law when financial matters were in question.

All the while I felt horribly bored with the whole lot of them, longing to be alone once more with Jean, and yet also in some odd manner almost dreading the moment when that time should come; one of those mixed sensations so characteristic of intense emotional excitement. There is always an element of unreality, perhaps even of slight absurdity, about someone you love. It seemed to me that she was sitting in an awkward, almost melodramatic manner, half-turned towards Quiggin, while she crumbled her bread with fingers long and subtly shaped. I seemed to be looking at a picture of her, yet felt that I could easily lose control of my senses, and take her, then and there, in my arms.

'But in these days you can't believe in such things as astrology,' said Quiggin. 'Why, even apart from other considerations, the very astronomical discoveries made since the time of the ancients have negatived what was once thought about the stars.'

We had returned to the drawing-room. Already it was obvious that the afternoon must be spent indoors. The leaden, sunless sky, from which sleet was now falling with a clatter on to the frozen snow of the lawn, created in the house an atmosphere at once gloomy and sinister: a climate in itself hinting of necromancy. The electric light had to be turned on, just as if we were sitting in the lounge of the Ufford. The heavy claret drunk at luncheon prompted a desire to lie at full length on the sofa, or at least to sit well back and stretch out the legs and yawn. For a second —soft and exciting and withdrawn immediately—I felt Jean's hand next to mine on the cushion. Quiggin lurked in the corners of the room, pretending to continue his examination of the pictures, his silence scarcely concealing the restlessness that had overtaken him. From time to time he shot out a remark, more or less barbed. He must by then have tumbled to the implications of his own status at the party. Nettled at Mrs. Erdleigh's capture of Mona, he was probably planning how best to express his irritation openly.

'Oh, but I *do*,' said Mona, drawling out the words. 'I think those occult things are almost always right. They are in my case, I *know*.'

'Yes, yes,' said Quiggin, brushing aside this affirmation with a tolerant grin, as the mere fancy of a pretty girl, and at the same time addressing himself more directly to Stripling, at whom his first attack had certainly been aimed, 'but *you* can't believe all that—a hard-headed business man like yourself?'

'That's just it,' said Stripling, ignoring, in fact probably not noticing, the sneering, disagreeable tone of Quiggin's voice. 'It's just the fact that I *am* occupied all day long with material things that makes me realise they are not the whole of life.'

However, his eyes began to start from his head, so that he was perhaps becoming aware that Quiggin was deliberately teasing him. No doubt he was used to encountering a certain amount of dissent from his views, though opposition was probably not voiced as usual in so direct and dialectical a manner as this. Quiggin continued to smile derisively.

'You certainly find in me no champion of the City's methods,' he said. 'But at least what you call "material things" represent reality.'

'Hardly at all.'

'Oh, come.'

'Money is a delusion.'

'Not if you haven't got any.'

'That is just when you realise most money's unreality.'

'Why not get rid of yours, then?'

'I might any day.'

'Let me know when you decide to.'

'You must understand the thread that runs through life,' said Stripling, now speaking rather wildly, and looking stranger than ever. 'It does not matter that there may be impurities and errors in one man's method of seeking the Way. What matters is that he *is* seeking it—and knows there is a Way to be found.'

'Commencement—Opposition—Equilibrium,' said Mrs. Erdleigh in her softest voice, as if to offer Stripling some well-earned moral support. 'You can't get away from it—Thesis—Antithesis—Synthesis.'

'That's just what I mean,' said Stripling, as if her words brought him instant relief. 'Brahma—Vishnu—Siva.'

'It all sounded quite Hegelian until you brought in the Indian gods,' said Quiggin angrily.

He would no doubt have continued to argue had not a new element been introduced at this moment by Jean: an object that became immediately the focus of attention.

While this discussion had been in progress she had slipped from the room. I had been wondering how I could myself quietly escape from the others and look for her, when she returned carrying in her hand what first appeared to be a small wooden palette for oil paints. Two castors, or wheels, were attached to this heart-shaped board, the far end of which was transfixed with a lead pencil. I recalled the occasion when Sunny Farebrother had ruined so many of Stripling's starched collars in a patent device in which he had a business interest, and I wondered whether this was something of a similar kind. However, Mrs. Erdleigh immediately recognised the significance of the toy and began to laugh a little reprovingly.

'Planchette?' she said. 'You know, I really rather disapprove. I do not think Good Influences make themselves known through Planchette as a rule. And the things it writes cause such a lot of bad feeling sometimes.'

'It really belongs to Baby,' said Jean. 'She heard of it somewhere and made Sir Magnus Donners get her one. She brought it round to us once when she was feeling depressed about some young man of hers. We couldn't make it work. She forgot to take it away and I have been carrying it round—meaning to give it back to her—ever since.'

Stripling's eyes lit up and began once more to dilate.

'Shall we do it?' he asked, in a voice that shook slightly. 'Do let's.'

'Well,' said Mrs. Erdleigh, speaking kindly, as if to a child who has proposed a game inevitably associated with the breakage of china, 'I *know* trouble will come of it if we do.'

'But for once,' begged Stripling. 'Don't you think for once, Myra? It's such a rotten afternoon.'

'Then don't complain afterwards that I did not warn you.'

Although I had often heard of Planchette, I had never, as it happened, seen the board in operation; and I felt some curiosity myself to discover whether its writings would indeed set down some of the surprising disclosures occasionally described by persons in the habit of playing with it. The very name was new to both the Templers. Stripling explained that the machine was placed above a piece of blank paper, upon which the pencil wrote words, when two or three persons lightly rested their fingers upon the wooden surface: castors and pencil point moving without deliberate agency. Stripling was obviously delighted to be allowed for once to indulge in this forbidden practice, in spite of Mrs. Erdleigh's tempered disparagement. Whether her disapproval was really deep-seated, or due merely to a conviction that the game was unwise in that particular company, could only be guessed.

Quiggin was plainly annoyed; even rather insulted, at this step taken towards an actual physical attempt to invoke occult forces.

'I thought such things had been forgotten since the court of Napoleon III,' he said. 'You don't really believe it will write anything, do you?'

'You may be surprised by the knowledge it displays of your own life, old chap,' said Stripling, with an effort to recover the breeziness of earlier days.

'Obviously—when someone is rigging it.'

'It's hardly possible to rig it, old chap. You try and write something, just using the board by yourself. You'll find it damned difficult.'

Quiggin gave an annoyed laugh. Some sheets of foolscap, blue and ruled with red lines for keeping accounts, were found in a drawer. One of these large sheets of paper was set out upon a table. The experiment began with Mona, Stripling and Mrs. Erdleigh as executants, the last of whom, having once registered her protest, showed no ungraciousness in her manner of joining the proceedings, if they were fated to take place. Templer obviously felt complete scepticism regarding the whole matter, which he could not be induced to take seriously even to the extent of agreeing to participate. Quiggin, too, refused to join in, though he showed an almost feverish interest in what was going forward.

Naturally, Quiggin was delighted when, after a trial of several minutes, no results whatever were achieved. Then the rest of us, in various combinations of persons, attempted to work the board. All these efforts were unsuccessful. Sometimes the pencil shot violently across the surface of the paper, covering sheet after sheet, as a new surface was substituted, with dashes and scribbles. More often, it would not move at all.

'You none of you seem to be getting very far,' said Templer.

'It may be waste of time,' said Mrs. Erdleigh. 'Planchette can be very capricious. Perhaps there is an unsympathetic presence in the room.'

'I should not be at all surprised,' said Quiggin, speaking with elaborately satirical emphasis.

He stood with his heels on the fender, his hands in his pockets—rather in the position Le Bas used to adopt when giving a lecture on wiping your boots before coming into the house—very well pleased with the course things were taking.

'I think you are horrid,' said Mona.

She made a face at him; in itself a sign of a certain renewed interest.

'I don't think you ought to believe in such things,' said Quiggin, nasally.

'But I *do*.'

She smiled encouragingly. She had probably begun to feel that occult phenomena, at least by its absence, was proving itself a bore; and that perhaps she might find more fun in returning to her original project of exploring Quiggin's own possibilities. However, this exchange between them was immediately followed by sudden development among the group resting their fingers on the board. Jean and Mona had been trying their luck with Stripling as third partner. Jean now rose from the table, and, dropping one of those glances at once affectionate and enquiring that raised such a storm within me, she said: 'You have a go.'

I took the chair and placed my fingers lightly where hers had been. Previously, when I had formed a trio with Mrs.

Erdleigh and Mona—who had insisted on being party to every session—nothing of note had happened. Now, almost at once, Planchette began to move in a slow, regular motion.

At first, from the 'feel' of the movement, I thought Stripling must be manipulating the board deliberately. A glassy look had come into his eye and his loose, rather brutal mouth sagged open. Then the regular, up-and-down rhythm came abruptly to an end. The pencil, as if impatient of all of us, shot off the paper on to the polished wood of the table. A sentence had been written. It was inverted from where Stripling was sitting. In fact the only person who could reasonably be accused of having written the words was myself. The script was long and sloping, Victorian in character. Mrs. Erdleigh took a step forward and read it aloud:

'Karl is not pleased.'

There was great excitement at this. Everyone crowded round our chairs.

'You must ask who "Karl" is,' said Mrs. Erdleigh, smiling.

She was the only one who remained quite unmoved by this sudden manifestation. Such things no longer surprised her. Quiggin, on the other hand, moved quickly round to my side of the table. He seemed divided between a wish to accuse me of having written these words as a hoax, and at the same time an unwillingness to make the admission, obviously necessary in the circumstances, that any such deception must have required quite exceptional manipulative agility. In the end he said nothing, but stood there frowning hard at me.

'Is it Karl speaking?' asked Stripling, in a respectful, indeed reverential voice.

We replaced our hands on the board.

'Who else,' wrote Planchette.

'Shall we continue?'

'Antwortet er immer.'

'Is that German?' said Stripling.

'What does it mean, Pete?' Mona called out shrilly.

Templer looked a little surprised at this.

'Isn't it: "He always answers"?' he said. 'My German is strictly commercial—not intended for communication with the Next World.'

'Have you a message? Please write in English if you do not mind.'

Stripling's voice again trembled a little when he said this.

'Nothing to the Left.'

This was decidedly enigmatic.

'Does he mean we should move the coffee tray?' Mona almost shouted, now thoroughly excited. 'He doesn't say whose left. Perhaps we should clear the whole table.'

Quiggin took a step nearer.

'Which of you is faking this?' he said roughly. 'I believe it is you, Nick.'

He was grinning hard, but I could see that he was extremely irritated. I pointed out that I could not claim to write neat Victorian calligraphy sideways, and also upside-down, at considerable speed: especially when unable to see the paper written upon.

'You must know "Nothing to the Left" is a quotation,' Quiggin insisted.

'Who said it?'

'You got a degree in history, didn't you?'

'I must have missed out that bit.'

'Robespierre, of course,' said Quiggin, with great contempt. 'He was speaking politically. Does no one in this country take politics seriously?'

I could not understand why he had become quite so angry.

'Let's get on with it,' said Templer, now at last beginning

to show some interest. 'Perhaps he'll make himself clearer if pressed.'

'This is *too* exciting,' said Mona.

She clasped her hands together. We tried again.

'*Wives in common.*'

This was an uncomfortable remark. It was impossible to guess what the instrument might write next. However, everyone was far too engrossed to notice whether the comment had brought embarrassment to any individual present.

'Look here——' began Quiggin.

Before he could complete the sentence, the board began once more to race beneath our fingers.

'*Force is the midwife.*'

'I hope he isn't going to get too obstetric,' said Templer.

Quiggin turned once more towards me. He was definitely in a rage.

'You must know where these phrases come from,' he said. 'You can't be as ignorant as that.'

'Search me.'

'You are trying to be funny.'

'Never less.'

'Marx, of course, Marx,' said Quiggin testily, but perhaps wavering in his belief that I was responsible for faking the writing. '*Das Kapital*. . . . The Communist Manifesto.'

'So it's Karl Marx, is it?' asked Mona.

The name was evidently vaguely familiar to her, no doubt from her earlier days when she had known Gypsy Jones; had perhaps even taken part in such activities as selling *War Never Pays!*

'Don't be ridiculous,' said Quiggin, by implication including Mona in this reproof, probably more violently than he intended. 'It was quite obvious that one of you was rigging the thing. I admit I can't at present tell which of you it was. I suspect it was Nick, as he is the only one who knows I am a practising Marxist—and he persuaded me to come here.'

'I didn't know anything of the sort—and I've already told you I can't write upside-down.'

'Steady on,' said Templer. 'You can't accuse a fellow guest of cheating at Planchette. Duels have been fought for less. This will turn into another Tranby Croft case unless we moderate our tone.'

Quiggin made a despairing gesture at such frivolity of manner.

'I can't believe no one present knows the quotation, "Force is the midwife of every old society pregnant with a new one," ' he said. 'You will be telling me next you never heard the words, "The Workers have no country." '

'I believe Karl Marx has been "through" before,' said Stripling, slowly and with great solemnity. 'Wasn't he a revolutionary writer?'

'He was,' said Quiggin, with heavy irony. 'He *was* a revolutionary writer.'

'*Do* let's try again,' said Mona.

This time the writing changed to a small, niggling hand, rather like that of Uncle Giles.

'He is sick.'

'Who is sick?'

'You know well.'

'Where is he?'

'In his room.'

'Where is his room?'

'The House of Books.'

The writing was getting smaller and smaller. I felt as if I were taking part in one of those scenes from *Alice in Wonderland* in which the characters change their size.

'What can it mean now?' asked Mona.

'You have a duty.'

Quiggin's temper seemed to have moved from annoyance, mixed with contempt, to a kind of general uneasiness.

'I suppose it isn't talking about St. John Clarke,' I suggested.

Quiggin's reaction to this remark was unexpectedly violent. His sallow skin went white, and, instead of speaking with his usual asperity, he said in a quiet, worried voice: 'I was beginning to wonder just the same thing. I don't know that I really ought to have left him. Look here, can I ring up the flat—just to make sure that everything is all right?'

'Of course,' said Templer.

'This way?'

We tried again. Before Quiggin had reached the door, the board had moved and stopped. This time the result was disappointing. Planchette had written a single word, monosyllabic and indecent. Mona blushed.

'That sometimes happens,' said Mrs. Erdleigh, calmly.

She spoke as if it were as commonplace to see such things written on blue ruled accounting paper as on the door or wall of an alley. Neatly detaching that half of the sheet, she tore it into small pieces and threw them into the waste-paper basket.

'Only too often,' said Stripling with a sigh.

He had evidently accepted the fact that his enjoyment for that afternoon was at an end. Mona giggled.

'We will stop now,' said Mrs. Erdleigh, speaking with the voice of authority. 'It is really no use continuing when a Bad Influence once breaks through.'

'I'm surprised he knew such a word,' said Templer.

We sat for a time in silence. Quiggin's action in going to the telephone possessed the force of one of those utterly unexpected conversions, upon which a notorious drunkard swears never again to touch alcohol, or a declared pacifist enlists in the army. It was scarcely credible that Planchette should have sent him bustling out of the room to enquire after St. John Clarke's health, even allowing for the importance to himself of the novelist as a livelihood.

'We shall have to be departing soon, *mon cher,*' said Mrs. Erdleigh, showing Stripling the face of her watch.

'Have some tea,' said Templer. 'It will be appearing at any moment.'

'No, we shall certainly have to be getting along, Pete,' said Stripling, as if conscious that, having been indulged over Planchette, he must now behave himself specially well. 'It has been a wonderful afternoon. Quite like the old days. Wish old Sunny could have been here. Most interesting too.'

He had evidently not taken in Quiggin's reason for hurrying to the telephone, nor had any idea of the surprising effect that Planchette's last few sentences had had on such a professional sceptic. Perhaps he would have been pleased to know that Quiggin had acquired at least enough belief to be thrown into a nervous state by those cryptic remarks. More probably, he would not have been greatly interested. For Stripling, this had been a perfectly normal manner of passing his spare time. He would never be able to conceive how far removed were such activities from Quiggin's daily life and manner of approaching the world. In Stripling, profound belief had taken the place of any sort of halting imagination he might once have claimed.

Quiggin now reappeared. He was even more disturbed than before.

'I am afraid I must go home immediately,' he said, in some agitation. 'Do you know when there is a train? And can I be taken to the station? It is really rather urgent.'

'Is he dying?' asked Mona, in an agonised voice.

She was breathless with excitement at the apparent confirmation of a message from what Mrs. Erdleigh called 'the Other Side'. She took Quiggin's arm, as if to soothe him. He did not answer at once, apparently undecided at what should be made public. Then he addressed himself to me.

'The telephone was answered by Mark,' he said, through his teeth.

For Quiggin to discover Members reinstated in St. John Clarke's flat within a few hours of his own departure was naturally a serious matter.

'And *is* St. John Clarke worse?'

'I couldn't find out for certain,' said Quiggin, almost wretchedly, 'but I think he must be for Mark to be allowed back. I suppose St. J. wanted something done in a hurry, and told the maid to ring up Mark as I wasn't there. I must go at once.'

He turned towards the Templers.

'I am afraid there is no train for an hour,' Templer said, 'but Jimmy is on his way to London, aren't you, Jimmy? He will give you a lift.'

'Of course, old chap, of course.'

'Of course he can. So you can go with dear old Jimmy and arrive in London in no time. He drives like hell.'

'No longer,' said Mrs. Erdleigh, with a smile. 'He drives with care.'

I am sure that the last thing Quiggin wanted at that moment was to be handed over to Stripling and Mrs. Erdleigh, but there was no alternative if he wanted to get to London with the least possible delay. A curious feature of the afternoon had been the manner in which all direct contact between himself and Mrs. Erdleigh had somehow been avoided. Each no doubt realised to the full that the other possessed nothing to offer: that any exchange of energy would have been waste of time.

In Quiggin's mind, the question of St. John Clarke's

worsened state of health, as such, had now plainly given place to the more immediate threat of Members re-entering the novelist's household on a permanent footing. His fear that the two developments might be simultaneous was, I feel sure, not necessarily based upon entirely cynical premises. In a weakened state, St. John Clarke might easily begin to regret his earlier suspension of Members as a secretary. Sick persons often vacillate. Quiggin's anxiety was understandable. No doubt he regarded himself, politically and morally, as a more suitable secretary than Members. It was, therefore, reasonable that he should wish to return as soon as possible to the field of operations.

Recognising at once that he must inevitably accompany the two of them, Quiggin accepted Stripling's offer of conveyance. He did this with a bad grace, but at the same time insistently, to show there must be no delay now the matter had been decided. This sudden disintegration of the party was displeasing to Mona, who probably felt now that she had wasted her opportunity of having Quiggin in the house; just as on the previous day she had wasted her meeting with him in the Ritz. She seemed, at any rate, overwhelmed with vague, haunting regrets for the manner in which things had turned out; all that unreasoning bitterness and mortification to which women are so subject. For a time she begged them to stay, but it was no good.

'But *promise* you will ring up.'

She took Quiggin's hand. He seemed surprised, perhaps even rather touched at the warmth with which she spoke. He replied with more feeling than was usual in his manner that he would certainly communicate with her.

'I will let you know how St. J. is.'

'Oh, *do*.'

'Without fail.'

'Don't forget.'

Mrs. Erdleigh, in her travelling clothes, had reverted to my first impression of her at the Ufford as priestess of some esoteric cult. Wrapped about with scarves, veils and stoles, she took my hand.

'Have you met *her* yet?' she enquired in a low voice.

'Yes.'

'Just as I told you?'

'Yes.'

Mrs. Erdleigh smiled to herself. They piled into the car, Quiggin glowering in the back, hatless, but with a fairly thick overcoat. Stripling drove off briskly, sending the crisp snow in a shower from the wheels. The car disappeared into the gloomy shadows of the conifers.

We returned to the drawing-room. Templer threw himself into an armchair.

'What a party,' he said. 'Poor old Jimmy really has landed something this time. I wouldn't be surprised if he didn't have to marry that woman. She's like Rider Haggard's *She—She who must be obeyed.*'

'I thought she was wonderful,' said Mona.

'So does Jimmy,' said Templer. 'You know, I can see a look of Babs. Something in the way she carries herself.'

I, too, had noticed an odd, remote resemblance in Mrs. Erdleigh to his elder sister. However, Mona disagreed strongly, and they began to argue.

'It was extraordinary all that stuff about Marx coming up,' said Templer. 'I suppose it was swilling about in old Quiggin's head and somehow got released.'

'Of course, you can never believe anything you can't explain quite simply,' said Mona.

'Why should I?' said Templer.

Tea merged into drinks. Mona's temper grew worse. I began to feel distinctly tired. Jean had brought out some work, and was sewing. Templer yawned in his chair. I wondered why he and his wife did not get on better. It was extraordinary that he seemed to please so many girls, and yet not her.

'It was a pretty stiff afternoon,' he said.

'I enjoyed it,' said Mona. 'It was a change.'

'It certainly was.'

They began to discuss Planchette again; ending inevitably in argument. Mona stood up.

'Let's go out tonight.'

'Where to?'

'We could dine at Skindles.'

'We've done that exactly a thousand and twenty-seven times. I've counted.'

'Then the Ace of Spades.'

'You know how I feel about the Ace of Spades after what happened to me there.'

'But I like it.'

'Anyway, wouldn't it be nicer to eat in tonight? Unless Nick and Jean are mad to make a night of it.'

I had no wish to go out to dinner; Jean was non-committal. The Templers continued to argue. Suddenly Mona burst into tears.

'You never want to do *anything* I want,' she said. 'If I can't go out. I shall go to bed. They can send up something on a tray. As a matter of fact I haven't been feeling well all day.'

She turned from him, and almost ran from the room.

'Oh, hell,' said Templer. 'I suppose I shall have to see about this. Help yourselves to another drink when you're ready.'

He followed his wife through the door. Jean and I were alone. She gave me her hand, smiling, but resisting a closer embrace.

'Tonight?'

'No.'
'Why not?'
'Not a good idea.'
'I see.'
'Sorry.'
'When?'
'Any time.'
'Will you come to my flat?'
'Of course.'
'When?'
'I've told you. Any time you like.'
'Tuesday?'
'No, not Tuesday.'
'Wednesday, then?'
'I can't manage Wednesday either.'
'But you said any time.'
'Any time but Tuesday or Wednesday.'

I tried to remember what plans were already made, and which could be changed. Thursday was a tangle of engagements, hardly possible to rearrange at short notice without infinite difficulties arising. Matters must be settled quickly, because Templer might return to the room at any moment.

'Friday?'

She looked doubtful. I thought she was going to insist on Thursday. Perhaps the idea of doing so had crossed her mind. A measure of capriciousness is, after all, natural in women; perhaps fulfils some physiological need for both sexes. A woman who loves you likes to torment you from time to time; if not actually hurt you. If her first intention had been to make further difficulties, she abandoned the idea, but at the same time she did not speak. She seemed to have no sense of the urgency of making some arrangement quickly—so that we should not lose touch with each other, and be reduced to the delay of writing letters. I suffered some agitation. This conversation was failing entirely to express my own feelings. Perhaps it seemed equally unreal to her. If so, she was unwilling, perhaps unable, to alleviate the strain. Probably women enjoy such moments, which undoubtedly convey by intensity and uncertainty a heightened awareness of their power. In spite of apparent coldness of manner her eyes were full of tears. As if we had already decided upon some definite and injudicious arrangement, she suddenly changed her approach.

'You must be discreet,' she said.

'All right.'

'But really discreet.'

'I promise.'

'You will?'

'Yes.'

While talking, we had somehow come close together in a manner that made practical discussion difficult. I felt tired, rather angry, very much in love with her; on the edge of one of those outbursts of irritation so easily excited by love.

'I'll come to your flat on Friday,' she said abruptly.

4.

WHEN, in early spring, pale sunlight was flickering behind the mist above Piccadilly, the Isbister Memorial Exhibition opened on the upper floor of one of the galleries there. I was attending the private view, partly for business reasons, partly from a certain weakness for bad pictures, especially bad portraits. Such a taste is hard to justify. Perhaps the inclination is no more than a morbid curiosity to see how far the painter will give himself away. Pictures, apart from their æsthetic interest, can achieve the mysterious fascination of those enigmatic scrawls on walls, the expression of Heaven knows what psychological urge on the part of the executant; for example, the for ever anonymous drawing of Widmerpool in the *cabinet* at La Grenadière.

In Isbister's work there was something of that inner madness. The deliberate naïveté with which he accepted his business men, ecclesiastics and mayors, depicted by him with all the crudeness of his accustomed application of paint to canvas, conveyed an oddly sinister effect. Perhaps it would be more accurate to say that Isbister set out to paint what he supposed to be the fashionable view of such people at any given moment. Thus, in his early days, a general, or the chairman of some big concern, would be represented in the respectively appropriate terms of Victorian romantic success; the former, hero of the battlefield: the latter, the industrious apprentice who has achieved his worthy ambition. But as military authority and commercial achievement became increasingly subject to political and economic denigration, Isbister, keeping up with the times, introduced a certain amount of what he judged to be satirical comment. Emphasis would be laid on the general's red face and medals, or the industrialist's huge desk and cigar. There would be a suggestion that all was not well with such people about. Probably Isbister was right from a financial point of view to make this change, because certainly his sitters seemed to grow no fewer. Perhaps they too felt a compulsive need for representation in contemporary idiom, even though a tawdry one. It was a kind of insurance against the attacks of people like Quiggin: a form of public apology and penance. The result was certainly curious. Indeed, often, even when there hung near-by something far worthier of regard, I found myself stealing a glance at an Isbister, dominating, by its aggressive treatment, the other pictures hanging alongside.

If things had turned out as they should, *The Art of Horace Isbister* would have been on sale at the table near the door, over which a young woman with a pointed nose and black fringe presided. As things were, it was doubtful whether that volume would ever appear. The first person I saw in the gallery was Sir Gavin Walpole-Wilson, who stood in the centre of the room, disregarding the pictures, but watching the crowd over the top of huge horn-rimmed spectacles, which he had pushed well forward on his nose. His shaggy homespun overcoat was swinging open, stuffed with long envelopes and periodicals which protruded from the pockets. He looked no older; perhaps a shade less sane. We had not met since the days when I used to dine with the Walpole-Wilsons for 'debutante dances'; a period now infinitely remote. Rather to my surprise he appeared to recognise me immediately, though it was unlikely that he knew my name. I enquired after Eleanor.

'Spends all her time in the country now,' said Sir Gavin. 'As you may remember, Eleanor was never really happy away from Hinton.'

He spoke rather sadly. I knew he was confessing his own and his wife's defeat. His daughter had won the long conflict with her parents. I wondered if Eleanor still wore her hair in a bun at the back and trained dogs with a whistle. It was unlikely that she would have changed much.

'I expect she finds plenty to do,' I offered.

'Her breeding keeps her quiet,' said Sir Gavin.

He spoke almost with distaste. However, perceiving that I felt uncertain as to the precise meaning of this explanation of Eleanor's existing state, he added curtly:

'Labradors.'

'Like Sultan?'

'After Sultan died she took to breeding them. And then she sees quite a lot of her friend, Norah Tolland.'

By common consent we abandoned the subject of Eleanor. Taking my arm, he led me across the floor of the gallery, until we stood in front of a three-quarter-length picture of a grey-moustached man in the uniform of the diplomatic corps; looking, if the truth be known, not unlike Sir Gavin himself.

'Isn't it terrible?'

'Awful.'

'It's Saltonstall,' said Sir Gavin, his voice suggesting that some just retribution had taken place. 'Saltonstall who always posed as *a Man of Taste.*'

'Isbister has made him look more like a Christmas Tree of Taste.'

'You see, my father-in-law's portrait is a different matter,' said Sir Gavin, as if unable to withdraw his eyes from this likeness of his former colleague. 'There is no parallel at all. My father-in-law was painted by Isbister, it is true. Isbister was what he liked. He possessed a large collection of thoroughly bad pictures which we had some difficulty in disposing of at his death. He bought them simply and solely because he liked the subjects. He knew about shipping and finance—not about painting. But he did not pose as a Man of Taste. Far from it.'

'Deacon's *Boyhood of Cyrus* in the hall at Eaton Square is from his collection, isn't it?'

I could not help mentioning this picture that had once meant so much to me and to name the dead is always a kind of tribute to them: one I felt Mr. Deacon deserved.

'I believe so,' said Sir Gavin. 'It sounds his style. But Saltonstall, on the other hand, with his *vers de societé,* and all his talk about Foujita and Pruna and goodness knows who else—but when it comes to his own portrait, it's Isbister. Let's see how they have hung my father-in-law.'

We passed on to Lord Aberavon's portrait, removed from its usual place in the dining-room at Hinton Hoo, now flanked by Sir Horrocks Rusby, K.C., and Cardinal Whelan. Lady Walpole-Wilson's father had been painted in peer's robes over the uniform of a deputy-lieutenant, different tones of scarlet contrasted against a crimson velvet curtain: a pictorial experiment that could not be considered successful. Through french windows behind Lord Aberavon stretched a broad landscape—possibly the vale of Glamorgan—in which something had also gone seriously wrong with the colour values. Even Isbister himself, in his own lifetime, must have been aware of deficiency.

I glanced at the cardinal next door, notable as the only picture I had ever heard Widmerpool spontaneously praise. Here, too, the reds had been handled with some savagery. Sir Gavin shook his head and moved on to examine two of Isbister's genre pictures. 'Clergyman eating an apple' and 'The Old Humorists'. I found myself beside Clapham, a director of the firm that published St. John Clarke's novels. He was talking to Smethyck, a museum official I had known slightly at the university.

'When is your book on Isbister appearing?' Clapham asked at once. 'You announced it some time ago. This would have been the moment—with the St. John Clarke introduction.'

Clapham had spoken accusingly, his voice implying the fretfulness of all publishers that one of their authors should betray them with a colleague, however lightly.

'I went to see St. John Clarke the other day,' Clapham continued. 'I was glad to find him making a good recovery after his illness. Found him reading one of the young Communist poets. We had an interesting talk.'

'Does anybody read St. John Clarke himself now?' asked Smethyck, languidly.

Like many of his profession, Smethyck was rather proud of his looks, which he had been carefully re-examining in the dark, mirror-like surface of Sir Horrocks Rusby, framed for some unaccountable reason under glass. Clapham was up in arms at once at such superciliousness.

'Of course people read St. John Clarke,' he said, snappishly. 'Though perhaps not in your ultra-sophisticated circles, where everything ordinary people understand is sneered at.'

'Personally, I don't hold any views about St. John Clarke,' said Smethyck, without looking round. 'I've never read any of them. All I wanted to know was whether people bought his books.'

He continued to ponder the cut of his suit in this adventitious looking-glass, deciding at last that his hair needed smoothing down on one side.

'I don't mind admitting to you both,' said Clapham, moving a step or two closer and speaking rather thickly, 'that when I finished *Fields of Amaranth* there were tears in my eyes.'

Smethyck made no reply to this; nor could I myself think of a suitable rejoinder.

'That was some years ago,' said Clapham.

This qualification left open the alternative of whether St. John Clarke still retained the power of exciting such strong feeling in a publisher, or whether Clapham himself had grown more capable of controlling his emotions.

'Why, there's Sillery,' said Smethyck, who seemed thoroughly bored by the subject of St. John Clarke. 'I believe he was to be painted by Isbister, if he had recovered. Let's go and talk to him.'

We left Clapham, still muttering about the extent of St. John Clarke's sales, and the beauty and delicacy of his early style. I had not seen Sillery since Mrs. Andriadis's party, three or four years before, though I had heard by chance that he had recently returned from America, where he had held some temporary academical post, or been on a lecture tour. His white hair and dark, Nietzschean moustache remained unchanged, but his clothes looked older than ever. He was carrying an unrolled umbrella in one hand; in the other a large black homburg, thick in grease. He began to grin widely as soon as he saw us.

'Hullo, Sillers,' said Smethyck, who had been one of Sillery's favourites among the undergraduates who constituted his *salon*. 'I did not know you were interested in art.'

'Not interested in art?' said Sillery, enjoying this accusation a great deal. 'What an idea. Still, I am, as it happens, here for semi-professional reasons, as you might say. I expect you are too, Michael. There is some nonsense about the College wanting a pitcher o' me ole mug. Can't think why they should need such a thing, but there it is. 'Course

Isbister can't do it 'cos 'e's tucked 'is toes in now, but I thought I'd just come an' take a look at the sorta thing that's expected.'

'And what do you think, Sillers?'

'Just as well he's passed away, perhaps,' sniggered Sillery, suddenly abandoning his character-acting. 'In any case I always think an artist is rather an embarrassment to his own work. But what Ninetyish things I am beginning to say. It must come from talking to so many Americans.'

'But you can't want to be painted by anyone even remotely like Isbister,' said Smethyck. 'Surely you can get a painter who is a little more modern than that. What about this man Barnby, for example?'

'Ah, we are very conservative about art at the older universities,' said Sillery, grinning delightedly. 'Wouldn't say myself that I want an Isbister exactly, though I heard the Warden comparing him with Antonio Moro the other night. 'Fraid the Warden doesn't know much about the graphic arts, though. But then *I* don't want the wretched picture painted at all. What do members of the College want to look at my old phiz for, I should like to know?'

We assured him that his portrait would be welcomed by all at the university.

'I don't know about Brightman,' said Sillery, showing his teeth for a second. 'I don't at all know about Brightman. I don't think Brightman would want a picture of me. But what have you been doing with yourself, Nicholas? Writing more books, I expect. I am afraid I haven't read the first one yet. Do you ever see Charles Stringham now?'

'Not for ages.'

'A pity about that divorce,' said Sillery. 'You young men will get married. It is so often a mistake. I hear he is drinking just a tiny bit too much nowadays. It was a mistake to leave Donners-Brebner, too.'

'I expect you've heard about J. G. Quiggin taking Mark Members's place with St. John Clarke?'

'Hilarious that, wasn't it?' agreed Sillery. 'That sort of thing always happens when two clever boys come from the same place. They can't help competing. Poor Mark seems quite upset about it. Can't think why. After all, there are plenty of other glittering prizes for those with stout hearts and sharp swords, just as Lord Birkenhead remarked. I shall be seeing Quiggin this afternoon, as it happens—a little political affair—Quiggin lives a very *mouvementé* life these days, it seems.'

Sillery chuckled to himself. There was evidently some secret he did not intend to reveal. In any case he had by then prolonged the conversation sufficiently for his own satisfaction.

'Saw you chatting to Gavin Walpole-Wilson,' he said. 'Ought to go and have a word with him myself about these continuous hostilities between Bolivia and Paraguay. Been going on too long. Want to get in touch with his sister about it. Get one of her organisations to work. Time for liberal-minded people to step in. Can't have them cutting each other's throats in this way. Got to be quick, or I shall be late for Quiggin.'

He shambled off. Smethyck smiled at me and shook his head, at the same time indicating that he had seen enough for one afternoon.

I strolled on round the gallery. I had noted in the catalogue a picture called 'The Countess of Ardglass with Faithful Girl' and, when I arrived before it, I found Lady Ardglass herself inspecting the portrait. She was leaning on the arm of one of the trim grey-haired men who had accompanied her in the Ritz: or perhaps another example of their category, so like as to be indistinguishable. Isbister had painted her in an open shirt and riding breeches, standing beside the mare, her arm slipped through the reins: with much attention to the high polish of the brown boots.

'Pity Jumbo could never raise the money for it,' Bijou Ardglass was saying. 'Why don't you make an offer, Jack, and give it me for my birthday? You'd probably get it dirt cheap.'

'I'm much too broke,' said the grey-haired man.

'You always say that. If you'd given me the car you promised me I should at least have saved the nine shillings I've already spent on taxis this morning.'

Jean never spoke of her husband, and I knew no details of the episode with Lady Ardglass that had finally separated them. At the same time, now that I saw Bijou, I could not help feeling that she and I were somehow connected by what had happened. I wondered what Duport had in common with me that linked us through Jean. Men who are close friends tend to like different female types; perhaps the contrary process also operated, and the fact that he had seemed so unsympathetic when we had met years before was due to some innate sense of rivalry. I was to see Jean that afternoon. She had borrowed a friend's flat for a week or so, while she looked about for somewhere more permanent to live. This had made things easier. Emotional crises always promote the urgent need for executive action, so that the times when we most hope to be free from the practical administration of life are always those when the need to cope with a concrete world is more than ever necessary.

Owing to domestic arrangements connected with getting a nurse for her child, she would not be at home until late in the afternoon. I wasted some time at the Isbister show, before walking across the park to the place where she was living. I had expected to see Quiggin at the gallery, but

Sillery's remarks indicated that he would not be there. The last time I had met him, soon after the Templer week-end, it had turned out that, in spite of the temporary reappearance of Members at St. John Clarke's sick bed, Quiggin was still firmly established in his new position. He now seemed scarcely aware that there had ever been a time when he had not acted as the novelist's secretary, referring to his employer's foibles with a weary though tolerant familiarity, as if he had done the job for years. He had quickly brushed aside enquiry regarding his journey to London with Mrs. Erdleigh and Jimmy Stripling.

'What a couple,' he commented.

I had to admit they were extraordinary enough. Quiggin had resumed his account of St. John Clarke, his state of health and his eccentricities, the last of which were represented by his new secretary in a decidedly different light from that in which they had been displayed by Members. St. John Clarke's every action was now expressed in Marxist terms, as if some political Circe had overnight turned the novelist into an entirely Left Wing animal. No doubt Quiggin judged it necessary to handle his new situation firmly on account of the widespread gossip regarding St. John Clarke's change of secretary; for in circles frequented by Members and Quiggin ceaseless argument had taken place as to which of them had 'behaved badly'.

Thinking it best from my firm's point of view to open diplomatic relations, as it were, with the new government, I had asked if there was any hope of our receiving the Isbister introduction in the near future. Quiggin's answer to this had been to make an affirmative gesture with his hands. I had seen Members employ the same movement, perhaps derived by both of them from St. John Clarke himself.

'That was exactly what I wanted to discuss when I came

to the Ritz,' Quiggin had said. 'But you insisted on going out with your wealthy friends.'

'You must admit that I arranged for you to meet my wealthy friends, as you call them, at the first opportunity—within twenty-four hours, as a matter of fact.'

Quiggin smiled and inclined his head, as if assenting to my claim that some amends had been attempted.

'As I have tried to explain,' he said, 'St. J.'s views have changed a good deal lately. Indeed, he has entirely come round to my own opinion—that the present situation cannot last much longer. *We will not tolerate it.* All thinking men are agreed about that. St. J. *wants* to do the introduction when his health gets a bit better—and he has time to spare from his political interests—but he has decided to write the Isbister foreword from a Marxist point of view.'

'You ought to have obtained some first-hand information for him when Marx came through on Planchette.'

Quiggin frowned at this levity.

'What rot that was,' he said. 'I suppose Mark and his psychoanalyst gang would explain it by one of their dissertations on the subconscious. Perhaps in that particular respect they would be right. No doubt they would add a lot of irrelevant stuff about Surrealism. But to return to Isbister's pictures, I think they would not make a bad subject treated in that particular manner.'

'You could preach a whole Marxist sermon on the portrait of Peter Templer's father alone.'

'You could, indeed,' said Quiggin, who seemed not absolutely sure that the matter in hand was being negotiated with sufficient seriousness. 'But what a charming person Mrs. Templer is. She has changed a lot since her days as a model, or mannequin, or whatever she was. It is a great pity she never seems to see any intelligent people now. I can't think how she can stand that stockbroker husband of hers. How rich is he?'

'He took a bit of a knock in the slump.'

'How do they get on together?'

'All right, so far as I know.'

'St. J. always says there is "nothing sadder than a happy marriage".'

'Is that why he doesn't risk it himself?'

'I should think Mona will go off with somebody,' said Quiggin, decisively.

I considered this comment impertinent, though there was certainly no reason why Quiggin and Templer should be expected to like one another. Perhaps Quiggin's instinct was correct, I thought, however unwilling I might be to agree openly with him. There could be no doubt that the Templers' marriage was not going very well. At the same time, I did not intend to discuss them with Quiggin, to whom, in any case, there seemed no point in explaining Templer's merits. Quiggin would not appreciate these even if they were brought to his notice; while, if it suited him, he would always be ready to reverse his opinion about Templer or anyone else.

By then I had become sceptical of seeing the Isbister introduction, Marxist or otherwise. In itself, this latest suggestion did not strike me as specially surprising. Taking into account the fact that St. John Clarke had made the plunge into 'modernism', the project seemed neither more nor less extraordinary than tackling Isbister's pictures from the point of view of Psychoanalysis, Surrealism, Roman Catholicism, Social Credit, or any other specialised approach. In fact some such doctrinal method of attack was then becoming very much the mode; taking the place of the highly coloured critical flights of an earlier generation that still persisted in some quarters, or the severely technical criticism of the æsthetic puritans who had ruled the roost since the war.

The foreword would now, no doubt, speak of Isbister 'laughing up his sleeve' at the rich men and public notabilities he had painted; though Members, who, with St. John Clarke, had once visited Isbister's studio in St. John's Wood for some kind of a reception held there, had declared that nothing could have exceeded the painter's obsequiousness to his richer patrons. Members was not always reliable in such matters, but it was certainly true that Isbister's portraits seemed to combine as a rule an effort to flatter his client with apparent attempts to make some comment to be easily understood by the public. Perhaps it was this inward struggle that imparted to his pictures that peculiar fascination to which I have already referred. However, so far as my firm was concerned, the goal was merely to get the introduction written and the book published.

'What is Mark doing now?' I asked.

Quiggin looked surprised at the question; as if everyone must know by now that Members was doing very well for himself.

'With Boggis & Stone—you know they used to be the Vox Populi Press—we got him the job.'

'Who were "we"?'

'St. J. and myself. St. J. arranged most of it through Howard Craggs. As you know, Craggs used to be the managing director of the Vox Populi.'

'But I thought Mark wasn't much interested in politics. Aren't all Boggis & Stone's books about Lenin and Trotsky and Litvinov and the Days of October and all that?'

Quiggin agreed, with an air of rather forced gaiety.

'Well, haven't most of us been living in a fool's paradise far too long now?' he said, speaking as if to make an appeal to my better side. 'Isn't it time that Mark—and others too—took some notice of what is happening in the world?'

'Does he get a living wage at Boggis & Stone's?'

'With his journalism he can make do. A small firm like that can't afford to pay a very munificent salary, it's true. He still gets a retainer from St. J. for sorting out the books once a month.'

I did not imagine this last arrangement was very popular with Quiggin from the way he spoke of it.

'As a matter of fact,' he said, 'I persuaded St. J. to arrange for Mark to have some sort of a footing in a more politically alive world before he got rid of him. That is where the future lies for all of us.'

'Did Gypsy Jones transfer from the Vox Populi to Boggis & Stone?'

Quiggin laughed now with real amusement.

'Oh, no,' he said. 'I forgot you knew her. She left quite a time before the amalgamation took place. She has something better to do now.'

He paused and moistened his lips; adding rather mysteriously:

'They say Gypsy is well looked on by the Party.'

This remark did not convey much to me in those days. I was more interested to see how carefully Quiggin's plans must have been laid to have prepared a place for Members even before he had been ejected from his job. That certainly showed forethought.

'Are you writing another book?' said Quiggin.

'Trying to—and you?'

'I liked your first,' said Quiggin.

He conveyed by these words a note of warning that, in spite of his modified approval, things must not go too far where books were concerned.

'Personally, I am not too keen to rush into print,' he said.

'I am still collecting material for my survey, *Unburnt Boats*.'

I did not meet Members to hear his side of the story until much later, in fact on that same afternoon of the Isbister Memorial Exhibition. I ran into him on my way through Hyde Park, not far from the Achilles Statue. (As it happened, it was close to the spot where I had come on Barbara Goring and Eleanor Walpole-Wilson, the day we had visited the Albert Memorial together.)

The weather had turned colder again, and the park was dank, with a kind of sea mist veiling the trees. Members looked shabbier than was usual for him: shabby and rather worried. In our undergraduate days he had been a tall, willowy, gesticulating figure, freckled and beady-eyed; hurrying through the lanes and byways of the university, abstractedly alone, like the Scholar-Gypsy, or straggling along the shopfronts of the town in the company of acquaintances, seemingly chosen for their peculiar resemblance to himself. Now he had grown into a terse, emaciated, rather determined young man, with a neat profile and chilly manner: a person people were beginning to know by name. In fact the critics, as a whole, had spoken so highly of his latest volume of verse—the one through which an undercurrent of psychoanalytical phraseology had intermittently run—that even Quiggin (usually as sparing of praise as Uncle Giles himself) had, in one of his more unbending moments at a sherry party, gone so far as to admit publicly:

'Mark has arrived.'

As St. John Clarke's secretary, Members had been competent to deal at a moment's notice with most worldly problems. For example, he could cut short the beery protests of some broken-down crony of the novelist's past, arrived unexpectedly on the doorstep—or, to be more precise, on the landing of the block of flats where St. John Clarke lived—with a view to borrowing 'a fiver' on the strength of 'the old days'. Any such former boon companion, if strong-willed, might have got away with 'half a sovereign' (as St. John Clarke always called that sum) had he gained entry to the novelist himself. With Members as a buffer, he soon found himself escorted to the lift, having to plan, as he descended, both then and for the future, economic attack elsewhere.

Alternatively, the matter to be regulated might be the behaviour of some great lady, aware that St. John Clarke was a person of a certain limited eminence, but at the same time ignorant of his credentials to celebrity. Again, Members could put right a situation that had gone amiss. Lady Huntercombe must have been guilty of some such social dissonance at her own table (before a secretary had come into existence to adjust such matters by a subsequent word) because Members was fond of quoting a *mot* of his master's to the effect that dinner at the Huntercombes' possessed 'only two dramatic features—the wine was a farce and the food a tragedy'.

In fact to get rid of a secretary who performed his often difficult functions so effectively was a rash step on the part of a man who liked to be steered painlessly through the shoals and shallows of social life. Indeed, looking back afterwards, the dismissal of Members might almost be regarded as a landmark in the general disintegration of society in its traditional form. It was an act of individual folly on the part of St. John Clarke; a piece of recklessness that well illustrates the mixture of self-assurance and *ennui* which together contributed so much to condition the state of mind of people like St. John Clarke at that time. Of course I did not recognise its broader aspects then. The duel between Members and Quiggin seemed merely an entertaining conflict to watch, rather than the significant crumbling of social foundations.

On that dank afternoon in the park Members had abandoned some of his accustomed coldness of manner. He seemed glad to talk to someone—probably to anyone—about his recent ejection. He began on the subject at once, drawing his tightly-waisted overcoat more closely round him, while he contracted his sharp, beady brown eyes. Separation from St. John Clarke, and association with the firm of Boggis & Stone, had for some reason renewed his former resemblance to an ingeniously constructed marionette or rag doll.

'There had been a slight sense of strain for some months between St. J. and myself,' he said. 'An absolutely trivial matter about taking a girl out to dinner. Perhaps rather foolishly, I had told St. J. I was going to a lecture on the Little Entente. Howard Craggs—whom I am now working with—happened to be introducing the lecturer, and so of course within twenty-four hours he had managed to mention to St. J. the fact that I had not been present. It was awkward, naturally, but I did not think St. J. really minded.

'But why did you want to know about the Little Entente?'

'St. J. had begun to be rather keen on what he called "the European Situation",' said Members, brushing aside my surprise as almost impertinent. 'I always liked to humour his whims.'

'But I thought his great thing was the Ivory Tower?'

'Of course, I found out later that Quiggin had put him up to "the European Situation",' admitted Members, grudgingly. 'But after all, an artist has certain responsibilities. I expect you are a supporter of the League yourself, my dear Nicholas.'

He smiled as he uttered the last part of the sentence, though speaking as if he intended to administer a slight, if well deserved, rebuke. In doing this he involuntarily adopted a more personal rendering of Quiggin's own nasal intonation, which rendered quite unnecessary the explanation that the idea had been Quiggin's. Probably the very words he used were Quiggin's, too.

'But politics were just what you used to complain of in Quiggin.'

'Perhaps Quiggin was right in that respect, if in no other,' said Members, giving his tinny, bitter laugh.

'And then?'

'It turned out that St. J.'s feelings *were* rather hurt.'

Members paused, as if he did not know how best to set about explaining the situation further. He shook his head once or twice in his old, abstracted Scholar-Gypsy manner. Then he began, as it were, at a new place in his narrative.

'As you probably know,' he continued, 'I can say without boasting that I have done a good deal to change—why should I not say it?—to improve St. J.'s attitude towards intellectual matters. Do you know, when I first came to him he thought Matisse was a *plage*—no, I mean it.'

He made no attempt to relax his features, nor join in audible amusement at such a state of affairs. Instead, he continued to record St. John Clarke's shortcomings.

'That much quoted remark of his: "Gorki is a Russian d'Annunzio"—he got it from me. I happened to say at tea one day that I thought if d'Annunzio had been born in Nijni Novgorod he would have had much the same career as Gorki. All St. J. did was to turn the words round and use them as his own.'

'But you still see him from time to time?'

Members shied away his rather distinguished profile like a high-bred but displeased horse.

'Yes—and no,' he conceded. 'It's rather awkward. I don't

know how much Quiggin told you, nor if he spoke the truth.'

'He said you came in occasionally to look after the books.'

'Only once in a way. I've got to earn a living somehow. Besides, I am attached to St. J.—even after the way he has behaved. I need not tell you that he does not like parting with money. I scarcely get enough for my work on the books to cover my bus fares. It is a strain having to avoid that *âme de boue,* too, whenever I visit the flat. He is usually about somewhere, spying on everyone who crosses the threshold.'

'And what about St. John Clarke's conversion to Marxism?'

'When I first persuaded St. J. to look at the world in a contemporary manner,' said Members slowly, adopting the tone of one determined not to be hurried in his story by those whose interest in it was actuated only by vulgar curiosity—'When I first persuaded him to that, I took an early opportunity to show him Quiggin. After all, Quiggin was supposed to be my friend—and, whatever one may think of his behaviour as a friend, he has—or had—some talent.'

Members waited for my agreement before continuing, as if the thought of displacement by a talentless Quiggin would add additional horror to his own position. I concurred that Quiggin's talent was only too apparent.

'From the very beginning I feared the risk of things going wrong on account of St. J.'s squeamishness about people's personal appearance. For example, I insisted that Quiggin should put on a clean shirt when he came to see St. J. I told him to attend to his nails. I even gave him an orange stick with which to do so.'

'And these preparations were successful?'

'They met once or twice. Quiggin was even asked to the

flat. They got on better than I had expected. I admit that. All the same, I never felt that the meetings were really *enjoyable*. I was sorry about that, because I thought Quiggin's ideas would be useful to St. J. I do not always agree with Quiggin's approach to such things as the arts, for example, but he is keenly aware of present-day tendencies. However, I decided in the end to explain to Quiggin that I feared St. J. was not very much taken with him.'

'Did Quiggin accept that?'

'He did,' said Members, again speaking with bitterness. 'He accepted it without a murmur. That, in itself, should have put me on my guard. I know now that almost as soon as I introduced them, they began to see each other when I was not present.'

Members checked himself at this point, perhaps feeling that to push his indictment to such lengths bordered on absurdity.

'Of course, there was no particular reason why they should not meet,' he allowed. 'It was just odd—and rather unfriendly—that neither of them should have mentioned their meetings to me. St. J. always loves new people. "Unmade friends are like unmade beds," he has often said. "They should be attended to early in the morning." '

Members drew a deep breath that was almost a sigh. There was a pause.

'But I thought you said he was so squeamish about people?'

'Not when he has once decided they are going to be successful.'

'That's what he thinks about Quiggin?'

Members nodded.

'Then I noticed St. J. was beginning to describe everything as "bourgeois",' he said. 'Wearing a hat was "bourgeois", eating pudding with a fork was "bourgeois", the Ritz was "bourgeois", Lady Huntercombe was "bourgeois"—he meant "bourgeoise", of course, but French is not one of St. J.'s long suits. Then one morning at breakfast he said Cézanne was "bourgeois". At first I thought he meant that only middle-class people put too much emphasis on such things—that a true aristocrat could afford to ignore them. It was a favourite theme of St. J.'s that "natural aristocrats" were the only true ones. He regarded himself as a "natural aristocrat". At the same time he felt that a "natural aristocrat" had a right to mix with the ordinary kind, and latterly he had spent more and more of his time in rather grand circles—and in fact had come almost to hate people who were not rather smart, or at least very rich. For example, I remember him describing—well, I won't say whom, but he is a novelist who sells very well and you can probably guess the name—as "the kind of man who knows about as much about *placement* as to send the wife of a younger son of a marquess in to dinner before the daughter of an earl married to a commoner". He thought a lot about such things. That was why I had been at first afraid of introducing him to Quiggin. And then—when we began discussing Cézanne—it turned out that he had been using the word "bourgeois" all the time in the Marxist sense. I didn't know he had even heard of Marx, much less was at all familiar with his theories.'

'I seem to remember an article he wrote describing himself as a "Gladstonian Liberal"—in fact a Liberal of the most old-fashioned kind.'

'You do, you do,' said Members, almost passionately. 'I wrote it for him, as a matter of fact. You couldn't have expressed it better. *A Liberal of the most old-fashioned kind*. Local Option—Proportional Representation—Welsh Disestablishment—the whole bag of tricks. That was just about as far as he got. But now everything is "bourgeois"—Liberalism, I have no doubt, most of all. As a matter of fact, his politics were the only liberal thing about him.'

'And it began as soon as he met Quiggin?'

'I first noticed the change when he persuaded me to join in what he called "collective action on the part of writers and artists"—going to meetings to protest against Manchuria and so on. I agreed, first of all, simply to humour him. It was just as well I did, as a matter of fact, because it led indirectly to another job when he turned his back on me. You know, what St. J. really wants is a son. He wants to be a father without having a wife.'

'I thought everyone always tried to avoid that.'

'In the Freudian sense,' said Members, impatiently, 'his nature requires a father-son relationship. Unfortunately, the situation becomes a little too life-like, and one is faced with a kind of artificially constructed Œdipus situation.'

'Can't you re-convert him from Marxism to psycho-analysis?'

Members looked at me fixedly.

'St. J. has always pooh-poohed the subconscious,' he said.

We were about to move off in our respective directions when my attention was caught by a disturbance coming from the road running within the railings of the park. It was a sound, harsh and grating, though at the same time shrill and suggesting complaint. These were human voices raised in protest. Turning, I saw through the mist that increasingly enveloped the park a column of persons entering beneath the arch. They trudged behind a mounted policeman, who led their procession about twenty yards ahead. Evidently a political 'demonstration' of some sort was on its way to the north side where such meetings were held. From time to time these persons raised a throaty cheer, or an individual voice from amongst them bawled out some form of exhortation. A strident shout, similar to that which had at first drawn my attention, now sounded again. We moved towards the road to obtain a better view.

The front rank consisted of two men in cloth caps, one with a beard, the other wearing dark glasses, who carried between them a banner upon which was inscribed the purpose and location of the gathering. Behind these came some half a dozen personages, marching almost doggedly out of step, as if to deprecate even such a minor element of militarism. At the same time there was a vaguely official air about them. Among these, I thought I recognised the face and figure of a female Member of Parliament whose photograph occasionally appeared in the papers. Next to this woman tramped Sillery. He had exchanged his black soft hat of earlier afternoon for a cloth cap similar to that worn by the bearers of the banner: his walrus moustache and thick strands of white hair blew furiously in the wind. From time to time he clawed at the arm of a gloomy-looking man next to him who walked with a limp. He was grinning all the while to himself, and seemed to be hugely enjoying his role in the procession.

In the throng that straggled several yards behind these mort important figures I identified two young men who used to frequent Mr. Deacon's antique shop; one of whom, indeed, was believed to have accompanied Mr. Deacon himself on one of his holidays in Cornwall. I thought, immediately, that Mr. Deacon's other associate, Gypsy Jones, might also be of the party, but could see no sign of her. Probably, as Quiggin had suggested, she belonged by then to a more distinguished grade of her own hierarchy than that represented by this heterogeneous collection, nearly all apparently 'intellectuals' of one kind or another.

However, although interested to see Sillery in such

circumstances, there was another far more striking aspect of the procession which a second later riveted my eyes. Members must have taken in this particular spectacle at the same instant as myself, because I heard him beside me give a gasp of irritation.

Three persons immediately followed the group of notables with whom Sillery marched. At first, moving closely together through the mist, this trio seemed like a single grotesque three-headed animal, forming the figurehead of an ornamental car on the roundabout of a fair. As they jolted along, however, their separate entities became revealed, manifesting themselves as a figure in a wheeled chair, jointly pushed by a man and a woman. At first I could not believe my eyes, perhaps even wished to disbelieve them, because I allowed my attention to be distracted for a moment by Sillery's voice shouting in high, almost jocular tones: 'Abolish the Means Test!' He had uttered this cry just as he came level with the place where Members and I stood; but he was too occupied with his own concerns to notice us there, although the park was almost empty.

Then I looked again at the three other people, thinking I might find myself mistaken in what I had at first supposed. On the contrary, the earlier impression was correct. The figure in the wheeled chair was St. John Clarke. He was being propelled along the road, in unison, by Quiggin and Mona Templer.

'My God!' said Members, quite quietly.

'Did you see Sillery?'

I asked this because I could think of no suitable comment regarding the more interesting group. Members took no notice of the question.

'I never thought they would go through with it,' he said.

Neither St. John Clarke, nor Quiggin, wore hats. The novelist's white hair, unenclosed in a cap such as Sillery wore, was lifted high, like an elderly Struwwelpeter's, in the stiff breeze that was beginning to blow through the branches. Quiggin was dressed in the black leather overcoat he had worn in the Ritz, a red woollen muffler riding up round his neck, his skull cropped like a convicts'. No doubt intentionally, he had managed to make himself look like a character from one of the novels of Dostoievski. Mona, too, was hatless, with dishevelled curls: her face very white above a high-necked polo jumper covered by a tweed overcoat of smart cut. She was looking remarkably pretty, and, like Sillery, seemed to be enjoying herself. On the other hand, the features of the two men with her expressed only inexorable sternness. Every few minutes, when the time came for a general shout to be raised, St. John Clarke would brandish in his hand a rolled-up copy of one of the 'weeklies', as he yelled the appropriate slogan in a high, excited voice.

'It's an absolute scandal,' said Members breathlessly. 'I heard rumours that something of the sort was on foot. The strain may easily kill St. J. He ought not to be up—much less taking part in an open-air meeting before the warmer weather comes.'

I was myself less surprised at the sight of Quiggin and St. John Clarke in such circumstances than to find Mona teamed up with the pair of them. For Quiggin, this kind of thing had become, after all, almost a matter of routine. It was 'the little political affair' Sillery had mentioned at the private view. St. John Clarke's collaboration in such an outing was equally predictable—apart from the state of his health—after what Members and Quiggin had both said about him. From his acceptance of Quiggin's domination he would henceforward join that group of authors, dons, and clergymen increasingly to be found at that period on political platforms of a 'Leftish' sort. To march in some public 'demonstration' was an almost unavoidable condition of his new commitments. As it happened he was fortunate enough on this, his first appearance, to find himself in a conveyance. In the wheeled chair, with his long white locks, he made an effective figure, no doubt popular with the organisers and legitimately gratifying to himself.

It was Mona's presence that was at first inexplicable to me. She could hardly have come up for the day to take part in all this. Perhaps the Templers were again in London for the week-end, and she had chosen to walk in the procession as an unusual experience; while Peter had gone off to amuse himself elsewhere. Then all at once the thing came to me in a flash, as such things do, requiring no further explanation. Mona had left Templer. She was now living with Quiggin. For some reason this was absolutely clear. Their relationship was made unmistakable by the manner in which they moved together side by side.

'Where are they going?' I asked.

'To meet some Hunger-Marchers arriving from the Midlands,' said Members, as if it were a foolish, irrelevant question. 'They are camping in the park, aren't they?'

'This crowd?'

'No, the Hunger-Marchers, of course.'

'Why is Mona there?'

'Who is Mona?'

'The girl walking with Quiggin and helping to push St. John Clarke. She was a model, you remember. I once saw you with her at a party years ago.'

'Oh, yes, it was her, wasn't it?' he said, indifferently. Mona's name seemed to mean nothing to him.

'But why is she helping to push the chair?'

'Probably because Quiggin is too bloody lazy to do all the work himself,' he said.

Evidently he was ignorant of Mona's subsequent career since the days when he had known her. The fact that she was helping to trundle St. John Clarke through the mists of Hyde Park was natural enough for the sort of girl she had been. In the eyes of Members she was just another 'arty' woman roped in by Quiggin to assist Left Wing activities. His own thoughts were entirely engrossed by St. John Clarke and Quiggin. I could not help being impressed by the extent to which the loss of his post as secretary had upset him. His feelings had undoubtedly been lacerated. He watched them pass by, his mouth clenched.

The procession wound up the road towards Marble Arch. Two policemen on foot brought up the rear, round whom, whistling shrilly, circled some boys on bicycles, apparently unconnected with the marchers. The intermittent shouting grew gradually fainter, until the column disappeared from sight into the upper reaches of the still foggy park.

Members looked round at me.

'Can you beat it?' he said.

'I thought St. John Clarke disliked girls near him?'

'I don't expect he cares any longer,' said Members, in a voice of despair. 'Quiggin will make him put up with anything by now.'

On this note we parted company. As I continued my way through the park I was conscious of having witnessed a spectacle that was distinctly strange. Jean had already told me more than once that the Templers were getting on badly. These troubles had begun, so it appeared, a few months after their marriage, Mona complaining of the dullness of life away from London. She was for ever making scenes, usually about nothing at all. Afterwards there would be tears and reconciliations; and some sort of a 'treat' would be arranged for her by Peter. Then the cycle would once more take its course. Jean liked Mona, but thought her 'impossible' as a wife.

'What is the real trouble?' I had asked.

'I don't think she likes men.'

'Ah.'

'But I don't think she likes women either. Just keen on herself.'

'How will it end?'

'They may settle down. If Peter doesn't lose interest. He is used to having his own way. He has been unexpectedly good so far.'

She was fond of Peter, though free from that obsessive interest that often entangles brother and sister. They were not alike in appearance, though her hair, too, grew down like his in a 'widow's peak' on her forehead. There was also something about the set of her neck that recalled her brother. That was all.

'They might have a lot of children.'

'They might.'

'Would that be a good thing?'

'Certainly.'

I was surprised that she was so decisive, because in those days children were rather out of fashion. It always seemed strange to me, and rather unreal, that so much of her own time should be occupied with Polly.

'You know, I believe Mona has taken quite a fancy for your friend J. G. Quiggin,' she had said, laughing.

'Not possible.'

'I'm not so sure.'

'Has he appeared at the house again?'

'No—but she keeps talking about him.'

'Perhaps I ought never to have introduced him into the household.'

'Perhaps not,' she had replied, quite seriously.

At the time, the suggestion had seemed laughable. To regard Quiggin as a competitor with Templer for a woman —far less his own wife—was ludicrous even to consider.

'But she took scarcely any notice of him.'

'Well, I thought *you* were rather wet the first time you came to the house. But I've made up for it later, haven't I?'

'I adored you from the start.'

'I'm sure you didn't.'

'Certainly at Stourwater.'

'Oh, at Stourwater I was very impressed too.'

'And I with you.'

'Then why didn't you write or ring up or something? *Why didn't you?*'

'I did—you were away.'

'You ought to have gone on trying.'

'I wasn't sure you weren't rather lesbian.'

'How ridiculous. Pretty rude of you, too.'

'I had a lot to put up with.'

'Nonsense.'

'But I had.'

'How absurd you are.'

When the colour came quickly into her face, the change used to fill me with excitement. Even when she sat in silence, scarcely answering if addressed, such moods seemed a necessary part of her: something not to be utterly regretted. Her forehead, high and white, gave a withdrawn look, like a great lady in a medieval triptych or carving; only her lips, and the elegantly long lashes under slanting eyes, gave a hint of latent sensuality. But descriptions of a woman's outward appearance can hardly do more than echo the terms of a fashion paper. Their nature can be caught only in a refractive beam, as with light passing through water: the rays of character focused through the person with whom they are intimately associated. Perhaps, therefore, I alone was responsible for what she seemed to me. To another man—Duport, for example—she no doubt appeared—indeed, actually was—a different woman.

'But why, when we first met, did you never talk about books and things?' I had asked her.

'I didn't think you'd understand.'

'How hopeless of you.'

'Now I see it was,' she had said, quite humbly.

She shared with her brother the conviction that she 'belonged' in no particular world. The other guests she had found collected round Sir Magnus Donners at Stourwater had been on the whole unsympathetic.

'I only went because I was a friend of Baby's,' she had said; 'I don't really like people of that sort.'

'But surely there were people of all sorts there?'

'Perhaps I don't much like people anyway. I am probably too lazy. They always want to sleep with one, or something.'

'But that is like me.'

'I know. It's intolerable.'

We laughed, but I had felt the chill of sudden jealousy; the fear that her remark had been made deliberately to tease.

'Of course Baby loves it all,' she went on. 'The men hum round her like bees. She is so funny with them.'

'What did she and Sir Magnus do?'

'Not even I know. Whatever it was, Bijou Ardglass refused to take him on.'

'She was offered the job?'

'So I was told. She preferred to go off with Bob.'

'Why did that stop?'

'Bob could no longer support her in the style to which she was accustomed—or rather the style to which she was unaccustomed, as Jumbo Ardglass never had much money.'

It was impossible, as ever, to tell from her tone what she felt about Duport. I wondered whether she would leave him and marry me. I had not asked her, and had no clear idea what the answer would be. Certainly, if she did, like Lady Ardglass, she would not be supported in the style to which she had been accustomed. Neither, for that matter, would Mona, if she had indeed gone off with Quiggin, for I felt sure that the final domestic upheaval at the Templers' had now taken place. Jean had been right. Something about the way Quiggin and Mona walked beside one another connected them inexorably together. 'Women can be immensely obtuse about all kinds of things,' Barnby was fond of saying, 'but where the emotions are concerned their opinion is always worthy of consideration.'

The mist was lifting now, gleams of sunlight once more coming through the clouds above the waters of the Serpentine. Not unwillingly dismissing the financial side of marriage from my mind, as I walked on through the melancholy park, I thought of love, which, from the very beginning perpetually changes its shape: sometimes in the ascendant, sometimes in decline. At present we sailed in comparatively calm seas because we lived from meeting to meeting, possessing no plan for the future. Her abandonment remained; the abandonment that had so much surprised me at that first embrace, as the car skimmed the muddy surfaces of the Great West Road.

But in love, like everything else—more than anything else—there must be bad as well as good; and by silence or some trivial remark she could inflict unexpected pain. Away from her, all activities seemed waste of time, yet sometimes just before seeing her I was aware of an odd sense of antagonism that had taken the place of the longing that had been in my heart for days before. This sense of being out of key with her sometimes survived the first minutes of our meeting. Then, all at once, tension would be relaxed; always, so it seemed to me, by some mysterious force emanating from her: intangible, invisible, yet at the same time part of a whole principle of behaviour: a deliberate act of the will by which she exercised power. At times it was almost as if she intended me to feel that unexpected accident, rather than a carefully arranged plan, had brought us together on some given occasion; or at least that I must always be prepared for such a mood. Perhaps these are inward irritations always produced by love: the acutely sensitive nerves of intimacy: the haunting fear that all may not go well.

Still thinking of such things, I rang the bell of the ground-floor flat. It was in an old-fashioned red-brick block of buildings, situated somewhere beyond Rutland Gate, concealed among obscure turnings that seemed to lead nowhere. For some time there was no answer to the ring. I waited, peering through the frosted glass of the front door, feeling every second an eternity. Then the door opened a few inches and Jean looked out. I saw her face only for a moment. She was laughing.

'Come in,' she said quickly. 'It's cold.'

As I entered the hall, closing the door behind me, she ran back along the passage. I saw that she wore nothing but a pair of slippers.

'There is a fire in here,' she called from the sitting-room.

I hung my hat on the grotesque piece of furniture, designed for that use, that stood by the door. Then I followed her down the passage and into the room. The furniture and decoration of the flat were of an appalling banality.

'Why are you wearing no clothes?'

'Are you shocked?'

'What do you think?'

'I think you are.'

'Surprised, rather than shocked.'

'To make up for the formality of our last meeting.'

'Aren't I showing my appreciation?'

'Yes, but you must not be so conventional.'

'But if it had been the postman?'

'I could have seen through the glass.'

'He, too, perhaps.'

'I had a dressing-gown handy.'

'It was a kind thought, anyway.'

'You like it?'

'Very much.'

'Tell me something nice.'

'This style suits you.'

'Not too *outré*?'

'On the contrary.'

'Is this how you like me?'

'Just like this.'

There is, after all, no pleasure like that given by a woman who really wants to see you. Here, at last, was some real escape from the world. The calculated anonymity of the surroundings somehow increased the sense of being alone with her. There was no sound except her sharp intake of breath. Yet love, for all the escape it offers, is closely linked with everyday things, even with the affairs of others. I knew Jean would burn with curiosity when I told her of the procession in the park. At the same time, because passion in its transcendence cannot be shared with any other element, I could not speak of what had happened until the time had come to decide where to dine.

She was pulling on her stockings when I told her. She gave a little cry, indicating disbelief.

'After all, you were the first to suggest something was "on" between them.'

'But she would be insane to leave Peter.'

We discussed this. The act of marching in a political demonstration did not, in itself, strike her as particularly unexpected in Mona. She said that Mona always longed to take part in anything that drew attention to herself. Jean was unwilling to believe that pushing St. John Clarke's chair was the outward sign of a decisive step in joining Quiggin.

'She must have done it because Peter is away. It is exactly the kind of thing that would appeal to her. Besides, it would annoy him just the right amount. A little, but not too much.'

'Where is Peter?'

'Spending the week-end with business friends. Mona thought them too boring to visit.'

'Perhaps she was just having a day out, then. Even so, it confirms your view that Quiggin made a hit with her.'

She pulled on the other stocking.

'True, they had a splitting row just before Peter left home,' she said. 'You know, I almost believe you are right.'

'Put a call through.'

'Just to see what the form is?'

'Why not?'

'Shall I?'

She was undecided.

'I think I will,' she said at last.

Still only partly dressed, she took up the telephone and lay on the sofa. At the other end of the line the bell rang for some little time before there was an answer. Then a voice spoke from the Templers' house. Jean made some trivial enquiry. A short conversation followed. I saw from her face that my guess had been somewhere near the mark. She hung up the receiver.

'Mona left the house yesterday, saying she did not know when she would be back. She took a fair amount of luggage and left no address. I think the Burdens believe something is up. Mrs. Burden told me Peter had rung up about something he had forgotten. She told him Mona had left unexpectedly.

'She may be taking a few days off.'

'I don't think so,' said Jean.

Barnby used to say: 'All women are stimulated by the news that any wife has left any husband.' Certainly I was aware that the emotional atmosphere in the room had changed. Perhaps I should have waited longer before telling her my story. Yet to postpone the information further was scarcely possible without appearing deliberately secretive. I have often pondered on the conversation that followed, without coming to any definite conclusion as to why things took the course they did.

We had gone on to talk of the week-end when Quiggin had been first invited to the Templers' house. I had remarked something to the effect that if Mona had really left for good, the subject would have been apt for one of Mrs. Erdleigh's prophecies. In saying this I had added some more or less derogatory remark about Jimmy Stripling. Suddenly I was aware that Jean was displeased with my words. Her face took on a look of vexation. I supposed that some out-of-the-way loyalty had for some reason made her take exception to the idea of laughing at her sister's ex-husband. I could not imagine why this should be, since Stripling was usually regarded in the Templer household as an object of almost perpetual derision.

'I know he isn't *intelligent,*' she said.

'Intelligence isn't everything,' I said, trying to pass the matter off lightly. 'Look at the people in the Cabinet.'

'You said the other day that you found it awfully difficult to get on with people who were not intelligent.'

'I only meant where writing was concerned.'

'It didn't sound like that.'

A woman's power of imitation and adaptation make her

capable of confronting you with your own arguments after even the briefest acquaintance: how much more so if a state of intimacy exists. I saw that we were about to find ourselves in deep water. She pursed her lips and looked away. I thought she was going to cry. I could not imagine what had gone wrong and began to feel that terrible sense of exhaustion that descends, when, without cause or warning, an unavoidable, meaningless quarrel develops with someone you love. Now there seemed no way out. To lavish excessive praise on Jimmy Stripling's intellectual attainments would not be accepted, might even sound satirical; on the other hand, to remain silent would seem to confirm my undoubtedly low opinion of his capabilities in that direction. There was also, of course, the more general implication of her remark, the suggestion of protest against a state of mind in which intellectual qualities were automatically put first. Dissent from this principle was, after all, reasonable enough, though not exactly an equitable weapon in Jean's hands, for she, as much as anyone—so it seemed to me as her lover—was dependent, in the last resort, on people who were 'intelligent' in the sense in which she used the word.

Perhaps it was foolish to pursue the point of what was to all appearances only an irritable remark. But the circumstances were of a kind when irritating remarks are particularly to be avoided. Otherwise, it would have been easier to find an excuse.

Often enough, women love the arts and those who practice them; but they possess also a kind of jealousy of those activities. They like wit, but hate analysis. They are always prepared to fall back upon traditional rather than intellectual defensive positions. We never talked of Duport, as I have already recorded, and I scarcely knew, even then, why she had married him; but married they were. Accordingly, it seemed to me possible that what she had said possessed reference, in some oblique manner, to her husband; in the sense that adverse criticism of this kind cast a reflection upon him, and consequently upon herself. I had said nothing of Duport (who, as I was to discover years later, had a deep respect for 'intelligence'), but the possibility was something to be taken into account.

I was quite wrong in this surmise, and, even then, did not realise the seriousness of the situation; certainly was wholly unprepared for what happened next. A moment later, for no apparent reason, she told me she had had a love affair with Jimmy Stripling.

'When?'

'After Babs left him,' she said.

She went white, as if she might be about to faint. I was myself overcome with a horrible feeling of nausea, as if one had suddenly woken from sleep and found oneself chained to a corpse. A desire to separate myself physically from her and the place we were in was linked with an overwhelming sensation that, more than ever, I wanted her for myself. To think of her as wife of Bob Duport was bad enough, but that she should also have been mistress of Jimmy Stripling was barely endurable. Yet it was hard to know how to frame a complaint regarding that matter even to myself. She had not been 'unfaithful' to me. This odious thing had happened at a time when I myself had no claim whatsoever over her. I tried to tranquillise myself by considering whether a liaison with some man, otherwise possible to like or admire, would have been preferable. In the face of such an alternative, I decided Stripling was on the whole better as he was: with all the nightmarish fantasies implicit in the situation. The mystery remained why she should choose that particular moment to reveal this experience of hers, making of it a kind of defiance.

When you are in love with someone, their life, past, present and future, becomes in a curious way part of your life; and yet, at the same time, since two separate human entities in fact remain, you merely carry your own prejudices into another person's imagined existence; not even into their 'real' existence, because only they themselves can estimate what their 'real' existence has been. Indeed, the situation might be compared with that to be experienced in due course in the army where an officer is responsible for the conduct of troops stationed at a post too distant from him for the exercise of any effective control.

Not only was it painful enough to think of Jean giving herself to another man; the pain was intensified by supposing—what was, of course, not possible—that Stripling must appear to her in the same terms that he appeared to me. Yet clearly she had, once, at least, looked at Stripling with quite different eyes, or such a situation could never have arisen. Therefore, seeing Stripling as a man for whom it was evidently possible to feel at the very least a passing *tendresse*—perhaps even love—this incident, unforgettably horrible as it seemed to me at the time, would more rationally be regarded as a mere error of judgment. In love, however, there is no rationality. Besides, that she had seen him with other eyes than mine made things worse. In such ways one is bound, inescapably, to the actions of others.

We finished dressing in silence. By that time it was fairly late. I felt at once hungry, and without any true desire for food.

'Where shall we go?'

'Anywhere you like.'

'But where would you like to go?'

'I don't care.'

'We could have a sandwich at Foppa's.'

'The club?'

'Yes.'

'All right.'

In the street she slipped her arm through mine. I looked, and saw that she was crying a little, but I was no nearer understanding her earlier motives. The only thing clear was that some sharp change had taken place in the kaleidoscope of our connected emotions. In the pattern left by this transmutation of coloured crystals an increased intimacy had possibly emerged. Perhaps that was something she had intended.

'I suppose I should not have told you.'

'It would have come out sooner or later.'

'But not just then.'

'Perhaps not.'

Still, in spite of it all, as we drove through dingy Soho streets, her head resting on my shoulder, I felt glad she still seemed to belong to me. Foppa's was open. That was a relief, for there was sometimes an intermediate period when the restaurant was closed down and the club had not yet come into active being. We climbed the narrow staircase, over which brooded a peculiarly Italian smell: minestrone: salad oil: stale tobacco: perhaps a faint reminder of the lotion Foppa used on his hair.

Barnby had first introduced me to Foppa's club a long time before. One of the merits of the place was that no one either of us knew ever went there. It was a single room over Foppa's Restaurant. In theory the club opened only after the restaurant had shut for the night, but in practice Foppa himself, sometimes feeling understandably bored with his customers, would retire upstairs to read the paper, or practise billiard strokes. On such occasions he was glad of company at an earlier hour than was customary. Alternatively, he would sometimes go off with his friends to another haunt of theirs, leaving a notice on the door, written in indelible pencil, saying that Foppa's Club was temporarily closed for cleaning.

There was a narrow window at the far end of this small, smoky apartment; a bar in one corner, and a table for the game of Russian billiards in the other. The walls were white and bare, the vermouth bottles above the little bar shining out in bright stripes of colour that seemed to form a kind of spectrum in red, white and green. These patriotic colours linked the aperitifs and liqueurs with the portrait of Victor Emmanuel II which hung over the mantelpiece. Surrounded by a wreath of laurel, the King of Sardinia and United Italy wore a wasp-waisted military frock-coat swagged with coils of yellow aiguillette. The bold treatment of his costume by the artist almost suggested a Bakst design for one of the early Russian ballets.

If Foppa himself had grown his moustache to the same enormous length, and added an imperial to his chin, he would have looked remarkably like the *re galantuomo*; with just that same air of royal amusement that anyone could possibly take seriously—even for a moment—the preposterous world in which we are fated to have our being. Hanging over the elaborately gilded frame of this coloured print was the beautiful Miss Foppa's black fez-like cap, which she possessed by virtue of belonging to some local, parochial branch of the Fascist Party; though her father was believed to be at best only a lukewarm supporter of Mussolini's régime. Foppa had lived in London for many years. He had even served as a cook during the war with a British light infantry regiment; but he had never taken out papers of naturalisation.

'Look at me,' he used to say, when the subject arose, 'I am not an Englishman. You see.'

The truth of that assertion was undeniable. Foppa was

not an Englishman. He did not usually express political opinions in the presence of his customers, but he had once, quite exceptionally, indicated to me a newspaper photograph of the Duce declaiming from the balcony of the Palazzo Venezia. That was as near as he had ever gone to stating his view. It was sufficient. Merely by varying in no way his habitual expression of tolerant amusement, Foppa had managed to convey his total lack of anything that could possibly be accepted as Fascist enthusiasm. All the same, I think he had no objection to his daughter's association with that or any other party which might be in power at the moment.

Foppa was decidedly short, always exquisitely dressed in a neat suit, blue or brown, his tiny feet encased in excruciatingly tight shoes of light tan shade. The shoes were sharply pointed and polished to form dazzling highlights. In summer he varied his footgear by sporting white brogues picked out in snakeskin. He was a great gambler, and sometimes spent his week-ends taking part in trotting races somewhere not far from London, perhaps at Greenford in Middlesex. Hanging behind the bar was a framed photograph of himself competing in one of these trotting events, armed with a long whip, wearing a jockey cap, his small person almost hidden between the tail of his horse and the giant wheels of the sulky. The snapshot recalled a design of Degas or Guys. That was the world, æsthetically speaking, to which Foppa belonged. He was a man of great good nature and independence, who could not curb his taste for gambling for high stakes; a passion that brought him finally, I believe, into difficulties.

Jean and I had already been to the club several times, because she liked playing Russian billiards, a game at which she was extremely proficient. Sixpence in the slot of the table brought to the surface the white balls and the red.

After a quarter of an hour the balls no longer reappeared for play, vanishing one by one, while scores were doubled. Foppa approved of Jean. Her skill at billiards was a perpetual surprise and delight to him.

'He probably tells all his friends I'm his mistress,' she used to say.

She may have been right in supposing that; though I suspect, if he told any such stories, that Foppa would probably have boasted of some enormous lady, at least twice his own size, conceived in the manner of Jordaens. His turn of humour always suggested something of that sort.

I thought the club might be a good place to recover some sort of composure. The room was never very full, though sometimes there would be a party of three or four playing cards gravely at one of the tables in the corner. On that particular evening Foppa himself was engrossed in a two-handed game, perhaps piquet. Sitting opposite him, his back to the room, was a man of whom nothing could be seen but a brown check suit and a smoothly brushed head, greying and a trifle bald at the crown. Foppa rose at once, poured out Chianti for us, and shouted down the service hatch for sandwiches to be cut. Although the cook was believed to be a Cypriot, the traditional phrase for attracting his attention was always formulated in French.

'Là bas!' Foppa would intone liturgically, as he leant forward into the abyss that reached down towards the kitchen, 'Là bas!'

Perhaps Miss Foppa herself attended to the provision of food in the evenings. If so, she never appeared in the club. Her quiet, melancholy beauty would have ornamented the place. I had, indeed, never seen any woman but Jean in that room. No doubt the clientèle would have objected to the presence there of any lady not entirely removed from their own daily life.

Two Soho Italians were standing by the bar. One, a tall, sallow, mournful character, resembling a former ambassador fallen on evil days, smoked a short, stinking cigar. The other, a nondescript ruffian, smaller in size than his companion, though also with a certain air of authority, displayed a suggestion of side-whisker under his faun velour hat. He was picking his teeth pensively with one of the toothpicks supplied in tissue paper at the bar. Both were probably neighbouring head-waiters. The two of them watched Jean slide the cue gently between finger and thumb before making her first shot. The ambassadorial one removed the cigar from his mouth and, turning his head a fraction, remarked sententiously through almost closed lips:

'Bella posizione.'

'E in gamba,' agreed the other. 'Una fuori classe davvero.'

The evening was happier now, though still something might easily go wrong. There was no certainty. People are differently equipped for withstanding emotional discomfort. On the whole women can bear a good deal of that kind of strain without apparently undue inconvenience. The game was won by Jean.

'What about another one?'

We asked the Italians if they were waiting for the billiard table, but they did not want to play. We had just arranged the balls again, and set up the pin, when the door of the club opened and two people came into the room. One of them was Barnby. The girl with him was known to me, though it was a second before I remembered that she was Lady Anne Stepney. We had not met for three years or more. Barnby seemed surprised, perhaps not altogether pleased, to find someone he knew at Foppa's.

Although it had turned out that Anne Stepney was the girl he had met on the train after his week-end with the

Manasches, he had ceased to speak of her freely in conversation. At the same time I knew he was still seeing her. This was on account of a casual word dropped by him. I had never before run across them together in public. Some weeks after his first mention of her, I had asked whether he had finally established her identity. Barnby had replied brusquely:

'Of course her name is Stepney.'

I sometimes wondered how the two of them were getting along; even whether they had plans for marriage. A year was a long time for Barnby to be occupied with one woman. Like most men of his temperament, he held, on the whole, rather strict views regarding other people's morals. For that reason alone he would probably not have approved had I told him about Jean. In any case he was not greatly interested in such things unless himself involved. He only knew that something of the sort was in progress, and he would have had no desire, could it have been avoided, to come upon us unexpectedly in this manner.

The only change in Anne Stepney (last seen at Stringham's wedding) was her adoption of a style of dress implicitly suggesting an art student; nothing outrageous: just a general assertion that she was in some way closely connected with painting or sculpture. I think Mona had struggled against such an appearance; in Anne Stepney, it had no doubt been painfully acquired. Clothes of that sort certainly suited her large dark eyes and reddish hair, seeming also appropriate to a general air of untidiness, not to say grubbiness, that always possessed her. She had by then, I knew, passed almost completely from the world in which she had been brought up; that in which her sister, Peggy, still moved, or, at least, in that portion of it frequented by young married women.

The Bridgnorths had taken their younger daughter's

behaviour philosophically. They had gone through all the normal processes of giving her a start in life, a ball for her 'coming out', and everything else to be reasonably expected of parents in the circumstances. In the end they had agreed that 'in these days' it was impossible to insist on the hopes or standards of their own generation. Anne had been allowed to go her own way, while Lady Bridgnorth had returned to her hospital committees, Lord Bridgnorth to his politics and racing. They had probably contented themselves with the thought that Peggy, having quietly divorced Stringham, had now settled down peacefully enough with her new husband in his haunted, Palladian Yorkshire home, which was said to have given St. John Clarke the background for a novel. Besides, their eldest son, Mountfichet, I had been told, was turning out well at the university, where he was a great favourite with Sillery.

When introductions took place, it seemed simpler to make no reference to the fact that we had met before. Anne Stepney stared round the room with severe approval. Indicating Foppa and his companion, she remarked:

'I always think people playing cards make such a good pattern.'

'Rather like a Chardin,' I suggested.

'Do you think so?' she replied, implying contradiction rather than agreement.

'The composition?'

'You know I am really only interested in Chardin's highlights,' she said.

Before we could pursue the intricacies of Chardin's technique further, Foppa rose to supply further drinks. He had already made a sign of apology at his delay in doing this, to be accounted for by the fact that his game was on the point of completion when Barnby arrived. He now noted the score on a piece of paper and came towards us.

He was followed this time to the bar by the man with whom he had been at cards. Foppa's companion could now be seen more clearly. His suit was better cut and general appearance more distinguished than was usual in the club. He had stood by the table for a moment, stretching himself and lighting a cigarette, while he regarded our group. A moment later, taking a step towards Anne Stepney, he said in a soft, purring, rather humorous voice, with something almost hypnotic about its tone:

'I heard your name when you were introduced. You must be Eddie Bridgnorth's daughter.'

Looking at him more closely as he said this, I was surprised that he had remained almost unobserved until that moment. He was no ordinary person. That was clear. Of medium height, even rather small when not compared with Foppa, he was slim, with that indefinably 'horsey' look that seems even to affect the texture of the skin. His age was hard to guess: probably he was in his forties. He was very trim in his clothes. They were old, neat, well preserved clothes, a little like those worn by Uncle Giles. This man gave the impression of having handled large sums of money in his time, although he did not convey any presumption of affluence at that particular moment. He was clean-shaven, and wore a hard collar and Brigade of Guards tie. I could not imagine what someone of that sort was doing at Foppa's. There was something about him of Buster Foxe, third husband of Stringham's mother: the same cool, tough, socially elegant personality, though far more genial than Buster's. He lacked, too, that carapace of professional egotism acquired in boyhood that envelops protectively even the most good-humoured naval officer. Perhaps the similarity to Buster was after all only the outer veneer acquired by all people of the same generation.

Anne Stepney replied rather stiffly to this enquiry, that

'Eddie Bridgnorth' was indeed her father. Having decided to throw in her lot so uncompromisingly with 'artists', she may have felt put out to find herself confronted in such a place by someone of this kind. Since he claimed acquaintance with Lord Bridgnorth, there was no knowing what information he might possess about herself; nor what he might report subsequently if he saw her father again. However, the man in the Guards tie seemed instinctively to understand what her feelings would be on learning that he knew her family.

'I am Dicky Umfraville,' he said. 'I don't expect you have ever heard of me, because I have been away from this country for so long. I used to see something of your father when he owned Yellow Jack. In fact I won a whole heap of money on that horse once. None of it left now, I regret to say.'

He smiled gently. By the confidence, and at the same time the modesty, of his manner he managed to impart an extraordinary sense of reassurance. Anne Stepney seemed hardly to know what to say in answer to this account of himself. I remembered hearing Sillery speak of Umfraville, when I was an undergraduate. Perhaps facetiously, he had told Stringham that Umfraville was a man to beware of. That had been apropos of Stringham's father, and life in Kenya. Stringham himself had met Umfraville in Kenya, and spoke of him as a well-known gentleman-rider. I also remembered Stringham complaining that Le Bas had once mistaken him for Umfraville, who had been at Le Bas's house at least fifteen years earlier. Now, in spite of the difference in age and appearance, I could see that Le Bas's error had been due to something more than the habitual vagueness of schoolmasters. The similarity between Stringham and Umfraville was of a moral rather than physical sort. The same dissatisfaction with life and basic melancholy gave a resemblance, though Umfraville's features and expression were more formalised and, in some manner, coarser—perhaps they could even be called more brutal—than Stringham's.

There was something else about Umfraville that struck me, a characteristic I had noticed in other people of his age. He seemed still young, a person like oneself; and yet at the same time his appearance and manner proclaimed that he had had time to live at least a few years of his grown-up life before the outbreak of war in 1914. Once I had thought of those who had known the epoch of my own childhood as 'older people'. Then I had found there existed people like Umfraville who seemed somehow to span the gap. They partook of both eras, specially forming the tone of the post-war years; much more so, indeed, than the younger people. Most of them, like Umfraville, were melancholy; perhaps from the strain of living simultaneously in two different historical periods. That was his category, certainly. He continued now to address himself to Anne Stepney.

'Do you ever go to trotting races?'

'No.'

She looked very surprised at the question.

'I thought not,' he said, laughing at her astonishment. 'I became interested when I was in the States. The Yanks are very keen on trotting races. So are the French. In this country no one much ever seems to go. However, I met Foppa, here, down at Greenford the other day and we got on so well that we arranged to go to Caversham together. The next thing is I find myself playing piquet with him in his own joint.'

Foppa laughed at this account of the birth of their friendship, and rubbed his hands together.

'You had all the luck tonight, Mr. Umfraville,' he said. 'Next time I have my revenge.'

'Certainly, Foppa, certainly.'

However, in spite of the way the cards had fallen, Foppa seemed pleased to have Umfraville in the club. Later, I found that one of Umfraville's most fortunate gifts was a capacity to take money off people without causing offence.

A moment or two of general conversation followed in which it turned out that Jean had met Barnby on one of his visits to Stourwater. She knew, of course, about his former connection with Baby Wentworth, but when we had talked of this together, she had been uncertain whether or not they had ever stayed with Sir Magnus Donners at the same time. They began to discuss the week-end during which both had been in the same large house-party. Anne Stepney, possibly to avoid a further immediate impact with Umfraville before deciding how best to treat him, crossed the room to examine Victor Emmanuel's picture. Umfraville and I were, accordingly, left together. I asked if he remembered Stringham in Kenya.

'Charles Stringham?' he said. 'Yes, of course I knew him. Boffles Stringham's son. A very nice boy. But wasn't he married to *her* sister?'

He lowered his voice, and jerked his head in Anne's direction.

'They are divorced now.'

'Of course they are. I forgot. As a matter of fact I heard Charles was in rather a bad way. Drinking enough to float a battleship. Of course, Boffles likes his liquor hard, too. Have you known Charles long?'

'We were at the same house at school—Le Bas's.'

'Not possible.'

'Why not?'

'Because I was at Le Bas's too. Not for very long. I started at Corderey's. Then Corderey's house was taken over by Le Bas. I was asked to leave quite soon after that—

not actually sacked, as is sometimes maliciously stated by my friends. I get invited to Old Boy dinners, for example. Not that I ever go. Usually out of England. As a matter of fact I might go this year. What about you?'

'I might. I haven't been myself for a year or two.'

'Do come. We'll make up a party and raise hell. Tear Claridge's in half. That's where they hold it, isn't it?'

'Or the Ritz.'

'You must come.'

There was a suggestion of madness in the way he shot out his sentences; not the kind of madness that was raving, nor even, in the ordinary sense, dangerous; but a warning that no proper mechanism existed for operating normal controls. At the same time there was also something impelling about his friendliness: this sudden decision that we must attend the Old Boy dinner together. Even though I knew fairly well—at least flattered myself I knew well—the type of man he was, I could not help being pleased by the invitation. Certainly, I made up my mind immediately that I would go to the Le Bas dinner, upon which I was far from decided before. In fact, it would be true to say that Umfraville had completely won me over; no doubt by the shock tactics against which Sillery had issued his original warning. In such matters, though he might often talk nonsense, Sillery possessed a strong foundation of shrewdness. People who disregarded his admonitions sometimes lived to regret it.

'Do you often come here?' Umfraville asked.

'Once in a way—to play Russian billiards.'

'Tell me the name of that other charming girl.'

'Jean Duport.'

'Anything to do with the fellow who keeps company with Bijou Ardglass?'

'Wife.'

'Dear me. How eccentric of him with something so nice at home. Anne, over there, is a dear little thing, too. Bit of a handful, I hear. Fancy her being grown up. Only seems the other day I read the announcement of her birth. Wouldn't mind taking her out to dinner one day, if I had the price of a dinner on me.'

'Do you live permanently in Kenya?'

'Did for a time. Got rather tired of it lately. Isn't what it was in the early days. But, you know, something seems to have gone badly wrong with this country too. It's quite different from when I was over here two or three years ago. Then there was a party every night—two or three, as a matter of fact. Now all that is changed. No parties, no gaiety, everyone talking in a dreadfully serious manner about economics or world disarmament or something of the sort. That was why I was glad to come here and take a hand with Foppa. No nonsense about economics or world disarmament with him. All the people I know have become so damned serious, what? Don't you find that yourself?'

'It's the slump.'

Umfraville's face had taken on a strained, worried expression while he was saying this, almost the countenance of a priest preaching a gospel of pleasure to a congregation now fallen away from the high standards of the past. There was a look of hopelessness in his eyes, as if he knew of the terrible odds against him, the martyrdom that would be his final crown. At that moment he again reminded me, for some reason, of Buster Foxe. I had never heard Buster express such opinions, though in general they were at that time voiced commonly enough.

'Anyway, it's nice to find all of you here,' he said. 'Let's have another drink.'

Barnby and Anne Stepney now began to play billiards together. They seemed not on the best of terms, and had perhaps had some sort of a quarrel earlier in the evening. If Mrs. Erdleigh had been able to examine the astrological potentialities of that day she would perhaps have warned groups of lovers that the aspects were ominous. Jean came across to the bar. She took my arm, as if she wished to emphasise to Umfraville that we were on the closest terms. This was in spite of the fact that she herself was always advocating discretion. All the same, I felt delighted and warmed by her touch. Umfraville smiled, almost paternally, as if he felt that here at least he could detect on our part some hope of a pursuit of pleasure. He showed no disposition to return to his game with Foppa, now chatting with the two Italians.

'Charles Stringham was mixed up with Milly Andriadis at one moment, wasn't he?' Umfraville asked.

'About three years ago—just before his marriage.'

'I think it was just starting when I was last in London. Don't expect that really did him any good. Milly has got a way of exhausting chaps, no matter who they are. Even her Crowned Heads. They can't stand it after a bit. I remember one friend of mine had to take a voyage round the world to recover. He got D.T.s in Hongkong. Thought he was being hunted by naked women riding on unicorns. What's happened to Milly now?'

'I only met her once—at a party Charles took me to.'

'Why don't we all go and see her?'

'I don't think any of us really know her.'

'But *I* couldn't know her better.'

'Where does she live?'

'Where's the telephone book?' said Umfraville. 'Though I don't expect she will be in England at this time of year.'

He moved away, lost in thought, and disappeared through the door. It occurred to me that he was pretty drunk, but at the same time I was not sure. Equally possible was the supposition that this was his first drink of the evening. The mystery surrounded him that belongs especially to strong characters who have only pottered about in life. Jean slipped her hand in mine.

'Who is he?'

I tried to explain to her who Umfraville was.

'I am enjoying myself,' she said.

'Are you?'

I could not be quite sure whether I was enjoying myself or not. We watched the other two playing billiards. The game was evidently war to the knife. They were evenly matched. There could be no doubt now that there had been some sort of disagreement between them before their arrival at Foppa's. Perhaps all girls were in a difficult mood that night.

'I've often heard of Umfraville,' said Barnby, chalking his cue. 'Didn't he take two women to St. Moritz one year, and get fed up with them, and left them there to pay the hotel bill?'

'Who is he married to now?' Anne Stepney asked.

'Free as air at the moment, I believe,' said Barnby. 'He has had several wives—three at least. One of them poisoned herself. Another left him for a marquess—and almost immediately eloped again with a jockey. What happened to the third I can't remember. Your shot, my dear.'

Umfraville returned to the room. He watched the completion of the game in silence. It was won by Barnby. Then he spoke.

'I have a proposition to make,' he said. 'I got on to Milly Andriadis just now on the telephone and told her we were all coming round to see her.'

My first thought was that I must not make a habit of arriving with a gang of friends at Mrs. Andriadis's house as an uninvited guest; even at intervals of three or four years. A moment later I saw the absurdity of such diffidence, because, apart from any other consideration, she would not have the faintest remembrance of ever having met me before. At the same time, I could not inwardly disregard the pattern of life which caused Dicky Umfraville not only to resemble Stringham, but also, by this vicarious invitation, to re-enact Stringham's past behaviour.

'What is this suggestion?' enquired Anne Stepney.

She spoke coldly, but I think Umfraville had already thoroughly aroused her interest. At any rate her eyes reflected that rather puzzled look that in women is sometimes the prelude to an inclination for the man on whom it is directed.

'Someone called Mrs. Andriadis,' said Umfraville. 'She has been giving parties since you were so high. Rather a famous lady. A very old friend of mine. I thought we might go round and see her. I rang her up just now and she can't wait to welcome us.'

'Oh, do let's go,' said Anne Stepney, suddenly abandoning her bored, listless tone. 'I've always longed to meet Mrs. Andriadis. Wasn't she some king's mistress—was it——'

'It was,' said Umfraville.

'I've heard so many stories of the wonderful parties she gives.'

Umfraville stepped forward and took her hand. 'Your ladyship wishes to come,' he said softly, as if playing the part of a courtier in some ludicrously mannered ceremonial. 'We go, then. Yours to command.'

He bent his head over the tips of her fingers. I could not see whether his lips actually touched them, but the burlesque was for some reason extraordinarily funny, so that we all laughed. Yet, although absurd, Umfraville's gesture had also a kind of grace which clearly pleased and flattered Anne Stepney. She even blushed a little. Although he laughed with the rest of us, I saw that Barnby was a trifle put out, as indeed most men would have been in the circumstances. He had certainly recognised Umfraville as a rival with a technique entirely different from his own. I looked across to Jean to see if she wanted to join the expedition. She nodded quickly and smiled. All at once things were going all right again between us.

'I've only met Mrs. Andriadis a couple of times,' said Barnby. 'But we got on very well on both occasions—in fact she bought a drawing. I suppose she won't mind such a large crowd?'

'Mind?' said Umfraville. 'My dear old boy, Milly will be tickled to death. Come along. We can all squeeze into one taxi. Foppa, we shall meet again. You shall have your revenge.'

Mrs. Andriadis was, of course, no longer living in the Duports' house in Hill Street, where Stringham had taken me to the party. That house had been sold by Duport at the time of his financial disaster. She was now installed, so it appeared, in a large block of flats recently erected in Park Lane. I was curious to see how her circumstances would strike me on re-examination. Her party had seemed, at the time, to reveal a new and fascinating form of life, which one might never experience again. Such a world now was not only far less remarkable than formerly, but also its special characteristics appeared scarcely necessary to seek in an active manner. Its elements had, indeed, grown up all round one like strange tropical vegetation: more luxuriant, it was true, in some directions rather than others: attractive here, repellent there, but along every track that could be followed almost equally dense and imprisoning.

'She really said she would like to see us?' I asked, as, tightly packed, we ascended in the lift.

Umfraville's reply was less assuring than might have been hoped.

'She said, "Oh, God, you again, Dicky. Somebody told me you died of drink in 1929." I said, "Milly, I'm coming straight round with a few friends to give you that kiss I forgot when we were in Havana together." She said, "Well, I hope you'll bring along that pony you owe me, too, which you forgot at the same time." So saying, she snapped the receiver down.'

'So she has no idea how many we are?'

'Milly knows I have lots of friends.'

'All the same——'

'Don't worry, old boy. Milly will eat you all up. Especially as you are a friend of Charles.'

I was, on the contrary, not at all sure that it would be wise to mention Stringham's name to Mrs. Andriadis.

'We had to sue her after she took our house,' said Jean.

'Yes, I expect so,' said Umfraville.

The circumstances of our arrival did not seem specially favourable in the light of these remarks. We were admitted to what was evidently a large flat by an elderly lady's-maid, who had the anxious, authoritative demeanour of a nanny, or nursery governess, long established in the family.

'Well, Ethel,' said Umfraville. 'How are you keeping? Quite a long time since we met.'

Her face brightened at once when she recognised him.

'And how are *you*, Mr. Umfraville? Haven't set eyes on you since the days in Cuba. You look very well indeed, sir. Where did you get your sunburn?'

'Not too bad, Ethel. What a time it was in Cuba. And how is Mrs. A.?'

'She's been a bit poorly, sir, on and off. Not quite her own old self. She has her ups and downs.'

'Which of us doesn't, Ethel? Will she be glad to see me?'

It seemed rather late in the day to make this enquiry. Ethel's reply was not immediate. Her face contracted a trifle as she concentrated her attention upon an entirely truthful answer to this delicate question.

'She was pleased when you rang up,' she said. 'Very pleased. Called me in and told me, just as she would have done in the old days. But then Mr. Guggenbühl telephoned just after you did, and after that I don't know that she was so keen. She's changeable, you know. Always was.'

'Mr. Guggenbühl is the latest, is he?'

Ethel laughed, with the easy good manners of a trusted servant whose tact is infinite. She made no attempt to indicate the identity of Mr. Guggenbühl.

'What's he like?' Umfraville asked, wheedling in his manner.

'He's a German gentleman, sir.'

'Old, young? Rich, poor?'

'He's quite young, sir. Shouldn't say he was specially wealthy.'

'One of that kind, is he?' said Umfraville. 'Everybody seems to have a German boy these days. I feel quite out of fashion not to have one in tow myself. Does he live here?'

'Stays sometimes.'

'Well, we won't remain long,' said Umfraville. 'I absolutely understand.'

We followed him through a door, opened by Ethel, which led into a luxurious rather than comfortable room. There was an impression of heavy damask curtains and fringed chair-covers. Furniture and decoration had evidently been designed in one piece, little or nothing having been added to the original scheme by the present owner. A few books and magazines lying on a low table in Chinese Chippendale seemed strangely out of place; even more so, a model theatre, like a child's, which stood on a Louis XVI commode.

Mrs. Andriadis herself was lying in an armchair, her legs resting on a pouf. Her features had not changed at all from the time when I had last seen her. Her powder-grey hair remained beautifully trim; her dark eyebrows still arched over very bright brown eyes. She looked as pretty as before, and as full of energy. She wore no jewellery except a huge square cut diamond on one finger.

Her clothes, on the other hand, had undergone a strange alteration. Her small body was now enveloped in a black cloak, its velvet collar clipped together at the neck by a short chain of metal links. The garment suggested an Italian officer's uniform cloak, which it probably was. Beneath this military outer covering was a suit of grey flannel pyjamas, mean in design and much too big for her: in fact obviously intended for a man. One trouser leg was rucked up, showing her slim calf and ankle. She did not rise, but made a movement with her hand to show that she desired us all to find a place to sit.

'Well, Dicky,' she said, 'why the hell do you want to bring a crowd of people to see me at this time of night?'

She spoke dryly, though without bad temper, in that distinctly cockney drawl that I remembered.

'Milly, darling, they are all the most charming people imaginable. Let me tell you who they are.'

Mrs. Andriadis laughed.

'I know *him,*' she said, nodding in the direction of Barnby.

'Lady Anne Stepney,' said Umfraville. 'Do you remember when we went in her father's party to the St. Leger?'

'You'd better not say anything about *that,*' said Mrs. Andriadis. 'Eddie Bridgnorth has become a pillar of respectability. How is your sister, Anne? I'm not surprised she had to leave Charles Stringham. Such a charmer, but no woman could stay married to him for long.'

Anne Stepney looked rather taken aback at this peremptory approach.

'And Mrs. Duport,' said Umfraville.

'Was it your house I took in Hill Street?'

'Yes,' said Jean, 'it was.'

I wondered whether there would be an explosion at this disclosure. The trouble at the house had involved some question of a broken looking-glass and a burnt-out boiler. Perhaps there had been other items too. Certainly there had been a great deal of unpleasantness. However, in the unexpected manner of persons who live their lives at a furious rate, Mrs. Andriadis merely said in a subdued voice:

'You know, my dear, I want to apologise for all that happened in that wretched house. If I told you the whole story, you would agree that I was not altogether to blame. But it is all much too boring to go into now. At least you got your money. I hope it really paid for the damage.'

'We've got rid of the house now,' Jean said, laughing. 'I didn't ever like it much anyway.'

'And Mr. Jenkins,' Umfraville said. 'A friend of Charles's——'

She gave me a keen look.

'I believe I've seen you before, too,' she said.

I hoped she was not going to recall the scene Mr. Deacon had made at her party. However, she carried the matter no further.

'Ethel,' she shouted, 'bring some glasses. There is beer for those who can't drink whisky.'

She turned towards Umfraville.

'I'm quite glad to see you all,' she said; 'but you mustn't stay too long after Werner appears. He doesn't approve of people like you.'

'Your latest beau, Milly?'

'Werner Guggenbühl. Such a charming German boy. He will be terribly tired when he arrives. He has been walking in a procession all day.'

'To meet the Hunger-Marchers?' I asked.

It had suddenly struck me that in the complicated pattern life forms, this visit to Mrs. Andriadis was all part of the same diagram as that in which St. John Clarke, Quiggin and Mona had played their part that afternoon.

'I think so. Were you marching too?'

'No—but I knew some people who were.'

'What an extraordinary world we live in,' said Umfraville. 'All one's friends marching about in the park.'

'Rather sweet of Werner, don't you agree?' said Mrs. Andriadis. 'Considering this isn't his own country and all the awful things we did to Germany at the Versailles Treaty.'

Before she could say more about him, Guggenbühl himself arrived in the room. He was dark and not bad-looking in a very German style. His irritable expression recalled Quiggin's. He bowed slightly from the waist when introduced, but took no notice of any individual, not even Mrs. Andriadis herself, merely glancing round the room and then glaring straight ahead of him. There could be no doubt that he was the owner of the grey pyjamas. He reminded me of a friend of Mr. Deacon's called 'Willi': described by Mr. Deacon as having 'borne much of the heat of the day over against Verdun when nation rose against nation'. Guggenbühl was a bit younger than Willi, but in character they might easily have a good deal in common.

'What sort of a day did you have, Werner?' asked Mrs. Andriadis.

She used a coaxing voice, quite unlike the manner in which she had spoken up to that moment. The tone made me think of Templer trying to appease Mona. It was equally unavailing, for Guggenbühl made an angry gesture with his fist.

'What was it like, you ask,' he said. 'So it was like everything in this country. Social-Democratic antics. Of it let us not speak.'

He turned away in the direction of the model theatre. Taking no further notice of us, he began to manipulate the scenery, or play about in some other manner with the equipment at the back of the stage.

'Werner is writing a play,' explained Mrs. Andriadis, speaking now in a much more placatory manner. 'We sometimes run through the First Act in the evening. How is it going, Werner?'

'Oh, are you?' said Anne Stepney. 'I'm terribly interested in the Theatre. Do tell us what it is about.'

Guggenbühl turned his head at this.

'I think it would not interest you,' he said. 'We have done with old theatre of bourgeoisie and capitalists. Here is *Volksbühnen*—for actor that is worker like industrial worker—actor that is machine of machines.'

'Isn't it too thrilling?' said Mrs. Andriadis. 'You know the October Revolution was the real turning point in the history of the Theatre.'

'Oh, I'm sure it was,' said Anne Stepney. 'I've read a lot about the Moscow Art Theatre.'

Guggenbühl made a hissing sound with his lips, expressing considerable contempt.

'Moscow Art Theatre is just to tolerate,' he said, 'but what of biomechanics, of *Trümmer-Kunst*, has it? Then Shakespeare's *Ein Sommernachtstraum* or Toller's *Masse-Mensch* will you take? The modern ethico-social play I think you do not like. Hauptmann, Kaiser, plays to Rosa Luxemburg and Karl Liebknecht, yes. The new corporate life. The socially conscious form. Drama as highest of arts we Germans know. No mere entertainment, please. *Lebensstimmung* it is. But it is workers untouched by middle class that will make spontaneous. Of Moscow Art Theatre you speak. So there was founded at Revolution both Theatre and Art Soviet, millions, billions of roubles set aside by Moscow Soviet of Soldier Deputies. Hundreds, thousands of persons. Actors, singers, clowns, dancers, musicians, craftsmen, designers, mechanics, electricians, scene-shifters, all kinds of manual workers, all trained, yes, and supplying themselves to make. Two years to have one perfect single production—if needed so, three, four, five, ten years. At other time, fifty plays on fifty successive nights. It is not be getting money, no.'

His cold, hard voice, offering instruction, stopped abruptly.

'Any ventriloquists?' Umfraville asked.

The remark passed unnoticed, because Anne Stepney broke in again.

'I can't think why we don't have a revolution here,' she said, 'and start something of that sort.'

'You would have a revolution here?' said Guggenbühl, smiling rather grimly. 'So? Then I am in agreement with you.'

'Werner thinks the time has come to act,' said Mrs. Andriadis, returning to her more decisive manner. 'He says we have been talking for too long.'

'Oh, I do agree,' said Anne Stepney.

I asked Guggenbühl if he had come across St. John Clarke that afternoon. At this question his manner at once changed.

'You know him? The writer.'

'I know the man and the girl who were pushing him.'

'Ach, so.'

He seemed uncertain what line to take about St. John Clarke. Perhaps he was displeased with himself for having made disparaging remarks about the procession in front of someone who knew two of the participants and might report his words.

'He is a famous author, I think.'

'Quite well known.'

'He ask me to visit him.'

'Are you going?'

'Of course.'

'Did you meet Quiggin—his secretary—my friend?'

'I think he goes away soon to get married.'

'To the girl he was with?'

'I think so. Mr. Clarke ask me to visit him when your friend is gone for some weeks. He says he will be lonely and would like to talk.'

Probably feeling that he had wasted enough time already with the company assembled in the room, and at the same time unwilling to give too much away to someone he did not know, Guggenbühl returned, after saying this, to the model theatre. Ostentatiously, he continued to play about with its accessories. We drank our beer. Even Umfraville seemed a little put out of countenance by Guggenbühl, who had certainly brought an atmosphere of peculiar unfriendliness and disquiet into the room. Mrs. Andriadis herself perhaps took some pleasure in the general discomfiture for which he was responsible. The imposition of one kind of a guest upon another is a form of exercising power that appeals to most persons who have devoted a good deal of their life to entertaining. Mrs. Andriadis, as a hostess of long standing and varied experience, was probably no exception. In addition to that, she, like St. John Clarke, had evidently succumbed recently to a political conversion, using Guggenbühl as her vehicle. His uncompromising behaviour no doubt expressed to perfection the role to which he was assigned in her mind: the scourge of frivolous persons of the sort she knew so well.

One of the essential gifts of an accomplished hostess is an ability to dismiss, quietly and speedily, guests who have overstayed their welcome. Mrs. Andriadis must have possessed this ingenuity to an unusual degree. I can remember no details of how our party was shifted. Perhaps Umfraville made a movement to go that was quickly accepted. Brief good-byes were said. One way or another, in an unbelievably short space of time, we found ourselves once more in Park Lane.

'You see,' said Umfraville. 'Even Milly . . .'

Some sort of a discussion followed as to whether or not the evening should be brought to a close at this point. Umfraville and Anne Stepney were unwilling to go home; Barnby was uncertain what he wanted to do; Jean and I agreed that we had had enough. The end of it was that the other two decided to accompany Umfraville to a place where a 'last drink' could be obtained. Other people's behaviour were unimportant to me; for in some way the day had righted itself, and once more the two of us seemed close together.

5.

WHEN, in describing Widmerpool's new employment, Templer had spoken of 'the Acceptance World', I had been struck by the phrase. Even as a technical definition, it seemed to suggest what we are all doing; not only in business, but in love, art, religion, philosophy, politics, in fact all human activities. The Acceptance World was the world in which the essential element—happiness, for example—is drawn, as it were, from an engagement to meet a bill. Sometimes the goods are delivered, even a small profit made; sometimes the goods are not delivered, and disaster follows; sometimes the goods are delivered, but the value of the currency is changed. Besides, in another sense, the whole world is the Acceptance World as one approaches thirty; at least some illusions discarded. The mere fact of still existing as a human being proved that.

I did not see Templer himself until later in the summer, when I attended the Old Boy Dinner for members of Le Bas's house. That year the dinner was held at the Ritz. We met in one of the subterranean passages leading to the private room where we were to eat. It was a warm, rather stuffy July evening. Templer, like a Frenchman, wore a white waistcoat with his dinner-jacket, a fashion of the moment, perhaps by then already a little outmoded.

'We always seem to meet in these gorgeous halls,' he said.

'We do.'

'I expect you've heard that Mona bolted,' he went on quickly. 'Joined up with that friend of yours of the remarkable suit and strong political views.'

His voice was casual, but it had a note of obsession as if his nerves were on edge. His appearance was unchanged, possibly a little thinner.

Mona's elopement had certainly been discussed widely. In the break-up of a marriage the world inclines to take the side of the partner with most vitality, rather than the one apparently least to blame. In the Templers' case public opinion had turned out unexpectedly favourable to Mona, probably because Templer himself was unknown to most of the people who talked to me of the matter. Normal inaccuracies of gossip were increased by this ignorance. In one version, Mona was represented as immensely rich, ill treated by an elderly, unsuccessful stockbroker; another described Templer as unable to fulfil a husband's role from physical dislike of women. A third account included a twenty-minute hand-to-hand struggle between the two men, at the end of which Quiggin had gained the victory: a narrative sometimes varied to a form in which Templer beat Quiggin unconscious with a shooting-stick. In a different vein was yet another story describing Templer, infatuated with his secretary, paying Quiggin a large sum to take Mona off his hands.

On the whole people are unwilling to understand even comparatively simple situations where husband and wife are concerned; indeed, a simple explanation is the last thing ever acceptable. Here, certainly, was something complicated enough, a striking reversal of what might be thought the ordinary course of events. Templer, a man undoubtedly attractive to women, loses his wife to Quiggin, a man usually ill at ease in women's company: Mona, as Anna Karenin, directing her romantic feelings towards Karenin as a lover, rather than Vronsky as a husband. For me, the irony was emphasised by Templer being my first schoolboy friend to seem perfectly at home with the opposite sex; indeed, the first to have practical experience in that quarter. But conflict between the sexes might be compared with the engagement of boxers in which the best style is not always victorious.

'What will they live on?' Templer said. 'Mona is quite an expensive luxury in her way.'

I had wondered that, too, especially in the light of an experience of a few weeks before, when sitting in the Café Royal with Barnby. In those days there was a female orchestra raised on a dais at one side of the huge room where you had drinks. They were playing *In a Persian Market*, and in that noisy, crowded, glaring, for some reason rather ominus atmosphere, which seemed specially designed to hear such confidences, Barnby had been telling me that matters were at an end between Anne Stepney and himself. That had not specially surprised me after the evening at Foppa's. Barnby had reached the climax of his story when Quiggin and Mark Members passed our table, side by side, on their way to the diners' end of the room. That was, to say the least, unexpected. They appeared to be on perfectly friendly terms with each other. When they saw us, Members had given a distant, evasive smile, but Quiggin stopped to speak. He seemed in an excellent humour.

'How are you, Nick?'

'All right.'

'Mark and I are going to celebrate the completion of *Unburnt Boats,*' he said. 'It is a wonderful thing to finish a book.'

'When is it to appear?'

'Autumn.'

I felt sure Quiggin had stopped like this in order to make some statement that would define more clearly his own position. That would certainly be a reasonable aim on his part. I was curious to know why the two of them were friends again; also to learn what was happening about Quiggin and Mona. Such information as I possessed then had come through Jean, who knew from her brother only that they had gone abroad together. At the same time, as a friend of Templer's, I did not want to appear too obviously willing to condone the fact that Quiggin had eloped with his wife.

'Mona and I are in Sussex now,' said Quiggin, in a voice that could almost be described as unctuous, so much did it avoid his usual harsh note. 'We have been lent a cottage. I am just up for the night to see Mark and make final arrangements with my publisher.'

He talked as if he had been married to Mona, or at least lived with her, for years; just as, a few months earlier, he had spoken as if he had always been St. John Clarke's secretary. It seemed hard to do anything but accept the relationship as a *fait accompli*. Such things have to be.

'Can you deal with St. John Clarke from so far away?'

'How do you mean?'

Quiggin's face clouded, taking on an expression suggesting he had heard the name of St. John Clarke, but was quite unable to place its associations.

'Aren't you still his secretary?'

'Oh, good gracious, no,' said Quiggin, unable to repress a laugh at the idea.

'I hadn't heard you'd left him.'

'But he has become a Trotskyist.'

'What form does it take?'

Quiggin laughed again. He evidently wished to show his complete agreement that the situation regarding St. John Clarke was so preposterous that only a certain degree of jocularity could carry it off. Laughter, his manner indicated, was a more civilised reaction than the savage rage that would have been the natural emotion of most right-minded persons on hearing the news for the first time.

'The chief form,' he said, 'is that he consequently now requires a secretary who is also a Trotskyist.'

'Who has he got?'

'You would not know him.'

'Someone beyond the pale?'

'He has found a young German to pander to him, as a matter of fact. One Guggenbühl.'

'I have met him as a matter of fact.'

'Have you?' said Quiggin, without interest. 'Then I should advise you to steer clear of Trotskyists in the future, if I were you.'

'Was this very sudden?'

'My own departure was not entirely involuntary,' said Quiggin. 'At first I thought the man would rise above the difficulties of my domestic situation. I—and Mona, too—did everything to assist and humour him. In the end it was no good.'

He had moved off then, at the same time gathering in Members, who had been chatting to a girl in dark glasses sitting at a neighbouring table.

'We shall stay in the country until the divorce comes through,' he had said over his shoulder.

The story going round was that Mona had been introduced by Quiggin to St. John Clarke as a political sympathiser. Only later had the novelist discovered the story of her close association with Quiggin. He had begun to make difficulties at once. Quiggin, seeing that circumstances prevented the continuance of his job, made a goodish bargain with St. John Clarke, and departed. Guggenbühl must have stepped into the vacuum. No one seemed to know the precise moment when he had taken Quiggin's place; nor how matters remained regarding Mrs. Andriadis.

Like Templer, I wondered how Quiggin and Mona would make two ends meet, but these details could hardly be gone into then and there in the Ritz.

'I suppose Quiggin keeps afloat,' I said. 'For one thing, he must have just had an advance for his book. Still, I don't expect that was anything colossal.'

'That aunt of Mona's died the other day,' said Templer. 'She left Mona her savings—a thousand or so, I think.'

'So they won't starve.'

'As a matter of fact I haven't cut her allowance yet,' he said, reddening slightly. 'I suppose one will have to in due course.'

He paused.

'I must say it was the hell of a surprise,' he said. 'We'd had plenty of rows, but I certainly never thought she would go off with a chap who looked quite so like something the cat had brought in.'

I could only laugh and agree. These things are capable of no real explanation. Mona's behaviour was perhaps to be examined in the light of her exalted feelings for Quiggin as a literary figure. Combined with this was, no doubt, a kind of envy of her husband's former successes with other women; for such successes with the opposite sex put him, as it were, in direct competition with herself. It is, after all, envy rather than jealousy that causes most of the trouble in married life.

'I've really come here tonight to see Widmerpool,' said Templer, as if he wished to change the subject. 'Bob Duport is in England again. I think I told you Widmerpool might help him land on his feet.'

I felt a sense of uneasiness that he found it natural to tell me this. Jean had always insisted that her brother knew nothing of the two of us. Probably she was right; though I could never be sure that someone with such highly developed instincts where relations between the sexes were concerned could remain entirely unaware that his sister was having a love affair. On the other hand he never saw us together. No doubt, so far as Jean was concerned, he would have regarded a lover as only natural in her situation. He was an exception to the general rule that made Barnby, for example, puritanically disapproving of an irregular life in others. In any case, he probably spoke of Duport in the way people so often do in such circumstances, ignorant of the facts, yet moved by some unconscious inner process to link significant names together. All the same, I was conscious of a feeling of foreboding. I was going to see Jean that night; after the dinner was at an end.

'I am rather hopeful things will be patched up with Jean, if Bob's business gets into running order again,' Templer said. 'The whole family can't be in a permanent state of being deserted by their husbands and wives. I gather Bob is no longer sleeping with Bijou Ardglass, which was the real cause of the trouble, I think.'

'Prince Theodoric's girl friend?'

'That's the one. Started life as a mannequin. Then married Ardglass as his second wife. When he died the title, and nearly all the money, went to a distant cousin, so she had to earn a living somehow. Still, it was inconvenient she should have picked on Bob.'

By this time we had reached the ante-room where Le Bas's Old Boys were assembling. Le Bas himself had not yet arrived, but Whitney, Maiden, Simson, Brandreth, Ghika, and Fettiplace-Jones were standing about, sipping drinks, and chatting uneasily. All of them, except Ghika, were already showing signs of the wear and tear of life. Whitney was all but unrecognisable with a moustache; Maiden had taken to spectacles; Simson was prematurely bald; Fettiplace-Jones, who was talking to Widmerpool without much show of enjoyment, although he still looked like a distinguished undergraduate, had developed that ingratiating, almost cringing manner that some politicians assume to avoid an appearance of thrusting themselves forward. Fettiplace-Jones had been Captain of the House when I had arrived there as a new boy and had left at the end of that term. He was now Member of Parliament for some northern constituency.

Several others came in behind Templer and myself. Soon the room became fairly crowded. Most of the new arrivals were older or younger than my own period, so that I knew them only by sight from previous dinners. As it happened, I had not attended a Le Bas dinner for some little time. I hardly knew why I was there that year, for it was exceptional for an old friend like Templer to turn up. I think I had a subdued curiosity to see if Dicky Umfraville would put in an appearance, and fulfil his promise to 'tear the place in half'. A chance meeting with Maiden, one of the organisers had settled it, and I came. Maiden now buttonholed Templer, and, at the same moment, Fettiplace-Jones moved away from Widmerpool to speak with Simson, who was said to be doing well at the Bar. I found Widmerpool beside me.

'Why, hullo—hullo—Nicholas——' he said.

He glared through his thick glasses, the side pieces of which were becoming increasingly embedded in wedges of fat below his temples. At the same time he transmitted one of those skull-like smiles of conventional friendliness to be generally associated with conviviality of a political sort. He was getting steadily fatter. His dinner-jacket no longer fitted him: perhaps had never done so with much success. Yet he carried this unhappy garment with more of an air than he would have achieved in the old days; certainly with more of an air than he had ever worn the famous overcoat for which he had been notorious at school.

We had met once or twice, always by chance, during the previous few years. On each occasion he had been going abroad for the Donners-Brebner Company. 'Doing pretty well,' he had always remarked, when asked how things were with him. His small eyes had glistened behind his spectacles when he had said this. There was no reason to disbelieve in his success, though I suspected at the time that his job might be more splendid in his own eyes than when regarded by some City figure like Templer. However, after Templer's more recent treatment of him, I supposed that I must be wrong in presuming exaggeration on Widmerpool's part. Although two or three years older than myself, he could still be little more than thirty. No doubt he was 'doing well'. With the self-confidence he had developed, he moved now with a kind of strut, a curious adaptation of that uneasy, rubber-shod tread, squeaking rhythmically down the interminable linoleum of our school-days. I remembered how Barbara Goring (whom we had both been in love with, and now I had not thought of for years) had once poured sugar over his head at a dance. She would hardly do that today. Yet Widmerpool had never entirely overcome his innate oddness; one might almost say, his monstrosity. In that he resembled Quiggin. Perhaps it was the determination of each to live by the will alone. At any rate, you noticed Widmerpool immediately upon entering a room. That would have given him satisfaction.

'Do you know, I nearly forgot your Christian name,' he said, not without geniality. 'I have so many things to remember these days. I was just telling Fettiplace-Jones about North Africa. In my opinion we should hand back Gibraltar to Spain, taking Ceuta in exchange. Fettiplace-Jones was in general agreement. He belongs to a group in Parliament particularly interested in foreign affairs. I have just come back from those parts.'

'For Donners-Brebner?'

He nodded, puffing out his lips and assuming the appearance of a huge fish.

'But not in the future,' he said, breathing inward hard. 'I'm changing my trade.'

'I heard rumours.'

'Of what?'

'That you were joining the Acceptance World.'

'That's one way of putting it.'

Widmerpool sniggered.

'And you?' he asked.

'Nothing much.'

'Still producing your art books? It was art books, wasn't it?'

'Yes—and I wrote a book myself.'

'Indeed, Nicholas. What sort of a book?'

'A novel, Kenneth.'

'Has it been published?'

'A few months ago.'

'Oh.'

His ignorance of novels and what happened about them was evidently profound. That was, after all, reasonable enough. Perhaps it was just lack of interest on his part. Whatever the cause, he looked not altogether approving, and did not enquire the name of the book. However, probably feeling a moment later that his reply may have sounded a shade flat, he added: 'Good . . . good,' rather in the manner of Le Bas himself, when faced with an activity of which he was uninformed and suspicious, though at the same time unjustified in categorically forbidding.

'As a matter of fact I am making some notes for a book myself,' said Widmerpool. 'Quite a different sort of book from yours, of course. So we may be authors together. Do you always come to these dinners? I have been abroad, or otherwise prevented, on a number of occasions, and thought I would see what had happened to everybody. One sometimes makes useful contacts in such ways.'

Le Bas himself arrived in the room at that moment, bursting through the door tumultuously, exactly as if he were about to surprise the party assembled there at some improper activity. It was in this explosive way that he had moved about the house at school. For a second he made me feel as if I were back again under his surveillance; and one young man, with very fair hair, whose name I did not know, went scarlet in the face at his former housemaster's threatening impetuosity, just as if he himself had a guilty conscience.

However, Le Bas, as it turned out, was in an excellent humour. He went round the room shaking hands with everyone, making some comment to each of us, more often than not hopelessly inappropriate, showing that he had mistaken the Old Boy's name or generation. In spite of that I was aware of a feeling of warmth towards him that I had never felt when at school; perhaps because he seemed to represent, like a landscape or building, memories of a vanished time. He had become, if not history, at least part of one's own autobiography. In his infinitely ancient dinner-jacket and frayed tie he looked, as usual, wholly unchanged. His clothes were as old as Sillery's, though far better cut. Tall, curiously Teutonic in appearance, still rubbing his red, seemingly chronically sore eyes, as from time to time he removed his rimless glasses, he came at last to the end of the diners, who had raggedly formed up in line round the room, as if some vestige of school discipline was reborn in them at the appearance of their housemaster. After the final handshake, he took up one of those painful, almost tortured positions habitually affected by him, this particular one seeming to indicate that he had just landed on his heels in the sand after making the long jump.

Maiden, who, as I have said, was one of the organisers of the dinner, and was in the margarine business, now began fussing, as if he thought that by his personal exertions alone would anyone get anything to eat that night. He came up to me, muttering agitatedly.

'Another of your contemporaries accepted—Stringham,' he said. 'I suppose you don't know if he is turning up? We really ought to go into dinner soon. Should we wait for him? It is really too bad of people to be late for this sort of occasion.'

He spoke as if I, or at least all my generation, were responsible for the delay. The news that Stringham might be coming to the dinner surprised me. I asked Maiden about his acceptance of the invitation.

'He doesn't turn up as a rule,' Maiden explained, 'but I ran into him the other night at the Silver Slipper and he promised to come. He said he would attend if he were sober enough by Friday. He wrote down the time and place on a menu and put it in his pocket. What do you think?'

'I should think we had better go in.'

Maiden nodded, and screwed up his yellowish, worried face, which seemed to have taken on sympathetic colouring from the commodity he marketed. I remembered him as a small boy, perpetually preoccupied with the fear that he would be late for school or games: this tyranny of Time evidently pursuing him no less in later life. Finally, his efforts caused us to troop into the room where we were to dine. From what I had heard of Stringham recently, I thought his appearance at such a dinner extremely unlikely.

At the dinner table I found myself between Templer and a figure who always turned up at these dinners whose name I did not know: a middle-aged—even elderly, he then seemed—grey-moustached man. I had, rather half-heartedly, tried to keep a place next to me for Stringham, but gave up the idea when this person diffidently asked if he might occupy the chair. There were, in any case, some spare places at the end of the table, where Stringham could sit, if he arrived, as a certain amount of latitude always existed regarding the size of the party. It was to be presumed that the man with the grey moustache had been at Corderey's, in the days before Le Bas took over the house; if so, he was the sole survivor from that period who ever put in an appearance. I remembered Maiden had once commented to me on the fact that one of Corderey's Old Boys always turned up, although no one knew him. He had seemed perfectly happy before dinner, drinking a glass of sherry by himself. Hitherto, he had made no effort whatever to talk to any of the rest of the party. Le Bas had greeted him, rather unenthusiastically, with the words 'Hullo, Tolland'; but Le Bas was so notoriously vague regarding nomenclature that this name could be accepted only after corroboration. Something about his demeanour reminded me of Uncle Giles, though this man was, of course, considerably younger. There had been a Tolland at school with me, but I had known him only by sight. I asked Templer whether he had any news of Mrs. Erdleigh and Jimmy Stripling.

'I think she is fairly skinning Jimmy,' he said, laughing. 'They are still hard at it. I saw Jimmy the other day in Pimm's.'

The time having come round for another tea at the Ufford, I myself had visited Uncle Giles fairly recently. While there I had enquired, perhaps unwisely, about Mrs. Erdleigh. The question had been prompted partly by curiosity as to what his side of the story might be, partly from an inescapable though rather morbid interest in what happened to Stripling. I should have known better than to have been surprised by the look of complete incomprehension that came over Uncle Giles's face. It was similar technique, though put into more absolute execution, that Quiggin had used when asked about St. John Clarke. No doubt it would have been better to have left the matter of Mrs. Erdleigh alone. I should have known from the start that interrogation would be unproductive.

'Mrs. Erdleigh?'

He had spoken not only as if he had never heard of Mrs. Erdleigh but as if even the name itself could not possibly belong to anyone he had ever encountered.

'The lady who told our fortunes.'

'What fortunes?'

'When I was last here.'

'Can't understand what you're driving at.'

'I met her at tea when I last came here—Mrs. Erdleigh.'

'Believe there was someone of that name staying here.'

'She came in and you introduced me.'

'Rather an actressy woman, wasn't she? Didn't stay very long. Always talking about her troubles, so far as I can remember. Hadn't she been married to a Yangtze pilot, or was that another lady? There was a bit of a fuss about the bill, I believe. Interested in fortune-telling, was she? How did you discover that?'

'She put the cards out for us.'

'Never felt very keen about all that fortune-telling stuff,' said Uncle Giles, not unkindly. 'Doesn't do the nerves any good, in my opinion. Rotten lot of people, most of them, who take it up.'

Obviously the subject was to be carried no further. Perhaps Mrs. Erdleigh, to use a favourite phrase of my uncle's, had 'let him down'. Evidently she herself had been removed from his life as neatly as if by a surgical operation, and, by this mysterious process of voluntary oblivion, was excluded even from his very consciousness; all done, no doubt, by an effort of will. Possibly everyone could live equally untrammelled lives with the same determination. However, this mention of Uncle Giles is by the way.

'Jimmy is an extraordinary fellow,' said Templer, as if pondering my question. 'I can't imagine why Babs married him. All the same, he is more successful with the girls than you might think.'

Before he could elaborate this theme, his train of thought, rather to my relief, was interrupted. The cause of this was the sudden arrival of Stringham. He looked horribly pale, and, although showing no obvious sign of intoxication, I suspected that he had already had a lot to drink. His eyes were glazed, and, holding himself very erect, he walked with the slow dignity of one who is not absolutely sure what is going on round him. He went straight up to the head of the table where Le Bas was sitting and apologised for his lateness—the first course was being cleared—returning down the room to occupy the spare chair beside Ghika at the other end.

'Charles looks as if he has been hitting the martinis pretty hard,' said Templer.

I agreed. After a consultation with the wine waiter, Stringham ordered a bottle of champagne. Since Ghika had already provided himself with a whisky and soda there was evidently no question of splitting it with his next-door neighbour. Templer commented on this to me, and laughed. He seemed to have obtained relief from having discussed the collapse of his marriage with a friend who knew something of the circumstances. He was more cheerful now and spoke of his plans for selling the house near Maidenhead. We began to talk of things that had happened at school.

'Do you remember when Charles arranged for Le Bas

to be arrested by the police?' said Templer. 'The Braddock alias Thorne affair.'

We were sitting too far away from Le Bas for this remark to be overheard by him. Templer looked across to where Stringham was sitting and caught his eye. He jerked his head in Le Bas's direction and held his own wrists together as if he wore handcuffs. Stringham seemed to understand his meaning at once. His face brightened, and he made as if to catch Ghika by the collar. This action had to be explained to Ghika, and, during the interlude, Parkinson, who was on Templer's far side, engaged him in conversation about the Test Match.

I turned to the man with the grey moustache. He seemed to be expecting an approach of some sort, because, before I had time to speak, he said:

'I'm Tolland.'

'You were at Corderey's, weren't you?'

'Yes, I was. Seems a long time ago now.'

'Did you stay on into Le Bas's time?'

'No. Just missed him.'

He was infinitely melancholy; gentle in manner, but with a suggestion of force behind this sad kindliness.

'Was Umfraville there in your time?'

'R. H. J. Umfraville?'

'I think so. He's called "Dicky".'

Tolland gave a slow smile.

'We overlapped,' he admitted.

There was a pause.

'Umfraville was my fag,' said Tolland, as if drawing the fact from somewhere very deep down within him. 'At least I believe he was. I was quite a bit higher up in the school, of course, so I don't remember him very well.'

A terrible depression seemed to seize him at the thought of this great seniority of his to Umfraville. There was a lack of serenity about Tolland at close quarters, quite different from the manner in which he had carried off his own loneliness in a crowd. I felt rather uneasy at the thought of having to deal with him, perhaps for the rest of dinner. Whitney was on the other side and there was absolutely no hope of his lending a hand in a case of that sort.

'Umfraville a friend of your?' asked Tolland.

He spoke almost as if condoling with me.

'I've just met him. He said he might be coming tonight.'

Tolland looked at me absently. I thought it might be better to abandon the subject of Umfraville. However, a moment or two later he himself returned to it.

'I don't think Umfraville will come tonight,' he said. 'I heard he'd just got married.'

It certainly seemed unlikely that even Umfraville would turn up for dinner at this late stage in the meal, though the reason given was unexpected, even scriptural. Tolland now seemed to regret having volunteered the information.

'Who did he marry?'

This question discomposed him even further. He cleared his throat several times and took a gulp of claret, nearly choking himself.

'As a matter of fact I believe she is a distant cousin of mine—perhaps not,' he said. 'I can never remember that sort of thing—yes, she is, though. Of course she is.'

'Yes?'

'One of the Bridgnorth girls—Anne, I think.'

'Anne Stepney?'

'Yes, yes. That's the one. You probably know her.'

'I do.'

'Thought you would.'

'But she is years younger.'

'She is a bit younger. Yes, she is a bit younger. Quite a bit younger. And he has been married before, of course.'

'It makes his fourth wife, doesn't it?'

'Yes, I believe it does. His fourth wife. Pretty sure it does make his fourth.'

Tolland looked at me in absolute despair, I think not so much at the predicament in which Anne Stepney had involved herself, as at the necessity for such enormities to emerge in conversation. The news was certainly unforeseen.

'What do the Bridgnorths think about it?'

It was perhaps heartless to press him on such a point, but, having been told something so extraordinary as this, I wanted to hear as much as possible about the circumstances. Rather unexpectedly, he seemed relieved to report on that aspect of the marriage.

'The fellow who told me in the Guards' Club said they were making the best of it.'

'There was no announcement?'

'They were married in Paris,' said Tolland. 'So this fellow in the Guards' Club—or was it Arthur's?—told me. My brother, Warminster, when he was alive, used to talk about Umfraville. I think he liked him. Perhaps he didn't. But I think he did.'

'I was at school with a Tolland.'

'My nephew. Did you know his brother, Erridge? Erridge has succeeded now. Funny boy.'

Sir Gavin Walpole-Wilson had mentioned a 'Norah Tolland' as friend of his daughter, Eleanor. She turned out to be a niece.

'Warminster had ten children. Big family for these days.'

We rose at that moment to drink the King's health; and Le Bas's. Then Le Bas stood up, gripping the table with both hands as if he proposed to overturn it. This was in preparation for the delivery of his accustomed speech, which varied hardly at all year by year. His guttural, carefully enunciated consonants echoed through the room.

'. . . cannot fail to be gratifying to see so many of my former pupils here tonight . . . do not really know what to say to you all . . . certainly shall not make a long speech . . . these annual meetings have their importance . . . encourage a sense of continuity . . . give perhaps an opportunity of taking stock . . . friendship . . . I've said to some of you before . . . needs keeping up . . . probably remember, most of you, lines quoted by me on earlier occasions . . .

And I sat by the shelf till I lost myself,
  And roamed in a crowded mist,
And heard lost voices and saw lost looks,
  As I pored on an old School List.

. . . verses not, of course, in the modern manner . . . some of us do not find such appeals to sentiment very sympathetic . . . typically Victorian in their emphasis . . . all the . . . rather well describe what most of us—well—at least some of us—may—feel—experience—when we meet and talk over our . . .'

Here Le Bas, as usual, paused; probably from the conviction that the word 'schooldays' had accumulated various associations in the minds of his listeners to which he was unwilling to seem to appeal. The use of hackneyed words had always been one of his preoccupations. He was, I think, dimly aware that his own bearing was somewhat clerical, and was accordingly particularly anxious to avoid the appearance of preaching a sermon. He compromised at last with '. . . other times . . .' returning, almost immediately, to the poem; as if the increased asperity that the lines now assumed would purge him from the imputation of sentimentality to which he had referred. He cleared his throat harshly.

'. . . You will remember how it goes later . . .

There were several duffers and several bores,
Whose faces I've half forgot,
Whom I lived among, when the world was young
And who talked no end of rot;

. . . of course I do not mean to suggest that there was anyone like that at my house . . .'

This comment always caused a certain amount of mild laughter and applause. That evening Whitney uttered some sort of a cry reminiscent of the hunting field, while Widmerpool grinned and drummed on the tablecloth with his fork, slightly shaking his head at the same time to indicate that he did not at all concur with Le Bas in supposing his former pupils entirely free from such failings.

'. . . certainly nobody of that sort here tonight . . . but at the same time . . . no good pretending that all time spent at school was—entirely blissful . . . certainly not for a housemaster . . .'

There was more restrained laughter. Le Bas's voice tailed away. In his accustomed manner he had evidently tried to steer clear of any suggestion that schooldays were the happiest period of a man's life, but at the same time feared that by tacking too much he might become enmeshed in dangerous admissions from which escape could be difficult. This had always been one of his main anxieties as a schoolmaster. He would go some distance along a path indicated by common sense, but overcome by caution, would stop half-way and behave in an unexpected, illogical manner. Most of the conflicts between himself and individual boys could be traced to these hesitations at the last moment. Now he paused, beginning again in more rapid sentences:

'. . . as I have already said . . . do not intend to make a long, prosy after-dinner speech . . . nothing more boring . . . in fact my intention is—as at previous dinners—to ask some of you to say a word or two about your own activities since we last met together . . . For example, perhaps Fettiplace-Jones might tell us something of what is going forward in the House of Commons . . .'

Fettiplace-Jones did not need much pressing to oblige in this request. He was on his feet almost before Le Bas had finished speaking. He was a tall, dark, rather good-looking fellow, with a lock of hair that fell from time to time over a high forehead, giving him the appearance of a Victorian statesman in early life. His maiden speech (tearing Ramsay MacDonald into shreds) had made some impression on the House, but since then there had been little if any brilliance about his subsequent parliamentary performances, though he was said to work hard in committee. India's eventual independence was the subject he chose to tell us about, and he continued for some little time. He was followed by Simson, a keen Territorial, who asked for recruits. Widmerpool broke into Simson's speech with more than one 'hear, hear'. I remembered that he had told me he too was a Territorial officer. Whitney had something to say of Tanganyika. Others followed with their appointed piece. At last they came to an end. It seemed that Le Bas had exhausted the number of his former pupils from whom he might hope to extract interesting or improving comment. Stringham was sitting well back in his chair. He had, I think, actually gone to sleep.

There was a low buzz of talking. I had begun to wonder how soon the party would break up, when there came the sound of someone rising to their feet. It was Widmerpool. He was standing up in his place, looking down towards the table, as he fiddled with his glass. He gave a kind of introductory grunt.

'You have heard something of politics and India,' he said, speaking quickly, and not very intelligibly, in that thick, irritable voice which I remembered so well. 'You have been asked to join the Territorial Army, an invitation I most heartily endorse. Something has been said of county cricket. We have been taken as far afield as the Congo Basin, and as near home as this very hotel, where one of us here tonight worked as a waiter while acquiring his managerial training. Now I—I myself—would like to say a word or two about my experiences in the City.'

Widmerpool stopped speaking for a moment, and took a sip of water. During dinner he had shared a bottle of Graves with Maiden. There could be no question that he was absolutely sober. Le Bas—indeed everyone present—was obviously taken aback by this sudden, uncomfortable diversion. Le Bas had never liked Widmerpool, and, since the party was given for Le Bas, and Le Bas had not asked Widmerpool to speak, this behaviour was certainly uncalled for. In fact it was unprecedented. There was, of course, no cogent reason, apart from that, why Widmerpool should not get up and talk about the life he was leading. Just as other speakers had done. Indeed, it could be argued that the general invitation to speak put forward by Le Bas required acceptance as a matter of good manners. Perhaps that was how Widmerpool looked at it, assuming that Le Bas had only led off with several individual names as an encouragement for others to take the initiative in describing their lives. All that was true. Yet, in some mysterious manner, school rules, rather than those of the outer world, governed that particular assembly. However successful Widmerpool might have become in his own eyes, he was not yet important in the eyes of those present. He remained a nonentity, perhaps even an oddity, remembered only because he had once worn the wrong sort of overcoat. His behaviour seemed all the more outrageous on account of the ease with which, at that moment on account of the special circumstances, he could force us to listen to him withcut protest.

'This is terrific,' Templer muttered.

I looked across at Stringham, who had now woken up, and, having finished his bottle, was drinking brandy. He did not smile back at me, instead twisting his face into one of those extraordinary resemblances to Widmerpool at which he had always excelled. Almost immediately he resumed his natural expression, still without smiling. The effect of the grimace was so startling that I nearly laughed aloud. At the same time, something set, rather horrifying, about Stringham's own features, put an abrupt end to this sudden spasm of amusement. This look of his even made me feel apprehension as to what Stringham himself might do next. Obviously he was intensely, if quietly, drunk.

Meanwhile, Widmerpool was getting into his stride:

'. . . tell you something of the inner workings of the Donners-Brebner Company,' he was saying in a somewhat steadier voice than that in which he had begun his address. 'There is not a man of you, I can safely say, who would not be in a stronger position to face the world if he had some past experience of employment in a big concern of that sort. However, several of you already know that I am turning my attention to rather different spheres. Indeed, I have spoken to some of you of these changes in my life when we have met in the City . . .'

He looked round the room and allowed his eyes to rest for a moment on Templer, smiling again that skull-like grin with which he had greeted us.

'This is getting embarrassing,' said Templer.

I think Templer had begun to feel he had too easily allowed himself to accept Widmerpool as a serious person. It was impossible to guess what Widmerpool was going to say next. He was drunk with his own self-importance.

'. . . at one time these financial activities were devoted to the satisfaction of man's greed. Now we have a rather different end in view. We have been suffering—it is true to say that we are still suffering and shall suffer for no little time—from the most devastating trade depression in our recorded history. We have been forced from the Gold Standard, so it seems to me, and others not unworthy of a public hearing, because of the insufficiency of money in the hands of consumers. Very well. I suggest to you that our contemporary anxieties are not entirely vested in the question of balance of payment, that is at least so far as current account may be concerned, and I put it to you that certain persons, who should perhaps have known better, have been responsible for unhappy, indeed catastrophic capital movements through a reckless and inadmissible lending policy.'

I had a sudden memory of Monsieur Dubuisson talking like this when Widmerpool and I had been at La Grenadière together.

'. . . where our troubles began,' said Widmerpool. 'Now if we have a curve drawn on a piece of paper representing an average ratio of persistence, you will agree that authentic development must be demonstrated by a register alternately ascending and descending the level of our original curve of homogeneous development. Such an image, or, if you prefer it, such a geometrical figure, is dialectically implied precisely by the notion, in itself, of an average ratio of progress. No one would deny that. Now if a governmental policy of regulating domestic prices is to be arrived at in this or any other country, the moment assigned to the compilation of the index number which will establish the par of interest and prices must obviously be that at which internal economic conditions are in a condition of relative equilibrium. So far so good. I need not remind you that the universally accepted process in connexion with everyday commodities is for their production to be systematised by the relation between their market value and the practicability of producing them, a steep ascent in value in contrast with the decreased practicability of production proportionately stimulating, and a parallel descent correspondingly depressing production. All that is clear enough. The fact that the index number remains at par regardless of alterations in the comparative prices of marketable commodities included in it, necessarily expresses the unavoidable truth that ascent or descent of a specific commodity is compensated by analogous adjustments in the opposite direction in prices of residual commodities . . .'

How long Widmerpool would have continued to speak on these subjects, it is impossible to say. I think he had settled down in his own mind to make a lengthy speech, whether anyone else present liked it or not. Why he had decided to address the table in this manner was not clear to me. Possibly, he merely desired to rehearse aloud certain economic views of his own, expressing them before an indifferent, even comparatively hostile audience, so that he might judge what minor adjustments ought to be made when the speech was delivered on some far more important occasion. Such an action would not be out of keeping with the eccentric, dogged manner in which he ran his life. At the same time, it was also likely enough that he wanted to impress Le Bas's Old Boys—those former schoolfellows who had so greatly disregarded him—with the fact that he was getting on in the world in spite of them; that he had already become a person to be reckoned with.

Widmerpool may not even have been conscious of this motive, feeling it only instinctively, for there could be no doubt that he now thought of his schooldays in very different terms from any that his contemporaries would have used. Indeed, such references as he had ever made to his time at school, for example when we had been in France together, always suggested that he saw himself as a boy rather above the average at work and games: that justice had never been done to his energies in either direction was on account of the unsatisfactory manner in which both these sides of life were administered by those in authority

The effect of his discourse on those sitting round the table had been mixed. Fettiplace-Jones's long, handsome, pasty face assumed a serious, even worried expression, implying neither agreement nor disagreement with what was being said: merely a public indication that, as a Member of Parliament, he was missing nothing. It was as if he were waiting for the Whip's notification of which way he should vote. Parkinson gave a kind of groan of boredom, which I heard distinctly, although he was separated from me by Templer. Tolland, on the other hand, leant forward as if he feared to miss a syllable. Simson looked very stern. Whitney and Brandreth had begun a whispered conversation together. Maiden, who was next to Widmerpool, was throwing anxious, almost distracted glances about him. Ghika, like Tolland, leant forward. He fixed his huge black eyes on Widmerpool, concentrating absolutely on his words, but whether with interest, or boredom of an intensity that might lead even to physical assault, it was impossible to say. Templer had sat back in his chair, clearly enjoying every phrase to the full. Stringham also expressed his appreciation, though only by the faintest smile, as if he saw all through a cloud. Then, suddenly, the scene was brought abruptly to a close.

'Look at Le Bas,' said Templer.

'It's a stroke,' said Tolland.

Afterwards—I mean weeks or months afterwards, when I happened upon any of the party then present, or heard the incident discussed—there was facetious comment suggesting that Le Bas's disabling attack had been directly brought about by Widmerpool's speech. Certainly no one was in a position categorically to deny that there was no connection whatever between Widmerpool's conduct and Le Bas's case. Knowing Le Bas, I have no doubt that he was sitting in his chair, bitterly regretting that he was no longer in a position to order Widmerpool to sit down at once. That would have been natural enough. A sudden pang of impotent rage may even have contributed to other elements in bringing on his seizure. But that was to take rather a melodramatic view. More probably, the atmosphere of the room, full of cigar smoke and fumes of food and wine, had been too much for him. Besides, the weather had grown distinctly hotter as the night wore on. Le Bas himself had always been a great opener of windows. He would insist on plenty of fresh air on the coldest winter day at early school in any room in which he was teaching. His ordinary life had not accustomed him to gatherings of this sort, which he only had to face once a year. No doubt he had always been an abstemious man, in spite of Templer's theory, held at school, that our housemaster was a secret drinker. That night he had possibly taken more wine than he was accustomed. He was by then getting on in years, though no more than in his sixties. The precise cause of his collapse was never known to me. These various elements probably all played a part.

Lying back in his chair, his cheeks flushed and eyes closed, one side of Le Bas's face was slightly contorted. Fettiplace-Jones and Maiden must have taken in the situation at once, because I had scarcely turned in Le Bas's direction before these two had picked him up and carried him into the next room. Widmerpool followed close behind them. There was some confusion when people rose from the table. I followed the rest through the door to the ante-room, where Le Bas was placed full-length on the settee. Somebody had removed his collar.

This had probably been done by Brandreth, who now took charge. Brandreth, whose father had acquired a baronetcy as an ear-specialist, was himself a doctor. He began immediately to assure everyone that Le Bas's condition was not serious.

'The best thing you fellows can do is to clear off home and leave the room as empty as possible,' Brandreth said. 'I don't want all of you crowding round.'

Like most successful medical men in such circumstances, he spoke as if the matter had now automatically passed from the sphere of Le Bas's indisposition to the far more important one of Brandreth's own professional convenience. Clearly there was something to be said for following his recommendation. Brandreth seemed to be handling the matter competently, and, after a while, all but the more determined began to disappear from the room. Tolland made a final offer to help before leaving, but Brandreth snapped at him savagely and he made off; no doubt to appear again the following year. I wondered how he filled in the time between Old Boy dinners.

'I shall have to be going, Nick,' said Templer. 'I have to get back to the country tonight.'

'This dinner seems to have been rather a fiasco.'

'Probably my fault,' said Templer. 'Le Bas never liked me. However, I think it was really Widmerpool this time. What's happened to him, by the way? I never had my chat about Bob.'

Widmerpool was no longer in the room. Maiden said he had gone off to ring up the place where Le Bas was staying, and warn them what had happened. By then Le Bas was sitting up and drinking a glass of water.

'Well, fixing old Bob up will have to wait,' said Templer. 'I want to do it for Jean's sake. I'm afraid you had to listen to a lot of stuff about my matrimonial affairs tonight.'

'What are your plans?'

'Haven't got any. I'll ring up some time.'

Templer went off. I looked round for Stringham, thinking I would like a word with him before leaving. It was a long time since we had met, and I was not due to arrive at Jean's until late. Stringham was not in the small group that remained. I supposed he had left; probably making his way to some other entertainment. There was nothing surprising in that. In any case, it was unlikely that we should have done more than exchange a few conventional sentences, even had he remained to talk for a minute or two. I knew little or nothing of how he lived since his divorce. His mother's picture still appeared from time to time in the illustrated papers. No doubt her house in the country provided some sort of permanent background into which he could retire when desirable.

On the way out, I glanced by chance through the door leading to the room where we had dined. Stringham was still sitting in his place at the table, smoking a cigarette and drinking coffee. The dining-room was otherwise deserted. I went through the door and took the chair beside him.

'Hullo, Nick.'

'Are you going to sit here all night?'

'Precisely the idea that occurred to me.'

'Won't it be rather gloomy?'

'Not as bad as when they were all here. Shall we order another bottle?'

'Let's have a drink at my club.'

'Or my flat. I don't want to look at any more people.'

'Where is your flat?'

'West Halkin Street.'

'All right. I shan't be able to stay long.'

'Up to no good?'

'That's it.'

'I haven't seen you for ages, Nick.'

'Not for ages.'

'You know my wife, Peggy, couldn't take it. I expect you heard. Not surprising, perhaps. She has married an awfully nice chap now. Peggy is a really lucky girl now. A really charming chap. Not the most amusing man you ever met, but a really *nice chap.*'

'A relation of hers, isn't he?'

'Quite so. A relation of hers, too. He will be already familiar with all those lovely family jokes of the Stepney family, those very amusing jokes. He will not have to have the points explained to him. When he stays at Mountfichet, he will know where all the lavatories are—if there is, indeed, more than one, a matter upon which I cannot speak with certainty. Anyway, he will not always have to be bothering the butler to direct him to where that one is—and losing his way in that awful no-man's-land between the servants' hall and the gun-room. What a house! Coronets on the table napkins, but no kind hearts between the sheets. He will be able to discuss important historical events with my ex-father-in-law, such as the fact that Red Eyes and Cypria dead-heated for the Cesarewitch in 1893—or was it 1894? I shall forget my own name next. He will be able to talk to my ex-mother-in-law about the time Queen Alexandra made that *double entendre* to her uncle. The only thing he won't be able to do is to talk about Braque and Dufy with my ex-sister-in-law, Anne. Still, that's a small matter. Plenty of people about to talk to girls of Braque and Dufy these days. I heard, by the way, that Anne had got a painter of her own by now, so perhaps even Braque and Dufy are things of the past. Anyway, he's a jolly nice chap and Peggy is a very lucky girl.'

'Anne has married Dicky Umfraville.'

'Not *the* Dicky Umfraville?'

'Yes.'

'Well I never.'

Even that did not make much impression on him. The fact that he had not already heard of Anne Stepney's marriage suggested that Stringham must pass weeks at a time in a state in which he took in little or nothing of what was going on round him. That could be the only explanation of ignorance of an event with which he had such close connexions.

'Shall we make a move?'

'Where is Peter Templer? I saw his face—sometimes two or three of them—during that awful dinner. We might bring him along as well. Always feel a bit guilty about Peter.'

'He has gone home.'

'I bet he hasn't. He's gone after some girl. Always chasing the girls. Let's follow him.'

'He lives near Maidenhead.'

'Too far. He must be mad. Is he married?'

'His wife has just left him.'

'There you are. Women are all the same. My wife left me. Has your wife left you, Nick?'

'I'm not married.'

'Lucky man. Who *was* Peter's wife, as they say?'

'A model called Mona.'

'Sounds like the beginning of a poem. Well, I should have thought better of her. One of those long-haired painter fellows must have got her into bad habits. Leaving her husband, indeed. She oughtn't to have left Peter. I was always very fond of Peter. It was his friends I couldn't stand.'

'Let's go.'

'Look here, do let's have another drink. What happened to Le Bas?'

'He is going to be taken home in an ambulance.'

'Is he too tight to walk?'

'He had a stroke.'

'Is he dead?'

'No—Brandreth is looking after him.'

'What an awful fate. Why Brandreth?'

'Brandreth is a doctor.'

'Hope I'm never ill when Brandreth is about, or he might look after me. I'm not feeling too good at the moment as a matter of fact. Perhaps we'd better go, or Brandreth will start treating me too. It was Widmerpool's speech, of course. Knocked Le Bas out. Knocked him out cold. Nearly knocked me out too. Do you remember when we got Le Bas arrested?'

'Let's go to your flat.'

'West Halkin Street. Where I used to live before I was married. Surely you've been there.'

'No.'

'Ought to have asked you, Nick. Ought to have asked you. Been very remiss about things like that.'

He was extremely drunk, but his legs seemed fairly steady beneath him. We went upstairs and out into the street.

'Taxi?'

'No,' said Stringham. 'Let's walk for a bit. I want to cool off. It was bloody hot in there. I don't wonder Le Bas had a stroke.'

There was a rich blue sky over Piccadilly. The night was stiflingly hot. Stringham walked with almost exaggerated sobriety. It was remarkable considering the amount he had drunk.

'Why did you have so many drinks tonight?'

'Oh, I don't know,' he said. 'I do sometimes. Rather often nowadays, as a matter of fact. I felt I couldn't face Le Bas and his Old Boys without an alcoholic basis of some sort. Yet for some inexplicable reason I wanted to go. That was why I had a few before I arrived.'

He put out his hand and touched the railings of the Green Park as we passed them.

'You said you were not married, didn't you, Nick?'

'Yes.'

'Got a nice girl?'

'Yes.'

'Take my advice and don't get married.'

'All right.'

'What about Widmerpool. Is he married?'

'Not that I know of.'

'I'm surprised at that. Widmerpool is the kind of man to attract a woman. A good, sensible man with no nonsense about him. In that overcoat he used to wear he would be irresistible. Quite irresistible. Do you remember that overcoat?'

'It was before my time.'

'It's a frightful shame,' said Stringham. 'A frightful shame, the way these women go on. They are all the same. They leave me. They leave Peter. They will probably leave you. . . . I say, Nick, I am feeling extraordinarily odd. I think I will just sit down here for a minute or two.'

I thought he was going to collapse and took his arm. However, he settled down in a sitting position on the edge of the stone coping from which the railings rose.

'Long, deep breaths,' he said. 'Those are the things.'

'Come on, let's try and get a cab.'

'Can't, old boy. I just feel too, too sleepy to get a cab.'

As it happened, there seemed to be no taxis about at that moment. In spite of what must have been the intense discomfort of where he sat, Stringham showed signs of dropping off to sleep, closing his eyes and leaning his head back against the railings. It was difficult to know what to do. In this state he could hardly reach his flat on foot. If a taxi appeared, he might easily refuse to enter it. I remembered how once at school he had sat down on a staircase and refused to move, on the grounds that so many annoying things had happened that afternoon that further struggle against life was useless. This was just such another occasion. Even when sober, he possessed that complete recklessness of behaviour that belongs to certain highly strung persons. I was still looking down at him, trying to decide on the next step, when someone spoke just behind me.

'Why is Stringham sitting there like that?'

It was Widmerpool's thick, accusing voice. He asked the question with a note of authority that suggested his personal responsibility to see that people did not sit about in Piccadilly at night.

'I stayed to make sure everything was done about Le Bas that should be done,' he said. 'I think Brandreth knows his job. I gave him my address in case of difficulties. It was a disagreeable thing to happen. The heat, I suppose. It ruined the few words I was about to say. A pity. I thought I would have a breath of fresh air after what we had been through, but the night is very warm even here in the open.'

He said all this with his usual air of immense importance.

'The present problem is how to get Stringham to his flat.'

'What is wrong with him? I wonder if it is the same as Le Bas. Perhaps something in the food——'

Widmerpool was always ready to feel disturbed regarding any question of health. In France he had been a great consumer of patent medicines. He looked nervously at Stringham. I saw that he feared the attack of some mysterious sickness that might soon infect himself.

'Stringham has had about a gallon to drink.'

'How foolish of him.'

I was about to make some reply to the effect that the speeches had needed something to wash them down with, but checked any such comment since Widmerpool's help was obviously needed to get Stringham home, and I thought it better not to risk offending him. I therefore muttered something that implied agreement.

'Where does he live?'

'West Halkin Street.'

Widmerpool acted quickly. He strolled to the kerb. A cab seemed to rise out of the earth at that moment. Perhaps all action, even summoning a taxi when none is there, is basically a matter of the will. Certainly there had been no sign of a conveyance a second before. Widmerpool made a curious, pumping movement, using the whole of his arm, as if dragging down the taxi by a rope. It drew up in front of us. Widmerpool turned towards Stringham, whose eyes were still closed.

'Take the other arm,' he said, peremptorily.

Although he made no resistance, this intervention aroused Stringham. He began to speak very quietly:

'Ah, with the Grape my fading Life provide,
And wash my Body whence the Life has died . . .'

We shoved him on to the back seat, where he sat between us, still murmuring to himself:

'. . . And lay me shrouded in the living leaf
By some not unfrequented garden-side . . .

I think that's quite a good description of the Green Park, Nick, don't you. . . . "Some not unfrequented garden-side" . . . Wish I sat here more often . . . Jolly nice. . . .'

'Does he habitually get in this state?' Widmerpool asked.

'I don't know. I haven't seen him for years.'

'I thought you were a close friend of his. You used to be—at school.'

'That's a long time ago.'

Widmerpool seemed aggrieved at the news that Stringham and I no longer saw each other regularly. Once decided in his mind on a given picture of what some aspect of life was like, he objected to any modification of the design. He possessed an absolutely rigid view of human relationships. Into this, imagination scarcely entered, and whatever was lost in grasping the niceties of character was amply offset by a simplification of practical affairs. Occasionally, it was true. I had known Widmerpool involved in situations which were extraordinary chiefly because they were entirely misunderstood, but on the whole he probably gained more than he lost by these limitations; at least in the spheres that attracted him. Stringham now lay between us, as if fast asleep.

'Where is he working at present?'

'I don't know.'

'It was a good thing he left Donners-Brebner,' said Widmerpool. 'He was doing neither himself nor the company any good.'

'Bill Truscott has gone, too, hasn't he?'

'Yes,' said Widmerpool, looking straight ahead of him. 'Truscott had become very interested in the by-products of coal and found it advantageous to make a change.'

We got Stringham out of the taxi on arrival without much difficulty and found his latchkey in a waistcoat pocket. Inside the flat, I was immediately reminded of his room at school. There were the eighteenth-century prints of the racehorses, Trimalchio and the The Pharisee; the same large, rather florid photograph of his mother: a snapshot of his father still stuck in the corner of its frame. However, the picture of 'Boffles' Stringham—as I now thought of him after meeting Dicky Umfraville—showed a decidedly older man than the pipe-smoking, open-shirted figure I remembered from the earlier snapshot. The elder Stringham, looking a bit haggard and wearing a tie, sat on a seat beside a small, energetic, rather brassy lady, presumably his French wife. He had evidently aged considerably. I wondered if friendship with Dicky Umfraville had had anything to do with this. Opposite these photographs was a drawing by Modigliani, and an engraving of a seventeenth-century mansion done in the style of Wenceslaus Hollar. This was Glimber, the Warringtons' house, left to Stringham's mother during her lifetime by her first husband. On another wall was a set of coloured prints illustrating a steeplechase ridden by monkeys mounted on dogs.

'What are we going to do with him?'

'Put him to bed,' said Widmerpool, speaking as if any other action were inconceivable.

Widmerpool and I, therefore, set out to remove Stringham's clothes, get him into some pyjamas, and place him between the sheets. This was a more difficult job than might be supposed. His stiff shirt seemed riveted to him. However, we managed to get it off at last, though not without tearing it. In these final stages, Stringham himself returned to consciousness.

'Look here,' he said, suddenly sitting up on the bed, 'what is happening? People seem to be treating me roughly. Am I being thrown out of somewhere? If so, where? And what have I done to deserve such treatment? I am perfectly prepared to listen to reason and admit that I was in the wrong, and pay for anything I have broken. That is provided, of course, that I was in the wrong. Nick, why are you letting this man hustle me? I seem for some reason to be in bed in the middle of the afternoon. Really, my habits get worse and worse. I am even now full of good resolutions for getting up at half-past seven every morning. But who is this man? I know his face.'

'It's Widmerpool. You remember Widmerpool?'

'Remember Widmerpool . . .' said Stringham. 'Remember Widmerpool. . . . Do I remember Widmerpool? . . . How could I ever forget Widmerpool? . . . How could anybody forget Widmerpool? . . .'

'We thought you needed help, Stringham,' said Widmerpool, in a very matter-of-fact voice. 'So we put you to bed.'

'You did, did you?'

Stringham lay back in the bed, looking fixedly before him. His manner was certainly odd, but his utterance was no longer confused.

'You needed a bit of looking after,' said Widmerpool.

'That time is past,' said Stringham.

He began to get out of bed.

'No. . . .'

Widmerpool took a step forward. He made as if to restrain Stringham from leaving the bed, holding both his stubby hands in front of him, as if warming them before a fire.

'Look here,' said Stringham, 'I must be allowed to get in and out of my own bed. That is a fundamental human right. Other people's beds may be another matter. In them, another party is concerned. But ingress and egress of one's own bed is unassailable.'

'Much better stay where you are,' said Widmerpool, in a voice intended to be soothing.

'Nick, are you a party to this?'

'Why not call it a day?'

'Take my advice,' said Widmerpool. 'We know what is best for you.'
'Rubbish.'
'For your own good.'
'I haven't got my own good at heart.'
'We will get you anything you want.'
'Curse your charity.'
Once more Stringham attempted to get out of the bed. He had pushed the clothes back, when Widmerpool threw himself on top of him, holding Stringham bodily there. While they struggled together, Stringham began to yell at the top of his voice.
'So these are the famous Widmerpool good manners, are they?' he shouted. 'This is the celebrated Widmerpool courtesy, of which we have always heard so much. Here is the man who posed as another Lord Chesterfield. Let me go, you whited sepulchre, you serpent, you small-time Judas, coming to another man's house in the guise of paying a social call, and then holding him down in his own bed.'
The scene was so grotesque that I began to laugh; not altogether happily, it was true, but at least as some form of nervous relief. The two of them wrestling together were pouring with sweat, especially Widmerpool, who was the stronger. He must have been quite powerful, for Stringham was fighting like a maniac. The bed creaked and rocked as if it would break beneath them. And then, quite suddenly, Stringham began laughing too. He laughed and laughed, until he could struggle no more. The combat ceased. Widmerpool stepped back. Stringham lay gasping on the pillows.
'All right,' he said, still shaking with laughter, 'I'll stay. To tell the truth, I am beginning to feel the need for a little rest myself.'
Widmerpool, whose tie had become twisted in the

struggle, straightened his clothes. His dinner-jacket looked more extraordinary than ever. He was panting hard.

'Is there anything you would like?' he asked in a formal voice.

'Yes,' said Stringham, whose mood was now completely changed. 'A couple of those little pills in the box on the left of the dressing-table. They will knock me out finally. I do dislike waking at four and thinking things over. Perhaps three of the pills would be wiser, on second thoughts. Half measures are never any good.'

He was getting sleepy again, and spoke in a flat, mechanical tone. All his excitement was over. We gave him the sleeping tablets. He took them, turned away from us, and rolled over on his side.

'Good-night, all,' he said.

'Good-night, Charles.'

'Good-night, Stringham,' said Widmerpool, rather severely.

We perfunctorily tidied some of the mess in the immediate neighbourhood of the bed. Stringham's clothes were piled on a chair. Then we made our way down into the street.

'Great pity for a man to drink like that,' said Widmerpool.

I did not answer, largely because I was thinking of other matters; chiefly of how strange a thing it was that I myself should have been engaged in a physical conflict designed to restrict Stringham's movements: a conflict in which the moving spirit had been Widmerpool. That suggested a whole social upheaval: a positively cosmic change in life's system. Widmerpool, once so derided by all of us, had become in some mysterious manner a person of authority. Now, in a sense, it was he who derided us; or at least his disapproval had become something far more powerful than the merely defensive weapon it had once seemed.

I remembered that we were not far from the place where formerly Widmerpool had run into Mr. Deacon and Gypsy Jones on the night of the Huntercombes' dance. Then he had been on his way to a flat in Victoria. I asked if he still lived there with his mother.

'Still there,' he said. 'Though we are always talking of moving. It has great advantages, you know. You must come and see us. You have been there in the past, haven't you?'

'I dined with you and your mother once.'

'Of course. Miss Walpole-Wilson was at dinner, wasn't she? I remember her saying afterwards that you did not seem a very serious young man.'

'I saw her brother the other day at the Isbister Retrospective Exhibition.'

'I do not greatly care for the company of Sir Gavin,' said Widmerpool. 'I dislike failure, especially failure in one holding an official position. It is letting all of us down. But—as I was saying—we shall be rather occupied with my new job for a time, so that I expect we shall not be doing much entertaining. When we have settled down, you must come and see us again.'

I was not sure if his 'we' was the first person plural of royalty and editors, or whether he spoke to include his mother; as if Mrs. Widmerpool were already a partner with him in his bill-broking. We said good-night, and I wished him luck in the Acceptance World. It was time to make for Jean's. She was reaching London by a late train that evening, again lodged in the flat at the back of Rutland Gate.

On the way there I took from my pocket the post-card she had sent telling me when to arrive. I read it over, as I had already done so many times that day. There was no mistake. I should be there at the time she asked. The events of the evening seemed already fading into unreality at the prospect of seeing her once more.

The card she had sent was of French origin, in colour, showing a man and woman seated literally one on top of the other in an armchair upholstered with crimson plush. These two exchanged ardent glances. They were evidently on the best of terms, because the young man, fair, though at the same time rather semitic of feature, was squeezing the girl's arm just above the elbow. Wearing a suit of rich brown material, a tartan tie and a diamond ring on the third finger of his right hand, his face, as he displayed a row of dazzling teeth, reminded me of Prince Theodoric's profile—as the Prince might have been painted by Isbister. The girl smiled back approvingly as she balanced on his knee.

'Doesn't she look like Mona?' Jean had written on the back. Dark, with corkscrew curls, the girl was undeniably pretty, dressed in a pink frock, its short sleeves frilled with white, the whole garment, including the frills, covered with a pattern of small black spots. The limits of the photograph caused her legs to fade suddenly from the picture, an unexpected subordination of design created either to conceal an impression of squatness, or possibly a purely visual effect —the result of foreshortening—rather than because these lower limbs failed in the eyes of the photographer to attain a required standard of elegance. For whichever reason, the remaining free space at the foot of the postcard was sufficient to allow the title of the caption below to be printed in long, flourishing capitals:

Sex Appeal
Ton regard et ta voix ont un je ne sais quoi . . .
D'étrange et de troublant qui me met en émoi.

Although in other respects a certain emptiness of background suggested a passage or hall, dim reflections of looking-glass set above a shelf painted white seemed to belong to a dressing-table: a piece of furniture hinting, consequently, of bedrooms. To the left, sprays of artificial flowers, red and yellow, drooped from the mouth of a large vase of which the base was invisible. This gigantic vessel assumed at first sight the proportions of a wine vat or sepulchral urn, even one of those legendary jars into which Morgiana, in the Arabian Nights, poured boiling oil severally on the Forty Thieves: a public rather than private ornament, it might be thought, decorating presumably the bedroom, if bedroom it was, of a hotel. Indeed, the style of furnishing was reminiscent of the Ufford.

Contemplating the blended tones of pink and brown framed within the postcard's scalloped edge of gold, one could not help thinking how extraordinarily unlike 'the real thing' was this particular representation of a pair of lovers; indeed, how indifferently, at almost every level except the highest, the ecstasies and bitterness of love are at once conveyed in art. So much of the truth remains finally unnegotiable; in spite of the fact that most persons in love go through remarkably similar experiences. Here, in the picture, for example, implications were misleading, if not positively inaccurate. The matter was presented as all too easy, the twin flames of dual egotism reduced almost to nothing, so that there was no pain; and, for that matter, almost no pleasure. A sense of anxiety, without which the condition could scarcely be held to exist, was altogether absent.

Yet, after all, even the crude image of the postcard depicted with at least a degree of truth one side of love's outward appearance. That had to be admitted. Some of love was like the picture. I had enacted such scenes with

Jean: Templer with Mona: now Mona was enacting them with Quiggin: Barnby and Umfraville with Anne Stepney: Stringham with her sister Peggy: Peggy now in the arms of her cousin: Uncle Giles, very probably, with Mrs. Erdleigh: Mrs. Erdleigh with Jimmy Stripling: Jimmy Stripling, if it came to that, with Jean: and Duport, too.

The behaviour of the lovers in the plush armchair beside the sparse heads of those sad flowers was perfectly normal; nor could the wording of the couplet be blamed as specially far-fetched, or in some other manner indefensible. 'D'étrange et de troublant' were epithets, so far as they went, perfectly appropriate in their indication of those indefinable, mysterious emotions that love arouses. In themselves there was nothing incongruous in such descriptive labels. They might, indeed, be regarded as rather apt. I could hardly deny that I was at that moment experiencing something of the sort.

The mere act of a woman sitting on a man's knee, rather than a chair, certainly suggested the Templer *milieu*. A memorial to Templer himself, in marble or bronze, were public demand ever to arise for so unlikely a cenotaph, might suitably take the form of a couple so grouped. For some reason—perhaps a confused memory of *Le Baiser*—the style of Rodin came to mind. Templer's own point of view seemed to approximate to that earlier period of the plastic arts. Unrestrained emotion was the vogue then, treatment more in his line than some of the bleakly intellectual statuary of our own generation.

Even allowing a fairly limited concession to its character as a kind of folk perception—an eternal girl sitting on an eternal young man's knee—the fact remained that an infinity of relevant material had been deliberately omitted from this vignette of love in action. These two supposedly good-looking persons were, in effect, going through the motions of love in such a manner as to convince others, perhaps less well equipped for the struggle than themselves, that they, too, the spectators, could be easily identified with some comparable tableau. They, too, could sit embracing on crimson chairs. Although hard to define with precision the exact point at which a breach of honesty had occurred, there could be no doubt that this performance included an element of the confidence-trick.

The night was a shade cooler now. Jean was wearing a white blouse, or sports shirt, open at the neck. Beneath it, her body trembled a little.

'What was your dinner like?' she asked.

'Peter turned up.'

'He said he would probably go there.'

I told her about Le Bas; and also about Stringham.

'That is why I am a bit late.'

'Did Peter mention that Bob is back in England?'

'Yes.'

'And that his prospects are not too bad?'

'Yes.'

'That may make difficulties.'

'I know.'

'Don't let's talk of them.'

'No.'

'Darling Nick.'

Outside, a clock struck the hour. Though ominous, things still had their enchantment. After all, as St. John Clarke was reported to have said at the Huntercombes', 'All blessings are mixed blessings.' Perhaps, in spite of everything, the couple of the postcard could not be dismissed so easily. It was in their world that I seemed now to find myself.